Windmills

by

ALAN CLEGG

To Julie
best wishes
Alan Clegg

5/3/95.

HORSESHOE PUBLICATIONS
KINGSLEY, WARRINGTON
CHESHIRE

ISBN 1.899310.26.6

British Library Cataloguing in Publication Data
A Catalogue record for this book is available from the
British Library

Printed and bound in Great Britain by
ANTONY ROWE LTD
Chippenham, Wiltshire

for the Publishers

HORSESHOE PUBLICATIONS
Box 37, Kingsley, Warrington,
Cheshire WA6 8DR

Cover designed and illustrated by TRACY WALKDEN

This story is dedicated
to the brave people of the Netherlands

Acknowledgements

I acknowledge the information provided by my family in the Netherlands. Particularly the memories given to me by my late mother and father-in-law, Annie Kingma-Jager and Harmen Kingma. Their names and the names of the other brave members of the Dutch Resistance movements should never be forgotten.

Bibliography

The Bibliography is limited by the number of books that are published in English. I have translated some from Dutch to provide the background for the story.

The Diary of Anne Frank, The Critical Edition, Viking. 1989.
Holland at War against Hitler, Edited by Foot, M.R.D.
                                    Frank Cass & Co. Ltd. 1990.
Gilbert, Martin, *Second World War*, FONTANA /Collins. 1989.
Maas, Walter, B, *The Netherlands at War*, Abelard-Schuman. 1970.
Middlebrooke, Martin, *ARNHEM 1944 The Airborne Battle*,
                                    Viking. 1994.
Philpott, Bryan, *History of the German Air Force*,
                                    Gallery Books. 1986.
Quarrie, B, *German Airborne Troops 1939-45*,
                                    Men-At-Arms Series, Osprey. 1983.
Waterford, Helen, H, *Commitment to the Dead*,
                                    Renaissance House. 1987.
Brongers, E.H, *De Oorlog in Mei '40*, Hollandia. 1963.
De Jong, L. *De Bezetting*, Querido's Uitgeverij N.V. 1966
Schaaf, Ype *Laarzen Op De Lange Pijp*, Van Wijnen. 1994.
Ypma, Y.N, *Friesland Anno Domini 1940-45*, J, Kamminga. 1953

Introduction

The Friesian Resistance Museum is located five minutes walk from the main railway station in Leeuwarden, the capital of the province of Friesland in the north of the Netherlands. I managed to persuade my Dutch wife that a quick visit would be interesting for the children, after all they were half-Dutch. We had agreed and as we all switched on our cassette players, the children left to walk round the exhibition on their own individual pilgrimages.

The story of the German invasion and occupation came over clearly and, as usual, the spoken English was excellent. I had heard the story many times and each time I was humbled by the sheer bravery and courage of the Dutch people. England was bombed and many died serving their country, but we were never occupied and nobody in England had any experience of occupation. I have only managed to feel something of what life must have been like through long, fascinating conversations with my Dutch relatives. The memories are fading, but the horrifying experiences are not.

After browsing through most of the exhibits and becoming deeply involved in Dutch life during World War II, I was brought to my senses by a hand tugging at my sleeve. I switched off the cassette-player only to see my son trying to drag me across the floor away from the main route of the tour. I stopped him and he excitedly explained that he had found something concerning his Dutch grandfather. As I was pulled through the exhibition, I realised for the first time that there could be something about my father-in-law in the museum.

The glass case was small and could easily have been missed but my son had found it and was gazing inside. The false identity card and documents said that the holder's name was Henk de Beer, the plain signet ring was inscribed with the initials of the same name

Now, my son looked at me questioningly and then pointed up at the wall above the case, and there, amongst all the yellowing posters, was a single postcard-sized certificate. Most of it was in English, which had helped him to find it; sharp young eyes always seek the unusual. I would never have noticed it. I was bombarded with questions.

'What about the funny writing?'

'Hebrew.'

'Where is the forest anyway?'

'In Israel.'

'And why did they plant trees for Dutch Granddad?'

'For saving Jewish lives.'

'Mum, Dad . . . why did Dutch Granddad and Grandma save Jewish people?'

PART ONE

Invasion

ONE

The fresh wind of spring rattled the rigging and flapped the furled sails of the Friesian *tjalk* as it lay hard against the wharf of the van der Meer Timber Factory. The cargo of Swedish timber had to be unloaded today or else the boat's *schipper* would be complaining loudly to Frank van der Meer himself.

By mid-morning most of the cargo was off-loaded and the men were beginning to tire. Almost in the nick of time the smell of hot coffee wafted across their perspiring faces.

'The coffee is klaar, gentlemen!' Aukje van der Meer stood with a tray holding seven cups of the steaming brown liquid. When Aukje was not at school she enjoyed carrying out small jobs, much to the delight of the men in the factory. Fifteen years old is an age when a growing girl can move easily between the world of children and that of adults. As she served the cups out to the semi-circle of men, there were one or two admiring glances. Her typically Friesian blonde hair and bright blue eyes set off an attractive, lively face; her smile was infectious.

'Milk for me, please, Aukje!'

'No sugar, thanks!'

She made her way to the kitchen and within a minute returned. Her voice was full of life as she glanced at each of the men, 'Would anybody else like more coffee?'

There were shaking heads and nodded thanks. The smile came back, she turned and, with a swirl of her skirts, disappeared into the house and left them to their discussions.

The *schipper* sat with the men and the talk was of the weather and canal life. Their short break was almost ended when another man approached.

'Good morning, everybody. I can see that you've done a good job. Well done.' He spoke Friesian, a local provincial tongue that was totally different from the national Dutch.

The man in front of them Frank van der Meer, the owner of the timber factory. He was in his late-thirties, tall, of medium build and casually dressed. The face was firmly set, friendly and the eyes a penetrating blue. A shock of strong, light-brown hair was his most dominant feature and it helped to frame the clean-cut face. His skin was vibrant and healthy, the outdoor life suited him well.

All the men answered in the same language. They were proud of their distinctive culture.

'Well, *meneer* van der Meer, we should be finished in another two hours and then we can load up your cargo. ... Is that it over there?' The *kapitein* pointed to a neat stack of completed door and window frames.

'That's it *Schipper* Schaaf. The way-bills are ready in the office. If you see my son he'll get them ready for signing.' The voice was deep and resonant and Frank flashed his famous smile. 'Please don't forget, half the load is for dropping off at Harlingen.'

As the factory men continued with their unloading, the two men walked back to the office. The factory was self-contained. At one end was a comfortable five-bedroomed house, built specially for the van der Meer family. The office was up a flight of wooden stairs that led to the first floor of the house as well as the office. From here, Frank was able to work and look down onto the timber yard and along each side of the river.

They climbed the stairs and walked in through the doorway. In the office sat Harmen, Frank's eldest son. He was a youthful version of his father. At seventeen he had worked in the factory since leaving school. Harmen dealt with the routine paperwork and on this morning he had the way-bills ready for signing.

He stood up from his desk, smiled and shook hands. 'Hello, *Schipper* Schaaf.' He was another Friesian speaker. 'Could you please sign here and then everything is clear.'

The *schipper* nodded, 'Yes, indeed I will.' He leant forward and used the proffered fountain pen.

Frank watched the signing, looked at the clock on the wall and said quietly, '*Schipper*, how about a bowl of soup and fresh bread and cheese before you leave us?'

The older man stood and nodded, 'A grand idea, *meneer*. That is, of course, if *mevrouw* van der Meer doesn't mind me dropping in like this?'

'Of course not.' The open friendly face split into a broad smile. 'I suspect that Aukje will have already warned Marieke of your arrival.' The three men laughed and walked towards the door leading to the stairway of the house. They made their way down to the main living-room of the van der Meer household.

The room was large and well furnished. Two big, French-windows faced onto the river and the brightly painted stern of the *tjalk* was clearly visible. The walls were faced with light wood, colour washed in green and the timber floor was polished to a deep, dark brown. Persian rugs lay casually scattered over the open spaces, adding more colour to the room. In front of the windows, arranged facing towards the daylight, were heavy comfortable sofas. They were complemented by lighter, wicker chairs with soft tapestry cushions dropped neatly in place. An open hearth-fire dominated one wall and logs burned gently in the grate. On the walls, paintings, some were local, some were modern; all of them were valuable, handed down by each preceding generation of van der Meers. Two enormous, classical brass chandeliers provided the main lighting and smaller lights on the walls gave more subtle tones. A large glass fronted antique cabinet contained silver and pottery *objet d'art*, each with a family story to tell. In pride of place hung an old wall-mounted, long-cased Friesian clock, its slow rhythmical tick the only sound in the room. Opposite the windows near to the door sat a large circular table, six places were already laid. The silver cutlery gleamed and reflected the colours of the room. The atmosphere was one of peace and tradition. This was a lived-in family room.

Marieke van der Meer was petite, the Friesian blonde hair and blue eyes had been passed on to her daughter. Her figure was excellent and she liked good clothes. The smooth fitting dress was modern and not at all provincial. A light gold chain looped round her neck set off her attractive face.

She stood framed in the doorway, her voice was quiet and pleasant on the ear. 'You're very welcome, *Schipper* Schaaf. How are your family?'

He inclined his head and smiled, 'They're fine, *mevrouw* van der Meer and they send their best wishes.' He stepped forward to shake a rather small hand. 'Thank you for the invitation for lunch.'

Frank moved towards the door and rang a hand-bell hanging on the wall. They sat down and Aukje brought in the large porcelain soup tureen and placed it in the middle of the table. There was a minute's silence as they all bowed their heads and Frank quietly recited a simple prayer of thanks. Marieke served out the hot pea soup with a silver ladle, each bowl was presented and each was filled. The freshly baked bread was cut into thick slices, just the right size for carefully dipping into the soup.

For the first few minutes of the meal there was silence as each person filled their mouths with the delicious soup. It was *Schipper* Schaaf who began the conversation.

'Well, *meneer*, things are not looking too good in Europe at the moment?' This was a question, not a comment.

Frank put his spoon onto the plate and looked up. 'You're right, *Schipper*, things don't look good. The *moffen* have taken over Poland,' he used the Dutch derogatory word for the Germans, 'and now they've invaded Norway. They had no trouble. Although the British are trying to fight them off, they just don't have the strength. I think we'll be next on the list for *Herr* Hitler. Our First World War neutrality won't save us now.'

The *schipper* nodded. 'You may be right. I've heard from other skippers that to the east of here in German Friesland there're massive numbers of soldiers and equipment beginning to pile up at their military camps. I'm sure they're not for defence of the Fatherland!'

Frank, looked up and said quietly, '*Schipper*, what concerns me most of all is the influence of my fascist country men.' This was a conversation that was going deeper and deeper and unusual for Frank, because normally he never discussed politics at the dinner-table.

The *schipper* took up the subject enthusiastically, 'You're right, *meneer*. Remember in 1935, 300,000 people voted for Mussert and his *Nationaal-Socialistische Beweging party*. I've never supported the *NSB*.' He shook his head and glanced at Frank. 'They'll look to Hitler; you can be certain of that!'

'What really annoys me, *Schipper*, is that Dutchmen are hoping to form a branch of the *SS*. They'll call themselves the *Nederlandsche SS*.' Frank took a deep breath, 'What an insult to our country, when you hear the rumours about what the German *SS* are doing to people in Poland.'

There was a silence in the room broken only by the deep tick of the Friesian clock. Marieke shifted uncomfortably in her chair and stared at her husband.

Harmen vehemently joined in, 'My friends are saying that they'll fight if they have to and I'll join them.' He glanced at his father.

'No you won't,' said Frank sharply, eyes flashing, 'You know that our Mennonite church preaches peace at all costs. Anyway, there's nothing that our small military forces could do. We're totally outnumbered.'

There was the sound of a spoon tapping on a plate, 'Come on you three, we don't want the talk of war to spoil our meal do we?' said Marieke, with a slight smile.

Schipper Schaaf gave his deep belly laugh, 'I'm sorry, *mevrouw* van der Meer, you're quite right, but outside this house that's what most of the people are talking about.' He carried on spooning the soup into his mouth.

There was silence for a few minutes as they all ate. The plateful of bread and the soup were quickly consumed and Aukje left for a brief minute to bring in more. The social conversation continued.

Again the subject returned, '*Heit*, if the Germans do invade, what will they do to us?' Aukje asked a child's question that was in all their minds.

Frank shook his head, 'I don't know, my *famke*. The country must survive somehow. Remember that many of our people support Hitler. I heard from the *dominee* in church last Sunday that Hitler is against minorities such as Jews, Gypsies and other groups, maybe even we Mennonites. Apparently the Jews in Germany are being treated very badly. Let's all pray that he doesn't invade Holland.'

'I hope so too, *Heit*. The de Bruin family are our best friends and they're Jewish.' For the first time Aukje's smile was replaced by a worried frown.

Frank shook his head and spoke with his usual authority, fingers tapping on the table. 'We could talk about this all day, but, it's no use worrying. The world wouldn't let the Germans invade and not help us. The British and the Americans are great friends of Holland and they won't stand by and watch.'

The room was absolutely silent, even the noises from outside had been strangely stilled. Someone had to break the heavy atmosphere that seemed to press down on the house. There was a quiet tap on the open window.

'Excuse me, *Schipper* Schaaf. We've finished loading and we're ready to leave in fifteen minutes.' The ship's mate smiled respectfully at the family. The reverie was broken and the relief was obvious. Marieke rose from her chair and began to gather in the plates; Aukje removed the empty soup tureen; Harmen stood with his father and the *schipper* and they walked towards the door.

The old man smiled and looked at their faces. '*Meneer* and *mevrouw* van der Meer, I must thank you for an excellent meal and now I really must get on my way.' There were nodding acknowledgements as they made their way through the house and back onto the river-side.

The early afternoon sunshine was rapidly being blotted out by a huge, dark thundercloud approaching from the east. The men shivered after leaving the warm house. The stack of off-loaded timber had been carefully covered with a tarpaulin. The *tjalk* was heavy in the water and some of the timber frames were secured to the deck because the holds were full.

Frank looked at the cloud, frowned and pointed at the deck cargo, '*Schipper*, will you cover those frames before the rain comes? They can sometimes warp before they're painted.'

He nodded, 'Consider it done, *meneer*. We'll do it when we cast-off and get on our way.' He turned and shook hands with father and son. 'Again, I must thank you for lunch. I'll see you again next week. *Tot ziens!*'

The family watched as the two great brown sails of the *tjalk* were heaved into place by the crew. They cast off and the beautiful old ship began to ease away from the wharf. The auxiliary motor was not needed as the wind freshened with the oncoming storm. With a wave from the crew, the ship creaked its way slowly down the river towards Leeuwarden. The wind began to rise as the sun blinked out behind the ominous storm clouds from the east.

TWO

The early May sunshine brought the good citizens of Leeuwarden out onto the streets of their town. Sunday was a time for walking and visiting, but only after families had attended church. All denominations were represented and the pealing of church bells was heard clearly throughout the town. The thirteenth century *Grote Kerk* was the oldest. Its rich Protestant history reflected in the carefully restored exterior. Soberly dressed families made their way through its great doors as the musical sound of the carillon almost drowned out their quiet chatter. There were a few cars but some people still arrived by horse and carriage and the horses waited patiently on the nearby *Kerkstraat*. Only a kilometre away the tall, slender spire of the Gothic Catholic church dominated the skyline. The same Sunday routines were followed and people made their way through the narrow streets to one church or another. It seemed as if the whole of the town's population was going to worship. Perhaps they had more reasons to attend on this particular day than on any previous Sundays.

The van der Meer family always walked from their house to church. It was three kilometres; but hail, rain or snow, they always walked. On this bright morning they dressed in Sunday best, after a small breakfast they left their home to arrive in good time. The first part of the journey was through the countryside surrounding the town. The Friesian landscape was the flattest in Holland. The horizon, a dead straight line punctuated by odd trees or farm buildings. The two predominant colours were the deep blue of the sky and the dark green of the pastureland. The regulated squares of the fields were dotted with an uncountable number of black and white Friesian cows. They were just part of the landscape and nobody paid them the slightest bit of attention; but without the cows, the province could not survive.

'What a lovely morning, Frank. It really feels as though summer is nearly here,' said a cheerful Marieke.

Frank liked to dress well and his dark grey suit fitted perfectly. The black shoes shone in the bright sunlight. 'Yes, *liefje*. You're right. It's a real pleasure to see the countryside waking up.' He turned round to look for Aukje. 'Come on, we haven't all day. Please keep up with us.' The family were in the outskirts of the town and the children were slowing to talk to friends.

Jan de Bruin was tall and eminently respectable. His younger son was desperately in love with Aukje van der Meer. All the signs were there; the excuses to walk past the factory; the best clothes, a bath every day; leaving for the town at the same time. His wife, Tineke, knew what was going on and thought it was wonderful.

She saw Frank van der Meer in front of her turn round and say something. She knew exactly what it was. He had said the same thing for the last six weeks. She called gently, 'David, stop chattering! Let Aukje catch up with her family. You'll make them late.' Her knowledge of his friendship and the loud voice made David blush with pleasure and he said his quick good-byes to Aukje. The de Bruins walked away towards their synagogue on *Sacramentstraat*. Their day of worship was on Saturday but they enjoyed walking in the peace of the Christian day of rest.

The van der Meers arrived in the town centre and they walked briskly along *Nieuwe Stad*, the main thoroughfare in Leeuwarden. Here were the best shops, the biggest banks, the police station and the *Waag*, a beautiful, sixteenth century building where the products of the town's Golden Age were once weighed and measured before being distributed along the excellent network of canals. A quick turn right into *Wirdumerdijk* and their church was in front of them.

The *Doopsgezinde Kerk* is a small building set back from the narrow street. It provided a centre for the followers of Menno Simons, a sixteenth century Protestant Lutheran cleric. Simons had a large flock in Friesland, his thoughts and creed had been exported to America where his followers were sometimes called the Amish. Other members of the congregation were already assembled outside the big double doors and the van der Meers met many of their friends.

Dominee Paul de Vries was clothed in the standard ministers' morning dress. He met them with an outstretched hand and a ready smile, 'Good morning, van der Meer Family. How are you all on this lovely morning?' The smile was genuine. The van der Meers were important leaders within the Church and their financial gifts were welcome. Four generations had been married within this very building.

The social pleasantries were exchanged and they took their place in their usual pews near the front of the church. The simple service and the litany of words from the Bible and the sermon were, as usual, appreciated by the congregation. The numbers were greater than normal and the *dominee* knew the reason when he made his brief announcements at the end of the sermon.

His voice was quiet but rang with authority. 'Brothers and sisters. I know that today the churches in our country are full.' He paused and waved his hand over the people below him. 'A great shadow hangs over Holland and our freedom to worship in the future may be threatened by invasion from the east.' The church was absolutely silent. He continued, slowly looking at every face in front of him. 'In our church we believe in non-violence and we believe in peace. Let us hold these two great beliefs close to our hearts and pray that our country will remain free.' Many of the heads in front of him nodded. The *dominee* had given his simple message. He stopped, said prayers and then stepped down quickly from the pulpit and made his way down the aisle to the open doors at the rear of the church.

The van der Meers did not leave, they made their way through a side door to the meeting-room of the elders. Frank sat down with his wife, his children and waited for friends and *dominee* Paul de Vries to arrive.

The aroma of coffee pervaded the large airy room and soon there were twenty or so people sitting in the comfortable leather chairs. The table was covered with a large Persian rug as was normal in meeting places and Dutch houses. Church magazines and pamphlets lay scattered around the table top and large potted plants stood in the centre. This was a normal gathering to bring people together in friendship. The business meetings were never held on Sunday.

There was no formal agenda and they just chatted to the people next to them and listened to the *dominee* talking about other Mennonite churches in Friesland.

The subject of the war in Europe was not mentioned until one older man said quickly in a loud nervous voice, 'If the Germans invade Holland then I shall certainly fight!' There was suddenly an awful silence in the room. Everybody looked at each other but nobody spoke.

Dominee de Vries broke the silence. 'Pim, I believe I know how you feel, but remember my words in church this morning.' He spoke gently and was full of understanding. 'Only your conscience can decide what you would do if invasion should occur. You know what the Church thinks.' He turned away and sipped his coffee making polite conversation with another of his parishioners. The man remained silent and the subject was not raised again.

Frank van der Meer had said very little during the meeting and he listened to what the other people had to say. Marieke was discussing with a friend about the timing of a church business meeting later in the week. The remaining coffee had gone cold and this was the usual signal for people to start leaving.

The walk from the church to their friend's house took only a matter of minutes as the Bokma family lived not far from the town centre on *Groningerstraatweg*. The family strolled past the old buildings on both sides of the canals.

Piet Bokma was really Frank der Beer's main competitor in the local timber trade but, somehow, they had always remained good friends. The two families usually met after church and Piet and Frank always talked business. The house was not grandly impressive, located in the middle of a row of substantial brick-built dwellings. It stood and looked solid and reliable.

The door was answered by the maid who led them through to the Bokma family sitting outside in the garden.

'Hello Marieke .... Frank .... Harmen... Aukje. How are you all?' He was short, stocky and radiated strength and dependability. He had no children and his wife, Sytske, rose to meet their friends. The two families sat and chatted with the friendly familiarity that only good friends can give. They drank more coffee and delicious slices of ginger cake and then Aukje and Harmen took the dog for a walk. Piet ran his business from an office upstairs. After the coffee had been drunk, both he and Frank excused themselves. They sat together in the comfortable office.

Frank frowned and began. 'Piet, is the war having any effect on your business?'

His friend replied, 'Not really, supplies are still arriving. Only last week I took delivery of a cargo of German timber with no problems at all. But ... I still keep hearing rumours and I feel helpless to do anything about them.' He nodded. 'I expect something to happen ... nothing does, and that I find the most worrying thing of all.' There was a pause in the conversation and then Piet suddenly banged his fist on the table in frustration and his eyes flashed. 'What the hell are the swines up to?'

Frank thought for a moment and shook his head. 'I really don't know, but I strongly suspect that they'll walk in anytime. What have they got to lose? Remember, the Rhine flows through their country and ends in ours. Our coast faces England, they can't take Europe completely unless they take England. So to me it seems obvious ... they'll invade! The only question now is when?'

Piet stood, took a deep puff on his cigar and looked through the window. 'If they come. Do we get our families out of the country ... or, just stay?'

Frank's face was set, 'I think it's too late now. From what I hear it's difficult to travel to England, most of the ships are full. Belgium won't let us in.' He looked across the small room towards his friend and shrugged. 'Why are we talking like this, Piet? We can't just leave everything behind. We've put all our lives into our businesses. If the Germans invade then they'll certainly need timber.'

Piet whirled round. He snatched the cigar from his mouth and his voice was edged with hardness, 'Frank, you're talking collaboration here. If it does happen, then we stay and trade as much as possible with our own people.'

Both men nodded.

They sat for a moment. Piet looked straight into Frank's eyes, 'You know, several people have said to me that if..... if they come, then we should form groups to oppose them whilst we have the time and energy to think about it. I've already started, I met some friends the other day in the *Hotel de Kroon* ...' He was quietly interrupted.

'Don't say any more Piet. You know my feelings, I'm a committed Mennonite I can't fight or take part in any violence whatsoever. Don't tell me anything that may be useful to the Germans ...' Frank shook his head, 'I just don't know! And that's worrying.'

'We do have our problems my friend.' Piet became serious, 'We've not been occupied for over a hundred years.'

' I know, I know,' said Frank, 'our neutrality in the First World War was respected. We're a small country. There's nowhere that we can hide, no mountains or forests. And I haven't the faintest idea where to find a gun, let alone fire one. Our coast is patrolled by German ships and our longest border is with Germany. I know all these things, but it doesn't help out situation now, at this very moment.' He shrugged his shoulders.

Their thoughts were interrupted and Marieke's cheery voice echoed up the stairs. 'Piet! ... Frank! ... More coffee ready in five minutes.' Both men smiled and stood.

Frank touched his friend's arm and his usual smile returned. 'Just a minute Piet. ... I hear there're several large cargoes of timber from Sweden arriving in Rotterdam on Thursday. If you agree, I'll go down, see our contractors and try and secure enough for what we need. I'll stay overnight and sort it all out. I can't see any big problems. ... What do you think?'

Piet turned to the calendar on the wall, 'An excellent idea.' He jabbed at the page and turned to face his friend. 'What date is that? ... I'll make a note of it?'

Frank took a slim leather covered diary out of his pocket and thumbed over the pages. With his pencil he made a small mark. 'That's the 10th of May. I think I'll leave on the 9th and stay overnight. I'll telephone you before I go. It should be an easy journey.' He laughed, 'Come on, I think the coffee will be ready.'

THREE

Life continued normally in the van der Meer house. The spell of fine weather had gone. Outside it was pouring down in blinding sheets and the rain blew horizontally from one side of the horizon to the other. Aukje bent her head over the handlebars and pedalled against the rain. It was hard work and the bike was heavy but she had been cycling nearly every day of her life and her muscles were well used to the daily journey. Today was the day her father had to leave for Rotterdam and she knew that she had to leave school as soon as possible and arrive back home. No visits to friends after school today.

'Be careful, Harmen, those doors have been closed for the last five years.'

His father's voice made him jump with surprise and he turned round to face him. He was angry. 'Yes! I can see that, *Heit.* ... Can you give us some help please? The doors are really heavy.'

Frank laughed, 'It's a job I've been promising to do for the last year. Those seasoning cellars need cleaning out and I'll certainly help you.'

The four men set to with a crow bar and a length of rope and very quickly the first door opened with a creak of warped wood and a loud crash. The other door moved easily and they leant over to look into the dark hole of the cellar.

'*Meneer* van der Meer, I didn't know that the cellars were so big,' said the younger of the two men. 'When were they last used?'

Frank wiped his brow, 'There are two cellars, one leads into the other. They're lit by electricity and normally dry. Come on, let's have a look down there.' He began to walk carefully down the narrow flight of wooden steps below the doors. Some of the light bulbs still worked and they cast a brownish light over the steps. The cellars were stone lined, unusual because there was little stone available for any construction in sandy Friesland.

Frank sniffed the cold air, 'No smell of damp in here. The ventilators have done their job well. If you look up there,' he pointed up to grills set in each corner of the wall, 'they vent naturally and come out somewhere near the sides of the house. The prevailing wind keeps the cellars fresh and clean.' His gaze dropped to the mess on the floor. 'Right, let's move these odd bits of timber and then you can lay out some new wooden slats and then I think the cellars will make an ideal storage place.' He looked at his watch. 'I'm sorry I can't stay, I've got to get on my way to Rotterdam and I don't want to drive in the dark.' Harmen nodded and the three men began to move the timber from the cellar.

The house was empty and Frank quickly washed, changed and packed his suitcase ready for the journey to Rotterdam. He did it without excitement. The weather was awful and although he usually enjoyed travelling, this time there was the nagging worry of the situation in Europe;

but he shrugged his shoulders; business was business.

Harmen had already backed the car out of the garage, the interior was warm and the windscreen was clean. The English Austin 10 had proved itself to be reliable. Frank enjoyed driving the car because it was just that bit different from most cars on the road, most of which were German or French. Marieke joined them, carrying a flask of hot coffee and a packet of sandwiches.

Her voice was concerned. 'Please be careful, Frank. It's a long way in such awful weather.' She hugged him closely and put the flask into the glove compartment.

'Have a safe journey, *Heit*. Watch the wind on the *Afsluitdijk*,' said Harmen. He smiled, loaded the suitcase into the boot and turned to shake hands with his father.

'You're right, son. I should go the long way round but the *Afsluitdijk* is always quicker.' Frank laughed, squared his shoulders and kissed his wife.

The giant dyke blocking off the *IJsselmeer* from the North Sea had shortened the journey to Rotterdam and Amsterdam by forty-five minutes. The only problem for Frank was the wind. The dyke was a thirty kilometre strip of narrow roadway. It was completely open to the elements and during strong storms, anybody driving or cycling on that road was likely to be drenched by sea spray or blown off the road.

The cargo waiting for him in Rotterdam was set at a good price and he could have ordered it by telephone. Frank loved timber and liked to inspect the cargoes as soon as they were unloaded at the docks. In the past his judgement had proved to be right and he always selected the best.

Frank quickly passed through the small port of Harlingen on the coast and made his way down to the start of the *Afsluitdijk*. As he approached the beginning of the dam, he felt the wind hammering against the front of the car. The clouds were heavy and rolled right down to the horizon. In front of him stretched the dyke; a long black strip of land disappearing into the horizon and lost in a mist of dark cloud. The water on both sides was pounded into a white froth and the North Sea on his right heaved with the heavy swell. There was not another vehicle or a living thing in sight and, for a moment, he was tempted to turn back, but he had made the journey many times and he pushed on. The strength of the head wind was so powerful that he had to drive in third gear at just fifty kilometres an hour. It was so cold that even though the car was labouring, the temperature gauge showed that the engine was only just warm. The noise of the wind, the rain lashing against the windscreen and the metronomic tick of the wipers allowed no calm thoughts and he just drove, concentrating on keeping the car in a straight line.

The wind eased a little as the road joined the main land mass of the province of North Holland and he followed the signposts that led towards the south and Rotterdam.

The rain was slowing and there was some traffic travelling in his direction. He drove carefully; the concrete roads were wet and greasy, sheets of spray flew up over the car whenever somebody passed him. There were gaps in the clouds and slowly some patches of blue appeared. Frank smiled and relaxed. He was not far from the outskirts of Haarlem.

Quite suddenly he braked hard. A man appeared directly in front of him with a flashing red lamp. As he skidded to a stop, he could see through the smeared windscreen that the man was in army uniform.

He waved him to the right and shouted, 'PULL OVER, NOW!'

Frank obeyed the order and drove onto the soft grass at the side of the road. He felt the car lurch into the deep mud. Climbing out he looked back. Even though it was only late afternoon the road was lit up by dozens of bright headlights. The huge lorries roared past. There was heavy spray but through it he could see that the rear tarpaulin flaps were fastened up and grim faced men in uniform stared back at him as they gripped their rifles. Some wagons towed light guns, others were completely sealed and packing cases bulged through the canvas sides. It was a long convoy and obviously in a great hurry. Their urgency was not lost on Frank and it took a few minutes after the last wagon had departed up the road for him to slowly realise that there was something unusual about this convoy; the colour of the vehicles, the briefly glimpsed uniforms, the position of the drivers. The last vehicle had confirmed his suspicions; it was flying a British flag! He knew that there were some British troops in Holland but these were sixty kilometres from Rotterdam. He jumped at the voice in his ear.

'Ja, meneer ... they're Tommies on their way to the docks at IJmuiden.' Frank was surprised when another driver forced to the side of road suddenly appeared behind him. The man continued, 'I hear they've British Royal Navy ships there, ... thousands of men and guns. I think we're going to need their help very soon!'

He was confused. 'Guns! ... Men! ... What for?'

The man stared hard, 'Haven't you heard? The Germans are massing on all borders. Our ships have seen their navy laying mines off the coast. The British are still landing their troops at IJmuiden ... It looks as thought this is it!'

Frank was speechless. His first reaction was to turn round and return to Leeuwarden. Then his disbelief made him go on. 'What's it like in Rotterdam meneer?' he shouted.

'I think it's all right from what I hear. Plenty of soldiers and sailors. If you've business there, then you must get in and get out as quickly as you can.' The man paused. 'I hear from your accent that you're from Friesland. ... What's it like up there?'

Frank was still thinking on his feet. All the time his family and the business flashed through his mind. 'Pardon, meneer, ... oh yes. ... It's very quiet. We hear nothing, only what's on the wireless.'

The man interrupted and laughed. 'You wouldn't hear anything ... All news is heavily censored. I only know because I live near Rotterdam. You can see things happening down there, believe me.'

A bright shaft of sunlight shone out of the sky. It brought Frank out of his thoughts. He looked at the man and smiled. 'If you'll excuse me? I must reach Rotterdam before nightfall.' Without reason he shook hands with the stranger. He was grateful. The man had made him realise the danger that he was in. Frank turned quickly and stepped back into his car. It started first time and he set off down the road. For some unexplained reason he kept glancing above him into the wide dome of the sky almost as if he expected the enemy to fall down upon him. In reality his thoughts were not far from the truth.

Stretched out on each side of the road was the flat landscape of North Holland. He noted the name of the smaller villages as he reduced speed to pass through them. Not far to Rotterdam now, no more than twenty kilometres. He noticed an unusually large number of police and soldiers at all the major cross-roads. Frank pushed his foot hard down on the accelerator. The car went faster and faster into the approaching dusk. He was desperate to arrive before darkness fell.

When in Rotterdam he usually stayed at the Maas Hotel on the main road near to the docks. It was comfortable and convenient and they knew him. The car's headlights stabbed into the darkening gloom. He just made it. As he drew up in front of the hotel, the doorman was ready.

'*Goede avond, meneer.*'

Frank returned the greeting and followed him to the small check-in desk near the main entrance.

The hotel was still managed by its owner and he smiled a welcome, '*Meneer* van der Meer, it's a pleasure to see you again. A good journey from Leeuwarden, I hope?'

Frank shook his hand. 'Thank you ... on the way down I had to stop for a British military convoy. What are they doing? ... '

Before he could continue, the manager raised his finger and winked. He lowered his voice. '*Meneer*, ... there're British everywhere ... Look!' He pointed towards the lounge. Sitting in the comfortable chairs were six British naval officers each holding a glass of beer. They chatted, apparently without a worry in the world. The whisper continued. 'They arrived two days ago and very graciously asked if they could stay here. How could I refuse ... they paid in advance!'

They both laughed loudly enough for two of the officers to turn round and smile at them.

'Your usual room is prepared for you, ... dinner is in thirty minutes,' added the manager.

Frank nodded and made his way up the stairs. The room was ready and his suitcase stood near the bed. He enjoyed looking after his clothes. He carefully unpacked and put them away neatly in the tall wardrobe. A quick wash and a change made him ready for the evening. Frank walked across to the window and opened the curtain. His thoughts were interrupted as the distant sound of a gong being struck signalled that dinner was being served. A quick glance in the mirror, a careful flick of a comb through his thick hair, and he walked to the door, opened it, and made his way downstairs.

The dining room was almost empty. The naval officers were already seated at their table. Frank waited and carefully surveyed the restaurant. The maître hovered and directed him to a table near the window. As he walked across the room, one of the British officers stood and intercepted his passage.

His voice was courteous, 'Excuse me, *meneer*. My Captain asks if you would like to join us for dinner?'

Frank faltered, his brain whirled. He spoke reasonable English, he had travelled to that country many times on business and on holiday, but he really wanted to be alone.

However, with a smile he quickly gave in and replied in English, 'I would be delighted, thank you.'

He followed the young lieutenant to the table. The other officers rose to meet him. They remained standing whilst the introductions were made. The names were a confusion and difficult to remember, but when he was introduced to the tall captain, the handshake was strong and one pair of blue eyes stared into another.

'Good evening, *meneer*. I'm Lieutenant-Commander Louis Mountbatten. A pleasure to meet you. I'm so glad you could join us.'

When they sat down, Frank's brain was working overtime but he remained cool. The name rang a bell and then he suddenly understood. Mountbatten was an English lord and a member of the British Royal Family. He ignored his thoughts and concentrated on the spoken English whilst regaining his composure.

His voice was polite and he composed his words carefully. 'Thank you gentlemen. ... Eh, yes. ... I'm a Dutch businessman. ... I have a timber factory to the north in the province of Friesland.'

The blue eyes looked at him again. 'Ah yes, *meneer*. Friesland ... I sailed many times on the Friesian lakes and my ship has been close to your islands in recent weeks. Friesland is a delightful province. You must be very proud of it?'

Before Frank could think, he started jabbering on about the lakes and the sea and other things Friesian. His chatter was interrupted by the wine waiter arriving at his shoulder.

The same quiet voice, '*Meneer*, would you like to join us for wine?'

Frank shook his head and smiled into the blue eyes. 'Thank you, no. I don't drink alcohol. Iced water will be fine for me.'

The soup arrived and the conversation was excellent. Families were discussed, sailing and the sea kept cropping up; but no mention of

Germany. Eventually Frank could not resist. As the last course arrived, he waited for a lull in the conversation. When it came he asked the question firmly. 'Sir, may I ask if you think that war is coming to Holland?'

All conversation immediately stopped. All eyes turned to the captain. He smiled politely and steepled his fingers. The broad gold rings of his rank gleamed on the dark sleeve.

'Mr van der Meer,' he paused, the other three diners glanced across the room. He continued in his quiet authoritative voice, 'In my opinion, total war in Europe is inevitable. I don't think that *Herr* Hitler will stop at your borders or, indeed, at the Channel. At this very moment, his ships are laying thousands of mines not ten kilometres from where we sit.' There was total silence. 'In three hours time, my ship will sail from harbour and attempt to disable those mines.' Another pause, he stood up, glanced around the room and raised his glass. 'Ladies and gentlemen. I give you a toast.' Everybody rose from their chairs. The hotel staff appeared in the doorways leading to the dining-room. Lord Louis Mountbatten did not need his uniform to give him that indefinable air of authority. His voice was calm and commanded immediate respect. 'God save Queen Wilhelmina of the Netherlands and King George of Great Britain.' The glasses lifted and the silence continued. Frank's heart skipped a beat as he raised the glass to his lips.

FOUR

Oberleutnant Ernst Kraft stood rigidly to attention. The pale blue uniform was immaculate and the late afternoon sun reflected off his gleaming jackboots. At his side were the remainder of his five-man crew, behind them, cleared for flight, was their twin-engined Heinkel 111 bomber.

The *Staffel* was ready. Nine He 111s' parked in perfect order down the taxi-way at the airfield near Emden. Their crews stood rigidly to attention as the *Luftwaffe* band played martial music. They were about to be inspected by the Chief of Staff of the German Air Force, *Generalmajor* Hans Jeschonnek.

The open top Mercedes-Benz car shone in the late afternoon sun and the journey round the aircraft and their crews was timed to take just fifteen minutes. The *Generalmajor* had already inspected four other airfields during the day and his Junkers 52 transport aircraft was waiting for him with its engines running at the end of the runway. The car was scheduled to make only two stops on its brief passage round the airfield. The first had already been made and the second was right next to *Oberleutnant* Kraft's crew. The band was at its loudest and drowned out the sound of the waiting aircraft.

He knew the military etiquette. When the Chief of Staff approached he remained staring straight ahead. His *Staffelkapitän* was with the inspecting group as they approached him.

'Sir, may I introduce *Oberleutnant* Ernst Kraft and his crew.'

Ernst remained ramrod stiff and saluted. The salute was briskly returned.

The Chief of Staff smiled. 'Please relax. What did you do before you flew Heinkels, *Oberleutnant*?' The voice was firm with a trace of comradeship.

'*Herr Generalmajor*, I was a maths teacher in Berlin.'

The staff officer nodded, reminding himself that time was short. 'What is your mission tomorrow?'

'*Herr Generalmajor*, the *Gruppe* take-off at 06.00 hours tomorrow, 10th May. My *Staffel* is to attack and bomb the Dutch airfield at Leeuwarden, in the province of Friesland.'

There was no enlarging of the facts. As he turned and walked back to his car, the Chief of Staff knew all the planned missions. He was in direct communication with *Luftflotte II* under the command of *Generalfeldmarschall* Kesselring. The *Generalmajor* knew it was going to succeed. The might of *Luftflotte II* was supporting von Bock's Army Group B in the north. They could not fail. He smiled grimly at the flashing salutes as the car made its way to the waiting aircraft.

As he climbed into the Junkers, he turned and glanced round at the assembled smiling faces of his senior officers gathered at the bottom of the metal steps. He sensed total victory from his men and felt sorry for the Dutch. They would be unable to hold back this flood that was going to be unleashed on them in the next twenty-four hours.

FIVE

Frank hardly slept on that night of May 9th 1940. He quickly stepped over to the windows and pulled back the curtains and opened the shutters. The bright early morning sunlight made him blink. There was some traffic below the hotel and the first horse and carts were beginning to clatter up and down the streets. He yawned, turned, and took off his pyjama-top ready to wash at the small hand-basin in his room. The water was cold and woke him up. The dry fluffy towel invigorated his skin. He stared at his face in the mirror. His eyes were bright and his skin glowed. It seemed to him that each moment of this morning was fresh and sharp. He was precise in his movements and every few minutes he was drawn back to the window. Each time he checked what was happening in the wakening streets below. Frank could not understand why he was feeling so unusually awake.

He thought it was the sound of a heavy canal boat, but this noise was a high pitched roar with a deep droning base. He could not place it and he stepped over to the window to see what could be causing the noise. The sight before him made his heart hammer and he knew why he had not slept. The deep blue sky above Rotterdam was full of patches of aircraft; bombers, fighters. All in perfect serrated formations. All marked clearly with the black cross of Germany. All obviously flying to assigned targets. As he stared out of the window, below him the streets became filled with people. Some stepping out of cars and buses, some still in night clothes, others running, not knowing where to go. Most were paralysed by what they saw in front of their eyes. Frank could not move as he watched the nightmare unfold before him. Suddenly puffs of smoke and flashes of gunfire were in the sky. It looked as though somebody was resisting. He caught the reflections of the twisting and turning wings, Dutch fighters by the look of it. One was so low as it flashed by he caught sight of the roundels on the wings, red white and blue, markings of the British Royal Air Force. What Frank was looking at was a Hawker Hurricane fighter of 22 Squadron based in northern Belgium. It was being chased by a German Messerschmitt fighter.

As he stared through the open window he jumped as the hotel manager rushed into his room and jabbed him on the shoulder. '*Meneer*, it's the invasion ... The Germans are everywhere ...' His breath came in short gasps and his words rattled against Frank's ears. 'There're parachutists landing at Waalhaven airfield south of the city ... My God, what can we do?'

Frank, in a flash, realised that if the Germans were attacking the airfield at Rotterdam then they would certainly be attacking the airfield at Leeuwarden. For a moment he panicked and stopped listening to the terrified hotel manager, the insistent tugging at his sleeve brought him back to earth.

'*Meneer ... meneer* ... look! ... look over there!' A shaking finger pointed to the far distance. There were bombs dropping somewhere near the main bridges over the River Maas. They could see them dropping from the bombers. Clusters of black specks falling to the ground and then followed by mushrooming clouds of dense black smoke. Within a few seconds the dull thump of the explosions reached them and they stood stock-still, utterly helpless to do anything but watch.

The noise of confusion rose from the streets below. People were still rushing around but the streets were now full of sirens from police and military vehicles as they drove to unseen destinations. Frank thought it strange that the ships and canal boats were still plying up and down the river and the canals. It made him realise that he still had an appointment. His personal self-discipline took over. He glanced at his watch; eight o'clock. He turned to look at the manager at his side who could do nothing but stare fixedly through the window. With incredulity Frank saw four sea planes land on the river. They taxied to the shore and disgorged German troops. He shook his head.

Frank struggled to control himself and said gently, 'Is breakfast ready yet?' No answer. He repeated the question.

The normality of his request in the midst of the nightmare brought the manager to his senses. His jaw opened as he tried to speak. He closed it and swallowed, his face chalky white. The voice shook. 'Ja, *meneer*, ... it should be. I'll go and check.'

Outside the sound of the bombers was beginning to fade, the sky was still a deep blue and, here and there, spirals of dense smoke gushed upwards. The roar of aircraft was replaced by the clamour on the streets. For some reason Frank began automatically to pack his suitcase. His brain was whirling with worry. His first thought was for his family.

A knock came at the door. A woman's voice came through the wooden panels.

'Breakfast is ready now, *meneer*.'

There were only three people waiting for breakfast and only one table laid. There was no sign of the British officers. Frank sat down and smiled calmly at the nervous guests. It was his nature to be cool under pressure. For a moment nothing happened and then they all started at once.

'The wireless said that the Germans were invading on all fronts ...'

'I heard from a man that the Government has fled from The Hague in a British navy ship ...'

'Our men are fighting and did you know that the Germans have invaded Belgium and France? ...'

'The telephones aren't working ...'

This last comment made Frank sit up. His quiet voice stopped the conversation. 'Excuse me, ... did you say the telephones were out? How do you know that?'

The smaller man of the three looked at him, 'I tried earlier ... before breakfast. The operator told me that all lines could only be used by officials. Many lines have been destroyed. They're having to use radio in some parts of the city.'

They all stopped talking as the manager entered and switched on the big Philips wireless-set in the corner of the restaurant. The sound of the Dutch National Anthem *"Wilhelmus van Nassau"* echoed around the empty room. Everybody stood, nobody spoke, each with his own private thoughts. When the music stopped the background crackle was soon replaced by an announcer.

'This is a special report from Radio Hilversum. This morning at seven o'clock German military forces invaded the Netherlands on all fronts.'

There was a long pause and the people at the table glanced self-consciously at each other.

'Bombers and fighters have attacked all airfields and landing grounds. Parachutists are landing in Rotterdam, airfields at Waalhaven, south of Rotterdam and Valkenburg, near Den Haag. The German Navy has shelled shore positions and their ships have continued laying mines in our coastal waters. British and Belgian military forces are assisting wherever possible. Our men are fighting against heavy odds. We are making tactical withdrawals wherever necessary. All males with previous military experience are asked to report to their local town halls as quickly as possible. Her Majesty Queen Wilhelmina asks that the Dutch people remain in their homes and to wait for future radio bulletins. The Government is limiting all non-essential journeys. We do not yet know which parts of our country have been occupied by German forces. Further information bulletins will be given every half hour.'

The National Anthem continued and the manager reached forward to turn down the volume.

The table was set with plates full of wafer thin slices of red meat and half round balls of red Edam and yellow Gouda cheese. Heavy chunks of dark bread and small oblongs of black granular *roggebrood* were piled-up on wooden platters. Fresh juices and hot dark coffee stood ready in the middle of the table. Everybody looked at the food in front of them but nobody started to eat.

Again Frank took the initiative. 'Gentlemen. Shall we pray?' Without hesitation heads bowed for a few precious moments of private peace.

'Amen', he said quietly. But still nobody began. 'Gentlemen! Come on, I think this may be the last good meal that we'll eat together today. Let's enjoy it.' They all nodded and hands reached forward to fill their plates.

One of the men spoke, 'And what, *meneer*, do you intend to do today?' All eyes looked at Frank.

He gave a brief smile, 'I'm not sure. I must contact my family and I must try and return to Friesland.'

The smaller man spoke again, 'I live in Arnhem and you can bet that the Germans have taken my town. After all, it's only fifteen kilometres from the border. I came by train and I doubt if it's running to schedule today!' There was a half-hearted smile from the men. The excellent time-keeping of the Dutch railway system was well known.

'I'm fortunate, I live only thirty kilometres away. I'll leave straight after breakfast,' said one of the other men.

Frank thought as he ate. There was now very little noise outside the hotel and nobody was speaking at the table. After a few minutes he stopped eating and looked up. The other men glanced at him expectantly. He smiled. 'Well, gentlemen, if the Germans are going to occupy our country, then business life will surely have to continue. We must carry on with our businesses.' There was a nodding of heads.

The first man spoke again, 'That may be so. But, I'm Jewish and from what I hear about life in occupied Poland, I don't fancy my chances of running a business!' More nods with no comments.

Frank continued, 'I can't sit in here all day and so, in a few minutes, I'm going to make my way to the docks and see if my cargo of timber has arrived. Then I'm going home ... if I can!'

As he spoke the hotel manager hovered near his guests and poured out the coffee. The aroma of the strong Mocha wafted around the table. The routine of coffee drinking is strong in Holland and each man at the table silently poured in the creamy milk and added tiny crystals of brown sugar.

'Gentlemen,' said the manager with a gentle smile on his face, 'the hotel will remain open. If you can't get home today, then I'll keep your rooms reserved for you.'

This comment re-assured Frank. He stood, 'Thank you, *meneer*. I'll leave my things in my room. Gentlemen, please excuse me.' He turned and left the room, his fellow guests sipped their coffee.

The Austin was just where he had parked it. The streets were strangely quiet. The police and the military were nowhere in sight. He sat in his car, its veneered wood dashboard and leather seats were familiarly reassuring. After switching on the ignition, the engine started at the first pull and he engaged first gear and pulled away from the hotel.

It was only a kilometre to the dock where his import agent was based. It was a journey he had made many times and as he turned into the entrance to the dock area, he saw with some dismay that the dock gates were wide open with no sign of the security guards. He slowed down to walking speed and drove carefully towards Number 3 Dock. It was a beautiful day and the seagulls were in their usual positions. There was not a person in sight and Frank became acutely concerned about his safety and thought about turning back. His stubbornness showed again and he continued the short drive towards the dock. Ships of all sizes were moored along the quay side. Nothing moved, even the canal barges had stopped.

For the first time, in Frank's experience, the Port of Rotterdam was silent.

He braked gently to a stop. For some reason he did not want the brakes to squeal. He climbed out of the car and walked to the door leading to the office. "*van Zuiden Exportbedrijf*" had been in business for many years and the van der Meer factory had benefited from their experience and knowledge of timber. The door to the office was open. Frank knocked and entered. There was nobody around, the room was empty. He walked towards the stairs leading to the manager's office. As he placed his foot on the first stair, he jumped with surprise. The door at the top suddenly opened and a frightened young woman appeared.

'*Meneer* van der Meer. We really didn't expect you to come this morning. *Meneer* van Zuiden is in his office. Please go straight in.'

The office smelt of timber, light pines mixed with heavy tropical. The desk was as big as the man seated behind it.

Albert van Zuiden stood and said excitedly, 'Frank van der Meer, you're the last man I expected here this morning.' He hesitated, and a smile dawned on his face. 'Although, on second thoughts, and knowing you, I should have guessed that you'd be here, and on time as well!' He offered his hand across the desk. 'You're more than welcome.' His face quickly changed. 'Before you sit down, come and look through the window.' The view stretched along the full length of the quay. Three ships were moored, waiting silently. The two men stared down at the scene in front of them. 'Frank, your cargo of timber arrived yesterday from Sweden. How it arrived I don't know, the entrance to the port is heavily mined. Only this morning I was told by a barge skipper that a British Royal Navy ship that was mine-sweeping was nearly sunk by a mine. Apparently, it's limping back towards England.'

Frank's stomach churned and he shook his head, 'Oh no. I think last night I had dinner with the captain of that ship and his officers. God help them.'

For a moment the room became quiet. Albert pointed through the window to the far end of the dock. 'If you look carefully towards the stern of that last ship, you'll see the reason why there's nobody about but us.'

In the bright sunshine, and clear to see, were about twenty German soldiers dressed in light blue jump smocks with steel helmets on their heads. They waited near a pile of timber. Two heavy machine guns poked round the sides of the pile, their ugly muzzles pointing directly at the office window. The soldiers looked completely at ease and there was no opposition.

Albert nodded towards the leather couch. 'I stayed at work last night and I was awake before the bombers came. I stood in this window and watched those bastards parachute down and land exactly where they are now. Not a shot was fired and they even brought sandwiches and a hot drink.' He handed over a pair of binoculars, 'Have a look for yourself.'

Frank pushed the binoculars against his eyes. The image was fuzzy but, with a quick twirl of the focusing knob, the image swung into view. The soldiers were casual in their attitude. They were eating sandwiches and one of them was drinking a bottle of beer. There were four men posted near the dock. Each had a sub-machine gun. Their rear was covered by the heavier weapons. As Frank took in the scene, he inhaled sharply.

Albert noticed, 'What's the matter?'

'I'm watching them, and one of them is watching me with his binoculars. ... Oh no! They've seen me.... They're moving towards us!' Four soldiers began to edge down the dock side dodging from side to side between mooring ropes and cargoes. Frank turned to his friend, 'They'll be here in two minutes. .... We've better do something!'

Albert pulled Frank away from the window. 'I suggest nothing. If we run they may shoot us down.' Both men nodded and sat and waited.

They did not have to wait long. The outside door opened quietly and the sound of heavy boots moved around downstairs. Both men looked at each other. Sweat lightly covered Frank's face. He tried to appear composed but his heart was racing. Albert looked calm and his hands trembled. gripping them harder made them worse. The heavy tread of boots on the stairs and suddenly the door smashed back against the wall.

The two men were tall. There was no indication of rank on their blue jump smocks. The taller man had a vicious looking 9mm sub-machine gun crooked in his arm. The other man held a similar weapon pointed directly at the two seated men. The muzzle moved in a slow arc from Frank to Albert and back again. Nobody moved, each man sizing up the men in front of him. The German's presence was terrifying.

The taller man spoke first. His voice was not unfriendly. '*Guten Morgen, meine Herren.*'

Frank and Albert both spoke German. Frank rose, the muzzle motioned him back towards the couch. He sat down.

Frank tried to appear composed, he opened his mouth but nothing came out. The Germans lowered their weapons. The soldier tried again, 'Good morning.'

Without thinking Frank said angrily, 'And what the hell do you think you're doing in Holland?' The guns rose again.

'*Meine Herren.*' Surprisingly the man smiled. 'We are following orders. Can we help you please?'

Frank could not resist, 'Yes, you can. Clear off out of my country!' There was anger on his face.

The German looked surprised. 'My men are taking over the whole of this dock. You must leave now.'

Before they could reply the other door in the office flew open and there stood Albert's secretary. The soldiers reacted instantly; one whirled round and crouched with his weapon at the ready; the other took one step forward and pushed the woman hard against the side of the door.

The taller twisted her arm sharply up her back, the echoing scream was cut off as he slapped her hard across the face. Albert was on his feet in an instant, but before he could take one stride to help he was knocked to the ground by the butt of the machine-gun. The scene was frozen, nobody moved. The weapons pointed unerringly.

After what seemed like minutes, but in fact was only a few seconds, the soldier said quietly, 'You have five minutes to leave this office and the docks.' He let go of the woman and she collapsed on the floor. Both men backed through the doorway and down the stairs.

Frank looked at his friend. Albert was slumped on the floor bleeding from a gash to his forehead. Frank leaned across to help and placed a handkerchief across the wound. The woman sat and stared. Frank spoke gently. 'Don't worry, they've gone away.' They were all conscious of the time limit that the German had set.

Albert slowly stood and grasped the back of a chair. 'We'd better leave as soon as possible.' He smiled at his secretary. 'Come on Ellie give yourself a shake.' He walked over to her. She smiled and slowly they made their way down the stairs.

The car was exactly where Frank had left it, he opened the rear door for Ellie, she climbed in and flopped onto the seat. He stared around. There were more Germans. This time they had removed their parachutists' smocks. Frank knew enough about the Dutch fascist uniforms to know that some of the soldiers were *Waffen-SS* troops. He could clearly see the silver runic flashes on the collars of their field grey uniforms. The troops were spread out across the entrance to the dock, their faces were impassive and they looked sharply at the car. The engine started and he slowly drove towards the line of men and the dock gates. When he was within touching distance of the line of field grey uniforms, interspersed with the lighter blue of the *Fallschirmjäger* airborne troops, they parted and he passed slowly through. The eyes under the rims of the steel helmets followed him as the car drove through the dock gates.

Nobody spoke as he drove down the deserted road. He thought for a moment that the next line of soldiers was another group of SS troops. This time he pushed his foot hard down on the accelerator. The car jumped forward straight at the line of approaching men.

Albert's voice shouted in his right ear, 'Stop, for Christ's sake! They're ours!'

He jabbed his foot hard onto the brakes and yanked up the handbrake. The car stopped an arm's length from the line of men.

'*Meneer*, where are you going to?' The British Sten gun re-enforced the question. Frank glanced along the men. They were a mixture of about fifty Dutch and British soldiers. Each was well armed and they looked as though they knew what they were doing.

He wound down the window, 'We're going to the Maas Hotel about a kilometre from here.'

The soldier nodded. 'Pass, *meneer*.' He waved them through the line.

Frank began to drive on, thought for a minute and reversed back towards them. The weary looking Dutch officer came up to the car. '*Kapitein* ... if you go back to Number 3 Dock, then be careful, there's about twenty German *Waffen-SS* in there. They've heavy machine guns and look well armed.'

'Thanks a lot ... we'll find them. Look out for about half a kilometre ahead. There's a small battle going on. Turn left here and then double back. Stop and wait if you see any action. Be careful, *meneer*, and good luck!'

Frank drove on carefully with both windows wound down and ears straining for the slightest sound of gunfire. Within two minutes he stopped. From behind them came the clatter of small arms fire and staccato bursts of heavy machine guns.

Frank said aloud, with some satisfaction, 'I think the Germans have met our men.' He shook his head and carried on. The three people in the car were silent as it slowly ground its way in first gear along the deserted road. There was the sound of gunfire but none within their sight.

The hotel looked totally deserted as they dashed up the steps. The doors were locked but a quick hammering on the glass brought the porter.

The manager was waiting and he was anxious, 'Come in, *meneer* van der Meer. Are you and your friends all right? Is there anybody hurt? ... Please sit down.'

The hotel was empty. Without thinking Frank straightened his tie and smoothed back his hair. His natural authority took over. 'Bring some hot water and something for this man's head. Strong coffee would be welcome.' The manager nodded and hurried away towards the kitchen.

For the first time Ellie spoke, '*Meneer* van der Meer, thank you for your help. I think it was just shock.' She looked at both men sitting opposite her. 'What are we going to do now?' There was fear on her young face.

The manager returned and walked quietly towards Frank, he raised his hand and broke the silence. 'Wait a minute, listen. They're going to broadcast a message from the Queen.' He walked over to the large Philips wireless-set. He turned up the volume, the static cleared.

The voice was clear and precise.

"My people.

After our country has, with scrupulous conscientiousness, preserved strict neutrality for all these months, and whilst we had no intention other than to adhere to this absolutely and consistently, the German Army last night, without the slightest warning, launched a sudden attack against our territory. This occurred in spite of the solemn undertaking that the neutrality of our country would be respected as long as we ourselves respected it. I hereby issue a fiery protest against this unexampled violation of good faith against the outrage done to conduct customary behaviour between civilised nations. My government and I

will now also do our duty. All of you must do yours, everywhere and in all circumstances, each one in the place assigned to you, with the utmost vigilance and with the tranquillity of mind and the assurance to which a clear conscience gives you every right."

The radio fell silent and the manager reached forward and switched it off.

SIX

His batman woke him at 03.00 hours with a cup of hot coffee. For a moment *Oberleutnant* Ernst Kraft lay back in his bed and stared at the ceiling before he realised that this was the day that he would take part in his first action of the war.

'Thank you, Hans,' was all he could say.

He quickly washed and put on his blue *Luftwaffe* uniform. He followed the instructions of his flight commander and left the envelope containing his last will and testament on top of the chest of drawers at the side of his bed. His flying boots fitted perfectly, a glance in the mirror and a tug at his thinning blonde hair and he was ready.

The walk to the operations room normally took fifteen minutes. But today there was a spring in his step and he tried not to appear to be too enthusiastic as he left the officers' block. It was a beautiful morning, dawn was streaking the clear sky and were the stars still shone brightly. The *Luftwaffe* station was unusually busy. All personnel ensuring that the aircraft would be ready to take-off on the scheduled hour. Timing was essential, the whole attack on Holland and Belgium was part of the *Blitzkrieg* technique; fast, organised movement of men, machinery and supplies.

The *Gruppe* briefing room was already packed. Everybody was talking and their chatter was almost drowned out by the martial music playing over two huge speakers at the front of the room. There were a hundred and twenty airmen squeezed into the hall, blue cigar and cigarette smoke swirled everywhere. The windows were wide open but nobody felt the chill on this particular morning.

Ernst sat next to another bomber captain and said quietly, 'Well, Johann, it's all happening now.'

A quick nod was the only reply. Before Ernst could say any more, two officers walked onto the raised platform at the front of the hall. Without any request the talking immediately stopped. The taller of the two men snapped out an order, with a scraping of chairs and a bout of nervous coughing everybody stood stiffly to attention.

A senior officer entered through the doors at the back of the hall and walked down the central aisle. *Oberst* Hans Teske was the *Fliegerführer* for the whole area under his command in this part of Germany. He knew the complete plans for *Fall Gelb* and he was about to give some of the details to his men.

He stepped smartly onto the platform and turned slowly round to face the aircrews. There was absolute silence. His voice was quiet but pin sharp. 'Gentlemen, we have been given the task of bombing the airfields in the north of Holland. This we will do for the glory of the *Führer* and the *Reich*.' He paused and there was a great cheer. His voice rose. 'Our armies are ready........ 2,500 aircraft, 136 German divisions and 20,000 airborne troops under the command of *Generalmajor* Kurt Student, all are on the move ... Even now, as I speak, our men are advancing into Holland and Belgium. ... Nothing can stop us. ... The enemy cannot match us. We will take Belgium and Holland within a day. The British and the French can only advance through France itself as they think we will accept Belgium neutrality.' There was another pause and another cheer. His voice continued to rise, 'The Dutch and the Belgians will present no opposition. By tomorrow we will be able to advance upon France and our men will be ready to take that country as well. ... This morning I want you to fly to your targets, bomb them and return to re-arm and bomb them again.' The voice quietened and he stared round the briefing room. 'Now, gentlemen, please sit. Your *Staffelkapitäne* will give the final briefing.' The crews sat. Not a word was spoken.

The officer was small and compact but he commanded immediate respect. He spoke quietly, in contrast to the previous speaker. '*Staffel* 1 will start engines at 06.00 hours. Take-off in flights of three aircraft will commence at 06.15 hours. You will steer the set course as laid down in your briefing instructions. Guns will be tested over the Ems estuary as ordered by your *Flugzeugführer*. Bombs will be armed five minutes before the target is observed. There is no need to observe radio silence.' He paused for effect, 'There will be no opposition. Bomb on line of sight. The weather forecast is clear and the target is only twenty-five minutes from this base. Gentlemen ... all stand ... ATTENTION!' He turned to the *Oberst* at his side. The man nodded and walked to the front of the platform.

He sprang to attention and the right arm pivoted upwards from the waist and his hand extended flatly downwards from the outstretched arm. It quivered with tension.

The voice was at full pitch and the eyes stared straight ahead. '*HEIL HITLER!*' The room echoed to the rafters with the response.

Ernst led his five man crew out of the briefing room to the waiting transport. The *Kübelwagen* just about fitted them all in and his navigator drove the small open car across the grass towards the waiting aircraft. This particular Heinkel 111 bomber was almost new but Ernst was one of the many pilots who had flown the aircraft type in the Spanish Civil War. The raid on Guernica had taught him much about bombing undefended civilian targets.

As he climbed the steps into the fuselage, his mind whirled with the details of the mission. There were nagging thoughts about bombing a neutral country and his military training did not stop such thoughts continually re-occurring. He knew he was good at his job, only six months previously the High Command had recalled him from his teaching position in Berlin. Ernst took all the commendations that his skills brought to him but his soul told him that he was not a Nazi. He obeyed orders and led his men. But, beyond that, he yearned to be back in his classroom. A thump on the back brought him back to his mission.

His co-pilot smiled across the cockpit at him. He nodded and they started the litany of aircraft checks. Ernst glanced out of the window to his left and waved to one of the ground-crew. The wave was returned and Ernst pointed to the starboard engine. With a clicking of voltage regulators and a whine of starter motors, the propeller of the Junkers Jumo engine slowly rotated. There was a puff of smoke and the beginnings of a high-pitched roar and within a few seconds the beat of the engine had settled down to a steady throb. The port engine started without any problems and the checks continued.

The co-pilot shook Ernst's arm. Away to the left of the airfield a green flare arced into the dawn sky. He nodded, gently opened the throttles and released the undercarriage brakes. The He 111 slowly moved forward from its parking area. The other two aircraft in the flight followed him along the taxiway. His aircraft was the first to take-off and, as he taxied, he felt a stab of excitement as the other thirty aircraft in his *Gruppe* slowly followed him towards the runway.

Another green flare gave the signal. He applied the undercarriage brakes and opened the throttles to maximum power. The aircraft was transformed into a living, shaking being. The roar of the two synchronised engines was totally deafening and the airframe shook and seemed to be crouching back against the confining effects of the brakes. Both pilots glanced at each other and nodded. Ernst released the brakes and the Heinkel leapt forward, free to fly. The airspeed indicator slowly began to creep round the dial, the vibrations on the flight deck lessened, the control columns began to lighten and within a minute, the tail-plane lifted the aircraft into its horizontal flying position. A sharp glance at the dials and Ernst knew that this was the moment. He gently pulled back the control column and braced his feet on the rudder bars. The end of the runway rose clearly into sight and, slowly but surely, the heavily laden Heinkel lifted free from its earthly confines. The thrill of flight for Ernst was ecstatic. He steered the aircraft tightly away from the end of the runway and began to circle, slowly gaining height. Through the window he could see the other Heinkels rising to meet him. Again, non-military thoughts flashed through his mind, so much beauty but with death as its mission.

Within ten minutes the *Gruppe* had assembled and began to fly off on the assigned route towards northern Holland. The dark waters of the Ems estuary reflected the fleeting shadows of the bombers as they flashed across the river. The chatter of the guns testing all round him made his skin prickle when, for a misjudged moment, he thought his aircraft was under attack. The steady drone of the engines settled and he concentrated on arriving on target at the correct time and in the right place. His position as flight commander made him bombing leader and his face was set against his oxygen mask. He automatically made slight adjustments to the aircraft track as the navigator fed route details to him through his headset. Time to target was only thirty minutes from base and Ernst felt that same twinge of guilt when he realised that he was flying over neutral Holland. The navigator continued intoning the route and times and the bomb aimer crept into his lonely position.

The flat land of the Friesian countryside was spring green and the sky a deep blue. The bright sun behind the aircraft cast long shadows on the ground and the shadows seemed to point arrow straight towards the target.

Underneath the leather flying gloves his hands became slippery with sweat, a normal reaction for Ernst: the remainder of his body was ice cold. The bomb aimer informed him that it was ten minutes to target. He realised that he was sitting on top of four two hundred and fifty kilos fully armed bombs, a disconcerting thought. All too quickly the target loomed into view.

The airfield near Leeuwarden was a grass strip. Rarely was it used by the Royal Netherlands Air Force, but this time two ageing Fokker biplanes had been hurriedly re-located to this remote part of Holland. On this particular morning intelligence had warned them of the massing of German forces near to the eastern border. Two ancient biplanes against the might of the *Luftwaffe*. It seemed that their position was symbolic of Holland's readiness for total war.

As the German air armada emerged over the flat horizon, the two Fokkers rose into the air to meet it. They skimmed over the trees and the deserted canals and slowly climbed to attack.

The leading Heinkel flashed over the countryside, its bomb doors wide open and ready to release the load of high explosive. Ernst's face was pale and drawn. For him this was the culmination of all the planning. He could only stare at the stretch of green grass below him. There were few buildings to attack and the aircraft continued to streak down its bombing line. His total concentration was shattered by the gunner above screaming down his headset. Shaking his head in disbelief, he scanned the horizon from side to side.

He shouted aloud, 'SOMETHING IS ACTUALLY ATTACKING MY AIRCRAFT!'

He knew it was impossible, military intelligence had told him so. The Heinkel lurched upwards as the bombs released. From the corner of his eye there was the fleeting glint of gun fire coming towards him from above and not from the ground. For a moment Ernst actually saw the rounds flying towards him. An ancient biplane twinkled past the nose of the Heinkel. His lungs sucked in oxygen through the face mask and his mouth froze open in shock. Three of his crew were shouted something about fighters, but again his brain informed him that the Dutch were not going to resist.

The first indication of the attack was the instrument panel shattering before his eyes. A jet of blood sprayed across his goggles and the redness made him involuntarily blink.

He screamed into his oxygen mask. 'JESUS CHRIST, I'M DYING.' But nobody heard him.

It was not his blood, he knew that for sure. In this brief moment of time the realisation of his aircraft being hit crashed through his consciousness. All was chaos. The co-pilot was a bloody mess, nobody else was shouting. The Heinkel stood on its nose and his eyes registered square fields that seemed to be getting bigger by the second. Training took over. With a jerk he smashed his fist into the release toggle of his seat harness. As he burst clear of the seat, he had the sense to push the bloody goggles off his face and tear himself loose from the oxygen pipe. The shattering roar of the engines and the rush of air told him that the front of the cockpit was missing. With a grunt of effort he fell sideways towards the floor of the fuselage. For some reason unknown to him, the emergency escape hatch was open. It probably saved his life. The Heinkel hit an air pocket and he lurched forward and fell through the hole, for one moment he thought there was no parachute. Again conditioning made him reach for the D-ring to release the silk canopy from its pouch. Ernst was falling and falling and falling. Suddenly there was a crack and the parachute blossomed open above his feet.

Silence everywhere. He stared at his feet above him. The feet made him understand that he was upside down. Somehow he had become entangled in the parachute shroud lines. With a massive heave he called out in the stillness of the morning.

'WRONG, WRONG! I MUST GET FREE!'

A shout of pain and he swung his legs over and through the nylon lines. At last he was gently swinging in the correct position below the green canopy. He hastily swivelled his head round from one side and kicked his body to the right. The view around him registered as quickly as a snap shot. Below him the fields were looming ever larger, to his left were mushrooming black clouds showing exactly where the bombs had struck. Even now other aircraft were delivering their bomb loads. Flying straight at him was a biplane with a single machine gun hammering away above the roar of its engine. He flinched as it passed over the parachute. Within a few seconds he saw tracer fly from a Heinkel belonging to his *Staffel*. The biplane had no chance. Its wings folded as neatly as a butterfly and it plummeted to earth in flames. He was a spectator to death and helpless to do anything.

The ground suddenly hit him hard and his legs folded under the impact. In the still of the morning the parachute canopy collapsed over him like a shroud and he lay motionless.

At first, Ernst thought he was unconscious. The green glow all around him made his situation unreal. For some unknown reason he turned to look at his watch: from attack to ground had taken no more than four minutes. An agonising stab of pain made him cry out. He felt towards the source of the agony. His left leg was thoroughly broken and a piece of his shin bone stuck out bloodily above his flying boots. He felt no pain, only concern to clear the parachute away from his head. Without any effort the green nylon was suddenly pulled away. Standing like an angel looking down at him was a beautiful blonde girl in a long, white night-dress.

Ernst said simply, 'Please help me?' and then fainted.

SEVEN

Marieke missed Frank more than usual on that particular night. For some reason she could not sleep. It also affected her family because at about five o'clock there was a gentle knock at the bedroom door.

A voice whispered, '*Mem* ... are you awake? Please can I come in?'

Marieke reached for the bedside light. For a moment she was dazzled and then she blinked her eyes to see. 'Yes, Aukje, I'm awake. Come in.'

Aukje crept on to the bed and looked at her mother. 'I couldn't sleep, I don't know why.'

Marieke smiled, she knew her family so well. 'Of course. ... Come on climb into bed with me.'

Aukje laughed sleepily and pushed the covers to one side. 'Oh *Mem* ... this brings memories back. It makes me feel like a little girl again.'

The house was totally silent and even the river outside the window was still. Normally, through the night, barges moved slowly past the house. The family usually slept through all the sounds, but, on this night, everybody seemed to be awake. The unusual silence had woken them.

A few minutes later another knock came at the door. Harmen stood there in his pyjamas. His voice was slurred with tiredness, 'I thought I heard you both talking. I can't sleep either.' He gazed at his mother and his sister. 'What's the matter with us?'.

Marieke looked at both her children. 'Come on, you two. Let's go downstairs and I'll make some hot cocoa. I think it's quite obvious that we're not going to get to sleep again.'

Aukje and her brother followed their mother down the stairs. The fire in the hearth still glowed a deep red and Harmen threw on some more logs. With a crackle and a shower of sparks the fire began to burn with life. They sat on the rug before the open hearth. One light glowed from the corner of the room. The tick of the Friesian clock was the only sound. For some unexplained reason brother and sister had nothing to say to each other.

The door opened, Marieke's voice was full of support. 'Right you two, ... here's the cocoa.'

She sat on the old leather chair near the fire and lowered the tray to the floor. As they leant forward to pick up the hot cups, the first greyness of dawn filtered through the curtains. She crossed the room to pull them open. The river was still and the single light from the house reflected off the black water. Everywhere seemed unnaturally quiet, normally at this time of the morning there was somebody about, even the cows in the fields made some noises at dawn.

Aukje spoke first, '*Mem*, is everything all right? Do you think *Heit* is safe?'

Marieke put her arm round her daughter's shoulder, 'Of course he's all right. He told me that he'd met some British Naval officers and had taken dinner with them. Yes indeed he sounded fine. I think we're all a bit worried about the future, but don't worry, the Netherlands was neutral in the First World War and I can't see us being any different if the war starts in Europe. The British are good friends to this country. They'll always help us if anything does happen.'

So far Harmen had been unusually quiet. '*Mem*, I don't trust the Germans,' he spoke with the clarity of youth, 'I'm sure that something is going to happen.' He stared hard at both of them, 'In fact I know that something is happening. ... I can FEEL it!'

Marieke put her arm on his shoulder. 'Don't be silly, Harmen. We're all a little worried and that's what makes you think too much about these things.'

'But, *Mem*,' said Aukje with a frown, 'I feel the same way.'

The cocoa was finished and they sat together on the long couch facing the windows. The sun was ready to rise and the deep blue of the early sky made everything fresh and new. Marieke stood in the window and looked towards Leeuwarden away to her left. The river in front of her was still and slowly into her view came a single barge. The steady beat of its diesel engine broke the silence. Her ears caught a different sound coming from behind the house. She assumed it was another barge coming the other way, but no, it was of a higher pitch. The heavy drone came nearer.

Marieke turned to her children. 'The *Luchtmacht* are up early this morning I never heard them take-off.'

Harmen joined her at the window. By now the house was beginning to shake with the noise. He had to shout. 'I've never heard this sound before, *Mem*. It's new to me.'

In front of them they watched two small aircraft take-off from the nearby airfield. They roared over the house just missing the trees. Marieke pushed open the windows and, in bare feet, they all stepped out into the garden. The grass was damp, but they did not notice. The whole sky echoed with noise. Shadows flashed past them. The horizon seemed filled with aircraft of different sizes and shapes. Quite suddenly the air was filled with the harsh thunder of explosions, cannon flashes from the smaller aircraft showed the attacker. The van der Meer family stood and watched. They were utterly helpless.

Marieke shouted above the cacophony of noise, 'Oh my God. They're German.' Her words grabbed away by the roar of engines.

They stood in the garden watching the bombers gather like locusts over the airfield. They saw it all. The bombs dropping like black confetti; the clouds of heavy smoke; the dull crump of explosions. They felt the ground shake as the bombs hit their targets. They were speechless. Aukje pointed at one of the aircraft. Above them one of the black bombers seemed to disintegrate. A single parachute emerged from its flames and drifted slowly downwards straight at the van der Meer house.

Aukje put her hand to her mouth. '*Mem* ... I'm going to see the parachute.'

Before her mother could say anything, Aukje darted through the garden and towards the timber yard. Marieke van der Meer was speechless, but she followed her daughter.

As the man hit the ground he let out a scream of pain. For a moment Aukje watched as the canopy flowed downwards and covered him. Without a moments hesitation she scrambled into the still billowing green nylon and began frantically to pull it to one side.

She stared at him. Blood was everywhere. His leg stuck up into the air at a painful angle. The concrete yard was hard and he lay in a difficult position unable to move.

His face was surprised and he looked at her. He only said one sentence, 'Please help me?'

She stared hard into his eyes and then her mother took over.

The voice was quiet but firm and her son had arrived. 'Harmen! Get the wheelbarrow from the factory. We must get him into the house. Don't touch him, his leg is broken.'

He hesitated and said with some venom, '*Mem*, why should we help him. The swine's just bombed our town?'

Marieke just turned and looked him straight in the eyes. 'Oh son, have you learnt nothing in church? This man has asked for our help and he'll get it.' She smiled and placed her hand on his shoulder. 'Now go on, do as I say. Please get the wheelbarrow.'

A frown crossed his face and then he nodded and strode off towards the factory.

EIGHT

The evening came quickly in the Maas Hotel. As well as Frank two of the guests from the previous night had returned. They all sat together in the dining room. On this particular night nobody had changed for dinner and they were all waiting for the next radio news bulletin. Albert van Zuiden and his secretary had left to return to their homes. For Frank a bath and something to eat helped him to concentrate. He knew that to return to Leeuwarden at this time would be impossible and, therefore, he desperately tried to contact Marieke and the family, but the telephones were still dead. Outside the hotel the occasional sound of gunfire could be heard and traffic seemed to moving again, but there was still an air of enormous expectancy. The hotel was a haven of peace and security. Nobody came through its revolving doors.

The table in front of him was covered by the traditional Persian carpet. Short stubby glasses of corn-coloured beer had been filled and refilled over the last two hours and, by now, the two other men at the table were becoming slightly drunk. Frank was a member of the Blue Button Society and dedicated never to drink alcohol.

'Well, van der Meer, what're you going to do now?' said the smaller man.

He answered politely. 'I really don't know, gentlemen. I can't get home and I can't telephone, so it looks as though I'm stuck here until something else happens.' He turned to look at the man. 'What about you? Do you have any plans?'

The man took another enormous mouthful of beer. He burped quietly and his eyes were dreamy, '*Ja, meneer*, ... I caught the train and got as far as the outskirts of Dordrecht, a journey of only twenty kilometres, but it took me over an hour. I watched the *moffen* attack the bridge over the River Waal. Bombers, fighters, parachutists, *verdomme*, it was like a nightmare.' He stopped to finish off the glass of beer. The hovering waiter had another one ready on the beer mat. 'I think the train driver must've got a bit worried. A locomotive with clouds of white smoke coming from its stack is quite a difficult thing to hide. The attack on the bridge only took about thirty minutes and then we began to move backwards fairly quickly.' He stopped talking and everybody at the table looked at him. He smiled with a look of fear in his eyes. The man hung over his glass of beer, the others stared at his face. He spoke in a hoarse whisper, 'One of their fighters, I think it was a Messerschmitt, flew at the same height as the train. I could see the pilot in his cockpit, I thought he was going to shoot at me personally ... you know what he did?' They all shook their heads. 'He waved at me, ... at me! I could see his eyes behind his goggles. It was only for a fraction of a second. It made me think, I can tell you. I'll never forget it. I came back here as fast as I could.'

He took a huge swig from the glass. 'And now I'm going to get drunk.'

Frank thought for a moment, 'There's no opposition to them really.' He banged his fist on the table in an uncharacteristic show of temper. 'How can we defend our country? We may be small in size but our frontier is long and most of it backs onto Germany. I'm sure that at this very moment their army is racing across our countryside. We can't do anything to stop them. I know about our defensive lines, but they'll only slow the Germans for a few days.' There was a shaking of heads.

The manager interrupted their conversation. 'Excuse me, gentlemen, I think there's a news broadcast about to start.' The manager walked over to the wireless and turned up the volume. All conversation stopped.

There was the same crackle of static and then the announcer's voice cut clearly across the still dining room.

"This is a special report from Radio Hilversum at eight o'clock Netherlands time."

A slight pause and the sound of rustling paper.

"The Netherlands is being attacked on all fronts. This morning at 10 p.m. Count Von Zech Von Burckersoda, the German Ambassador, handed over the declaration of war to our Foreign Minister. Our Government has not accepted the declaration and has asked for time to make a response. No time limit has been given. German regiments of the *Waffen-SS* and *Fallschirmjäger* airborne troops have taken some positions but our men are fighting back bravely. Units of *Waffen-SS* have taken control of parts of Rotterdam and The Hague. The Government advises all civilians to remain in their homes and not to attempt to move outside unless absolutely necessary. Strong German forces have also attacked Belgium to the South and there is evidence that their forces are moving into France through Belgium.

Further news bulletins will be given when information is available."

There was stunned silence and two glasses of beer were quickly emptied. As the manager sat down with his guests, food arrived at the table. Trays of sandwiches and fresh meats were laid out neatly around the bowl of flowers. The normal evening meal was out of the question. Frank sipped at his tonic water and collected sandwiches onto his plate.

The manager looked apprehensive. 'I heard this afternoon that the German Ambassador actually cried when he spoke to our Foreign Minister. Can you believe that? They bomb us and the bastard cries! ... Our men are fighting back.' He paused. He had the attention of the people at the table. 'Somebody told me that the sluices to the east have been opened and we're flooding roads and railways to stop them.' He waved his fist in the air. 'Fortress Holland is resisting.'

Between mouthfuls of food Frank said, 'Tomorrow, I intend to try and travel back to Friesland. I can't just sit here. I've just got to try!'

One of the men added with a smile, 'I understand, *meneer*. But be careful. Nobody seems to know where the Germans are. Just go carefully.'

Frank agreed and continued to eat his meal. The evening wore on and the men in the restaurant were obviously intent on getting completely drunk. He wanted none of it, and after another hour, he quietly excused himself from the table and left the dining-room.

The bedroom was in darkness and he stood near the open window. The air was still and his nose caught the faintest whiff of burning and another indefinable odour; the stink of war. The docks were quiet and not a ship or a barge was moving. There was no enforced blackout but the streetlights were out and there was little traffic. His mind was strangely at rest, Frank knew he could do no more in Rotterdam, he had to return to his family. Later, as he lay in bed, dreamless sleep came quickly.

He awoke with the dawn chorus and mused that birds sing regardless of war. The hotel was as quiet as the streets outside and he moved out of the room towards the bathroom at the end of the corridor. Without thinking he ran a bath of hot water and lay deep in its enveloping warmth, planning the day in front of him. A gentle knock at the door brought him out of his concentration.

'*Meneer*, please, I must talk to you urgently' The manager's voice was quiet and insistent.

'Yes, of course. Please wait in my room.' Frank dried himself briskly, put on his dressing gown and walked quickly back into his room.

The manager was sitting near the window with a concerned frown crossing his face. He rose as Frank entered.

'*Meneer* van der Meer, I have good news.' He watched his guest's face change with expectancy. 'During the night your wife telephoned the hotel. I was only able to talk to her for a brief minute. She's telephoning back,' he glanced at his wrist watch, 'in about half an hour at seven o'clock. Please take the call in my office. You'll be quite alone.' The manager nodded his head, brushed past Frank and left the room.

He sat with a thump on the bed. His mind was whirling and his logical brain took over. He quickly cold-shaved in the wash-basin and dressed in his best suit. He checked his wrist-watch; five minutes to go, dashed to the door, yanked it open and flew down the stairs to the hotel foyer. There was nobody around and, as he strode towards the manager's office, he heard the shrill ring of the telephone. Without knocking he walked into the office and the manager was smiling at him holding the telephone in his hand.

'*Mevrouw* van der Meer, for you.' He passed the handset over and left.

Frank took a deep breath and spoke first in the quietest of tones, 'Well, *liefje*, how are you and the children?' There was a long pause and for a brief moment he thought the connection had not been made. Then, quite suddenly, he heard Marieke's voice; it was chillingly clear.

'Frank, I'm so glad to hear you. How are you?' Before he could reply she continued and her voice sounded unreal. 'I was worried about you ... yesterday the Germans attacked the airfield near Leeuwarden ... Frank there're German soldiers in the town and one of them is in our house. Please come ho- ....' There was a loud click as her voice was cut off in the middle of her plea. Frank looked at the handset and tears filled his eyes. His shoulders heaved and he slumped into the chair.

NINE

As Ernst began to slowly return to conscious life he soon realised that he was safe, warm and seated in a comfortable leather chair. In front of him was a large open fire, the flames licking up the back of the chimney breast. The pain was intense and it centred on his left leg. He squeezed out a long groan. As he tried to move, his memory flashed back to the sight of the young woman that he had seen watching him under his collapsing parachute. He shook his head, hallucinations did strange things to the imagination. But the fire and the room were real and so was the pain. He moved his arm and touched the leg. The break was bad, even the slightest touch of his fingers on the bandage made him shudder with agony. He could just feel the edges of the bone and he knew he was in trouble.

The slightest movement at the boundary of his vision caused him to glance sideways. Marieke and Aukje were sitting opposite the chair, staring at the German pilot. Nobody spoke. All three sat looking at each other. Nobody moved.

Ernst broke the silence. He spoke in German. Still nobody answered, Aukje shook her head. He realised that probably neither of the two women facing could speak German. Or, if they did, they certainly were not going to speak to him in his mother tongue. His school-teacher English came back to him.

'Please, where am I? Who are you?' His voice was softened by pain and shock.

Marieke stared hard at the young German's pale face. Her English was halting but carried some authority. 'Just sit and be still. You're in a Dutch house not far from the airfield that you bombed.' She paused to gather her vocabulary. 'Your leg is broken and you must rest until help arrives.'

Waves of pain kept flooding across the whole of his body and he was utterly helpless. Marieke leant carefully across his still form and extracted the grey pistol out of the shoulder harness on his uniform. He felt nothing.

Aukje whispered, '*Mem*, why did you take that gun?'

Her mother nodded knowingly and answered quietly, 'Aukje, my dear, men can do strange things when they're in pain.'

Aukje nodded, failing to understand why adults said, and did, certain things.

They sat for a few moments and watched the pilot go from flickering consciousness to open-eyed pain. The knock at the front door made them jump. Their patient hardly stirred. Marieke, still clutching the gun, motioned Aukje to remain quiet and then she rose and walked quickly across the room. Before leaving she stopped near the Friesian clock on the wall and, with only a moment's hesitation, quickly opened the clock's long case and slipped the gun into its dark recesses.

Before opening the front door she glanced through the side window. With an audible sigh of relief, she unbolted the heavy door and opened it wide.

Her voice showed her emotions, 'Jan de Bruin! You don't know how glad I am to see you ... Please, come in.'

Jan was full of questions and his eyes darted over her shoulder, 'Marieke! What's going on here? We saw a parachute land in the factory yard. Are you all right? Where are the children? Have you heard from Frank?' He stopped for breath. Marieke took his arm and guided him in through the front door and closed it behind her. She put a finger to her lips. He obeyed.

'Jan,' she whispered, 'there's an injured German pilot in my living room, and yes, the children are safe. Now please be quiet.' They both stood in silence. Outside the morning was strangely still. There was no sounds of war.

They continued talking in urgent whispers. 'Marieke, if you've got a German in there,' he pointed to the closed door of the living room, 'then you'd better make up your mind about what you're going to do with him, and pretty damned quick. If other people find out then you could be in trouble for harbouring the enemy.' He stared at her face and grasped her arm. 'Let's telephone the police ... now.'

Marieke stared straight back into his eyes. 'You may be right, but this man is badly injured. If I hand him over his injuries will get worse and then I'll be responsible for what's happened to him.' The tone of her voice changed. 'Now, what's happening outside? I presume the Germans have invaded Holland.'

He nodded, 'Yes, they crossed over the border everywhere early this morning. From what I hear, Groningen is occupied. The Queen broadcasted a message last night and the wireless this morning said that German parachutists had landed at airfields near The Hague and Rotterdam.' He stopped and looked anxiously at her face. 'Have you heard from Frank yet?'

She shook her head. 'Last night I spoke to him and all seemed well. But this morning all lines are engaged. I'll just keep trying.' For a moment her composure dropped and her shoulders slumped forward. Her voice remained resolute. 'I'm so worried about everything. What are we going to do?'

He smiled gently and put his arm around her shoulder, 'Well, for one thing, Marieke, I'd love a cup of coffee.'

She raised her hand to her mouth, 'Of course, we've not yet had breakfast. Aukje, Harmen, ... breakfast time.'

The routine of daily life began to take over and they both made their way to the kitchen.

The table was quickly laid and the plates were filled with bread and slices of cheese and cooked meats.

Jan smiled at his friend. 'Just coffee for me Marieke.' He wanted to change the subject. 'Do you expect the men to turn up for work today?'

She nodded her head, 'I can't see why not. What else are they going to do all day?'

'I suppose you're right. I'll be leaving for the bank soon, but I was worried about what had happened to you all.'

Harmen had sat quietly without saying a word. He could not keep his feelings bottled up any longer. He banged his knife down hard on the table. They all stopped talking and looked at him in amazement.

He was upset. 'How can you all sit here eating breakfast and talking about work as though nothing has happened?' His eyes blazed with anger. 'We've a German pilot in our living room, our town has been bombed and the *moffen* have invaded our country. Why don't you all, ... just, ... do something!' His fists clenched tightly.

Marieke placed her knife and fork carefully onto her plate. She looked at her son and spoke softly. 'You see, Harmen, there's nothing else that we can do. I'm sure that the police and the army have everything under control in the town. The German will stay here until I decide what to do. The fact that he's here will remain a secret.' She glanced at her daughter. 'Aukje, please make up a plate of food and pour out another cup of coffee and then take breakfast to our patient.' Aukje nodded, collected a tray and left the room.

Harmen's voice grated across to her, 'Don't expect me to do anything for him *Mem*, I just want him to get out of our house. I don't care what happens to him.' His clenched fists lay on the table.

Jan took up the conversation, 'I have to say it again, Marieke. You must move him as soon as possible. He's dangerous when he's in your house.'

She looked steadily at his face. 'Jan, I've said what's going to happen and that's it.' He knew her well enough not to argue when she had made her mind about something.

'Right, everybody, it's time to get dressed and ready for work and school. Come on, Jan, there's extra coffee.' She paused, 'Perhaps you'd like to meet the German in our living room?'

He hesitated and nodded. Curiosity got the better of him. 'Yes I would.'

Harmen began to clear the table and turned his back on his mother and their friend.

The fire was beginning to die back and the room was flooded with morning sunshine. Ernst lay slumped on the chair with one leg resting on a footstool. His face was ashen and he ate with little relish. Aukje stood opposite him watching his small eating movements. The light blue *Luftwaffe* uniform was creased and torn across the chest, the white collarless shirt was exposed and there were specks of blood on his trousers. He still wore his heavy, black flying boots and he looked very uncomfortable.

As the door opened, his body jerked with surprise and he dropped the plate of food onto the floor. His head swivelled round to face Marieke and Jan. They both stood and looked at him.

Jan was the first to speak, this time in German. 'What's your name?' A question that previously no one had thought to ask.

Ernst took a minute to answer. 'I am *Oberleutnant* Ernst Kraft.' He spoke in a hushed voice. The two men looked hard at each other. He tried to pull himself into a sitting position and, with a grunt of pain, failed.

Jan moved forward and looked at the injured leg. Ernst stared back at him. Jan glanced at Marieke. 'This leg needs urgent treatment. I think we should contact Doctor Bergsma, take him into our confidence and see if he'll help.'

Before she could answer, Ernst looked at Marieke and spoke again. 'First of all, madam, thank you for saving my life. I owe you a great favour. May I ask that you keep me in your house. Please don't send me to your police, they'll probably kill me.' He saw Marieke exchange glances with Jan as he translated.

Jan's eyes glittered. 'Tell me, *Oberleutnant*, why should we keep you in this house?'

Ernst looked at his leg and then appeared to make up his mind, 'By early this evening, forces of the German *Wehrmacht* will be in your town. Please hand me over to them. I can assure you that they'll treat you well for looking after me.'

Jan signalled Marieke to leave the room. They turned and left, closing the door firmly behind them.

He faced her, 'Look, Marieke, the information that he's just given us must be passed on to the right authorities as soon as possible.'

She took his arm, looked at his face and said patiently, 'Jan, don't you think that the authorities will know all this by now. If the Germans were in Groningen early this morning, then surely they'll be here by tonight?'

Shrugging his shoulders he replied, 'Marieke, as usual, you're probably right.'

She interrupted his thoughts, 'If the Germans are here by tonight then it's obvious that I'll hand him over to them. If I hand him over to our police now and the Germans find out, then my family could be in real danger, couldn't they?' She neatly turned the question over to him.

'OK ... I'll go and see old Doctor Bergsma and find out if he'll come round as soon as possible.' A movement made him glance through the glass window near the front door. 'By the way Marieke, I think you should get dressed soon, your workmen are arriving.'

She took her arm away from his, 'Thank you, maybe I'll see you later?'

He nodded and kissed her gently on the cheek.

When she returned to the living-room the pilot was fast asleep. She looked down at him. The leg of the uniform was stained by the blood seepage from the injury. His eyelids were tightly closed and flickered as though he was about to waken. There was a sheen of sweat over his forehead. The fists were tightly clenched and she could see slight trembling movements over the whole of his body. Without a thought she leaned over and put her palm over his forehead. The man was certainly running a temperature and Marieke knew that the doctor must come soon or else the German would be beyond any help. As she waited silently. Aukje returned.

'*Mem*, what can we do?'

She turned, and smiled. 'Aujke, we have to wait and trust in God, please find Harmen and tell him to inform the men in the factory that Frank has not returned.' She inclined her head slightly. 'It may help if you get dressed and I'll go and see them for myself.'

Aukje nodded and left the room. Marieke waited for a moment with her thoughts divided between her family and her worries about Frank. She made up her mind, touched the pilot again on his head and left the room.

The knock at the front door echoed through the house and Marieke ran quickly down the stairs from her bedroom to answer it. She glanced through the window and saw the comforting figure of Doctor Bergsma silhouetted against the afternoon sunshine.

She opened the door. 'Hello, Doctor. Please come in.'

He closed the door behind him and for a moment felt the atmosphere in the house. He looked Marieke straight in the eye, 'Good afternoon, *mevrouw* van der Meer.'

She returned the greeting. He was elderly and had been the van der Meer family doctor for many years. 'Jan de Bruin tells me that you have a ... Er ... shall we say a "special patient" for me to see?'

'Follow me please, Doctor.' She turned and led him towards the living room.

He took in the scene without a word. Within a minute his case was open and with a scalpel, in one swift movement, he cut open the trouser leg and began feeling the broken bone. He poured iodine over the gaping wound and applied a bandage pad. Ernst stirred and his eyes flickered open. He muttered something in German. Doctor Bergsma ignored him and took out a small steel container from his case. The hypodermic needle was carefully cleaned with a wad of cotton wool soaked in surgical spirit. He filled the syringe from a small phial and swiftly injected the contents into the exposed left leg of his patient. Again Ernst tried to speak. The Doctor spoke gently in German.

'*Oberloutnant*, I've given you a shot of morphine to deaden the pain and to make you sleep.'

Ernst tried to nod. Within a few seconds his body sagged as the drug took its effect.

The Doctor turned and spoke softly, 'Now look here, Marieke, I know what you're doing. But, this man needs treatment fast. His leg is badly broken and he'll get worse if we leave it any longer.' By the set of her folded arms he knew what was coming.

'Thank you for helping his pain, Doctor. I will not have him moved from my house until the Germans arrive. Let them deal with him.' Her gaze penetrated his thoughts.

He shook his head. 'All right, if that's how you feel, then it's your problem. I've got to go now, I think I'll be needed in the next few hours. The Germans will be here sooner than we think, I was told an hour ago that they were twenty kilometres away to the east in Kollum.' He turned away and left her standing in the hall.

Harmen came into the kitchen and faced his mother. '*Mem*, the men want to speak to you in the factory.'

Marieke took off her apron, hung it on the hook near the door, fluffed her blonde hair and followed her son out of the house.

The large door leading to the workshop was wide open. The fifteen men of the van der Meer factory waited in a semi-circle.

The foreman, Henk Wiersma, waited for Marieke to stand in front of them, 'Good afternoon, *mevrouw* van der Meer. Thank you for coming to see us.' He was a young man, recently promoted by Frank. 'Have you heard from *meneer* van der Meer yet?' Marieke shook her head. He continued quietly. 'We've heard that the Germans are only a few hours away from Leeuwarden. All the men here would like to leave and go back to their homes. They want to be with their families when the *moffen* arrive. We hope you can agree with this request?'

Marieke with a smile said, 'Of course you can all go home. Thank you for coming to work today. Please stay with your families until something is sorted out with the Germans. Remember, your jobs are still safe here. If I can help any of you in any way, then please contact me.' She paused and took a deep breath. 'You asked about my husband. Well, I keep on trying to contact his hotel in Rotterdam. As yet there's no reply. But you know what Frank is like. I'm sure he'll come back safely as soon as he can.' Marieke glanced at all the men in front of her, she had known them all for many years. 'Good luck to all of you and your families.' There were nodding smiles. The men left and the factory became strangely silent. Marieke waited for a moment and then returned to the house.

Dinner was ready and the van der Meer family ate quietly, not knowing what was happening outside their home. Aukje took a tray of food to Ernst. He was conscious, but his eyes were sleepy.

'You should really eat something,' she said.

He looked at the tray of food and finally picked up a piece of bread. His hand could not move it to his mouth. Aukje shook her head and sat down beside him. She took the bread, dipped it in the bowl of hot soup and slowly placed it near his lips. He ate carefully, each small mouthful was chewed and swallowed. He tried to speak, but Aukje merely put more bread near his mouth.

She looked at him. He said, '*Danke.*' His eyes closed and he slept again.

She stayed with him and wiped his forehead with a table-napkin.

Marieke went quietly into the living-room. She smiled, Aukje was fast asleep in the chair. Marieke left the room closing the door behind her.

Harmen was sitting in the kitchen reading. He looked up as his mother came back. '*Mem*, I think I'm going to catch the train to Rotterdam and see if I can find *Heit*.'

For the first time that day she became angry. She put her hands on her hips and raised her voice. 'You'll do no such thing, Harmen van der Meer. Don't you realise that Rotterdam is probably already occupied by the Germans.' She quietened. 'You must stay here. I need a man in the house if the Germans come.'

'What do you mean, *Mem*? ..... If the Germans come. I'm surprised that they're not walking through that front door right now.' There was fire in his eyes.

The knock at the door was loud and made the house shake. Marieke jumped up, Harmen dropped his fork. She stood stock-still.

'I'll answer the door. Harmen, don't say anything. Stay here.' She turned and walked slowly and deliberately out of the kitchen and into the hall. Marieke threw open the front door.

'Hello! ... Quick let me in!' Jan de Bruin pushed his way through and closed the door behind him. 'Let's just sit somewhere away from your German.' She shrugged, turned, and he followed her to the kitchen. He sat down and began his story. 'The *moffen* have stopped some distance from Leeuwarden. Most of our army has dropped back to the *Afsluitdijk*. They can take up a better defensive position there and try and stop the Germans joining forces north of Amsterdam. From what I can gather, they've taken our airfields near The Hague.' He nodded and added shrewdly, 'It looks as though they're trying to kidnap the royal family. I just hope for God's sake that the Queen has escaped.' Jan paused, Marieke remained silent. 'The best thing that I've heard today is what happened at the station in Leeuwarden.' Another pause. Marieke stared at him curiously and his voice rose with excitement. 'The men at the station have run their biggest engine off the lines. It's tipped over onto its side and is now blocking the main rail route into the town from the east. The Germans will never be able to arrive at the station. They'll have to come by road.'

Marieke shook her head. 'Jan, the road from the east is closer to here than the town. They may very well see this factory and try and come past it to get into Leeuwarden.'

'I don't think so, Marieke. They'll want to control the town council as quickly as possible and they'll head straight for the centre. There're no soldiers to stop them. I hear that some of our beloved citizens are actually putting out flags of welcome. The *NSB* are wearing their uniforms and they're waiting outside the *stadhuis*.' She tried to hide a yawn. He took the hint, his voice became softer, 'I'm sorry, Marieke, if I bore you. But remember, you do have a German in your living-room. Somebody will find out sooner or later... I must go back to my family.' Before he left, he turned to face her, 'Have you contacted Frank yet?' She shook her head. He put his hand on her arm. 'Keep trying, some people have got through to relatives in other parts of Holland. Telephone me if you need any help.' She silently nodded her thanks and he left the house.

Thoughts teemed through her mind as she returned to the kitchen. As she sat down to gather her thoughts Aukje came into the room.

'*Mem*, it's time for dinner. Let's just have some sandwiches. I really don't feel hungry.' She glanced around the room. 'Where's Harmen?'

'He's in the factory. I don't know what he's doing. Please go and look for him.' Aukje nodded and left.

He was standing in the middle of the deserted factory floor. The woodworking machinery was silent. Dust still hung in the air, swirling in the late evening sunshine that slanted in through the windows. She watched him for a moment and tried to read his thoughts. Something must have alerted him. He whirled round in surprise.

His voice was indignant, 'Aukje! Don't creep up on me like that again. What's the matter?' His voice changed. 'I thought you were looking after your German.'

She did not rise to his sarcasm. 'Harmen, *Mem* wants us back in the house, now.' She did not wait for his reply. He followed her, kicking a piece of scrap timber out of his way.

The house was as silent as the factory.

On that night Marieke slept fitfully without getting changed into her night dress. She lay on the bed and stared at the ceiling. She was a strong minded woman but the problems that now faced her seemed to be insurmountable. She knew that Frank must be contacted so that he could help. Marieke made up her mind quickly. Swinging her legs off the bed she stood and quietly made her way down the stairs. The hall was in total darkness and the only sound was the ticking of the clock. Reaching for the telephone she called the Maas Hotel in Rotterdam. As the telephone clicked and connections were made she shook her head in disappointment. In the last twelve hours she had tried at least a dozen times and there was sometimes not even a dialling tone. She placed the telephone back on its cradle. For some unknown reason she clasped her hands in prayer and stood motionless for several minutes. With a deep breath she slowly reached for the telephone and carefully re-dialled the numbers. Her heart leapt as the twin tones of the connection clearly rang out. She let it ring and ring: quite suddenly.

'Good evening. Maas Hotel. This is the manager speaking.'

She could not get the words out and began to stutter. 'This ... is *mevrouw* van der Meer ... speaking. ... Please can I speak to my husband?'

'Hello, *mevrouw*, nice to hear from you again.' There was a pause. Her heart sank. The manager's calm voice continued. 'I think you'll be cut off in the next minute. That seems to be happening to all calls that are connected with the hotel. By the time that I've woken your husband you'll lose the connection. May I suggest that you call me in a couple of hours time on my private number at about seven this morning?

Before she could reply the line clicked and she was left again in silence. She returned to her bedroom, set the alarm clock and slept solidly for three hours until morning.

TEN

Frank had to do something, he stepped over to the washbasin and rinsed his face in cold water. Scribbling a quick note he left it on the bed and dashed out of his room.

The Austin was waiting exactly where he had left it. He pulled out the road-map from the car's glove-compartment and scanned it for a possible route back towards Leeuwarden.

The Germans were invading on all fronts and one of the keys to their occupation was the taking of the *Afsluitdijk* to the north. Frank was a pacifist by nature and by upbringing and he knew little of military tactics. He decided to travel north via The Hague and Amsterdam and attempt to enter Friesland back over the long dyke. Little did he know that he was heading straight into the area where German paratroopers had landed in some strength. Their target was the taking of Queen Wilhelmina and thus the quick capitulation of the Dutch Government located in The Hague.

It was Saturday morning, the 11th of May, and the roads were unusually quiet. He encountered his first road block when he neared the northern outskirts of Rotterdam. It was a simple affair, an old car and two policemen on bikes. They waved him down, both had rifles slung over their backs. He stopped and wound the window down.

The taller one glanced at the registration plates and then stared hard at Frank. The voice grated. 'Papers!' There was no sign of courtesy.

Frank produced them and smiled. There were a thousand questions on his lips. They gave him no time to ask them.

'You'll have to turn back. This road is closed.'

He was about to protest when he noticed a small brass pin glinting in the breast-pocket flap of the man's uniform. The letters *NSB* were tiny but clearly seen against the coarse black material. Frank had seconds to make up his mind. The *Nationaal Socialistische Beweging* were Dutch supporters of Hitler's Nazi Party. There was a moment's silence. The card was flung back through the window. He made his decision.

'Thank you, gentleman, for your advice.' Frank's voice was calm and he gripped the steering wheel with suppressed anger.

They unslung their rifles and watched the car as it reversed down the road. Frank executed a neat turn and headed back the way he had come, but not for long. When he was out of sight of the *NSB* roadblock he turned left and again proceeded northwards. Some farm traffic trundled past but he avoided any sort of contact and drove quietly for about an hour. There was not a person in sight.

Somehow he could feel that all was not right, the hustle and bustle of the Dutch countryside was missing; cows a plenty but no people. He remembered the wireless broadcasts in the hotel and suddenly felt the prickle of fear. Another road block emerged at the beginning of a bend.

This time it was manned by Dutch soldiers. Surprisingly they waved him on without stopping the car. He managed to find his way back onto the main road to The Hague. He quickly passed through the outskirts of Delft and thought that he would make good time before finding somewhere for lunch. Overhead he could see a low-flying aircraft. For a moment he ignored it. Then suddenly it turned and seemed to be flying straight at him. Faster and faster it approached and he could hear the snarl of the engine through the open window. He stood on his brakes and the car shuddered to a halt. The plane screamed overhead and, as its shadow flashed by, he stared upwards. The black crosses on the wings imprinted on his consciousness.

Everything occurred very quickly. The road block was manned by ten heavily armed German soldiers. A machine-gun was sandbagged into place in the middle of the road. He stopped without being asked, five men surrounded the car. One of them fingered the Austin sign on the bonnet.

This time they were courteous. The officer spoke Dutch perfectly. 'Please, step out of the car, *mein Herr.*' Frank obeyed.

The young *Leutnant* stood ramrod straight and wore the same kind of uniform that Frank had seen at the docks in Rotterdam only yesterday. He did not know that this officer was a member of the 22nd Air Landing Division of the German Airborne Forces. Their comrades in the 7th Air Division had landed at the same time in Rotterdam.

'Your papers, please.' The handsome face had a genuine smile. He took the papers and glanced through them. He handed them back and saluted smartly.

'*Meneer* van der Meer. Please return to your car and follow me.' He turned round and assumed that Frank was following, he was.

The officer climbed into a small military vehicle and drove it down the road. Frank remained at a respectful distance behind the car. Following him were two soldiers sitting astride BMW motor-bikes. One of them drew level with Frank and stared hard through his heavy goggles. He ignored him.

He followed for two kilometres and then realised where he was going to. Frank had passed by the small airfield at Ypenburg many times. He drove along the narrow road. After another two hundred metres the German vehicle turned sharply right. He had time to glance to his left. Parked neatly in the open were eight German twin-engined aircraft. His surprise almost made him lose control of the steering wheel. The motorcyclists sensed his surprise and moved up to the side of the car. They waved him forward.

The car in front stopped outside a group of buildings. Frank parked the Austin neatly behind the German vehicle. A motor-cyclist drew up at the side of the car and blocked his way out. He waited and watched the officer disappear into a small wooden house. It gave him time to look around. There appeared to be hundreds of German soldiers. They were well dug-in and there were signs of battle. He noticed the still smoking wreckage of an aircraft. Some of the buildings were damaged, there were holes through the walls and collapsed roofs. He could see no sign whatsoever of Dutch troops. There was no panic, only an immense feeling of orderliness. A feeling that Frank was going to experience for the next five years.

There came a tap on the window. The young man waited as the motor-bike pulled out of the way. His voice was polite but firm.

'*Meneer* van der Meer. Follow me, please.'

Frank climbed out of the Austin and walked towards the building. Before he entered he was stopped by another soldier. Without being asked he was given a quick body search. As his anger rose, the Leutnant again smiled.

'My apologies. Security is necessary.'

The officer knocked on a door at the end of a long dark passage. They both entered. The room was square with windows on two sides. It was bare and functional. In front of the windows was a long table behind which sat two men. A single light bulb shone down weakly. They both wore blue *Luftwaffe* uniforms, their white and gold collar tabs indicated high rank. Behind them two armed paratroopers stood rigidly to attention. One of the men seated at the table rose as Frank entered. He introduced himself.

'I am *General* Graf von Sponeck, commanding general of the 22nd Air Landing Division.' He waved towards the other man at the table. 'This officer is *Generalmajor* Student, commanding general of the 7th Air Division. Please sit down.' He waved towards a single chair. 'May I offer you coffee or a cold drink?'

Frank did not know what to say, so he decided to say nothing.

General Student began, his voice was soft and with an accent that Frank could not place. '*Meneer*, you're probably wondering why you have been brought here to meet us?' Frank nodded. 'Our troops parachuted into here and into Rotterdam yesterday against brave opposition from your army. They didn't stand a chance. The British Royal Air Force attacked us with their outdated Hurricane fighters. They were no match for our Messerschmitt 109's. We shot them all down. No doubt you saw the wreck of one of them on the way here.' He paused to watch Frank's face. 'We have the whole of this immediate area cordoned off and under supervision from the air. I want to know how you managed to get so close to this airfield without being stopped.' Before Frank could answer, the *General* continued, 'You're the first Dutch civilian that I have met since I arrived yesterday.' He paused and glanced down at neat piles of documents on the table. The voice was smoothly reassuring, 'I can see from your papers that you are a businessman from Leeuwarden in Friesland.' This time Frank nodded. 'I must ask, have you seen any sign of our troops near

Rotterdam and particularly have you have met any of your own soldiers? Or, indeed, seen anything of British military forces?' The *General* stopped talking and waited.

Frank was by now boiling with anger. He had met German soldiers twice in the last twenty-four hours. He stood and tried to keep his temper. One of the guards raised his machine pistol. *General* Student motioned him back.

Frank spoke slowly in Dutch, his voice edged with anger, 'I want to know why you've brought me here? I want to know why you've invaded my country and I want you to let me go now ... *bitte!*' The young *Leutnant* translated.

The silence was almost touchable. Nobody spoke or moved for a full minute.

The soft voice resumed. 'I have asked you some questions, *meneer*. I need those answers. I can only assume that you wish to continue on your journey as soon as possible?' He left the question hanging in the air and arched his eye-brow whilst he stared hard at the angry Dutchman in front of him.

Frank knew he was trapped. If he refused to answer the questions then there was little chance of him continuing with his homeward journey. He decided that there was little harm in telling the Germans what they wished to know. He sat down and the atmosphere in the room relaxed.

He spoke quietly and glanced at both of the men in front of him. 'I saw some of your soldiers dressed like those men.' He pointed to the two guards behind the generals. 'They were near the docks in Rotterdam. I left this morning and I passed through a large Dutch roadblock about an hour from here. I have seen no British Forces.' He deliberately did not mention his meeting with Lord Mountbatten. He thought for a moment and added, 'I'm as surprised as you are that we have met here this morning. Now, perhaps, you'll answer my questions?'

General Student glanced at his colleague and they both smiled.

'Thank you, *meneer*. I must believe what you have told me. We are here in your country to protect you from British and French forces that are attempting to stop our advance. We had to come through the Netherlands to attack them on a broad front.' He leant back in his chair and relaxed. 'You see the Germans and the Dutch are from the same stock. We almost speak the same language. Our countries have the same border. Your political parties have the same beliefs as ours. Therefore it is obvious that our two countries should unite against a common enemy.' Before Frank could reply the *General* glanced at some of the documents on the table. 'I see you are trying to get home. I would advise you not to go over the *Afsluitdijk*. It is at this moment being taken by German forces. I must add, *meneer*, that your home town has been occupied by units of the 2nd Cavalry Regiment under the command of *Oberstleutnant* von Saucken.' He saw Frank stiffen. 'Before you ask, there has been little civilian bloodshed.' Both generals stood and looked down at Frank. 'Now, I think you must be on your way. Return to your hotel and wait until our forces have stabilised and then you will be free to return home.' He pointed towards the *Leutnant* who was waiting quietly near the door. 'This officer has prepared a pass for you to get back through our lines to Rotterdam.'

Frank knew he had been dismissed and he rose and walked towards the open door. He paused and glanced back into the room.

There was a smile on the *General's* face. 'Oh, by the way, *meneer* van der Meer. Driving an English car will not endear you to our soldiers. I suggest that you get rid of it as quickly as possible. Buy a good Opel! ... *Auf Wiedersehen.' Generalmajor* Kurt Student gave a half-salute.

There was a group of soldiers around his car. They parted as he approached. Neither Frank nor the Germans spoke. As he climbed into the car, he noticed an official-looking document lying on the driving seat. A quick glance showed it be an officially printed military pass. He was surprised to see that it was written in Dutch as well as German. Through his mind flashed the knowledge that this invasion had been well prepared.

The journey back down the main road was full of events. He encountered five road-blocks. Each was carefully organised with large signs written in Dutch, warning all people to stop and for papers to be produced. Frank noticed that at each stopping point there were at least two or three members of the Dutch *NSB*. All were dressed in their black uniforms. The pass that he had been given at Ypenburg airfield worked like magic. He now merely waved it through an open window. It brought salutes from the Germans and the *NSB*'ers alike. Overhead flew waves of German aircraft; bombers, fighters and reconnaissance planes. There was no opposition that Frank could see as he drove slowly down the road. It was late afternoon and he suddenly realised that he was hungry. He decided to stop at the next hotel for something to eat.

Loosduinen is a small village astride one of the main roads from The Hague to Rotterdam. Frank parked his car near the front entrance of its only hotel and walked through the open doors. The cafe was almost empty apart from two men drinking beer. He sat down at the large table and began to look at the newspapers. The waiter came up to him.

'Yes, *meneer.'*

Frank looked up, 'Can I have ham and cheese and coffee, please?'

There was a confirming nod and the waiter scurried away towards the kitchen.

'Well, *meneer*. Where've you come from? You're certainly not from round here are you?' said the larger of the two men.

The question was left hanging and there was a feeling of mistrust in the air. The room was standard Dutch hotel. Old paintings and photographs on the walls, gleaming parquet floors and tables covered with heavy oriental rugs. There were two half-full spittoon near the doors to the toilet. Frank could smell the old cigar smoke and stale beer.

He briefly explained his situation but left out his meeting with the Germans at Ypenburg. One of the two men nodded.

'You're not an *NSB*'er are you? Because if you are you can piss-off out of here, now!' He seemed the worse for drink.

Frank gave his charming smile, 'No, *meneer*. I'm not an *NSB*'er and all I want to do is to get home as soon as possible but the Germans won't let me.' He wanted their confidence. 'Just what's going on around here?'

The other man looked up from his glass. 'About half a kilometre from here is a small airfield. The Germans took it yesterday but by God our men fought like crazy. The Germans are still there.' He paused and took another swig from his glass. 'Do you know not an hour ago a German officer walked through that door and ordered a cup of coffee. He drank it and left. He never spoke a word to either of us, did he Dirk? And he paid in Dutch money.'

The other man nodded and drank deeply from his glass.

'Of course, *meneer* ... you know what they're after don't you?'

Frank shook his head.

The man gave a conspiratorial wink and lowered his voice, 'They're after our Queen. They've taken most of the ports and every airfield round The Hague has been occupied by parachutists. There were hundreds of 'em dropping yesterday. I've heard that the Queen and her cabinet have left the palace and are hiding on the roads somewhere near here. I've also heard that she's trying to get to England through Rotterdam on a British ship. After all we've still got most of Rotterdam.' He nodded. 'Our men are doing well there.'

The ham and cheese arrived and Frank began to eat. The men remained silent. The meal quickly disappeared. He left the money for the bill, nodded to the men at the bar and left the hotel.

Roadblocks were everywhere and it was not until he reached the centre of Rotterdam that they changed from German to Dutch. He passed through all of them easily. Each time he stopped he could hear the occasional crackle of gunfire in the distance. Each time he was given further information about the state of the invasion and the occupation of his country. Around him were clouds of billowing black smoke towering into the late evening sky.

It was approaching darkness as he climbed out of his car and trudged wearily up the steps into the hall. It was almost as if the manager had been waiting for him.

'Good evening, *meneer* van der Meer. Welcome back to the hotel. There's fresh coffee in the lounge and your room has been kept for you.'

ELEVEN

The alarm clock rang for a full minute. Instantly alert, Marieke sat up and turned it off. In a few brief seconds all the problems came flooding back into her mind. She stared at her heavily creased cotton dress, each crease reminding her of what was happening to herself and her family. With a decisive mental snap, she swung her legs off the bed and walked towards the bedroom door. In a moment she was by the telephone in the hall and she dialled the numbers of the hotel manager's private office. The lines connected immediately.

The voice was clear, 'Maas Hotel. This is the manager speaking.'

For a moment she did not know what to say, then words came tumbling out. 'This is *mevrouw* van der Meer. I must speak to my husband as soon as possible. Please find him for me.' There was a moment's silence.

His voice was so welcome and her heart leapt with joy. 'Frank, I'm so glad to hear you. How are you?' Before he could reply she continued and her voice sounded unreal. 'I was worried about you ... yesterday the Germans attacked the airfield near Leeuwarden ... Frank there're German soldiers in the town and one of them is in our house. Please come home ...'

She was interrupted as the line was suddenly disconnected. A strained voice crackled into her ear.

'All telephone calls are now prohibited until further notice. No contact can be made with the rest of the Netherlands. Please wait for pronouncements by the German Occupying Forces.'

The line went dead.

Marieke stared at the telephone in total disbelief. She was still holding it when Harmen and Aukje came and stood silently behind her.

Aukje spoke first, 'Did you manage to speak to *Heit*?' Marieke nodded dumbly. 'Is he all right? *Mem* ... is he all right?'

Marieke placed the receiver carefully back on its cradle and turned to look at her children.

'Yes, he seems to be all right. But I was disconnected before I could speak to him.'

'What did he say, *Mem*?'

Marieke glanced at the clock in the hall and shook her head. 'Let's have some breakfast and then we can decide what to do.' She turned away and walked towards the kitchen. The atmosphere was strained.

Aukje opened the living-room door quietly and looked in. The German pilot was awake. He looked up and smiled, his face grey with fatigue. He nodded and Aukje quickly returned the smile. She left the door open and went back to her bedroom to get dressed.

The breakfast-table was quickly laid and the three quietly sat down. Marieke sensed her children's anticipation. Knowing that she must provide stability and guidance for her young family she spoke decisively, 'Today is Friday. The men won't be at work and I think the schools will be closed. After breakfast, Aukje, take something to eat to our German guest. We'll then invite the de Bruins round and find out what's happening.' She raised her hand. 'Before you ask, Harmen. ... It's silly waiting for *Heit* to telephone. The lines will be disconnected for some time. We'll try again later today. The German can wait.'

'Is there anything else I can do?' asked Aukje. Marieke shook her head.

'Do I have to stay in the house, *Mem?*' Harmen looked distinctly uncomfortable.

She glanced at him. 'Yes, you do. Today we stay together all the time. We need each other. You can telephone the de Bruins and ask them to come round as soon as possible.' He wilted under her enforcing smile. Marieke stood and looked at them each in turn. 'Right, let's clear the table. I need a quick bath and a change of clothes.'

Their tasks completed, Aukje carried a tray of food and coffee through to the living-room. She laid the tray on the small table near to Ernst's raised legs and walked over to the windows to open the curtains. The early morning daylight flooded into the room and made her blink. She gazed into the garden and beyond to the river. It was as though nothing had happened during the last twenty-four hours. The sky was cloudless, a deep innocent blue that made everything stand out as clear and as sharp as a newly painted picture. Her thoughts were interrupted.'Miss van der Meer. Could you please tell me what is happening?' The voice was quiet and respectful.

Aukje quickly turned round. 'I've brought you something to eat and drink.' She bent down to look at his injuries. 'How's the leg, *Oberleutnant?*'

'Can you please call me Ernst? It sounds so official when you use my rank. I feel better than last night but it still hurts.' She gave no reply. 'What's going on out there?' He waved his arm towards the open window.

'Your comrades are in our town. Some friends are coming to see us and then we'll tell you what's going to happen to you.' She glanced at his leg but moved no closer. 'Please eat your breakfast, I'll see you later.'

Aukje left the room without turning round. She closed the door behind her and waited in the hall for her mother to come downstairs. Harmen joined her.

'Well, sister, how's the German this morning?' The voice was sarcastic and he stood near her with arms firmly folded.

She stared hard. 'He's a bit better. But this morning I really don't care how he is. I keep thinking that it's his friends that are stopping *Heit* coming home.'

Harmen smiled, 'So, you're beginning to think like me are you? ... And about time.' He put his arm round her shoulder and her erect stance softened. 'Well let's give *Mem* a shout and see what's happening in the big wide world ... If there's one left when we get outside?'

Marieke was ready quickly and she smiled at them as she came down the stairs. She wore a simple blue summer-dress and her face was devoid of make-up. Her blonde hair was neat and tied in a bunch at the nape of her neck. Around her slender throat was a small Mennonite cross hanging from a thin gold chain. She followed her children outside. They stood together and looked at the view in front of them.

Little traffic was on the road and a tractor pulling a load of freshly cut hay chugged past the end of the factory entrance. They expected to see some signs of the invasion but there was nothing to be seen. The earlier clouds of black smoke had disappeared. They waited for the de Bruins to arrive. They said little to each as they looked into the distance. Eventually their friends cycled round the corner and they pulled up near the van der Meers.

Marieke went straight up to Tineke de Bruin and put her hand on her arm. 'Hello, do come in.'

There were pale smiles from everybody, though David grinned when he saw Aukje looking at him.

Marieke broke the strained feeling. 'We'll sit somewhere else, our living-room is otherwise occupied.' They all looked towards the closed door as Marieke led them through the hall and into the kitchen.

The room was heavy with anticipation. The table was full of clean cups and fresh coffee bubbled ready in the tall Friesian pewter urn. With a quick flick of her wrist Marieke turned the small brass tap and hot coffee filled the waiting cups.

'Tineke, what are we all going to do?' Marieke asked the question with a calm expression on her face.

Tineke attempted a smile. 'I don't really know. I think we just have to sit and wait.'

'I'm not waiting,' Harmen was sitting next to David. The tone of his voice made them all turn towards him. 'I'm going to get on my bike and go into Leeuwarden and see exactly what's happening. I'm just fed-up with sitting around and doing nothing.' He stared hard at everybody and quickly rose from his chair. 'Anybody coming with me?'

Jan shrugged his shoulders and looked at the two families in front of him. 'I think he's got an idea. It sounds peaceful enough out there and I for one would like to know what the hell is going on. But I want David to stay here.'

Marieke looked at Aukje and Tineke, they looked back at her. She nodded her head. 'I suppose I have to agree, although I don't like it I think the two men should go and have a look.' She glanced at the wall clock. 'Let's have a quick cup of coffee and then go. But please, no longer than an hour or else we'll get really worried.'

Eventually they left.

Jan chose the narrow path at the side of the Dokkumer Ee river to arrive into Leeuwarden. They cycled side-by-side along the river path. The day was mild with huge clouds scudding along the skyline. Both men were worried, they gripped the handlebars and pedalled hard into the light wind.

'Where shall we go, Uncle Jan?'

'I think, Harmen, it's time now that you dropped the "uncle".' They both laughed and the sound was carried away by the wind. 'We'll go straight to the town centre. If we don't see anything there then we'll head out to the east and see if we can see any activity.'

Harmen nodded and pushed the pedals even harder.

The nearer the centre the more people appeared on the streets. There was a look of both concern and curiosity on their faces. Whole families walked arm-in-arm down the pavements. The police had set up road blocks but cyclists were allowed through. Everybody was heading in the same direction. Eventually Jan turned to Harmen.

'We'll never get through. Come on, turn left down *Woud Straat*. It's a short cut onto the main Groningen road.'

They rode in single file. All around them people stood in doorways or gathered in chattering groups. At times they had to stop and push their way through dense crowds of people. Eventually, they arrived on the *Groningerstraatweg*, the main road into the town. It was a boulevard with tall trees lining its straightness. From where Harmen stood with his bike he could see Piet Bokma's house over to his left. For some unknown reason nobody was using the road. It was completely empty but crowds lined the sides and some even stood in the gardens of the houses. Eventually they managed to move into a decent position very close to the road. Slowly they made their way towards the Bokma house at number 94. Piet was already standing on the low wall at the end of his garden. He recognised them immediately.

'Hello Jan, Harmen. ... put your bikes in our hallway. They'll be safer there.'

'Thanks, Piet. ...' The bikes were quickly pushed into place.

Jan stared around him. 'What the hell's going on here? Have the Germans arrived yet?' They joined him on the wall. There was a clear view over the crowd.

'There's a small group of German soldiers near the town hall. I hear they're well protected by *NSB*'ers.' Piet was having to shout over the general noise. 'There's a strong rumour that the main German invasion force is coming down here at any time now.'

'The swines,' muttered Harmen in a voice that was heard by most of the people near to the wall.

Two men swiftly turned round and looked up at him. One of them was tall and powerfully built. His voice was loaded with menace. He pointed a finger straight at Harmen's face.

'You! ... watch what you're saying. The Germans are our best friends. We're here to welcome them. Where's the Dutch Army and the British?'

Harmen's youthful pride was about to reply when he felt his arm being squeezed.

'Not now ... some other time,' whispered Piet in his ear. They all stared up the road to the right.

The crowd did not have to wait long. The sun was obscured by a dark cloud. It was as if the Germans had waited for this omen. As the sky darkened the crowd suddenly became silent. In the far distance there was the roar of motor-bikes and the heavy throb of motorised vehicles.

Somebody whispered hoarsely, 'Oh my God, here they come.'

Four BMW motor-bikes with side-cars straddled the road and led the invading force. The riders' field-grey uniforms were immaculate. The two men on each bike were heavily armed. They looked straight ahead and drove at a slow speed. Following them was a black open-topped Mercedes-Benz tourer. Its bodywork gleamed and it looked as it though it had just driven out of a garage instead of across sixty kilometres of dusty Friesian countryside. One man sat in the back draped across the deep leather seat. *Oberst* von Saucken glanced from side to side and occasionally said something to his driver. Behind him followed a stream of open, tracked troop lorries each containing thirty armed soldiers sitting stiffly to attention. The column continued to flow, armoured personnel carriers towing heavy guns, wheeled mortars, bridge building equipment; all the paraphernalia of war was there. The roar of engines, each throwing out great clouds of heavy blue and black smoke, made the crowds cough and splutter. Finally, two columns wide, marched over three hundred German soldiers. They were in perfect step, a single drum at the front gave the pace. There was a feeling of total organisation. The crash of their shiny black jackboots on the *Groningerstraatweg* was in total contrast to the sound of the engines. It was a perfectly organised piece of stage management. The sounds and sight of the invading army hit the emotions of the onlookers very hard. Many were crying and most hung their heads. But, the worst was to come.

'I've had enough,' said Piet, 'Let's go back into the house.'

'No!' said Jan sharply. 'Look at the bastards!' He pointed back up the road.

Two minutes after the last German soldier had marched past a new group appeared. There were over a hundred men. Each was dressed in uniform with the standard German steel helmet sitting low over their foreheads. They wore black jackboots to compliment the uniforms. On their left arms was the black and red "wolfs-hook" symbol of the *NSB*. These were Dutchmen and their faces wore smirks of power. They carried their weapons stiffly in front of them and to hurt the Friesians even more they were not marching, they were goose-stepping.

There was total silence from the crowd as they marched past. Harmen nudged Jan. In front of them the two men held their arms out stiffly in the Hitler salute, their faces flushed with excitement. Harmen glanced up and down the road, there were many others who were following their example.

Piet shook his head. 'That's it! ... I've had enough. Come on you two into the house.'

Harmen and Jan followed him silently through the front door. The three men paused and looked at each other. Outside the crowds began to melt away.

'What do we do now, Jan?' said Harmen with tears in his eyes.

Piet answered the question, 'There's nothing we can do but sit tight and wait and see what they do.' He smiled grimly. 'I think that you should both go back home. How about a drink of something before you go?'

They shook their heads.

Jan spoke, 'No thanks, Piet. I think we've seen enough today. It's something I'll never ever forget. It's been good to have you with us.'

'That's no problem, you know what my feelings are about the *moffen*.'

They waved and set off back up *Groningerstraatweg*.

On the return journey neither of them spoke. It was late afternoon and the evening chill made them hunch down over their bicycles. A few people were about but most were anxiously waiting in their houses for the future to unfold.

They were within sight of the factory when Jan noticed something. Nearly all the houses had the national flag hanging from their small flagpoles. On top were long streamers of orange, the colour of the royal house.

Marieke's largest flag flew at full stretch from her tall flagpole. The broad red, white and blue colours flapped proudly. The two men smiled at each other and wheeled their bikes into the shed at the back of the house.

Tineke and Marieke greeted them at the door and the four of them stared out across the flat countryside.

'What about all the flags, *Mem*? Who told you to put them up?' said Harmen.

'It was David who saw the first one,' she replied. 'The house down the road had theirs flying and since then nearly every house has put out its flag.' Like the mother of old, she laughed loudly.

Before they entered the house they heard a car approaching from the distance. Harmen jumped into the air.

'I bet it's *Heit*. I knew he would come!' He began to run down the garden path towards the road.

Marieke glanced through the window. 'STOP!' she shouted, with terror in her voice. 'It's not Frank! It's the police!' Aukje and David were outside. They froze and watched the black car draw up outside the gate. Within a minute another car arrived. Both of them stopped. As if by an unseen signal all the doors opened. Out of the first stepped four policemen, their holsters unfastened. From the other car emerged four members of the NSB, rifles unslung. All eight made their way up the path. Jan stared in horror at their approach. Marieke put her arm round Aukje, and Harmen took one stride back towards the door. A policeman stepped forward.

'Good evening, *mevrouw* van der Meer, and *meneer* and *mevrouw* de Bruin.' His voice was polite.

One of the *NSB* men pushed the policeman out of the way. 'Don't be nice to those people, they're Jews.' His face was a picture of hatred. 'It's that woman we need to speak to.' The voice was at full strength and his arm pointed towards Marieke.

The whole group remained motionless and stared at the *NSB* man. Marieke remained absolutely still. Her shoulders were square and her eyes blazed with anger. She did not speak or cringe in front of him, which infuriated the man even more.

'You ... woman! We've been informed that you're hiding an injured German pilot. Where is he?'

'Who told you?' asked Marieke quietly.

The man stared at her with disbelief in his eyes. His shouted comment surprised them all and he sneered down at them. 'You think you can trust your best friends don't you and that includes your own doctor. He was only too pleased to help.' The smile was more like a grimace. He raised his rifle and pointed the black hole of the muzzle straight at Marieke. 'I'll only ask you once again. If you refuse to answer you'll be arrested immediately.' The rifle did not waver.

The silence continued. Eventually, Jan spoke, 'Marieke, for all our sakes I think you'd better tell him. After all, what is it to you? From what I saw this afternoon, it's only another injured German?'

The rifle butt caught him behind his left ear and, with blood flowing from the gash, he dropped to the ground. Tineke stepped forward and the rifle pointed at her, the man drew back the rifle bolt. She stopped in her tracks.

'Just try it ... Jew!' His voice was now strangely quiet.

Marieke's presence seemed to calm the situation. She did not want any more trouble for either of the two families.

'All right, I'll take you to our German guest.' The tone of her voice was cool and collected.

The policeman whirled round on the *NSB* man. His voice was full of authority. 'Calm down you and for God's sake put the safety catch on that bloody rifle before you kill somebody.' The man lowered his eyes and the rifle, but his body remained stiff with anger.

One of the other men pushed past her and strode into the house. She laughed, 'There's nobody else here. My husband's in Rotterdam.' Now she pushed past the man and opened the living-room door.

The pilot was sitting-up and in a great deal of pain. He stared in amazement at the scene in front of him.

The four *NSB* men sprung to attention and gave the Hitler salute.

'*HEIL* HITLER!'

Ernst just waved his arm.

Marieke took control. 'Now, gentlemen, this man needs urgent medical treatment. As you can see, he has a broken leg and must go to hospital. And, what's more, you'll need an ambulance. You can't move him in your car because you'd probably kill him.' She placed her hands on her hips and with eyes flashing stared at each man in turn.

'Now, ... will one of you telephone the hospital? Or shall I?'

'*Mevrouw* van der Meer,' began the policeman, 'Please will you telephone and we'll wait with you.'

She left the room and dialled the hospital.

The big *NSB* man desperately needed to re-assert his authority. He left the room and his loud voice could be heard clearly.

'*MEVROUW* van der Meer, now you WILL come with us to the police station to answer questions.' Before Marieke could reply, he grabbed her arm and propelled her through the door.

'What am I to be charged with?' she shouted.

The man smiled in victory, 'We don't need any charges to take you away.'

The rifles of the other three men raised menacingly as the two families looked aghast at what was happening before their eyes.

The policeman called out, '*Mevrouw* I'm sure that this is a mere formality. I can assure you that you'll be brought home as soon as possible.' He remained with one of the men and the others left to take Marieke to their car.

Jan rose to his feet. His face was bloody but there was still some light in his eyes. He was seen.

'Out of the way, Jew!' The *NSB* man pushed him roughly to one side.

Jan helplessly watched Marieke being pushed into the back seat of the car. There was a black uniformed man on either side of her. She was looking straight ahead, trying to distance herself from the horror. Jan watched the car move off and then he returned to the kitchen and was joined by the two families. Tears flowed and Jan tried to calm them.

Marieke soon discovered that the man on her left had the most appalling bad breath. It diverted her thoughts from her desperate situation. She hoped that the man would stop glancing round at her. Every time he did a wave of stench hit her. He must have felt her stiffen.

'Worried a bit ... are you?' He rasped at her with a lopsided grin.

To make matters worse he spoke with a harsh, Rotterdam accent and this, linked with the breath, made her visibly wince. She hardly noticed the journey into Leeuwarden. The familiar streets flashed by and within ten minutes she was travelling down the sides of the canals in the centre of town.

The police station was on the northern side of the *Nieuw Stad*. It was a typical, provincial, canal-side building. Twin steps arrived at a main door some three metres from street level. The lower windows were barred, the upper ones heavily curtained.

A large Dutch flag hung from a horizontal flagpole, at its side was a blood red and black swastika. Even though there was a breeze it remained stiffly straight.

The car drew to a stop and the door was flung open, Marieke emerged into the evening sunshine. She had time to look around her. The streets were almost deserted apart from some children on bikes. The cafes were closed and the town centre had lost its life. She was surprised to see a black German staff car parked in front of the police station.

Marieke climbed up the steps and the heavy door opened in front of her. She had never been in a police station in her life. A young policeman pointed her towards a low wooden bench in the corner of the entrance hall. One of the escort stood at her side. She sat down primly and looked around her. The hall was spotlessly clean and smelled of disinfectant. She did not to have to wait long. An elderly inspector came from an office and crooked a finger at her. She stood and followed him.

The room was large with a single desk set in front of the window. Various chairs were positioned near to the table. Marieke was not told to sit. The late evening sunshine came in through the tall window. There were strong bars hidden behind thick lace curtains. What surprised Marieke was the German officer sitting in the corner. The black uniform was perfectly tailored and silver piping edged the collars. The black peaked hat placed beneath his seat had a single badge in its centre. By screwing up her eyes she was able to make out two small bones behind a silver skull. It meant nothing to her. She waited patiently, but her heart began to beat faster. Without looking she could feel the German's eyes boring into her. But she refused to move her head.

'*Mevrouw* van der Meer, I'm *inspecteur* Koopman.' He waved his hand towards the corner. 'This gentleman is *Hauptsturmführer* Müller of the German *Schutzstaffel*. We would like to talk to you.' His voice was not unfriendly and Marieke knew him from somewhere. She decided to speak.

'Thank you, *inspecteur*. May I sit down?' Without waiting for an answer she walked to an upright seat near to the desk and furthest away from the German *SS* officer. He remained motionless.

The policeman continued, 'We know that you've had an injured German pilot hidden in your house. At this stage I don't want to know how he got there. But I've been informed that you kept him there against his will.' Marieke opened her mouth to interrupt, but he raised his hand to silence her. 'My men are carrying out further investigations. Naturally our German colleagues are very interested in this matter.' He glanced towards the other man and took a deep breath. He did not move. 'I won't ask any more questions and you must remain here until this incident is investigated more fully. Meanwhile, you must stay in the police station overnight.'

Marieke was indignant and very upset. She sat stiffly in the chair and fought back the tears. She said quietly, 'Why am I being held here? I have committed no crime.'

For the first time the German stood and said in perfect Dutch, 'You're being kept here because I cannot guarantee your safety outside the police station. After all your own people will be thinking that you have helped a German officer. They will think of you as .... ' He hesitated and then the cultured voice continued, 'Shall we say .... a *moffenmaiden*.'

Marieke shuddered. This man knew exactly how to use the enmity that many Dutch were feeling towards the German invaders. She turned her head sideways a fraction to look at him, took a mental snapshot of his face and looked away again.

He was quite young and very good looking. He had a deep tan and a handsome face. The impeccable uniform fitted his physique perfectly. It was the eyes that gave away his occupation. They were a penetrating blue but as cold as ice. Before she could think he collected his hat, turned and left the room. She gave an involuntary shiver.

Marieke stared at the policeman sitting at the desk in front of her. She was speechless.

The man felt her fear. '*Mevrouw* van der Meer, in this case my hands are tied.' To emphasise the point he stood and shrugged his shoulders. 'Yes, we've met before. You were with your husband at a lunch for members of the *SDAP* Workers Party.' He nodded, 'I would help you if I could.'

Marieke understood: the Germans had already taken over the police force.

'Follow me, please.'

She expected a prison cell. There was a single barred window, the glass was opaque. A wooden bed in the corner had clean sheets and a blanket, all neatly folded. There was no toilet or washbasin. As the substantial door closed behind her, she noticed that there was no handle on her side. The bolt being driven home reminded her that this indeed was a prison.

Marieke had never felt so utterly helpless. She slumped on the hard bed and gazed around the room. There was nobody to talk to and she was totally alone.

TWELVE

Early in the morning of the 13th May 1940, Queen Wilhelmina telephoned a sleeping King George VI at Buckingham Palace. She begged for aircraft to be sent to help Holland. The King replied that he would tell the right people and then he went back to bed.

Frank also had a bad night's sleep. It was pure frustration that made him restless. Eventually he threw the sheets back and climbed out of bed. He again stood near the open window. There was the sound of distant gunfire and the odd cloud of smoke drifted away quickly on the stiff breeze. Below him life seemed to be as normal as it possibly could be. He quickly dressed, locked his room and walked down the stairs.

Two women were laying the table for breakfast. They glanced at him and smiled. He moved past them and found the manager's office.

'Good morning, *meneer* van der Meer,' said the manager and he knowingly nodded. 'I see that you didn't sleep too well either.' Both men laughed hollowly. The hot coffee was brought by one of the kitchen staff. The manager continued, 'The latest news is that the Queen and her family have left Holland.'

Frank stared hard at the manager. He was upset. 'I can't believe that. If it's true then all is lost. What happened?'

'She asked King George for help. I think the British are doing all that they can do at this time. She then set off in a British ship to see our Army in the south at Zeeland. They're still fighting hard there. Apparently, the bombardment was so bad that she was forced to sail on to England. She landed at Harwich on the east coast. King George met her in London and explained how hopeless it was for her to return. She's stayed there. Anyway, from what I hear, The Hague has been overrun and the Government have left.' He scratched his head. 'I think it's rats leaving the sinking ship.'

Frank nodded, 'Yes, I saw signs of that yesterday. Up near The Hague the Germans are everywhere. At least the Queen and her family are safe, but I don't hold out much hope for our country now.'

The two men sipped their coffee in silence.

As the day wore on Frank prowled round the hotel. Meals came and went. Several times he left and each time he was told by the police and the army to go back. There was a spirited defence of Rotterdam taking place, he saw the occasional Royal Air Force fighter pass overhead but there was no sign of the conflict that was obviously taking place in the outskirts of the city. It was as though there was a ring around the hotel preventing him from leaving. In reality there was. It was the German 9th Panzer Division, *SS-Standarte "Adolf Hitler"* and the 7th Airborne Division.

Frank was the only remaining guest and he had the whole building to himself. He spent most of his day listening to the wireless in the restaurant.

The manager seemed to be a mine of information and they drank coffee whenever he had more news to report. He walked outside on the old streets as often as he could. He was watched all the time by the police patrols. Several times the gunfire drew closer and then it faded. On that night he climbed into bed and knew that tomorrow he had to try again to reach his family.

Sunday the 14th May dawned slowly. It was overcast with the promise of later rain. Frank ate breakfast alone. His bag was packed and already loaded into the boot of the Austin. He had made up his mind not to return to the Maas Hotel no matter what happened during the day. If necessary he was prepared to use the German pass to get through anything or anybody that tried to stop him. Frank ate more than usual, he realised that it may be some time before he could eat another decent meal. As he drained his last cup of coffee, the manager appeared at his elbow.

'*Meneer* van der Meer, I've had a packed lunch prepared for you and your thermos flask is filled.' He placed the basket of food carefully on the floor close to Frank's chair. 'Don't worry about the bill, you may need your money later. I'll post it to you within the next week.' Frank nodded and looked at him. '*Meneer*, it's been a pleasure to have you as a guest in my hotel. If I can help you in the future, then please don't hesitate to contact me. God's speed for your journey, I'm sure that you'll be successful this time.'

They shook hands for the last time.

Frank sought out a small garage near to the hotel. He was lucky, only one petrol pump was operating and the price had doubled in the last two days. When the tank was full the man cleaned the windscreen. Frank followed him into the small office and paid for the fuel.

The man seemed friendly enough. 'Where are you going to, *meneer*?'

Frank smiled. 'I'm hoping to drive to Friesland today. That is, if I can get through the road blocks.'

The man shook his head, 'That could be difficult. From what I've heard we're surrounded. The best way might be to go east from here, away from the Maas bridges. Most of the fighting seems to be going on near there.'

Frank shrugged his shoulders and left the garage. He drove slowly and carefully to the east, following the man's suggestion. He kept away from the main roads but every time he moved a half kilometre forward there was yet another road block. He travelled two kilometres in an hour. The last road block was the biggest. Two armoured cars guarded the road and a burnt-out truck blocked the main route. Yet again he was waved to a stop. The soldier was Dutch and looked exhausted.

'Sorry, you can't come this way. Nobody is allowed through at all.' He pointed, 'Pull over behind that armoured vehicle, switch off your engine and get out of your car.'

Frank wearily did as he was told. The armoured car looked immense.

He stood near it and looked up at the turret not quite knowing what to do. The hatch opened and a young officer climbed out. His face was sweating. He sat on the short barrel of the gun and called down to Frank.

'Well, *meneer*, what's your name and where've you come from?'

Frank explained what he was trying to do and only when he spoke about the meeting with the Germans at the airfield did the young man show any interest. He climbed down from the tank and called over some more of his men to listen. Frank remembered the food and the coffee. He reached into the Austin and brought out the basket and offered its contents to the men around him. Within ten minutes the food had gone. An older man with a single major's star on his uniform joined the small group.

He looked at Frank and was obviously tired and depressed. '*Ja*, the Germans have surrounded us. What weapons they have. ... This thing,' he patted the side of the armoured car, 'is over fifteen years old. It's outgunned and bloody slow.'

Before Frank could answer, a voice called down from the turret hatch. The *majoor* turned, climbed up the side of the armoured car and slid down inside the turret. After a few minutes he emerged. He motioned his men to join him. Around twenty stood in a semi-circle round the car. Frank tried to move away but the men waved him over to join them. This simple act made him proud to be with them.

The *majoor* cleared his throat, 'Men, *Kolonel* Scharroo, Commander of the Dutch garrison in Rotterdam, has been called upon by the Germans to surrender. I have been informed that he's seeking authority to agree to this surrender with the High Command in The Hague. Meanwhile, we sit and wait and do not engage enemy forces. ... That's all.'

The men shook their heads and their shoulders sank. Frank went back and sat in his car.

About ten minutes later he heard that almost familiar drone of engines overhead. As he climbed out of his car, the sound came from the east. By shading his eyes he could clearly see masses of German bombers and fighter escorts approaching their position. He had time to count them as they flew towards him.

The *majoor* was standing at his side, 'Jesus Christ, there must be a hundred bombers out there! ... They're flying straight towards the centre of Rotterdam.' He banged his fist on the side of the tank. 'Don't they know we've been offered surrender terms?'

'Sir, ... look!' One of the soldiers pointed towards the city.

Three red flares arced into the sky. It was obviously some kind of signal. Thirty of the bombers peeled off and turned to the south, probably seeking another target. The men held their breath as the armada roared over their heads. The ground shook, forcing Frank to put his hands over his ears. There was something awesomely fascinating about such power. The *majoor* crumpled against the side of his armoured car, he was shouting loudly over the roar. 'OH NO! JESUS CHRIST! ... THEY'RE GOING TO DO IT!'

He pointed with both hands as the bombers flew straight over the city. 'LOOK! ... OH MY GOD! ... LOOK!'

The bombs fell like rain. Even at this distance the soft, sandy ground shook and within seconds, the concussion waves hit the group of men. Dense black clouds of smoke jetted upwards and rolled back towards them. Within a minute the clouds were over them blotting out the sun. The stench of burning fell about them and they were covered in speckles of black dust. The crump of heavy explosions hit them in waves and the men dived for cover. The screaming of the Stuka dive bombers penetrated everything.

The *majoor* made the decision, 'Right men, on the cars! Head back to the city, they'll need our help there! ... Come on, hurry up!' His parade ground voice clearly heard by everybody.

Frank stood near his car. The *majoor* caught his eye. 'Van der Meer, stay here. It's safer.'

'*Verdomme, majoor*! Like hell! I'm coming with you!' He leapt into his car and started the engine. The armoured cars roared away, exhaust plumes belching from their rear. The Austin followed in second gear.

The streets were full of people staring from their houses towards Rotterdam. The heavy armoured cars cleared the way and Frank had to peer through the smoke and dust. He followed them for about ten minutes and then suddenly he turned a corner and they were gone. He could not reverse as there were other cars behind him. He managed to keep going towards the River Maas and then he pulled off at the side of the road. When the other cars passed him all was quiet.

He put his head on the steering wheel and prayed. He did not know what to do next. His prayers were answered. There was a tap on the window. He wound it down.

'*Meneer*, what the hell are you doing here? Get out of your car.' The man was another Dutch army officer.

Frank wearily climbed out of the Austin and gazed around him. Somehow he had ended up in a small square to the south of Rotterdam. Smoke still hung in the air and there were little signs of movement. Around stood large crowds of Dutch soldiers. Most of them looked exhausted and over them hung an air of defeat. Their equipment lay on the ground and they stood in small groups. Outside a tall brick building were two armoured cars. Frank recognised the *majoor* immediately and walked over towards him.

'We meet again, *meneer*.' He smiled grimly, his face ashen. 'Do you realise what we're sitting in the middle of?' Frank shook his head. The *majoor* let out a hollow laugh. 'You're watching history, my friend. This is the surrender of the City of Rotterdam to the enemy. ...... Look over there.' He nodded towards a small building in a row of non-descript houses.

Near the largest group of Dutch soldiers were three tanks but these had great black crosses on their sides. Close to them, smartly dressed ranks of German soldiers stood to attention. They wore immaculate black uniforms and looked as though they were on parade. Everybody followed their movements.

Frank's heart missed a beat. Appearing on the steps of the building was the German *general* that he had met two days previously. Kurt Student put his hands on his belt and stared round at the Dutch soldiers. There was a look of intense satisfaction on his face. He glanced again towards Frank and frowned with curiosity. Making up his mind, he marched towards the *majoor*. All eyes, both Dutch and German, were upon him. The late afternoon sunlight reflected off the Knight's Cross that hung at his throat. He paused again and glanced around. There was total silence.

'Why is he coming here?' whispered the *majoor*.

'We've met before,' answered Frank.

Generalmajor Kurt Student stopped directly in front of the two men. Realisation dawned on him. The voice was neutral with an element of surprise.

'*Meneer* van der Meer, if my memory serves me correctly. What, may I ask, are you doing here?

The question demanded an answer. There was still total silence.

The *majoor* stiffened to attention and saluted the senior officer. Frank remembered the bombing. He managed to wait for just the right moment. He looked directly into the eyes under the high peaked hat.

'I've come to help the people of Rotterdam after you deliberately broke the terms of the proposed surrender.'

For a moment the *General*'s eyes flickered. He stared intently into Frank's face. The voice took on a new tone.

'I am not used to explaining things to civilians. But in this case I will do. We did not break the surrender arrangements. Due to communications problems, *Luftflotte 2 HQ* was unable to contact the squadrons in time. Thirty aircraft were diverted with the red flares. The remainder, I'm sorry to say, bombed their targets. Meanwhile, you must leave this area. I assume that you still have the pass that I gave to you?' There was no response. 'Use it!'

Without waiting for a reply he turned on his heel. Frank did not quite remember how it started. From the corner of his eye he saw groups of heavily armed German troops crawling through piles of rubble off to his left. The sound of tank engines ticking-over drowned out further noises. They came from all directions with machine-guns chattering and men diving to the ground. Everywhere there was utter confusion. The Dutch were unable to defend themselves. The enemy in the immediate area were not sure whom to fire at.

General Student knew instantly what had happened. He ran forward with his arms outstretched shouting at the top of his voice.

'Hold your fire! ... HOLD YOUR FIRE! The Dutch are surrendering to ME!'

He kept repeating the order but the crash of small arms fire drowned out his words. Frank stood rooted to the spot as bullets buzzed around his head. It was unreal and his legs froze. He almost saw the flight of one single bullet that flew straight at the General's head. He saw the hat fly off and he saw the spurt of blood just below the ear. The officer's mouth snapped shut and he dropped to the ground. Without hesitation, Frank ran forward and knelt beside the body.

The firing stopped suddenly as quickly as it had begun. Nobody moved and then there was a rush from both sides to where the *General* had fallen. His head lay cradled in Frank's arms. The eyes flickered for a moment and then the body slumped back. A German officer pulled Frank to one side. A medical orderly rushed up with a stretcher and first-aid equipment. Within a minute *General* Student was surrounded by his men. One of them was obviously his doctor who attempted to revive him. Eventually Frank stepped forward. He was the only civilian present and probably for this reason alone the soldiers on both sides let him through.

His voice was calm and his German was clear. 'There's a hospital three kilometres from here. ... My car will be better than a tank. ... Get him in quickly, ... now!'

The Germans stood back incredulously and just stared open-mouthed at this imposing Dutchman. Some of the soldiers began to edge forward but the doctor realised what had happened.

'He's right, I'll go with him. Come on now, lift the *General* into the back of the car.'

Four men stepped forward and gently lifted their commander, they carried the stretcher towards the waiting Austin.

The *majoor* said, 'I'll come as well. With me you stand a better chance of getting past the Dutch lines.'

There were hurried nods all round and the three men closed the car doors carefully behind them. Frank started the engine and the car moved slowly away towards the outskirts of the city. As it drove carefully through the silent streets the *majoor* gave directions.

The car suddenly burst into the beginning of the bomb damaged areas. Total desolation greeted them. Whole blocks had disappeared to be replaced by heaps of fiercely burning rubble. People were running round scrabbling with their bare hands at the ruins. The heavy stench of burning wood and other unimaginable odours flew in through the open car window. The sounds of shouting and crackling timber made them all wince. The three men felt the horror that was in front of them. Frank turned round to look at the German doctor. Not a word passed between the two men, their exchanged looks said it all.

The Austin reversed away from the burning centre of old Rotterdam and moved down a clear side-street. They had only travelled a hundred metres.

'QUICK! ... STOP!' screamed the *majoor*.

The car was surrounded by scores of soldiers. They were German, green uniformed members of the *Waffen-SS*. Frank noted the black arm bands with the words *"Adolf Hitler"* woven in silver. Their fully cocked sub-machine guns pointed in the same direction. The doctor was quick enough to wind down the rear window. He shouted something that Frank did not hear. One of the SS men stuck his head in. A glance at the uniform and the blood was enough. He jumped to attention and shouted to the other men. They parted and Frank drove on.

Huge Red Cross flags hung outside the hospital. Frank drove straight through the gates to the main entrance. Two orderlies came out and looked at the man on the back seat. They shook their heads. The *majoor* said something that Frank did not hear. The orderlies quickly walked away. A tall man in a white coat appeared and looked through the open door of the car. Again the *majoor* explained. The man looked grimly at the occupants of the car, turned and waved the two orderlies back to the car.

The doctor's voice was weary. 'You two. Put him on that stretcher and take him to Theatre 3.'

Frank thought twice, removed the keys from the ignition and locked the car. They moved through the corridors and the two doctors separated and continued with their patient through tall swing doors. Frank and the *majoor* sat down to wait.

An hour later and the Dutch doctor returned. His face was straight and expressionless. He looked closely at the two men. His voice was quiet, 'We'll be able to save him. The bullet is lodged near the base of the skull. I'm not so sure whether I should thank you or not because another fifteen minutes and he would've been dead.' The message was obvious.

The *majoor* turned, 'Van der Meer, what're you going to do now?'

Frank shook his head. 'I'm going to set off again and this time try to get through to the north. Last time I travelled quite some way before I was stopped.' He thought about the German pass that was still in his car. 'If Rotterdam has surrendered then I think the rest of Holland will soon be taken by the Germans.'

The *majoor* nodded wearily. 'I think you're right. When I see the weapons that the Germans have I don't think it'll be long.' He shook his head. 'You know some of my men are using guns that were made before the First War.' He stood and looked at his watch. 'I'd better get back to my unit. Any chance of a lift?'

Frank nodded. As they were about to leave the German doctor returned. He still wore the white operating gown. It was bloody. He pulled of his gauze mask.

'Gentlemen, the *General* owes you his life. The surgeon has removed the bullet and his condition is stable.' He paused and looked at each man in turn. 'I'm sorry that your beautiful city has been bombed. If either of you ever needs any help in the future, then please telephone this number.

It's the number of the *General's* Headquarters in Germany.' He pulled out two small cards from under his gown and gave one to Frank and the *majoor*. Without another word they quickly left the hospital.

It was late evening and for a moment they waited near the entrance to the hospital and looked at the devastation around them. Near the Austin there was a small group of disconsolate-looking Dutch soldiers. They were covered in dust and had no weapons. As soon as they saw the *majoor* they stood stiffly to attention and saluted. One of them stepped forward.

'What do we do now, sir?'

He returned the salute and smiled gently at them, 'Return to your units as soon as possible.'

The men shook their heads, 'We don't know where our units are, Sir.' They saw the look on his face. 'Did you know, Sir, that Holland has surrendered?' He shook his head and Frank showed no surprise. 'That's right, Sir. At 20-30 hours tonight our High Commander, Generaal Winkelman, formally surrendered.'

He gave them a grim smile and saluted. 'Go to your families and good luck!'

He turned to Frank, 'Come with me. The least I can do is find you a bed for the night. My divisional headquarters are north of Rotterdam. By the way, it's about time you stopped calling me *majoor*, my name is Marius Hofstra.' Frank only had the strength to nod a reply.

He was back on the same stretch of road that he had travelled on only days before. They saw no road blocks, only weary columns of walking Dutch soldiers. The biggest problem of the night was encountered after about an hour of slow driving. Slued across in the road and illuminated by car headlamps were four German Ju 52 bombers. Their undercarriages were damaged but the aircraft were well guarded by German soldiers and light tanks.

'Must have missed the runway!' said the *majoor* with a lopsided grin. For the first time that day both men laughed.

The muzzle of the tank's gun pointed menacingly down towards the Austin's bonnet.

'Van der Meer, I think we have trouble,' he spoke with a whisper.

'Papers! Now!' The voice was hidden behind the bright light, but the meaning was clear.

'I've got just the thing,' said Frank with a slight smile.

He produced the German pass from his pocket and waved it through the window whilst still staring straight ahead. The effect was instantaneous. The tank's gun barrel swung out of the way and the light switched off. The car was saluted by four German soldiers and they were waved away.

'Christ, van der Meer! What is that and just who the hell are you? You follow my car into Rotterdam. Rescue a German general. Save his life and now you can pass through their roadblocks, with salutes! What is it with you.' His voice was incredulous and just tinged with a hint of menace.

Frank laughed again and told his story. The remainder of the journey was uneventful.

The Dutch army headquarters was ringed by German troops but they let them in. Marius Hofstra was as good as his word. He did find a bed for him and Frank ate a snack meal in his room. The bed was hard but after a hot bath he slept like a baby for ten hours with no questions asked.

When he awoke he found his suitcase ready at the side of the bed. His clothes had been neatly cleaned and ironed. Frank washed and shaved in the small wash-basin. Before he had finished there was a quiet knock at the door and *Majoor* Hofstra entered.

'Good morning, *meneer*. Had a good sleep I presume?' He looked at his watch, 'You know it's eleven o'clock!' He laughed when he saw Frank's reaction. 'I know you want to be on your way so I've returned the meal you gave to me yesterday. On your back seat there's a basket of food and a flask of coffee, courtesy of the Dutch Light Division.'

Frank saw the *majoor* for the last time when he shook hands with him at the gate to the camp. They parted company without really ever getting to know each other. The roads were quiet and, for Frank, there was no turning back.

He stayed off the main auto-routes and followed the coast roads. Occasionally German aircraft flew overhead. They ignored him. Only once did he see a British plane. It was flying low and back towards the coast. He planned to cross the North Sea Canal at IJmuiden and then continue towards the *Afsluitdijk*. He stopped once for a snack and was wise enough to pull off the road under some trees. It was lucky for him that he did because a whole column of German tanks and troop carriers rolled past. He waited for a short while and drove on.

IJmuiden is an important port at the entrance to the North Sea Canal that leads from the North Sea to Amsterdam and the internal canal network. Frank entered the town through a small side road that ran parallel to the sand dunes on the coast. The port was busy. There were large groups of people standing around looking completely lost. He drove the car through the crowds and, to satisfy his curiosity, he stopped near to the docks.

As he stepped out of his car, he had a real surprise, moored at the docks were four British torpedo boats and a large civilian freighter flying the Dutch Flag. Stepping down the gangway were British soldiers. He could not believe his eyes. He rushed over to them and tried to speak to the officer near to the Dutch army vehicles.

'Hey! You must listen to me!' The soldier ignored him. He tried again. This time a Dutch soldier came to his side.

'*Meneer*, you must leave now! The Germans are outside the town.' His voice was not unfriendly.

'I know, they've just driven past me. Tanks and troops. Hundreds of 'em!' shouted Frank.

The man stared hard and then turned and called to the other soldiers, both British and Dutch, to Frank's side. They listened to what he had to say about the surrender of Rotterdam and the German troop movements. The English officer was more forthright.

'You may've surrendered but we've not. We're trying to support some of your men near The Hague. But, from what you say, if they've surrendered then we may be wasting our time.'

'I'm not a military man, but from what I've seen over the last few days you don't stand a chance.' Frank said with conviction.

The soldiers just shrugged their shoulders and turned away. There was nothing else that Frank could do. He decided to leave as soon as possible. He had seen the speed of German troop movements too many times.

He quickly noticed six buses coming through the dock gates. They braked to a halt nearby. What surprised him more than anything was the gold writing down the side of each bus, "STAD-AMSTERDAM". He was filled with curiosity. What on earth were buses from the city of Amsterdam doing in the docks at IJmuiden? The first bus stopped in front of him just as the last British soldiers disembarked from the ship. He glanced along its length. The windows were open and at every one were children's faces. There must have been thirty or forty jammed into each bus. But these children were not real. They were sad-faced and drawn and appeared unconnected with the chaos outside their buses. Most of them had dark hair and dark skins. To Frank they seemed out of place and then he realised why. There were no signs of their parents, just a few adults who sat separately from the children. As thoughts raced through his mind, the door swung open and a woman stepped down. He knew instantly that she was the leader of the children.

She was slim and in her mid-forties. To Frank there was a fleeting resemblance to Marieke and his heart yearned for home. She had enormous brown eyes and these fixed straight onto his. The voice was soft and melodic and bore a slight accent that he could not place.

'Meneer, are you in charge here?' Before he could shake his head she continued, 'If you're not, then where's the kapitein of that ship?' She remained staring at his face and pointed at the ship behind him.

He was captivated and for a moment, and unusually for him, he could not find the words. Then they came, 'No, I'm not in charge and no, I don't know where the kapitein is?' He somehow felt inadequate.

She laughed and her body trembled. 'Well, you're not much good to me are you?'

He had to reply, 'Look here. ... What can I do to help? Why are all these children on the buses and why? ...'

She held up her hand and he closed his mouth. 'Right, my name is Geertruida Wijsmuller. I'm Jewish and so are these children in the buses. They need our help to get away from Holland and that ship looks about the right size. If you really want to help?' Frank nodded and flashed his charming smile.

She grasped his hand and hurried on, 'Let's go onto the ship and let's see what the *kapitein* says.' She turned and called out. 'Harry Jacobi, come with me!'

A boy about fourteen years old joined her on the quayside. He was painfully thin and his huge brown eyes fastened on Frank.

'*Guten Abend, mein Herr.*'

The simple fact that he spoke German shocked Frank. He thought that all the children were Dutch. The boy instinctively came and stood at his side.

At the top of the gangway was a lone ship's officer. He was no match for Geertruida.

She smiled at him, put her hand on his shoulder. 'Take us to your *kapitein* please.' He saluted her and asked her to follow. They did.

The *kapitein* rose from behind an old desk and welcomed them into his cabin. It was wood panelled with three brass portholes let into one wall. Various paintings of ships adorned the walls.

Geertruida walked straight up to him, looked him in the eye and with a slight smile on her face said, '*Kapitein*, I need your help. I have two hundred Jewish children on my buses and some adults. Please can you take them to England?'

The *kapitein* slumped back into his chair. The group remained standing and looked down at him. He raised his hands. '*Mevrouw*. This is impossible. I've just sailed from England with British troops. I've done my job and I must return to my home port in Rotterdam.' He shook his head. 'It's really out of the question.'

Unasked, Geertruida sat down directly opposite the table. She spoke in a voice so quiet that the *kapitein* had to lean forward to hear. 'I'm Jewish and so are the children. They've travelled from Germany to Holland chased all the way by the Nazis. Harry, here,' she waved a hand, 'used to live in Hamburg. The Germans are sending all their Jews to resettlement camps, including Harry's parents. All of them will never return. We thought that Holland would be safe but I know exactly what they will do when they take over the whole of this country. WE must save them or else they will die!'

The *kapitein* hesitated for a moment. Frank saw his chance. He spoke for the first time. 'If your home port is Rotterdam then you no longer have a home port. I saw it yesterday. It's been completely bombed by the *Luftwaffe*. The city centre and the docks are flattened. There're probably thousands killed. I've seen at first hand how the German forces operate. If you've just finished ferrying British troops then there is not a hope in hell of you even getting to your home port. The entrances to the rivers near Rotterdam are mined. They've also complete control of the air. You have no other choice but to take these people to England.'

Now Frank sat down and looked and waited for a response.

The man drummed his fingers on the table and gazed at the group of people in front of him. His eyes came to rest on Harry Jacobi. They examined each other in silence. He looked away and the drumming stopped. As if by coincidence through the open portholes came the sound of heavy explosions. The sound seemed to convince him.

He nodded and for the first time smiled, 'All right, I'll take you. From what I can hear outside you'd better hurry up and load your children.'

Geertruida rose, went round the table and kissed the *kapitein* on the cheek, 'In God's name, thank you,' she murmured.

As they walked out of the cabin, she turned to Frank. 'Thank you, and I don't even know your name. Are you coming with us?'

He shook his head, 'No, my family live in Friesland and I've been trying for five days to reach them. I must leave you when the children've boarded.'

They reached the gangway and looked at the scene set out below them. All the children had left the buses and were standing in a huge crowd around the bottom of the gangway. Their eyes seemed to bore into the adults watching them. The explosions came ever nearer. Not a word was spoken and then, suddenly, Harry stepped to the top of the Gangway. His eyes lit-up and his voice had new strength.

'COME ON! ... All of you, NOW!'

The children needed no second bidding. With a roar of delight they surged up the narrow gangway and flooded past Frank. He stood there and unashamedly cried. Looking down he found that Harry Jacobi was holding his hand. The big brown eyes said it all. Suddenly, Frank was alone. Without looking back he strode down the gangway and onto the dockside. When he glanced upwards, the children were in a line along the side of the ship. He waved and they cheered.

Within five minutes the ship cast off and began to move. Frank watched it leave the dock. The black smoke from its funnel left a dark smear across the blue sky. He sighed, another symbol. As he walked back to his car shells began to fall into the nearby town. He climbed into the cool leather seat and put his head on the steering wheel. A tap came on the window. He looked up. It was the same Dutch officer that he had met earlier.

'*Meneer*, you must leave this area now. We're going to blow up the oil storage tanks to stop the Germans taking them.' He glanced at his wrist watch. 'You have about fifteen minutes. Go north towards Alkmaar. It's quieter up there. Good luck!' As a second thought he touched Frank's shoulder, 'And thanks for helping the kids. We all saw what you did.'

Frank nodded and started the engine. The officer returned before he could travel a hundred metres.

His face was full of sadness, 'We've just heard on the wireless that Holland has capitulated to the Germans. God help us all.'

Frank thought for a moment and drove the car right out of the town without even realising what he had done. His brain was numb and he drove like a robot. It was the ground shaking under the car that made him stop and look back towards IJmuiden. There were dense clouds of billowing, black smoke. They had indeed blown up the oil storage tanks. Frank shook his head and drove on.

THIRTEEN

Food arrived regularly. Each time the door opened and the same young policeman walked in and placed the food on a low table near to Marieke's bed. By the quick glances that he gave he was obviously embarrassed. Whenever she wanted to go to the toilet she knocked on the door and the man escorted her down the corridor. He waited outside but she was not allowed to lock the door. Nobody spoke to her and nobody else came to see her. She began to despair.

By looking up at the window Marieke saw that night had turned to day and day had turned to night. She tried to wash but each time she was so concerned that at any moment the policeman may just walk in. Exploration of her cell had proved fruitless. There was nothing but bare walls and a single light bulb. The air was heavy, the window was never open. Time seemed to slow until eventually she began to stop thinking about how long she was to be imprisoned. Her only solace was her belief in the Church. Eventually she started to recite out aloud all the verses of the Bible that she could remember. At night she forced herself to sleep by singing her favourite hymns.

Sleep was never deep. She was awoken by the slightest sound from the slamming of a door to the creak of a floorboard. This sound was different. It was the sound of a voice. She swung her legs off the bed and stood. Just in time because the door creaked open. The policeman beckoned her forward. She meekly followed. This was something new. The only time she had left the room was to go to the toilet. She turned the corner and saw the open door of the office.

The room was empty. She waited, this time not daring to sit. A glance at the clock showed it to be six-thirty in the morning. Marieke shook her head. She had to think twice to remember what day it was.

Behind her there was a slight cough. The *inspecteur* walked past her and sat down. He was followed by another man. For a moment she was only conscious of his shape and then her heart gave a massive leap of joy. It was Frank!

Without a moment's thought she reached out and threw her arms around him and clung onto his body. She cried and the tears flowed down her cheeks as her chest heaved with emotion. She was speechless.

The *inspecteur* saw their joy and smiled. As Marieke let go of her husband she glanced around the room. *Hauptsturmführer* Müller was sitting in exactly the same chair as at their previous meeting. Her joy faded and the fear returned.

Frank did not wait for anybody. He stood. His voice was resolute. 'I demand to know why my wife is being kept here without charges being brought against her?' He glared at the two men.

The *inspecteur* said nothing and turned to the SS officer.

The *Hauptsturmführer* steepled his fingers and the cold eyes surveyed the two people in front of him. His legs were crossed and the black leather jackboots gleamed. The crossed leg swung backwards and forwards, backwards and forwards. Not a sound.

The voice was so quiet that Frank had to turn slightly.

'Your wife will stay here as long as I say.' A pause. 'I have not yet finished my investigations. After all, she is safer here.'

He bent over and picked up his peaked hat and then stood. Frank was tall but this man was five centimetres taller and looked down into Frank's eyes. He felt the chill of cold terror. Neither of the two men flinched. He felt Marieke's hand in his. Even though he was exhausted this gave him the strength to speak. He took a step back and reached into his pocket. Quick as a flash the SS man reached for his pistol.

'Before you do anything else, look at this!' Frank's hand held the small oblong of card that had been given to him by *General* Student's doctor. He offered it to Müller.

With a look of utter contempt he gave only a peremptory glance at the card. When his eyes settled on the tiny eagle with the swastika clutched in its talons, his body stiffened. As he reached for the card Frank took it back.

His eyes held the German's and then glanced down. 'I'll read it for you. It says, **"Given with the compliments of *Generalmajor* Kurt Student. Commanding *General* 7th Flieger Division. Headquarters Templehof-Berlin. Telephone 0223-42134."** Now, I would like you to telephone that number and see what the *General* has to say.' Frank put the dagger in and turned it. 'I'm sure he won't mind you telephoning at this hour.'

Müller physically shivered. His voice had lost its menace. 'Give me the card and I'll telephone immediately.'

He took it and walked round the desk to pick up the telephone. He barked the numbers and waited. It took a few minutes but eventually he was connected. Marieke still clutched Frank's hand. He briefly glanced into her eyes and winked. She looked totally amazed.

Müller spoke in sharp grunts, '*Jawohl, ... jawohl .... nein ... nein ...* I will wait, *Herr Oberst.*' He looked up at Frank. 'I am being re-connected to a hospital in Rotterdam.' There was total silence in the room. Again he began, '*Bitte ... ja ... ja!*'

Suddenly he made them all jump with surprise as he sprang to attention. He spoke quickly and Frank realised that he was telling *General* Student about Marieke's imprisonment.

With one hand clutching the telephone he shouted, '*Jawohl, Herr Generalmajor.* I will obey your orders.'

He put the telephone back on its cradle and stared hard at Frank. His voice was silky and Frank noted that there were one or two mistakes in his Dutch pronunciation.

'I have spoken to the *Generalmajor* and I have decided to release *mevrouw* van der Meer immediately. I must apologise for any inconvenience.' He paused and attempted to understand the depth of Frank's relationship with the *General*.

Frank knew that the man was so desperate to ask questions, but mentally he dismissed him. His inherent good manners took over.

'Thank you, we will now leave. May I have the *General's* card back please.' It was returned without a sound. He turned to the silent policeman. 'Good bye *Inspecteur*,' grasped Marieke firmly by the arm and tried to leave the room. He was stopped by Müller.

'*Meneer* and *mevrouw* van der Meer, please allow me to provide you with my staff car for you to travel home.' His eyes glittered.

'No thanks. I have my Austin waiting outside.' Frank smiled at both men and brushed past the *Hauptsturmführer*.

Reaching the door he turned round. He could not resist. He gave his most charming smile, '*Mein Herr* how is the *Generalmajor*? He was not too well the last time we met.'

It stopped Müller dead. His eyes dropped and then lifted again. It was a question that over the telephone he had not dared to ask. He made up an answer.

'The *Generalmajor* is much better, thank you.' The words ground out from between compressed lips.

Frank smiled and walked arm in arm with his wife through the main hall of the police station. He was conscious of the stares and smiled at everybody that he saw. Nobody noticed just how tightly the couple clung to each other.

Marieke wanted to ask a thousand questions but she knew that they had to reach the car first. As they descended the steps of the police station she was surprised to see that life had returned to the streets of Leeuwarden. The dusty Austin was waiting and Frank opened the car door for her and she sank into the seat. As he walked round to open his door, the *inspecteur* appeared at his shoulder.

'Good bye, *meneer* van der Meer. May I say to you, privately, well done. You really caught him out! ... I'm sure we'll meet again.' Both men nodded to each other. The bond was established.

The journey home meant so much to both of them. They exchanged smiles and their arms were interlocked, but neither of them spoke.

As they reached the end of the narrow road to the factory the sun broke through the clouds and shone out clear and sharp. As the car arrived at their home, and before he had time to switch off the engine, their children came running down the path excitedly followed down by the de Bruin family. There were hugs and kisses everywhere but underneath the smiles and the laughter there were flashes of worry and apprehension.

An enormous breakfast had been prepared and they all sat down to eat. It took over three hours for the stories to finish.

Soon after breakfast the de Bruins left, David and Aukje took longer to say good-bye. For the remainder of the day the family sat about the house. Frank was exhausted and after a full dinner he and Marieke went to bed early. They both had a long bath and climbed into bed.

She lay on her side and looked into Frank's eyes. 'Darling, I just had to wash that prison stink off me. Even now I still feel dirty.'

'I know exactly how you feel, *liefje*. I will never wash away what I feel until our country is free again.'

They clung to each other and shared their thoughts without speaking.

PART TWO

Occupation

ONE

During the first week of German occupation, life in Leeuwarden appeared to return to normal and for the van der Meer Factory, business re-started. Marieke picked up the newspaper.

'Frank, please, read this.'

He shook the paper and glanced over the front page. Over the top of the headlines was the statement.

"The uncensored publication of this paper is due to the generosity of the German troops."

There was a photograph of a Rotterdam suburb. One house was slightly damaged and another had some broken windows.

He was red with anger. 'Marieke, this is absolutely untrue. I saw the damage with my own eyes. The whole of the city centre was bombed flat.' He threw the flimsy sheets on the floor. 'Who's going to believe anything that the newspapers print from now on.'

'Some people will Frank and we have to be very careful what we say about anything that's written in the papers.'

They both sat in the office and waited for the day to unfold.

As usual, *Schipper* Schaaf came and loaded up with the next batch of wooden frames. Again he stayed for a quick lunch. It was as though the last week had never occurred. The table was laid just as before and Marieke had made ginger cakes especially for the kapitein. She knew he loved them.

He tried not to raise the subject but it was too difficult for him to hold in his thoughts any longer. He chose his moment. 'Now, *meneer* van der Meer. I hear you had a very interesting time last week?'

Frank looked up from his meal, *Schipper*, it's something I prefer not to talk about. If you don't mind?' He saw the old man's face drop and he smiled. 'Some other time perhaps, but not now.'

'You see, *Schipper*, what happened was a shock for us all,' added a smiling Marieke.

'Yes indeed, *mevrouw*. What the Germans did to you was disgraceful. Do you know who informed on you?'

She exchanged a glance with Frank. He gave an imperceptible shake of his head. Marieke looked down at her plate and then lifted her head and smiled at their old friend. 'I presume they just put two and two together and came up with me. After all one of the other bombers must have seen the parachute land in the factory yard and, therefore, they only had to come looking.'

He waved his fork angrily. 'I think it was one of your neighbours. There's many people about now who want to gain favours with the *moffen*. You mark my words, we'll have to watch ourselves all the time from now on.' He muttered something and carried on eating.

There was a pause in the conversation. Even Harmen kept his mouth firmly shut. But the *schipper* had to continue, after all the van der Meer family had become famous.

He delved into his trouser pocket and with a flourish produced a sheet of paper. 'I assume that you've all seen one of these? I picked it up in Leeuwarden on the way here this morning.' They all leant forward.

'I haven't, *Schipper*. What is it?' said Frank curiously.

'I'll read it for you. It's an order to all town *burgemeesters* from the Queen's Commissioner in Friesland. This is what they have to make sure is happening.' His voice took on an official tone.

'All bridges and roads must be repaired.
It is forbidden to use petrol and diesel oil.
Coal must be used sparingly.
It is forbidden to increase prices and hoard food.
Report all strangers.

What do you think of that?' He rubbed his grey beard. 'I'm lucky. I've got enough diesel oil for my boats to last me for months. But it's going to be hard for some people. I've heard that the Germans have plenty of money. They've been giving their troops sack loads of the occupation notes.'

Frank looked at the sheet of paper and shook his head. 'It's starting now. This is just the beginning.' He threw it on the table in disgust and picked up his knife and fork. 'I don't get paid at the moment. My last bill to the Province for timber was paid by a note saying that I would be reimbursed in the future. How long the "Queen's" Commissioner can last for, I don't know. Something has to break soon.' He placed his knife and fork on the plate, pushed it away and glanced at his friend.

There came a tap on the window. The *schipper* waved an acknowledgement.

'If you don't mind, *mevrouw* van der Meer, I'll miss the coffee. I want to get home before it goes dark. Thank you for your usual hospitality.' He smiled at them. 'There was a time last week when I thought I would never see either of you again.'

He stood, nodded to the family and Frank walked with him to the *tjalk*. As they approached, the *schipper* took his arm and said quietly, '*Meneer*, a word of warning. You should know that some people believe that you're far too friendly with the Germans. They want to know why you had one in your house and how your wife got out of prison. I don't believe these rumours. But ... ,' he bent even closer, 'be careful. ... Please be careful.'

Frank could do nothing but thank him. He returned to the house with the warning ringing through his brain.

They all helped to clear the table and it was Marieke's suggestion that really cheered them up. 'Come on, let's get on our bikes and go and see the de Bruins. We haven't seen them for days.'

Aukje's eyes lit up.

'Do I have to come, *Mem*?' said Harmen with a bored look on his face.

It was Frank that answered, 'Yes you do. Until things settle down, we must keep together.' He was mindful of *schipper* Schaaf's warnings. 'I should stay at the factory, but,' he glanced at the clock, 'Jan will be home soon and the workmen can look after themselves.'

The farmhouse was typically Friesian, strong and functional. A large square barn with a high sloping roof laid with red pantiles. At each end of the ridge, soaring above the roof line, stood a wooden carving of two intertwined swan's necks, painted in green and white. A narrow tiled building led to the farmhouse itself at the front of a barn. Two storeys with high narrow windows and wrought iron decoration on the dark red brickwork. The neat gardens at the front led down to a small canal. Flat green fields surrounded the farmhouse. It had long since stopped being used as a farm. Jan de Bruin had inherited it from his father and had quickly sold off the land. Banking was much more lucrative than farming.

As they cycled up the narrow road Tineke emerged from the front door. She waved a greeting.

'Hello everybody. We were half expecting you. Do come in.'

They stepped into the cool interior. It was full of old Dutch furniture that blended in perfectly with the atmosphere of the house. David jumped up from the sofa. It was obvious that he wanted Aukje to sit next to him, and she did.

Tineke smiled at them, 'Please sit down, surely I don't have to ask you?' They all laughed.

Tineke looked at her friends and said gently, 'How are you both feeling now?'

Marieke sighed, 'We may be recovered physically, but it's something we'll never forget. Frank has nightmares about it.'

Tineke wanted to talk to them. Before she could say anything the front door opened and they heard Jan walking quickly down the hall and into the living-room. He put his brief case down in the corner and greeted everybody.

Frank looked up. 'How are things, Jan?' His voice was steady.

Jan undid his tie and collar-stud. 'Well, it's a bit hectic. We're still issuing the promissory notes like there was no end. The Germans keep coming in for bagfulls. I think we'll be moving into real occupation money soon. That'll replace the notes. They'll have to get rid of the Queen's head on all our currency as quickly as possible. That's not my real worry.' He dropped his head and then lifted it again quickly.

Frank caught the worry. 'What is it, Jan? Come on, I know you. What's really bothering you?'

He took a deep breath, 'The Rabbi came to see me privately in my office this morning. It seems that the rumours from Germany are coming in thick and fast and there'll be big problems for the Jews of Leeuwarden. Already some of our clients who are members of the NSB are starting to move their accounts. They've not said anything to me directly yet but I can feel their hatred. I'm worried for all my family.' He shifted uncomfortably in his chair. 'Where can we go to? It's the same everywhere.'

'How many Jewish people are there in Friesland?' asked Frank.

'From what I know, about nine hundred. Not many really. In Amsterdam and the immediate area we number about ninety thousand.'

Frank spoke in that voice that always seemed to calm people. 'I think you have to wait and see. Although I'm not Jewish, I do have a business and we all just have to see what happens. You have some time on your side. But, I think that you should start thinking about what to do with your family and your assets.'

'Come on you two,' interrupted Marieke, 'let's make the best of what we have now. I think a good talk will do us a lot of good. Then it's back home for dinner.'

David smiled at his parents, 'Aukje and I are going on our bikes *Mem*, we'll see you later.' They stood to leave the room.

Marieke returned the smile. 'That's fine, Aukje. But please be back in the next hour, and keep away from the town.'

'I assume that you don't want me with you?' said Harmen. The glare from his loving sister was sufficient.

The two families continued talking and, eventually, after half an hour, the van der Meers rose to excuse themselves.

'Thanks for your company. I think for the next couple of weeks we ought to try and meet as often as we possibly can,' said Frank.

Jan looked at his wife and they nodded, 'We agree.'

The three of them cycled back home. As they turned into the factory yard Marieke suddenly took a deep breath, 'Oh no! Not again!'

Along the road came a black vehicle, the dust cloud rose behind its wheels. They waited silently.

It was an official car. The door opened and a German soldier climbed out. He walked round the car and opened the rear door. Out stepped a young man in light blue *Luftwaffe* uniform. A side-arm was clipped onto his black leather belt. Marieke stared hard and then realised whom she was looking at.

'Good evening, *mevrouw* van der Meer.'

Oberleutnant Ernst Kraft stood with one leg in plaster and supporting himself with two crutches.

He looked at Frank and Marieke, '*Mevrouw* van der Meer, I have come to thank you for saving my life.'

He remained motionless and looked at the people in front of him. Harmen audibly let out a low moan and walked quietly off towards the factory.

Marieke shrugged her shoulders and decided that this German meant no harm. She introduced him to Frank. 'Thank you. *Oberleutnant*, may I introduce my husband?' They looked closely at each other.

Kraft leant against the car, took away a crutch and saluted. He then waited and there was a continuing silence.

'I think *Oberleutnant*, that you'd better come in,' said Marieke politely. She turned and went back into the house.

For some reason Frank went forward to help the man. He took his arm and found himself looking into a face that was still pale and drawn.

'*Danke*, I can walk but it's still a little painful.' They went into the living-room. He sat down in the chair near to the fireplace and Marieke found a foot-stool.

There was an embarrassed silence and then Kraft quietly spoke, 'After I went away in the car I was taken straight to the hospital.' He took a deep breath, '*Mevrouw* van der Meer, I tried to protest about your arrest, but nobody listened and then I don't remember much after that. Nearly two days later I regained consciousness. They told me I had compound fractures of my leg and I was suffering from severe shock.' He turned again to look at Marieke. 'Without your help I would have died and I can never thank you enough.'

'I only did what any good Christian would have done,' she replied.

He nodded and smiled, 'My *Gruppe* commander flew in to see me yesterday. It seems my comrades had given me up for dead. I had permission from him, and my doctor, to come and visit you today, and so here I am.'

He shrugged his shoulders and shifted his leg painfully on the footstool. Kraft accepted Marieke's cup of coffee and sat with the cup on his lap. There was pride in his voice as he spoke.

'I have received some wonderful news. This morning I was informed that I'm to be the *Luftwaffe* liaison officer for the airfield near Leeuwarden. I shall have my own quarters at the base.'

Frank listened carefully and said quietly, 'You say you'll have your quarters at the airfield. Do I understand my German translation correctly? I didn't know there were so many buildings there.'

The returned smile was full of intrigue. 'I shouldn't really tell you, *meneer*. My role is very important.' He hesitated and then decided. 'The airfield is to be named "*Fliegerhorst*-Leeuwarden". It's to be massively developed and soon it will be the most important night-fighter base for the whole of Holland. I'm telling you about this because your factory will be asked to make the timber frames for some of the new buildings.' He looked at Marieke for a moment. 'I suppose this is my way of thanking you.'

Frank inwardly groaned. 'Thank you, *Oberleutnant*. But I think that I'll be more than happy to take part in the normal tendering process. I do have to work with other people in the town.' He was unsure as to just how naïve this young man really was. He was even more unsure after the next comment.

'I spoke with *Hauptsturmführer* Müller the other day and he told me about your conversation with him. He was most impressed with both of you.' Kraft winked and he smiled. 'He's a very important man you know. It will pay to keep on the right side of him.' He looked directly at Frank and the look on his face changed to that of curiosity. '*Meneer* van der Meer, he said that you were a personal friend of *Generalmajor* Student. He's one of our most famous generals. How on earth did you get to know him?'

Frank's mind whirled. He was still unsure whether this young, and apparently innocent man, was really laying traps for him and he spoke carefully. 'I made his acquaintance some time ago and it's really not important how we met.'

But the man held on. '*Meneer*, you seem to know all the right people.' He took a deep breath and his eyes flashed. 'Very soon the Third *Reich* is going to be the most important country in the world. With your business and your contacts you could go far and I would be honoured to be of any assistance to you.'

Frank carefully folded his arms and paused for a moment. He knew that he could be on very dangerous ground and therefore he proceeded with caution. 'Thank you, *Oberleutnant*. I'm flattered that you think I could be of assistance. But, I just want to remain as a normal Dutch businessman. I'm sure that you would want to keep matters as straight and as legal as possible?'

Kraft nodded, 'Of course, you're absolutely right,.' He glanced towards Marieke. '*Mevrouw* van der Meer, I would welcome another cup of your delicious coffee.'

Marieke quickly realised that this meeting was not going to be brief and she decided to use it to their advantage. She put the coffee-cup on the saucer and placed it carefully on the table at the side of his chair. She gave her most charming smile.

'*Oberleutnant*, perhaps you could tell us what is going to happen in Friesland, now your soldiers are here?'

He picked up the cup and nodded again. A broad smile crossed his pale face. 'The German and the Dutch people are very closely related and we have so much in common.' Frank had heard this all before but he let him carry on. 'The Germanic race is pure and not corrupted by other inferior races. When I look at the van der Meer family I can see the Aryan blood from my forefathers in all of you. Our two countries must work together to improve our lives. The British and the French are mongrel people and much inferior to ours. When I remember your daughter I see how close we all are. With German organisation, strength and your co-operation, Holland must surely succeed. Nothing can stop us.'

Frank cringed when he heard his daughter mentioned.

'Which reminds me, *mevrouw*, where's Aukje?' Kraft said with a frown. Frank did not like this man calling his daughter by name and he answered sharply. 'She's out with a friend at the moment. I don't think she will be at home until much later.' Unfortunately, as he spoke he heard two bikes banging against the wall outside the house. He was helpless to warn his daughter.

The door opened and she came into the room followed by David. Her blonde hair fell into natural curls round her face and Frank's heart leapt with pride. She saw Kraft sitting in the chair. Aukje stopped dead and her mouth fell open. She quickly closed it and looked at her father.

'Hello, Aukje, how are you?' Kraft's face turned red and he tried to sit up, but then slumped back. 'I was just asking after you.' His eyes caught sight of David standing quietly near the door.

She was flushed with the effort of cycling. Aukje quickly summed up the situation and remained calm. 'Hello, *Oberleutnant* Kraft. I see you're feeling much better.' She caught her father's stare. The apology was ready. 'I'm sorry I can't stay and talk. I have to prepare dinner.'

'Surely not, *Fräulein*, I think we have much to talk about.' He stared at David. '... And who is this young man?'

He stepped forward, 'My name is David de Bruin.' He held out his hand.

Kraft looked as though he had been burned and said sharply, 'Er ... yes. I see. ... *Mevrouw*, I would like, perhaps, one more cup of coffee and then I must go.' He avoided eye contact with David.

Frank knew exactly what the problem was, his voice was brisk. 'David, perhaps you could help Aukje in the kitchen.'

They left without saying another word.

There was silence in the room and Frank knew the reason why. He was determined not to be the first to speak. Kraft looked at Marieke and then at Frank.

His voice was firm, 'I must say that I'm surprised to see your daughter with that boy ... .'

'And why is that?' interrupted Frank sharply.

Kraft was trying to be polite. 'Well, I happen to know that he's Jewish. They're an inferior race.' His face was expressionless. 'I must strongly urge you not to be friendly with the de Bruin people. It can only mean trouble.'

Frank wanted to know more. 'Yes, I understand, *Oberleutnant*. I would welcome your advice. Perhaps you could explain what kind of trouble?' He ignored Marieke as she arched her eyebrows in concern.

Kraft smoothed away an invisible crease on his tunic. 'The Jews are inferior and the reason for all our problems. Very soon you will find out what we intend to do about them.'

'How soon?' pressed Frank.

Kraft eagerly continued, 'In the near future orders will be issued to say that Jewish children will not be able to attend your schools. They will be banned from public transport and public places. All Jews will be required to wear a symbol of their inferiority.'

'What will that be?' said Marieke quietly, her blue eyes flashing.

'A yellow, six pointed Jewish star sewn onto their clothes. It must be worn day and night.'

'You mean in bed?' said an incredulous Frank, with a cynical smile on his lips.

Kraft did not rise to the bait. 'No, that will not be necessary. But, they will have to wear it when they are outside their house or at their place of work. If they are found without it then they will be placed in prison or in a special place. If they cause any difficulties in conforming with these arrangements then they will have their property confiscated. We are carrying out our orders to protect you from the influence of these people. I can assure you that we have proceeded with such measures in the Fatherland and our country is now functioning much more efficiently. You know at least half a million Jews have already left for other places.' He took a deep breath and his smile returned. ' ... And so you see, *meneer* and *mevrouw* van der Meer, I'm helping you to settle into your new way of life. In fact, much of what I have said is still secret. But, I'm sure I can trust you not to reveal anything. It would be unpleasant, to say the least, if you had to be arrested again.' He glanced at the clock, 'Now I must leave.'

Swinging his leg off the footstool he slowly stood. Crutches in position he looked hard at Marieke and the smile came back to his face.

'Thank you, *mevrouw* van der Meer for the coffee and for allowing me back into your lovely house.' He looked at both of them. 'I'm sure we'll meet again. Perhaps, *meneer* van der Meer, you would call my batman from the car to assist me.'

Frank was glad to leave the house and take a deep breath of fresh air.

The soldier was leaning against the car smoking. When he saw Frank's wave he stamped out the cigarette and walked up the path to the house. He smiled, Frank ignored him.

Dusk rapidly approached as the car drove down the narrow road and out of sight.

Aukje rushed back into the living-room and faced her parents. She was white with anger, 'I heard everything that idiot said. I just can't understand that sort of attitude. How can he believe such rubbish?' She turned towards David behind her. 'What do you think about it?'

David was a highly intelligent boy. He stood quietly for a moment. 'I've heard it all before. When you're Jewish you're well used to anti-Semitism. I just keep out of the way. It's impossible to understand men like the *Oberleutnant*. Germany's plans have been known for some time. My family have heard the rumours. These things are happening in Germany and so it's bound to happen here.' He shrugged. 'There's nothing we can do about it.'

Frank listened. 'David, I'll cycle back with you. I want to tell your parents about what Kraft has said. You're right. There's little we can do about it ... yet!' He thought for a moment and scratched the tip of his nose. 'We may not like our new found German friend, but he may prove to be very useful in the times ahead. I shan't be long Marieke, tot ziens.' He left the house and climbed onto the bicycle.

They both left the house and disappeared into the darkness.

TWO

Work made time pass quickly and Frank absorbed himself into his business. Orders were coming in as usual and he fulfilled the long held contracts with the provincial authorities. Kraft had been right, the airfield was being massively expanded. Piet and Frank had most of the timber contracts for "*Fliegerhorst*-Leeuwarden". Jan had also been right. Within two weeks of the occupation the Germans had issued guilder banknotes without a sign of the Queen's head. Frank's worries about unpaid promissory notes were unfounded. His bills were paid in full in the new currency.

Frank and Piet agreed to visit the airfield and check on the requirements of their contracts in more detail. They met at Piet's house and decided to travel together in one car to save petrol. Although, as contractors working for the Germans, they were allowed fuel.

There was the usual smiling welcome. 'Good morning, Frank. How are you?'

Piet showed his friend through to the living-room. Frank knew that Piet wanted to say something to him in private. This was the first occasion that they had been alone for some time.

'I hope that Marieke is now fully recovered?'

Frank nodded and ran his hands through his thick brown hair. 'It was quite a shock for both of us and I think that we'll both need some time to recover.'

'I don't believe the rumours about you,' said Piet quietly.

Frank quickly smiled. 'I'm sure you know me better than that Piet. I still can't believe what's happening to our country and I still can't forecast what's going to happen in the future.'

Piet shook his head. 'The Germans have nearly taken France and I don't think that anything will stop them. The British are retreating on all fronts.' He was suddenly quiet.

'What's the matter?' asked Frank.

His friend's usual smile had gone. 'It makes me so angry that we have to deal with the Germans. I wish I could find some other way of doing business without them.'

'I know exactly how you feel. But we're the lucky ones, we have some choice. I think that many people have just had to fall in with them. After all, they're bringing more employment to the area. I don't like it, it's not our country anymore.'

Piet hesitated, 'Frank, I know I can trust you. I've been meeting some other men who think the same way as me. We're organising a movement to oppose the German occupation.'

Frank quickly sat up and his face was stiff with anger. 'No! No! ... I can't agree with that. I'm a pacifist and I will not put my family at risk.'

Piet placed his hand on Frank's shoulder. 'It's not violent. Just a little bit of information here and a whisper there. After all you're in an excellent position. You seem to have their trust. Just pass on anything that may be of use to us.'

Frank's face was set. 'No, I'm sorry. I can't compromise my beliefs, no matter what's happening. But I'll do nothing to stop you. I believe that the best way to stop the Germans is to wait for the British to come to our help. After all, we know that they're bombing Germany, you've seen them flying over Friesland.'

Piet stood, his voice was weary, 'All right, Frank. I understand but for God's sake be careful. You're walking a dangerous tight-rope.' He walked towards the door. 'Come on, let's go and see what the swines are up to.'

Frank and Piet discussed business as the Austin travelled the short distance to the airfield. The entrance was lightly guarded. Two men with rifles stood casually at ease.

'Not particularly good security,' muttered Piet.

'Who've they got to worry about? Their nearest enemy is about a thousand kilometres away,'

Piet nodded with a twisted smile. 'They may have enemies a little nearer than they think.'

Frank glanced sharply at him.

'*Passe, bitte!*' One of the guards bent over near the car's side window. Frank passed out the letter from the German base commander.

'*Alles in Ordnung!*' The guard jumped back and let them through.

The amount of activity surprised them both. There was a mass of movement over most of the airfield. Men and materials seemed to be arriving from nowhere. Internal security was better, they were stopped twice before they arrived at a low wooden building.

Piet looked around and smiled. 'The last time I was here, Frank, I flew in a KLM biplane to Amsterdam. It was a grass runway with two wooden buildings.'

They parked the car near to the entrance of the largest building. Frank cast an experienced eye over the wooden structure as they walked in through the single door.

'This lot needs replacing, the timbers are rotten right the way through.'

Piet agreed. 'I built this fifteen years ago. That was at a cheap price, even for those days.' They both laughed.

Frank pushed the small bell near the inner door. An elderly soldier appeared. Before he could say anything, another man pushed past him. With an ornate walking stick clasped in his right hand he gave a slight bow.

'Good morning, gentlemen. *Meneer* van der Meer, nice to see you again.'

Oberleutnant Ernst Kraft stood casually to one side and waved the two men through the door. He was dressed in *Luftwaffe* uniform. Around his right arm he wore a yellow arm-band. The jackboots were buffed to a high gloss and there was no sign of his injury. He saw the direction of

Frank's glance. '*Ja*, apart from a few aches, my leg has totally recovered. I shall be cleared for flying in two weeks.' He fingered the arm-band. 'I'm now one of the senior, management. We all have to wear these things.' He beckoned to them. 'Do come in and sit down.'

He introduced himself to Piet and continued, 'I'm so glad that you were awarded the contracts. I did say to the contracts' manager that your timber factory only produced the best.' He banged the tip of his stick on the floor. 'Gentlemen, the Third *Reich* only wants the best.' He paused for a moment. 'Now, what can I do for you? I presume that you would like to see where your timber will be used?' They shrugged their shoulders. 'Follow me please.'

They followed him into a large room that was obviously the old passenger waiting hall. In the middle stood a large table covered with a dust-sheet. Kraft walked over and with the point of his stick carefully removed the cover. He saw the astonishment on their faces.

'Ha ... Ha, a complete surprise for you both. This .... ' he waved the stick over the table, 'is a model of what "*Fliegerhorst*-Leeuwarden" will look like when it's finished.' The model was perfect in every detail.

Both men were speechless.

There was pride in his voice. 'Three, very long, concrete runways. Brick barrack blocks large enough to house a thousand men. Hangars for seventy aircraft. Even now our engineers are building a railway to connect the airfield with the Harlingen main line. The administration building will be built as soon as possible. We have one of Germany's leading military architects designing the whole project.' The stick waved again. 'All round Friesland there will be flak positions to protect the airfield.' He walked over to a map hanging on the wall. 'We will have our new aircraft locating devices positioned here at Sondel, on the island of Terschelling and over near the coast at Den Helder.' Kraft paused for breath.

Frank interrupted and he forced a smile. 'It looks wonderful, *Oberleutnant*. What buildings are we providing materials for? I see only brick being used here. Our contracts were not too specific ... just lengths and types of timber.'

Kraft gave a cat-like smile. 'Notice, I said hangars. Gentlemen can you see them?' He waved his stick over the model. Frank and Piet shook their heads. He pointed. 'There are six typically Friesian farmhouses in these locations.' He jabbed the tip at each model. 'They're not farms, gentlemen, they're hangars camouflaged to look like farms. The front of the barns are hangar doors. It will be easy to store aircraft inside them. Each hangar will have piped fuel and full communications with headquarters. All fuel will be stored underground and will be invisible from the air. Your contract is to provide the timber for each of the farms and all other buildings. We will expect you to erect them on site.'

Piet nodded and added, '*Oberleutnant*, those runways are massive. There's not enough stone in the whole of Friesland to build them. Where are you getting your materials from?'

For the first time Kraft looked uncomfortable. Eventually he took a deep breath and said, 'The cement is coming from Germany. The hard-core rubble is coming from Rotterdam.'

Frank thought for a moment and said quietly, 'Whereabouts in Rotterdam?' He knew the docks were closed to the outside world.

'The hard core is from the rubble of damaged buildings in the city centre.'

Piet could hardly control his anger and he clenched his fists, 'You mean you're building runways for the defence of Germany from the rubble of our city that you bombed?'

Kraft could not look at them but merely stared at the model. '*Meneer*, it's for your defence as well as ours. It's a waste not to use all that rubble. At this very time fully laden barges are moving through the Friesian canals to off-load near the airfield. This project is giving a lot of work and money to many of your business colleagues.' He changed the subject. 'Do you have any more questions?' Without waiting for a reply he continued. 'You'll also be required to build two other buildings at the village of Menaldum ten kilometres to the east. We are building a false airfield there and we need hangars that look real. The idea is that any British bombers will think it's the main airfield and bomb it first.'

Frank could not help himself. 'You mean that the British know that you're developing the airfield here at Leeuwarden, *Oberleutnant*?'

Kraft pondered for a moment. His answer was simple. 'I think the British know that fact, gentlemen.'

Frank wanted to get out of the room. The sight of the model nauseated him, it represented all the things that occupation signified. Piet felt the same. As they left, Kraft diverted them to another room. He knocked respectfully at the door. A voice answered, they entered.

Frank tried not to flinch, he gently nudged Piet. *Hauptsturmführer* Müller stood behind the desk. There was the same cold look on his face that Frank had seen before and his presence radiated power.

The same quiet voice, 'Good day, gentlemen.' This time the Dutch was faultless. 'Please sit down, I have something to say to you and there is something that you must do before you leave.' He waited until they sat and then slowly lowered himself into his high backed chair, subtly higher than the other chairs in the room.

The hard blue eyes moved slowly from man to man and he spoke very quietly. 'The model that you've just seen shows what we are capable of achieving. You are joining in that success and you will become part of it. I'm sure that you are both loyal to your country and the *Reich*, but there are temptations for you. Two of your business colleagues believed otherwise. They installed new drains for the runways. They deliberately made them from sub-standard materials. Fortunately the faults were spotted by our inspectors. The two men were called Joop Heemstra and

Jan Sipma.' He paused for the names to sink in. 'You may know them? ... Yes or no?' Frank looked at Piet, they both nodded. 'They were arrested on charges of sabotage against the Third *Reich* and placed in the prison in Leeuwarden.' Again he paused and then glanced at his wristwatch. 'One hour ago they were executed by firing squad directly over the new drains that their men had built. I think that the lesson must be learned. To oppose us is to be a traitor, and that is punishable by death.'

Frank's mind was whirling. He knew Joop Heemstra well. His company always laid the foundations for van der Meer buildings. The message that Müller was giving was obvious. There was nothing left for him to say and a surge of anger welled up inside him.

Müller continued, 'Any contractor will be required to sign a quality pledge to the *Reich*.' He stood up to dismiss them.

As they left Kraft appeared near their car. 'Follow me. I have something to show you.' It was not a request.

Piet took a quick step towards their waiting car. 'I think I've had enough Frank. Let's go home.'

Frank winced, 'No, I think we have to follow him. Remember what happened to our two colleagues?' Piet resignedly nodded.

The Austin followed the green staff car. It weaved its way through lorries carrying materials and gangs of men operating machinery. They stopped near the end of the grass runway. It was a calm, clear day. The grass was green and fresh, the skyline pin sharp. Kraft stepped out of his car and walked back towards them.

'Just watch this.' He smiled, placed his peaked hat on the ground and put his hands on his hips. He stared into the blue sky.

Frank knew that sound. From the east, in the general direction of his home, came the steady drone of aircraft. This time the pitch was slightly higher and then he suddenly knew why. These were fighter aircraft. They came over in ten waves of four. The sleek planes flew straight over their heads, turned, and lined up with the end of the grass runway. The formation flying was perfect. They landed in the same precise way that they flew. Each wave passed so close to Frank that he ducked. He could see the pilots' faces as the aircraft settled onto the runway. The noise was shattering even with his hands over both ears. There was the pungent smell of exhaust fumes.

Kraft's face shone with excitement. 'Well, gentlemen, that was the first squadron of fighters to arrive at "*Fliegerhorst*-Leeuwarden". They're brand new Messerschmitt BF 109's, the latest type. Now you know why we need to build this airfield so quickly.' He replaced the hat. 'I'll escort you back to the entrance, that is if you don't have any more questions?'

Both men shook their heads and turned towards their car.

As they drove across the airfield Piet's eyes were everywhere. Several times he stopped and stared at some particular work detail. Frank nudged him. He smiled and followed Kraft's car.

They reached the gate and the guards saluted as *Oberleutnant* Kraft waved goodbye.

A kilometre from the airfield and Frank stopped. He switched off the engine and turned to look at his friend. He shook his head. 'Piet I've been thinking. You know what surprises me? That model must have taken months to build. It shows that the *moffen* have been planning this occupation for years. For the last five they've been re-assuring us about our neutrality. I just can't believe it.'

Piet put his hand on his friend's shoulder and looked him straight in the face, 'Frank van der Meer! You're a great business man, a good friend, but, very naïve. Ever since Hitler came to power, the Germans have been planning to conquer Europe. Only one person saw all of this happening and that was the English politician, Winston Churchill. Thank God they've just made him Prime Minister.' He smiled again. 'Now Frank, are you ready to join us?' He removed his hand.

Frank shook his head, his mouth was resolute. 'I'm sorry, I'm not ready for this yet. I need to discuss it with Marieke and the *dominee* at church.'

'Wouldn't bother talking to the *dominee*,' smiled Piet, 'He joined us last week! Look here, before you say any more let me tell you what happened in Rotterdam on the day of the bombing.' He took a deep breath. 'Four men sat down and decided to do something about the Germans. Apparently, one of them said, "One should be able to do something about this riffraff; help to throw them out again." These men shared their thoughts and soon a local teacher started to copy their feelings onto paper. It was the first call to Resistance. One or two of us in Leeuwarden did the same thing. I managed to get hold of a copy of their second message. I learnt it by heart, it goes, **"*Geuzen* Action - Message Number Two. The Geuzen Action has started on 15th May in Amsterdam. All our stores will be taken away: food, clothing, shoes ... Our young people will be taken elsewhere for the usurper. We'll soon be getting a new Duke of Alva and Margaret of Palma. Courage and trust. The Geuzen action will gradually bring an organisation into being, and one day we will recapture our liberty, just as happened in the 80-years war. Our country shall not become part of Germany. Secret agents are being placed everywhere. Copy this message. You will soon hear more. Let everyone do his duty as a Geus!"'** His eyes shone and he gripped Frank's arm. 'There's a need for absolute secrecy Frank.'

Frank understood his friend's excitement. 'Yes, I understand. But what is a *Geus*?'

Piet relaxed. 'In 1572 when we were occupied by the Spanish, a group of freebooting seamen took a small Dutch town away from the Spanish occupiers. These men were called the sea beggars or *Water-Geuzen*. I think it's an excellent name.'

Frank shook his head and there was sadness on his face. 'I'm sorry, the answer is still "no". I need longer to think about it.'

'All right I understand. But come and tell me when you want to talk about it.'

Frank leaned forward, started the engine and the car slowly pulled away.

As they arrived back at Piet's house Sytske was waiting for them. They could tell that something was wrong.

'Piet, there's been an urgent telephone call for you. Your friends want you to call back as soon as possible.' He nodded and walked over to the table in the hall.

Frank could hear the murmuring of the one-sided conversation through the closed door. With Sytske he waited for Piet. The door opened and his usual cheery disposition had gone.

'All right Piet, what is it?' said his wife.

He sat down and spoke quietly, 'It seems that our naval base at Den Helder was attacked and bombed by the Royal Air Force, civilians have been killed. The German newspapers are putting it on their front pages as, **"Murderous RAF attack Dutch towns"'**

'I don't believe it,' said Frank indignantly.

Piet continued. 'The interesting point is that people in Den Helder actually saw German crosses on the wings of the aircraft. There were others with no markings at all. Before you say anything this can only mean one thing. The Germans are stepping up their propaganda by claiming that our Allies are killing Dutch people. My contact also told me that there are German troops in Den Helder port but they're billeted with Dutch families and not in the old naval barracks. Also their military supplies are stored near the main hospital in the town.' He stared hard at Frank. 'Does all this convince you of the need to take action against them?'

Frank bit his lip and said nothing.

THREE

The *Nieuwe Stad* main thoroughfare was full of life. Families strolling along the side of the canal. Children cycling past the shops. People window shopping and there was plenty to look at. The cinema had opened again and was showing a Dutch film with German sub-titles. All appeared absolutely normal. The only difference was that German soldiers were walking up and down the *Nieuwe Stad*. The men were unarmed and most of them were in small groups. They looked happy and carefree.

'Frank,' said Marieke, 'look at that. Some of our girls are actually walking arm in arm with the Germans.' He shook his head and they pedalled on.

It was the 29th of June and nearly everybody was wearing a white carnation. The van der Meer family had collected their flowers from a small stall near the centre of town.

'*Heit*, tell me the story again,' said Aukje, with a quick smile.

He laughed and fingered his silk tie, 'Prince Bernhard always wears a white carnation when he appears in public. As it's his birthday we've decided to wear his flower. I think it's a wonderful idea. The Germans won't like it.'

Almost before the word had left his mouth there was a commotion on the other side of the canal. Two *NSB* men were trying to pull the flower out of a man's buttonhole. There was a brief struggle, the man escaped. The two men turned on another group. There was a scream from one of the *NSB* men and he dropped to the ground with blood pouring from his hand. The group surrounded the men and began to bludgeon them with fists and boots. Two German soldiers appeared from around the corner, they were unarmed but the sight of their uniforms caused the Dutch group to turn and run. The *NSB* man climbed to his feet and wrapped a white handkerchief round his hand. Even from across the canal the blood could be seen soaking through the white material.

Frank pushed the pedals harder. 'Come on, let's get away from here, quickly.' As they hurried away the wail of a police siren came down the *Nieuwe Stad*.

Jan turned off into a side street and they followed. Frank knew exactly where he was going to. At the end of a narrow street, and round the corner from main railway station, was a small hotel. They often went there. The owner was a close friend and his restaurant was excellent.

As they walked through the door he was waiting. 'Good evening, everybody. It's nice to see you all again.' Their host smiled a welcome. 'Your usual table I presume?'

Dirk Haan's father had established the *Hotel de Kroon* fifty years ago and his son made sure that it was going to survive. The food was excellent and the hotel was well run. There was always a table for his guests and

Frank often spent time there for business meetings.

They walked to their seat near the window. Before they sat down the coffee cups were on the table.

'Please join us, Dirk,' smiled Tineke.

He was dressed in a hoteliers' dark morning suit and he fitted it perfectly. The slicked back greying hair shone with pomade and his face wore a perennial broad smile. His voice was clear with a trace of the local accent. 'Well, how are things my friends? Improving, I hope?' He sat down.

Tineke explained, 'We're all right now, thanks. But we saw a rather nasty incident a few minutes ago.'

He smiled mischievously. 'Ah yes. You've just witnessed a little Dutch resistance. It's happened several times today. Our *NSB* friends have been going around snatching the white carnations off people. But some of our naughty citizens have been hiding razor blades inside the flowers. A good trick really!'

Marieke shook her head. 'That's not a good idea Dirk. Someone will get hurt.'

'Only the Nazis, Marieke.' He laughed out aloud.

Frank looked around him and changed the subject. 'The hotel seems to be full, business must be good?'

Piet replied, 'Well, the occupation hasn't done the hotel any harm. The Germans pay well and are no trouble whatsoever. Their manners are perfect and I have no complaints. They're always smiling, it's as though their last order was, "smile at the natives"! Every time a woman comes into the restaurant a German will stand and offer his seat.' He looked at his friends and shook his head. 'The big question is, will it last? Your personal experiences may prove things otherwise.'

Jan explained his concerns, 'My worries at the bank are unfounded at the moment. The *NSB*'ers withdrew their accounts and that was it. Head office in Amsterdam are happy, so I'll just hold on and see what happens.'

Frank spoke quietly, 'I think we now know why the Queen left Holland.' There was a nodding of heads. 'I keep hearing people saying "never submit". I'm inclined to think the same.'

The waiter appeared with more coffee and Dirk glanced over his shoulder. 'Have you seen the announcement from the new Reichs Commissioner yet?' There was a shaking of heads. 'I'll tell you a story. Hitler has appointed an Austrian traitor as our lord and master. He's a doctor of something or other, an ardent Nazi and his name is Arthur Seyss-Inquart.'

For a moment there was an incredulous silence. Tineke laughed first and then they all joined in. Their laughter echoed round the hotel. Frank realised it was the first time that he had laughed so hard for days.

'Do you think he knows what his name means in Dutch?' said Marieke.

'Just imagine being Hitler's man in Holland and having a name that translates as six and a quarter!' laughed Frank. At the mention of the name he set off into another roar of laughter.

Dirk continued, 'You can't trust the wireless to give out truthful news at this time, but I hear a lot of rumours from my guests. Apparently when Hitler told Six and a Quarter that he wanted him to govern Holland, the Doctor said to his good wife, **"Trudi, you must listen, the Führer wants me to plant tulips, get ready for it."** He lives in Holland but his wife has stayed in Austria. I smell trouble. But, his first edict sounds reasonable and you have to read between the lines to see what he's really saying.' He paused and pointed towards the entrance. 'If you look near the check-in desk you'll see the notice. I've been told that it must be where everybody can see it. Apparently every public place has to display a copy.' Dirk waved to one of the waiters to bring the poster over to the table. He held it up in front of him.

'Very impressive,' said Tineke.

Piet continued. 'He announced this in the Hall of the Knights in the Hague. That's where the Queen normally opens parliament. I think it was a calculated insult to our people. They brought the Radio Cologne orchestra to play, another insult. I'll read it out to you.' And Dirk began speaking in his most official voice :

TO THE DUTCH PEOPLE IN THE OCCUPIED TERRITORIES

With effect from today I have taken on supreme powers over the civil authority in the Netherlands.

The magnanimity of the Führer and the might of the German Army have made it possible that even after a few days we have restored the damage caused by the enormous catastrophe brought about by the previous government and we will make it possible that some degree of order in public life will be restored.

As the Reichs Commissioner I will exert the highest power over the civil authority within the Dutch territory protected by the German Army, in order to secure public order and public life.

I shall take all necessary measures and create legislation to see that my orders are carried out. It is my wish to respect Dutch Law as much as possible and to consult the Dutch civil authorities wherever necessary. I expect, in return, that all members of the judiciary and civil servants will carefully comply with my instructions and that the Dutch people will follow my leadership with understanding and self-control.

The Dutch soldier has shown bravery in the fight. The Dutch civilians have behaved correctly towards the adversaries. So, therefore, nothing can stop us treating each other with respect and consideration.

The German people, led by their Führer, are fighting for their existence, a struggle that was forced upon them by the hatred and envy of their enemies. This struggle is forcing the German Nation to use all of its might and power and it justifies all possible measures in reaching their goal. This duty, and necessity, will also influence public life in the Netherlands. Therefore, I will ensure that the Dutch people, being of the same blood as the German people, will not have their quality of life diminished further than is unavoidable under the fateful circumstances and our enemies' intention to destroy us.

As Reichs Commissioner I have to safeguard the Reich's interests in the Dutch territories protected by Germany and I will safeguard them. In fulfilling the duties that result from our common fate the Dutch people will secure their territory and their freedom in the future.

THE HAGUE
29th May 1940

signed
Seyss-Inquart

There was a moment's silence. Frank was the first to speak. 'What it really means is that we have a dictator who can do anything that he wants to. I can't see the Dutch Government really opposing him.' He shrugged. 'The majority are *NSB*'ers anyway.'

He stopped talking when Dirk kicked his foot under the table. Through the main entrance walked two German soldiers. They stared about them, removed their hats and sat at the next table. They saw Dirk and nodded politely. One of them beckoned the waiter over and ordered two glasses of beer. The conversation between the two families died. They glanced at each other and began talking about everyday matters. One of the Germans stood and approached Dirk. He bowed slightly from the waist

'Good evening, *meneer* Haan. May we have the honour of buying a drink for you and your friends?'

Dirk's face was impassive. 'That's very nice of you. My friend here does not drink alcohol and therefore coffee will be fine.' He snapped his fingers and the waiter dashed away to the kitchen.

The soldier sat down and continued talking to his friend. The coffee arrived and they all nodded their thanks.

'See what I mean? ... Perfect gentlemen,' whispered a grinning Dirk.

They continued talking, occasionally laughing and the soldiers drank more beer. Two other men, accompanied by two girls, came into the hotel. They wore the black uniform of the *NSB*. A quick glance at the people in the cafe and they sat together near the window. Drinks and cakes were ordered.

Marieke felt eyes burning into the back of her head. She turned quickly and saw one of the *NSB* men staring at her. He dropped his eyes and continued talking to the girls sat opposite him. A minute later she could feel the same eyes looking at her. She nudged Frank.

He stopped talking to Dirk, 'What is it, *liefje*?' But, before she could answer, the man stood, put his hands on his belt and swaggered over towards her.

He glared down at them from one end of the table. Jan and Tineke sat with their backs towards him. As the man began to talk, Jan turned round.

'*Mevrouw* van der Meer, I see you've managed to escape from the police station. We met at your house, remember? I'm sure ... !'

He stopped talking and turned his gaze onto Jan. Surprise came over his face which rapidly changed into contempt. He took a step backwards.

'My God! It's you de Bruin and your woman!'

Jan stood with red-faced anger beginning to surface. Dirk pulled him down.

The *NSB*'er pointed his finger and shouted. 'You're a Jew, you must leave now! ... immediately! We will not stay in the same room as Jews.' He sneered.

Frank was not a violent man but he was big. He stood, as did Marieke, and Tineke. The atmosphere in the cafe suddenly became tense and explosive. The other *NSB* man came over to the table and stood at the side of his friend. Frank noticed from the edge of his vision that the two Germans had stood and were becoming intensely interested in the situation.

'Did you hear what I said, JEWS?' repeated the man. His voice climbed higher in volume, 'Leave this hotel, ... NOW!' Dirk could not hold Jan down. He jumped up and lunged at the tall *NSB* man. Frank managed to reach him and hold him back but not without them falling over onto the floor. The table upended and the cups, saucers, flowers and newspapers crashed over everybody. The smashing of crockery only increased the tempers of the people at the table.

Dirk stood, his face was pale. He said quietly, 'Come on, my friends, our meal is waiting next door in the restaurant.' He took Marieke's hand and threaded it through his arm. He did the same with Tineke's. Like the Pied Piper he stepped across the wreckage of the table and led them across the floor of the cafe. Frank and Jan managed to rise from the floor and they followed. The worried waiter held the door open and they walked into the empty restaurant.

They flopped into chairs. The door remained firmly closed.

Dirk began, 'I'm sorry, but this is going to start happening all the time. I'm just ashamed that it happened in my hotel.'

Tineke refused to cry. She held Jan's hand tightly.

'Well, so much for Six and a Quarter and him treating us with "self respect and consideration",' commented Frank.

Jan had calmed a little but sweat poured off his face. His voice trembled with anger, 'What really annoys me is the fact that they're Dutch. From a German, I could maybe have understood.'

'What you must remember, my friend,' continued Dirk, 'is that these people are controlled by Germans. We must expect the worst. I've heard that rules concerning the welfare of Jewish people are soon going to be enforced.'

Jan nodded slowly, 'I've heard the same things and, if that is one example of what may happen, then God help us all.'

They ate their meal with little enjoyment. The conversation was slow and lacked the usual enthusiasm. Even Dirk's humour failed to revive their hopes for a pleasant evening. He refused to present them with the bill and they parted with a shaking of hands and faint smiles.

He whispered to them quietly as they left. 'By the way my friends, the 31st August is Queen Wilhelmina's birthday. Wear an orange flower, a marigold will be just right.' His look said it all.

As they left the hotel there were few people on the footpaths and, pushing their bikes, they walked down the main street. It was almost dusk and the street lights illuminated their way. There seemed to be more soldiers than when they had arrived earlier. It was Frank who noticed the difference.

'Just keep walking, but look at the Germans. This time they're carrying rifles.'

It was true, each man had his rifle slung casually over his shoulder. Gone were the grey field service caps, they were replaced by the *Stalhelm*. The men with the rifles had their steel helmets pulled down low. It cast their faces in heavy shadow and Frank was unable to make out their features.

'I think they're worried about the dark,' commented Jan. 'We'd better get on our bikes and ride as quickly as possible.'

They agreed and cycled swiftly past the groups of soldiers.

FOUR

Business for the van der Meer factory boomed. Every contract was legally tendered for and each time Frank was successful, he had no idea whether or not the success was based on his relationship with the Germans or not. He took on extra men to keep up with the work. But not for one moment did he consider that the Germans were right in what they were doing.

His friend Piet Bokma never competed with him. They shared their bids for business and each was pleased with the results. Their frequent meetings in the *Hotel de Kroon* were purely for business and their friendship was never interrupted. It was a letter that Frank received that morning that prompted the next meeting.

They met at the van der Meer factory. The sound of the bell on Piet's bike made Harmen stand and look down from the office window.

'*Heit*, Piet's here. I'll ask *Mem* to make some cold drinks and a tray of biscuits.'

The footsteps on the wooden stairs forced Frank to stand up from his desk but not before he had closed up his account books. After all Piet was a competitor as well as a friend. He buttoned his jacket and straightened his tie.

He smiled a welcome. 'Morning, Piet. I'm glad you could come. I suppose you've had one of these letters as well?' He held up a bulky brown envelope.

'Morning, Frank. Yes, you're right. Mine came in the post this morning. What do you think about it?' He smiled.

Harmen returned with a carefully laid tray. He placed it gently on the table and passed out the glasses and sat down. He was curious. '*Heit*, what letter are you talking about? I didn't see that envelope in the post this morning.'

Frank weighed the envelope thoughtfully in his hand. 'My letter was delivered personally by messenger. I have no idea why. It contains an invitation. I'll read it out.'

He withdrew the contents and laid them out on the table in front of him. He took a long drink from the glass, selected the letter and began to read it aloud.

'The letter is headed,

THE GERMAN-DUTCH ASSOCIATION

This association, with great pleasure, invites meneer and mevrouw van der Meer and their children Harmen and Aukje, to attend a reception to be held in the Friesian Museum on the 1st July 1940 at 5 p.m.

The occasion for this reception is a visit to the museum by our

Reichs Commissioner of the Netherlands, Dr. Albert Seyss-Inquart.
He has requested that all prominent people from the Province of
Friesland should attend. The Reichs Commissioner will be speaking
on the bond that exists between our two great countries.

signed

Theo Hulpman
Chairman'

Frank took a deep breath. 'That seems about it. The other part of the package is a list of who's been invited and a map showing where the museum is, and that's an insult. Who in Friesland doesn't know where the Friesian Museum is?'

'You're right, Frank,' Piet was scanning the list, 'and there's something else. Nowhere in the list are there any German names. Most of the Dutch names are members of the *NSB*.' He passed the list over to his friend.

Frank looked at the list again, 'Er ... yes. They've not invited the de Bruin's either. In fact, there're no Jewish names at all.'

'What else did you expect?' said Piet, with a cynical smile. 'I don't know about you but I'm going. I really want to see Six and a Quarter, I've heard so much about him. After all what harm can it do? We're stuck with the Germans for some time to come.'

Harmen interrupted, 'You can be sure I'm not going. I don't want to be anywhere near them. After all, we don't have to go, do we, *Heit*?' He faced his father.

Frank ignored him. 'I agree, Piet, there's no harm in attending and it could be useful. At least we'll know whom the Germans regard as the "prominent" people in Friesland.' He turned to his son and said quietly, 'Harmen, it's true we don't have to go. But you're part of this family and part of the business and, therefore, I think you should go. As a young man, you've much to learn about the politics of diplomacy.'

Harmen squared his shoulders, glanced downwards and remained silent.

Frank turned to his friend. 'Piet, we'll cycle to your house and then we'll walk into town together. It'll save petrol and give us time to weigh up the situation.'

Marieke shouted up the stairs, 'Quick come and listen! It's the Queen. It's from England.'

There was total silence as everybody listened. The voice was strong and clear.

'It is a source of great satisfaction to me that, that as a result of
the willing co-operation of the British authorities, facilities have
now been secured from the British Broadcasting Company for this
Dutch quarter of an hour.

I hope that many of our compatriots, wherever they may be, will henceforward regularly listen in to the voice of their country as it comes to them through this new channel.

And now I take great pleasure in being the first to address a few words to you in our Dutch quarter of an hour.

First of all, I wish to join you in a solemn commemoration of the homeland that has been so heavily afflicted by the calamity of war. Deeply moved, we think at this moment of the endless sorrows that have come upon our people and that continue to weigh upon our hearts.

We render homage to the heroes who fell in the execution of their duty to the homeland, to the courage of our armed forces on land, at sea, and in the air, who with their exertion of their utmost strength resisted the overwhelmingly powerful assailant much longer than he expected.

After all that has already been said and written about the war in which we have become involved, you will not expect me in these few moments to deal with the war itself and its many related problems.

But what we must do is to realise that the war reveals itself more and more clearly as being essentially a war between good and evil, a battle between God and our conscience on one side and the forces of darkness now in the ascendant on the other side.'

Frank found himself with his arms locked around Marieke and Aukje's shoulders. Piet was sitting absolutely still. Harmen stared intently at the wireless. His eyes were alight.

'It is a battle, I need hardly tell you, which belongs to the realm of the spirit fought in the deepest recesses of the human heart, but now, in the most distressing and loathsome manner, has come to the surface in the form of this immense world struggle of which we have become the innocent victims; and all our peoples suffer.

What is at stake in this war is the liberty of those all the world over, who wish to work for the good of mankind, and to do so without being frustrated by the evildoers.

Those who think that the spiritual values acquired through the ages can be destroyed by the sword, must learn to realise the idleness of such beliefs. They must be made to understand that crude violence cannot deprive a people of its conviction.

Just as in earlier days neither force of arms, nor the flames of the stake, nor impoverishment and suffering have ever succeeded in exterminating our love of liberty, our freedom of conscience and religion, so I remain convinced that once again we and all of those of whatever nation, who think like us, shall emerge from the ordeal strengthened and chastened through our sufferings.

May the knowledge, that already thousands of our brave

compatriots gave their all for this high purpose, and that this sacrifice has not been in vain, be a source of solace to their kith and kin and to all of us.

Even though the enemy has occupied our sacred soil, the Netherlands will carry on the war till the morrow of a free and happy future dawns for us. Our beloved flag flies proudly on the seas, in great Netherlands in the East and the West. Side by side with the Allies, our gallant men continue the struggle.

The Empire overseas, which has given such striking proof of its sympathy in the calamity which struck the motherland, is more closely attached to us in its thinking and feeling than ever before. With unshakeable unity we intend to vindicate our freedom, our independence and all our territories.

I call on my compatriots at home and wherever they may be, however dark and difficult the times may be, to keep faith in our cause, a cause which is strong, not only because it is served by strength in battle but also because of the profound belief that our most sacred values are at stake.'

Marieke found tears streaming down her face. She clenched her fist. 'She was right to leave Holland. She'll become an inspiration to us all. We must listen every day.'

Frank was more practical, 'You're right Marieke. But I don't think the Germans will let us listen for long. We must continue with our lives. To oppose them will be difficult.'

Piet nodded and glanced at the clock. 'I agree. But to hear the Queen talking to us from England is really amazing. I knew that something was going to happen. My contacts told me that there would be a broadcast but I never thought that the Queen would be the first to speak to us.' He took a deep breath, 'I really have to go now.'

Piet rose to leave. The three men walked down the steps past the open doors to the factory. The roar of the machinery stopped any conversation. There was dust in the air and sawdust lay thick on the concrete floor. Any onlooker could see that the factory was working flat out. One or two men shouted a greeting to Piet as he glanced round the machinery. He waved back to them. He wandered whether Frank realised that most of the men that he employed were already members of the fledgling Resistance movement.

The factory continued working as Frank left his office to be ready for the reception. Marieke had laid-out his best suit. The bath was hot and he immersed himself in it, soaking the dust of the factory from his pores. As he lay with his eyes closed, revelling in the luxury of a mid-afternoon bath, the door opened. He opened one eye, Marieke stood in the doorway. He opened the other eye. She looked wonderful. Her blonde hair was cut short and the natural curls surrounded her face. She wore no make-up, with her complexion it was unnecessary. The dark blue dress showed off her figure to perfection. It was nipped at the waist and flowed down over her hips to just above her calves. The sleeves were short and there was a neckline that gave space for a simple gold chain that rested just before the slightest suggestion of her cleavage. The dress was sober enough for the occasion but reflected perfectly Marieke's natural beauty. Her eyes laughingly looked at him.

She waited. Frank continued staring, motionless.

'Well, *meneer* van der Meer, what do you think?' Her voice was husky.

He stirred in the bath and sat up, '*Mevrouw* van der Meer, you look beautiful. It's a great pity that we have to go out!' She laughed at his insinuation. He continued, 'I think you're wasted on the Germans. Let's just go out for dinner, shall we?'

'Certainly not, Frank. I want to see just who our great conquerors are and how they behave.' She pouted her lips, turned and swirled out of the bathroom. Over her shoulder she said, 'Do hurry up. For a change I'm ready before you. Oh! and by the way. If you think I'm going on my bike in my new dress, then think again, *meneer*. We're going in the car!'

Frank climbed out of the bath, dried himself, shaved for the second time that day and began to dress. As he shaved he realised that he had not seen that blue dress before. He smiled. He knew how much Marieke liked shopping. He also liked good clothes and his suit was made in pre-war England and was of the softest Yorkshire wool. The silk tie completed the scene and he was ready. He paused in front of the mirror and squared his shoulders. With a smile he pushed his thick brown hair carefully back over his ears.

The house was strangely quiet as he strode down the stairs. He knew why when he walked into the living-room. Marieke was sitting in her chair, with legs primly crossed. There was a cat-like smile on her face and he soon found out why. Harmen was in a new suit. He was not smiling. To his left Aukje entered through the French windows from the garden. She took his breath away.

There was laugher on her lips, 'Hello, *Heit*. What do you think?' She twirled round in one neat movement.

Aukje's face was radiant and her blue eyes were full of happiness. The dress was almost a copy of her mother's. The neckline was cut more deeply showing her young breasts and Frank felt himself flushing from the neck upwards. The skirt was shorter and the stockings were the faintest of brown. The seam at the rear was arrow straight down her slim legs. He realised that he was now looking at his daughter for the first time as a woman and not as a child.

His family just looked at him and laughed.

Marieke was the first to speak, 'For the first time, for as long as I have known you, Frank van der Meer, you appear to be speechless. Whilst you're thinking what to say, the car is ready and we're about to leave. Don't forget the invitation!'

He felt Marieke hook his left arm in hers and Aukje took the other. Harmen led the way and they left the house. As they approached the car, a group of the men from the factory came to open the doors to see them off. Frank was still in shock. He automatically started the engine and drove slowly away.

Eventually he took a deep breath and spoke, 'My family always surprise me. I suppose you three have been out shopping because you're all wearing new clothes. Or, at least, I can't recall having seen them before.' He turned and looked at a smiling Marieke. 'That perfume smells like expensive French?' She nodded and her face lit up. He glanced backwards, 'And as for you young lady, who said you could wear a dress like that?' His voice was full of banter. 'If David de Bruin sees you he'll probably have a heart attack.' Frank wished he could have swallowed his words.

'*Heit*, you know that the de Bruin's will not be at the reception,' said Harmen quietly.

For a moment there was silence in the car.

Marieke squeezed his arm, 'Frank, I didn't buy this dress. I thought about what to wear for quite a while and then I discussed it with Tineke de Bruin.' She smoothed the blue silk with her hand. 'This is her dress. It was made by an old Jewish seamstress in Leeuwarden. Tineke had it altered for me. The same old woman made another dress for Aukje.' She nodded and looked at Frank as he drove carefully towards the town. 'I think it's rather appropriate that I wear this dress for this occasion, don't you?' Her husband could only nod. There was a moistening of his eyes as he gripped the steering wheel. Marieke never failed to surprise him.

Harmen sat with his arms folded and stared into his Father's eyes in the rear view mirror. They exchanged quick smiles. 'My suit, *Heit*, was a gift from Jan de Bruin. It was made by his tailor and he's Jewish too!'

Frank tapped the horn. 'I saw Jan yesterday in Leeuwarden and he gave me this and asked me to put in my pocket.' All eyes focused on Frank's hand as he reached inside the jacket of his suit. He produced a small, gold six-pointed star of David. As he held it up, it reflected the rays of the late afternoon sun.

The reception was a big occasion. They passed other smartly dressed people walking in the same direction. They nodded and smiled at one or two acquaintances. As they arrived at the Bokma's house, Piet and Anneke were waiting for them. Frank parked the car and they stepped out to meet their friends.

Piet let out a low whistle. 'The van der Meer ladies look wonderful. It's good to see you all looking so happy and well.'

Anneke took Frank's hand and the two families set off down the *Groningerstraatweg* towards the town centre.

There was strict security for the reception. As they approached within a kilometre of the Friesian Museum their invitation was checked by plain clothes' policemen. Down *Turfmarkt* Street they were met by a wall of

German soldiers. All in dress uniform and most of them were armed. As Frank produced his invitation, for the third time, the wall parted and they made their way towards the entrance to the museum. It was an old town house situated almost opposite the *Kanselarij*. Large flags bedecked the houses and the old chancellery office. It shocked Frank to see the long, blood red German banners with their ugly black swastikas. They almost covered the whole of the front of the buildings. The smaller Dutch flags were at street level.

As they walked forward, Marieke gripped his hand. To Frank there was that same feeling of complete organisation and total domination. There were German soldiers everywhere. Several huge, open-topped Mercedes-Benz cars lined the street outside the Museum. He involuntarily shuddered and grasped Marieke's hand even harder. There was not a human sound apart from a small army band playing military music. The smiles on the faces around them were that of acceptance.

The doors to the Museum were wide open and they walked through together. A soberly dressed councillor showed them down the long corridor to the rear of the building.

Frank had been in the Friesian Museum many times. He loved the Friesian culture. Many of the exhibitions re-created complete rooms from the past. He had given a gold skull cap from his grandmother to help with one of the displays. They passed through a gallery filled with blue porcelain. Much of it was priceless, Chinese, brought back by the early Dutch explorers and traders. The later Delft exhibits were in another room. They followed other guests and not a word was spoken.

The van der Meers entered the large hall. They were guided by the museum staff towards a long table loaded with German and Dutch delicacies. They looked at each other. They had lost their appetites.

Dirk Haan approached. 'Nice to see you all. Not hungry by the look of it?' His usual smile cheered them up.

Frank said, 'Why is it, Dirk, that when I'm in the vicinity of Germans I always feel so miserable. They always look so official and humourless.'

Dirk grinned, 'I know exactly what you mean, my friend. It's the Wagnerian tradition you know. They like to put on the big show. Everything has to be grand and just right.' Another smile, ' "Alles in Ordnung", controls everything. It doesn't bother me. I'll eat their food for free and I'll find out what's going on. We business men must find out how the monster ticks.' He gave large wink. 'Let's forget our troubles. Marieke, you look wonderful, and Aukje ... well, words fail me.'

Marieke glanced quickly at her daughter, she smiled, 'With that dress, young lady, goes control. Just you learn very quickly how to keep the bees from humming around you.'

Aukje frowned with a lack of understanding. She soon learnt exactly what Marieke meant. Two young German officers approached. They were handsome and their field-grey uniforms a perfect tailored fit. She hid a smile as they actually clicked the heels of their jackboots.

Their Dutch was passable, 'Excuse me, *Fräulein*, may we get a drink for you and perhaps a sandwich?' Their smiles were full of excited interest.

Frank wanted to interfere, but he just stood back and watched his daughter perform.

She coolly looked them up and down from head to foot, turned her head slightly, pursed her lips and, with the faintest touch of annoyance, said, 'No, thank you, gentleman. I'm with my parents.' She turned round and left them standing with red faces. They returned to their grinning comrades.

Frank shook his head. He thought to himself just where his daughter had leant how to handle men. He saw the answer when Marieke looked at him with her blue eyes full of laughter.

The hall was packed. Everybody was looking at everybody else and Frank was forced to acknowledge their greetings. His arm ached with so many hands to shake. Smoke filled the room and the drink flowed but he could feel a sense of foreboding.

'Good evening, *meneer* and *mevrouw* van der Meer. It's so nice to see you again.'

He knew the voice and could sense the presence. *Hauptsturmführer* Müller stood at ease, the black peaked hat under his arm. He was in full dress uniform. The black riding breeches fitted perfectly and the jackboots shone. The dress tunic was creased in all the right places and the silver buttons and piping gave a touch of hardness. The black swastika in the white circle on the red armband was the only indication of any real colour. Müller knew exactly the effect that he was creating. He still radiated that immense feeling of power. His face was split by a smile that was painted into place. The cold blue eyes were quite still and stared directly to the depths of Frank's heart.

Frank knew that this was a battle of stage managed posturing. It took him just ten seconds to size up the situation. He took a step to one side covering Müller's view of his wife and daughter. The well-known smile came over his face and he returned the stare, eye for eye. '*Hauptsturmführer* Müller, what a pleasure to meet you again.'

Marieke moved directly into Müller's view. '*Hauptsturmführer*, that uniform looks wonderful. I'm sure it's a difficult job to keep clean. It must show every little mark?'

He was taken off guard, 'Well ... yes I suppose so. But, I have a servant.'

Marieke leant forward and the cross on the necklace swung slightly outwards making his eyes follow its movement. She kept going. 'Why don't you have any medals? I can see that many other officers here have medals.' She could feel her husband's hand pressing gently on her back. Without realising the fact she had struck Müller to the heart.

'*Mevrouw* van der Meer. ... Thank you for your kind attention,' the voice was icy and his eyes flashed, 'I am a man of diplomacy and politics.

I do not have to pander to life for mere baubles.' He bowed from the waist, stepped sideways and was gone into the crowd.

The look on his face had said it all. Marieke knew that she had struck home.

Frank was not a man to take the Lord's name in vain, but this time he did. His face smiled for the audience and he muttered, 'For God's sake, Marieke, be careful. He's a dangerous man.'

She laughed loudly staring at people around her and whispered, 'Frank, I couldn't resist. I hate the man and all that he represents.'

As the family moved through the various groups, Frank became interested in just who was present. As the invitation had said, the most prominent people in the province were present. The majority of the Germans were in uniform and he realised just how much as a race they adored uniforms. There were other men in dark suits. They were quiet and withdrawn and watched everybody carefully. They were the advanced group of *Geheime Staatspolizei*, the Gestapo, the German secret police. The family kept together. At times they held hands and sometimes stood back to back.

Marieke was talking to a friend from the Church. Half way through a sentence she was stilled into silence by the blast of two trumpets sounding a brief fanfare. A man in a dark suit stepped into the middle of the room. Everybody turned to listen.

'Ladies and Gentlemen. The Reichs Commissioner of the Netherlands, Dr. Seyss-Inquart, has just arrived. May I please ask you to charge your glasses in preparation for a toast after his speech. You must all stand when he enters.'

People looked at each other unsure of what to do next. The Germans set the example. The man walked alone through the door and all the Germans flung out their hands and roared, '*HEIL* HITLER.' It was followed by total silence.

Frank drew his family back into a corner.

The Reichs Commissioner walked across the room and shook hands with notable Germans. He was in turn introduced to local Frieisan councillors and certain businessmen. In one swift movement Seyss-Inquart found Müller, flashed the Nazi salute and greeted him with a large smile. They spoke briefly and then Müller glanced round the room and his eyes settled on Frank. He beckoned the family forward. Marieke pulled Frank back, but all eyes were on them. They walked forward, hand-in-hand.

Frank could feel the hairs on his neck prickle and his hands suddenly became cold. Seyss-Inquart was of average height and wore the brown uniform of the Reichs' administrators. The hair was closely cut and he wore steel-framed glasses. There was a slight limp. His face was straight and showed little sign of feeling. He faced Frank and waited for the introductions.

Müller began, '*Herr* Reichs Commissioner, may I introduce *meneer* and *mevrouw* van der Meer and their two children.'

Seyss-Inquart remained erect. There was no formal bow. His voice was soft with just the faintest Austrian accent. Frank understood his German. 'It is a pleasure to meet you, *meneer* and *mevrouw* van der Meer.'

Before he could move on, Müller continued in a loud voice that could be heard all over the stilled room, '*Ja, Herr* Reichs Commissioner. This man and his family are supporting the German war effort magnificently.' Frank inwardly heaved. 'I must also say, *Herr* Reichs Commissioner, that he is a personal friend of *Generalmajor* Kurt Student. They have met on more than one occasion.'

Seyss-Inquart's eyes glinted behind the steel frames. 'It is always good to make the acquaintance of real friends of the *Reich*.' He stuck out his hand and Frank had no choice but to take it. The grip was limp and slightly damp. The two Germans nodded and moved on. The van der Meers felt their friends staring at them. There were even disapproving looks. The Bokmas stood close to them and together they managed to outface the other people at the reception.

Within ten minutes of his arrival, Seyss-Inquart mounted a small dais and, without notes, began to speak. The room was hushed and the invited guests heard his words clearly. Frank listened. He heard nothing new. The same old stories of the bonds between the German and the Dutch and the need to fight for the *Reich* against the mongrel races of Europe. The speaker's voice droned on and on. Frank felt a dig in his side.

Harmen whispered, 'Wake-up, *Heit*, you're nearly asleep!'

He shook himself and stared ahead. A quick glance at the clock on the wall showed that the speech had lasted almost an hour. Somehow, he still had the glass of lemonade in his hand. He heard a voice proposing a toast and he raised the glass, although he had no idea what the proposal was. There was a cheer and a round of applause. With hardly a glance to left or right Seyss-Inquart, strode past Frank, followed by army officers and German administrators. There was a vacuum of silence that was suddenly filled by the sound of a barrage of rifle shots. Most people remained standing with open mouths, some became anxious. Within a moment a man appeared at the door, glanced at the scene before him and announced that an honorary salute had just been fired by German soldiers of the *Waffen-SS*. There were embarrassed coughs as people tried to smile. Some even laughed in a halting way.

'Come on, Frank, I've had enough of this,' said Marieke. She led her family towards the exit and down the corridor towards the main entrance. Within a minute people were following them and the reception quickly drew to a close. In the street outside she stopped and took a deep breath. 'I didn't enjoy that at all.'

Frank shook his head. He looked rather pale. 'At least we went through with it and I must say it was exactly what I'd expected. Not one Dutchmen was allowed to say anything. The Germans have complete control.'

Dirk invited them back to the hotel but Marieke declined. They were beginning to become used to disappointment. The journey back home was punctuated only by brief conversations.

It was unusual for Aukje to cry. Marieke found her in her bedroom with tears streaming down her face. 'What is it darling? What's wrong?'

She stopped crying. '*Mem*, I didn't tell you this but two weeks ago they took all our books away at school. The teacher told us that the Germans are censoring them. Some of our books came back today, they've totally changed. Some of the best books have gone completely. No English or Jewish authors are allowed. And *Mem* .... A lot of the books are now in German.' She held her mother's hand firmly. 'Why are they doing this to our school and our teachers?'

Marieke shook her head. She had no reply to give and she held her daughter close. The day had not been happy.

FIVE

Orange was the colour of the week. The rumour had flashed around Holland and everybody was trying to buy flowers. But this time the stall holders were ready: they gave them away. The Reichs Commissioner was also ready. Seyss-Inquart ordered that no orange flowers were to be sold or worn near to the Queen's birthday. The citizens of Leeuwarden carried them in their pockets or hidden in their hands.

Frank and Marieke walked into Leeuwarden to see what was happening. They walked past the *stadhuis* and onto *Wilhelmina Straat*. They were surprised to see, directly underneath the street sign, piles of orange flowers of all types. The single colour standing out starkly against the deep red of the old bricks. There was a small crowd standing nearby. They all had broad grins. Two *NSB*'ers stood near the flowers, unsure what to do next. A German car drew up and a *Feldwebel* said something to the two men. They strode towards the flowers.

Frank and Marieke both flinched as the roar of aircraft engines passed low over the centre of Leeuwarden. Everybody froze and looked at the sky. The aircraft returned and Frank thought it must be German from the air base. He was wrong.

He shouted at the top of his voice, 'Look Marieke! Look at the roundels on the wings! It's British!'

The twin engined Wellington bomber flew in a lazy circle almost over their heads. Frank was sure he could see the pilot waving to him.

'Look at the bomb doors! They're opening!' They needed no prompting. They both dropped flat on the ground. The lone German just stood and stared.

Marieke saw it first, 'Oh my God, Frank ... Look! ... Look!'

The sound of the engines faded into the distance. A shower of orange confetti cascaded gently over the centre of the town. It covered everybody and everything in tiny pieces of bright orange paper. People appeared from nowhere and rushed to pick up every scrap. Even Frank found himself pushing pieces in his pocket. Scrambling to his feet, he reached down to pick up Marieke. Her face was radiant and her hair was thick with orange.

'Frank, this is wonderful!'

SIX

The *Hotel de Kroon* was busy. The tables in the restaurant were occupied by German officers and their *NSB* brothers, whilst the bar and the reception area were full of Leeuwarders. Piet Bokma sat in a corner with his friend Dirk. They were hidden by a screen. If the Germans next door could hear what the two men were discussing then they would indeed have saved themselves a great deal of trouble in the years to come.

Dirk had his usual earthenware jug of claret in front of him. He filled Piet's glass and his own to the brim. The long heavy curtains were tightly closed and Dirk had given instructions that they were not to be disturbed. Their lightly grilled steaks were ready to eat.

Dirk began, 'The flower protest went well and that RAF bomber was wonderful. But I've since heard that the *dominee* from the village of Hindeloopen was imprisoned. Apparently, his daughter was caught by the *NSB* for wearing an orange flower. He got six months. We must be careful. We don't want children involved with our activities.'

Through the busy noise of the hotel Piet pondered for a moment. 'I think we have even bigger worries at this time. The Germans have introduced their secret police. Seyss-Inquart has appointed a German called Hanns Albin Rauter and made him *SS-Brigadeführer* for public security. He's responsible for the *Sicherheitsdienst*, the *SD*, and the Gestapo. They're a secret civilian police force. They can go anywhere and do anything.'

'Yes, I've heard of Rauter. My other worry is our own police. Most of them have sided with the Germans and the *NSB*. Some are already with us. The big problem is making sure that we protect the police who are with us.' He paused and took a folded newspaper from his pocket. 'This smaller article is interesting. The Germans are introducing special military courts called the *Landesgericht*. They'll try any offences against Germany, the Führer, the German Army, the German State and all its leaders.' He continued reading. 'It will also cover offences against black-out regulations. ... *Verdomme!*' Piet banged his fist on the table. Dirk raised his eyebrows. 'Do you know Dirk, the principal *Landesgericht* is to be located in Princess Juliana's palace. What an insult!'

Dirk could see his friend's rage and changed the subject. 'All right Piet, I understand. Let's have a look at what we've got so far?'

Piet calmed himself but he was still white with anger. His voice was edgy. 'At this stage we have fifteen active people, a few guns and no radio communications. But, I feel that it wouldn't take too much to involve others. The people that we do have hold good positions in Leeuwarden.'

Dirk took a long drink from his glass, nodded in satisfaction. 'The big question is what are we going to do. We've tried cutting a few telephone cables and letting down car tyres. What we need is something really big.'

'I agree, the Germans aren't fools. They're well used to dealing with a little local resistance. From what I hear about Poland they've got real problems there.' He thought for a moment. 'We need to spread our network over the whole of Friesland. I have some contact with other groups and one of our people is in the printing business so he's agreed to print copies of the *"Vrij Nederland"*. It's only a small paper, two pages long. At least it shows people that there's some organised resistance. *Dominee* de Vries put me in touch with the group in Amsterdam that writes the newspaper and every week a single copy is brought up by *schipper* Schaaf. It does have a Calvinistic viewpoint, but we've not been able to produce anything like it. We need something that can be brought to us much more quickly.' He scratched the tip of his nose. 'We can't use the normal postal services because the Germans would know the addresses. I think at this stage we have to depend on the good *schipper*. We need somebody to help us to organise and we both know who that must be, don't we?' Piet smiled and sat back in his chair. The buzz of conversation and the rich smell of cigar smoke drifted over the screen. 'We've got to have Frank van der Meer. He's a good friend and well respected. He travels widely over Friesland and travels frequently over the whole country. His dealings with the Germans have been excellent. They seem to trust him, although I know for a fact he deeply hates their occupation.'

Dirk glanced over his glass, 'I've got to say this, Piet. There are some people who doubt his patriotism. He's escaped from German clutches twice and he has those massive contracts.'

Piet nodded. 'I understand what you're saying. But, remember what Marieke went through in the police station? That takes some courage, believe me.'

'I have to believe you and, as a friend, I like him and his family tremendously. I suppose I just can't understand why he won't join us. You've asked him often enough.'

'Believe me, he'll join us. Just give him a little more time.' Piet gave a grim smile, 'Wait until he sees what the Germans do to our Jewish friends.'

They carried on discussing potential members before a gentle tap came on the screen. The hotel manager put his head round the ornate panel and apologised. 'Gentlemen, I'm sorry to disturb you, but there's been a man waiting to speak to both of you for the last hour. Perhaps you could see him.'

Piet and Dirk stared hard at each other. Dirk shrugged his shoulders. 'Let's see him.' He nodded to his manager, stood and walked towards the reception desk.

A tallish man in his mid-thirties stood near the desk, dressed in a neat suit and carrying a case. There was a larger suitcase on the floor near his left foot. The face was slightly tanned with blue eyes set in dark sockets. His dark hair was smoothed back over his head. He looked tired. Dirk could size-up people in an instant. It was his business. He liked this man the moment he saw him. Their eyes locked and the stranger gave a quick smile. His eyes remained fixed on Dirk's face.

'Good evening, do I have the pleasure of addressing *meneer* Haan?' The voice was quiet and his Dutch was well accented.

His old-world manner struck Dirk as slightly quaint and he soon realised why.

'I am Dirk Haan. Who, may I ask, are you, *meneer*?'

He inclined his head slightly, 'I'm *luitenant* van Hamel. It's urgent that I speak to you immediately, in private.' He saw Dirk's hesitation. 'It's on a matter of national importance.'

'Follow me please, *luitenant*.' He turned and led the way back to the table.

'This is my friend, *meneer* Bokma. Piet, may I introduce *luitenant* van Hamel.'

Piet was taken aback. He motioned the men towards a seat. 'I'm sure, *luitenant*, that you wouldn't mind showing me some kind of identity?'

The man reached into his pocket and produced a folded piece of card and handed it to Piet. He glanced at it carefully and passed it to Dirk who scrutinised it closely.

With a brisk nod he pointed to the chair. 'Please sit.' The man sat opposite them with his back to the screen. 'Now, *luitenant*, why do you want to see us?'

The quiet voice started to speak, 'I'm a *luitenant* in Her Majesty's Navy ...'

Piet interrupted, 'You mean you were a naval officer. Our armed forces have been disbanded.'

The man's voice turned hard, 'No, you're wrong *meneer*. I'm still a serving officer in Her Majesty's Navy.'

Piet leaned forward and stared into the blue eyes. They stared back at him. 'Just exactly what do you mean?' He put his hand below the table and onto the bottom of his jacket. Dirk knew that he was touching a small revolver.

'I mean exactly what I say, gentlemen. I'm a member of Her Majesty's Navy in exile.'

Piet sat back in his chair and glanced at Dirk.

The man put both hands palm down on the table. 'I've been informed that you two gentlemen are setting up a small resistance movement in Friesland. I would like to help you.'

Piet laughed loudly, 'I really don't know what you're talking about. My friend and I are two successful Friesian businessmen. My friend's hotel serves the Germans and my timber business builds their houses. Why should I be opposing them?'

'Don't play with me, *meneer*.' His voice became tense but he still spoke in a whisper. 'I know from your contacts in Amsterdam and The Hague that you're both active against the Germans in this province.'

Piet again smiled, '*Luitenant*. Prove it!'

All three men glanced at each other. It was the *luitenant*'s turn to smile. He reached over the side of the table and pulled his case onto the white table-cloth. Taking a key-ring from his pocket, he swiftly opened both of the small brass locks. With a flick of his wrist, the lid was thrown open. There was a white towel. He lifted one end of it to reveal a wireless transmitter.

'Jesus Christ!' muttered Dirk. 'Close the damned thing, quick. Do you realise half the German High Command in Friesland is sitting only ten metres away from here?' Piet was pushing the lid closed.

'Gentlemen,' he pushed Piet's hand away and gently half-opened the lid. 'If you look at the brand-mark near to the tuning dial you'll see the name "**Pye of London**". Believe me, I didn't buy it on the local market.'

Piet folded his arms and took a deep breath, 'All right, *luitenant* van Hamel you'd better tell us your story.'

He closed the case with a snap, locked it and placed it on the floor under the table. He spoke quietly, watching their faces. 'After some troubles at Dunkirk I was evacuated by the British to England. In London I met Prince Bernhard and he asked me to work with the British Secret Intelligence Service to help to contact *Orde Dienst* in Holland. There are not many military men left in Friesland but *OD* consists mainly of ex-military officers. Our aim is to provide law and order when the German occupation of Holland ceases.'

'You've got a long wait, my friend,' said Dirk.

The man continued, 'I want to help you to get organised in Friesland. London wants intelligence on anything concerning the occupation.'

'Like what for example?' said Piet, quietly.

'Troop movements. Names of high ranking officers. New construction, particularly at the airfield near Leeuwarden.' Dirk's glance towards Piet confirmed the man's suspicions. 'I need to know how the *NSB* is working with the Germans. Everything you can find on fortifications on the coast.' He caught Piet's frown. 'Oh yes, *meneer* Bokma, they're already fortifying our coast down in the south west, near to the Belgian border. They're going to fortify the whole of the Dutch coast line. It'll take many hours of hard work from good Dutch men.'

Piet was still curious. 'How did you get here, *luitenant*?'

The man leaned back in his chair. He smiled. 'Well, as a sailor, I hate flying but the British have their way of doing things. I was given a two-day parachute course and dropped into a field near Leyden and here I am!' All three smiled.

Dirk rang a small hand-bell on the table. The manager appeared. 'Another glass for our visitor here.' He turned to van Hamel. 'Perhaps a tray of sandwiches would help, *luitenant*?' There was a nodded agreement.

The talk was of the occupation and they all ate well. The three men revealed little of anything that was important.

' ... and do you know, gentlemen, in Amsterdam people have the heads of matches sticking out of the matchbox. It symbolises keeping our heads above the Germans. Coins with the head of our Queen on are in fashion as necklaces. ...'

The wine flowed. There was a tap on the screen and a man stepped round the side. *Hauptsturmführer* Müller, in full dress uniform, stood and looked at Dirk.

The voice was pin sharp, '*Meneer* Haan, I really must compliment you on such excellent cuisine and your wine is superb.' He stared hard at Piet and van Hamel. 'Gentlemen ... I have not had the pleasure.'

Dirk introduced the two men, he did not mention his visitor's rank. Müller glanced briefly at them, bowed from the waist and left.

Dirk frowned. 'That man will remember your name, *luitenant*. I hope for God's sake that your papers are in order.'

Van Hamel smiled. 'The Dutch Register of Population is the best in Europe. I'm on the card index in Leeuwarden and in the central office in The Hague. Don't worry. They can check up all they like. My cards were placed in the system long before I arrived in Holland.'

Piet shook his head, 'I envy your planning and resources. It's just the sort of thing that we need in Holland.'

'That's why I'm here, gentlemen. My wireless can be hidden somewhere in Leeuwarden. I'm expected to make contact within the next week. *Radio Oranje* will tell me when.'

Dirk glanced at his watch, '*Luitenant* van Hamel. Tonight you'll be a guest in my hotel. Tomorrow we'll find more permanent lodgings for you.' He turned to his friend. 'Piet, I don't know about you but I've had enough excitement for one night. Perhaps we could meet early tomorrow and we can make arrangements for our guest.' The three men smiled politely at each other.

On the following day Piet made a special point of being early at the van der Meer factory. He almost beat Frank to his office but not quite.

He smiled a welcome, 'Hello, Piet, nice to see you. Have a seat. Is there something special I can do for you?'

'I was hoping you could do me a favour for a few weeks?' Seeing his friend smile he pressed on. 'I have a colleague visiting me from Amsterdam. He's something to do with shipping and needs somewhere to stay for a few weeks. I'd normally put him up myself but I'm out of the house so often now that it wouldn't be fair to Sytske to offer him our spare room.'

Frank raised an eyebrow and thought for a moment, 'I need to talk to Marieke and the children about it but I can't see any problems. Perhaps I could meet him?'

'I thought you might say that. As a matter of fact he's sitting in my car waiting to come in. May I bring him in?'

Frank laughed. 'Piet Bokma. I should know you by now after all these years. Bring him in, I'll ask Marieke to come up.'

As Piet stepped out of the office, Frank used the telephone to talk to his wife. Harmen appeared from the factory and his father explained what was happening.

Van Hamel returned with Piet. Frank had chairs ready for them. There were handshakes all round. Van Hamel stood and Piet made the introductions.

'Marieke, Frank. May I introduce Lodo van Hamel. He's a colleague from Amsterdam. Can I ask that you please accommodate him for a couple of weeks?'

Marieke looked at the visitor, 'Perhaps, *meneer* van Hamel, you could tell us a little about yourself?'

He looked a little uncomfortable. He was not used to women questioning him. '*Mevrouw* van der Meer, I'm working for a transport company in Amsterdam. We're hoping to expand our business in Friesland. You have an excellent canal system that links with Germany.'

She nodded and one eyebrow raised questioningly. 'Thank you, *meneer*. I want to know a little about yourself not about your work.'

'Of course, I quite understand. I'm a bachelor, twenty-six years old. I can very easily look after myself, I don't eat a great deal and for most of the time I'll be travelling round Friesland. I may be late back some nights and sometimes I will stay away. I will naturally pay a rent for my room.' He stopped talking and looked Marieke straight in the eye.

Frank recognised Marieke's uneasiness. He respected her intuition. '*Meneer* van Hamel, what do you think of the proposed new canal connection between Leeuwarden and Germany?' It was a lie.

Van Hamel knew that something was wrong. He had been treated in this way before. He tried to bluff his way through. 'An excellent proposition. A great deal of business will be flowing through the two countries. We must take our share in the business.' He looked at Frank's face.

Frank was upset. He turned to his friend. 'Piet, I've got to say this to you. Just exactly who is this man?' He pointed his finger at van Hamel and his voice held a trace of anger. 'I strongly suspect that he has something to do with ... shall we say ... your, "other" business.'

Van Hamel shrugged his shoulders and turned to Piet. 'I think, *meneer* Bokma that if you trust this man and his family that you'd better tell him the truth about me.'

'I knew it,' said Marieke grim-faced.

Frank closed the office door and Piet retold the events of the previous night. Van Hamel watched. 'Frank, Marieke, I can only apologise for not trusting you. I have to be careful. But again I must ask you if Lodo can live with you.' He paused for a moment and continued, 'Because your house is away from town then there is little chance that the Germans will be suspicious. They know me in a different way than you.' He looked uncomfortable. 'Am I making myself clear?'

Frank's face was serious, his voice tinged with worry, 'I know exactly what you're trying to say to me.'

Marieke recognised the uncomfortable situation and arrived at instant decision. '*Meneer* van Hamel, we would be delighted to let you live with us. You'll be more than welcome. But! .... On one condition.'

'*Mevrouw?* ...' He let the question hang.

'You must promise me for any reason whatsoever, that you will never put this family in danger.'

He nodded. 'I agree.'

She watched him and waited for a full minute before answering. Van Hamel was conscious of a pair of blue eyes staring intently at him. He lowered his head and folded his arms and smiled. He knew when he had met his match.

Marieke organised. 'Now, let's get down to details. Where are you staying at the moment?' They discussed where he would sleep and the van der Meer household routine. Harmen had remained silent until just before van Hamel was about to leave.

His voice was excited, '*Meneer!*'

Van Hamel turned and looked him in the face. 'Yes, young man.'

'You really are a spy, aren't you? ... Tell me about England. They're not going to win the war are they?' the questions came tumbling out. Nobody else interrupted. Harmen was voicing all their thoughts. When he stopped the room was silent.

Van Hamel stood and looked through the window. He spoke carefully in measured tones. 'The British will win the war. Maybe not this year and probably not the next but, with our help, they will win. Hitler must be defeated. He's evil and threatens our way of life. I saw their spirit after Dunkirk. I saw their fighter pilots fight the *Luftwaffe*. I saw their people prepare to fight. I've met and listened to Winston Churchill.' He turned and faced them. 'I met our Queen and I had many meetings with Prince Bernhard. He's now Commander-in-Chief of all Dutch forces. I've no doubt at all that we will win. But, by God, we'll have to fight them in any way that we can.' He remained standing. The conversation was finished.

Piet and van Hamel left the factory leaving the van der Meers sitting in the office.

Frank turned to his wife, 'Thank you, Marieke, for taking him in.'

'*Liefje*, I knew exactly what you were thinking and somebody has to help him. He's in great danger.'

'And so are we.' added Harmen. Nobody added anything to that final comment.

SEVEN

Jan de Bruin continued with his job at the bank. It had taken him many years to reach the senior position that he now held. Most of his wealth was in his property and investments. His gentile friends still treated him in a friendly and courteous way but he could feel some animosity from many people who used the bank.

Tineke was waiting as he arrived home late one evening. She heard him come through the front door and called out, 'Hello, Jan. How are you? ... There's a drink ready.' He took off his wet coat and scarf and came into the kitchen and sat down.

He stared at the table and shook his head. 'You know they're damned clever, the *moffen*.'

'What is it darling?' She smiled.

Jan folded his arms, 'This is how their financial system works. If a Dutch man owes money to a Belgian firm he doesn't pay it directly, he pays it through the bank to the Dutch Clearing Institute. They then pay it to the Germans in Berlin who then send the money to the Belgian Clearing Institute who then pay the money to the Belgian company. It's said to be a model of German administrative genius. But really it means that they control all the money in occupied Europe and can pay bills anytime that they want to at any rate of exchange.'

He sipped at the coffee. Tineke, for the first time, noticed that his hair was beginning to grey around the temples. She felt concern for him.

'Jan, darling, try not to worry. There's nothing that you can do. Just keep out of the way of people at work and do your job.'

He looked thoughtful and his voice was weary. 'It's the money I'm worried about. I can't take anything out of the bank and if I lose my job, which seems likely, then how do we live?' He drained the coffee, put it on the table and stared hard at the empty cup.

Tineke pulled her chair over towards him and put her arm around his shoulders. For the first time in their marriage she saw that he was crying. Tear drops rolled down his cheeks.

'Jan, there's something that I must tell you and now seems a good enough time.' He shook himself, stopped crying and looked at her face. She continued. 'The day before the invasion, I emptied my private account ... '

He interrupted, his eyes were clear, 'What account? ... Why? ... I didn't know anything about it.'

She had his full attention. 'I'm sorry, Jan. I kept it for emergencies. When my mother died she left me some of her money in an account opened in my maiden name. It's been there for seventeen years and I've never touched it.'

His jaw dropped and he stared at her. 'I know all the accounts at the bank. Your name is not on any account.'

She smiled mischievously, 'Actually the account was at another bank in Groningen. On the day before the invasion, I caught the morning train to see Aunt Judith. Whilst I was there, I emptied the account and closed it. It had been a good investment. I went to a business friend of my mother's family and changed it into gold. I got a very good rate because my family friend said there was a bit of a rush on gold at the time.' She placed her hands on her hips and her long black hair swirled round her shoulders. 'You're not angry are you, darling?'

Jan stood. Suddenly she had become very desirable. 'I'm not angry, just totally amazed. How much have you got?'

'You mean, how much have we got, darling? I changed 100,000 guilders into gold coins.'

'You did what?' shouted Jan. 'Where the hell is it?'

She walked out of the room and returned with a leather handbag. Her smile was bright. 'Remember that old bag of my mother's that you're always asking me to throw away? Well, here it is.' She flipped open the flap and tipped the bag upside down. Dozens of gold coins poured onto the wooden table top. Some rolled onto the tiled floor and spun away into dark corners.

Jan stared at the heap and ran his fingers through the bright coins. 'I can't believe it. I'm a banker and I never thought for one minute that you had any money from your mother. I know she died before we met ... but this, ... this is unbelievable!' Without thinking he began to count the coins and stack them into neat heaps. Tineke crawled round the floor finding the odd lost coin.

They sat at the table holding hands staring at the neat piles of gold. Each heap gave out a dull yellow gleam.

'Where shall we hide it?' She spoke in a hushed whisper.

'In a hole underneath the biggest pile of cow shit that I can find!'

They laughed until they cried and then they laughed some more. Eventually Jan rose from the table and gathered the coins back into the bag. 'Tomorrow, I'll find somewhere to hide this little lot.' As he walked to the back of the house, the front door opened. David and Aukje walked into the hall.

'Hello, *Heit ... Mem*,' said David. Aukje smiled.

Tineke took a deep breath. 'I was getting worried about you two.' She glanced at both of them, 'Why are you so dry when it's raining so hard?'

David looked distinctly uncomfortable. 'Well, *Mem* ... we were sheltering in the barn to keep dry ... and well ... time went so quickly.'

'I hope you don't smell of cow muck,' said Jan over his shoulder. Aukje blushed.

Tineke glanced at the clock, 'I think, David, that it's time you took Aukje home. Say hello to Marieke and Frank from us.' They scuttled out of the house into the rain and Marieke watched them cycle away into the dark.

Next day the sound of a heavy lorry drawing into the factory yard did not surprise Frank. Lorries came and went all day. But this time he heard the sound of German voices. It made him stand and walk over to the office window. Within a minute he heard somebody hammering on the front door. In a flash he was into the house and arrived in the hall at the same time as Marieke. He opened the door.

'*Guten morgen,*' said a young German *Wehrmacht* officer. He glanced at the paper clipped to a board. 'Are you *meneer* van der Meer?'

'Yes, why?' was Frank's terse response.

The man stepped inside, without invitation, followed by four soldiers. The smile appeared genuine. 'I'm here to requisition certain items for German Headquarters in Leeuwarden. ... .' He stared through the door into the living-room. 'Ah yes, ... I can see the items that I need.' Frank and Marieke watched speechlessly.

He stood in the middle of the room and pointed with his board. '*Ja*, ... the two silver candlesticks.' One of the men stepped forward and took the candlesticks off the fireplace and placed them into a bag. The officer jotted something onto the paper.

He waved his hand towards the wall. 'Also the two paintings ... street scenes in Leeuwarden, ... *ja.*' Again the scribbled notes.

Frank came to his senses, 'What the hell do you think you're doing! Get out of my house!'

The officer turned towards him and smiled, 'We're only borrowing these things for a short time. See ... ' He waved the paper. 'You'll be given a receipt for everything and you'll be able to apply for compensation if anything is damaged.'

Marieke touched his foot with hers. Frank glanced sideways. One of the soldiers had unslung his rifle. The meaning was obvious. The officer continued.

'Now let me see, ... two of those carpets.' He bent down, '*Ja* ... 19th Century Kashmir, I think. ... *ja*, take them.' The soldier rolled them up carefully. More notes.

He scrutinised the room. 'I think that's all for now. Thank you for your co-operation, *mein Herr.*' He clicked his heels, turned smartly and walked towards the front door. His men followed. Almost as an afterthought he snapped his fingers. 'Oh, ... *ja*, I almost forgot. *Hauptsturmführer* Müller sends his kind regards.'

EIGHT

Lodo van Hamel settled in well at the van der Meer house. He proved popular with the family. He came and went on his bicycle and, occasionally, Frank let him use the Austin. Nobody made any enquiries. In Friesland many people were on the move. The Germans were organising things in a big way. A strip of coastal land one kilometre wide was declared military property and it was compulsorily bought. Many people lived with relatives and the roads were busy. It provided a perfect cover for Lodo's work. When Piet visited the factory on business he always talked to Lodo after any meeting with Frank.

He pushed the plate away. 'Marieke, that was a beautiful meal. Thank you.'

She smiled with pleasure, 'I don't know what you do all day, Lodo. But you eat enough food for three people.' She waved away his apologies.

'*Meneer* van Hamel, would you like to play cards with me,' said Aukje, with her most charming smile.

He loved playing cards and enjoyed her humour and sense of fun. She reminded him of his younger sister back in his home town. He knew he dared not make contact with her, so he played cards with Aukje.

He glanced at the clock, 'I'm sorry, Aukje, tonight I have some work to do in my room. Maybe tomorrow?'

'Tomorrow, I'm going to see David de Bruin. It'll have to be Friday,' she laughed.

Lodo excused himself and climbed the stairs to his room at the top of the house. He was fortunate, the room was quiet and he could be perfectly alone. The family rarely disturbed him. It was five minutes to ten and he had four minutes to prepare his wireless for transmission.The case was stacked with other boxes in the corner of the room. Every night for the last five weeks he had sent signals to the British Secret Intelligence Services in London. Usually from as many locations as possible. The Germans were not stupid. When he was away the case came with him, securely fastened to the carrier on the rear of his bicycle. The case had enough room for overnight changes of clothes and toilet articles. Nobody had stopped him to examine its contents. Life in Holland would only remain so easy for another two months.

He closed the door securely and lifted the case onto the table near the small window. Glancing through the small panes of glass pleased him. With the clear night-sky, no clouds meant good reception. Carefully, he unreeled the aerial and threaded it across the roof beams and down towards the window. The orientation was perfect. He plugged the end of the copper wire into the brass contact on the front of the wireless. The small adapter was connected into the wall socket. Batteries were precious and he saved them for emergencies. He withdrew the Morse key from its canvas pouch. It was a sensitive instrument especially tuned for his touch. All was ready. He slipped the headphones over his ears, checked his watch and switched on. A gentle whine came into his ears and a needle on a dial flickered and steadied. He nodded. The carrier wave was established. At precisely ten o'clock he started to tap the Morse key. First the dits and dahs of his personal code. Within ten seconds a single modulated tone was transmitted from England. They were ready. At the side of the wireless were three sheets of paper containing columns of single letters. He had already encoded the information that his agents had provided for him in the last twenty-four hours. Piet Bokma had proved as good as his word. His information was top quality. Piet always gave that extra piece of news. This time precise time-tables of trains to Germany from Leeuwarden. It was all there. It took him exactly three minutes to transmit everything. Speed was essential. He knew that there was at least one wireless-tracking vehicle in Friesland.

He tapped his end of message signal and waited. His code came through again and he wrote the message onto his pad. The stream of letters took fifteen seconds. He had them all. He knew exactly what the last group meant and his heart raced even faster.

Lodo switched off and removed his headphones. As he reached up to pull down the aerial, he jumped and dropped the thin wire. Behind him stood Frank and Marieke. Their faces pale with anger.

Frank angrily began, 'MENEER van Hamel! One of the reasons why we allowed you to live in our home was that you promised that you would not put my family in danger.' With an unwavering finger he pointed at the wireless. 'That! ... that! ... could mean death for us all.' He remained stock-still and Marieke was silent.

Lodo stood up. There was little he could say or do. The meaning of the last group of codes flashed again into his mind.

Gone was the informality, 'Meneer and mevrouw van der Meer, I can only apologise. I beg you to forgive me. Before you say anything else,' he waved the notepad in his hand, 'this signal tells me that I'm wanted back in England. They've decided that they're going to fly me out in two days time. I've nowhere else to go in those two days.' He shrugged his shoulders and stared appealingly at Marieke. 'What more can I say?'

Frank calmed but his voice remained icy. 'Lodo, I understand what you're going through. But I will not have my family placed in danger.' He felt Marieke's hand on his arm, took a deep breath and shook his head. The voice was decisive. 'You can stay here for the two days. But do not use the wireless.' They both turned and without another word left the room.

Piet was having lunch in the *Hotel de Kroon*. It always amazed him just how much information the Germans gave away when they were eating or drinking in the hotel. His memory ferreted away anything that was useful. As he drank a glass of beer Piet was surprised to see Dirk beckoning him from behind the reception desk. He put the glass back on the table, rose and walked casually towards him. He passed two groups of German officers. He nodded at one of them; there was a business connection.

Dirk smiled and talked quietly, 'Piet, make your way down to the wine cellar. Lodo needs to talk to us urgently.'

Dirk knew that that this was important. They had never met like this before. He waited for a couple of minutes and then made his way to the long velvet curtain that concealed the entrance to the cellar. The door opened silently and he made his way down the narrow brick stairs. He walked into the smallest of the three cellars. A single candle lit the barrel-vaulted chamber. It cast flickering shadows over the bottles that lined the walls and atmosphere was cool and dry. Dirk and Lodo were waiting. There was no time to waste.

He whispered as though in church, 'I've some important news. The British want me to return to London with all the written information that I've collected so far.' Piet and Dirk glanced at each other. 'They will land on the night of the 13th November and fly me out.'

'Just where are they going to land?' said Piet. 'Friesland has only small fields and at this time of the year they're usually waterlogged,'

'They're using a seaplane. It'll look for my signal and land on the *Tjeukemeer*.'

Piet nodded, 'Yes ... that is one of the bigger lakes. I hope they only need a short length of water. What are the arrangements?'

The candle flame dipped for a moment and all three men straightened up. Dirk gave a nervous laugh. 'Don't worry. It's only air from the ventilation tunnel behind the wine rack.'

Van Hamel hunched down over the small wooden table and extracted a piece of paper from his pocket. '23.30 hours. The signal is three short flashes followed by three long and then continually repeated. It's to be flashed as near as possible to the start of the longest stretch of water.' He turned to Piet. 'I'll need your help to get there.'

There was a moment's silence. Piet said, 'I think it's silly for the three of us to wait at the lake with you. We'll go on bikes, that'll look innocent enough. When we get there Dirk and I'll set up the light and wait away from the lake. In that way if there's a problem, only one of us will get caught.' The men nodded.

Van Hamel thought for a moment. 'I'll make sure that the information contains no local names. One small suitcase should be enough. London has told me to leave the wireless in your hands. Before I leave, I'll show you how to use it.'

Dirk had a question. 'Lodo, we'll miss you. You're the only person from England that's ever come here. Will they send you back to us, or will it be somebody else?'

Lodo shook his head, 'I don't know what'll happen. Collecting intelligence is useful for London but I think they want more action and possibly some acts of sabotage. There're rumours that Churchill wants to set up a new organisation especially for that purpose. I heard the name Special Operations Executive mentioned. Maybe I'll have to join that department.' He shook his head again. 'I don't really know. I'll just have to wait until I get back to London.'

The candle had nearly burnt its full length and Piet stood and looked at his two friends. 'All right, gentlemen. Lodo and I'll leave through the back door. We'll make our separate ways to Vierhuis to the east of the lake and meet at the end of the road that goes through the village.' He looked from one face to another. 'Any questions?' There was no reply.

As they quietly left the cellars, the candle spluttered into darkness.

Tjeukemeer is four hours hard cycling from Leeuwarden. The weather on the night of the 13th November was atrocious. Gales and rain lashed Dirk's face as pushed the pedals to get his bike to make headway. As he passed through the small town of Sneek there were two German soldiers near the railway station. He passed them without a second glance. As he pushed himself hard, the cobbles were slippery and several times he nearly fell off the bike. There were no lights to be seen in the open countryside and no living soul moved along the narrow roads. The dead flat landscape allowed every gust of wind to come straight at him. As he approached the open water of the *Tjeukemeer*, the wind gained in strength and it rained horizontally. Even in his thickest clothes he was soaked to the skin and very cold.

Lodo was standing under a tree and as Dirk waved to him Piet arrived from the other direction.

Lodo was the first to speak, 'Good timing, gentlemen. I've been here for over an hour and I haven't seen anybody.' He shook himself and water cascaded onto the sodden ground. 'It's another twenty minutes before zero. When we hear the sound of the aircraft, I'll take up my position over there.' He pointed to a small spit of land that disappeared into the black waters of the lake. 'I think you should cycle to that group of trees just beyond the spit. I've checked it already and there're plenty of places to hide.' He looked into the black sky. The moon was hidden by enormous thunderous clouds. The water was whipped into a seething froth by the wind. 'I don't think that they'll come tonight anyway, but it's good practice for tomorrow.' There was a grunt from his friends.

Zero time came and went. They waited under the trees in the hope that the storm would pass. They crawled about in the mud at the side of the lake and strained their ears for the slightest sound. There was nothing.

Dirk delved into his pocket and produced a silver hip flask. 'Best Dutch gin. Four sips for each of us.' It helped them a little.

As dawn approached, they scrambled their way back through the trees towards the hidden bikes.

'HALT! DON'T MOVE! ... WHAT ARE YOU DOING?' The voice grated through the silence.

Lodo pulled a pistol out of his pocket.

'Don't! ... put it away!' snapped Piet.

Lodo took the initiative and whispered, 'You two stay where you are. I'll see who it is.' Before Piet and Dirk could do anything, Lodo stepped forward away from them.

The man was alone and dressed in a dark green uniform. The polished peak of his hat gleamed. He was armed. The loud voice was demanding, 'Give me your papers now! What are you doing here?'

As Lodo reached in his pocket, the man placed his hand on the open flap of his leather holster. Lodo was tempted to reach for his own pistol and shoot him, but he hesitated, realising that it was a Dutchman that he would kill.

He spoke loudly and respectfully, 'Yes, of course. ... Here are my papers.'

As he pulled out his wallet, he glanced at himself in the early morning light. He was a mess. Thick mud and water dripped from his clothes and his face was streaked with dirt. The man took the wallet and stepped backwards. His eyes flickered downwards, a glance at the papers and a glance at Lodo.

Dirk was flat on the ground behind a small bush. 'Come on, Piet,' he whispered, 'let's take him now.' He began to rise. He was pushed firmly back into the mud.

Lodo recognised the uniform of a village policemen. He took off the sodden hat and pushed his hair back. He gave a broad smile. '*Meneer*, My name is Lodo van Hamel and I'm one of those crazy bird watchers.' He waved his arms around. 'This is the time of the month for observing the flight of the Canada goose. If you look over there ...' He pointed over the lake. 'There's a flock just about to take-off. I've been watching them all night. This is the best place in the whole of Friesland to see them.' There was a flock just gaining height above the lake.

The policemen folded the papers and stuffed them back into the wallet. He stared at Lodo for a full minute. Eventually he made his decision.

'*Meneer*, you were seen and heard at five o'clock this morning. A local farmer's wife reported you to my office.' He paused. 'She said she saw more than one man. Where are the others?'

Lodo laughed out aloud. 'There's only me. After all, *meneer*, who else would be so crazy to sit in this mud and rain all night?'

The man handed the wallet back. There was a sneer on his face. 'You must leave the area now. Do not return.' He turned away and walked back towards the road.

Lodo stood stock-still. Underneath his soaking clothes sweat was pouring off him. He realised that the man could be waiting and he waved the palm of his hand downwards in a waving motion to warn his friends. He walked back to his bike and waited silently. The clouds had cleared and the early morning sunshine made steam rise from his clothes. Piet and Dirk rose from the bushes.

'Come on, Lodo, Dirk ... ,' said Piet hoarsely. 'Let's get out of here, ... quick!'

Lodo stayed at Dirk's hotel and, after a good bath, he slept for most of the day. They met again in the wine cellar late in the afternoon. They were quiet and the conversation was subdued.

'Lodo, you can't go back there again. That policeman will certainly report what he saw this morning.' Dirk had his hand on his friend's shoulder.

'I agree,' added Piet.

Lodo was adamant. 'He's a Dutchman and he wasn't suspicious. We have to go back tonight. The plane will most certainly return to pick me up. I insist that you stay here.' He saw the look in their eyes and added, 'I can go myself.'

'Oh no! We're coming as well. We'll not leave you alone under any circumstances.'

Lodo stood up and began to pace round the small cellar. The candle cast dancing shadows over the racks of wine. He spoke confidently. 'This time we'll separate the moment we hear the aircraft. I'll hide the case until the very last minute.' He raised a hand in warning. 'You must keep clear. I don't want anything happening to you.'

Dirk produced a stone bottle from under the table. 'This is better than my hip flask. Let's drink some now and more later. I won't forget that weather last night.' He pulled out three glasses and filled them to the brim. 'A toast, my friends. ... To the Royal Air Force and the Queen!' Three more toasts were drunk in quick succession. For the last thirty minutes the conversation lightened.

It was a crystal-clear calm night. The moon was full, casting long shadows as Piet coasted down the cobbled roads through the Friesian countryside. He sang out aloud as he neared the *Tjeukemeer*. Apart from a lone cyclist there was nobody about. They met at a place half a kilometre from their last waiting point. The feeling between them was totally different. There was almost an atmosphere of relief.

They waited long past midnight and the temperature dropped.

'Oh no!' said Lodo quietly. 'Look over the lake.' They all watched the still waters.

Slowly, curls of mist began to rise from the black surface. They spiralled upwards and seemed to have a life of their own. Within an hour the whole lake was covered in a fog that was head-height. They watched it roll backwards and forward in time to the gentle waves on the lake's surface.

'That's it!' said Piet emphatically. 'They won't come now.'

'Patience, my friend,' nodded Dirk.

It was absolutely still. Not a sound could be heard. The mist deadened everything.

Lodo sat upright. He took his hat off and turned his head from side to side. 'Listen ... listen! Can you hear it? That slight droning from the north-west.' They all stood. The three men turned and strained to hear the sound.

'Lodo, you're right. I can hear it,' said Piet, excitedly.

'Right, quick! You two hide in the trees. I'll signal and collect my case when the plane lands. Don't move until I've left.' He paused for a moment. The sound of the engines grew louder. He looked at Piet and Dirk. 'I suppose this is goodbye. I hope to see you again soon.' There was no time for handshakes. He turned and ran towards the lake.

Piet pulled Dirk into the darkness under the trees. Just in time. The footpath to the lake was suddenly illuminated by a shaft of bright light.

'Oh no! No! I knew it!' breathed Dirk. They froze and watched the scene unfold before them. Six armed men jumped out of the undergrowth. All had bright torches in one hand and pistols in the other. Lodo was caught in the middle of their trap. He made no movement and slowly raised his hands over his head. One of the men rushed forward and pushed his gun into Lodo's stomach. Another quickly searched him from top to bottom. He flourished Lodo's pistol in the air. They could see the look of triumph on the man's face.

The shouting began. 'Why are you here? ... Not for bird-watching this time I'm sure. ... Don't move.' It was the same policeman from the night before. He turned to the other men. 'Come on! Search the area. I think he's up to no good.'

The men began to spread out, poking the bushes and the water's edge. It did not take long.

'I've found it!' The man shouted in his Friesian dialect. 'A case. ... It's locked.' He dragged the dripping case out of the bushes.

'Leave it locked and bring it with you.' The men stood together with Lodo caught in the beams of their torches. His head was erect and he stared into their eyes.

'Take him to the village. I'll have to get in touch with my *inspecteur* as soon as possible.' The policemen began to walk away.

Dirk writhed in the mud. 'My God! ... Oh my God! They've got him.'

'And they've got the case full of information,' said Piet grimly. 'There's absolutely nothing we can do about it. We'll wait here for an hour and then move back to Leeuwarden.'

He looked into the clear sky. There was no sign of the aircraft, just a fading drone to the north-west.

NINE

'This third time is wrong. I can feel it. The Germans aren't fools, they're bound to be waiting for us.'

The smell of the rubber oxygen mask pervaded his words as he spoke down the intercom.

'But we have to try,' was the reply into his head-set.

The aircraft was a twin-engined Fokker seaplane pressed into service with a Dutch crew and RAF markings. Flight Lieutenant Schaper was worried. He knew for certain that they would be waiting for him. His corporal telegraphist, van Tongeren agreed but they had to try and rescue their countryman. The Secret Intelligence Service desperately needed the information that van Hamel was bringing out.

The night was clear and the bright moon sent reflections around the cockpit. The synchronised drone of the engines was strangely calming as the aircraft flew at two thousand metres above Texel, one of the Wadden islands to the north of the Dutch coast.

'We'll just have to be vigilant and be prepared for a quick take-off if needed.'

'Sir. Ten minutes to *Tjeukemeer*,' intoned van Tongeren.

Schaper adjusted the throttles and the aircraft began a slow descent towards the flat countryside. The moon cast long shadows upon the land. They passed over several of the Friesian lakes and eventually he spotted the larger *Tjeukemeer* to port. He cruised over the lake once, at a height of five hundred metres. There was no sign of any signal.

'I'm taking her lower.' The engines throttled back and the nose of the aircraft dipped.

'Sir! Directly ahead. A flashing light. Can you see it?'

'Yes, ten degrees to port.' He counted the flashes. 'They don't look right. What do you think Corporal?

The Fokker was only two hundred metres high and turning in a slow circle. The weather was perfect with a slight headwind.

'I agree Sir. It doesn't look right. But if he's down there we can't leave him.'

Schaper was worried. It felt all wrong and his earlier suspicions kept repeating in his brain.

He lowered the landing flaps. 'We have to take a chance. Prepare to land. Corporal, unstrap and go down and open the access hatch.' He slid back the small perspex window at the side of his seat. He sucked in the jet of fresh air. It made him realise that fresh water smelt different to sea water. He passed low over a village, weaving slightly to miss a small group of trees. He braced himself and gently lifted the nose of the aircraft. With a whooshing sound the floats touched the water and sent back streams of white froth behind the wings.

He was not conscious of the sound of guns but he was blinded by the searchlights. They stabbed through the darkness across the lake from shore to shore. He covered his eyes, but his night-sight was gone..

'Sir! ... Sir! ... They're firing at us from both sides.'

He shouted at the top of his voice, 'DAMN! ... DAMN! ... I WAS RIGHT! THE BASTARDS!'

Now, even above the roar of the engines, he could hear the staccato cracks of heavy gun-fire. There was the rapid chatter of machine-guns and the search-lights followed their every move. The aircraft became stationary and rocked in the slight swell, the engines just ticking over. He had never felt so alone and terrified in his life. But soon reason and training took over.

He aimed towards the darkest part of the lake. His voice was strident. 'Take-off! ... Take-off! ... Close the hatch ... be quick about it. Strap in! ... Strap in!'

He gunned the engines, flipped the rudder and jockeyed the aircraft in a tight half-circle. He felt bullets ripping though the fragile fabric skin of the fuselage. One explosion rocked the Fokker from wing-tip to wing-tip. He prayed that the fuel tanks were safe. The seaplane roared along in a welter of spray. Red and green tracer fire arced through the sky from shore batteries. He jinked from side to side in the vain hope of escaping the concentrated fire. Gone was the normal routine of take-off.

A quick glance at the air-speed indicator showed that he was way off the correct speed. Schaper yanked at the control column, pulling it sharply into the pit of his stomach. His feet wrestled with the rudder bars.

'Come on you bloody thing! ... Come on! ... Lift, for Christ's sake, lift!' He squeezed the words through clenched teeth.

The aircraft pitched and yawed, climbed off the water and then crashed back with a sickening thud. His left hand held the twin throttle levers hard against the control gate. The guns continued their hammering. Somehow he remembered to switch off the landing lights and then he just aimed himself towards the darkest strip of land in the distance. Another yank on the column and another crash onto the water. Time seemed to slow down. Suddenly the skyline disappeared and the engines roared in harmony. The sound of rushing water was replaced by rushing air. He raised the flaps and levelled off. His brain told him to keep low and fly fast. Trees skipped past the window and he was conscious of the glare of searchlights behind him.

'Thank God. Corporal, how bad is the damage?' The North Sea had loomed over the seaplane and he slowly began to climb into the welcoming black sky. There was no answer to his request.

He glanced down in front of him into the perspex nose canopy. Instead of his crew member seated in the normal observation position he could see an arm extended over the seat. Schaper tried again.

'Corporal! ... Can you hear me?'

The arm moved and his crewman dragged himself into a sitting position. 'Sir, I've been wounded. A piece of shrapnel is stuck in my leg. I'm bleeding pretty badly.' There was a pause. 'I think I'll be all right. I'll make a tourniquet out of my tie. Hang on a minute. I'll be all right. ...Oh my God! ... I've just realised. It means they've got him.'

There was a brief minute's silence. The aircraft climbed back to two thousand metres and, at full throttle, headed back towards the English coast.

TEN

Frank heard the footsteps on the stairs to his office. It was a pale-faced Piet who confronted him.

'Frank, I bring bad news. This morning Lodo was taken by the Dutch police. He was about to be picked up by a seaplane to be taken back to England. Dirk and I only just escaped.'

Frank shook his head and banged his chair. 'I half expected something to happen. When I saw that wireless set, I knew he was living on borrowed time.' He looked at his friend. 'Are you and Dirk all right?'

'Yes, we're fine.' Piet fingered the button on his coat and took a deep breath. 'I'm worried about you and your family. It seems that our policemen took him to the Germans. I can't say that he won't talk. They've also got his case and it was full of information.' Frank raised his hand but Piet continued, 'I checked the contents. There were no incriminating names. Only information about German coastal defences and other building work.' He looked up at his friend. 'I thought of trying to rescue him. My group does have some weapons but I'm sure the Germans would take reprisals. Anyway, tomorrow they're taking him under heavy guard to the prison in Scheveningen. From what I hear, people never get out of there.'

'Why are you worried about me?' said Frank quietly.

'The Germans will know that he lived with you. It said so on his papers. I expect them to visit you at any time. Frank,' he said with a worried expression, 'you must stick to your story. Tell them that he came to Dirk's hotel and that you put him up in good faith. After all, they can't prove that he did anything wrong whilst he was in your house.'

Frank remained calm. 'Piet, I knew that this was going to happen. I'm ready and so are my family.' He stood. 'Thanks for warning me. I'll talk to Marieke.'

Piet walked towards the door of the office. He turned, 'Frank, you could join us, you know. At least that way we can co-ordinate these problems that'll keep on occurring as long as you're my friend.'

Frank shook his head and remained silent. They parted.

The family did not have to wait long. Within twenty minutes of Piet leaving, a black Opel car came round the corner of the yard and drew to a halt. *Inspecteur* Koopman stepped out, followed by one of his men. He waited for a moment looking up towards the factory office. He made up his mind and climbed the steps. Frank was waiting for him with Marieke at his side.

'Good afternoon, *inspecteur*. What can I do for you?' His voice was polite.

The *inspecteur* was dressed in uniform with a long, dark greatcoat stretching below his knees. His face was not unfriendly and he returned the politeness, '*Meneer* van der Meer. You must accompany me to police headquarters in Leeuwarden.'

'May I ask why?'

The *inspecteur* took a deep breath. 'This morning, my men arrested a man by the name of Lodo van Hamel. He was attempting to escape from Holland in a British seaplane. He had with him a case of highly incriminating documents. Unfortunately, I had no other choice but to inform my German superiors. Van Hamel had this address as his place of residence and my superiors wish to discuss this matter with you.' He turned to the policeman standing near the door and waved him away. He took a pace forward and took off his leather gloves. He glanced from face to face. This time he spoke in a whisper. '*Meneer*, whatever you do, be careful. Müller is very upset. Even Berlin has been on the telephone about this arrest. It means that he must find the other agents. Van Hamel is the first such man to be caught in Friesland and Müller wants success. He knows that other people helped van Hamel.' He thought for a moment and turned to Marieke. 'In another twenty minutes, *mevrouw*, a lorry load of Germans and two *SD* men will be here to search the house. In other words you have twenty minutes to, shall we say, ... "tidy" your house.'

Marieke gave Frank a squeeze on the arm, nodded and left the room.

The *inspecteur* pulled on his gloves and straightened his back, 'And now, *meneer*, please follow me.' Frank followed without a sound.

During the short journey, he was sitting at the side of the *inspecteur* and there was no conversation. Frank felt a slight pressure on his arm. He followed the *inspecteur's* gaze. Coming the other way was a large military lorry. As it swept past, he could see the rows of German soldiers sitting erect inside the rear of the vehicle. It was followed by a black Mercedes-Benz saloon. There were two dark suited men silhouetted on the back seat.

The car arrived at the rear of the police station in *Nieuwe Stad*. He was ushered through the massive wooden door, along a dark passage to a short corridor. There were two benches. Frank was surprised to see a dejected Dirk sitting on one. At his side was a policeman. His friend lifted his head, winked and then turned away. Frank was pushed down onto the other seat, but not before he was given a quick body search. The policeman sat so close that Frank could smell the lunch on his breath.

He waited for over an hour. A door opened and Dirk was summoned into a room at the end of the corridor.

A minute later, another door opened. A voice shouted, 'Van der Meer!' He stood and walked into the room.

There was one light and no windows. There was a single chair and a small table in the corner. There was another door deep in the shadows. He waited with the policeman at his side. He thought he could hear raised voices but the walls were thick. The smell in the room was of carbolic cleaning fluid and after a while it made him sneeze. He must have stood for another hour. The policeman said nothing.

The door opened quietly. A man entered. He was dressed in a black suit with a white shirt and a dark tie. A single gold swastika badge in his lapel was the only bright spot on his otherwise sombre suit. He walked clockwise, slowly, around Frank and finally came to a stop one metre in front of him. His eyes were brown and they bored into the man stood opposite him. The voice was soft and the Dutch was heavily accented.

'Sit!'

'I prefer to stand, thank you.' Frank knew he had to gain the upper hand. The *SD* man shrugged his shoulders and turned away.

'Why did you have the traitor van Hamel in your house? Why did you not tell us who he was?' The voice remained soft.

'I did tell you,' said Frank equally quietly, in German.

The man turned round and the voice became louder. 'Explain!'

'I was asked by a business friend to take van Hamel in as a paying guest. On the day that he arrived, I followed your regulations. I came to this station and registered him in the visitors' book. I also registered the fact that he was not a relative or a family member.' He reached into his pocket and the policeman stepped forward. The *SD* men motioned him to stand still.

Frank continued, 'Here is a copy of the documents appertaining to van Hamel. They're signed by one of your men. I also have receipts for his rent. You can see that he paid cash every week.' Frank shook his head. 'I really can't believe that he was an agent for another country. He was a very pleasant young man, even my daughter liked him. Now, *mein Herr*, as I've committed no crime, may I go now, please?'

The other door opened and through the darkness emerged another figure. Frank did not recognise the shape but he knew the voice.

'Good evening, *meneer* van der Meer,' said *Hauptsturmführer* Müller.

Marieke heard the sound of the engine as the lorry drew into the yard. She waited near the front door. The knock was heavy. She waited another minute and then opened the door.

The *SD* man stood in front of a row of *Wehrmacht* soldiers, all standing to attention and all armed with light machine-pistols.

'*Mevrouw* van der Meer. I have orders to search this house. Step to one side, *bitte*.'

Without a sound she moved.

The soldiers crashed through the door and she shuddered as the heavy jackboots marched across her floors. One *SD* man stayed with her, the other followed his men. They made their way directly upstairs. Aukje appeared at the door of her room and one of the young soldiers smiled at her and pushed past. She watched as he strode towards a chest of drawers at the side of her bed. He slung his weapon over his shoulder and began to pull open the drawers. Aukje was white faced as he lifted up her underclothes. He gave another smile. There was a sparkle in his eyes.

She walked up, to him grabbed his shoulder and shouted, 'How dare you! Get out of my bedroom.' What surprised her was that he laughed, turned round and left the room.

They found nothing. Marieke watched every move they made. Not a word was spoken. They paid particular attention to the attic rooms. After thirty minutes they left. She followed them outside. Marieke was surprised. All the men from the factory were lined up and watching the soldiers like cats watching mice. They looked ominous and for a moment, she was concerned for their safety. The Germans totally ignored them, clambered back into the lorry and left in a cloud of blue diesel fumes.

'*Meneer* van der Meer, we do keep meeting, don't we?' The voice was silky smooth. He stood to one side of the *SD* man. There was long thin cigar dangling from his fingers. The black uniform was, as usual, immaculate. Frank was glad that the cigar smoke cancelled out the stink of carbolic.

'We let you work for us and we pay you well. ... It would appear that you have nothing to do with this man van Hamel. Your business colleague, Haan, says the same as you. ... It seems everybody is innocent and ... yet, I suspect that everybody is guilty.' He slowly placed the cigar to his lips and drew in a lungful of smoke. It was exhaled across the room in Frank's direction. '*Meneer* van der Meer, I cannot prove a thing and until I can, you are free to go.' He motioned with his cigar to the man. 'Show him out.'

As Frank turned to leave, the voice called after him. He froze.

'Van der Meer! Other people, more expert than me in these matters, are questioning van Hamel in Scheveningen at this very time. Maybe we will be meeting each other again in the near future.' He watched him leave the room. Frank walked home. The air refreshed him.

Marieke was waiting in the doorway of the house. She threw her arms round him. 'Frank, I heard you were all right. How was it?'

He thought she smelled better than the police station and held onto her. Finally letting go, he stood back. 'I'm getting used to being questioned by the Germans.' He thought for a moment. '*Liefje*. How did you know I was all right?'

'*Inspecteur* Koopman, telephoned me twenty minutes ago.'

'I think that man is going to very useful in the future,' said Frank softly.

'Why, darling, you're beginning to sound like Piet Bokma,' she replied with a smile on her lips. 'And he's been on the telephone every hour for the last four hours.' She paused and stopped smiling. 'Before you ask, I didn't enjoy having visitors.'

He banged his head with his hand. 'Sorry, Marieke, I forgot to ask.'

The stress showed and she answered in a jerky staccato way. 'They were awful. No manners. I feel as if the house has been desecrated. They didn't find anything. Aukje was wonderful. Harmen stayed in the factory. They didn't go near there.' She led him through into the living-room and they both sat down.

He sat in the leather chair opposite her and looked closely into her eyes. 'Marieke, Piet keeps asking me to join this movement to oppose the Germans. But, in my heart, I just don't know what to do. What do you think?'

Her heart went out to him. 'I know it's been worrying you, Frank. If you take part, then it involves the whole family. Deep down I feel that we must help in any way that we can.'

He nodded and looked into the blue eyes. 'Yes, as usual, you're right. But, I'm a committed pacifist and resistance means violence and that I can't agree to.'

Marieke looked at her husband's face and felt that she must help him. 'Frank, talk to the *dominee* in church on Sunday.'

The day of rest arrived. They made their usual way to Leeuwarden chatting with the de Bruins. Although it was the middle of winter, it was a fresh sunny morning and people were out walking to church.

They waited in line to move slowly through the big doorway. *Dominee* de Vries met them. 'Good morning, van der Meer family. Welcome. How are you all this morning?'

Frank nodded a reply and asked, '*Dominee*, after the council meeting, Marieke and I would like to meet you privately. We would like your advice on a rather special matter.'

Dominee de Vries was a small, well-built man. He was grey and his eyes reflected an inner strength. He was well liked by his congregation but he was very stubborn when it came to matters of principle. His Friesian was perfect and he lowered his voice, 'I think I have an idea what you wish to talk to me about.' He glanced over Frank's shoulder at the waiting queue of people. Behind them stood Piet and Sytske Bokma. As they walked down to their usual pew, Aukje nudged her father in the ribs. He was just about to speak to her sharply when he noticed whom she was looking at.

Oberleutnant Ernst Kraft was dressed in a dark suit and sat at the end of a pew, totally alone. He caught Frank's surprised glance and stood. The van der Meer family had to pass him.

'*Oberleutnant*, I'm surprised to see you in this church.' He left the comment hanging in the air. Kraft grabbed it.

'Good morning, *meneer* and *mevrouw* van der Meer and Aukje and Harmen.'

Frank could feel all eyes in the church boring into him. The congregation had quietened. Kraft continued, 'I thought I may surprise you. I do have a right to be here.' He saw Frank's eyebrows rise. 'You see, I'm a Mennonite. I used to attend a small church in Berlin.' He smiled, 'Remember, Luther was German.'

Frank nodded briefly and the family walked past the German officer and sat in their pew.

The simple Mennonite church was packed. The service was excellent and the *dominee's* sermon went down well. Marieke always sang with great gusto much to Aukje's amusement. At the end of the service they joined the queue to shake hands with *dominee* de Vries and their friends. They walked out of the big double doors and turned right to the meeting rooms. Aukje and Harmen went home.

The council room was only half-full. The coffee was ready and its pungent aroma pervaded the room. As a council member Frank took notes and contributed to the discussions about the organising of the Christmas activities. He was really only just listening and the picture of Kraft in the church kept flashing through his mind.

'Now, Frank, I believe you wanted to talk to me.' *Dominee* de Vries's voice in his ear interrupted his thoughts. He glanced around and the room was empty. There was just the three of them.

He took a deep breath, 'Yes, Paul. I'm very worried about some of things that are going on in Leeuwarden.' He looked hard at the *dominee*. 'Many people support the occupation of Holland and I must add from the start that I'm not one of those people. I can see enormous wrong-doing by the Germans and I feel that I must do something to help against those wrong-doings. But, as you know, I'm a committed Christian and a pacifist.'

The *dominee* held up his hand and smiled. 'Frank, like me you have very strong principles. I too am a committed pacifist. I see and hear more than you do. The churches of all denominations are very strong. For example, I know that your very good friends the de Bruins are increasingly worried about their future. Before you say anything, Rabbi Jacobs and I have many private meetings. We both know how you feel about the Jewish citizens of Leeuwarden.' He raised his hand again. 'I also know that Piet Bokma has told you that I'm a member of his group. At this stage I'm useful for information. For example, I shall tell him about the *Luftwaffe* officer who was present in the church this morning. But information is as far as I'm prepared to go at this stage of the occupation.' He sat back and folded his arms.

Frank looked at Marieke and spoke quietly. His eyes were fixed on the *dominee*. 'Paul, I respect how you feel. I've seen the Germans operating at first hand in Rotterdam and here in Leeuwarden. They control everything and everybody. Many of our people welcome them. Do you know that unemployment in Friesland has dropped by over fifty per cent?' He paused and leaned forward. 'But! ... but! ... at what cost? If we actively resist the Germans, they will extract revenge upon us. I know what has happened to some of my business colleagues. Don't think that members of the clergy will escape from them. At *IJmuiden* I saw what they tried to do to children.'

Their friend smiled at them and laid his hands on the table. His eyes were sharp and bright. They belied his true feelings. 'Frank, Marieke, you can only do what you believe in. The Mennonite church preaches non-violence and peace. It's been our watchword for three hundred years. But, the cost as you say, Frank, may be too much to bear. This country is one of many that will be occupied. Hitler will not stop at Europe. He aims to conquer the world. We may have to .... shall we say, adjust our beliefs to deal with so great an evil.' He saw Frank's eyebrows rise. 'I'm helping to oppose the Germans by providing information. If ... If, I say, the Germans raise the stakes, then I will have to pray for guidance. But, my friends, I will not see our church and our country delivered into the hands of these invaders without opposition.' He rose and walked to the tall stained-glass windows at the end of the room. He turned and looked back at them. There was total silence.

Frank clasped his hands and stared at the patterned table top. His mind was in a turmoil. He had expected the *dominee* to be against any resistance. Marieke glanced at him and put her hands over his. The silence continued. *Dominee* de Vries walked slowly towards Frank. He placed his hand upon his shoulder.

Frank took a deep breath, 'I understand you, Paul. But I cannot possibly join in this movement ... yet. I will help my friends, but I will not spy and I will not raise my hands against the Germans.' He let go of Marieke's hands and stood. He was sad. 'I feel that I have a family to care for.'

The *dominee* very quietly said, 'So do I, Frank. My family and the family of the Church.'

They smiled together, shook hands and left the church.

ELEVEN

The van der Meer family celebrated Christmas with an air of unreal normality. Frank collected the tree on Christmas Eve as he had always done. They were quieter than usual, as they tried to ignore their occupiers. *Oberleutnant* Kraft had arrived with small gifts for everyone and the family, with Christian humility, had accepted them.

Marieke came to Frank in his office. 'I've just heard some awful news on the radio.'

He put down his pen. 'What is it, *liefje?*'

'Jews are not allowed to go to the cinema and they must all register with the civil authorities in Leeuwarden. Oh, Frank! Something is starting. I feel so worried about the de Bruins. Let's go straight away and see them!'

Frank sat back in his chair. 'Marieke, don't panic. Things have got much quieter over the last three months. The Nazis seem to have settled down.' He picked up his pen. 'I just can't spare the time at the moment. The factory is very busy. Perhaps you could go and see them?' For a moment he thought that she would argue but instead she turned and quietly left the office. He put his head down and continued with the paper work.

Marieke was not put off. She put on her coat and left the house. Tineke saw her coming and the door was open. She was smiling, which surprised Marieke. 'Hello, do come in.' There was another woman sitting in the living-room.

'Marieke, may I introduce Lottie Cohen. She's a very good friend of mine.'

She was younger than Marieke. Slightly built with long black hair framing her very attractive face. There wore a quizzical expression that, Marieke realised, was permanent. She spoke Dutch with a strong Friesian accent.

'*Mevrouw* van der Meer, I've heard such a lot about you from Tineke. We've met before, but it was some years ago.' She saw Marieke about to speak, she smiled and continued. 'My husband used to be in timber, the same as yours. I think they occasionally met before my husband died.' She sat back in her chair, folded her arms and looked at Marieke.

'*Mevrouw* Cohen ...' She was interrupted.

'Please, call me Lottie.'

Marieke was unused to quick familiarity but she continued, 'Lottie, Tineke. I heard on the radio about the restrictions that are being placed on the Jews in Holland.' She stopped talking and watched Lottie Cohen.

'Really, Marieke, I'm not surprised,' said Tineke. 'It's not a real problem. Most of us never go to the cinema, anyway.'

'What about registering?' replied Marieke. She sensed a change in her friend's attitude.

Lottie answered, 'I think that it's common knowledge who the Jews are in Holland and Leeuwarden. Registration is just a formality. I've heard that a Jewish Council will be formed in each province and that means that we'll have to look after ourselves.' She gesticulated with her small hands. 'After all, we Jews have been looking after ourselves for years.' She laughed in a peculiarly nervous way. There was a silence.

Marieke thought for a moment, unsure what to say. 'Lottie, I'm sure you've heard the rumours about other Jews in Europe?'

For a moment a frown of worry passed over Tinneke's face. She spoke quietly with a slight tremor to her voice. 'Lottie, I've heard those rumours as well. What do you really think about them?'

Lottie uncrossed and re-crossed her slim legs. The smile returned to her face and there was that same quizzical expression. 'Believe me, there's nothing to worry about in Leeuwarden. We're only a small community but we have a long history of involvement in Friesian life. From what I've heard, there's never been any anti-Semitism around here.'

Marieke was still unsure of herself. 'But, I'm sure you've heard about Adolf Hitler's beliefs. He doesn't like Jews.'

Lottie looked her straight in the eye. There was an air of impatience in her voice. 'It will just not happen here. I have to say that the Jews of Holland control most big business. They control the whole of the diamond industry in Amsterdam ... and,' she added carefully, 'a great deal of the business in Leeuwarden.' She paused and laughed. 'Really *mevrouw* van der Meer, there's nothing to worry about.' She leaned forward towards the table. 'Do have some chocolate cake. It's fresh from the bakers.'

Marieke watched Tinneke's face light up as Lottie spoke. She realised that her friend believed everything that Lottie said. She did not want to interfere. She knew what she believed in.

'The cake is delicious. Thank you,' Marieke said with a polite smile.

The social conversation continued for another half hour. Eventually Marieke excused herself and returned to her home. But Lottie's pale face kept returning to her thoughts.

It appeared to Frank that more and more people wore uniforms. It re-enforced his belief that the occupiers were uniform crazy. He was therefore pleased when he met *Inspecteur* Koopman for lunch that he was dressed in a dark suit. it was the *inspecteur's* suggestion that they met. He said they must discuss something that was mutually beneficial. They met in the *Hotel de Kroon*. Dirk had arranged for them to meet privately behind one of the screened dining areas.

'Good morning, *meneer* van der Meer. It's a pleasure to meet you under better circumstances than the last time we met.' There was a broad smile on his face.

'I agree,' replied Frank with a similar smile.

Joop Koopman was about the same age as Frank. But he was smaller and more compact. For his own security he had delayed this meeting for some time. He looked at the man sitting opposite him. He was composed, well dressed, with an air of inherent calmness. Good looking, but not handsome. He had heard much about him, some good, some bad. Apart from the trouble with the Germans, his police file was completely clear. He was successful in business and a dedicated family man.

They shook hands across the table as they looked at each other.

'*Inspecteur*, you asked to meet me. Well, here I am.' Frank's smile had gone.

'Yes I did. I'll come straight to the point, *meneer*. I know what people say about you. Some don't trust you. Your closest friends do and, I must add, so do I. Dirk Haan and *dominee* Paul de Vries speaks highly of you.' He watched Frank's reaction. There was none.

'*Inspecteur*, I hope you aren't another one of these people who want me to oppose the Germans? If you're a friend of Dirk's, then you know what my answer will be.' He was being polite.

'Not at all.' He scratched his chin and spoke quietly. 'I must tell you something. The very fact that I'm telling you puts me in the greatest danger. If the *moffen* found out then I would be quickly inside one of their prisons.' Still Frank sat motionless. 'Müller has ordered an inquiry into your activities. At this very moment the *SD* are collecting information on you.' He put his hands two centimetres apart. 'At this time ... your file is that big.' Frank leaned forward. 'For the sake of your family, *meneer* van der Meer, I must ask you to be very careful.'

Frank nodded. 'Why are you telling me this?'

'People always mistrust the police. It's part of the job.' He sat back and smiled. 'Since the start of the occupation, many policemen have joined with the Nazis. I have not. I know which of my men I can trust, probably about eighty per cent of my total force. My chief is not with them, thank God. But, my *sergeant* is. Müller knows who he can trust and he uses me as much as he can. In two weeks time the Germans will introduce their own police force all over Holland. They'll be dressed in green uniforms and will be answerable only to the *SD*. I'll have no control over them at all. The *NSB* have formed a new group with money from the Nazis. It's a military organisation and the biggest collection of bullies that I've ever seen. They dress in black shirts like the other fascists. So now you can see that the Germans have total control over all civilian and military activities. Forget the courts, their *Landesgericht* can do anything. I'm telling you all this because it's vital that you tell our Jewish friends. The Germans will be particularly looking out for Jews who break the new regulations.'

'You mean not going to cinemas and registering?' asked Frank, who by now was leaning over the table. 'Surely not major crimes, *inspecteur*?'

Dirk appeared around the screen, smiled and left hot coffee.

Both men sipped at their cups. Joop Koopman continued, 'Within the next two weeks, and about the same time as the green police are introduced, new stringent laws will be introduced that will seriously affect the Jewish community. I'm not party to the details, but Müller has been to

Berlin twice in the last three weeks. I must ask you again. Tell your Jewish friends what's going to happen. Meet them, talk to Rabbi Jacobs if you have to. Warn them, because things are going to happen that I can't control or resist.' He sat back in his chair and drained the cup. He glanced at his wrist-watch. 'I must leave you now.' Hesitating for a moment he added. 'By the way, *meneer*. If I was you I would hide that damned English car of yours and get another one. It's recognisable ten kilometres away.' He stood and extended his hand to Frank. He clasped it.

'Thank you, *inspecteur*. I will try and do what you ask.' It was the second time that he had been advised to part with his car. The men went their separate ways.

TWELVE

The winter was harsh. Frank felt its penetrating chill as he cycled back from a meeting with Piet Bokma. A sudden blast of cold wind from the north rushed up the Dokkumer Ee River and caught him full in the face. He stopped for a minute and looked around him. The fields were empty and the grass was a dull green. Trees bent in the gusts of wind and there were no birds. Over the horizon loomed ever-darkening clouds, rolling towards Frank at a speed that showed that rain was on the way. Shrugging his shoulders, he climbed back onto the bike and pedalled home even harder.

The woodworking machinery was still operating at full tilt and he glanced through the half-open doorway of the factory. A few waves and nods and he turned back to the house. Before he opened the door, Marieke was waiting.

'Frank, I tried to telephone you at Piet's house, but you'd already left.'

He could see by the look on her face that something was wrong. He took off his coat and placed his hand on hers. 'Come on, Marieke, what the matter?'

She shook her head, 'I don't know, Frank. Tineke just telephoned and asked if just the two of us could go round and see them straight away.'

He glanced at his wrist-watch. Something must be wrong. He knew that Jan never came home from the bank before six-thirty.

She read his thoughts. 'Tineke's made sandwiches for us. We'll leave now.'

There were a few heavy drops of rain as they cycled to the de Bruins' farmhouse. They were ready for it with heavy clothes and hats pulled low. Neither of them spoke as they put their bikes in the barn at the back of the house. The door was open and Tineke stood ready for them. The clouds were just bursting as they stepped over the threshold.

'You made it just in time. Take off your coats and come through to the living-room.' Her usual welcoming smile was missing and she looked worried.

Jan rose to meet them, shaking hands with Frank he kissed Marieke on the cheek. 'Please sit down.' He waved towards a pile of sandwiches on the low table. 'Help yourselves.'

Outside, the rain began to hammer against the windows. The room darkened and Tineke switched on the soft lights of the brass chandelier. The storm appeared to be hovering over the old house. Marieke involuntarily shivered and glanced at Jan. He was sunk in his leather chair and his face was pale. Frank waited for Jan to choose his moment, but Tineke prompted him.

'Tell them, Jan. For God's sake let's share it with somebody.'

He took a deep breath, 'It's started. Today I was told by an officer of the *NSB* that our children can no longer be educated at the public schools in Leeuwarden.' He raised his hand as Frank tried to interrupt. 'With effect from the start of the school year, all Jewish children must be educated within the Jewish community... And there's worse to come. All Jewish employees working for the council and provincial authorities will be dismissed and replaced by gentiles.' He stopped for a moment and sipped at his drink. His eyes were closed and there was a frown on his forehead. 'All people of Jewish nationality must register their gold and wealth with the State. Within a certain period, all the declared wealth will be confiscated by the Reichs Commissioner.' The coffee cup and saucer rattled back onto the table. He looked up and there were tears in his eyes. 'What the hell am I going to do? If I don't conform, then both my family and I will be resettled in a German camp.'

Marieke said, 'Tineke, I knew that this was going to happen. Kraft told me some time ago. But I never believed him. All that he said is beginning to take place.' She touched Tineke's arm. 'When I met your friend Lottie, I couldn't believe how naïve she was.'

'I know, Marieke. But she's a brave person. She always looks on the good side of things.' She shrugged her shoulders. 'I have to try and believe her. But, it's difficult when she's such a nice person.' Marieke smiled reassuringly at her friend.

Frank knew he had to pass on the warnings to his friends. It took him five minutes to explain Koopman's message. 'And so it's vital that you discuss this with the Rabbi and make sure that the Jewish community know the facts.'

There was silence in the room, broken only by the noise of the rain on the windows. Frank steepled his fingers as his mind raced. He put his hand into the inside pocket of his suit. He withdrew a single sheet of paper.

'Jan, my friend. It's happening to all of us. I received this yesterday and it's remained in my pocket ever since. I'll read it.

DECLARATION

The undersigned

....

Born in...

Date of Birth ....

and living in Leeuwarden

Works (a) full time (b) temporarily (c) with a contract of employment for the Municipality of Leeuwarden as

....

declare that he/she is/is not of Jewish Blood * as defined in this circular of the Secretary General, Acting Head of Department of the Ministry of the Interior. Circular Number 47176, Department of Civil Affairs.

At the same time he/she declares that his/her spouse born in ....

on...

is/is not of Jewish blood.

LEEUWARDEN .... 194 .....

(*A definition of non-Jewish blood for this circular is when he/she has four grandparents not of the Jewish faith.)

Because my factory has contracts for the Municipality and the Provincial Reichs Commissioner, I have to sign the form. I don't know whether any of my employees is Jewish or not and, personally, I don't care. I'll sign tomorrow, return it and see what happens.' He carefully folded the sheet of paper and returned it to his pocket.

Frank continued looking at his friends. 'Jan, Tineke, ... you have big problems. But, let's be positive. I think that the Rabbi could quickly organise a Jewish school. There're plenty of spare buildings in Leeuwarden that are ideal for that purpose. Your banking connections would give you access to properties.' He became thoughtful. 'I presume you've heard of the refugee camp at Westerbork?'

'I know of it, Frank,' nodded Jan. 'I make donations towards its running costs. But that's as far as my knowledge goes.'

'Yes, I've heard about it. But not a great deal,' added Tineke.

'I supplied some of the timber for its construction. It was built to house Jewish refugees from Germany,' continued Frank. 'At the start of the occupation there were over a thousand people there from Nazi Germany and it was funded partly by the Dutch Government and by contributions from the Jewish Council in Leeuwarden. Since the Germans came I'm not sure what it's used for now. Apparently they've put up high fences and nobody is allowed to enter.' He paused for a moment and looked at Jan. A slight smile came over his face. 'As far as your wealth is concerned, hide it!'

Jan sat up and began to take notice. 'All right, I agree about the school but where can I hide my money and these things?' He waved his arm around the room.

Frank smiled. He was relishing the problem. 'Jan, it's easy. I'll leave you a load of timber and some shovels. If anybody asks, you can say you're doing some repairs on the house before the winter. Go into your barn, Harmen and I will come and help you. Carefully lift the brick floor. We'll dig a hole, line it with timber, make a false floor covered with the old bricks and then put all your things in the hole. Nobody will see us because the barn only has one door and we'll close it.' Frank laughed, 'It shouldn't take too long!'

Jan tried to protest. Frank let him chatter on. 'I really can't ask that of you Frank, it's too much for you, really it is. If they find out, then you could have real trouble. Anyway, they'll know I've put our belongings somewhere.'

Frank nodded, 'Yes, Jan, you must give them something. I'll find some old furniture from somewhere. We can use it to replace yours. Whatever you do, don't start withdrawing money from your account. The NSB'll be watching the banks.' He scratched his head, 'I'll buy some things from you for a fair price. You can hide the rest in the hole in the barn. You'll certainly lose out, but not everything.'

Tineke leant over and flung her arms around his neck. 'Oh, Frank, I love you. You've made it all sound so much better.' She let go and frowned, 'What if they catch you helping us?'

Frank stood up and looked down on his friends. 'For some time now I have been wanting to harm the Germans in a non-violent way. To me this is a perfect way of doing just that.' He rubbed his hands, 'Let me think. I have some lovely English oak in store. I was saving it for some new frames for the house. But, never mind!' His smile took over. 'I tell you what Jan, let's go into the barn now and measure it out. Tomorrow I'll cut the timber myself and bring it round tomorrow night.' With an expectant look on his face, he moved towards the door. Jan followed him. Marieke and Tineke shook their heads and there was a smile on their lips.

The rain had eased slightly and a wan sun was setting. There was a tinge of redness that reflected in through the windows of the short passage that led from the barn to the house.

The floor size of the barn was huge although it was partitioned off for farm animals. Above them were the massive wooden floors that could hold enough fodder for the winter. Jan hardly used the barn apart for his car and odds and ends from the house. Frank marched around, moving junk from one side to another. Jan could see his eyes looking at everything around him. Suddenly Frank stopped.

'Jan, this is just the right place.' He pointed at a long deep channel still partly blocked with old cow dung.

Jan wrinkled his nose. 'We can't dig there, Frank. That stuff stinks. The drains are blocked up and that muck has not been cleared out for years.'

Frank raised his hands, 'It's perfect, Jan. The Germans won't like to get their nice uniforms dirty. We can dig it out, bury your things and then cover it over after with the old cow muck. They might search the barn but they would never think of moving this mess.' He patted his pockets and found what he was looking for. He withdrew a short ruler that unfolded into a metre in length. Jan looked surprised. 'You always carry a pen, Jan. But a good timber man always carries a ruler. Let's measure it out now.' He dropped to his knees. 'I think about three meters square by the same deep.' He continued nodding writing details into a small note pad, 'That'll be just about right. The soil we can dump in the canal at the bottom of your garden. Nobody will ever see it.' His eyes shone and he looked at his friend, 'What do you think?'

'Frank, you always amaze me. I would never have thought of this.'

Both men whirled round as they heard the sound of applause. Marieke and Tineke had crept into the barn unnoticed. Their claps and smiles were well received. Tineke placed her hands on her hips, 'Don't think you men are doing all of the digging, we're helping as well.'

For the first time that night they laughed together.

Frank rose early and decided to prepare the timber himself. He crept out of the house and made his way to the factory. He switched on the lights and walked through the silence of the still machines. The oak lay neatly stacked in a corner covered by a sheet of tarpaulin. He pulled it off and began to move the lengths of timber across the floor towards the band-saw. The ruler appeared out of his pocket and he swiftly marked off the correct lengths and laid them out ready for work. A quick walk back to the main switchboard and he located the control for the band-saw. He set it for "ON".

The sweet smell of freshly cut oak rose above the ripping sound of the saw. He inhaled it, relishing in its pureness. Oak was his favourite wood.

A slight sound made him whirl round, making him almost slip into the spinning blade. Before him stood a young man. At first he failed to recognise him and then he realised who he was. Arnold Kuipers had only worked in the factory for a year. Frank was unsure about him, but he had helped out a friend who asked him to take this young man on. He had been down on his luck and Frank was always helping such people. The saw stopped.

'Good morning, *meneer* van der Meer. Can I help you?'

'All right, Arnold, you can help. Pull those pieces across here and slide them into the saw.' Frank was curious. Within an hour the job was finished and Kuipers helped him to move the timber to the door.

His voice was oily, 'But, *meneer*, why do you need the wood at this time of the morning?' It was a question that not one of his other employees would have dared to ask. Frank knew he had to answer.

He smiled, although inwardly his brain was whirling. 'It's for a little job that I'm doing on the house. It's a lovely morning and I felt like doing it myself.'

The man nodded with a smile, '*Meneer* van der Meer, may I ask a favour?'

Frank thought he knew what this man was up to. 'Yes, you may.'

'I came in early to ask if I could have the day off. My mother is not well and she wants me to visit her sister in Groningen. If I leave now, I can catch the 7-30 train.'

Frank was still unsure what the man's motives really were. 'Of course, that'll be all right. Give your aunt my best wishes.' He nodded. 'I'll see you in the morning.'

Harmen came down to the factory woken by the sound of the saw. He saw Kuipers leave.

'Morning. What was Kuipers doing here?' Frank explained. 'I don't like that man, *Heit*. He works well but he worries me.'

'I know what you mean son, but he helped me without any problem whatsoever.' He paused, 'Help me to load this timber on the trailer and I'll tell you what we're going to use it for.'

As they filled the trailer, Harmen listened carefully. They pushed the trailer towards the back of the yard and covered it with the tarpaulin.

'I'll help in any way that I can, *Heit*. You know you can trust me. It makes me feel good to be doing something against the *moffen*.' His bright face beamed with pleasure.

By the time Frank had entered the house, the men from the factory were just beginning to arrive. The day passed normally and he waited for dusk to fall before they set out for the de Bruins' house.

The trailer was hitched onto the back of the Austin and he knew it would take two journeys to move the full load. The drive took five minutes. As he swung into the dirt track at the back of the barn, Frank switched off the car lights and glanced around. Jan had the heavy doors open and the Austin drew into the barn.

'Close the doors, Jan, before we put the lights on. We don't want anyone to see us.'

Jan said, 'I still can't believe this, Frank. But here we are. Shall we have a drink first?'

Frank shook his head, 'I think not. Let's get something done and then we'll stop for a break.'

They were all in old clothes and he helped Frank to pull the tarpaulin off the trailer. Spades, pickaxes and other assorted tools were laid neatly on top of the pile of timber. Frank produced the ruler and a piece of chalk from his pocket. He sized up the floor, used a length of the timber as a straight edge and drew a square over the edge of the trough leading from the cow milking stalls. He struck the first blow with a heavy crowbar. With some difficulty he drew the first brick out of place. The others followed in quick succession.

As the others joined in he gave directions, 'Watch the bricks, put them down in a row over there in exactly the same pattern as you took them out. If you can, take the mortar out with them. We'll have to match the whole thing up later.'

They worked in thirty minute shifts with breaks, until two in the morning. They managed to dig a metre deep. But it was hard going. The earth had been compacted down over two hundred years of use. Marieke and Tineke watched them.

'Come on, you two,' said Frank with a smile, 'take the timber out of the trailer and stack it behind that old cow stall. We'll then fill up the trailer with the earth and dump it in the canal on the way home.'

Drinks and food came and went. David and Aukje disappeared for half an hour, but nobody noticed. When they returned they were both slightly flushed and had to take the sarcasm that was directed at them. The final shovelful was thrown into the trailer and Frank stood back.

'We've done a good job tonight. Two more nights should do it. We'll take a rest tomorrow and come back the night after.' He glanced at Jan. 'You both need to decide which items you put in there first.'

Jan agreed, 'You're right. I'll put the smallest and most valuable objects in first. They won't be missed if somebody visits the house. The larger items of furniture I'll put in last.' He saw Frank looking at him.

'As I said, we'll look after some of your better pieces.' He turned to his wife. 'No problem at all, is it, Marieke?'

She joined in, 'Whatever you want to lend to us will be safe.'

Aukje looked curious, 'I can't understand this, *Mem*.'

'What's the matter, my *famke*,' said Frank.

'Why are we storing everything and how long will it be for?' Her voice was quiet and everybody stopped and listened. 'Who's going to stop the Nazis and how will they do it? I have so many worries and so many questions. What's going to happen to us?' She suddenly burst into tears and Marieke placed her arm round her daughter's shoulder.

'Aukje, we're all tired. These questions are difficult to answer at this time of the morning.'

'Look, everybody,' said Jan, 'The Germans can't treat the people of Europe in this way. We know that they plan on dealing with the Jews and they've already conquered other countries. Britain and her friends will not let this continue. That, Aukje, is what we have to hope for. Sooner or later, the Germans will come up against something or somebody. Until then we have to make plans for the future and pray to God that help will come soon.'

Frank looked at his friends. It was two in the morning. 'Jan, what you've said is absolutely true. Let's silently pray for the future.' They stood in a circle and bowed their heads. For a full minute they were motionless until, eventually, Frank said, 'Amen.' He walked towards the trailer. 'Come on, van der Meers. Let's tow this lot away and shovel it into the canal.'

Tineke switched off the barn lights and Jan opened the heavy doors. Frank reversed the car out with its loaded trailer. With a quick wave they were off down the track driving on sidelights. Aukje pointed out a good place where a side track dipped towards a canal.

'Down there, *Heit*. David and I often sit near the canal when we go for a walk.'

'Oh yes,' leered Harmen from the front seat.

'Be quiet you two,' said Marieke with a smile faintly illuminated by the dashboard lights.

Frank reversed the trailer carefully back until its rear opening was just over the canal. 'Come on, Harmen, two shovels should do the job in no time.'

Fifteen minutes later they stowed the tools away under the tarpaulin and started to leave.

'One moment, just a little thing to finish the job.' He drove the car down the track for fifty metres and stopped. He climbed out of the car, reached into the trailer and produced a brush. Walking back to the canal-side he brushed away the last traces of earth. Reaching over the side of the canal, he pushed small pieces of mortar into the black waters. A quick check in the darkness, a nod to himself and he returned to the car. The journey back to the house was completed in exhausted silence.

Frank was up at his usual time. He let Marieke sleep as he left the bedroom for a bath. As he walked towards the factory and then to his office, he saw Kuipers waiting for him.

The young man's eyes fixed on his. 'Good morning, *meneer* van der Meer. Thank you for letting me have the day off. My mother sends her thanks.' Before Frank could speak, Kuiper's eyes switched to the trailer. 'I see you've moved the oak, *meneer*. It's good timber. I hope that it's not wasted?' The question hung in the air.

Frank was not in the mood to discuss matters. He glanced at his watch, 'Good morning, Arnold. The foreman will be upset, you're two minutes late.' He turned on his heel and walked away to his office.

THIRTEEN

Frank sat in the *Hotel de Kroon*, reading the paper after a good lunch. Dirk appeared at his elbow and flopped into the leather chair. He grabbed Frank's arm. Trembling with excitement, he said. 'It's happened!'

'Dirk, what are you talking about?' Putting his paper down and glaring at his friend.

Dirk's voice quivered with anger, 'Last night *NSB* black shirts attacked Jews in the streets of Amsterdam. I heard from a friend. ... He's just telephoned me. They dragged people from buses and in the Jewish district they went into restaurants and pulled people onto the streets and attacked them. Dozens have been injured.' He squeezed Frank's arm and looked at his face. 'You know what happened next, my friend?' Frank shook his head. 'Action groups of gentiles and Jews retaliated against the Nazis. They fought them openly in the streets. ... Can you imagine that?' Dirk sat back and clenched his fists. 'Jewish action groups went out and tackled Dutch Nazis. ... Unbelievable! Some black shirts were injured and one was killed.'

Frank looked up sharply. His voice was full of worry. 'If one of them was killed then you can expect real trouble. Don't think that Rauter will let the Jews get away with it.' He mentioned Seyss-Inquart's chief of security. 'Keep well away, Dirk. It'll spread now. That I'm sure of.'

Frank was right. The paper the following day was full of big black headlines.

TERRORISTS MURDER NSB MAN.

One paragraph caught his notice.

"Jewish and Dutch terrorists attacked Members of the NSB last night in the streets of Amsterdam. The attacks were unprovoked and unnecessary. The dead NSB man fought against overwhelming odds but finally he was murdered by a single bite through the jugular vein. — — — — — — — — — — — — — "

Frank shook his head, he knew it was beginning.

Events happened quickly. The following week Dirk called Frank and Piet to lunch at the hotel. They sat down and waited for the information. Dirk always had the right contacts.

His voice was quiet and matter of fact, 'You were right, Frank. It's the start. The German "Green Police" raided an ice-cream cafe in *van Woustraat* in Amsterdam. That's in the Jewish quarter. I know exactly where it is, a colleague has a hotel nearby. There was a huge battle. The Jewish action groups sprayed acid over the Germans. The Green Police arrested the owners and one was executed.'

Frank put his hands on his head and stared into the distance. 'It won't stop now, Dirk.'

His friend answered, 'I know Frank. The worst is to come. Masses of the Green Police invaded the area and arrested 425 young men all under 35 years old. I was told it was awful to watch. The police brutally beat them up and set dogs on them in the middle of the street. Some had awful injuries and were dragged away and thrown into the back of lorries. There was nothing that anybody could do. The Nazis were armed with machine-guns. There were hundreds of them.' He dropped his head for a moment. 'Yesterday there were red posters stuck all over walls in Amsterdam. I don't know why they printed them in red. They told us that the arrested men would be transported to a concentration camp in Germany. The posters explained in great detail that the arrests were in retaliation against the attacks on the police. Nobody believes that.' Frank noticed that Dirk was very upset.

'What's a concentration camp?' asked Piet quietly.

'It's a place where they put people with no hope,' Frank answered. 'I've heard of these places before. Germany is full of them.' His blue eyes looked at both men. 'Koopman told me that the Nazis are going to deal with the Jews.' He thought for a moment and put his hands on the table. 'We know that van Hamel was executed at Scheveningen without trial. I've since heard that the Germans have opened other prisons at Vught and Amersfoort. It seems, gentlemen, that the Germans have a variety of places that they can send us to.' He looked up at his friends. 'You talk about opposing them and forming groups. What can you do about police with machine-guns? You can't hide anywhere and you've no organisation whatsoever.'

Dirk watched Frank carefully, 'You're right about most things and I respect you for that. But things are happening. Since the arrests of the young men the streets of Amsterdam have been busy and there have been meetings in the docks .'

Piet nodded and smiled. He said warily, 'When you mention the docks, Dirk, what you're really talking about are Communists. We all know that Amsterdam Harbour is a hot-bed of Communism. Who wants to join up with that crowd? Some say they're worse than the Nazis.'

Frank shook his head and interrupted with a gentle smile, 'Now, you're wrong Piet. The Communists hate the Nazis and many of them are Socialists.'

Dirk shrugged his shoulders and saw the gleam in Frank's eye, 'Frank, we know that you're a strong Socialist.'

'That's true. But, I'm not a Communist.' He sat back.

Dirk said, 'Anyway, the upshot of all this is that the Communists are urging a one day strike in protest against the ill-treatment of the Jews.'

Piet shook his head incredulously. 'Dirk, how do you know all this?

I'm pretty close to all the organised labour movements and I've not heard about a strike.'

An expression of sheer cunning crossed Dirk's face. He glanced around the restaurant and delved into his inside pocket. He produced a much crumpled sheet of folded paper. 'This, my friends,' He laid it on the table and smoothed it down with the flat of his hand, 'Is the secret Communist newspaper "THE TRUTH". Brought to me, fresh this morning, by the trusted *schippen* Schaaf.' He enjoyed the surprised looks and pulled another piece of paper out of the other pocket. 'This is a pamphlet that's freely available on the streets of Amsterdam. Schaaf tells me that thousands of copies are on their way to Friesland. It tells us about the strike and what's more it asks for wage increases and higher unemployment benefits.'

'Typical!' interjected Piet.

'I think,' continued Dirk, 'that we must support this strike here in Leeuwarden. When the leaflets arrive we can see what effect the call to strike has upon the good citizens.'

'It won't work,' Frank said quickly. 'It may work in the big cities but not here in the north. People are just not like that, most of them are happy to have a job.' He stopped and thought for a moment. 'The most important thing is that people know that something is happening to oppose the Nazis. This is the first real resistance to their occupation.'

Piet coughed gently and smiled, 'You know Frank, it's the first time I've heard you call them "Nazis" and it's the first time I've heard you mention the word "resistance" with any real feeling.' A ghost of a smile crossed Frank's face and he remained silent.

'Well, I'm going to Amsterdam myself on the next train. I want to see this with my own eyes,' said Dirk.

Frank was quick to warn him, 'Be careful, you know that the Germans are watching everybody.'

The usual smile returned and Dirk rubbed his hands. 'Business, my friends, business. The greatest reason for travelling ever invented.' He checked his watch. 'I'll have to leave now, or else, I'll be late.' He reached down, folded up the papers and returned them to his pocket.

Frank could not resist having a little jab at his friend, 'Dirk, I didn't know that you were so interested in what happens to Jews.'

Dirk froze and his normal smile disappeared. He stared hard at Frank and tapped a single finger on the table. His voice was surprisingly cold. 'They may be Jews. But they're our Jews and we'll decide how to treat them! ... Not the Nazis! Don't forget that, Frank van der Meer!'

Frank arrived home late and parked the Austin in the corner of the workshop. Within a few minutes he found what he was looking for. The green tarpaulin just covered the car. He weighted it down all around with lengths of timber and then stood back. His thoughts were interrupted.

'Frank, what are you doing?' shouted Marieke from the other side of the factory

He turned round and walked towards her. 'I've been told twice not to use this particular car so I'm storing it for future use.' He saw the question on her lips and smiled. 'Don't worry. I've bought a second-hand Renault. I'm collecting it tomorrow.'

'I'm not worried about the car. But, I am worried about our son. I think you'd better come upstairs.' She saw concern on his face and added, 'Don't worry, he's safe.'

Frank followed her into the house. He was surprised to see Jan sitting on the chair near the fire. Harmen and Aukje relaxed on the long couch. The fire roared up the chimney.

'Hello, Frank,' smiled Jan. He glanced at Marieke. She nodded. 'I think you'd better sit down. I've got an interesting problem for you.' He reached under the chair and produced a can of paint and a paintbrush. He placed them in the middle of the floor. 'Just as it was going dark this afternoon, I was leaving the bank on my bicycle to come home. As I passed the town hall I saw Harmen with another person, a girl I think, painting a large "V" sign on the wall. Fortunately, nobody else saw him but me. I shouted and he ran off. He left the evidence.' He pointed at the paint. 'Eventually, I caught up with him. The girl had disappeared and I came straight here.' He stopped talking and there was a silence.

Frank looked at Jan and then his head swivelled towards his son. The voice was neutral. 'I think, Harmen, that you'd better explain ... Now!'

Harmen had been gazing at the floor and now he looked up and proudly stared his father straight in the eye. He took a deep breath. '*Heit*, the V sign is the sign for victory against the Nazis. I've been painting it everywhere. ... It's quick and easy to do. ... I'm not the only one doing it. Most of my friends have areas of town where they operate. I work near the town hall.' He paused and his eyes flashed. 'Somebody in this family has to do something to resist them'

'That's enough!' snapped his mother.

Frank held up his hand and the room fell silent. He spoke quietly. Harmen was totally surprised. 'Son, I understand your feelings completely. Have you read the papers recently?' No response. 'I know about the "V for Victory" campaign and I know about part of Beethoven's Fifth Symphony used as Morse for the "V". But, Goebbels, Hitler's Minister of Information, has decreed that the "V" means victory for the Germans. I don't believe that propaganda.'

He stopped talking and thought for a moment. His face was inscrutable. The calm voice continued. 'Just carry on doing it, and,' his voice rose theatrically, 'DON'T GET CAUGHT!' He leaned over and picked up the can of paint. The silence continued. He read the label. 'I'm angry about one thing though. Don't use this paint. It's hard to get hold of. In the factory I have some old cans somewhere, use those and take some for your friends.' He put the can down and glanced from face to face. Jan was the first to smile. Harmen was the next. Marieke was unsure. Aukje remained silent. Frank turned, 'Jan, did you say there was somebody else with him?'

'Correct.'

He ground out the words as he stared into the fire. 'I have the strongest suspicion just who that may be.' He turned and looked at Aukje. Two pairs of blue eyes met, they were unwavering. Eventually her eyes dropped and she winced.

'*Heit*, somebody had to hold the paint can.' She put on her sweetest smile and it worked.

Frank rose and took a deep breath. 'Thank you, Jan. I think this subject is now closed. Would you like to stay for dinner?

FOURTEEN

'Frank, Dirk's on the telephone for you,' shouted Marieke.

He walked to the hall and picked up the receiver. 'Hello, Dirk, I presume you're back?'

'Yes, I arrived twenty minutes ago.' His voice sounded strangely distant. He added tersely. 'Frank, we've got to talk.'

'I understand. Look, later today Marieke and I are going to the de Bruins' house. Perhaps we could meet there? Please ask Rinske if she'll come with you,' replied Frank.

There was a pause, 'A good idea. We'll see you about four-thirty.' There was a click as he hung up.

Frank stared at the receiver and placed it back on the cradle.

'What is it, *liefje*?' asked Marieke, seeing his hesitation.

He turned, 'I think Dirk's had a bad time in Amsterdam. That's why I asked him to come with Rinske to the de Bruins.'

It was cold and raining and so Frank drove in the Renault. As they arrived at the de Bruins' farmhouse he noticed more bicycles than usual outside.

The living-room was softly lit by tall candles and the open-fire cast dancing shadows around the walls. There were just enough seats. Frank smiled to himself when he realised where most of the furniture was now safely stored. Jan rose to meet him and shook hands.

'Hello, Frank, Marieke. Dirk and Rinske are here already.' Frank saw him sitting near the fire, cigar in hand. Rinske beckoned Marieke to sit next to her. Jan stepped back and continued, 'I believe you haven't met Lottie Cohen before?' He waved towards a low comfortable chair. 'Lottie, may I introduce Frank van der Meer.'

She remained seated and looked up at him. Frank was used to attractive women but Lottie made his back stiffen, Marieke noticed.

Her voice was soft and he had to bend slightly to hear the words. 'Frank, what a pleasure. I've heard so many interesting things about you.'

She extended her hand palm down and Frank was forced to stoop and kiss the back of her fingers in the old-fashioned way. His eyes met hers for a second and parted. What surprised him most of all was the slim cheroot that dangled from her other hand. She was the first woman that he had ever seen smoking a cigar. He sat down hard in the chair opposite her.

Jan said, 'Soft drinks and biscuits are on the table in the corner, please help yourselves.' Nobody moved. He folded his arms and took a deep breath. 'Our little group is not yet complete. When I heard that so many of our friends were coming, I decided to ask Rabbi Aron Jacobs to join us.'

Tineke looked up. 'I know that most of you have seen him in Leeuwarden but, maybe, have never met him personally.' He checked his watch. 'He's due in ten minutes. If anybody wants to leave then it certainly won't bother me and I know it won't bother the Rabbi.' He moved over to the table and began pouring out the drinks. Nobody moved, everybody seemed to be staring at the fire. Jan carried the tray of drinks round and the tension in the room dropped. Before he had served the last drink there was a knock at the door. Tineke rose and walked into the hall.

Frank had seen him before but he had never been introduced. The Rabbi was of medium height, erect, with a head that sat on a short neck. He was dressed in the customary black clothes and exceptionally shiny shoes. He had long, very dark hair, a small pointed beard and gold-rimmed glasses. The face showed strength. Wide open, brown eyes that scanned everything with slow head movements. The mouth had a ready smile that flashed across the room. Frank noticed that this man sized everybody up in the time that it took him to shake hands. They appeared to have much in common.

'*Meneer* van der Meer, I'm very pleased to meet you,' the voice was deep and melodic. He walked around the room, shook hands and had a brief word for everyone.

For a few minutes the social exchanges continued. Jan stood again. People stopped talking. He spoke in a lowered voice, 'I think there's only one person we want to listen to tonight.' All eyes turned to Dirk.

He remained in his seat and took in a deep lungful of smoke from the cigar. He exhaled and blew the smoke into the fire. A quick glance around the room. 'I've been going to Amsterdam for many years.' He threw the cigar butt into the fire. 'It's a great city, full of life and friendly people. I've not been since the occupation. I don't know what I expected, really. The same as my last visit, I suppose.' He stared at the floor and then lifted his eyes towards the fire. 'It's now totally different. When I got off the train there were Green Police everywhere. My identity card was asked for every five minutes.' He produced it from his pocket and stared at it intently. 'We never had these damned things when we were free. They'll be the end of us.' He dropped it at his feet and was surprised to hear Lottie quietly interrupt him.

She reached into a small leather hand-bag. 'At least yours doesn't have a big letter "J" stamped on it like all Jews in Holland.' She threw hers down on the floor to join his.

He glanced at the identity card. The black "J" was indeed big. He continued, 'If it wasn't the Green Police at me, then it was the *NSB* black shirts. I walked to the Jewish quarter. I had to walk. There wasn't a tram or a bus operating. Everybody was on strike. There were big crowds everywhere, shouting and demanding that the Germans go home. I couldn't believe it. I met gangs of dockers milling about and carrying placards urging more strikes.' For the first time he smiled. 'I know one thing. Our own police did nothing. They stood by and let us march on. By the end of the afternoon some men were pasting posters on walls telling us that demonstrations were prohibited. I can remember a little of what one poster said. **"If we all co-operate, we shall end today's confusion with a united effort"** ' The smile turned to a forced laugh. '"Confusion"! We weren't confused, we knew exactly what we were doing. Anyway, they told us there was a curfew and eventually we packed up and went to bed. I found my friend's hotel. It was in the Jewish quarter.' He glanced at the Rabbi. 'They're scared stiff there, but they want to fight. ... I drank a lot that night. The bar was packed full. ... I don't remember going to sleep.' He closed his eyes and his head sank onto his chest. The silence continued. Suddenly Dirk shook himself and his eyes snapped open. 'The following morning I found out why we were allowed to march. Six and a Quarter was in Vienna.' His voice rose, 'You know what, my friends? It's the first strike anywhere in occupied Europe. No German worker has ever dared to strike since 1933 when Hitler came to power. ... Wonderful! I knew it couldn't last. By mid-day the Germans declared a state of siege. It was a military order signed by our traitor, *General* Christiansen. By this time, we received news that the strike had spread to Haarlem and Zaandam. The Germans threatened us.' Dirk rose to his feet and his eyes roamed round the faces in front of him. He was silhouetted against the fire. 'Rauter called in SS troops and the Green Police. ... There were hundreds of them.' His voice rose higher. '... I was with a crowd near the station. ... They marched forward. The Germans were in long lines. ... We were shouting and cheering. ... There was no warning. The SS opened fire with machine-guns. ... Jesus Christ! Machine-guns! ... People fell around me. ... There were women with us.' With one swift motion he bared his arm. There was a bloody bandage. 'They hit me and I was bleeding badly. There was panic and I was pushed to the ground. The bastards still kept firing. I could hear the bullets overhead. Somebody fell on top of me. I could see it his eyes. He was dead.' Dirk froze and slumped back into his chair. Tineke tried to rise but Frank, with a wave of his hand, stopped her. 'How I got back to the hotel, I don't know. Somebody bandaged me. I slept all night. In the morning I felt better. They told me that the swines killed seven in Amsterdam with forty-five wounded.' He shook his head and his eyes burned. 'I'm one of those forty-five. ... They killed two more in Zaandam. Everybody went back to work. You can't argue with SS troops and machine-guns.' Suddenly Dirk abruptly stopped talking.

The Rabbi was the first to speak. His voice cut through the awful stillness. '*Meneer* Haan,' he said gently. 'Nobody in Leeuwarden has done what you did in Amsterdam. We all respect you for it.' He stood and moved towards him. 'You must get that arm seen to by a doctor as soon as possible.' Dirk allowed him to lift up the shirt sleeve.

Rinske was at his side, 'Darling. It needs attention. You must go to the doctor.'

He waved them away. 'Jan, give me something stronger than

lemonade.'

'Dirk, please, you shouldn't,' she said.

Jan opened the cupboard near the door. He called back across the room. 'A little cognac will help.' He couldn't help smiling. 'After all I've had many a glass in your hotel, Dirk.' He glanced at his guests. 'Who else would like a cognac?' The Rabbi and the van der Meers shook their heads. 'Well, I'm having a big one.' He filled the balloon glasses and handed them out.

Dirk continued, 'Rabbi, your people will not survive this occupation. I saw the looks on the faces of the SS.'

'*Meneer* Haan. The Jews are strong. We've seen anti-Semitism before. We'll struggle through.' He nodded gently, as if wishing to re-enforce his words.

Lottie joined in, 'Rabbi, I agree with you.' He smiled at her. 'I think that if we follow what the Germans want of us. Then we'll manage somehow.'

Dirk interrupted and almost shouted across the room. 'You've no idea what you're talking about. ... I saw Jewish people being shot and killed without question.' He smacked a fist into his palm. 'For the first time Dutch and Jew stood side by side and resist, ... resist together! The Germans will never forgive us for that! Never!'

Lottie's smile was utterly charming, 'Dirk. Maybe you're right. But one thing that you said is true. At least we have shown them that we can resist.' He did not answer.

Frank listened to every word and watched every movement. He rubbed his smooth chin and his voice was steady, 'Friends, I think we must do everything that we can possibly do to help anybody that is oppressed by the Germans. We can achieve much by peaceful means. All of us are not without influence and we must work together as much as we can. Although I understand what Dirk is saying. I saw the Germans bomb Rotterdam.'

Dirk spoke wearily and stared hard. 'Good old Frank. Forever the optimist. Listen, my friend, we can help each other. But at the same time we've got to fight these swines. We've got to organise and we've got to organise, now!' He banged his fist hard on the arms of the chair.

Rinske walked across the room and laid her hand on her husband's shoulder. 'Darling, I think that's enough for tonight. You must rest.' She looked at Frank. 'I don't know how he cycled here tonight with that arm. Could you take us home in your car, ... please?'

The night was finished. As they all left, the rain hammered down and the moon disappeared behind black clouds.

PART THREE

Resistance

ONE

'Frank, I told you so,' said Dirk, 'Listen to the BBC.'

'I did,' replied his friend, 'and I can't believe it.'

'In Poland, the Germans are putting the Jews into vans, closing the doors and then gassing them with the fumes from the engines.'

Frank shook his head, 'Impossible, it's just not true. ... It's inhuman. No person could ever do that to anybody. It must be Allied propaganda.'

'Over the last year I've come to believe the BBC. They don't report anything that's untrue.' Dirk gave a grim-faced nod, 'I, too, find it hard to believe,'

The three men were sitting in Frank's office. Piet had joined them earlier.

'I agree,' added Piet. 'My movement says that worse things are coming. We must prepare to help our Jewish friends.'

'Oh yes, and what can we do? Tell the Germans to go away and not be bad boys,' added Dirk, sarcastically.

Piet shook his head, 'As usual, Dirk Haan, what you say has the ring of practicality.'

Frank leaned back in his chair. Clasping his hands round the back of his head, he said, 'I feel strongly that the matter will soon be taken out of our hands. The Germans have been strangely quiet for the last two months. When that happens they're usually up to something. Jan has asked me to visit the bank later. He has some news and when Jan has news it's normally bad.'

Dirk remained silent for a few moments and then looked sharply at Frank. 'Some terrible things happen that are never broadcasted. I know you're not in our group. But I'm going to tell you something that will shock you. Two days ago, twenty members of the Friesian OD were murdered by the German police. They were shot in cold blood in the courtyard of the prison in Leeuwarden. The sound of machine-guns was clearly heard by people living near the prison. Their bodies have disappeared.' There was a shocked silence.

'Dirk, how can you be so sure?' As Frank spoke there was an edge to his voice.

'Most of the people in the prison aren't criminals, they're men and women who oppose the Germans. Some of the men shot were officers in the Dutch army. They'd committed no crime apart from belonging to Orde Dienst. Other men in the prison saw the murders and passed the message out.' Piet stopped talking and stared at the floor.

Frank was speechless. His brain refused to accept what he had just heard.

Perhaps Frank was used to the sound but it came to him through a faint trembling of the wooden floor of his office. The vibrations passed to his ears. He then immediately knew what he could hear. Jumping to his feet, he shouted loudly.

'Oh NO! ... Bombers coming! Outside everybody! Down to the cellars in the house!' Dirk and Piet froze. Frank repeated his instruction. 'Come on, NOW! ... Outside.' He didn't wait for them and rushed down the stairs to the house, shouting for Marieke. It was too late, the drone grew to a roar and the bombers flashed overhead. In the yard outside the men from the factory just stood and watched. They were joined by Dirk and Piet. Marieke had made up her mind, she joined the men outside. Frank soon came to her side.

'Look! Bombs dropping!' shouted somebody. They all stared into the sky.

'They're not German. Look! They're American and British. ...You can see the bombs!' Nobody moved. They were transfixed.

'Not for here. ... It must be the airfield!'

'No! ... They're dropping in Leeuwarden.'

The crashing of anti-aircraft fire joined with the noise of the planes and the dull crump of the exploding bombs. Marieke put her hands over her ears. Soon there was the scream of German fighter planes overhead.

It was over in five minutes. Silence returned and there were plumes of black smoke blacking out the sun over Leeuwarden.

'I suppose we should cheer,' said Marieke and all the men stared at her, 'but, I'm sure there must be some people hurt in the town.'

'I hope they killed some of the *moffen* bastards,' muttered somebody. Frank turned to see Arnold Kuipers smiling at him. Everybody looked at the insignificant little man.

Frank cycled to the town and on the way saw the damage caused by the bombs. He arrived at Jan's bank on time and was ushered into his office.

He rose from behind his wide desk, 'Hello, Frank, I'm glad to see you. Do sit down.' His face was expressionless. 'I'm sorry to drag you down here. And you probably know it's bad news. It always is from me.' He put his face in his hands.

'What is it now, Jan?' Frank asked quietly.

He opened a drawer in his desk and withdrew a newspaper. The voice was weary, 'This is the latest copy of the "Jewish Chronicle", published by the various Jewish Councils. We Jews find out what is going on through the "Chronicle". It says here,' he jabbed his finger onto the front page, 'that this bank and all its branches will have to collect all the money from other Jewish banks. When the other banks have moved their money they will then be closed down and the staff declared redundant.' He looked up. 'Frank, can you see what this means?' Before his friend could answer he continued. 'When we've got all the money the Germans will do the same thing to us. Then there'll be no more Jewish banks or Jewish bankers.' Jan threw the paper down and banged his fist hard on the table. 'It's damned clever and there's nothing we can do about it!' Frank tried to talk but Jan picked up the paper again. 'There's more. All unemployed Jews will be deported for labour in eastern Holland.' Frank again tried to interrupt. Jan unexpectedly began to cry and his voice shook with anger. 'You know what it means? David will be taken away from us. We wanted him to go to university, but all Jews are forbidden to go there.' He leaned over the table and grasped Frank's hand. His brown eyes were filled with tears. 'What in God's name am I going to do?'

Frank tried to remain calm but his heart was beating fast. He tried to smile, 'David could come to work for me, Jan. But the SD would soon find out because I would have to declare him on my records.' Frank thought for a moment and nodded. 'I think that when the leaving date approaches he'll have to come and stay with us for a while.'

'What will I say to the Germans?' said Jan, raising his hands.

Frank gave his most re-assuring smile and gripped his friend's hand even tighter. 'Don't worry. We'll think of something.' Jan loosened his grip and collapsed back into the chair.

There was no further time to think. The telephone on the desk rang. He picked up the receiver angrily and Frank saw a flash of the old Jan.

'I told you, I'm not taking any calls.' There was a pause and he nodded. He handed over the receiver to Frank. 'It's Marieke. She needs to speak to you urgently.'

She did not give him time to say anything. 'Frank, come home quickly. The Green Police have just been here to the factory. They've arrested Arnold Kuipers.'

Frank arrived back at his office as soon as he could. Marieke and the foreman, Henk Wiersma, were waiting.

She spoke first and said quite simply, 'He's been arrested for treason.'

Frank was puzzled and said incredulously, 'How can that be possible? He's just a young man who works at the factory. I know he's a bit strange, but ...'

Henk Wiersma interrupted him. '*Meneer* van der Meer, the police say that somebody informed them that Arnold had said openly that Germans should have been killed by the bombers.'

Frank was silent for a few moments. The foreman nodded his head. 'I'm ahead of you, *meneer*. It means that somebody in this factory told the Germans. It also means that you have a traitor working for you.' Frank shook his head and bit his lip. Marieke put her arm around his shoulders.

TWO

The de Bruins sat in Lottie Cohen's house. The Cohens lived on Perkstraat, one of the wealthiest parts of Leeuwarden. There were six people in the room. They all knew why they were there.

Lottie waited for a few moments and began. 'Well, everybody, thank you for coming. I've got the parcel here.' She reached under her leather chair and brought out a small package wrapped in string.

'Do open it, Mother,' said her eldest child.

Lottie gave a brief smile and gently pulled the string. The paper fell open to reveal a small cardboard box. She lifted the lid and everybody craned over to look inside.

'It's the stars. I bought enough of them for all of us,' said Lottie.

'I don't like the colour,' interrupted another of her children, 'it's not a nice yellow. I thought it would be a lovely deep yellow.'

Jan was the first to move. He leaned over and picked up a piece of cloth between two fingers. He examined it closely and let it fall back on top of the other stars. He sat back without a word.

Lottie laughed, 'I think it's going to look awful on my yellow dress. The colours clash terribly.'

'Mother, have we got to wear one on all our clothes?'

'Yes,' interrupted Tineke, 'but only when you go outdoors.'

'Mother,' said her eldest son, 'I read in the newspaper yesterday that you have to wear them on the left side.'

Lottie replied, 'Yes, I've heard that as well.' She stared intently at the piece of cloth, 'The lettering on the stars is so small that nobody will be able to read them.'

'It won't matter,' said David quietly from his chair, 'everybody knows what's written on them.'

Tineke held one in her hand. She looked at it closely. 'It'll be difficult to sew on. All those little points. I'll have to do it by hand.' The Jewish stars were passed round.

Lottie stood and held one against her left breast. 'I'm proud to wear mine because I'm proud to be Jewish. I'm going to sew mine on straight away.'

As she left the room the two families stared at her in disbelief. During the whole conversation Jan had remained totally silent. As he watched Lottie leave there was a single tear in the corner of each eye.

THREE

Within an hour of hearing about Albert Kuipers, Frank was at the police station. He was angry and felt utterly helpless, but his determination to free the man was strong. The road outside the building was clear of all traffic and he leaned his bicycle against the wrought iron rails lining the steps. He climbed upwards and pushed open the heavy door and stepped into the waiting hall. The familiar carbolic smell hit his senses and, for a moment, it made him pause. A lone Dutch policeman sat behind the counter. He looked slightly bored and continued writing as Frank stood in front of him. Neither of the two men moved. Frank was determined not to let the man get the upper hand. He waited one more minute, turned, and strode towards one of the doors opposite the counter.

The voice was strident, 'Where do you think you're going to?'

Frank turned round slowly and said clearly, 'It's obvious that you can't deal with me and so I'm going to see *inspecteur* Koopman or *Hauptsturmführer* Müller.' He turned round again but before he had walked one step the man was at his shoulder.

'*Meneer*! Why didn't you tell me that you wanted to see my superiors?'

Frank merely stared at him.

'Please take a seat. I'll see if the *inspecteur* is available.' He rushed away through one of the doors. Frank remained standing.

Within a minute the man returned, 'Follow me please, *meneer*.'

Frank did so, he knew exactly where he was going.

Inspecteur Koopman rose from behind the desk and waved Frank to a seat. His tone was not what Frank had expected.

'*Meneer* van der Meer, I know exactly why you're here and there's nothing that you can do about it.' As he spoke he scribbled something on a piece of paper and pushed it over the desk. The single written word made Frank look up for the microphones. Joop Koopman pointed above his head to the light-fitting. Frank nodded.

'I really must complain most strongly about the arrest of one of my workmen on a false charge of treason.' He was indignant.

The official tone continued, 'This office was informed that during the bombing of the town by the British and American terror fliers,' Frank winced, 'he was heard to speak treason against our German brothers.' Frank put his hand over his mouth to cover up a smile. 'He will be detained for further questioning.'

Frank was about to reply when Joop put a finger to his lips. Just in time. Müller walked in through the door behind Frank. He could smell the man, cologne and cigar. His physical presence was awesome.

Müller stood behind Frank's chair. The voice was patronising. 'Ah, *meneer* van der Meer. A pleasure to see you.' Before Frank could say a word, the man continued as though he was not there. 'No doubt you've come rushing to the rescue of the traitor Kuipers. It's not possible. He's in Leeuwarden prison and later tonight he will be taken to Scheveningen for trial before a *Landesgericht*. He's most certainly guilty.' He walked round the chair and looked down at Frank. Frank knew his methods and quickly stood. Müller took a step back and continued. 'He admitted it to me personally. I see no reason why you should try and protect such a man.'

Frank's gaze flickered over the *SS* officer in front of him. Their eyes locked for a few seconds and he paused for a moment before replying. 'In my country, *Hauptsturmführer*, a man is proved that he is guilty by the due process of law. Not by the police.'

Müller gave a mocking laugh, 'But, *meneer* van der Meer, this is your country and it's mine as well.' His stare bored into Frank's eyes. Quickly Müller glanced at his wrist watch and added. 'Now, the *inspecteur* and I have more important things to do than stand here and chatter about such minor matters.'

He strode over to the door and opened it wide. The meaning was obvious.

The hand raised and stiffened, '*heil* Hitler!' he said quietly.

Frank glanced at Joop Koopman's impassive face and left the room.

By the time Frank was home, it was dark. He put his bicycle in the shed and opened the front door. As he stood in the hall to hang up his coat Marieke appeared from the kitchen.

'How was it, Frank?' she said with concern in her voice.

'Useless,' he replied. 'It sounds as though Albert Kuipers was boasting to Müller. He doesn't stand a chance. He's in Scheveningen prison and nobody gets out of there.'

Marieke shook her head.

Frank glanced in the hall mirror and reached into his inner pocket for a comb. As he began to push the thick brown hair back into place, a small piece of paper fluttered to the floor. Marieke reached down to pick it up.

'Is this yours?' She held it carefully.

'Ah yes. Joop Koopman gave it to me.' He took it from Marieke's fingers and was about to throw it onto the hall-stand. A quick glance made him freeze.

'Oh no!'

'What's the matter?' she asked anxiously.

'Look at this.' He passed it back to her.

'I don't understand.' She turned it over with her fingers. 'On one side it says "microphone" and on the other it says,' she held it up to the hall light, '"your foreman". What does it mean?'

He put his arms around her waist and drew her to him. He held her close and breathed into her ear. 'It means, darling, that Henk Wiersma is an informer. Joop Koopman passed this message to me not an hour ago.'

She sprung back and stared at him. 'Don't be silly! He's been with you for fifteen years. It can't be him!' she exclaimed.

His face was grim. 'Marieke, I have to believe Koopman.'

They ate dinner quietly and nobody was in a mood to make conversation. Aukje had wanted to clear her mind for some time. She waited until the table was cleared.

'*Heit*, ... *Mem*. I've decided that I want to leave school as soon as I can.'

Marieke was the first to reply. 'Aukje, I'm not surprised. I've been expecting you to tell us for the last month.'

'I don't blame you,' added Harmen, 'I always hated the place.'

Aukje turned to her father, '*Heit*, what do you think?'

Frank needed time, 'Let us pray so that we can leave the table.'

There was a minute's silence as they bowed their heads. 'Amen,' intoned Frank. He took a deep breath and looked at his daughter. He always used the Friesian word of endearment when he wanted to speak to Aukje about something personal. '*Famke*, perhaps you could tell us why you want to leave?'

She folded her arms tightly and frowned. Finally she smiled and looked her father full in the face. '*Heit*, the last six months haven't been easy. We're told exactly what we can and cannot learn. There's an unhappy feeling all over the school and I'm fed up with hearing about the "Glorious Reich". Some of our teachers have been forced to leave and the new ones are obviously *NSB*. I really think that I could be of more use to you here in the office.' She turned to her brother who was just about to speak. 'Harmen, I know you hate the paper work and the typing. Well, I love that sort of thing and I'm quite happy to learn how to type. ... Please can I try?' Harmen shrugged his shoulders and looked at his father. Marieke just smiled in her knowing way.

Frank cleared his throat, needing more time to think. 'Aukje,' gone was the personal touch, 'I understand how you feel. Marieke and I had hoped that you would go on to university, you've a good brain you know.' He tapped his fingers on the table-cloth and looked at her. He saw a composed and beautiful young woman. He almost smiled, she would be an asset to any office. 'All right, I agree.' Aukje gave a whoop of delight. 'But, ... on one condition.' She nodded eagerly. 'That you attend evening classes to learn how to run an office properly.' He turned in his chair and stared thoughtfully at his son. 'Harmen, there's a condition for you as well. For the last two years I've been very pleased with your hard work.' His son blushed. 'It's about time that you went back to college to learn about managing a business. After all, I won't be here for ever.' Before Harmen could reply, Frank turned to his wife. 'Marieke, what do you think?'

Her reply was immediate, 'I totally agree.' The sidelong glance at her two children made Frank think that the whole thing had been planned some time ago. For the first time in weeks the family laughed together.

Six forty-five brought them closer as they sat near the wireless. The regular time for the Radio Orange broadcast was the hour when all windows in Holland were tightly shut. It was always a time when Marieke cried. It remained for her, fifteen minutes of what Holland was like before the occupation. There was not much said of any consequence but warnings about the Jewish community came across loud and clear. Frank rose and switched off the wireless when the broadcast was finished. Aukje opened the windows.

The late evening sunshine cast shadows across the garden. Frank and Marieke stood arm-in-arm. Aukje appeared at their side.

'*Heit, Mem,* David's told me that he'll have to come and live with us. Is it true?' She looked at their faces.

'Yes,' replied Marieke, 'It's true, and I'm sure that if David told you that, then he must have told you the reason why.' Aukje nodded.

Frank interrupted. 'It must be an absolute secret and it's going to be very difficult to hide him in the house. He'll live in the same room that Lodo van Hamel used.' He grasped Aukje's arm firmly. She saw her father in a new light. 'Nobody, nobody, must ever know that he's there. Only the four of us and his family will know. As far as anybody else is concerned, he's ran away.' He released her arm. 'If the house is searched, then he'll be hidden in the chimney on the roof. Up there it's safe.' Aukje turned and looked at the high chimneys on the house. They towered over everything and she shivered again.

FOUR

Frank became used to the monotonous drone of heavy bombers overhead. Every day and night huge numbers of aircraft flew over Friesland. Radio Orange told them all about it. The Allies were bombing German cities. People knew where the bombers were going to and it gave them greater strength and lifted their spirits. Many thought that liberation would soon be at hand. They were false hopes.

The factory continued to prosper. *Fliegerhorst*-Leeuwarden was complete and Frank had moved on to the timber needs of the coastal defences. Every Sunday he saw Ernst Kraft at church and every Sunday they exchanged brief nods and the minimum of greetings.

It was after the normal church meeting on a Sunday in June 1942 that *dominee* de Vries beckoned Frank and Marieke to remain. They waited until the last person had gone. Without a word the *dominee* walked across the church and opened the door to his private office. Frank jumped with surprise. Rabbi Jacobs strode across the meeting room and shook hands with them. The cloth yellow star on the left pocket of his dark suit shone out. The word "JEW" was crystal clear.

'Good morning, *meneer* and *mevrouw* van der Meer. I'm sorry to have to meet you like this.' He sat down opposite them.

'Frank,' said a sad Paul de Vries, 'Rabbi Jacobs is here on urgent business. He has been told, in secret, some unbelievable news. I think it best if he tells you himself.' He turned to his friend. 'Rabbi.'

He fingered his small beard and his eyes were cast downwards. For a moment he was silent and then he clasped his hands together and his head lifted. He began slowly and the deep voice trembled, 'My friends. ... The Germans never stop issuing edicts against us. We can tolerate a special curfew in the evenings for Jews. ... We can deal with not being able to travel on public transport. There are plenty of places to go to where there are no "Jews Forbidden" signs. They've even taken our bicycles.' He brushed the six-sided star on his chest. 'We can even treat these with contempt. We can run our own schools. We can even find jobs for people so they're not deported, and ...,' the faintest of smiles passed over his face, 'we can say thank you to our friends for helping us. Last night I saw a copy of the latest "Jewish Chronicle". This morning I confirmed the details with the Jewish Council in Amsterdam.' He took a deep breath. 'All Jews, I repeat all Jews - everybody, women, children and babies - will be transported to Germany for resettlement. Nobody will be excused. Leading Jews will go first.' As he spoke, tears flowed down his face and his voice became stronger. 'We have no other choice. They've also said that once the labour needs have been met that we'll return to our homes. Many of our people will believe that, but, I do not.' He abruptly fell silent.

Paul de Vries spoke very quietly, 'Rabbi, the Christian churches will strongly protest. We will stop this inhuman behaviour. The Nazis cannot do this to the Dutch people.'

'Oh yes they can,' said Frank. 'We've seen what they've done already. I know people that they've murdered without trial. I was there at the bombing of Rotterdam. My friend was in Amsterdam during the strikes and I've seen my Jewish friends being degraded daily.' He banged a clenched fist hard on the table and there was determination in his voice. 'We've got to save our people. Somehow we have to do it without violence.'

Marieke leaned over and clasped Frank's fists. '*Liefje*, what can we do?'

Paul de Vries stood and walked to the end of the room. He thought for a minute, turned and came back to the table. He remained standing. 'Frank, I know how you feel about violence. The Mennonite church has many contacts with other churches. In 1939 I went with a friend to stay at Woodbrooke College in England.' He saw his friends frown with misunderstanding. 'It's a college that's organised by the International Quaker movement. I think you know a little about their beliefs?' Frank nodded, he had read some of their books and knew of the work of their founder, George Fox. Paul continued. 'They have similar beliefs as us about non-violence and peace. But, ... Frank, but, ... they also believe that if there's an evil that is so great that it cannot be vanquished by normal means then they can decide personally to use passive violence to beat that greater evil.' He folded his arms tightly and gave a gentle smile of understanding. 'I believe that God, here this morning, has given us this right to make that decision. I've already made it. I will give my fullest support to the Resistance movements in Friesland.' He put both hands on the table and leant over, looking Frank full in the face. 'God will understand if you make this decision.'

They walked home through Leeuwarden. The streets near the synagogue were quietly full of people. The Jewish community was out on the streets. Frank nodded to some friends. The yellow stars were everywhere. It was as though on this particular bright sunny day the stars had blossomed like summer blooms. Frank could sense that most of the people had heard what Rabbi Jacobs had told him only an hour ago. Marieke had the same feeling.

'Bad news travels fast,' she said, quietly. He nodded.

They sat down on a bench at the side of a small canal. Marieke turned to him.

'Will the Germans really transport all these people?' she said, waving her hand at the streets around them.

'Of course they will. I haven't the slightest doubt about what they intend to do.'

Grasping his hand she looked at his face. 'Frank, have you thought about what *dominee* de Vries said about violence?'

He appeared not to hear and gazed into the dark waters below. In a whisper that she could just hear her husband said, 'I have decided to join Piet Bokma's group. I want to help our Jewish friends and to support Paul de Vries.' He straightened his back and turned to look Marieke in the face. His voice was stronger and he spoke with determination. 'But, I will not kill, or carry a gun.'

They sat for ten minutes without speaking. Occasionally Frank closed his eyes and appeared to doze in the sunshine. Marieke knew that his mind was in turmoil. She squeezed his hand and broke his thoughts.

'Frank, I'm so pleased that you've decided to oppose the Nazis. I want to help you in any way that I can.'

'*Liefje*, thank you. It's the biggest decision that I've ever had to make.' He smiled into her eyes. 'I'll go and see Dirk and Piet as soon I can.'

'Why not now, darling?' asked Marieke. 'Look around you. I think that people will need help after the news hits the whole of Holland.'

He laughed, 'You're right, as usual. Let's walk to the *Hotel de Kroon* and see if Dirk is there.'

There were not many people in the hotel. A mixture of local businessmen and uniformed German soldiers. The manager recognised them immediately and steered them towards a table near to the window.

'Good day, *meneer* and *mevrouw* van der Meer. Coffee will be here in a moment.' He answered Frank's unasked question. 'I will inform *meneer* Haan that you're here.'

As they waited, Marieke nudged Frank. He followed her glance. *Oberleutnant* Kraft was sitting alone on the other side of the foyer. He had not seen them. Dirk brought the coffee and set it out for them.

'Hello, you two. What brings you here on this lovely day?' His face was straight and the usual grin was missing.

Marieke began, 'Dirk, Frank and I need to talk to you urgently.'

He sipped the coffee. He held the cup with both hands and looked at them. 'If you're talking about the Jews being transported to Germany, then I know all about it.' He saw the look on Frank's face. 'Paul de Vries telephoned me half an hour ago. I thought that you might be coming here so I took the liberty of inviting Piet Bokma. ... He's on his way.' Frank and Marieke glanced at each other.

Dirk watched through the window and saw Piet arrive. They exchanged brief smiles as he leant his bike against the outside wall.

The manager placed a screen around the group and their conversation began.

'We all know what's going to happen. How do we prepare for it?' said Piet.

Frank tapped gently on his coffee cup. 'Before we discuss anything, I have to tell you about a decision that I've made.'

'WE have made, Frank,' added Marieke.

'We've decided to join your group.' He caught the smile on Piet's face. 'On two conditions.' He folded his arms. 'I will not knowingly take part in murder and I will not carry a gun.'

Piet's smile was quickly replaced by that of pleasure. 'Congratulations to both of you. Thank you, you don't know how much we've wanted you with us and we accept your conditions.'

Dirk placed his hands on the table. 'Now you're with us I have some important information.' Conversation stopped. 'I've been told that the refugee camp at Westerbork will be used as a transit camp before people are transferred to Germany. The first group of eight hundred Jews will be moved by train on the 10th July. A special branch line has been built from the main line to connect Westerbork with express routes to Germany.'

Frank interrupted, 'Dirk, I only found out this morning about transporting Jews to Germany. How on earth do you know so many details?'

He shrugged his shoulders, 'I can tell you now that we've somebody very close to the *SD* here in Leeuwarden. I can also tell you both, that although the Resistance is generally poorly organised and there are not many of us, we do communicate very well with each other. The Churches are with us and they're much better organised. Now back to the immediate problem. German efficiency is not as good as people think it is and therefore the Jewish Councils will inform each Jew by post when they have to go. The Council then tells the Germans. The transport is already arranged.' He sipped his coffee, swallowed and took a deep breath. 'By the end of next week, Jews living outside Leeuwarden will be told to move into the town and await instructions. It's expected that the first people will be moved from Amsterdam within the next three weeks.'

Marieke had listened quietly but now she spoke. 'I still can't believe it. ... You can't make a whole group of people just pack up and leave their own house and ... and their country! Nobody will take any notice. The Germans can't just march into towns, round them up like cattle and then send them on their way.'

There was silence. Frank put his arm around Marieke's shoulders and said quietly, 'That's what people will think. It's a psychological trap. We know that they've been told that they'll return when they've completed their work in Germany. But I've never believed that, not since I first heard the rumours from Kraft two years ago.'

'All right, if it happens, or when it happens, just what do we do?' asked Marieke. 'We can't tell the Germans not to do it. We've tried that before and innocent people get killed.' Her face was pale and she gripped the coffee cup tightly.

Piet was calm and composed. 'At this stage, we can't blow up railway lines and we can't stop them in any other way. All we can do is see what happens and offer our help. I'm sure the Church and the Jewish Community themselves will soon ask for help in their own way.'

Frank smiled, 'I think the good people of Leeuwarden will soon say how they feel when all this is printed in the newspapers over the next few days.' He paused. 'Today I need time to think about it.' He paused for a moment. 'Aukje and Harmen will be worried about us. We really must get home.' They rose to leave. Piet shook hands with everybody and they walked through the main doors and out onto the street. As they passed the main windows of the hotel, Frank glanced in. He was surprised to see Dirk leaning over a table quietly talking to Ernst Kraft.

FIVE

'Coincidence is a strange thing, Marieke,' said Frank. Aukje had already opened the morning mail and it was waiting on his desk. The sight of the swastika on the envelope made him take the letter downstairs. They stood together in the kitchen.

'What do you mean?' she replied.

He was reading it for the third time. 'They want me to tender for a new contract. They're going to expand the facilities at Westerbork and they want my factory to make the new buildings.'

'What're you going to do?'

He nodded and weighed the document in his hand. 'I may be the only civilian non-Jew in the whole of Holland who has a chance to see Westerbork from the inside.'

Before he had time to climb the stairs back to his office, the telephone rang. It was Aukje. '*Heit*, Piet on the line. I'll put him through.'

The message from Piet was simple. He asked Frank to find out as much as possible about the camp at Westerbork. He explained to Marieke. She was very insistent.

'Frank, this time I'm coming with you. I remember your journey to Rotterdam only too well.' He had to agree.

Frank easily obtained permission to travel. They left on a dull, rainy day for the two hour drive. Westerbork is situated on an area of heathland twenty-five kilometres from the German border and south-east of Leeuwarden. As they approached within a kilometre there were Green Police patrols on the road. Each time he showed his pass and the car was let through. He suddenly found himself on a narrow stretch of deserted road. To his left was a small rise partly surrounded by trees. He parked the car and stepped outside. They both walked up the hill and stood looking silently at the camp in front of them.

A huge half kilometre square of sandy soil with high barbed-wire fences all around. Tall watch towers at each corner with another half way along each side of the square. Long single-storey, wooden barracks, parallel but facing in all directions. Running through it like an artery, was a single railway line. Within the camp, the line was bounded on one side with a long building, higher than the barracks on the other side. In the middle of it all was a tall, brick chimney linked to a square, single-storey structure. Outside the fence were two modern, detached houses surrounded by small trees. Close by were three other houses backing onto extensive vegetable gardens. There was another noticeable building. It resembled a church, a high sloping roof with a small entrance hall at one end. Mingled with the barracks were oblong plots of darker coloured soil growing tall, yellow lupins. He could, once again, feel that sense of total organisation.

'Frank, look!' Marieke nudged his arm and pointed over to their left.

A plume of white smoke rose into the air. Within a few seconds the puffing of a train came to their ears. They watched it trundle down the line towards the perimeter fence. One locomotive pulling ten passenger coaches. There were faces at the windows. It slowly stopped, the double gates were opened and the train passed through.

'WHAT'RE YOU DOING HERE?' The voice was loud and strident. Frank spun round. He saw a black car on the road. The sound of the train and their complete concentration had blotted out any sound of its approach.

The question was repeated. 'What're you doing here?" There were three of them. German Green Police, all armed with machine-pistols. Their menacing looks worried Marieke but she matched them stare for stare.

Frank had seen this approach before. The charming smile flashed. He answered in faultless German. 'Good afternoon. My wife and I are travelling to Westerbork. I have business there, ... with I believe.' He fumbled in his pocket for the letter, ' ... yes, ... eh, ... here we are. An *Obersturmführer* Gemmeker.' He held out the letter. The taller man shouldered his weapon, took the letter off Frank and began to read it. He thrust it back into his hand.

'This is a prohibited area. Move, now!'

'We're not sure how to get in to the camp. Perhaps you could take us to the gates?' Frank stepped towards his car.

The man grunted a reply. 'Follow us. Don't stop, and park outside the gates.'

At the main entrance two SD guards checked his papers and opened a small gate in the fence.

The man was expressionless and he shouted orders at them. 'This letter only lets you in! The woman must stay in the car!'

Marieke looked at Frank frantically. He smiled and squeezed her arm. 'Don't worry, *liefje*. I shan't be long.'

Frank could feel the atmosphere. It weighed down on him at every step. He was conscious of people staring at him. Then he realised why. He was not wearing a yellow star.

The camp was full of people. They were smartly dressed, as though going to work. Many of them carried a suitcase or a rucksack. Babies in their mothers' arms. Children running here and there. Old people in black with hats. Young people smiling and linking arms. Men and women clutching at each other. Overall was the smell of humanity and the sweat of the unknown. Standing erect, with hands behind their backs and high hats with peaks reflecting the afternoon sun, were the uniformed men of the SS, clad in grey with gleaming black jack boots and leather gloves. Their eyes saw everybody and everything. The only sound was the babble of fear. Chattering, shouting and whispering. It could all be heard with every second of listening.

Frank trembled as the wave of humanity parted.

'This way, *meneer* van der Meer,' ordered the Green Police guard. He followed as meekly as a lamb.

The room was well furnished. Comfortable arm-chairs, polished parquet floor and long curtains. With that same smell of carbolic. It was insulated from the world outside. Frank slumped into a chair and tried to gather his senses. A door opened and a man approached. He was SS. There was a smile on the handsome face. The hair was grey and he was tall and distinguished. In his green uniform he stood at ease in front of Frank. Under his left arm were rolls of paper.

'*Guten Tag, mein Herr. I'm Obersturmführer Gemmeker,* Camp Commandant. Thank you for coming here.' The voice was precise and almost friendly. 'I have the plans for you to examine.' He unrolled blueprints on the floor in front of Frank's feet and then sat next to him. He pointed with a small leather swagger stick. 'We need to increase the number of wooden barrack blocks by thirty per cent. They're a standard pattern and we pay a standard price.' He waved his finger, 'This time no heating or water. Only the original barracks that your countrymen built had water and heating.' He pointed at spaces on the plan, 'Here ... and here. Also a new administration building ... here.' He looked up and smiled at Frank. 'I think it's good business for you? ... *Ja,* ... I think so.' The officer relaxed and sat back in the deep leather chair. There was pride in his voice. 'Soon this camp will be very busy. We're expecting a transport in every two days and then one out every Thursday.' Frank could only nod, he was speechless. The man read his face. '*Ja, Herr* van der Meer, I can see that you're interested.' He stood up and beckoned. 'Come with me. A guided tour will help you to appreciate our little problems.' There was that same smile. He placed the green peaked hat on thinning grey hair and twitched it to a jaunty angle. Frank meekly followed.

They walked together into the late afternoon sunshine. All the guards stiffly saluted the SS officer as he marched through the crowds. The German Green Police were everywhere. Frequently he stopped and pointed with a short stick. Frank heard the words and watched the people.

'Here is the meeting hall. ... See, the Jews are holding some sort of ceremony. ... Over there is one of our gardens. Lupins, they're popular here.' He stopped and said some words to a yellow-starred woman. '*Mevrouw* Akker, please will you make sure that we have enough milk for the children. *Ja* ... thank you.' She smiled at him. He threw open a door. 'This is our crèche, specially for young children whilst they're waiting for transport to Germany.' He smiled at Frank. 'Beautiful ... eh? I'm very proud of this place.' He slapped his riding breeches with the stick and strode off. The church-like building appeared in front of them. Gemmeker marched in. Neat rows of tables full of people completing forms. Some rose as he entered. He waved them down. 'This is our administration building. The Jews do all their own paperwork. They do everything for themselves. In the evenings it's a theatre. Wonderful music, excellent poetry readings. ... We'll need a new building like this one but bigger.' He looked at Frank questioningly. 'You saw the space on the plan? .... *Ja?*'

'Yes, of course,' he answered weakly.

Frank could smell the acrid smoke from the train. Within a minute they were at the sidings in the middle of Westerbork. Gemmeker stood astride the shining steel railway line. There were hundreds of people all around him. Smoke swirled over his body. Nobody took any notice, they just plodded forward following the person in front of them.

He held up his arms and shouted, 'This is the best organised railway station in the whole of Holland. We can process 800 people in two hours. It's magnificent. ... Don't you agree?' Frank waited in silence. 'Soon, we'll be able to handle over a 1000 people per train. For that we need more handling facilities.' He pointed to another open space. 'You build it there. ... *Ja?*'

It was the faces that affected Frank. Total disbelief, tinged with acceptance. Some were smiling as they met old friends. Others were white-faced and saw nothing. But there was no panic, only organisation. The train load of humanity was thinning, pushed and directed into the correct barrack blocks by Jewish men and women with sheaves of papers. All medically checked and fed.

Gemmeker pointed to wooden houses, detached with small gardens. 'Here live our guards and civilians, ... *Ja* ... necessary people for the efficient running of the camp.' He steered Frank towards one of the wooden barracks. It was 80 metres long and 10 wide. As Frank walked through the single door the solid wall of humanity hit him. Endless rows of bunks, three beds high. Suitcases piled near the beds. People chattering; children crying; groups playing games. And the smell of 900 people living together.

Some waved a greeting to Gemmeker. He smiled back at them. 'There's somebody you must meet. ... *Moment* ... *bitte.* ... Here he is.' He pulled a man out from a group playing cards. 'Babinski looks after all the contracts for the camp. When he comes to Leeuwarden next week, I'll make sure he meets you.'

This time Frank was surprised, 'He comes out of Westerbork?'

Gemmeker looked surprised, '*Ja* ... of course! ... All *Prominents* are given leave from the camp. ... It makes them work harder.' He laughed, 'They always return. It's so good here.'

Frank walked back to the gates alone. He was confused. On the way, for some reason that he could not understand, the guards saluted him. Marieke was waiting for him near the car. She rushed up and threw her arms around his neck. He froze and she stepped back and looked at him.

'What's the matter, Frank? ... Are you all right?'

He grasped her hand and they quickly walked to the car. They drove back down the narrow road. It was half an hour before he spoke. He glanced sideways at her. His face was pale, 'I don't care what information Piet needs, but I'm not going to tender for the contract.'

Marieke said slowly, 'I love you, Frank, and I understand, and I agree with you.'

SIX

It took some days for Frank to tell Marieke what he had seen at Westerbork. The experience was something that he found difficult to talk about. Piet needed to know about his trip when he asked Frank to meet him at his house on *Groningerstraatweg*.

He came straight to the point and began sympathetically, 'Frank, you have to tell me what you saw.'

His voice was almost a whisper and he shook his head. 'I can't describe it.'

Piet pushed his friend harder. 'But what was it that upset you? I've spoken to other people that've been there and they say that it's just like a railway station. The only big difference seems to be that you sleep there. There's been no rumours about cruelty or torture.' He stopped talking and tried to look into Frank's face. 'Come on, old friend,' he said quietly, 'we have to know what we're dealing with here.'

Frank lifted his head and looked at Piet. The whisper continued and his eyes burned, 'What you say is correct. I didn't see any signs of mistreatment. It's not that that concerns me. You have to be there to feel it. It's not something that you can see from the outside.' With a finger he wiped globules of sweat from his forehead. 'It's the feeling of utter desperation.' He searched for words. 'It's ... it's ... the helplessness of the unknown.' He sighed, 'You know, Piet, they transport them to Germany in cattle wagons. Great bare wooden things, sliding doors, one grill for light and air; you can see dozens of them waiting in the sidings. And the people in the camp just know they're going to be transported. There's no resistance, no protest, no light in their eyes. They sing and dance to pass the time. They treat it all as if it's ... if it's ... NORMAL!'

Piet jumped at the sound of Frank's voice. He had never heard him shout before. Tears rolled down his friend's face and his body shuddered. He put an arm round his shoulders. 'All right, Frank, that's enough. I'll stop.'

The late summer sunshine helped Frank as he cycled home. The warmth on his face and the cool wind in his hair brought him back to some level of normality. As he arrived home the men from the factory waved a greeting to him as they passed on their way home to their families. Henk Wiersma shouted something which Frank did not hear. The man's smiling face made Frank disbelieve Joop Koopman's word.

The sight of more bicycles than usual outside the house made him sigh. Every day seemed to bring another crisis.

Marieke greeted him, 'Hello, darling, the de Bruins are here.' The expression on her face told him that there was more trouble ahead. He straightened his tie in the mirror and physically shook himself. He knew that very soon his support and help would be needed.

No words of welcome, just a wan smile from Tineke. Frank sat down in his usual leather chair.

Jan's voice was calm, 'Frank, Marieke ... it's happened.' He tried to smile and pulled a grey envelope from out of his pocket. He passed it to Frank.

Piet had shown him such an envelope not an hour ago and he knew exactly what it was.. He held it in his hand for a moment and looked across at his family. They were white faced. Frank withdrew the three sheets of paper. Apart from the names at the top, they contained the same information. He pushed them back into the envelope.

'Before I read these letters, I want to say something to you all.' They waited. He looked at each of the de Bruins in turn. 'Tineke, Jan, David. You've been our friends for many years and we love you dearly. We've shared much happiness and much sadness. I can remember the joy that Marieke and I felt when David was born. Before the war came to Holland I thought that this happiness would continue for ever. I've seen Aukje and David become fond of each other and that has made us all full of hope. David has been hiding here for six weeks and there's never been a complaint from him, or from us. We've been happy to have him here.' He paused and twisted his wedding-ring. 'I know I don't have to ask Marieke, but if you both want to come and stay with us, then we'll hide you and protect you.' He paused again and this time he was too emotional to speak anymore. He withdrew one of the three letters from the envelope.

'Frank, I'll read it,' Jan said quietly and took the letter from Frank's hand.

den Heer Jan de Bruin,
(born. 11 - 6 - 1901)
Oude Lekkummer Straat
Leeuwarden.

CALL UP!

The German labour authorities inform you that on Tuesday 18th October 1942 you must report to the work camp at Westerbork.

You may take with you the following articles:
1 suitcase or rucksack
1 pair of work-boots or shoes
2 pairs of socks
2 sets of underwear
2 sets of bed linen (sheets and pillow-cases)
2 shirts
2 pairs of underpants
2 woollen blankets
1 pair of overalls
1 complete set of cutlery
1 drinking beaker
3 handkerchiefs
2 towels
1 pullover

On Tuesday 18th October 1942, you must, at precisely 06.35 hours, report to the main railway station for processing.

The Burgomeester of Leeuwarden.
Herman Wilders

J 1064

Harmen spoke for the first time. 'Do you have to go, Jan? I mean ... can't you just ignore the letter?'

Jan shook his head, 'That's not possible. If you miss the call-up, or try to hide, then they come looking for you. In Amsterdam, whole streets of people have refused the letters or have just thrown them away. The Green Police put a cordon around the whole street and the German *SD* went in with guns and lorries and forced the people to go.' He frowned. 'I've been told that if you resist, you don't go to Westerbork. You go to the concentration camp at Amersfoort. Usually those people are never heard of again.' He looked worriedly at Frank and Marieke. 'I can't risk that: Tineke and I will have to go.'

'You're most certainly not going,' said Marieke determinedly. She stood up, placed her hands on her hips and faced Jan. Her voice was crystal clear. 'We'll hide you here in the house. If we can't do that, then we'll find somewhere else to hide you. We've plenty of friends in Friesland and they'll help, the Church will as well.' She leaned over and kissed Jan gently on the cheek. 'It's another two weeks before you have to leave. We can make plans and find a good place to hide you.'

Harmen gave a low laugh and everybody stared at him. 'I know just the place, don't you, *Heit*?' Frank raised his eyebrows and Harmen continued. 'The cellar under the factory is ideal. A bit noisy in the day time. But quiet enough at night, You'll have electricity and fresh air.' He jumped up. 'After dark, you could come into the house and eat with us.' He clapped his hands. 'I know it'll work. The *moffen* will never find out.' He looked imploringly at his father. 'Come on, *Heit*, say you'll agree?'

'We could never ask you to do that,' interrupted Tineke. Her lips compressed into a thin line. 'If the *SD* found out then they'd put you in prison with us.' She shook her head. 'No, we can't let you do it. It's out of the question.'

Jan grasped his wife's hand and kissed her gently on the forehead, 'Tineke, we must survive, for David's sake at least. The Germans tell us that we'll come back, but nobody really believes that. Anyway, what would we come back to? They're already selling Jewish businesses in the town and the bank closes next week. Our friends have made us a wonderful offer. I think we should accept it with gratitude. We've no other choice.'

The two families in the room were silent. It was now almost dark and Marieke stood and switched on the lights.

Frank glanced at the letters again and put them back into the envelope. His smile returned. With a flick of his wrist he threw the envelope into the embers of the fire. It flared for a moment and curled into ashes. He said, 'Well, that's it everybody. Jan, you never even received the letters, did you?' Jan shook his head in disbelief.

They made plans and for over two hours discussed the details. The ideas seemed to give them new vigour and soon they were laughing and chattering like the old days. The de Bruin family eventually returned to their home in the early hours of the morning.

Frank thought he had solved one problem but another nagged away at his mind. It was his factory foreman. If the cellar was to be used, then it was a matter of life and death for the workmen to be trusted. There was only one man who knew the answer.

Two days later, Frank arranged to meet Joop Koopman at the *Hotel de Kroon*. As he waited, Piet walked over and sat down with him.

'Hello, Frank, I see he's late.'

'Yes, that's unusual for our *inspecteur*. He's normally very punctual.'

commented Frank. He sipped at the cold drink that Piet had brought. 'I suppose you've seen the latest transport details for Westerbork?'

'Rabbi Jacobs showed me the schedule,' his face was full of sadness, 'Frank. I'm sorry to see that your friends are on the list.'

Frank smiled, 'Thank you. But you see, Piet, they're not going.'

'They don't have much choice. You know the consequences if they refuse.'

'I now know what we can do to help them,' said Frank. 'We can hide the Jews and save them from the Germans.'

Piet scratched his head, 'What you're suggesting would be impossible. Where can we hide so many? Who would do it?' ... Frank, you and I are businessmen and I've got to say this, who the hell would pay for it? It'll cost an awful lot of money.'

Frank warmed to the argument, 'This is the one big thing that many people would take part in. It gives them something that they can fight the Nazis with. There're plenty of houses in remoter parts of Friesland where we could hide people. I know at least a dozen families that would help.' Frank was now really excited and he rubbed his hands together. Piet noticed a light in his eyes that he had not seen for some time.

'Frank, we may have to hide them for years. We've no idea how long the war will last. I think that your idea is all right in theory but difficult in practice.' He shook his head, 'I really don't know ... I don't think it would work.'

Piet heard a slight knock at the back door. He glanced through the window and saw Joop Koopman smiling at him. He waved him in.

'Hello, gentlemen. It's good to see you.'

Piet poured out two glasses of beer and a soft drink for Frank.

'Joop, I'm glad you could come.' He turned to glance at Frank. 'I've just been hearing about Westerbork from Frank. It's not good news.'

Joop nodded, 'I've heard about that place. Some of my men accompany the Jews on the trains to the camp. Their stories are mixed, depending on whether they support us or the NSB.'

'Is there anything we can do?' asked Frank.

He sighed, 'Nothing at all. The trains are heavily guarded and the camp is patrolled by German SS and SD. Frank, you're the only one from the Resistance group who's been inside.' He paused for a moment and smiled. 'By the way, our little band is now called Group "Uncle". Uncle has looked at ways of stopping the trains. There's no way at all that we can stop them. The Germans aren't stupid, they're very well organised.'

'I know, I've seen it for the last three years,' added Frank quietly.

'Well, there's one good thing,' continued Joop. 'At least we're now armed.'

'When did that happen?' said Frank sharply. 'I've not been told anything about weapons.' His eyes opened wide.

'It's not something that we felt you should know,' Piet added quickly.

'You know how I feel about guns. Anyway, where've you got them from? I thought only the Germans were armed.'

Joop swirled the last of the beer around the glass and in one gulp tipped the yellow liquid down his throat. '*Orde Dienst* is nearly all military or police. As you know. When we surrendered in 1940, many weapons were deliberately hidden in caches all over Holland. Piet and I asked OD for guns some weeks ago. I was given the information and last weekend six of us met near the coast at Harlingen and dug up a cache of small pistols and ammunition. It should be sufficient for our immediate needs. There's plenty of weapons of all kinds, we only have to ask.'

Frank was angry, 'I still don't like it.' He thought for a moment and stared at Piet. 'Do you have a gun in this house?'

Piet uncomfortably shifted in his chair. 'I'll be honest with you, Frank. ... Yes, I do have a gun, in fact two. One is under the chair where you're sitting and the other is hidden behind a fresh air duct at the top of the stairs.' He saw his friend glance at the floor as though looking for the gun. 'I've got to say, Frank, if I'm threatened by anybody, I'll protect my family and my house.' Piet was surprised at the response. Frank nodded calmly and sat back in his chair.

'What about my proposal to save our Jewish friends?' said Frank. The normal, charming smile had returned.

The two men looked at each other and Joop spoke. 'I think that this will have to be put to the whole group. It's not something that we can decide upon here. We need a place to meet outside the town, somewhere where we can't easily be watched.'

'Why not at the factory?' said Frank quickly, 'It's not easy to observe without being seen. We've plenty of room. How much space do you need?'

'We won't all meet, only the cell leaders,' replied Piet.

Frank laughed and clapped his hands. 'Cell leaders! You sound like a bunch of Communists, surely not?'

Joop was serious, 'Frank, the SD know that active groups are forming. Some people in Friesland have already disappeared. We know that executions have taken place in Scheveningen and Amersfoort. We can't afford to be careless with our organisation.' He paused. 'Anyway, to answer your question, I would think space for about eight people will be sufficient. I could arrange a meeting for next Tuesday after dark.'

There was a break in the conversation for a few minutes as Piet left to bring more drinks.

When he returned he looked Frank straight in the face. 'There's a job that needs doing and we'd like you to do it.' There was an edge to his voice.

'What exactly do you want me to do?' asked Frank calmly.

'I believe that you've kept all the plans for the new buildings at the airfield?' said Joop. He glanced at Piet.

'Yes, I have,' answered Frank, 'why?'

'Every day and night we can hear the British and American bombers flying over Friesland. The airfield has one of Germany's best night fighter squadrons based there.' Frank nodded. 'At precisely midnight tomorrow night we need to cut the main telephone cables that link the airfield with Germany. There's a big raid coming over and cutting communications will stop the fighters being warned by their radar.' Frank opened his mouth to protest and then shut it tightly. 'Piet will help you. He'll be round at about eleven o'clock. It's best if you cycle to the airfield and wait until about ten minutes to midnight.' He paused. 'I presume you've some good wire cutters at the factory?' Frank found his voice.

'I'm really rather pleased. It's good to be doing something positive. But I know the man that laid those cables.' Frank had a broad grin on his face. 'At least he'll get some more work!' They all laughed.

The following day Marieke listened carefully to Frank as he explained his task.

'Darling, I don't like it. It's dangerous. Are you sure you have to do it?' she asked nervously.

'Marieke, we have to resist. If we're in the group then we have to take part in what's happening. At least this is not direct violence and in a way I'm glad that I can contribute something. Anyway, Piet is with me.'

'I think he's as bad as you. What does he know about sabotage?' asked Marieke.

'Piet always seems to know what's going on. He must be in contact with somebody, how else did he know about the raid tonight?' Frank thought for a moment, 'And he has guns in the house. I would never, never allow guns in this house.'

For a moment Marieke nearly told Frank about the gun still resting in the case of the Friesian clock. She bit her lip and remained silent.

Both their thoughts were interrupted by the shrill ringing of the telephone.

'I'll take it,' said Marieke.

'Hello, *mevrouw* Wiersma, it's nice to hear from you.' Frank listened, Marieke was talking to his foreman's wife. She suddenly stiffened and her voice was sharp. 'Oh no! ... That's terrible ... How did it happen? ...' There was a long silence as she listened. 'Can I help you with anything? ... I'll come and see you first thing in the morning. ... Of course I'll tell Frank. ... Yes, ... yes, ... of course.' Marieke put the receiver back on its cradle and turned to face him. There were tears streaming down her face. Her voice was full of panic.

'Frank, Henk Wiersma, ... He's dead!'

'What!' shouted Frank. 'How can that be? I saw him leave the factory not two hours ago.'

'Henk was nearly home and a car came round the corner and knocked him off his bike. The car didn't stop. His wife says that nobody saw it happen, they walked out and there he was on the road. He was killed outright. Oh Frank it's awful.' Marieke thought for a moment and frowned. 'He's worked for you for years and I know that you suspect him because of Kuipers. ... ' A look of sheer horror passed over her face. She covered her mouth with her hand and then dropped it to her side. 'Oh my God, Frank! ... It couldn't be. ... surely not?' Her expression changed to that of anger. 'Did you know that this was going to happen? Did you?' She clenched her fists at her sides.

Frank's brain was in a turmoil. He had jumped to the same conclusion, but he could not believe what he was hearing and thinking. He snapped back at her. 'Marieke, don't be silly. I knew absolutely nothing about it.'

They both stood, shaking with frustration. Eventually Frank spoke, 'Come on. Let's sit down and think it through.' He nodded and put his arm around her shoulder and led her into the living-room.

'*Liefje*, we don't know if this is true. The Germans won't have killed him and therefore it could be the Resistance. Or, just sheer coincidence.'

She stopped crying but her eyes were wide open. Her voice was hoarse with shock. 'I just can't believe it, Frank. It can only be the Resistance and they're our ... our ... friends? How can they do things like that?'

'We can ask Piet.' He glanced at the clock, 'He's due here in thirty minutes.'

They were quiet and even though they sat close to each other, there was suddenly an emotional distance between them.

The knock at the front door echoed round the house. Before Aukje answered the door she turned to look at Frank. '*Heit*, I don't understand what's happening. I heard you and *Mem* arguing. Please talk to me about it.' He nodded and she opened the door.

'Come in, Piet,' she said. '*Mem* and *Heit* are expecting you.'

Piet felt the atmosphere when he walked into the room. It was electric. He had no time to talk. Marieke flew at him with fists waving. Her face was stiff with anger.

'Piet, we've just heard that Henk Wiersma has been killed by a car. What do you know about it?'

He pushed her away. 'I'm sorry to hear that. I don't know anything about it.' His face must have said what he was really thinking.

'Piet Bokma,' said Frank quietly, 'I know you and I know when you're lying. I can see it in your face. Come on, man, you've got to tell us the truth!'

'But, Frank, ... Marieke.'

He recoiled as Marieke stood and pushed him hard in the chest. 'LIAR!' she shouted. 'How dare you come into this house and deny murder! ... How dare you!' Frank took her gently by the arm and returned her to the sofa. He turned to face a white-faced Piet.

'I think you'd better tell us the truth, ... now!'

Piet slumped into the chair. 'We didn't want you to know. We didn't want to upset your beliefs about violence.' He looked up, 'You and Marieke are a great asset to the group. We respect you for what you're doing for the Jews.' He glanced upwards and pointed to the ceiling. 'I know that you're hiding David de Bruin up there. And I bet a million guilders that you've offered to take in Jan and Tineke as well.' He caught their glances. 'Wiersma had to go. He was becoming a danger to you and the group. What you don't know, is that some months ago his son was arrested for some minor infringement of German regulations. The boy is in Scheveningen prison. *Hauptsturmführer* Müller knew that Wiersma was close to you and therefore they blackmailed him to pass on information. There was nothing, nothing, that Wiersma could do about it. His son's life meant more than yours. Frank, you now know a lot about the Group.' He shrugged his shoulders. 'If it helps, the execution was not carried out by Uncle. It was done by a group from Harlingen. In that way, nobody locally knows anything about it. Marieke,' he looked towards her pleadingly, 'perhaps you could go and see his widow tomorrow. Soon she'll be told about what happened and she'll be financially well-supported for the rest of her life.' He saw the look in Marieke's eyes and he emphasised the point with his finger. 'You've both got to realise that we're now at war with the Nazis. Look at what they're doing to the Jews. Marieke, you think that they're going to Germany. But they're not, they're going to Poland through Germany. God knows what happens to them when they get there. Believe me, it's going to get much harder than this. When the groups get really organised the *moffen* will have something to deal with.' Piet glanced at the clock and stood. 'Frank, we have to leave. It's time.'

Frank was pale-faced but calm. Without a word he walked across to Marieke and kissed her on the lips. She clutched the back of his head with her hand. 'Frank, for God's sake be careful,' she said softly.

SEVEN

It took Frank five minutes to collect the tools that he had laid out earlier in the day. As they climbed onto their bicycles neither man spoke a word. The journey to the airfield took only twenty minutes. There was no moon but both men knew exactly where they were going. For the last half kilometre they left their bicycles in some bushes and walked quickly towards their target.

Fliegerhorst-Leeuwarden was busy. From where they waited at the end of the runway they could see sparkling lights and rows of parked aircraft. Frank pulled a plan out of his pocket, unfolded it and laid the paper on the damp grass. Piet switched on a small torch and shielded its bright light. Carefully he shone it onto the plan.

'The line of the duct is marked with wooden markers,' Frank whispered. 'It's capped with concrete slabs. The duct leads back to the main cable-ways.' He leant closer and pointed to a line of black ink. 'This is it. We need to cut it in three places.'

'That's a bit risky, isn't it? After the first cut they'll know what's happened and they'll be looking for us,' said Piet.

Frank carried on whispering, 'I don't think so.' He delved into the large pockets of his overcoat. 'You see I brought two pairs of wire cutters. We both cut at exactly the same time and then we get out as quickly as we can.'

There was a faint smile on Piet's face. 'Frank van der Meer, you're getting more like a real resister every day.' There was no reply.

It was pitch-black but Frank knew his way. Only once did he stop to check the duct markers. There was not a guard in sight. He stopped and waved Piet to his side. He dug his toe into the black earth. It hit something solid and Frank grunted. Quickly he slipped his fingers under a small slab of concrete and heaved. Piet flashed his torch into the cavity.

'Wonderful!' he breathed.

There was a thick bunch of shiny coloured wires disappearing into the darkness of the duct. Frank whispered into his ear. 'Give me the torch. When you see me give one flash, cut everything you can see and then run like hell towards me.' Piet squeezed his arm in confirmation.

A quick breeze had sprung up and the sound of chattering Germans came across the airfield and then all was still. Two minutes seemed like ten. Piet strained his eyes into the darkness. He reached into the cavity and for a moment the wires felt like slippery snakes. He shivered, recoiled and reached in again. With one hand he pulled the thickest bunch of wires off the dusty concrete bottom and forced the jaws of the wire-cutters over the cable. He glanced up, just in time. There was the briefest flash of light. With all the force he could muster he squeezed the arms of the cutter. Nothing happened.

'*Verdomme,*' he said aloud and used all his strength.

A huge blue flash knocked him backwards. It blinded and stunned at the same time. The wire-cutters became red hot and he dropped them. The nearest lights on the airfield went out and, within a second, wailing sirens cut through the night.

Frank saw the flash as he cut through the lines. He stuffed the wire-cutters in his pocket, covered the ducting and crawled back towards Piet. He flashed the torch on his face. He was sitting up and shaking his head.

'Frank, I think I cut through power cables as well as the telephone lines.' There was a smooth smile on his blackened face.

'You most certainly did,' laughed Frank. 'It looks as though you cut through the cables for the runway lights.' The sound of sirens was getting nearer. 'Come on ... we've got to get out of here, ... right now!' He grabbed the wire-cutters and dropped them.

'OUCH! They're damned hot.' He used his cap to pick them up. He lowered his voice. 'Piet, how are your hands?'

'I think they're okay. Thank God I had my leather gloves on.' He stood quickly and looked at Frank. 'Let's go!'

'Quickly now, I'll cover the duct and scrape the soil over,' said Frank. 'Run like hell and keep down!' They ran like hares back towards their bikes. They found them and as their chests heaved they clambered onto the saddles.

'Frank, ... that was ... bloody ... good! ... You were ... great! ... Pedal like hell!'

They arrived at the house and collapsed like two great giggling children into the hallway. Marieke, in her night-dress, just looked at them. She shook her head. There was a smile on her lips. 'I presume that you two boy scouts have achieved what you set out to do?' Aukje and Harmen joined her. David sat at the top of the stairs.

Frank's eyes were shining and he was holding his stomach. 'Marieke, it was wonderful. I really enjoyed myself. Look at him.' He pointed at Piet who was black-faced and covered in mud. 'He cut through one of the power cables as well as the telephone lines.' He let out another roar of laughter.

Marieke brought them down to earth. There was banter in her voice. 'Piet Bokma, I think I've had enough of you tonight. Now, get on the phone to Sytske and tell her you're all right. Frank, get those clothes off and run the bath. You look as bad as him.' She turned to the children, 'You three, off to bed. We don't want anybody noticing that our lights are on at this time of the morning.' Her mind was working out the risks. 'Piet, you'd better stay in the spare room and leave early in the morning. I think, after your escapade, the Germans'll be searching every road in Friesland.' As she spoke, the sound of bombers droned overhead.

Frank hugged her. He could feel the warmth of her body against him.

He found it strangely exciting as though the danger had aroused him. She felt the same and clung to him.

'Marieke, you're wonderful. I love you.'

She looked into his eyes and touched his hair. The smell of his sweat aroused her. 'Darling, go and have a bath. I'll go upstairs.'

EIGHT

The cell leaders arrived one by one. Most walked, some cycled. They all came from different directions. The living-room was full. Frank was surprised by some of the faces as much as they were to see him. Marieke waited by the door and welcomed them all. The recent events had clearly brightened her whole personality. She wore a simple dress that made men look twice. The perfume was best French and she radiated excitement.

Dominee Paul de Vries began the meeting. 'Ladies and Gentlemen of Group Uncle, welcome to our first cell meeting. Before I start. May I thank Frank and Marieke for allowing us to gather here.' There were muttered thanks. 'I have posted look-outs all around the factory. They were in position before first light this morning. Young Harmen is on the roof at this time watching for any signal that they may give. This rope,' he pointed to a piece of string that came through the open window and was attached to the dinner bell, 'will be pulled if there's any sign of danger. Needless to say, the reason why we're here tonight is to hold a prayer meeting.' There was subdued laughter. He gave a brief smile. 'We have certain items to agree upon. However I'm sure that you would like to compliment Piet and Frank on the great job that they did at the airfield last night.' He paused for a moment to shake hands with the two men. He then turned and continued addressing the group. 'All the information that you've been passing along the system, must continue. London wants as much as we can get. I'm the only one who knows where van Hamel's transmitter is hidden and it's vital that we keep in contact with each other and at the same time keep our mouths firmly shut. Never mention names, never make idle chatter, but I think that you know all that.' He looked at all the faces in front of him. 'Now, the real reason why we're here is to listen to a proposal from Frank van der Meer.' He motioned to Frank. 'Would you like to explain?' Paul de Vries sat down on the edge of the circle.

Frank stood, folded his arms and looked at each person in turn. He spoke with his usual conviction, 'Firstly, I must say that I never thought that I would have a meeting like this in our house.' He glanced at Marieke and she smiled back at him. 'You know my beliefs and I think most of you know me. Yes, we can interfere with the German organisation and yes, we can carry out minor sabotage. But soon they'll take reprisals and I dread to think how they'll do that. But,' He waved a finger at the faces, 'is that really helping our people? Friesians are proud and independent. What was our watchword six hundred years ago? "Better dead than slaves". Some of our people want to be slaves and we will deal with them after the war is over by the due process of law. But, there is a group of our people in Friesland who are already being persecuted by the Nazis, and we know who they are, don't we?' There were united nods of agreement. 'We must save our people, whether they be Jew or gentile. I know we can't stop the trains. But we can stop people getting on them.' He saw the curious stares. 'Let's hide them! Let's take them into our homes! Let's build secret rooms! Let's feed and clothe them! Let's save them from the unknown! Let's help them to escape.' There was total silence. He took a deep breath. 'And that, Uncle, is my proposal.' He sat down and folded his arms.

For a moment the silence continued. A young man in blue overalls was the first to speak, '*Meneer* van der Meer, I think it's a great idea. But we could be dealing with hundreds, if not thousands of people. We just don't have the expertise to do this.'

Paul de Vries's quiet voice interrupted. 'The Church will support this proposal. I already have agreement from the other church leaders in Friesland.' He looked at Frank. 'I have to say this to you, Frank, other people all over Holland have been thinking along the same lines.'

The man spoke again, 'What we need are names of people who will help, and money. Yes, we'll need lots of money.'

'Money isn't a problem. Some people will do it as a duty to their country and others will do it because they believe it's right,' said Frank.

Joop Koopman shook his head, 'This could be organised chaos. We could have people hiding all over Friesland.'

'Yes, that's right,' said Paul simply. 'Our Government in London will give us money via bank loans here in Holland. We only have to ask.'

Joop continued, 'I can see the sense of it. I still say that you could have people diving into different houses on different days and not knowing where they are.'

'Yes, that's right,' Paul said again. 'I think the word "diving" is a good way of understanding what this proposal means. At least let's give it a try. Let's ask the people we trust to save at least one family.' He felt the atmosphere in the room. 'All right, I think we'll take a break for a few minutes. That'll give us time to discuss the matter amongst ourselves.'

They argued together for over an hour. Marieke spoke to a woman who was one of the cell leaders. They knew each other from somewhere.

'Marieke, I remembered where we met,' she said with a smile. 'It was at my daughter's wedding four years ago. You came with one of the guests.'

Marieke tapped her forehead, 'That's it! You're Mia Santema. How are you?'

'I'm fine. My daughter has settled down and I'm about to become a proud grandmother.'

Marieke laughed and all the men glanced at her. 'Where's she living now?'

Her friend's face quickly changed and she lowered her voice, 'She and her husband are living in Balk village, in the south of Friesland.'

'I know it well,' said Marieke with a tinge of curiosity on her face. She knew that Mia Santema had something else to say. Marieke was right.

'They have a German *Luftwaffe* officer billeted with them.' Marieke's heart froze. 'I think you may know him? His name is *Oberleutnant* Ernst Kraft.'

She nodded, 'Yes, I do know him.'

'Marieke, he's been absolutely superb. He brings food for the family and he's ever so helpful. If he wasn't German I could very easily get to like him.'

Their conversation was interrupted. Paul rose to his feet. 'Comrades, from what I can gather, I think we ought to put this matter to the vote. All those in favour of Frank's proposal please raise their hands.' Everybody looked at each other. Frank watched them carefully. Slowly the hands went up. It was unanimous. 'Comrades, I think the vote says it all and this meeting is now officially over. Good luck to all of you.' One or two stood.

'A minute of your time, ladies and gentlemen,' said Paul de Vries. They waited. 'Since we formed this group two years ago, I've been proud to lead it. But, I think the time has now come for me to step down.' He gave a broad smile. 'If I'm to help the Church to assist the "divers", as Joop calls them, then I would like to propose that Piet Bokma becomes the leader of Group Uncle.' There was only a moments hesitation. The nodding heads said it all.

Piet was straight faced and said quite simply, 'I agree.' There was spontaneous applause.

At the same time as Group Uncle met, another meeting was being held. Berlin had telephoned *Hauptsturmführer* Müller one hour after the raid on the airfield. Piet's blue flash had knocked out links with all the air attack warning outposts in Friesland and also to *Luftwaffe* Communications Headquarters in Arnhem. The raid had caused total chaos. Even as Müller listened to the tirade coming down his telephone, the search teams had failed to find the location of the attack. That task had to wait until daybreak.

Müller was furious. Leeuwarden had promised to be a nice easy job for him. He came to Friesland with the knowledge that the Dutch were civilised people, easily malleable to the ideas of the German Reich. With an impatience born of frustration he had summoned his advisors. There were three of them assembled in his new office. Recently the combined services of the SS had taken over a large insurance building on the south side of *het Zaailand*, the main square in the centre of Leeuwarden.

Oberleutnant Ernst Kraft stood stiffly to attention. At his side was the leader of the military wing of the NSB in Friesland. One other man stood casually to attention. He was dressed in the field-grey uniform of the SD. *Sturmscharführer* Hofmann was in charge of all secret police in the Leeuwarden district. This gathering made him apprehensive.

'*Heil* Hitler,' said Müller quietly. The hand merely waved the Führer salute. 'All sit.' His voice was edged with steel and he sat with arms tightly folded and looked at each man in turn. He began calmly. 'You know what happened last night. The airfield was sabotaged by Dutch terrorists. The damage to the *Reich* is enormous. Three bomber raids flew over Friesland to bomb the homeland before repairs could be made.' He unfolded his arms and banged a fist on the table. 'How did it happen? It must never happen again, NEVER!' The hands clasped tightly until the knuckles turned white. His handsome face was impassive but the eyes glowered and stared at each person in turn. 'You! ... You! ... and you, are all responsible for what happened last night.' One hand unclenched and a single finger pointed unwaveringly. 'Where was the airfield security? How did they get in? How did they know where the lines were? Who did it?' He lowered his eyes and the finger tapped on the table. 'I expect them caught and executed within the next twenty-four hours.' He stopped tapping and the finger pointed again. '*Sturmscharführer* Hofmann, what have got to say for yourself? You have enough men to police the whole of Berlin and yet it happened, why?' Before the man could open his mouth Müller continued, 'Go to your contacts, see if they can tell you who did this. If you don't have them within the next twenty-four hours, then I want a proclamation posted on every door in Leeuwarden. Tell them that if the terrorists are not handed over in twenty-four hours then the eight people presently being held in Leeuwarden prison will be executed.' He stood and looked down at them. 'Tell them that! Any questions?' He sat down.

Hofmann answered in his harsh Berlin accent, '*Hauptsturmführer*, the terrorists are getting worse. Over the last eight months terrorist groups have been springing up everywhere. Their newspapers get to everybody. Whatever we do they seem to find out about in advance.' His voice lowered respectfully, 'I agree with you, I've plenty of men, but most of them spend a lot of time looking for Jews. The Jews will soon become a big problem for us.' A smirk crossed his coarse features He thumbed at the man at his side. 'Ask our *NSB* comrade here, he's closer to the locals than I am.'

The *WA* was the military wing of the *NSB*. They dressed in the black uniforms of the *SS* and had the same ranks, although they were always outranked by their German comrades. *Obersturmführer* Postma was a fanatic. He was even more feared by his countrymen than the *SS* themselves. His German was faultless.

'*Hauptsturmführer* Müller, kill them now! Don't wait. Shoot the swine and put their bodies on the streets. We have to set an example of what happens to people who attack the *Reich*.' His eyes shone and he fingered the gold buckle of his belt.

Müller smiled, the voice was silky smooth. 'Postma, you don't yet understand the effects of calculated terror. You see, time is of the essence. Twenty-four hours makes them worry and they feel threatened. As the deadline approaches, the relatives of these eight men will start asking questions. The pressure will mount and who knows what things will come crawling out onto the streets. Time is on our side, use it Postma, ... use it!'

He turned to the *Oberleutnant*. 'What have you to say for yourself, Kraft?

This happened on your territory. Your Commanding Officer is furious. As *Luftwaffe* liaison officer he holds you partly responsible and so do I.' The hard edge had returned to his voice. The finger resumed its tapping.

Ernst shifted in his seat. '*Hauptsturmführer*, fences are already being re-enforced. Guards are being doubled and extra security lights have been brought in.' He took a deep breath. '*Fliegerhorst*-Leeuwarden is massive. It's one of the biggest bases in the Greater *Reich*. For the first two years the Dutch welcomed us. It took 7,500 local labourers to construct it and we brought much work and business to the area. I believe that this resistance is only small and we should use that fact to our advantage.'

Hofmann interrupted, '*Oberleutnant*, that's rubbish. I know of terrorist acts happening all over Friesland. They're increasing and they're becoming very clever.' He patted the *NSB* man on the shoulder. 'I agree with *Obersturmführer* Postma, hit them hard, all the time.' His dislike of the *Luftwaffe* was obvious. 'What do you people at the airfield know about what goes on around here? You sit in your nice warm offices and fly aeroplanes. You don't know what real work is all about.' With a wave of his gloved hand he dismissed him. 'Get out there and deal with them.'

Ernst looked at the man, 'I live with a Dutch family and I hear what they're saying.'

Postma said loudly, with his eyes flickering towards Müller, 'If they're saying anything against us, then arrest them and if you can't do it, then tell me. I'll have them into prison before you can say, "HEIL HITLER".'

Müller again stood. 'Gentlemen, you have your orders, now leave. Remember you have twenty-four hours.'

With his final words ringing in their ears, they rose from their seats, saluted and left his room.

Sturmscharführer Hofmann had no idea where to look for the saboteurs. The posters were displayed everywhere. He was given two names by the Green Police but they proved to be of no use. He still gave them three months in prison. Hofmann knew what he really wanted to do. From his office he telephoned to the next floor.

The telephone was picked up immediately, '*Obersturmführer* Postma speaking. ... Ah! ... *Sturmscharführer* Hofmann. It's good to hear from you. What can I do for you.' He lounged back in his chair.

'Postma, come to my room immediately.'

'*Jawohl, Sturmscharführer.*'

Two minutes later they were seated casually in Hofmann's office. Cigarettes dangled from their fingers. Through the wreaths of blue smoke Hofmann was the first to speak. There was a cat-like smile on his face. 'Postma, I presume you've found out nothing about the attack on the airfield?' He raised his thick eyebrows.

'No, ... apart from the two names that I gave to you, nothing. But I'm sure that ...'

'Forget it Postma. ... Just, forget it.' Hofmann leaned forward and an inane grin came over his face. 'But when we were with the *Hauptsturmführer*, I liked your idea about setting an example. Now that I really like.' He sat back. 'Let's arrange the execution now. Shall we?'

The Dutch-man nodded and his face was alight. '*Jawohl, Sturmscharführer*. I have an even better idea.' He received an affirmative nod. 'In the past we carried out executions in the yard at the back of the main prison in Leeuwarden. Nobody ever sees it happen. For these eight men I suggest that we blindfold them and take them into a field near the town. We can then shoot them in the open and the good citizens of Leeuwarden can watch.' He clenched his fist. 'Then they'll believe what we say. It'll be the best example that we can set.' He relaxed for a moment. 'But, we don't leave the bodies. They can be buried later at our convenience. We don't want martyrs. '

'Excellent, Postma.' Hofmann stubbed out the half-finished cigarette and clapped his hands. 'Excellent, we'll do it tomorrow. Now go and organise it. Tell Koopman of the Dutch Police to leak it to some of his men. It'll be around town in no time at all.'

'It's impossible. They can't do it.' Frank's face was deathly white. 'We've got to stop them.'

Joop looked at him, 'I'm so sorry Frank. There's nothing we can do about it. There'll be *SS* everywhere. Even the convoy is being heavily guarded by Green Police. It's set to take place at 6-30 tomorrow morning.' He glanced at his wrist-watch. 'That's in another six hours.'

Frank stood in the hall of his house in his dressing-gown. The knock at the door at this time of the night had set his heart beating fast but Joop was by himself.

'Don't blame yourself, Frank, it's not your fault. The Nazis were looking for an excuse to do something like this. It's sheer coincidence that your raid came at this time.'

Frank looked helpless, 'Do I know any of these men?' he said imploringly.

Joop shook his head, 'It's better that you don't know the answer to that question.'

'Joop, wait here, I'll tell Marieke.'

'You don't have to, Frank. I heard every word.' She was sitting at the bottom of the stairs. He turned, she was crying.

'I want to be there. Where will it take place,' said Frank softly.

'I can't tell you not to go, but I understand why you must.' There were tears in his eyes. 'I've already let Piet know. It'll take place on the road to Jelsum village near the airfield. For God's sake, Frank, be careful.' He left and closed the door quietly.

There was no sleep for either of them that night. Frank was up at four o'clock. He bathed and dressed and sat in front of the embers of the fire in the living-room. He prayed silently for over an hour until Marieke gently shook him.

'Frank, it's time to go. Please have some breakfast, it's cold outside.' He shook his head and stood. They embraced for a long time. He pushed himself away, took his coat off the hat-stand and left the house.

He was not the only person to stand in the half-light of the early dawn. There were small groups of people near some bare trees. It was a damp miserable place, close to a small farm at the side of a country lane. The winter green of the field had been churned into mud by the lorries of the SS. They were parked in a half-circle. Their headlights shone onto a small area of green. Blue exhaust smoke and white mist mingled to form a hellish halo around the set stage. A hundred soldiers were on guard.

Frank stood alone, hands in his pockets and a scarf wrapped tightly round his neck. He noticed neither the thick mud nor the creeping cold. He caught a movement off to his left. Piet gave a half-wave, Frank nodded. They remained alone.

The first car was a black Mercedes. Behind it two heavy lorries were followed by another black car. The first lorry pulled into the circle. The tarpaulin flap was raised, the tail-flap dropped with a crash. The interior was jet black. The doors of the first car swung open. Two men stepped out, Hofmann and Postma. Frank gripped the pockets of his coat and bit his lip. He could hear their laughter. The last car waited with its headlamps dipped. He knew who the lone occupant was.

There was no ceremony, the few people there edged forward from the trees. The back of the second lorry was thrown open by two SS. One by one the black- hooded men emerged out of the darkness of the lorry and into the glare of the headlights. Each one of them was guided forward by two soldiers. They put them in a rough line and left them. They wore prison clothes and were indistinguishable from each other. Their heads twisted and turned as they sought the comfort of each others presence. Suddenly there was an awful silence. A voice shouted above the sound of the running engines.

'TAKE AIM!'

Their bodies stiffened to attention and abruptly their ragged voices cut through the still, cold air, 'ORANGE ABOVE ALL! LONG LIVE THE QUEEN!'

'FIRE! damn you, FIRE!' Hofmann stepped forward and took over the execution.

From within the darkness of the rear of the first lorry, stabs of flame shot out. The staccato ripping sound of a single machine-gun clamoured through the air. The six men fell where they stood. Hofmann and Postma drew their pistols, walked forward and placed single shots into each one of the black hoods. Within a minute, a group of soldiers rushed forward picked up the bodies and threw them like rag dolls into the back of a lorry. The convoy left the murder site as quickly as it had arrived.

Frank waited until everybody had gone. He was motionless. His eyes saw the mud, the blood and the absolute horror of it all. The scene kept flickering through his brain in a never ending nightmare. He had no idea of how long he stood there.

Marieke was on one side of him and Piet on the other. They gently put their arms around him and together moved him out of the field. As they put him into the car he looked at Marieke.

'Why does God allow this to happen?' he said softly.

NINE

Lottie Cohen prepared herself for the arrival of her letter. It never came. She was curious and invited Rabbi Jacobs to visit her. She liked him and even in these difficult times of strict food rationing she laid out the best delicacies she could find. Tiny pieces of home-made cake and a single apple, sliced so thinly that it was transparent. The tea in her small tea-pot had been used twice before. She sat and waited for the doorbell to ring. Her children were out and she had a moment to gather her thoughts. Already some of her friends had left for Westerbork. On her book-shelf were the post-cards that they had sent before leaving for Germany. She kept them as mementoes of friendship. Some of her relatives had just disappeared into thin air. She found it hard to comprehend what was happening.

The aroma of the tea rose from the tea-pot on its stand as the small candle flame underneath kept it warm and ready.

She wore a simple, dark blue velvet dress that reached just below the knees and showed off her calves and small feet to their best advantage. Her long black hair shone with the careful brushing that she carried out each day. Childbirth had not affected her figure and she was as slim as the day she was married.

The gentle tap on the front door brought her back to reality.

'Do come in, Rabbi Jacobs,' she called from her chaisé-longué.

There was a moment as the sounds from the busy street outside came into the house, then it ceased as the door closed.

He came into the room and smiled down at her, '*Mevrouw* Cohen, you really must keep that front door locked. There're many people nowadays who would take advantage of a single Jewish woman.' She merely smiled and extended her hand towards him. He gently touched the back of her fingers with his lips.

'Nonsense, Rabbi. They can take what they like and, any way, I've my housemaid to look after me.' She waved to a strategically placed chair. 'Please sit down.' He made himself comfortable.

'I understand that you wanted my advice, *mevrouw* Cohen.'

She smiled, 'Please, oh please, Rabbi, call me Lottie. I'm not a terribly formal person.' He returned the smile and nodded. 'I have some tea here. May I pour you a cup?' She leant over and poured the tea into two delicate china cups and handed him one. His nose caught the delicate swirl of her perfume.

She continued, 'Yes, I do need your advice. Perhaps you could tell me why I've not yet received my letter? All my friends have had one.' Her legs on the chaisé-longué suddenly tucked themselves under the skirt of her dress and she patted the velvet into shape.

He watched her and took a deep breath, Rabbi or not, he was still a man. 'I too haven't received a letter, ... eh, ... Lottie.' She nodded. 'I think I know why.' He reached into the pocket of his sombre suit and opened two pages of printed script. 'You were born in Germany in Breslau, I gather.' He looked up at her.

She frowned. 'Correct, Rabbi. But I came to live in Leeuwarden ten years ago. I saw what Hitler was doing to the Jews.'

He continued reading, 'Your father was a senior officer in the German Army in the First World War. It says here that he was awarded the Iron Cross, First Class.'

'Yes, quite right.' She pointed to a small picture-frame hanging on the wall near to the door. 'There it is. It was given to him by the Kaiser himself. But, my dear Rabbi, that's all over now. He died some years ago and now I'm a naturalised Dutch citizen.'

He nodded respectfully and put the folded papers back into his pocket. 'I'm sure that's why you've not yet received your letter. You're fortunate. The longer it takes the better for you. You know that the Germans are having problems with their attack on Russia. Yesterday they lost Stalingrad and a million men. The Allies have taken North Africa and there're are rumours of a landing in Italy. The war can't last for much longer and then the persecution of our people will stop.'

'All Dutch people are being persecuted, Rabbi.' She reminded him. 'I'm quite willing to take my place in the queue for the labour camps.' Lottie gave that peculiarly nervous laugh. 'I may look a bit thin but I'm really very strong. A year working for the Germans won't do me any harm. I can then return and carry on where I left off. As you say, by then the war may be over.'

He shook his head and smiled, 'Lottie, you're a wonderful woman. Warm and a good mother. You're also very naïve. I've not heard of any of our people returning from Germany. They just disappear.'

'That can't be true, Rabbi. Look,' she pointed at the post-cards, 'I've had so many of these. They're all the same, happy and excited about the journey.'

'Lottie, have you ever had a postcard from Germany?' She shook her head and a frown crossed her face. 'We know that our people are not staying in the German resettlement camps. They're actually going to camps in Poland.'

Lottie shrugged her shoulders and pouted her lips, 'Germany, Poland, who cares? Work is work no matter where it is.'

Rabbi Jacobs was becoming a little exasperated with her. 'If you're that keen to help, then I have a job for you.'

She clapped her hands and her face lit up, 'Oh, please tell me. I really want to work.'

'At Westerbork the Jewish Administration needs help. Your German is excellent and the amount of paperwork there is enormous. I received a letter only yesterday asking me if I could supply somebody who could help them. It means that you'd be made an official of the Jewish Council and it means travelling to Westerbork three times a week to help with the documentation.' He looked at her questioningly. 'Can I put your name forward?'

'Of course, Rabbi. When do I start?' She swung her legs off the chaisé-longué.

'Next week will be fine. But what about your children?'

'They're old enough to look after themselves. Anyway, other people live near here and I'm not the only one who's having difficulties.'

Rabbi Jacobs placed his cup and saucer back on the small table and rose from his chair. 'Lottie, I hope I've been able to help.'

'Yes, Rabbi,' she smiled again. 'You've given me a sense of purpose. Thank you very much. At least I'm going to be doing something useful.' Lottie rose to her feet.

'No, please, ... I'll see myself out.' He kissed the proffered hand, smiled, and left the house.

The plans that Frank and Marieke had made appeared to be working. Jan and Tineke de Bruin had merely locked their front door and, to all intents and purposes, just disappeared. They had been in the underground room at the factory for a month. The New Year had been and gone. They celebrated it with the van der Meer family behind closed curtains and to the strains of music broadcast by the BBC.

Their routine was the same each day. Rise at 7-30, eat a small breakfast. Read, talk and study until midday and then eat, rest and read. Only at seven in the evening were they allowed to creep quietly into the van der Meer house.

Frank had provided some comforts for the family. He had made wooden partitions and Jan had helped to erect them in the room. It gave them two bedrooms and a small toilet. During the harshest part of the winter the stone floor had proved to be very chilly and they had laid old planks of wood down to prevent the cold striking up through the stone slabs. Boredom was the main problem and each of them had to find his own way of avoiding it. They played every game they could think of including some that had not been seen before. They knew the factory routine. The machines above them each had their own noises and vibrations that came down through the ceiling of their abode. Some were soothing and helped them to sleep, others hammered away and they had to put cotton wool in their ears. Even though the three access doors were a tight fit, dust still showered down like a fine mist and by the end of a busy day in the factory they were covered in tiny white particles. The only advantage of living under a noisy factory was that during the day they could make as much noise as they wished. At night it was another matter. They crept about and whispered. The stone room acted as an echo chamber and in the early days Frank had to warn them about noise. Perhaps the greatest relief to them was the electricity supply. It gave them light, heat and warmth. David had discovered quite by accident that one of the ventilation shafts was wide enough for him to squeeze down. It was cold and damp but eventually it came to a dead stop against an iron grille hanging over the waters of the Dokkumer Ee. On one dark night from the river side Frank and Jan had loosened the securing rivets and left the grill hanging by a single bolt. It was a simple matter for David to unscrew the nut from the inside and there was a ready-made escape route. Frank had moored an old rowing boat just below the exit to the shaft to make any possible escape easier.

It was time for dinner and Aukje went from the house to the factory via the office entrance. In that way nobody could see her movements from outside the building.

The boxes over the trap doors looked heavy enough but Aukje was able to move them with ease. They had small wheels beneath and would only move in one direction. Three short bangs on the door and one long gave the well-known Victory sign to the de Bruins below. It took two minutes to free the door upwards and they stepped out.

'Another day, Aukje,' said Tineke, with a wan smile, 'and another night.'

Aukje had made up her mind to always be happy when she saw the de Bruins. She smiled, 'The showers waiting. Whose turn is it this time, Tineke?'

'Mine, please,' replied a dusty Jan. His smile was genuine. The twice weekly shower was something not to be missed. David helped Aukje to secure the doors and put the boxes back into place. As his parents crept through the darkness of the factory, he stole a quick embrace from her.

Frank made sure that all the doors were securely locked, something that he never had to do before the war. The curtains were tightly closed and they sat down for dinner. Jan said prayers and then intoned the Jewish prayer of thanksgiving.

'We're lucky being with you,' said Tineke, looking at Marieke. 'Good food is becoming scarce and you always seem to eat well.'

'It's a pleasure,' said Marieke, 'Friesland is full of good things and we must share them.' She did not mention that for the rest of the day they ate hardly anything at all.

'Tineke, I think I should add,' said Frank, 'that the resistance is, shall we say, "redistributing" ration stamps. Anybody who's hiding a "diver" gets extra stamps.' The soup was finished and Marieke spooned out the vegetables.

'How many people are hiding now, Frank?' said Jan as he put a forkful of carrots into his mouth.

'It's hard to say. At this stage, hundreds I would think.' Frank sipped from a glass of water. 'We're also hiding students from Amsterdam. The Germans have ordered that all students be rounded up for labour. Some have gone, some have got jobs. A lot have dived under. I know at least twenty not a kilometre from here.' He laughed making them all look up.

'What is it, *Heit*?' asked Aukje.

'Who would have thought a year ago that Friesland would become a huge hotel for people from all over Holland. We supply the food and the rooms.' There were nodding smiles from their guests.

'David and Aukje, quickly now, the dishes,' said Marieke. The table was precisely laid for four. The de Bruins used plates and cutlery that were extra to the table. When they had finished a course the extra three sets were quickly washed and put away. If the house was raided, or somebody visited them, then the table was laid just for the family. Anyway it gave more time for the two of them to be alone in the kitchen.

'What's the news outside, Frank?' said Jan as he finished eating.

Frank placed his knife and fork back on the plate. 'Not good. The round up of Jews is getting bigger and more efficient. Rabbi Jacobs told me that the transports to Westerbork are increasing. Jews are only allowed in certain provinces. Soon there will be none of your people in Friesland. He also told me that Lottie Cohen has volunteered to help at Westerbork. She's travelling to the camp three times a week. In that way she's avoiding her call up.'

'Frank, I'd love to see her again,' Tineke said. 'It's been a long time since we last met. Down in our cellar we're starved of company. Is it safe for her to come here?'

He looked at Marieke, 'I can't see a big problem. If she comes here then she won't know that you're hiding in the factory. I'll contact the Rabbi tomorrow.'

'Oh, thank you, Frank. I don't know how we would live without you.'

'Exactly,' said Jan quietly.

Frank moved in his chair and changed the subject. 'I want to tell you about a little something that Harmen and I have made over the last couple of weeks. Son, perhaps you could explain?'

Harmen stood up and his face glowed with pride. 'It was my idea really. I thought that if the Germans ever raided this house and you were still here then there's no way out of this room apart from the French-windows into the back garden. I'm sure the *moffen* would have that covered. So this is what we've done.' He casually walked over to the fireplace, peered at the brick work and suddenly aimed a kick at the third course of bricks. There was a soft click, and a knee-high hole appeared. Harmen continued. 'The chimneys are very wide, the flue for the smoke only takes up half the space of the chimney breast. If you climb through this hole and stand up you'll see that there's a small ladder going upwards. Climb it and when you reach the top you end up with a trap door on your left. Push it and you're on the roof. By keeping to the edge of the roof you can walk to the inspection ladder that leads down to the factory. From there it's only a minute to your room.' He gave a satisfied grin. 'I wouldn't recommend staying in the chimney very long. Although the ladder access is separate to the flue it can be hot.' He pushed the brick panel back into place.

'Can I try it?', said Jan. Harmen nodded.

They all heard the soft click. Jan bent over and in a flash he disappeared. They waited and waited. There was a tap on the office door at the top of the stairs. Harmen strode towards the door of the living-room and dashed upstairs.

'You're right! It works,' shouted Jan. He faced them with black sooty marks all over his face. They all laughed loudly. But it was the laughter of tension and not of happiness.

TEN

Rabbi Jacobs was as good as his word. He arranged for Lottie to travel to Westerbork and it was three weeks before he saw her again. He had also accepted Frank's invitation and late one evening he cycled with her to the van der Meer house. When she arrived they were all shocked. The change was obvious. She had aged more in those two weeks of her life than in the last ten years.

Lottie's smile was as pale as her face and she spoke softly, 'Hello everybody, I must apologise for my appearance. I've hardly had any time to look after myself.' However Rabbi Jacobs noticed that she still wore that same perfume. Her dress was plain white cotton, loosely made and her beautiful hair was tied up in a tight bun that nestled in the nape of her neck. The jet-black hair contrasted sharply with the whiteness of her skin.

Lottie refused to sit on the comfortable sofa. Instead she sat starkly upright on an antique wooden chair. There were no social pleasantries. She began slowly, 'Rabbi, everybody, I have to tell you. I have to.' She paused and crossed her long legs. 'It's not what I imagined. It's, ... it's, ... well, ... different to what I expected.' They waited patiently. Her voice was faint but grew angrier. 'My job is completing forms, thousands of them. White ones, grey ones and rubber stamps. Oh my God! Rubber stamps, ... red, green, black, ... every colour of the rainbow. ... Duplicate, triplicate, carbon copies. Stapled, paper-clipped, checked, double checked. ... Referenced, cross referenced. ... Filed, stored, and bound. Yes, Rabbi, bound in leather. There's a book binder in the camp.' She paused for a moment in her obvious frustration and then gathered some strength. 'Everybody that comes off the trains has to fill in forms, pages of them.' She put her hands to her face, rubbed her eyes and continued. 'I don't know why they have to complete them. When they get on the transports to Poland the escort guards just take the list, not the files. We have one whole block full of files. All catalogued, in long rows on shelves. It's a, ... it's a catalogue of Dutch Jews.' She stopped talking abruptly, as though waiting for questions. There were none. Marieke handed her a glass of water. She took it and sipped, her eyes stared into the distance. 'I love them all, I love them all. My people arrive, a thousand at a time in cattle wagons. They stink and they're lost, totally lost. We sort them into men for the men's barracks and women for the women's barracks; the children go to the crèche. If they're sick, we have a hospital with a thousand beds. If they're hungry, we feed them; there's plenty of food. They only stay a week or so and then they wait for the lists. All life is controlled by the list. We all wait for the list, even I wait for the list, although I'm a *Prominent*.'

'What is it, Lottie? What is the list?' said Frank, in a voice that was so gentle.

She looked at him with curiosity. 'It's the list Frank. ... It's the list.' She thought about his question and then understood. 'Every Monday night, although it's usually the early hours of Tuesday morning, the Germans and the Jewish section leaders decide who's leaving and then I have to type the list. There's usually about a thousand people on it. The section leaders then go round the barracks and post the lists on the walls. Within thirty minutes after I've typed it out everybody knows who's on the transports. When I first arrived I didn't know what the transports were, so one morning I went to see for myself. You're not allowed near the wagons but I was able to watch from the nearest barracks. ... I wish I hadn't gone.' Again she stopped talking. Frank could see that her face was wet with perspiration. She fidgeted on the chair and her hands kept fluttering to her face and then back onto her lap.

'About thirty, unpainted cattle wagons in a long row with a locomotive at one end. There's a coach for the guards. The doors of the wagons were open and I could see inside. Even from where I was standing I could smell the stink of excreta and ... something else, ... it was, ... Oh my God, human suffering. There were names and dates gouged into the woodwork. There's a single bucket in the middle of each wagon and some had piles of straw in the corner.' Again she stopped and this time her eyes were filled with a deep fire. 'You know, they even transport sick people and they have the luxury of paper mattresses to lie on.' Lottie stood for a moment, looked around the room and then sat down again. 'I waited for my people to arrive. The railway line has an asphalt path running down one side of its sidings. It's swept clean every day. I watched and the first people to arrive were men in brown overalls pushing barrows of luggage. Suitcases and rucksacks full with things from another list.' Frank glanced at Jan and received a haunted look. 'Some of the men are known to all of us. One of them sings popular songs. Another is a wonderful piano player. They say he can play Beethoven's Ninth as jazz. Both of them are favourites of the commandant, *Obersturmführer* Gemmeker. He's put them in special houses with their wives.' Her description came out in staccato sentences. 'As I watched, I saw the people beginning to arrive. They came in long organised columns. The children looked so innocent. The Green Police appeared everywhere. They had guns over their shoulders and looked ... oh, ... so casual. They load them carefully, so many per wagon. Sometimes families travel together but for most times they could be anywhere on the train. It doesn't take long. The guards check the names over and over again. They use the lists that I typed. ... I typed, ... I can't believe it. It's as though it's because of me that they're going.' She stopped for a moment searching for inner strength. Her voice was almost a whisper. 'The final act of terror is when the commandant appears. He's handsome. Rumour has it that he's quite young.' She looked Aukje full in the face. 'My dear, he could be your teacher.' She looked away again. 'His face is straight, he shows no feeling. Gemmeker walks the full length of the train and then back again. He seems to look through you, I imagine that he can see me, but of course he can't. He has a secretary. She's Jewish and she follows him everywhere. Everybody hates her. I saw another group appear. They're the other *Prominent* Members of the Jewish council in the camp. They strut about trying to be like Germans. We all know that one day they'll be transported as well.' She stopped and her face froze and she added softly, 'Just like me.'

Marieke came up to her and grasped her hands. Lottie forcefully pushed her away, 'I've not yet finished telling you,' she said sharply. Marieke retreated to her chair.

'The last man to join the ceremony of departure is the *Oberdienstleiter*. He's a German Jew. Massive, dressed in black and he still wears his yellow star. I'm ashamed of him. He marches around and stands next to the commandant. He dwarfs him. The doors are banged tightly shut.' She moved her hands from her face to her ears, 'I can still hear that awful noise. The commandant uses a bike to cycle up and down the train for his final check. When all is correct he gives a brief wave and the train's whistle gives a penetrating scream. That made me cringe. It's like ... a trumpet call from the devil. I saw the train move out of Westerbork. Through the small, steel grills I could see hands waving and eyes staring at nothing. That was my first transport of 956 people that I saw leave Holland.' She shook her head and the black hair shone. 'There are only 140,000 Jews in the whole country. At this rate they'll all be gone in three months.' Lottie slumped back into her chair and her thin body sagged with exhaustion.

The Rabbi stepped forward. He produced a silver hip flask from his pocket and looked questioningly at Frank. The returned nod made him lift the flask to her lips. She sipped and a little colour returned to her face. She grasped the flask firmly and took a full mouthful. Lottie spluttered and sat up, a little of her old sparkle returned.

'Rabbi Jacobs, where the hell do you get French brandy from in times like these?' He smiled at her.

She ate a little and for some time said nothing.

'Lottie, we can hide you. Why don't you become a diver?' said Frank.

'Frank,' she said with that gentle smile, 'my people need me. I couldn't possibly hide from them.'

'But what can you do, one person to help so many people?' said Tineke.

'I can help the sick. I can talk to the old. I can feed the children and, most importantly, I can try and give them some hope. You see,' she turned to Rabbi Jacobs, 'it's not the spiritual leaders that can help all those people. Of course, we're allowed to hold our religious ceremonies. No, it's the personal things that one human being can do for another. I can move through the camp freely, so I can deliver a little coffee here, and some milk for a baby, there. I've been writing letters and cards for people to post to friends. And the people I meet, artists, doctors, lawyers, philosophers and everybody from everywhere. It's like seeing the Jewish nation all in one place.' There was a brief smile. 'So you see everybody, I must keep going. Rabbi, I'm staying for five days a week now. I have my own tiny space in the *Prominent* barracks. When I return there tomorrow, I know that there'll be messages waiting for me and people to see.'

Harmen had been watching. Lottie had seriously affected him, '*Mevrouw* Cohen.' She turned to face him. 'What happens after Westerbork? Where do people go to? Does it worry you?'

She thought for a moment and gave him a wonderful smile, 'Young man, questions, questions. Why do the young always want answers? There's a belief amongst my people that they all go to heaven, as one day we all will.' She shook her head, 'They go to Poland to labour for the Nazis. I hear that they go to a big work camp near a village called Auschwitz. There're rumours that many of them die there in the bad work conditions.' She shrugged her narrow shoulders. 'But, again, we don't know for sure. There're some awful things said about these camps but we can't prove any of them. However, there's some hope. Members of our intelligentsia are sometimes sent to a castle in the village of Barneveld in the middle of Holland. I know of some who have gone directly there instead of Westerbork. The Germans have also set up a Jewish family centre at another castle in a place in Germany called Theresienstadt. I want to persuade the *Oberdienstleiter* to try and arrange for some of our older people to go there.'

Harmen remained silent but Frank asked again. 'Lottie, most of the Jews in Leeuwarden have now gone to Poland ....'

'I know, Frank. I see all their names, I can tell you exactly how many have left,' she said brusquely.

'No, you miss my point ...'

Again she interrupted, 'No, I don't! I know exactly what your point is and the answer is still, no!'

Frank persisted. 'Lottie, you must save yourself. Somebody has to live to tell the story about what's happening to your people. After all, there're so few of you who have actually lived through life at Westerbork.'

Lottie's presence dominated the room. She was a contrast of black and white. 'Frank, you'll never understand, never. I'll go when my time comes. I look forward to seeing all the friends that I've made. We'll meet again, either in Poland, or in heaven and I don't really mind which.'

'What about your children and the rest of your family?' said Marieke, almost in a whisper.

The question shook Lottie's composure. She took a deep breath. 'That's something that I've thought about a great deal. When my time comes I'm sure that then I'll make the right decision. My family are with me and we pray to God for guidance. We'll never split up. We'll all go together when the time comes.' She reached in her bag and produced her identity card. 'At the moment I have a red stamp saying *"Stammliste"*, I'm exempt from transportation. I don't know how long that exemption will last for.' She shook herself. 'Frank, I'm sorry, but I'm very tired. Could I go home now, please?'

'Of course,' said Rabbi Jacob, 'I'll take you.'

Marieke asked, 'Lottie, you haven't eaten tonight and I've made up some sandwiches for you. Aukje, could you get the parcel please? I hope you don't mind, but I've taken the liberty of packing some other things for you to take to Westerbork with you.'

Lottie's face lit up and she clapped her hands. 'Oh Marieke, you're wonderful. Thank you so much. Frank, may I ask a favour of you?' He nodded. 'Could you let me have some writing paper and stamps. The people always forget to take stamps for letters.' She fumbled with her black leather hand-bag. 'Of course, I'll pay for them.'

Frank reached over and closed her bag. 'Don't be silly. It's the least I can do.' He stopped and thought for a moment. 'Listen, I can arrange for things to be collected. Let me know what you need and I'll make sure that they're delivered.'

'Thank you, very much,' she said with her eyes shining out of dark sockets.

When they had gone, Tineke looked at Frank, 'Somehow, we've got to save the Cohen family.'

Frank smiled, 'It's going to be difficult. Lottie's a stubborn person, she'll find it hard to resist.'

'I know exactly what you mean,' said Marieke with a knowing smile. For the first time that night Frank relaxed and laughed.

ELEVEN

In Leeuwarden it was a hot day and the sun reflected harshly off the narrow canals. Frank never liked to linger in the centre of town, there were too many uniforms and too many dangers. As he turned a corner into the main street his way was blocked by two men. They were quite obviously Gestapo. He recognised their dark suits immediately. He stopped his bike and faced them.

'*Passe, bitte!*'

Frank thought to himself that they never bothered to speak Dutch anymore. He reached in his pocket and pulled out the pink identity card. They snatched it off him. One stared into his eyes without moving. The other scrutinised the card closely. He held it up to the light and ran a dirty fingernail over the photograph.

'Van der Meer, where are you going?' The voice was totally disinterested.

Frank carefully explained that he was on his way to the *Hotel de Kroon*. They pushed the card back at him and he cycled off down the street. He could feel their eyes watching him. His heart sank as he approached the main railway station. There was a line of Green Police. Before he even stopped pedalling, he again produced the identity card. Not a word was spoken between them and they returned the card and waved him on.

Lottie's words rang in his ears, "We'll all go together when the time comes." Frank watched the scene in front of him. There must have been a hundred people. They all wore their yellow stars, even the children. The queue was quiet and infinitely patient. Nobody spoke. Outside the station in the midday sun sat twelve yellow starred civilians behind six long wooden tables. They were bent in concentration and every minute or so, without heads lifting, hands stabbed out and more papers were handed over by the people at the front of the queue. Frank watched the process and it chilled his heart.

He saw the families move off together towards a special siding near the station entrance. It was well away from the main platforms. He gripped the handlebars tightly. They were being pushed into cattle wagons. He counted fifteen and Lottie kept flashing into his mind, he was watching what she had described and it was being repeated here, in his town. It did not take long. The sound of the heavy sliding doors crashing shut made him shiver. He wanted to cry but he held the tears back. The Green Police watched him and took no action. Frank understood. They wanted him to see what was happening. Frank could take no more and he turned away towards the hotel, pushing his bicycle in front of him.

His way was barred by a man and a woman. They were ordinary looking and about the same age as himself and quite well dressed. As he tried to wheel his bicycle past them they merely moved to block his way.

This slow dance went on for a minute. Frank was a patient man but his exasperation was beginning to show.

The man saw this and spoke. '*Meneer*, please help us?' He spoke in a whisper.

Before Frank could reply the man slowly stretched out a clenched hand and, for a moment, he thought that the man was asking for money and, with a sigh, he reached for his wallet. The hand opened to reveal a crumpled yellow star. It quickly closed again. Their eyes followed Frank's every move.

The Green Police were still behind him. Frank was quick. The war had sharpened his instincts. He grasped the outstretched hand.

'*Meneer, mevrouw*. It's so good to see you again. I was just going for tea in the hotel.' He waved to the right. 'Perhaps, you'd like to join me?' Before shock could register on their pale faces, he linked the woman's arm and began to walk away. The smile and the voice soothed them. ... 'And how's your mother? ... Well, I hope?' She nodded dumbly. Frank looked at the man's astonished face. '*Meneer*, I hear you've been ill? You'll soon be better.' He continued the one-sided banter. A Green Policeman suddenly appeared from the right blocking his way. Frank realised that if he wanted identity cards then all was lost, the "J" would be a death sentence for all of them.

The flashing smile worked again. 'Good day to you, a lovely day it is as well.'

Frank just walked straight past him leading his new found friends. The policeman nodded and actually smiled. Frank swore that the man could hear his heart pounding away under his ribs.

They reached the steps of the hotel. Frank parked his bike and ushered the man and woman up the steps and through the door. Dirk was waiting.

He grasped Frank's arm and said quietly, 'I watched it all. Wonderful. How the hell did you get away with it! ... Quick, you two, follow me!' He led them through the empty foyer and behind the curtained cellar door. 'Wait down there,' he whispered. Dirk turned back to Frank, 'My friend, I know exactly what's just happened. For God's sake act normally and sit down at the table.'

Frank wanted to sit and relax. He couldn't. He felt exhilarated, the adrenaline still coursed through his body. The words ground out through clenched teeth. 'We've got to help them, Dirk. We've got to!'

Dirk held his arm. 'All right, Frank! All right! Just calm down and let's think logically.' He grabbed the jug of water and two upturned glasses from a tray and filled them. He pushed one into Frank's trembling hand.

'Dirk, I watched them loading the wagons. It's beyond belief. Why? Oh why, do they just stand and take it?' He drank the whole glass of water in one gulp and it seemed to calm him.

'I watch it every week through the side window of the restaurant and I ask myself the same question. But, Frank, you saw it. There's nothing that you or I can do to stop it happening.' They stopped talking.

Eventually Dirk stood and said, 'Come on, I've got a surprise for you in the cellar.' They pushed open the heavy door and walked down the steps.

The man and woman were standing nervously near the wine racks. They held each other's hand and looked anxiously at Dirk.

'*Meneer*, we're sorry if we put you in any danger. ...' Before he could finish, Dirk laughed.

'Don't worry about it. Help yourself to a glass of wine.' He pointed to the open bottle. 'That should calm you down a bit and then please sit down.' Dirk smiled at the woman and guided her towards the chair and gently pushed her down onto the seat. He turned to Frank, 'Follow me, my friend.' He walked past the still shocked couple and through a small archway into the next cellar.

It was cooler and pitch black. Dirk struck a match and reached up to light a candle mounted high on the brick wall.

'For my next trick, watch this,' he whispered secretively. Frank stood and watched. As Dirk walked across the brick floor his shadow cast dancing patterns on the walls of the cellar. He dragged an empty wine-rack to one side to reveal a heavy wooden door. 'Give me a hand, my friend. It's a bit heavy.' He began to pull on the rusty iron handle. Frank leant over and added his strength. For a moment nothing happened, and then it burst open. Dirk reached up and took down the candle holder off the wall. He crooked his finger and motioned Frank to follow.

What he saw made him jump. In the flickering light of the single candle, sitting hunched together, were eight people. Four adults; two young, two old and four children. Even by the pale light of the candle, Frank's eyes immediately focused on the yellow stars.

'May I introduce the Levisson family. Grandfather and grandmother, mother and father and sons and daughters. Levisson family may I introduce my friend, Frank van der Meer.' He bowed theatrically. They rushed forward to shake hands with Frank. Dirk watched the look on his friend's face. The children were young and their wide open eyes reflected the candle flame. They clutched at their mother.

Dirk was happy. 'I'll tell you about it.' He lifted the candle. 'The cellars of this esteemed hotel were once served by boats from the canal. They arrived at a small opening in the wall of the canal, undid the door and carried food and drink down this passage and into the cellar. It's not been used for years. I only opened it up some months ago to let in a bit of fresh air.'

Frank was curious, 'But how did the family get here? Surely not through the hotel foyer?' He smiled at them.

Dirk became serious, 'Like you, I've seen the loading of the trains for Westerbork. I got so angry about it that I've started waiting near the street where this cellar access is located. If you open the door at the other end then you can stand in the shadows of the canal wall and nobody can see you. All I had to do was to wait until I knew that there was a transport leaving. If I saw somebody coming down the street. ... a quick check, it's only a narrow street, up like a Jack-in-the-box grab a family, and down again.' He beamed with pleasure, 'So far nobody has refused my hospitality.'

The Levissons gazed in amazement. Frank looked just as amazed. 'Dirk, how long have you been doing this for? ... And how many?'

His friend raised his hand, 'Well, let me think now. Over the last two months,' He scratched his head, 'Eh, ... probably about a hundred and twenty people.'

Frank clapped him on the shoulder, 'That's amazing. I can't believe it.'

'Before you ask, Frank. A lot of the hotel rubbish is collected by a barge twice a week. The skipper is well-known to me. He collects the extra, shall we say, "goods", and passes them along the line. A free bottle of gin works wonders. Although I am getting a little short. As far as I know, all my new friends have new homes in the villages of beautiful rural Friesland.'

The two families joined them in the cold passage and shook hands. Dirk gave out cigars. Grandfather Levisson waited for a quiet moment.

He coughed politely, there was silence. 'Meneer Haan and Meneer van der Meer. On behalf of both families, I would like to thank you for saving us.' Dirk tried to wave his hand but the grey-bearded old man grasped it and held it to his face and gently touched the fingers with his lips. 'God will be with you, my son, for ever.' Still holding Dirk's hand he continued. 'I think, about now, the train will be leaving for Westerbork. Let us silently pray together for our brothers and sisters.' The narrow cellar, the light from the one candle and the utter silence made the prayer more powerful. For some minutes they stood, until the candle flickered out. There was a splutter of light as Dirk lit a match.

'Amen. Back into the cellar everybody until I can find some more candles.' They held onto each other and in single file, followed the light.

Frank was sitting in the restaurant, alone, drinking tea. It was a beautiful day and for once he felt that he had done something to make the day even more beautiful. Even though he had not eaten since breakfast he felt no hunger. He had come to the *Hotel de Kroon* for a purpose. Piet and Dirk had asked for a business meeting and Frank knew what that meant. He played with the teaspoon and drew circles of tea on the white table cloth. As he looked up he saw Piet arriving on his bicycle at the entrance to the hotel. He saw Frank and waved.

'So this is why my laundry bills are so high,' said Dirk with a wry smile as he sat next to his friend. Frank put the spoon back on the saucer and looked decidedly guilty.

Piet, unusually for him, was casually dressed. An open necked shirt and rolled-up sleeves.

Frank smiled, 'Hello, Piet. Before we start there's something I must tell you about our friend here.' He held Dirk's arm.

Dirk tapped on the table, 'Not now, Frank, not now. Some other time maybe. Let's get on with our business. ... Piet, I believe you wanted to say something to us?'

'Yes, indeed I do,' he replied. 'There are awful things happening all over Holland and nearly every day we hear of atrocities against our people. But,' he looked at his friends, 'it mustn't stop us continuing with active resistance.' Frank looked curious. 'However,' said Piet, 'there's an important matter to discuss.'

'Is the murder of innocent people not important enough?' said Frank quietly.

Piet glanced at him, 'Frank, we all know how you feel about violence and neither of us disagrees with you. The difference is that some of us need to fight these swines.'

'I know exactly what you mean,' said Frank,' you just want to take part in more killing. I believe, ...'

'Frank, listen to what I'm about to say,' interrupted Piet impatiently. 'You're not the only who's worried about the killings. Other people all over Holland believe in non-violence. I think that any members of the group who oppose violence should join the group that deals with divers and food supplies. It's known as the organisation of rural resistance, or the L.O.' He saw Frank look sharply at him. 'If you join them, then I don't see any reason why we shouldn't continue meeting together. In that way we can co-ordinate our activities. The L.O. is accepted by our people.' Frank remained silent. 'I've met with other group leaders in Friesland. It is the unanimous decision of all present at that meeting that you should be the leader of the L.O. here in Friesland.' He held up his hand, 'Before you say anything I must remind you that we'll work together on all projects and that you'll not be expected to use or carry weapons.' He sat back and folded his arms.

Frank tapped his finger on the table, 'I understand what you're saying and I take it as a compliment that I've been asked to take on this job as leader.' He paused for a moment and raised his head. 'My answer is a definite, yes, and I'm sure that my family will be behind me.'

'That's fine then,' said Piet. 'Group Uncle expects you to call a meeting of "Auntie" as soon as possible.' For the first time that day the three men laughed.

'However, gentlemen,' he continued, 'there's a task that I've offered to take in hand on behalf of our group. As I'm sure we all know, there's a problem with moving divers around the province.' Frank nodded. 'It's all a matter of identity cards and ration books. If we can somehow gain control of part of the administration of these documents then we can help even more people. So here is my plan. Firstly, we hit the administration offices that hold all the paperwork relevant to people living in Friesland. As you know the office is located three buildings down from Müller's headquarters on *het Zaailand*. For that reason it's lightly guarded.' He produced a sheet of paper from his pocket. 'I know this, because I've just cycled to the offices for a copy of my birth certificate.' He quietly laughed. 'I walked into the main entrance, no guards. I went to the counter, no guards, only a very attractive young lady who was so willing to help. She said it would take twenty minutes so I walked all over the three stories of that building from top to bottom as easy as a fly and nobody asked me what I was doing. I got my copy and here I am.' He paused and sat back 'By the way, I walked passed Müller's building and there were guards everywhere. I was stopped three times. Now for the second part,' and he held up two fingers. 'Once we've destroyed the offices then we form a forgery group.' He saw Frank and Dirk glance at each other. 'Yes, I can see you're surprised but we must start making false identity cards and other necessary documents. Without the documents section in Leeuwarden the Germans will be in a real mess.' He turned to Frank and tried to speak. Before he had even opened his mouth, Frank interrupted.

'Piet, I know exactly what you're going to say. You want me to help you to do the job.'

He laughed, 'How did you guess? It's on our territory in Leeuwarden and you've not been active for some time now,' said Piet.

'Not been active!' snorted Frank. 'I've got a house full of divers and goodness what else.' He shrugged his shoulders and smiled resignedly. 'All right, where and when?'

Dirk was worried. 'Hey, listen, you two. This is bloody dangerous. How are you going to break in, set the place on fire and then get out? The Germans are only a hundred metres away and they aren't stupid.' He thought for a moment. This is far too risky, you'll be caught. I don't like it'

Frank took the point, 'Piet, he's right. I can't see a way of doing this job properly. Anyway, the Germans can pick up the telephone and check with the national archives in The Hague, so what's the use of destroying the offices in Leeuwarden?'

Piet unfolded his arms and looked mysterious. There was an impish smile on his face. 'Well, you see, gentlemen. The only thing we need are five cans of red paint and then the job is done.' He waited for the response and it came from Frank.

'All right, all right, enough of the mystery. What's red paint got to do with it?'

'You and I are going onto the roof, it's flat you know, and then we pour the paint all over and then we leave the building.'

'Right,' continued Frank, 'how do we get on the roof to pour the paint?'

The same smile, 'We get in through the building next door. Remember, Frank, it's the old offices of the Friesian Timber Company, before we bought them out two years ago. And ......,' he reached into his pocket, 'I still have a key to the back door.' He placed the brass key on the table-cloth.

Dirk was slightly angry, 'Look, Piet, get to the point!'

'All right, I'll tell you. The Royal Air Force are going to bomb the offices in Leeuwarden at the same time as they bomb those in The Hague and Amsterdam.'

'How?' they said, almost simultaneously.

Piet lowered his voice, 'Paul de Vries has been in touch with British Intelligence in London several times over the last few weeks. They'll use a low level attack aircraft called a Mosquito. Apparently it's very fast at low level and has pin-point accuracy.'

Frank snapped his fingers, 'Ah! The red paint. Now I understand!'

'Exactly,' said Piet. 'and you'd better get ready. The raid's at six-thirty the day after tomorrow.' A smile crossed his face, 'I presume, Frank, that you've got some red paint?'

Frank thought for a moment, 'Well it's not quite red, more like orange. I suppose that's patriotically better!' The three men laughed.

The manager was at his elbow, '*Meneer* van der Meer, your wife is on the telephone. Perhaps you would like to take the call in *meneer* Haan's office?'

Frank looked up quickly. He suddenly felt a shiver of apprehension pass through his body. In an instant he was on his feet and running towards the office. He grabbed the receiver.

'What is it, Marieke?'

'Frank, come quick! They're searching the house.' Her voice was strained. The line clicked dead.

Frank had never pedalled so hard before. He crossed every junction without looking and raced across short cuts to get home. With a heaving chest and his legs numb he arrived fifteen minutes later.

There were the usual black cars and a troop lorry. Marieke was standing in the doorway waiting. She looked composed but her face was deathly white. As he stared at her, her eyes swivelled quickly sideways. Frank followed her glance. Seated in the garden on their wooden bench was *Obersturmführer* Postma in full uniform. He saw Frank and stood.

'*Meneer* van der Meer, we've not had the pleasure before. My name is Postma.' He removed his brown glove and extended his hand.

Frank tried to calm his breathing and ignored the hand. 'I know full well who you are. What do you want in my house?'

Postma's attitude changed. He straightened and his eyes glazed. 'We know that you're a Jew lover. Your friends have disappeared recently and I think that you may be hiding them.' He tilted his head and the sun caught the silver runic flashes on his coat lapels. 'I presume you know that if you're hiding them then you'll be removed to a labour camp and your property confiscated.' He looked over Frank's shoulder as the sound of breaking glass came clearly through the front door. '*Hauptsturmführer* Müller tells me that you've friends in high places.'

His eyes narrowed and he took a pace closer to Marieke. She could feel his breath on her face. The stink of recently-eaten fish made her nose wrinkle. For some unexplained reason she wanted to laugh and her face turned a bright red. Frank knew the signs and rushed to the rescue.

'Yes, that's right,' he said very quietly, '*GeneralMajor* Kurt Student. I always carry his card.' He patted his jacket pocket. It was a lie.

Postma stepped back and diverted his eyes. 'Let's go and see if my men have finished searching the house.' He walked past them and through the front door. Frank had time to squeeze Marieke's hand and flash her a supportive smile.

There were two Gestapo men in the living-room. Overhead heavy footsteps made the ceiling shake. Postma walked straight over to the fireplace leant over it and stared hard at the picture over the mantelpiece. He walked round to the side of the chimney breast, stared at the picture again and grunted.

'That's a de Hoogh landscape, isn't it?'

'Yes,' replied Frank.

He leant against the fireplace and tapped the toe of his jack boot against the side of the chimney breast.

'I'll give you a thousand guilders for it.' The thick eyebrows rose questioningly.

Frank saw the toe striking the second course of bricks. He had to get the man to move. Marieke solved the problem with flattery.

She put her hands on her hips and straightened her back. Her breasts stood out against the thin summer dress. Postma's eyes swiftly turned away from the picture and homed in on Marieke's body.

She smiled sweetly, 'Actually, *Obersturmführer*, it's a fake.' She lowered her hands and neatly twirled around. She pointed at the Friesian clock. 'Now, this clock is something special.'

It worked, Postma stepped away from the fireplace. 'I'm not interested in clocks,' he snarled.

Marieke felt that he knew exactly what she was doing. She demurely lowered her eyes. Frank marvelled at her composure. At just the right moment a soldier entered the room.

'Nothing, *Obersturmführer*.'

'Van der Meer, your factory.' His face resumed its hardness. 'Let's have a good look in there, shall we?' Without a second glance, Postma strode past Marieke and through the door. They followed him with the Gestapo men bringing up the rear.

The factory was working at full tilt and the noise of the machinery was deafening. Postma ordered the main doors open and the dust and the heat hit him in the face. He took a step backwards.

'SEARCH IT!' he shouted.

The men in the factory totally ignored the Germans. Frank gave a grim little smile as he saw one of his men wink and turn on two more machines. There was not much to search. They stamped round the walls and pushed over some stacks of timber and one of them kicked at the box over the trap door. Nothing happened, so he moved on. It did not take them long. Within five minutes Postma was climbing the steps to the office. As Frank followed him, one of his men waved him into the workshop. He smiled, walked over and shouted in Frank's ear.

'DIDN'T FIND 'EM, DID THEY!'

Frank could only shake his head in total wonderment.

'Now, you're nice, aren't you?' Postma had his boot on Aukje's office chair. She was unsure what to do next. He reached over and fingered the edges of the short sleeve on her dress.

'Come over here, Aukje,' said Marieke quietly. She quickly rose, slipped away from the chair and stood by her mother.

His eyes greedily followed her. The voice was oily and his face was sweating, 'Now, what a pretty picture you two make, don't you?' He stared at Frank. 'You're a lucky man, van der Meer. I bet your nights are never lonely, are they?' He licked his lips and laughed.

Frank was rigid. For a moment the sound of Postma's laughter forced an image of the execution to flash through his mind. He felt Marieke's foot press on his. Postma was goading him. They had luck on their side.

'*Obersturmführer* Postma,' one of the Gestapo men was on his knees rifling a cupboard near Frank's desk. There were papers all over the floor, 'look at this.' For a moment Frank's heartbeat rose again. He triumphantly held up a wooden box. 'Sir, best Havana, and it's unopened.' Frank relaxed, a gift from a business friend from before the war.

Postma strode across the room totally ignoring Marieke and Aukje. 'Ah! ... Ah! van der Meer.' He snatched the box from the man's hand and stared hard at the label. His eyes shone, 'I've got you. You can only get these on the black market.'

'They were a gift before the war. Look at the label, damn you!' said Frank squeezing Marieke's hand.

Postma tapped his boot on the floor. His eyes raced from the box to Frank's face and from there to Marieke. He lowered his gaze a fraction and then stared at Aukje. He scanned her from head to foot and again he licked his lips. The foot still tapped and the eyes completed another circuit. He stopped tapping and made up his mind.

'I'll take these. They may be needed for evidence later.' He pointed at Frank. 'Watch it, van der Meer, or next time you'll lose more than a box of cigars.' He leered at Aukje, stamped his boot, walked out of the office and down the stairs. They heard the slam of car doors and the roar of engines.

The three van der Meers looked at each other. Aukje was the first to speak. 'Oh, *Heit*, his breath was absolutely awful.' She said it with such a look of relief that for three full minutes they all roared with laughter.

When Marieke had calmed down she added, 'You know, Aukje, I've noticed the same thing.'

TWELVE

The sound of bombers always made Frank's skin prickle but recently he had become immune to the noise that passed daily over his head. The Allies were increasing their bombing offensive and Friesland was one of the main routes for the Ruhr.

The reality came home to him early on a Saturday morning when he was awoken by somebody hammering at the front door. He sat up, instantly awake. Marieke was already out of bed and peering through the curtain.

'Is it a search?' he whispered loudly, as he swung his dressing gown over his shoulder.

'I can't see any cars. There aren't any people either.'

Frank hesitated as he opened the bedroom door. Harmen and Aukje waited on the landing. Suddenly the hammering began again. It convinced Frank and he tip-toed down the stairs. He squinted through the stained-glass panel at the side of the door. There were two people standing close together. He opened the letter box.

'Who is it? What do you want?' he whispered loudly.

One of the figures leant closer. 'Frank, ... it's me. Joop Koopman. For God's sake, open the door! ... Quickly, man!'

Frank released the lock and stepped to one side. Joop was in uniform and so was the man with him. Frank did not recognise him or the uniform.

'You were the nearest, I had to bring him here. I was on my way home and I found him in a ditch, or, should I say, he found me,' said Joop, anxiously.

The three men stood in the darkened hall and stared at each other.

'Frank, bring them in here,' called Marieke. 'I've checked the curtains.' The lights from the living-room shone through into the hall.

Joop was the first to speak, 'Before you ask, he's English.' He pulled off his peaked hat. 'I found him wondering around in a field. How he got there, I don't know. Frank, you speak to him, I think your English is better than mine'

Frank looked his guest up and down. Shortish, stocky, probably about twenty-five, with brown hair and a pale complexion. His uniform was blue with a matching shirt and a black tie. The trousers were tucked into flying boots which were well made but very muddy. His tunic was covered by a waist length sheepskin jacket. He wore heavy brown leather gloves. The face was set and serious and the green eyes coolly glanced from Frank and back to Joop. Eventually they settled on Marieke who was leaning casually against the door. She smiled and for a moment his face lifted and then settled back into seriousness.

'Who are you?' said Frank gently in English. 'Where are the rest of your crew?' There was no answer.

'Wait a minute,' Marieke stepped forward, 'the poor man's been shot down and he's probably scared to death. Frank, ask him if he would like a drink of something.' She drew her dressing gown around her waist and smiled at the Englishman. He was looking a little unsure.

Frank said, 'We can offer you some coffee, well it's not real coffee, only ersatz. We may have some tea.' He looked questioningly at Marieke. She nodded.

She gently placed her hand on the man's arm. 'Please sit down.' He frowned and she guided him to the leather chair. He shook his head and remained standing. There was a long period of silence. The door opened and Aukje and Harmen came into the room.

Aukje looked at him. 'Hello,' she said casually, in English, as she sat down near the table.

'Hello,' he replied and then shook his head. 'Christ,' he muttered.

'Come on,' said Frank, 'who are you? We can't stand round here all night. The Germans will be looking for you by now.'

The Englishman made up his mind. 'My number is 102435, my rank is Flight Lieutenant and my name is Richard Johnstone. That's all I have to say.' He stared at the ceiling.

Frank translated and Marieke took the pilot's arm, 'Flight Lieutenant Johnstone. You can't stand here all day. Now take off your gloves and jacket and sit down. That can't do any harm can it?'

He appeared not to understand but her intention was obvious as she tugged at his gloves. He carefully caught her arm and moved it to one side. He removed the gloves and placed them on the table in front of Aukje. She just smiled at him. He reached to his chest and drew down the brass zip of his leather jacket and removed it. He laid it on the floor and stood up.

Frank nodded when he saw the flying eagle of the Englishman's pilot's wings sewn just above his left breast pocket. Frank did not know what the blue and white striped medal ribbon was or the other two ribbons at its side.

Joop quickly stepped forward. He put out his open hand and said in English, 'Please, give it to me, now.'

Frank saw what he was looking at. The khaki shoulder harness was under the tunic but the butt of the Webley service pistol was sticking out above the undone top button. The pilot shook his head and remained motionless. Joop undid his long police greatcoat. He unfastened the leather flap of his gun holster and raised his eyebrows questioningly. The meaning was obvious. The pilot very slowly unclipped the pistol from its canvas pouch and removed it from under his uniform. He held it by the long, black barrel and handed it across to Joop. He took it by the butt, stepped back, spun the chamber and flipped out the six brass bullets into his palm. He put the pistol and the six rounds into separate pockets.

'Thank you, Flight Lieutenant Johnstone.' He smiled and turned to

Frank. 'I think you'd better explain to our friend here just what the situation is.'

Frank began, 'You know we're not Germans. But we don't know what you are. You say you're English and in the Royal Air Force. How can we believe that?' He saw the look of curiosity in the man's eyes. 'Yes, we can help you but only if you answer some questions for us.' He nodded towards Joop. 'This man is a Dutch police *inspecteur*. If you are not what you say you are, then he will hand you over to the Germans.' Frank shook his head. 'They're not very nice in this part of the world. They have a habit of shooting people, particularly pilots of planes that have been bombing their fatherland.' He waited for a moment. 'Now, Flight Lieutenant, answers to a few questions, please.'

Richard Johnstone's brown eyes turned full beam onto Frank's face.

'I have nothing more to say.' It was said with a slight smile but with deadly intent.

Marieke had returned with a tray of drinks. She laid the tray on the table, selected a cup and saucer, filled the cup with tea and held it out for her guest. He turned to look at her and she laughed. 'Oh, I'm so sorry. If I remember rightly the English take milk with their tea.'

She pushed the cup and saucer towards him and half-turned back to the table. She smiled and came back with a delicate porcelain jug half-full with milk. 'Do help yourself, Flight Lieutenant.' She offered him the jug.

He took it and added a few drops to his cup. 'Thank you, madam,' he said quietly.

'My name is Marieke van der Meer. I'm afraid I don't have a number, but my rank is *mevrouw*.' She laughed and he shook his head. She continued. 'This angry man is my husband, Frank van der Meer. The young lady at the table is Aukje, our daughter. The quiet young man in the corner is our son Harmen.'

Harmen had been waiting for the opportunity and he bounded forward. His English was halting, 'Welcome to our house, Flight Lieutenant Johnstone. Eh ... You're the first Allied officer we've met.' He grabbed the pilot's hand and pumped it up and down. The cup rocked precariously on the saucer. The Englishmen was unsure how to take such enthusiasm.

'Thank you, ... eh, I'm pleased to meet you.'

It was Aukje who broke the ice. Her face was flushed with the excitement of the meeting. She slowly rose from the chair and crossed the floor. Richard Johnstone was rooted to the spot. He held onto the cup and saucer with his left hand and watched Aukje approach.

She looked him up and down, 'Flight Lieutenant, I think the Royal Air Force uniform is very smart. You look much more, ... much more ... she sought for the word in English. She nodded and swept her blonde hair away from her eyes with a flick of her hand. 'Human, yes that's the word, ... human.' Their eyes met and then it was his turn to laugh.

'That's a nice compliment to my tailor, Miss van der Meer. Remind me to tell him when we next meet.'

For a moment the purpose of the meeting was forgotten but Frank brought things back to normality. 'Flight Lieutenant, I still need to know the answers to my questions and,' he glanced at the clock, 'time is moving on.'

The pilot took a deep sigh and placed the cup and saucer back on the table, 'All right, I need your help and I don't want the Germans to capture me. But, I can't tell you anything about my mission.'

Frank shook his head, 'I still need to know about the remainder of your crew. I could have them knocking at my door with the SS behind them. I can't expose my family to any sort of danger. .... Surely, you can understand that?'

'Yes, Mr van der Meer. I do understand.' He pulled his left ear lobe with finger and thumb. 'Suffice it to say that my crew bailed out long before I did. I left it to the last minute before I crashed my aircraft. Your friend here,' he nodded to Joop, 'found me and that was thirty minutes after I'd landed. I'm pretty sure that nobody else saw me, so you have no worries about the Germans.' His face suddenly lit up, 'Nobody is more surprised than me. It was a piece of cake to get out of my aircraft.'

Frank looked worried, '"A piece of cake", I don't understand.'

He laughed in a slightly boyish way, 'It's RAF slang for ... eh, ... something that's easy.'

Frank nodded and smiled. Joop nudged him and said in Dutch. 'I still don't trust him. He could be a German plant. We know what they're like. A lot of Dutch agents have been murdered recently. Try him in German and see what his response is.'

Before Frank could speak, Richard Johnstone turned towards him and took a step closer. He spoke very quietly, 'There's no need to speak in German. You'll just have to trust me.' It took Frank some time to understand, Marieke was quicker. 'Frank, he's speaking Dutch!'

Joop took in the situation and yanked his gun out of its holster. His hand was rock steady. 'Don't move. Stand over there near the fireplace, NOW!' The gun followed the Englishman as he stepped back towards the wall. 'Start talking. Why do you speak Dutch? Just who the hell are you?' He pulled the firing hammer back on the pistol. The click echoed round the room. Everybody froze apart from Richard Johnstone.

He laughed again, 'Yes, I do speak your language. You see my mother is Dutch. She's a relative of your Prime Minister in exile, *meneer* Gerbrandy. But I suppose I've no way of proving that.' He raised his hands and shrugged his shoulders. It caused Joop to lift up the pistol.

Frank intervened, 'Wait a minute, wait a minute. ... Joop, let's just think about this for a moment. He looks English, he acts English, he's in RAF uniform and he claims to have dropped out of the sky over Friesland. Where's his 'plane? I've not heard one crashing near here.'

Joop lowered the gun a fraction, 'I know you won't hold my gun, Frank. So you'll have to make the telephone call. Dial Leeuwarden 236, mention my name and ask if a British bomber is down near here.' He saw his friend's concern. 'Don't worry, you won't have to give your name. The number's safe anyway.'

Frank left the room and went up the stairs to his office. The number answered straight away.

'236.'

'Koopman asked me to call.'

'*Ja*,' came the laconic reply.

'Has a British bomber crashed in this area of Friesland in the last hour?'

'*Moment*.' There was a muffled conversation.

'*Ja*, a Lancaster bomber crash-landed at Giekerk. There were no survivors that could be seen. It's still there. The Germans have surrounded it.' The line clicked and went dead. Frank returned to the living-room and repeated the message.

'Anything to say, Flight Lieutenant?' said Joop, 'Giekerk is only six kilometres away and none of us have heard anything.' His gun was locked into position.

Richard Johnstone remained calm and he leant against the fireplace. He again squeezed his left ear lobe. 'Your information is correct. I did crash in a Lancaster bomber. I switched off the engines and the fuel cocks just before landing. I simply ran out of fuel. My crew had parachuted out twenty minutes before me. I'm surprised the old bird lasted so long.' He yawned and looked at his wrist-watch. '*Meneer* van der Meer, did you say that the aircraft was surrounded by Germans?' Frank nodded. 'In about four minutes I think they're due for a surprise, that is if my watch is accurate. Which it usually is.'

Before he could continue, a flash of light penetrated the heavy curtains and there was a thunderclap of an explosion. The widows rattled.

'What the hell was that?' cried Joop.

The pilot laughed, 'It seems my watch is correct but my aircraft isn't. You see I had to abort my mission, the release mechanism for the bomb load had failed. What with that and no fuel, I couldn't land with my crew so they left me earlier. I had hoped to crash land in the sea, but the old bird decided she didn't have enough juice for that. It scared the hell out of me, landing with a full bomb load. I thought I was a goner, believe me.' He paused for a moment and looked at their faces. 'Oh yes, the big bang. ... When I'd landed on dead engines I managed to get back into the bomb bay and arm one of the bombs. It was guess work really, but not too bad. You just heard the results of my little trap. I only hope that none of your people were killed.'

'Unlikely,' said Joop, 'we're not allowed anywhere near crashed aircraft.'

'I think that we have to believe what our guest has been telling us,' said Marieke. 'It's unlikely that any German could plan that in such detail. Now, Flight Lieutenant Johnstone, I think it's time that you did sit down.'

Richard smiled and collapsed into the chair. Marieke noticed that his hands were trembling and there was that same nervous movement to his ear lobe.

'Frank, he'll have to stay in Lodo's room for a couple of days.'

Frank nodded, 'As usual, Marieke, you're right. But, Flight Lieutenant, ...'

He interrupted, 'Please call me Richard. And, by the way, I don't want to cause you any trouble. I can quite easily sleep in the garden shed.'

'I'll get the room ready,' smiled Aukje and, with a smile, she darted out of the room.

'Well, *meneer*,' said Joop. 'The first thing is to get out of that uniform. I'm sure that Frank can find something for you.' He looked at Harmen who had been taking everything in. 'Perhaps, Harmen you've something that would fit your guest?

'I certainly have, *inspecteur*.' He walked across the room and stood at Richard's side. 'Please follow me.' There was a touch of excitement in his voice.

'Of course,' said Richard.

'I've got to ask you,' Harmen leant over and touched the blue and white medal ribbon. 'What's that for?'

'Don't be bad mannered,' said Marieke crossly.

'Oh no, I don't mind him asking,' smiled Richard. He glanced down at his chest. 'It's nothing really. They give them out when you've done so many hours flying.'

Harmen nodded.

Joop had put away his pistol and was just preparing to leave. He turned and spoke very quietly. 'I don't think so, Flight Lieutenant. The blue and white striped ribbon is, I believe, a Distinguished Flying Cross. The British certainly don't give them away. The other ribbon's a Distinguished Service Order.' He suddenly stood to attention and saluted Richard. 'I think I'm saluting a very brave and modest young man. I must wish you the best of luck. We'll certainly meet again.' He left the room quickly and was gone before Frank or Marieke could say good bye.

THIRTEEN

Richard's Dutch was excellent and within the three days in the van der Meer house he had picked up a Friesian accent, which was not surprising, considering the amount of time that he spent chattering to Aukje. Frank decided that Richard was to stay as a diver for a little longer as the number of Allied aircrews seeking refuge in Friesland was increasing daily. Having an English-speaking Dutchman was proving to be an invaluable resource for both Uncle and *L.O.*

Richard was provided with a complete new identity and given a job in Frank's factory. The foreman had accepted him completely and he nodded when Frank sent Aukje with a message for Richard to go to his office.

'Good morning, Gerard Kiestra,' said Frank with a big smile. Richard looked the part; clogs, baggy blue overalls and a cap at a jaunty angle.

Piet sat in the corner and gave a slow handclap at a beaming Richard. 'You look the complete Dutchman. Why, you even stand like a Friesian.'

'It's these damned clogs,' muttered Richard, clumping them together.

'Actually,' said Piet, 'if you push a handful of straw in each clog before you put them on, then you'll find them much more comfortable. ... At least that's what the farmers tell me!'

Richard glared at him, shook his head and sat down.

Piet continued laughing but then became serious. 'We have an operation planned for tomorrow morning and we need your advice.' He saw Richard's eyebrows lift with curiosity. 'There's a British air attack on the administration offices in Leeuwarden.' Now Richard was really interested and he sat forward to listen to Piet's explanation.

Richard thought for a moment and took his cap off. 'The Mosquito is an excellent aircraft. A low-level attack is really low-level, probably roof-top height at least. They'll probably use a cluster of fifty-pound incendiary bombs. I would certainly recommend that you're three hundred kilometres away, minimum, from the bombing point.' He smiled, 'Perhaps I could help a little more?'

Piet and Frank looked at each other. Piet spoke first, 'I can't see why not. We're marking the roof during the night and the attack is at 6-30 tomorrow morning. Meet us here at eight o'clock tonight. We're waiting at the *Hotel de Kroon*.' The smile returned, 'And please don't wear your clogs, you'll wake up everybody in Leeuwarden.' Even Richard had to laugh.

They sat in one of Dirk's hotel rooms and played cards. Frank found it fascinating to listen to Richard talking about life in wartime Britain. Richard could not believe what was happening in Holland.

'Frank, are you sure about the transporting of the Jews to Poland?' Frank nodded. 'In England I've heard some rumours about forced labour but not on the scale that you're talking about. Can you prove anything of what you're saying?'

'Nobody comes back to tell us, if that's what you mean,' said Frank. 'We can only go on information that comes through the resistance groups in other countries,'

'Where're you hiding all these people?' asked Richard incredulously.

'Everywhere,' replied Frank with a grim smile, 'houses, factories, canal boats. We've even dug holes underground to hide people in. At one stage we had four Jewish families hiding on the German airfield in Leeuwarden but we moved them because of the noise!' He grinned and paused for a moment. 'We move people around to different places at different times. Some get caught in German round-ups.' He saw Richard about to speak. 'Round-ups are our biggest worry. The Germans surround a village or a street and carefully check every house and person in the street. We lose quite a few divers like that.'

'Fortunately,' interrupted Piet, 'we're usually informed about where raids are going to take place and we can then warn people in the area.' He raised a warning finger. 'Don't ask me how we know. We do have good intelligence from within the German command in Friesland.'

Richard was really interested, 'Okay, I accept your security. But how the hell do you know if there are Germans in any particular area? I mean, ... we left the factory and never saw a German. How's that possible?'

Piet glanced at Frank. He shrugged his shoulders. 'All right, I'll tell him.' He cleared his throat, 'Our lovely country is famous for clogs, which you know all about, and windmills. A windmill is a wonderful thing. Once you've seen one in a village, you never notice it again. It blends into the landscape perfectly. Some villages have two or three. They're usually on the outskirts, in that way they catch the wind. You can see the big windmills from ten kilometres away on a clear day.' He stood up from the table and crossed his arms over his chest. 'If you see the sails set in a vertical position, like this, twelve o'clock to six o'clock, it means no Germans.' He changed the position of his arms, 'If the sails are set diagonally, then beware, there're Germans in the village.' Piet sat down.

Richard was amazed, 'That's damned clever. Does it work?'

'Only when the weather's clear,' replied Piet. 'There are other signals from the windmills as well. It's a tried and proved system that's been used for hundreds of years.'

They all tried to sleep but it proved to be difficult. They dozed and occasionally Dirk came into the room with drinks and food.

Eventually Piet made the decision. 'Come on, let's go. It's time.'

The streets were totally deserted. Dressed in dark clothes they moved quietly, one at a time, from corner to corner. The administration building was only half a kilometre from the hotel and they reached it within twenty minutes. Piet pushed them back against a wall.

'Freeze,' he hissed and darted into a dark passage.

Around the corner appeared a German patrol. The two men were laughing loudly and talking. They passed within two metres of the passage and continued on their noisy way.

'Idiots,' muttered Frank as they walked through the passage to the rear of the building. He glanced quickly up and down the narrow road, walked forward and then threw himself flat on his stomach with his head hanging over the narrow canal. Piet did exactly the same and Richard watched from the shadows.

Frank grunted as he reached with both arms over the lip of the canal wall. With a low cry and a heave he pulled a piece of sodden rope out of the water. The two men pulled with all their strength and a large canvas bag came to the surface. It stank. The canals of Leeuwarden were rarely cleaned. They dragged it over to Richard.

'What the hell's in that, a body?' he whispered.

Frank pulled out his penknife and slashed at the canvas. 'No, it's a little present from *schipper* Schaaf. He left it there the other day when he passed through the town on his *tjalk*.'

Richard suddenly understood. The bag burst open and four huge paint cans spilled out onto the alleyway.

'Right, one can and a paintbrush each. Let's move.' Piet's voice was firm as he quickly threw the remains of the bag back into the canal and started to walk towards the rear door of the building.

It was still a very calm night. There was nothing moving and it seemed as if they were the only people in the world. Piet dropped his can onto the ground and crouched in the doorway entrance. He fumbled in his pocket and found the key. The door was massive and looked solid. Gently he pushed the key into the key-hole and turned it. Nothing happened. He tried again. Still nothing. He pulled the key out and examined it by the light of a small torch.

'What's the matter?' whispered Frank.

'I don't know,' grunted Piet as he tried the key again. He banged his fist against the door in frustration. He turned to face Frank. 'Oh my God, they've changed the lock.'

'Try again,' said Frank patiently.

Piet shook his head, 'It's no good. We'll never get it open.' He thumped the door again.

'Stop!' said Richard. 'The patrol's coming! Back into the alley!'

Quick as a flash, they dashed into the welcoming darkness. The regular clatter of nailed boots came down the narrow street. The two soldiers were quiet and the three men withdrew deeper into the shadows. One of the Germans was silhouetted in the alleyway arch, his rifle levelled towards the men. Piet put his hand inside his coat and withdrew a vicious-looking knife and quickly hid it away from Frank's line of vision. Richard was conscious of Piet's hand gripping his shoulder. With infinite care he reached up and unclamped the fist. The soldier disappeared and the sound of boots faded away down the street. They rose out of the shadows and crept to the end of the passage.

Piet was the first to whisper, 'What the hell are we going to do now? No key, no plan.'

'If we don't mark the roof, there'll be no attack but they'll bomb the other targets and then they'll guard this one. Damn! ... Damn!' said Frank angrily.

Richard suddenly dashed out of the passage. Piet looked at Frank and shook his head. Within a minute he appeared back at their side.

'All is not lost, gentlemen. Follow me.' They did.

He pointed to a small window two metres up the wall. 'That has only a slip catch. If somebody has a knife or a screwdriver?' He looked questioningly from one man to the other, 'Then I could stand on Frank's shoulders and open the window.'

Piet sheepishly withdrew the knife and handed it, hilt first, to Richard.

'Very nice,' said Richard.

'For sharpening pencils, I presume?' said Frank sarcastically.

'Oh shut up, you two,' grinned Richard, 'let's move!'

The plan worked. Richard was in the building for two minutes before he pulled Frank and Piet after him, complete with paint cans. They padded along the corridors and up the stairs. The way to the roof was blocked by a solid door. They stopped.

Richard let out a whoop and body charged the door. He rebounded and dropped to the floor, 'Ouch!'

'Be careful, Richard,' said Frank, 'you'll damage it.'

Richard stood up and let out a roar of laughter, 'Don't be bloody silly, Frank. It'll be in a million pieces in an hour and a half. Come on, charge!' He rushed at the door again. They were all roaring with laughter as they took turns in attacking the door. Eventually it splintered open and they rushed onto the roof.

Richard gazed all around him. He pointed to the east and squinted into the blue sky, 'I think they'll come in from there. They'll miss the two church steeples and that old building.' He nodded his head. 'Yep, that's the only way.' He picked up a can of paint. 'We'll paint this section of the roof and that bit of wall on the chimney. I don't think they'll miss it.'

Frank, forever the perfectionist, in short sharp movements, began to carefully paint whole bricks Piet started on the other side. Richard watched them.

'What the bloody hell are you two doing? You're not a pair of Rembrandts you know. That way'll take you hours. Look! just slosh it on.' He picked up the can and poured great puddles of bright orange paint all over the roof. 'Come on now,' he whispered loudly, 'don't mess about. There's only an hour to go.'

The job did not take long but by the time that they had finished there were bright splashes of orange all over their clothes. They stood back to look at their work.

'I think there's more paint over us than the roof. I just hope the RAF don't spot us. We make an ideal target.' Richard's face was deadly serious and then it split into a broad grin. Frank and Piet looked at each other and smiled.

Frank put his arm on Richard's shoulder, 'Why is it, Flight Lieutenant Johnstone, that whenever I'm with you, you always make me laugh?'

Richard smiled, 'It's because you Dutch are always so bloody serious about everything, that's why.'

'We have a lot to be serious about, my young friend,' said Piet quietly, 'and if we don't stop chattering your friends will bomb us. There's only thirty minutes left.'

They dashed down the stairs and made their way back to the window. Frank carefully lifted it. He gently closed it and shot down back onto the floor.

'*Verdomme!* The patrol is right outside the door. They're having a smoke and a good chatter. We can't move.'

'Fifteen minutes to go,' breathed Piet.

They heard them move and they could hear their voices.

'There's only one thing we can do.' Both men turned to Richard. 'If we make a run for it, the Germans will certainly kill us. We just have to wait for the raid. I'm pretty certain the Mosquitoes will make a sighting pass before they attack. That'll scare our two friends outside and then we can get out and run like bloody hell back to the hotel.'

There was no protest, only nodded agreement.

At precisely 6-25 a.m. Frank nudged Richard. They heard the sound. 'Two of 'em,' whispered Richard. 'I think another half minute.'

He was right. The roar of four Rolls Royce Merlin engines at an altitude of fifty metres was enough to wake the whole of Leeuwarden. Richard was on his feet in an instant. He reached for the window just as the two aircraft screamed overhead at what seemed like roof-top height.

'Come on,' he shouted, 'the bastards have gone, scared shitless I shouldn't wonder.' He jumped to the ground and turned to help his friends. They were ready and landed at his side. 'Run like hell!' They did just that as the aircraft began to return.

The street was empty and to Frank it was like Rotterdam all over again. One minute nothing and then one of the Mosquitoes appeared over the top of the bridge on the canal. He saw the twin-engined, stubby-nosed fighter-bomber fly straight towards him. He grabbed his friends and forced them to stop running. They turned with wide open mouths. The camouflaged Mosquito flashed over the roof-tops and Frank saw its nose lift; wide open bomb doors, screaming engines. Four black specks, four massive explosions. White fire and searing heat blasted down the narrow street where Frank stood. He was transfixed as the sound assaulted his senses. The blast knocked him off his feet and he ended up in a heap on top of Richard.

Before he could stand, from the corner of his eye he saw the second

Mosquito, exactly the same flight path and exactly the same effect. Frank covered his ears and tried to push himself into the cobbled street. He was so numbed he felt and saw nothing.

'FRANK! RUN! GERMANS!' Richard was pulling him off the ground.

His reaction was slow but he saw a rain of bricks, timber, and dust. The dust was everywhere, everywhere. He crawled to his feet and tried to move. His legs were glued to the road and he desperately tried to run.

'COME ON! COME ON! JESUS CHRIST, MOVE!'

The roar of the aircraft had gone. It was replaced by another roar, the roar of flames and fire. The heat-flash caught Frank full in the face as he turned to face the wrecked building. It was completely gone. Nothing, apart from flames. The slap on the face hurt him. He shook his head, another slap and he saw Richard about to hit him again. It had the required effect and he began to run, pushing Piet and Richard out of the way.

They had not gone far before Piet fell to the ground. Frank could see why, there was a neat hole through the arm of his jacket. Almost without stopping he bent down and scooped Piet off the ground, Richard grabbed his legs.

'THEY'RE CATCHING UP WITH US!'

Frank slowed with the extra weight, his brain was beginning to clear. He looked around him. To the rear, what looked like ten men in uniform. In front, a fire engine with sirens screaming. They were trapped. They stopped and looked at each other. Richard was silent but there was a desperate look on his face.

'Leave me,' said Piet quietly.

Frank let out an un-Christian oath. 'Jump into the canal. Now man, now!'

Richard looked puzzled. There was the chatter of a machine-gun. He jumped and dragged Piet and Frank with him.

It was like black ink, Frank felt his feet touch the bottom and sink into a hundred years of mud. He kicked himself free. He surfaced. His friends were with him. He paddled his way to the side of the canal wall and stopped for a moment in its welcoming shadow.

'What next?' spluttered an angry Richard.

'Just swim to the next corner of the canal. It's only twenty metres.'

It seemed to take an hour. The water was like treacle. Frank's chest heaved and slowly Piet began to drag him down. He took a gulp of air and grabbed at a hook in the brick wall of the canal. He saw the steps let into the bricks before Richard. What surprised him most of all was the sight of Dirk Haan's anxious face staring down at him.

It only took a minute and they were heaved, like floundering fish, into the dank passage.

Richard sat up, 'What the hell is this place? Dracula's castle?'

Frank was panted like a dog and he was absolutely exhausted. Without thinking he swallowed the drink that Dirk put to his mouth. There was a splutter and a retching sound and he emptied the canal water from his stomach. He took another swig from the bottle and sat bolt upright.

'I'm sorry, Frank. I know it breaks all your rules but it is recommended by the doctors. Anyway, it's a drop of my best Napoleon. I've been saving it for a special occasion.' Dirk beamed down at him.

It took thirty minutes before the three men recovered. Piet's flesh wound looked worse that it was. They were back in the hotel room, bathed and sitting in borrowed clothes. From the window, in the early morning sunshine, they could see the fire still burning. The fire engines were surrounded by armed Germans and there was a feeling of panic in the air as well as thick black smoke.

'Richard, I think you were a great help, thank you,' said Piet. His arm was in a sling but he was smiling.

'I enjoyed it,' he replied simply. 'When you're sitting in a bomber at fifteen thousand feet you get no idea of what's happening down below. This morning really showed me war at first hand.'

Dirk came into the room with hot drinks and a late breakfast. Frank looked at him. 'Dirk, I'm worried. If we found the door in the canal wall then I'm sure the Germans will as well.'

He placed the tray on the table, 'Don't worry, the tunnel from the door slopes up into the hotel cellars. One of my friends has been raising the water level on that stretch of canal ever since I picked you up. By now the door is covered. They won't find a thing.' He smiled, 'You did a great job and,' he turned to Richard, 'so did the RAF. The buildings nearby are a little damaged. Most of the windows in Müller's headquarters have gone. I think, on the whole, my friends, you can say that this was a great success for Uncle.' He produced the bottle of brandy from his pocket. 'Let's drink to that before we eat.' He glanced at Frank, 'I'll excuse you from this one.' Frank just shook his head and filled his cup with coffee as the bottle was passed round.

They slept like babies until dusk. Each man left separately at half-hour intervals. There were no police or Germans around the area. They were too busy clearing up the damage.

Frank arrived home weary, with a buzzing head and aching limbs. As he walked into the hall Marieke was waiting.

'Frank, darling, I'm so glad to see you. Are you all right? Dirk telephoned, he explained why you were so late.' The excitement on her face was obvious. 'We could see it all from here. It looked wonderful.'

Frank put his arms round her waist and pulled her towards him. She held him close and he could feel her body against him.

'Where are the children?' he asked gently.

She stepped back for a moment from his embrace. 'Harmen is staying with a friend and Aukje is working in the office.' She gazed at his face. 'Darling, you look so tired.'

'Marieke, I feel exhausted. You're right, it was very successful but they nearly caught us.' He thought for a moment, 'I suppose I should feel guilty about destroying somebody else's property but I don't.'

'Frank, don't worry about it. You're safe and that's the most important thing.' She put her arms around his neck and pulled herself close to him. For a moment he was going to push her away, but the warmth of her body surprised him and he drew her into his arms. He felt his blood coursing and he knew why. The danger had become an aphrodisiac for both of them. He looked at her face and saw her wide-open eyes staring back up at him. He laughed out aloud and kissed her on full on the mouth. She pulled his head round and returned the kiss. There was a deep moan from within her and he found himself rising to meet her demands. This was not the Marieke that he knew from the past, this was a new woman. He fought to control his desire but he knew that he would give in to her. Somehow they found their way up the stairs and onto the bed. Their lovemaking did not last long but it was instant and fulfilling.

They certainly did not hear Aukje tapping on the door, or her closing the curtains. They slept the sleep of the exhausted.

FOURTEEN

Their house was searched three times in a week. The de Bruins had to stay in the cellar almost continuously. Only with careful observation from the factory roof were they able to emerge and rush into the house, take a bath and see their friends. The pressure was beginning to tell on the family. Frank knew that his son was active in the Resistance. Sometimes Harmen did not return home at night and he worried about him. Even more worrying was Aukje, she was now a courier for Uncle. She cycled around Leeuwarden carrying messages. She very much kept things to herself. The timber business was beginning to take second place as Frank and Marieke were drawn deeper into Uncle's activities.

Frank knew what was going to happen when Rabbi Jacobs knocked at the front door on a cold winter's night. His face said it all.

'Good evening, Frank. May I talk with you?'

Marieke was sitting in the living-room. She sensed what the Rabbi had come for. Together they waited for him to speak.

'I think you know why I'm here.' He spoke without a trace of emotion. 'I've received my call-up letter for Westerbork. The Germans are winding up the Jewish Council in Leeuwarden and I'm one of the last to be called.' He sat down wearily. 'I've no choice, I have to go. My people have gone and if I hesitate then they'll take hostages.' He looked at his friends and rubbed his beard. 'They might even take you or your children.' Frank opened his mouth to protest. The Rabbi raised his hand. 'It's no use, I've heard all the arguments.'

'When do you have to go?' said Marieke quietly.

'In three days. The usual procedure, I think you know what happens.' He stopped talking and then finally made up his mind. 'I know that Lottie would like to have told you herself,' Marieke inhaled sharply. 'She got her call up at the same time as me.' He smiled grimly, 'Now, there's one person you'll never stop going.'

'How is she?' asked Marieke.

'She's as well as she can be with the responsibility that she takes on her shoulders. You know she's met, and comforted, every Jewish person from Leeuwarden as they've passed through Westerbork. The Germans are strange. They could've just kept her at the camp. But, oh no! They told the Council to send her a letter in the normal way.'

'Where is she now, ... at this moment?' said Marieke.

'At home packing things that seem to pour into her house almost daily. She never stops. When I saw her today she asked how you all were.' The Rabbi became silent for a moment and then he quickly glanced at the clock. 'I'm short of time. I really can't stay any longer. There's the curfew for Jews and I don't want any more trouble.' He hesitated and raised and eyebrow. 'How are your friends?' The nod of re-assurance came from

Marieke and Rabbi Jacobs, for the first time during their brief meeting, smiled.

'I presume,' added Frank, 'that you're reporting at the usual time on Thursday?' The Rabbi nodded. 'Naturally, Marieke and I will be there to help you and Lottie.'

He looked angry, 'That's not necessary Frank. It'll put you all in danger if the Germans spot you.'

Frank smiled and shook his head. 'We're just as stubborn as you are. ... We're coming!' He put his arm on Marieke's shoulder, 'Aren't we, *liefje*?'

She held his hand. Her voice was soft. 'We'll be at the station, Rabbi. There's no doubt about that.' There was a hesitation in her voice, 'It may be the last time that we'll ever see you and Lottie again.'

The Rabbi shrugged his shoulders and his eyes filled, 'I pray to God that we will meet again.' Quite spontaneously they stood near each other for a minute in silence. He lifted his head. 'I must go now.'

Marieke kissed him gently on his cheek and Frank grasped his hand. Rabbi Jacob gave one great shiver, turned and walked out through the door. Frank and Marieke stood rooted to the spot. They were unable to speak.

The following day Marieke called at Lottie's house several times but there was nobody at home. She tried the door. It was open. The house was immaculate, everything was where it should be. She felt that she was interfering and quietly left.

Marieke cycled slowly through the streets of her town. She passed through the old Jewish quarter. Most of the houses were closed up. Some even had boards nailed to the window frames. There were no people around and the streets were silent. For a moment she stopped and looked around her. The wind swept along the canal and she felt the damp chill strike her in the face. Two German soldiers walked towards her. In the past they would have raised their caps but now they stared stonily ahead. It was as though she did not exist.

She stepped onto her bicycle and cycled a little further along the cobbled street and arrived at the site of the bombed administration building. She stopped. There was nothing left. The ground was clear, apart from a few German vehicles parked on the rubble. For the first time that day Marieke smiled, the memories of the attack still excited her. She moved on and passed by SS Headquarters. As she slowed down to pass a staff car, she was suddenly faced by a uniformed *Hauptsturmführer* Müller. She could not help staring at him, he was standing immediately in front of her. She had to stop.

He was utterly charming, '*Mevrouw* van der Meer, so nice to see you again. How are you and your family?' The voice was patronising to the extreme.

The car was obviously waiting for him and Marieke was trapped. The driver had the door open and she could not retreat. Müller waited for her reply. She gripped the handlebars, determined to be calm and looked at his handsome face. He reminded her of a hooded cobra waiting to strike.

'Good day, *Hauptsturmführer*, I'm fine, thank you.' She tried not to smile.

His legs were braced apart and his hands were hooked over his belt; the posture was pure SS. There was a slight smile on his face and Marieke felt that he was waiting for something.

'I trust that your husband is busy in his business? ... After all, he is still working for us.' He remained stock still. She remained silent, unsure what to say.

Muller straightened his shoulders and the blue eyes stared intently into hers. The voice was calm but he spoke with deadly intent. 'I hear that your friends have been called up to work for the *Reich* in the east.' For a moment Marieke thought that he was talking about the de Bruins and then she realised that this could be a trick. Around her the whole world fell silent and she felt desperately alone.

'I'm not sure who you mean, *Hauptsturmführer*. Which friends are you talking about? We have many friends.'

He waited for a brief moment and touched the shiny peak of his black hat. His voice had an edge of hardness. 'The Cohen woman of course and the Rabbi.' He saw Marieke's eyes flicker. 'They will be almost the last of your Jews to leave Leeuwarden. Good riddance, I say. When they've gone there'll be more business for your husband.' He took a step towards her and Marieke shook herself.

'Excuse me, *Hauptsturmführer*, I'm busy,' she mounted her bicycle and tried to move past him. He remained immobile and put his hands behind his back. She felt the loneliness pressing down on her.

'What's the hurry, *mevrouw*? Perhaps we can walk together to the *Hotel de Kroon* for a snack. ... I know you're always welcome there.' He bent forward and touched Marieke's hand. She physically recoiled at his cold contact. 'In fact your husband nearly lives there. You know, from my office I can see him coming and going into the hotel nearly every day.' He folded his arms and a smile passed over his face and went as quickly as it came. 'Yes, I think that's a wonderful idea.' He half turned, 'Driver, take the lady's bike to the hotel.'

A shocked Marieke could do nothing. She let go of the bike and found Müller at her side.

'Come on now. It's only a short way.' He laughed and stared straight ahead, 'Now what shall we talk about?'

His voice was quiet and the perfectly-spoken Dutch confused her. She had no option but to walk at his side. Müller strode out with purposeful steps and he removed his hat and pushed it under his arm. Marieke could feel everybody in Leeuwarden looking at her. She felt like a *moffenmaiden* but there was nothing that she could do about it. He continued talking to her.

'It's a pity about your other Jewish friends, the de Bruins,' he glanced sideways at her. 'They seem to have disappeared. Have you any idea where they might be?' He left the question hanging as he strolled down the street.

Marieke drew her coat around her, trying to avoid any eye contact with the devil at her side. She kept her head high and stared straight ahead. The *Hotel de Kroon* loomed up in front of her and she forced herself to walk quicker.

'What's the hurry, *mevrouw* van der Meer? Surely you're not that hungry are you?'

Marieke wanted the ground to open up and swallow her but nothing happened. The distance to the steps of the hotel seemed to become longer and longer. When she at last reached them, Müller marched past her and stood near the open door, legs astride. He placed his hat back on his head and folded his arms.

They walked inside together. The usual mid-day crowd was there and she saw Dirk standing near the bar. He looked both anxious and curious. She blinked a warning to him. The chatter around her suddenly stopped and she found herself the centre of attention for all the wrong reasons. Müller placed his hands on her shoulders and she steeled herself.

'Please allow me to take your coat, *mevrouw* van der Meer.' He peeled it away off her shoulders and held it out with one hand. Dirk stepped forward, slipped it onto a coat hanger and hung it on the rack. Marieke was motionless, unsure what to do. In a flash it came to her.

'Excuse me, *Hauptsturmführer*, I must go and comb my hair.' She turned on her heel, knowing that it would leave him standing alone. Before she had walked one step he spoke to her in that quiet voice that everybody could hear.

'I know that you're a regular church attender, *mevrouw* van der Meer. But your church doesn't have any bells, does it?'

The question surprised her. It threw her off balance. She turned, shook her head and stared back at him.

He didn't wait for an answer. 'Bells are wonderful things. They wake you up in the morning and stop you going to sleep at night.' He now addressed a larger audience. Everybody was listening to him and watching Marieke. He continued, 'Yes indeed, bells. ... Holland has many bells. But I think you can manage without the noisy things. Reich Commissioner Seys-Inquart has passed a decree that from midnight tonight all bells in Holland will cease ringing.' The chatter resumed but in a moment subsided. 'Now that you don't need them anymore, the *Reich* will take all the bells into safe custody. You will start removing them tomorrow.' He laughed, 'You Dutch are such practical people, I'm sure you can live without your bells.' He looked at his wrist watch and clapped his hands. The sound echoed around the hotel foyer. 'Now look at the time. I really must leave you, *mevrouw* van der Meer. I'm terribly sorry.' He turned round and walked towards the door of the hotel. He stopped, snapped his fingers and faced Marieke. 'Oh dear me. ...' There was a half smile on his face. 'If you're thinking of going to tell *dominee* de Vries about the bells. Then save yourself a journey, *Obersturmführer* Postma arrested him forty minutes ago for being in your futile Resistance movement.'

He strode through the hotel door and left Marieke frozen to the spot.

Dirk was the first to reach her. 'The bloody bastard! He used you to get in here. I could kill him.' He gripped her arm.

Marieke was recoiling from the shock but her pride took over and she lifted her chin and took Dirk's hand off her arm. 'I need somewhere private to sit down and I need a cup of real coffee, ... now!' Within a minute she was in a small private room at the rear of the hotel. Dirk sat with her.

'Marieke, one of my men will let us know in a moment if it's true about *dominee* de Vries. He's just making a telephone call.' They sat together without saying a word. It only took two minutes and a man appeared with a note. Dirk scanned it. He took a deep sigh. 'I'm sorry, Marieke, it's true. He was arrested at the church whilst he was praying. There are no charges. Ha! ... as if they need them nowadays. Our contact says that he's not in Leeuwarden. He was taken under heavy guard straight onto a train that left ten minutes ago.'

Marieke slowly began crying. She clenched her fists but still the tears flowed. Dirk put his arm around her shoulder and she turned and clung to him.

'Oh Dirk, what are we going to do?'

'There's nothing we can do, to save Paul de Vries. I know that he would want us to resist as hard as we can.' He let go of her and slumped into an easy chair.

What to do next was taken out of their hands. There was a knock at the door and before Dirk could stand, it burst open. It was his manager.

'It's a search. It's Postma and his gang!'

'Marieke, ... stay here. Leave this to me.' He dashed away from her side. Again she was alone.

Obersturmführer Postma stood in exactly the same spot where Müller had stood not twenty minutes previously. His face was twisted into a grin and he aped his superior's stance. The Luger pistol was in his hand. He pointed it at the people in front of him.

'Now, my good citizens. I'm looking for anybody with the wrong papers.' The voice suddenly changed. 'STAND UP! ... ALL OF YOU! ... NOBODY MOVES!' He waved his pistol to the Green Police at his side. Nobody moved as the three men began to search the guests and methodically check their papers. Postma glared at each person in turn. He scratched the side of his face with the muzzle of his gun and carefully levelled the weapon at Dirk's head.

'Haan! Where's the van der Meer woman? I know she's here.'

Dirk was about to speak when the door to the back room opened and Marieke appeared. She walked towards Dirk and stood at his side.

Postma's eyes lit up. He took three steps towards her and licked his lips. She saw his mannerism and her heart chilled. Dirk took a step forward and she nudged him to remain still.

'Ah, ah, the beautiful *mevrouw* van der Meer. No husband here I see,' he wet his lips again. 'Where is he?' He strode towards her and his face reddened. 'What've you been doing with *meneer* Haan? ... A bit on the side, eh! ... They say you Mennonites are cold. ... But, I bet you're as hot as hell on the inside.' He let out a roaring laugh and stood very close to Marieke. She could taste his breath. The room was totally silent. She watched the barrel of the Luger rise from waist height and it hovered near her throat. In a fraction of a second she could see the dirt in Postma's fingernails. She stared straight into his eyes. They darted in all directions. The muzzle was like a circular black hole pointing at her face. Postma's face was working hard, all movement and sweat. She clenched her fists. The muzzle lowered and slipped between the buttons of her dress. She felt its icy coldness press against the top of her left breast. She prepared herself to kick him between the legs

'YOU DISGUSTING BASTARD!' screamed a voice near her ear. Dirk's manager pushed Marieke out of the way and he stood there, shaking, with a long carving knife clutched in his hand.

Postma's face straightened. He did not hesitate. The Luger moved in a slow arc from his belt to the man's head. She heard the click of the firing pin hitting the cartridge. The bang echoed round the room. The bullet entered the man's skull dead in the centre of his forehead and exited with a bloody plop through the rear. The eyes remained fixed open and they stared at Marieke as he twisted to one side and sank in slow motion to the floor.

She looked at herself. There was a surrealistic splattering of blood all over her dress. Her hands were sticky with the grey matter of the man's brain. She did not know what to do. Her anger took over. She strode up to Postma and slapped him very hard across the side of the face, and again, and again, and again. Postma stood there with his mouth wide open. Dirk stepped forward. Marieke stopped and saw the Luger rise. It covered a slow arc as it came down as he pistol-barrelled her across the face.

'BITCH!' were the last words that she heard before a curtain of darkness descended over her vision.

FIFTEEN

'Frank, I can't stand any more of this, ... just look at me!'

Marieke was sitting in Frank's car. He had used the last drops of his precious petrol ration to collect her from the hotel. He drove one-handed with his arm round her shoulder.

'Oh no!' he moaned, jabbing at the brakes, 'I don't believe it.'

In the lights of the headlamps a black police car blocked their way. Two men stood in the middle of the road. One was waving a torch.

'Out of the car, both of you! Quickly!' They were Gestapo, standard black leather coats and hats. Frank could not see their faces.

'Papers!'

The other man stood with a hand in his pocket. The threat was obvious.

Frank produced his identity card, driving licence, and the German driving permit for using his car.

There was a minute's silence. The voice was harsh. 'Are you on official *Reich* business?'

Frank patiently and quietly explained. At the mention of Postma's name one of the men laughed.

'Don't cross *Obersturmführer* Postma. He's worse than us.'

Frank did not know what to say.

The other harsh voice continued, 'You're not allowed to use this car for unofficial business. We'll report you to the German authorities. ... On your way. ... No stopping.'

When they got home Aukje and Harmen were waiting.

'Oh *Mem*, look at you.' said Aukje.

Marieke was a mess. The gun barrel had hit her over her the left ear. The scalp was cut and her hair hung matted with congealed blood. Dirk had done a good job. The wound was clean and the plaster held everything tightly in place. Frank was white-faced with anger.

'Marieke, this is getting worse. Every day something happens. I can't sleep and I can't concentrate on my work.' He looked at his family. 'All of you are involved in something that's either illegal or dangerous. We live on a knife edge and I can't see an end to it.' He shook his head and pushed his hand back through his thick hair.

Marieke sat quietly in the leather chair. She was composed, her hands crossed neatly in her lap. Her voice was steady, 'I agree with your feelings, Frank, but there's nothing we can do about it. We have to believe that God will not let this evil continue for much longer.' She touched the plaster and flinched. 'That man Postma will not survive. When we're liberated, justice will deal with him.'

Harmen watched his mother. He leant over and held her hand. '*Mem*, the Resistance will take care of him long before we're liberated. Anyway, there's no sign of the Allies doing anything about Holland.'

His Father looked at him. 'Son, I will not have anything to do with violence. You know my feelings on that matter.'

Harmen jumped to his feet, 'Your feelings! ... Your feelings! ...You've not just been beaten up.' He was upset. He stood over his father and pointed, with a trembling finger, at his mother, 'Look at her! ... Just look! If you were a man then you'd do something about Postma.' His face was suffused with rage. '... How can you allow somebody to do that to your own wife? And then just sit there and talk about, ... talk about non-violence. How? ... How can you do it?'

For a moment Frank thought that his son was actually going to hit him. An inner calm flowed through his body. He rose and put his hands firmly on his son's shoulders. Even through the thick shirt, he could feel the heat of Harmen's anger.

His voice was soft and he was gentle in his touch, 'Son, I feel exactly the same way as you do. My beliefs are my strength. Marieke is right. There will be a time to deal with the Postmas of this world and that time is not now.' 'If we match violence with violence then we cannot win. They're much stronger than we are. What innocent lives would be taken if Postma was killed. We would have to carry that in our hearts for the rest of our lives.' He gently touched his son's hair and looked carefully into his eyes. 'Be at peace. Let's oppose them as we're doing now and let's continue helping the weak and the innocent. This family has achieved so much without using violence. Look at the de Bruins. Look at all the people who've passed through this very room. We've managed to help them all and saved their lives. God would ask nothing else of us.'

Marieke stood quietly at Harmen's side. She kissed him on the cheek, 'Frank's right. We must keep calm and trust in God.'

Harmen's eyes moved from face to face. He shook his head and took a deep breath. '*Verdomme*, it's difficult for me to follow your beliefs. My God,' he put his arms round the necks of his parents and drew them close to him, 'I don't know how you control yourselves. But I love you so much.' Aukje reached out and touched her mother's arm. The family clung to each other. Marieke broke the circle.

'Frank, tomorrow you and I are going to Lottie Cohen's house and we're going to stop her going to Westerbork.'

'Yes, I know, *liefje*. Patience, I have a way of stopping her. Just leave it to me.'

They all managed to sleep and Marieke was the first to rise. She carefully showered and carefully washed her hair. As she finished she saw Frank standing quietly in the doorway. He watched her with concern.

'Marieke you look dreadful. Stay at home, I'll see Lottie.'

She gave a knowing smile. Frank shrugged his shoulders. He knew what that smile meant.

They left quietly and on a cold, dark morning cycled towards Leeuwarden. Neither of them spoke. They had their own thoughts and worries. Lottie was up and ready. She heard their bicycles clatter against the wall of her house. The front door was already open.

'Come in,' she said.

'I'm sorry we're late,' said Frank quickly, almost before he saw her.

The living-room was neat and tidy. They were surprised by Lottie's appearance. She was standing by the window. Her face was radiant and she was dressed in a beautiful black coat. The six-sided star of David, with the word "Jew", neatly sown in position. The fur collar trimmings framed her head and neck and she smiled at them. Marieke felt Frank stiffen at her side.

'Lottie, you ... you look ... beautiful.' She echoed Frank's thoughts.

She smiled her most charming smile and for a moment the old Lottie shone through. 'Thank you, I don't want those Germans to see me as they've known me. I'm in my very best and I shall stay like this as long as I can.' She saw Frank's mouth open. She quickly waved her finger. 'Frank van der Meer, don't you even try!' She laughed in that special, endearing way. His mouth closed. 'I'm meeting my family at the station and I want you to say good-bye to me, here, in my own house.'

It was Frank's turn, he waved his finger, 'Lottie Cohen, don't you even try!'

Their laughter echoed out into the empty street.

Lottie left her room and returned a few minutes later holding a small leather handbag. She walked up to Marieke, kissed her gently on the cheek and pressed the bag into her hand. 'I want you both to have this.' She stepped back. 'Now come on, let's get on our way, we're late. You know their trains always leave on time.' When they had left the house, she produced a key, locked the door and then gave the key to Frank. 'Look after this for me. I may need it.' Her eyes were watery. She was fighting back her emotions. With head held high she took Marieke's arm and walked away from her home. Frank followed carrying the regulation suitcase.

In the town morning life was beginning. Bicycles everywhere, people walking and Germans checking. They nodded to one or two acquaintances.

'Lottie, let's go past the *Hotel de Kroon*. I'm sure Dirk Haan will want to see you,' said Frank.

She spoke sharply, 'Frank, that's the long way round. That means going over the *Prins Hendrik* Bridge. It's quicker over the other bridge.' She saw his smile and took a deep breath, 'All right, but only if we walk quickly. My family are waiting.' Marieke gave Frank a sharp glance. He smiled at her as well.

He deliberately walked along *het Zaailand*, the large square where Marieke had met Müller. They passed *SS* Headquarters without a second glance. Marieke firmly linked Lottie's arm in hers. Lottie stared straight ahead. They saw no other people wearing yellow stars.

They turned left out of *het Zaailand* and into *Prins Hendrikstraat*. It was strangely quiet and only the three of them were in the narrow street. As they emerged into the early morning sunlight they heard the shrill whistle of a train.

Lottie looked at Frank and tugged Marieke's arm. 'Come on, hurry up. That means fifteen minutes before the train leaves.'

They walked towards the *Prins Hendrik* Bridge that spanned the broad canal. Marieke saw Frank glance at the bridge keeper's cabin. There was a clanking bell, the barriers lowered and the bridge began to rise. They stopped.

Lottie's composure was gone, 'Come on, quickly, to the other bridge!' She pulled Marieke.

'No time, Lottie, ... look!' said Frank. There was the gentle beat of a diesel engine and a Friesian *Tjalk* began to move very slowly from their right towards the bridge. 'By the time we reach the other bridge, it'll be closed.'

They watched the stately progress of the boat as it avoided the moored barges along the canal. Occasionally the throb of the engine changed as it slowed to negotiate the narrow strip of water. The bridge was still clanking into its fully open position. The boat stopped. Frank looked at the stern. *Schipper* Schaaf gave a half salute, leaned on his tiller and waited.

They took Lottie back to her house. Frank produced the key and let her in.

The house was strangely quiet. The sounds of the street were stilled.

She put her hands on her hips and stared at him, 'Frank van der Meer, I think you planned it all.'

He smiled his charming smile. 'Lottie, it was all pure coincidence. I think you could call it God's work.'

Her pale face was set. 'Don't think that this will stop me. There's another transport next week; they'll just put me on the next list.'

Marieke looked at her, 'Lottie, I'm sorry that you missed your family.'

'Don't worry. I'll see them next week.'

'Here's your bag back,' said Marieke as she pulled it out of her coat pocket.

'Don't be silly, use it to help others,' she snapped tersely with a quick shake of her head.

'What do you mean?' interrupted Frank.

'Open it,' she said simply.

Marieke walked over to the table and undid the leather strap. As she peered inside she gasped.

'What is it, Marieke?' said Frank.

She emptied the contents of the bag onto the table. The single electric light bulb caught the flashes of the diamonds as they rolled onto the dark polished wood. There were twenty of them, each with a life of its own. As she shook the bag a leather pouch dropped out. Marieke carefully pulled open the draw strings. She shook her head and upended the bag. Heavy gold coins dropped into a gleaming heap at the side of the diamonds.

Lottie spoke in the quietest of whispers, 'They're no use to me where I'm going.' She looked carefully at Marieke and then switched her gaze to Frank. 'Sell the diamonds in Amsterdam. I know somebody there who will buy them off you for a good price. The gold is easily used.'

Marieke started to talk, 'We can't ...' Lottie put her fingers over Marieke's lips and shook her head. 'Now, my two very good friends. Please leave me. I'm not feeling too well. I need to rest.' She scooped up the contents of the bag and handed it back to Marieke.

Dirk was on the telephone two days later. Aukje connected the call to her mother in the hallway.

'Marieke, one of the surgeons at the hospital dines at the hotel. He's just told me that your friend, Lottie Cohen, had emergency surgery this morning.'

'What!' exclaimed Marieke.

'Don't worry, it's her appendix. She'll be in for a couple of days. I won't say anymore.' The telephone clicked as she was cut off and she dashed up the stairs to Frank.

Richard Johnstone was sitting in the chair opposite Frank's desk. She explained what had happened.

'You'll have to rescue her. When she's well the Germans will take her,' said Richard, after only a moment's thought.

'What do we do?' said Frank. 'Walk right in and kidnap her?'

'Exactly,' he replied. He then went on to outline his plan.

'I've got say it, Frank,' said Marieke with a smile, 'it sounds a good plan to me.'

'*Mem*, anything to do with the *moffen* is dangerous,' interrupted Aukje, looking up from her desk.

Frank shrugged his shoulders and nodded.

Lottie was segregated from everybody else. She was in a side room to the main ward. There was a screen in front of the open door. It was the day after her operation and she still felt waves of nausea. Nobody came to see her and she was not surprised. As she lay in bed with pillows piled high behind her head, the yellow star on her night-dress made her a leper in the hospital. The nurses and the doctors did what they could but they dare not spend time with her. Their own lives would be at stake if they did. Already a German had been to check up on her. She knew that when the hospital released her the SD would be waiting at the main door. This time there was no escape from Westerbork and she lay quietly in the knowledge that it would soon all be over.

Lottie drifted into sleep and out again. The same dream kept re-occurring. She was on a train from Westerbork to Poland. It was as though she was with her people but they did not see her, she was invisible. She saw the horrors of the journey. She watched them die. She could see in the distance two queues of people. They split into two, one to the right one to the left. She could see towering columns of flames and thick black smoke intermingled with white snowflakes. Each time she awoke from the dream she was soaked in sweat and there was a cry on her lips. Each time the same nurse quietly wiped her brow. She could not understand the dream.

'Lottie, wake-up,' said the whispered voice. She ignored it.

'Lottie, WAKE-UP!' The voice was louder. She could see the white nurse's uniform.

'Go away! let me sleep!' She pushed the face away.

She felt the nurse shaking her and pulling her upright against the bank of pillows.

'Lottie, it's me!' whispered Marieke frantically.

Lottie stared unbelievably. The shock of it all brought her to full consciousness. At the side of the bed was Marieke in a nurse's uniform. The lace starched bonnet was perfectly in place and the black shoes shone.

'What are you, an angel?'

Marieke smiled, 'No, I'm not. I've come to take you out of here.'

She shook herself, 'Don't be silly, they'll stop you.'

Marieke was in no mood to listen, 'Now look here, you silly woman. I'm risking my life to get you out of here. Frank's waiting outside and if you don't come now then he's in danger as well.' She pulled the bedclothes away from Lottie and swung her legs off the bed.

'Marieke, how are you going to do it?'

'I'm not, you are. Put on your robe and get into that wheel-chair. Don't look at anybody, don't talk to anybody and don't touch me. Just act the part of being the only Jew in the hospital.'

Lottie looked straight into Marieke's eyes and said very quietly, 'My dear, I am the only Jew in the hospital.' She quickly moved the star from the night-dress to the robe.

They moved past the screens and out onto the ward. Nobody even glanced at them as Marieke pushed the chair between the rows of beds and into the corridors. A single white-coated doctor looked at them curiously and then Marieke realised he was looking at her and not Lottie. She knew that look, some men used it all the time. She gave her sweetest smile and passed him by. The main reception desk loomed up in front of them and Marieke turned to the left and away from the waiting patients. She stopped outside a door, pushed it open and pulled in Lottie after her, leaving the wheel-chair in the corridor.

The broom cupboard was full of cleaning equipment.

'Lottie, put these clothes on quickly.' Without a word Lottie immediately did as she was told. Marieke removed her uniform and pushed it behind a pile of buckets. As she stood there in her underslip the door was thrown open. The doctor stood there and stared at them. He took in Marieke's half-nakedness and a pale-faced Lottie standing in the corner. He said nothing and quickly closed the door.

'Oh my God, Marieke. What are we going to do?' moaned Lottie. She was worried but certainly not scared. Marieke admired her composure. She pulled out a bag from off the top shelf and they both began to dress.

'Nothing, let's get out of here.' She gripped the door handle for a moment, turned it and walked out into the corridor; Lottie followed her.

A quick glance up the short corridor, nobody there. She took Lottie's arm and they walked away from the cupboard. After five paces they passed an open door. The doctor was waiting.

'Ah, ladies,' he said in a loud voice, 'I'm glad you're on time. Do come in.' He grabbed Marieke's arm and yanked her into his office. The three people stared at each other. Not a word was spoken. He put a finger to his lips. They all heard the heavy footsteps. A German soldier walked past the door without a second glance. 'Ladies,' he whispered, 'you have three minutes before he returns.' He gently pushed them back into the corridor.

Within a minute they were at an emergency exit. Marieke pushed the door open. It was raining heavily and Frank and Richard waited patiently. Lottie burst into laughter. Frank scowled at her and wheeled a bicycle towards her. They slowly left the yard near the exit and began to pedal down the short street. They looked like any two married couples cycling home at the end of a busy day. Richard pushed Lottie along following the tradition of husband helping wife; it aroused no curious stares.

They turned down a narrow alleyway between two rows of houses. As they approached a gate it quickly opened. Richard looked at Lottie, smiled, gave her a quick kiss on the cheek, which surprised her, and quickly pedalled away.

The kitchen was small but it was warm and welcoming. Marieke made the introductions. 'I'd like you to meet *mevrouw* Lok. You'll be living in her home from now on. She lives by herself. The SS murdered her husband six months ago.' The two women shook hands and scrutinised each other.

'You're very welcome in my home, Ilse,' Lottie looked at Marieke.

'That's your new name. Forget about your old one until the war is over.'

Frank put his hand on Lottie's shoulder and she turned to look at him. 'Lottie, these are your new papers.' He gave them to her one at a time, 'Identity card, no Jewish "J", ... Ration stamps, ... and some money. *Mevrouw* Lok will be paid each week for your keep, so don't worry about that.' He caught her looking at him and smiling.

'I've got to thank you for saving my life,' she paused and the smile returned, 'Frank, why do you have to wear that ridiculous false moustache? It makes you look like a real villain.'

He looked very uncomfortable, 'I was told that I was easily recognisable and so I bought this thing as a disguise.' He could see Marieke starting to go red and he knew that very soon she would start laughing. With a grimace he peeled off the piece of brown hair from his lip and threw it on the table. He joined in with the laughter.

They ate together and Lottie left them early to rest in her room. They were both tired and left as darkness descended. They were home in time to see the men from the factory finishing work. Richard gave a wink as he cycled past them. It was a cold night and the wind was blowing hard as they wheeled their bikes into the shed. Aukje was waiting at the door. The smiles on their faces said it all.

'Oh, *Heit, Mem*, I'm so glad it was successful.' She threw her arms around them. 'I've got hot soup ready and the table is laid.' They put their coats over the stand in the hall and walked into the living-room. The fire was burning brightly and the curtains were tightly closed. Marieke sat next to Frank on the couch and put her head on his shoulder.

'I feel good. I'm so glad that we saved her. She took it so well, ... didn't she?'

'Yes, *liefje*, I think that she's seen the light. All we can do now is make sure that she's safe.'

Marieke looked at her husband. ' Thanks for sending that doctor to us in the hospital. Without him, one of the guards would have caught us.'

Frank sat up and grasped her hand. 'Marieke, I didn't send any doctor to you!'

She sighed, 'At least there are some good people left. Oh dear,' she stifled a yawn, 'I'm really tired. This excitement is really too much for me.' Frank raised an eyebrow, he was unsure of her motives.

Aukje came through the open door, 'Dinner is ready. Please take your seats.'

They sat at the table and Aukje ladled out the soup. Before any of them could lift the first spoonful to their mouths the telephone rang.

Frank stood up with a deep sigh, 'Always just when we start to eat.'

The telephone gave its usual click. He recognised Harmen's voice. It was high-pitched and echoed into the earpiece.

'*Heit*, get out of the house, NOW! You're totally surrounded!' There was another click as the line went dead. For a moment Frank stared at the telephone and then he let it drop. It swung on its cord from side to side. He whirled round and shouted.

'For God's sake, get out! ... The Germans are here!'

Marieke stood with a spoon in her hand, mouth wide open. Aukje just sat and stared. Frank banged his fist hard on the door.

'COME ON! ... NOW!'

She dropped the spoon with a clatter and ran towards the hall. Frank grabbed her and yanked her away from the door.

'NO!' he hissed. 'That's the first place they'll come to.' He pulled her towards the fireplace. 'Use the escape route.' He kicked the brick, the panel clicked open and he pushed her through. 'Climb like hell!' Aukje was ready behind him. Her face was expressionless.

Frank put his hand on her shoulder, 'I'll see you in a minute.' He dashed out of the living-room up to the office, groped around in the dark and found what he was looking for. Through the windows he could see and hear nothing.

The space up the side of the chimney was stifling. By hanging upside down Frank was able to push the trap door closed. He popped out onto the roof. Below him the house was in darkness. Even though there was a slim moon it was hidden by scudding black clouds. He crawled along the gully between the roof and the factory and jumped.

'Frank, thank God, we were worried.' Marieke crouched in the shadows.

He could just about see their silhouettes as they clutched the ridge tiles of the factory roof. They grabbed him and hugged each other and the wind moaned around their bodies.

'*Heit*, look down there,' whispered Aukje into his ear.

There were shadowy figures in the factory yard. As the clouds parted for a split second he could see a column of darkened vehicles parked in the road leading to the house. At that precise moment two flares arced into the sky. The small parachutes opened and the pure white light cast a pale glow over everything. Frank scanned the scene in front of them. He could see a vast circle of soldiers surrounding the house and the factory. Three men were trying to kick the front door down. He smiled, solid oak with triple locks; it would take some time.

'Right, down the ladder and into the factory. ... Quickly now!'

He was the last down the ladder. They ran past the massive sliding door of the factory and through the shadows of the machinery.

'Both of you! Move the packing cases! ... Heave! ... again, ... heave!'

They moved to one side and the door was pushed upwards from the inside. Jan peered up at them.

'What's the matter?'

'*Moffen*, hundreds of 'em,' snapped Frank as he pushed past a startled Jan. 'They've surrounded the house. Come on Aukje, ... Marieke, down into the cellar. ... Jan, the doors! Pull them back.'

They locked back into place and the two families looked at each other. There was a stench of body odour and excreta. The de Bruins were pale-faced and looked tired. They had been hiding for nearly two years. Aukje was shivering, Marieke had an arm round her shoulders. David rushed forward and lifted Aukje's head. He kissed her gently on the cheek.

Jan rushed back up the step. As he left them they clearly heard the rattle of machine-gun fire. 'Quiet!' he shouted back at them. He had his ear against the door.

'They're in the factory. ... They've shot the locks off the doors. ... I can hear them shouting.' He looked down at them and smiled grimly. '*Moffen* always shout.'

Frank made up his mind. 'I've been thinking. Let's all get out of here. They'll see our footprints in the dust on the factory floor. It won't take them long to work out where we are.'

David stepped forward. 'I know the way out. I often lie in there for fresh air.'

He started towards the second cellar. 'Follow me.' The oblong aperture was in the darkest corner and not easily seen.

David pushed a box into place under the small opening and stepped up towards the lip of the air shaft. Overhead there was the sound of heavy boots.

Frank looked up at him and said quietly, 'Hurry up, there's not much time.'

David pulled himself upwards, slithered away on his stomach and disappeared into the black hole.

'Aukje, you next, then Tineke, Marieke and Jan. I'll go last.'

'*Heit*, what happens if the rowing boat's not there?' said Aukje. Her blue eyes were huge and Frank knew she was covering up her terror.

'Swim, my *famke*, swim.' He squeezed her arm and pushed her onto the box.

The cold night air blasted out of the air shaft and Frank grabbed some coats and threw them at Jan. 'Take these and hurry.'

As he waited for Jan to disappear, he darted into the other cellar and heard the packing cases above him creaking and sliding across the upper surface of the door. He leapt back across the floor and placed his foot on the box. For a moment he hesitated, kicked the box to one side and jumped to catch the edge of the shaft. He missed. Another jump and he made it. He pulled with all his strength and managed to get his chest over the edge. With a final grunt he pulled his body along the slippery stones and began to wriggle along the inky-black, narrow tunnel. Just in time. Behind him he heard the machine-gun blast away the lock on the door. It made him move faster. His knuckles were scratched as he clawed his way along. He stopped for a brief second. He knew the voice: Postma!

'They're in here somewhere. Search everything!'

It gave Frank the final impetus to clear the last stretch of the air shaft. He saw the oblong of lighter darkness at the end. He saw two hands reaching for him and he was pulled bodily out into the cold night air like an extracted bad tooth. Frank fell into the boat. He glanced around him. They were all there, huddled together round the side of the small boat. Jan thrust an oar into his hands. He had no time to think.

'Frank! Row like hell!' he whispered hoarsely.

SIXTEEN

They were the de Beer family, Henk and Kitty and their two children, Ninke and Hendrik. Their new identity cards were new but looked well worn. Disguise was useless so they had their hair cut in a different way. Frank was so upset; they wore farmer's clothes, blue overalls, clogs and heavy skirts.

They had escaped from the factory but only just. After an hour they had eventually reached the little village of Birdaard. A knock on a door and they were safe. Piet had organised everything. Within twelve hours the de Bruins were whisked away to the north of the province and the van der Meer family were taken to the south.

The village of Bakhuizen was only a hundred souls but they were tight-knit and fiercely independent. The nearest German was fifteen kilometres away in the town of Lemmer. Leeuwarden was half a day to the north. They were now divers and Frank knew the routine. Their guardian was an old business colleague, Wim Visser and his wife Hennie. Elderly and well-established they preferred living in the Friesian countryside rather than near the towns. Wim's small timber business, apart from farming, was the only employment in the village. They made their new house guests very welcome.

'We're delighted to see you,' smiled Hennie, 'and so glad you escaped from the *moffen*.'

The van der Meers had slept for a whole day and they were now looking and feeling much better.

Frank relaxed for the first time for months, 'It was a close thing, believe me.' He glanced towards Harmen, 'If it wasn't for my alert son here, then I think we'd all be in a concentration camp, ... or dead.'

'I was on my way home, *Heit*. They passed me at a terrific speed, it was obvious where they were going to. I followed them until I saw our neighbour's house and then I stopped and telephoned you.'

Marieke laughed just as she used to. Her face was flushed, 'Harmen, just this once I'm glad you were late for dinner.'

'I could hear them shouting and shooting from the field nearby. I thought you may've gone along the canal so I cycled about for an hour looking for you. I couldn't find you so I went to Piet's house and told him what had happened.'

'What about the curfew?' questioned Aukje.

He gave her a superior stare, 'Curfew! ... Curfew! ... I never bother about the curfew, I go where I want to go. It's my country.' He turned away.

Wim folded his arms and leant forward, 'Frank, about your factory?' the room fell silent. 'I went there the day after your escape. The men had turned up for work and then, apparently, went home again. I got in touch with the Friesian Timber Association and they've contacted the provincial German Economic Bureau and offered to run the factory as a going concern for the war effort. Surprisingly enough they've accepted the proposal and the Association have asked me who I would like to manage it. So really, Frank, it's over to you. ... Although I have a good man here that I can recommend.'

Frank accepted the recommendation without question. Wim looked uncomfortable, 'I don't know how to say this to both of you. ... I suppose I just have to give you the straight facts. Your house was ransacked by the Germans after they realised you'd escaped. Most of the furniture is still there but your personal things have gone.'

Marieke shook her head. She was saddened 'Material things we can live without. We're alive and that's the important thing.'

'They didn't get everything,' said Frank and he reached into his overalls. 'I managed to save a few things.' He tossed the package to Marieke. She opened it. There was a small collection of jewellery, including a beautiful gold skull cap.

'Oh, Frank, they mean so much to me. They belonged to my grandparents, thank you!' She turned and kissed him on the cheek.

'The Friesian skull cap is wonderful, Marieke,' said Hennie. 'I have one as well but it was hidden long ago when the *moffen* invaded Holland.' She carried on with her knitting.

'I'm hopeful for the future,' nodded Wim. 'The Germans are having a bad time in Russia. That's the one big mistake that Hitler made.'

'Have you still got your radio, Wim?' asked Marieke.

He laughed quietly and his well-proportioned stomach bobbed up and down. 'Yes, mine's the only one left in the village. Banning radios was another mistake they made. I suspect that half of them are hidden. The biggest problem is the batteries.' He nodded again, 'Now, they're difficult to find.'

Frank was more serious, 'The Allies' advance through Italy means that Hitler is fighting a war on two fronts. He'll find it hard work to cope with that situation.'

Suddenly the ground shook and the windows rattled. They instinctively glanced upwards.

'They fly over here all the time,' said a relaxed Wim. 'We're closer to the flight path that you are in Leeuwarden. There's three anti-aircraft batteries about five kilometres away.' He spoke directly to Frank as the wave of bombers continued overhead, 'Your group has saved about a hundred Allied airmen so far and at this rate,' he gripped the arms of his chair, 'it'll be double that by the end of the year.'

'Does it ever stop?' shouted Marieke.

There was pride in his voice. 'Some of the raids on the Ruhr must be nearly a thousand planes. Now, they take hours to fly across here.'

The sound of the aircraft engines almost drowned out the heavy knock at the door. Aukje jumped up and put her hand to her face. Frank whirled round in his chair.

Hennie smiled at them, 'Don't worry. We very rarely see *moffen* down here unless one of the planes has crashed. Anyway, if it was a German, somebody from the village would've warned us.'

She walked into the hall and pulled open the door. She returned with her visitors.

'Hello, everybody. Good to see you all again!' There was clapping from the van der Meers. Piet and Richard took a bow. There was a lot of kissing and shaking hands.

'I know now why you Dutch are so damned fit. The amount of cycling that you all do must be more than the rest of the world put together,' complained Richard, rubbing his calves. 'It's taken us three hours to cycle from Leeuwarden to here. I hope it's not something we'll have to do every day!' There was laughter.

Wim stood, 'Please excuse me for a moment.' He left the room.

The chatter was relaxed and for a moment they all forgot about the war. Richard was sitting next to Aukje and Marieke noticed the glances that they kept exchanging. She smiled to herself. Her daughter was indeed beautiful and at nineteen years old she knew that she would have problems ahead. Marieke looked away: she had problems of her own.

The living-room door opened again and Wim returned. He stood quietly and all eyes turned towards him. '*Meneer* Kiestra,' he used Richard's false name, 'would you like to meet a fellow countryman?'

Richard was totally surprised. From behind Wim's bulky body emerged a young man. He was wearing a huge overcoat and an old cap covering short ginger hair. It was the shiny black boots that gave him away. He glanced around the room and smiled nervously. He was even more nervous when Richard spoke to him in English.

'Taking a spring holiday in the lovely province of Friesland, are you?' The man stood with his mouth open. 'I'm Richard Johnstone, RAF. Who are you?'

'Pilot Officer McDonald, eh, ... Sir.'

Richard bounded across the room and introduced himself. 'Forget the "Sir".' He looked his comrade up and down. 'Dear, oh dear, you've broken the first rule about coming into a Dutch house.' He waved his finger theatrically, 'Never, never, old boy, wear your shoes.'

The young man blushed, bent down and began to untie the shoelaces. Hennie did not speak English but she saw the young airman's dilemma. She quietly took his arm and sat him down next to her on the couch. There was a quiet moment. Wim delved into his pocket and passed the man an enormous cigar.

'Thank you, sir. I ...eh, ... don't smoke.'

'I bet he drinks,' commented Richard with a smile.

Wim beamed, put the cigar back in his pocket and reached into the oak cupboard at the side of his chair. He pulled out a bottle and filled up four glasses with a dark brown liquid. He handed them out to the four men.

'*Proost!* Winston Churchill!' toasted Wim. He threw his head back and drained the glass.

The young man followed and nearly choked. His face went a bright red and he spluttered. Wim patted him on the back and roared with laughter.

'It's pretty strong stuff,' said Richard licking his lips. 'What is it?'

'Best Friesian *Berenburg.* A local poison made from herbs and alcohol,' said Wim as he re-filled the glasses.

It did not take long. Pilot Officer McDonald soon became extremely voluble and began to laugh with the others. After the fourth glass he fell asleep and his head lolled back against the chair.

Wim looked at him and spoke quietly, 'As far as I know, he's the only survivor from a British Wellington bomber that crashed in the *IJsselmeer* two days ago. He's been living in a hole under my cabbage patch since then. I'm going to move him on tomorrow and he should be back in England within six weeks. No doubts the swines'll shoot him down again. They don't survive a second crash.' He inhaled a deep lungful of aromatic cigar smoke and turned to Richard. 'Your countrymen are very brave and so young.'

Richard looked into his glass, 'Not as brave as the Dutch people. They can't go safely home every night.'

Piet spoke for the first time, 'Come on, everybody. This is not a time to be miserable. I think this year is going to bring better news than the last. Although, I think we've a lot to go through before things really improve.'

'I'll drink to that,' said Richard and the glasses were refilled again. He downed it in one gulp and then took a deep breath, 'I've been instructed to return to London next week. I'll be collected by a courier aircraft.'

'Why?' said Aukje. Frank saw her concern.

'Well,' replied Richard, cautiously, 'something is on the boil ...'

'You mean the second front?' interrupted Wim excitedly.

'I don't know, really. But, I've been here for over a year and they wouldn't call me back unless it was for something serious.' Richard smiled at everybody and deliberately changed the subject. He turned to Frank. 'There's something I've always wanted to ask you.'

Frank smiled, 'You may, young man. And I think I know what the question may be and so I'll answer it. I don't drink, because my father was an alcoholic. Twenty years ago he drank himself to death. On that day I swore on his grave never to drink alcohol. It's a promise that I've kept and one that I'll never break.' He turned his palms upwards, 'But, don't let my moral views stop you drinking. After all, we are guests in Wim and Hennie's house.' Their hosts smiled and Richard nodded.

'I think, everybody,' said Hennie, 'that the time has come to let the van der Meer family be alone.' She turned to her friends, 'I'm sorry your accommodation is only two rooms and you have to share washing with my family, but it's all we can do at the moment and I hope it'll be all right for the four of you.'

'Five,' said Marieke ever so quietly. All heads swivelled towards her and she looked at her hands resting neatly in her lap.

Aukje was quicker than all of them. '*Mem!*' she screamed and flew across the room and threw her arms around Marieke's neck.

Frank was totally nonplussed and sat with his mouth open.

'I think congratulations are in order here,' said Richard with a huge smile.

Frank found his tongue, 'Marieke, are you sure?'

'I think so, darling. ... Yes, I'm sure!' She waited for her family to come to her and they did. She was bombarded with kisses and her hand was shaken until it ached. Even the British airman had woken up and Richard told him what was happening. He stood up, a little shakily, and offered his congratulations. Another bottle of *Berenburg* was produced. Hennie found some real coffee and home-made biscuits and there was a small party. Marieke realised that it was their first celebration for three years.

Piet stood and Frank knew that he was going to become serious.

'I'm sorry to spoil this party but I've come with other news and soon Richard and I will have to leave.' He nodded to Richard who said a few words to the British airman. He rose, shook hands with everyone and quietly left the room. Piet continued, 'Frank, since you all escaped it's got worse. Yesterday, Birdaard, the village that sheltered you, was surrounded by SS troops. They took away fifty men, women and children. We don't know where they are. They've disappeared off the face of the earth. We must think the worse.' Aukje began to cry and she clung to Marieke. Frank's head sank onto his chest. Piet continued, 'The *dominee* spoke to me only this morning. He says that the people in the village are praying for you and your family.'

The room was totally silent for several minutes.

Piet began again, 'I'm sorry to bring even more bad news. But, last night I was told that *dominee* Paul de Vries was executed at Amersfoort concentration camp.'

Frank stood up and looked at the people in the room, 'Let us silently pray and at this time remember our friends who are no longer with us.' They all stood and bowed their heads. After a few minutes Frank looked up.

'Amen,' he said softly.

SEVENTEEN

Frank, as leader of *L.O.*, was even more directly involved with providing food and money for the divers of southern Friesland. He cycled once a week to Leeuwarden. He kept away from the *Hotel de Kroon* and the group meetings were normally held in a private house in the south of the town. He never cycled along the same route twice. On each journey he followed trackways and old roads and watched the villages very carefully. The windmills helped him considerably and he knew where he could stop and ask for help. He always travelled alone. The SS had put a price on his head, 10,000 Reichs Mark. Frank took it is a compliment. His false identity was complete. He wore a signet ring engraved with the initials H.D.B. His pink identity card was original, part of a number stolen from the town hall in Leeuwarden. The name, Henk de Beer, was pure fiction, but now he was beginning to act the part. His address was a real house, although he didn't live there. He lived in a boarded-off room in the Vissers' home. Frank's beard was flecked with grey and it was real. Marieke had carefully dyed his hair to match but Frank knew that he was quickly going grey. There was nothing that he could do about it, the war was taking its toll.

The sun had just risen and there were flecks of mist across the flat green fields. As he pushed the pedals round and round and stared at the never-ending horizon he had time to think. He was always alert, looking for the slightest indication of danger. The sails of the windmill in the small village were in the upright position. He was safe. He entered through a farm track from the south. As he turned the corner a man emerged out of the back of a house and hailed him.

'*Meneer*! ... Stop!'

Frank pulled over and leant his bike against the side of the house.

'*Ja*, ... what's the matter?'

The man was dressed in blue overalls and looked a carbon copy of Frank. He took his arm and roughly pulled him round to the front of the building. They crouched down together in the bushes and watched the scene in front of them.

'I thought there were no Germans here,' whispered Frank.

'They came before dawn. We didn't see them.'

The field-grey uniforms of the *Wehrmacht* soldiers matched the early morning mist. Fifty of them, with a smattering of Green Police and two or three SD. They were scattered around the small village square and lolled against their vehicles. Some were smoking, others quietly talking in small groups. There was a casual feeling about their behaviour. There was not a sign of any local people, curtains were tightly drawn; even bicycles were off the streets.

'What's going on?' said Frank. The man shook his head and remained silent.

They crouched behind a bush for over twenty minutes before Frank heard the sound of an engine. The black German car passed within twenty metres of them and braked to a stop in the middle of the tiny square. Its appearance changed the behaviour of the gathered Germans. Cigarettes out, lined up in rows, weapons at the ready and all stiffly to attention. A German *SS* officer climbed out of the car. There was a cigar dangling from his gloved hand. From the other side of the car appeared another *SS* officer. Frank inhaled sharply and clenched his fists. The two men strolled casually across the square and returned the salute from the *Wehrmacht* officer. *Sturmscharführer* Hofmann and *Obersturmführer* Postma were ready for something. They stood the men at ease and patiently waited. Frank heard their occasional laughter and his nose caught the whiff of their cigar smoke as a gentle breeze cleared the mist away from the square.

The village was waking up. Curtains were drawn and faces appeared at the windows and then just as quickly disappeared. The man nudged Frank. Postma crushed out his cigar with his jackboot and walked slowly towards the small church.

As usual, the church was built on a mound of earth, an old tradition to protect the most important building from the frequent floods of the Middle-Ages. The road through the village split down either side of the mound. The mist had gone and the day promised to be warm as the early sun stared from a cloudless blue sky. The first person to appear along the road was an old man, walking slowly with a dog on a lead. Postma nodded and pointed with an outstretched finger. Quickly two soldiers ran forward and grabbed the old man and pulled him back into the square. The dog ran off into the church yard, yapping. Next, were two children. They were ignored: they walked open-mouthed past the lines of soldiers. A man appeared on a bike. He was knocked to the ground and taken. In all nine people entered the village square, six were men, the remainder were women and children.

Frank began to tremble. He had heard about reprisals but had never seen the crime take place. They watched the scene in front of them. The six men stood together in a ragged line, totally bewildered but with fear on their faces. Postma climbed on to the bonnet of his car. He held a megaphone to his mouth. His voice echoed round the empty streets.

'People of Woudsend! ...One of you has admitted to being a terrorist and a member of the Resistance. ... Reprisal is necessary to convince you that such acts against the Third Reich will not be tolerated. ... In precisely ten minutes the six men from your village will be shot as a lesson for you to learn.' He jumped off the car and handed the megaphone to his driver. Postma waved to one of his men.

The men were marched through the narrow church gates to the entrance of the church. It was the highest point of the village and a vantage point for everybody. They stood together and their hands were bound behind their backs. Not a word was spoken as ten soldiers stood in a precise line facing the men. The six villagers backed up against the solid wooden doors of the church. Postma held up his arm and examined his wrist-watch. He looked around him, staring at the streets and the rows of houses. Slowly doors opened and people emerged. Men and women ran towards the village square. The *Wehrmacht* were positioned in exactly the right places. Nobody could get near the church. Postma lit another cigar and stood casually leaning against the door of his car.

Frank rose. The man grabbed at him but he pulled away and joined other small groups of people walking in the same direction. The only sound was the clatter of wooden clogs on the cobbled streets. All movement stopped. Again Postma checked the time. Frank had to break the awful silence. He lifted his head and, in Friesian, began to slowly recite the Lord's Prayer. The first few words echoed back from the church. Within a minute the people began to intone the prayer. The voices swelled in volume. The six men joined in, their eyes alight with new strength. Postma looked at them and then at the crowd. He turned away, waved his cigar and a volley of machine-gun fire rang out. The crescendo of sound went on forever. Nobody stopped praying. The men in front of the church door twisted and turned as the bullets tore into them. They ended up as a ragged heap on the ground.

'Amen!' said Frank loudly.

The firing squad turned round smartly and left the church yard. There was a murmur from the small crowd and they pressed against the confining circle of soldiers. Postma unfastened his holster flap and withdrew his pistol. He fired three shots into the air in rapid succession.

His voice rang out. He spoke in Friesian, not Dutch. 'CLEAR THE SQUARE! IMMEDIATELY!'

Frank knew what could happen next and he was the first one to turn away. The people left the sides of the square and walked towards the windmill at the edge of the village. Some of the women were crying and they were consoled by their friends. Frank found the man at his side and they looked at each other. They were both crying, anger and hatred on their faces.

Engines were started and the Germans left as quickly as they had arrived. The crowd cried out, turned and ran back towards the church. The men were all dead. The wounds were terrible to see and men pushed their womenfolk away from the scene. The doors of the church were bloodstained and the old oak door was split by great gashes torn into it by the machine-gun bullets.

Frank let out a wail of anguish and put his head into his hands. He knew nobody and yet he felt as close to these people as to his own family. The men were tenderly lifted off the ground, the doors of the church were swung open and they were carried inside. The six were laid peacefully on the pews and people gathered around them. They looked at Frank, for a reason he did not understand. He began again to quietly recite the Lord's Prayer. His was the only voice and as the sunlight streamed through the windows over the altar he could hear his words echoing back at him from the brick walls of the old church.

How he got away from the village he never knew.

EIGHTEEN

He arrived at the house long after the group had started its meeting. As he entered the room they looked up at him. Piet was the first to speak.

'Frank, we've been worried. Are you all right?' There were anxious looks as he sat down.

He told them what had happened and the eight men did not know what to say.

Frank sensed their feelings and it took a few moments for him to gather his strength. 'Life must go on and we must help our people. Gentlemen, I've come to this meeting because *L.O.* is having problems. What I saw today demonstrates that problem. I cannot move my people around with any sort of security. Over the last two weeks I've lost three Jewish families to round-ups. We don't know where they're going to strike next. There are spies everywhere and I need your help.'

Piet replied, 'Look, Frank, we'll help you as much as we can. Our main problem in the past was Rauter's decree about ration stamps and identity books.'

Commissioner-*General* Rauter's decree was specifically designed to stop divers and their helpers from moving around Holland and to control the issuing of ration books. In the middle of 1943 he issued a decree saying that ration books would only be issued to people presenting their identity cards to the distribution offices. Before issuing the ration book, the identity card itself had to be stamped and a seal was affixed to the book. It was only valid for six months. It meant, therefore, that the German authorities could check the whole Dutch population twice yearly. Rauter did not trust the Dutch administrators and he had the stamps and ration books printed in Austria.

Piet continued, 'I've got to say that our countrymen have been wonderful. Many of our officials have just handed the new books over to us. The Dutch police have helped us to steal the books and the official stamps.' He shot a quick smile at Joop Koopman, 'I'm glad to say that some of the police in Friesland have now become divers themselves and their uniforms and weapons have been more than useful. Many documents have been stolen and, as I am sure you all remember, this group single-handedly attacked the train from Germany when we stopped it near Leeuwarden. We emptied a freight wagon full of six months supply of documents.' He looked questioningly at Frank, 'I think that you've just about used them all up by now?'

Frank nodded, 'I have used them and that's the problem. I need more.' He rose to speak, as was his way, 'However, I've heard that the ration books are not being examined as closely as before. The books are being handed out with the briefest of checks.'

'You're right, Frank.' said Joop Koopman quietly from his corner chair.

Frank sat down. 'I have information that Rauter could not control the administration of these important documents. My informant also told me that Rauter will soon inform all provincial authorities that any offence regarding identity cards or other documents will mean being brought to trial and that, gentlemen, as we all know, means certain death. So, Frank, for God's sake, be careful.' Joop shifted his feet and looked at each of the men in turn. They knew he was going to say something important.

'What I'm going to say now is absolutely secret.' He spoke almost in a whisper. 'It has been brought to my notice that the Germans have begun a new policy, code-named "Operation Silver Fir". ... Whenever a Nazi, either Dutch or German, is killed by a Dutch citizen, then the Germans will secretly avenge that death by the killing of three prominent citizens from the same area or town. The executioners will be Germans dressed in civilian clothes. They will then be protected and helped to move out of Holland and so avoid reprisals by our Resistance. It seems that some famous people have already been murdered because of this policy.' He looked at the faces around him. 'Gentlemen, most of us here are "prominent people" and when we take part in any action against the Nazis then, in the future, we can expect such things to happen to us. We must be on our guard at all times and protect our families as well as ourselves.'

'That policy would explain some of the activity that has taken place in other parts of Holland,' said Piet. 'But, it should not stop what we're doing. I've heard of other actions by the Nazis.' He looked at the group. '*Generalfeldmarschall* Keitel of the German High Command, has signed a decree called, "*Nacht und Nebel*". It effectively means that if any person acts in any way against Germany then that person should only be brought to trial if the death sentence is a certainty. If their guilt is in doubt then they will be taken at night and in secrecy to a German concentration camp. The arrested people will disappear completely and even their burial place will be unknown.' He folded his arms and his lips formed a thin line. 'I think we now know exactly what we're dealing with, both morally and legally. These German swine will not get away with it forever.' The heads nodded.

'No matter what we do, either way they've got us,' said Frank. 'I don't know how long we can keep it up for, ... but, I know one thing.' his eyes were alight, 'I'll fight them to the last drop of blood in my body.'

There was a quiet knock at the door and the group of men stiffened with anticipation. Joop leapt from his chair and gently moved the curtain.

'Nobody there,' he whispered. Frank was surprised to see four of the men withdraw guns from inside their coats.

Piet eased the door open. The lady of the house whispered in his ear. He smiled and closed the door. 'Relax, which one of you brought his dog to the meeting?' They looked at each other and shook their heads. 'Well, there's been a dog sitting on the front door step for the last hour.'

'Bring it in,' said one of the men. Piet left the room.

He returned holding a lead. At the end of it was a small terrier, very muddy and exhausted. Without a moment's hesitation it padded across the floor leaving a trail of wet prints. It sat in front of Frank, put a paw on his leg and gave one sharp bark.

Frank leant forward and stroked the terrier behind its ears. He suddenly snapped his fingers. The men were watching him.

'It's the old man's dog, from Woudsend, ... he was the first one to be taken, ... I can't believe it. He's followed me for over twenty kilometres and found this house.' As he spoke, the terrier jumped onto his lap and began licking his face.

'I think, Frank,' said Joop with a smile, 'that you've got yourself a new friend.'

The meeting broke up in the usual way. They left at brief intervals and Frank and Piet scrambled through the roof space into the adjoining house. They were let out through the back door into the passage-way that connected the houses. The terrier was waiting for them and Piet laughed aloud.

Frank made good time back to Bakhuizen. The wind was behind him and it pushed the bike along. He only had to stop for the dog. It trotted along at the side of the rear wheel of his bicycle and occasionally flopped to the ground. Frank knew it was tired and he stopped and stroked its head as the dog sprawled in the damp grass. The brown eyes followed his every move.

It was late evening and dusk had just descended as he cycled through the woods near the village. The trees were fresh with the spring and the light green leaves cast a faint glow onto the track with the last light of the day. He walked for a time, pushing the bicycle with the terrier at his heels. He realised that he did not know what to call the poor animal. There was no collar only the lead. He pulled it out of his pocket and looked at it. There was a small brass plate sewn onto the looped handle. By bringing it close to his eyes in the fast fading light he was able to read, "Dempsey". Frank smiled, an appropriate name for a dog that was going to help him resist the Germans.

He threw his bicycle in the bushes and walked the last hundred metres to the Vissers' house. A precaution, it was easy to cycle into a trap. The house was silent and he knocked at the back door. Four short taps.

The door opened quietly and Frank stepped inside. The silence was uncanny and then he realised why. Everybody was upstairs in the top two bedrooms only used by his family. He sensed danger and his skin prickled. He followed a grim looking Wim up the steep stairs. Marieke and Aukje were waiting for him. She was pale faced and she clasped her hands tightly. She stood quietly and her voice was almost a whisper. 'Frank, they've taken Harmen.'

He threw his arms around her and felt her body heave as she began to cry. He looked into her eyes. There were few tears. He knew that she had cried before his arrival. He led her to the bed and sat down at her side. Aukje stood and looked at them. She was composed and quiet.

'Marieke, tell me about it.' She shook her head and nodded to Wim.

He stood in the doorway and looked at the three van der Meers. 'Harmen has been working for Uncle for some time, as we all know. He took part in the raid on the train and yesterday a small group from within Uncle robbed the main post office in Leeuwarden. Frank, he knew that you were desperately short of ration books. They were very successful and nearly got away with it. They went to ground in the de Bruins' old house near to your factory.' He paused and shook his head, 'Somebody must've informed the Germans. They surrounded the house this morning. The group fought well, several Germans were injured and one of the group was killed. Eventually they were overwhelmed and six were taken prisoner, Harmen was one of them.'

'Where is he?' asked Frank.

'He's in *SS* headquarters on *het Zaailand*. We don't know for how long. They'll probably move him to the prison in Leeuwarden. He'll be in good company. There's over forty of our men in there.' He gave a quick smile of re-assurance. It was not returned by Frank.

Wim pushed back his thinning grey hair, 'Frank, I've got to say this. I spoke to Piet and he thinks the same way as I do. They may torture Harmen to make him tell them about you and Uncle's activities. We could all be at risk.'

The small bedroom was silent. Hennie knocked at the open door, she spoke quietly, 'Let's all go to the living-room and talk about this awful thing.'

Slowly they all stood and helped each other down the stairs. Nobody felt like talking as Wim pulled the curtains tightly closed and sat in his old leather chair. The telephone rang loudly and everybody jumped. Wim left the room. A few minutes later he returned.

'It was Piet. The *moffen* have let it be known that Harmen will be executed unless the rest of the van der Meer family give themselves up within the next forty-eight hours.' Frank put his head into his hands and rocked backwards and forwards. Wim continued, 'Müller has doubled the price on your head to 20,000 *Reich* Marks. They want you, Frank, and they want you badly.'

He looked up at Wim, 'Why me, oh my Lord above, why me?'

Marieke put her hand on his, 'Because, my darling, at first they trusted you. You worked for them, you met them socially and they thought they could depend on you. They now know what you're really doing. They can fight the Resistance but they can't fight what you believe in. They know that you're more dangerous than any man with a gun. Pray with me, Frank, please.'

NINETEEN

Things happened quickly. Harmen was taken by four men of the *Waffen-SS*. They carefully smashed him in the kidneys with the butts of their machine-pistols and threw him into the boot of a car. He was not conscious of the journey, the excruciating pain in his back made him curl up like a ball and he hugged his knees to his chest trying to lessen the agony. As the boot opened and the daylight flooded in he knew exactly where he was. Two Green Police dragged him across the pavement and kicked him up the steps of *SS* headquarters. He fell down the flight of steep stairs to the cellars and was pushed into a dark room.

It was pitch-black. Only a sliver of light came under the bottom of the door. He lay for a moment, unsure what to do. The pain eased slightly, when he tried to stand, it hit him again and he dropped onto the cold floor. He crawled on his hands and knees and explored the cell. About three metres square with a door on one side. As he felt the rough surface with his fingers, a single light bulb above him burst into life. It blinded him and he covered his face with his hands. Slowly he let his eyes adjust to the brightness and only then was he able to look around.

A brick-lined cube, dazzling white paint, no windows and not one item of furniture. The light was recessed behind a thick glass lens on the ceiling and let into the brick floor was a small iron grille. He sat back against the wall and then abruptly, total darkness. His eyes blinked and he lifted up his arms, nothing. As he tried to relax, through the door of his cell he heard a shrill scream. It was a scream of pure agony and after a moment it subsided into a sobbing moan. Total silence returned.

The stories about what happened in the cellars of this building began to flash out of his memory. He knew of only one person who had walked out of this building and that person never spoke again. Harmen was a brave young man, toughened by the vagaries of war. But now, shivers of fear began to rack his body. He began to shake in uncontrollable waves that made his teeth rattle.

He forced out a wretched shout, 'NO! ... NO! ... NO!' The shaking stopped.

A few minutes later the light clicked on again. He stood and reached out for it: it went out. Harmen forced himself to stand with his back against the wall to concentrate on what was happening to him. He knew that he was going to die. All people who attacked Germans eventually died. He knew that he was going to be tortured. His father was too well known to the Germans for them to do anything else. He found himself clenching and unclenching his fists and his palms bled through his fingers. The light came on again and he closed his eyes and waited for it to go off: it remained on. The door slammed open and two *SS* men watched him from the doorway. He was unsure what to do. They said nothing and motioned for him to follow. He surprised himself by meekly obeying.

There was one of them on each side of him. No shackles, no chains, no harsh treatment. For a moment he thought he was dreaming. Up the stairs and onto a normal corridor. The wooden floor gleamed with a high polish and he fleetingly saw the lights of the high chandeliers reflecting off its surface. They stopped opposite the last door and one of the guards knocked.

'Come!' announced a voice from within.

Harmen saw *Hauptsturmführer* Müller sitting behind a massive desk. He was immersed in a book. The guards left and quietly closed the door. It was a comfortable office in the Dutch style with Teutonic touches. On the wall behind Müller's chair was a huge portrait of Adolf Hitler in military pose. At its side was a blood red and black swastika flag. There was music playing, something that Harmen could not recognise, but it was definitely classical. Still Müller continued reading. He let his gaze spread further round the room. His eyes passed it for a moment and then returned. The painting was so familiar and then he understood. It was his father's de Hoogh landscape. Somehow the sight of this blatant theft gave him an inner strength that was not there before.

On the hat stand near the window hung a black belt with a shoulder strap. The holster on the belt was unfastened and the butt of the black Luger gleamed in the soft lights. For a moment Harmen thought of making a lunge for the weapon and he gauged the distance.

'Don't even think about it, van der Meer,' grated the voice without looking up from the book. 'You would not get two paces across this room. My reflexes are even faster than yours.' The head never moved but the free hand did, 'I would shoot you through the right knee cap, with this.' The hand brushed away a pile of papers to reveal another gun. Both men hesitated and then the book closed with a snap and Harmen physically jumped.

Müller sat back in the chair and folded his arms. The blue eyes stared intently at the young man in front of him. He pursed his lips and nodded, 'I remember you,' Harmen was surprised at the perfection of his high Dutch. 'We last met many years ago at the first reception given by the Reichs Commissioner at the Friesian Museum.' They matched each other stare for stare. 'I've had the pleasure of meeting your mother and father under different circumstances.' Harmen stared harder at the man sitting in the chair in front of him. He was handsome and his uniform was immaculate. He somehow began to doubt the awful things that he had heard about him. This fleeting moment of relaxation was instantly felt by Müller. The fist crashed down on the table and the voice whiplashed across the room.

'You have tried to kill my men! ... I don't like that! ... You will be executed tomorrow! ... Now, get out!'

The raised voice brought the guards. Harmen whirled round, too late.

One black jackboot caught him behind the knee, the other at the base of his spine and he buckled to the floor. They dragged him out of the room, kicking him over and over again. Before the door closed he caught a snapshot glimpse of Müller. He was reading the book.

They kicked him all the way back to his cell. He crawled down the corridor past the offices. He saw secretaries looking at him. The click-clacking of their typewriters seemed to be in harmony with the kicks that hammered into him. The guards pushed him into his cell. The last kick was aimed at his head. He saw it coming and twisted away from the blow. The boot was quicker than him and his brain exploded into darkness.

It was the icy cold temperature of the water that brought him back to life. The light bulb shone into his single open eye. Harmen was flat on his back. He moved his head away from the light and saw the bloody water trickle away down the grille. Realising it was his blood, he forced himself to sit up. The pain washed over him from a dozen places and his mouth felt gritty from the dried blood on his lips. He moved his hands to his face and felt the bruised, wet patches with his fingers. One eye was firmly closed and the other only half-open. Even so, the light was blinding. He squeezed the eye open a little more and saw Müller looking down at him. The peaked hat was set at an angle and he had his hands deep in the pockets of his black riding breeches. The eyes under the peak watched him as though he were a fly. Harmen tried to compose himself. He sat up, wanting to look back at Müller.

The voice was almost friendly, 'Young man, I've been thinking. That death sentence could be commuted to long term imprisonment.' Somehow Harmen knew exactly what Müller was going to say. 'You're not important to me but your mother and father are. All you have to do is to tell me where they are and then you can go to a normal prison. A trial will come much later and there will be no death sentence.'

Harmen did not hesitate. The reply was in foul Friesian.

He replied in passable Friesian. 'I also speak your gutter dialect.' Müller turned, nodded to the men standing behind him and left.

Obersturmführer Postma looked at his prisoner. His tie was slack at the neck and he wore no hat. The face was red with excitement and it poured with sweat. He stood with his hands behind his back and his legs were spread wide apart. The smile was one of pleasurable anticipation.

For a moment Harmen thought of raising himself and head-butting the man in the crotch. He should have known Postma. From behind him appeared four other men. They were stripped to the waist and their boots were black and shiny. Their faces were expressionless. It was the boots that Harmen feared most of all. Postma licked his lips like a snake. The men sat down at the four corners of the cell. In one united movement they grabbed their prisoner's wrists and ankles and pulled him into a cross on the floor. He was helpless to do anything. He saw Postma bring his hands from behind his back. One hand held a long, flexible leather cosh and he whacked it into the palm of his hand. Each time he hit the hand he grunted, another slap another grunt. He quickly worked himself into a sadistic frenzy. The whacking stopped and he nodded to the men. They smiled with the knowledge of what was to come and leaned back, stretching their victim as though he was on a rack.

Harmen closed his eyes tightly and tried to stiffen his muscles. A grunt, the first blow was to his testicles. The pain was excruciating and lances of pure agony shot through his body like hot knives. A grunt, the second blow fell on his stomach. The third was to his arms. The fourth to his feet. Legs, arms feet, stomach, head, ears, testicles; and over and over again. He was hardly conscious. The first screaming pain had left him and now he felt detached. It was the sounds that came through to his consciousness. Postma's grunt signalled another blow. His body gave off different sounds as the cosh struck him. His belly gave off a hollow thwack but his legs sounded solid and the leather crackled as it hit the exposed bone. He blacked out and the darkness gave him blessed relief.

He felt the water again. It sluiced over his body and it produced no response. He was sprawled on the floor and he made no movement. Hands pulled him to his feet and he was dragged along the brick floor and up the stairs. The typewriters were still at work and, as ever, the floor gleamed. A thought flashed through his mind that the *moffen* would have to polish it after they had dragged him down it. He wondered how on earth he was able to think such improbable things at such a time.

They sat him in a chair. This time *Hauptsturmführer* Müller stood near the window with his back to the room. Harmen drew strength from the bright sunlight and the green of the trees outside. He was a mess of pain and pride and unable to sit still. Each bruise and cut was desperately uncomfortable. His swollen eyes caught sight of a tray of food on the ornate desk. The aroma of hot coffee and the pungent smell of freshly cut oranges seemed to overpower his senses. He was so tempted to reach forward and take the coffee. His memory of the last time that he met Müller stopped him but his eyes lingered.

Müller walked across the room and sat against his desk. He lifted the cup to his lips and sipped noisily. He placed the cup back on its porcelain saucer and put a slice of the orange into his mouth. He made a gentle sucking sound and swallowed.

'Orange is such a delicious fruit and so refreshing.' He stood and withdrew his gun from the holster on the desk. He walked to Harmen. 'Oh dear, I see your countryman, Postma, has made quite a mess of you.' Carefully he poked the barrel of the Luger into Harmen's ear.

Müller watched his prisoner cringe but saw that the eyes still blazed. He kept the barrel in the same position and drew back the hammer with his other hand. The voice quietly continued, 'I have the power of life or death. Now, tell me, where is your father?'

Harmen could hear the birds singing outside the window and in a brief second he whispered a short prayer. It surprised him. It was something that he had never done before.

'Appealing to your God, will do you no good. I have the gun, not him.'

He felt the barrel pushing him sideways off the chair. Still the cold steel bored into his battered head.

He fell in a heap and Müller was on him in a flash. The muzzle moved to his forehead. He forced him to lie flat, his foot planted firmly in the middle of Harmen's chest. 'Now, tell me!' There was no response. 'NOW!' he screamed.

He did not know how he did it. It was probably the bitter taste of blood in his mouth and the loose tooth. He rolled the sticky wad of spittle around his tongue and spat it out full into Müller's face. He had the satisfaction of seeing it hit the target. The man recoiled and the gun lifted for a moment and the hammer clicked home. He felt nothing. If this was death then he was still conscious. Harmen realised that the click of the falling hammer was all that he had heard, no pain above what he already felt. He promptly fainted and felt no more. He did not feel Müller kicking him over and over again.

Harmen awoke on the brick floor of his cell. The light was on and he was alone. The pain was a high throbbing ache, with stabs of ferocity in different parts of his battered body. He managed to sit up and the stench hit him. He looked down and nearly cried with shame. His bowels and his bladder had emptied all over him. He was soaked in his own excreta and urine and he stank. With something like anger boiling within him, he ripped off his clothes, wiped his body and threw them into a corner. He looked at himself. He was bleeding in several places and there were welters of bruises all over his body. Hardly a spot was untouched. He pushed his finger into his mouth and felt his gums. One of his teeth fell out onto his hand. He felt again. There was another bloody hole. It hurt him to smile, but he did when he realised that the other tooth was in the wad of spittle that he had blasted into Müller's face.

He was desperately cold but nothing would make pick up his clothes. He drifted in and out of consciousness and time meant nothing.

Harmen did have to wear the stinking clothes. In the middle of the night they moved him to the prison in Leeuwarden.

PART FOUR

Liberation

ONE

They all gathered in another safe house. There were people in the small room whom Frank had never met before but they were all there for a common purpose.

Piet began, 'Ladies and gentlemen, we're here to make a plan to rescue Harmen van der Meer and our comrades from the Central Prison in Leeuwarden.' He looked around the room and at each face, 'Time is very important. Our people could be moved or executed at any time.' Frank's face remained expressionless. Piet continued, 'The rescue must take place tomorrow, or not at all. Suggestions please.' There was silence and everybody glanced at each other.

Frank raised his hand. His voice was quiet and respectful, 'Firstly, I must thank you for trying to save my son's life. Secondly, I think that to use violence will serve no purpose whatsoever. If we kill any *moffen*, then they'll take reprisals. If we fail, then they'll certainly kill our comrades in the prison. Therefore, let's make a plan that will kill nobody and work first time.'

One of the group was the next to speak, 'Frank, I agree completely. But we'll need a good plan to achieve such success.'

Piet sat down and the various members of the Resistance groups present began to talk amongst themselves. After thirty minutes of frantic discussions Joop Koopman stood. There was a respectful hush.

He spoke with authority, 'I know the prison well and I know how it works. It's part of my job to take criminals into custody, either before they go to court or when they've been sentenced. The prison has Dutch police inside but they're there mainly for administration. The German Green Police and the SD do all the dirty work.' He paused for a moment, scratched his chin and nodded, 'I think we could use the police uniforms that we've got already. Two of us would be disguised as policemen who could then escort three of us disguised as prisoners and therefore gain entry in the normal way. The necessary documents could be easily and quickly forged.' For a moment he smiled, 'The drunks of the town are normally taken into the prison around midnight, usually when the police cells are full. And, knowing my comrades here, some of you don't need to act the part of being drunkards.' There was a ripple of laughter and some of the group turned to nod and smile at each other.

'Right,' said Joop, 'I can't come with you, because I'd be recognised immediately. The prison staff don't know every policeman in Friesland, so let's say that you've come from another town. You arrive at midnight. Some of the staff will be asleep. You gain entry with the three men accused of petty crimes, drunkenness or something else. The guards let you in, you overpower them and put them in a cell, release our friends and escape through the back entrance. I'm sure that Frank's organisation can hide them all before dawn.'

Dirk raised his hand and asked quietly, 'Joop, the prison has a moat around it. Will that be a problem for the escapees?'

'You're right, there is a moat. The main entrance is a permanent bridge. The rear entrance is only for emergencies. Believe it or not, it's a small drawbridge that's lowered electrically. I don't see that as a problem.' He looked around for other questions. Piet stood and joined Joop at the front of the room.

'I think this is a good plan. It's the only one that we have and we have to make it work.' A woman raised her hand. Eyes turned towards her.

'I'm a part-time cleaner at the prison,' she said simply.

Piet hit the side of his head in frustration, 'My God, Jean, of course you are. Why the hell didn't I remember that?'

She spoke quietly, 'Probably because you've a lot to think about. I only work there for three mornings a week. The *moffen* ignore us cleaners, probably because we're women as well as mere cleaners. I don't clean the cells but I know how to get information to the guards and the prisoners.'

'How?' asked Joop.

'In their food. It's cooked by women in the kitchen and then picked up by the guards. They never check, they just take it straight to the cells. I could arrange for any message that you want to be sent. But, you'll have to hurry. I'm due at work at six tomorrow morning.' She smiled at the men around her.

The discussions continued for another hour. Eventually Piet raised his hand for silence and then began to speak.

'Ladies and gentlemen, I think we've sorted out most of the details. Perhaps if I cover the most important parts of the plan it will help all of us. All right, I'm one of the police, Dirk's the other. Frank is one of the drunks,' roars of laughter, 'all together, six of us. As the prison is near the main canal in town we'll be taken away by barge. I think *schipper* Schaaf will help with that, I'll contact him later.' He turned to his friend, 'Joop, you wanted to say something ... ?'

Joop nodded and waved his finger, 'You've got to look the parts that you're playing. It'll be dark but the entrances are well lit. Some of my men work in the prison, I'll brief them. We'll meet two hours before midnight and I'll have a plan of the prison ready for us.' He looked across the room. 'Jean, if you see me before you go I'll give you the messages. I want only three of our comrades informed. Any more and the whole atmosphere inside the prison will be affected. The Germans are very good at spotting such changes.' He looked around the group, 'Remember Frank's point. It's vital that we don't kill anybody. A bash on the head is all right but no shooting, absolutely no shooting.' He turned as there was a hammering at the door. Piet jumped forward, gun in hand and unbolted the back door of the small terraced house.

Richard Johnstone burst in and whispered something to Piet. He pushed

Richard forward into the centre of the room.

'You tell them, it's your news,' he said, with a smile.

Richard could not contain himself. 'An hour ago I heard some wonderful news from one of my contacts in Amsterdam. I had it confirmed by radio twenty minutes ago.' He took a deep breath and his voice quivered with excitement, 'This morning the Allies, in great strength, landed on the beaches somewhere in Normandy and they've made good progress so far!' His voice was drowned out by the cheers. Everybody stood and there was handshaking and backslapping. Piet calmed them down.

'I think that today, the 6th June 1944, will go down in history and I feel that the end for us may be in sight.'

Frank never pushed his faith into meetings but this time he felt compelled to do so. When he stood, everybody knew what he was going to say and they rose and listened to his words.

He spoke emotionally and with a great sense of occasion, 'Comrades and friends. This is a time of great happiness. Let us pray in silence for a few moments for our gallant Allies and for our friends who are no longer with us. Let us think about the mission tomorrow and pray to God that it is successful without death.'

The assault on the prison was launched from the cellars of the *Hotel de Kroon*. Before they left Dirk laid on a wonderful meal. So far the plans had worked. They were gathered together and they were ready. Piet and Dirk looked the part, their police uniforms fitted and, in the brief time that they had to prepare, Joop had carefully coached them.

Piet strutted up and down the cellar, 'Frank, you'll never look like a drunk. Why don't you be a curfew breaker instead?'

'No, I'll be a drunk. Nobody will ever recognise me,' he said, grinning from ear to ear.

'Twenty minutes to go,' said Dirk quietly. 'Frank, you may not drink but you've got to smell like a drunk. Close your eyes.' He upended a whole bottle of his best gin over his friend's head. 'Now, at least you smell like one!'

Dirk led the group down the passage to the canal. Dusk had gone but it was still a light summer's evening. Joop took them down the narrow cobbled street. All along their path members of Group Uncle checked the route and waved them on. They saw no patrols and it took them twenty minutes to reach their target. They waited in the shadows of the moored barges on the canal.

The prison was nineteenth century Gothic; spires and archways, all built in red brick and it was stark and functional. No architectural style could hide its purpose. The barred windows looked down on the moat and the main doors were securely closed. The prison was surrounded by bright security lights. A huge swastika flag hung limply from a tall flagpole. To the citizens of Leeuwarden the building was a symbol of their occupation.

Frank made the decision. He looked at his watch, 'Gentlemen, time to go. Good luck to everybody.' He stepped out of the shadows and onto the quayside and they followed him. Piet took over and he and Dirk began to escort the three men.

The bridge to the main door loomed up in front of them. It was a calm, summer's night, with not a breath of wind and nobody about. Frank clutched at Dirk's arm and began to stagger. The smell of gin was making him feel quite ill. Dirk nudged him.

'Sing!'

What Frank sang totally surprised the men. It was the dirtiest song that had ever been written in the Dutch language. He was really enjoying himself and the other two men joined in with gusto. They crossed the bridge and approached the doors.

Piet saw the flap on the spy-hole move to one side. His heart began to beat faster. He pressed the door bell. The small window in the door opened.

'*Ja*, what do you want?'

Piet calmed. The voice spoke in Dutch.

'Three prisoners. To be placed in cells for the night,' he replied brusquely.

'Papers!'

He reached into the pocket of his leather jacket and pulled out the wad of documents and waved them at the face.

'All right, come in.' There was a clicking of locks and bolts. The door swung open. In front of them stood the high wooden counter and away to their left down a short corridor, another door, this time barred and locked.

The man behind the desk was a Dutch police *sergeant*. Frank started singing again and lurched towards the counter.

'Jesus, get him away from me,' muttered the Dutchman. Behind him stood a man in the uniform of the Green Police.

'What are the charges against these men?' he said in German.

'Drunkenness and breaking curfew,' replied Piet, casually.

Frank was unused to gin. He suddenly vomited all over the counter.

'Pardon me,' he said wiping his mouth.

'*Scheisse*! ... Why don't you keep these animals in the police station?' shouted the German.

'Sorry, we're full up,' replied Piet.

Dirk started coughing, mainly to cover up his smile. He had never seen Frank perform like this before.

The German came round to the front of the counter. 'Leave your papers on the other counter and get a bucket for this swine to clear up his mess.' He turned round away from Piet, a fatal mistake. Dirk clubbed him neatly on the back of the head with the butt of his pistol. The man collapsed without a sound. He reversed the gun and pointed it at the *sergeant*.

'Quickly now, where are the keys?'

The *sergeant* raised his hands, walked slowly round the counter and kicked the German very hard between the legs. 'I've been waiting for years to do that to this bastard.' He turned to face them with a smile on his lips. 'I know why you're here and I'll help you in any way that I can. I'm leaving this bloody police force, I've had enough.'

He slammed the main door closed and opened a cupboard on the wall. Rows of labelled keys hung from brass hooks. He selected several bunches, 'Follow me.' He quietly led the way down the passage and stopped in front of the heavy, barred door, turned to the men, put his fingers to his lips and whispered, 'On the other side of here are three Germans and two Dutchmen. One of our men can't be trusted, I'll deal with him. Look out for the alarm on the wall to the left of the door. It's connected to SS headquarters and the barracks.'

Frank could not believe their good luck. Everything seemed to be going to plan. The smell of his vomit and the gin made him feel quite giddy and strangely detached from reality.

The *sergeant* put a key in the door and turned the lock. The door opened. The Germans were sitting playing cards. One of the Dutchmen sat with them. It was a normal scene. There was the smell of coffee and a pile of old newspapers.

'Three prisoners for remand,' intoned the *sergeant*. They carried on playing. The Dutchman stood up. With his back to the card players he gave an enormous wink and a huge smile.

The smallest German at the table stared hard at his hand, 'Cell 20. ... Feitsma, take them down.'

Dirk walked up behind one of the Germans and tapped him on the shoulder. The man turned, with curiosity on his face. It was over in two minutes. Frank surprised everybody, one of the men tried to draw his gun. Frank punched him neatly on the jaw and without a sound the man slumped over the table. They dragged the men down the passage towards the cells.

'There're two more guards, but they're ours. They'll ignore us,' said the *sergeant*.

There was no panic. They walked along each row of cells and the beaming prisoners were released.

After the last man had been freed Frank turned to the *sergeant*, 'Where's my son?'

'He'll be in solitary. There're are three of them down there. Come on, I'll show you.'

He walked back towards the guard office, turned left and opened a heavy door. The steps led down below the prison. A shiver went down Frank's spine. It was like descending into hell.

There were six doors. The locks turned easily. The first two men limped out. Frank knew one of them. They shook hands without a sound. The last door was opened. At first he thought it was empty. The light was faint and he could see little. He turned to leave. A voice croaked from the darkest corner.

'*Heit!*'

Frank whirled round and stared hard. He could just hear the voice.

'It's me, Harmen. ... For God's sake, help me. ... Please, *Heit*, help me!'

He dashed to the corner and reached down into the pile of stinking clothes. A hand grasped his and he pulled his son into the dim light.

'Oh my Lord in heaven above,' whispered Frank. 'What have the swines done to you?'

'*Heit*, I didn't tell them anything,' whispered the voice.

He could not see his face, it was just a bloody mess. Matted hair in clotted blood. The eyes were closed and surrounded by heavy bruises. Harmen tried to lift himself and with a moan of pain fell back onto the brick floor.

'I need help! Come here quickly. Help me to carry him!' shouted Frank.

It took three of them to carry him gently out of the cell and up the short flight of stairs. There, many hands helped their comrade towards the rear of the prison.

Time was short. So far the assault was going well, but rescuing Harmen had slowed the operation. Piet followed the *sergeant* down a maze of short corridors. Still doors were being unlocked and released prisoners joined the column. Hardly anybody spoke and the tension was beginning to rise minute by minute. They stopped in front of a heavy door. A key was produced and it swung open. Behind was a narrow hatch-way secured by massive padlocked bolts. Piet was became impatient as the men began to push from behind.

'Come on man, for God's sake, get it open! Quickly!

The *sergeant* fumbled with the keys and tried four or five. Each failed to fit.

He turned to face them, 'I don't have the keys. They must've changed the padlocks.'

Frank held his son close to him but his brain was still functioning. 'Piet, Dirk use your guns. Blast the locks off.' He saw their hesitation. '*Verdomme*, we've got no other choice. Do it! ... NOW!'

They withdrew their weapons and waved the men back. The crash of shots echoed deafeningly around the confined space but it worked. The padlocks shattered and dropped off the bolts. Dirk yanked the bolts back and pushed the hatch.

'No ... wait,' said the *sergeant*, 'it's electrically operated. Wait a minute!'

He reached to a small panel at the top of the hatch-way, flipped it open and pushed a switch. There was the low whining of an electric motor and the hatch began to lower away from them. A louder clanging reached their ears as the fresh air rushed in at them through the open hatch.

'Oh my God, it's the alarm!' shouted the *sergeant*. 'It must be connected to this emergency door. I never knew it.' The men pushed forward as panic began to set in. Piet and Dirk held them back as the hatch dropped into place on the other side of the moat.

Piet led the way, 'Come on! ... All of you. ..... Follow me!' He dashed over the small bridge. The wailing of sirens seemed to fill the narrow streets and gave added impetus to the running men.

Dirk stayed and helped Frank to half-carry and half-drag Harmen. He must have been in the most awful pain but his lips remained firmly shut. Hands helped them as they crossed the bridge and out onto the street. They followed the men in front of them as they all raced though a short passage towards the canal.

It was still dark and the black strip of water was a welcome sight. The first men were already boarding two low barges, their gang-planks held firmly in position by the crew. The first boat was full and it quickly chugged away down the canal. The second one was just as fast and it travelled in the opposite direction.

'*Meneer*, quickly down here!'

Frank knew that voice. Two strangers took his son away from him but he held on and followed them into the dark hold of the barge.

'*Schipper* Schaaf! You don't know how glad I am to see you,' said Frank.

The sight of the smiling *schipper*, lit by the oil lamps swinging from the deck beams, gave him new heart and he collapsed onto a pile of sacking. He felt an arm around his shoulders as the *schipper* welcomed him.

'*Meneer* van der Meer, have you started drinking?' The deep voice cut through the silence.

Frank was confused and then from within him arose an inane giggle. It changed to a smile and he suddenly began to laugh. He could not stop. He laughed until his stomach ached. All around him men were joining in and it was Piet who eventually stopped them.

'BE QUIET! ... BE QUIET! ... We're passing houses, somebody may hear you.'

The silence was even more pronounced as they waited in the slowly moving barge. Frank could feel the boat making way along the canal. He knew exactly where they were going and occasionally he looked down at Harmen cradled gently in his arms.

'Listen,' said Dirk. Over the sound of the barge's engines they could all hear the wailing of sirens as vehicles passed by near the canal.

'The Germans are looking for us,' said *schipper* Schaaf. 'Another ten minutes and we'll be in open countryside. Then we should be safe.'

Most of the twenty or so men were sprawled flat in the belly of the hold. Some were asleep. Others just stared around them in disbelief. Frank glanced at his watch. The assault had taken exactly twenty-five minutes from leaving the *Hotel de Kroon* until clambering on the barge. That was eight minutes longer than planned.

Schipper Schaaf knelt close to Harmen. His voice was gentle, 'Well, young man, you've been very brave. I'm proud to have taken part in your rescue.' He tenderly stroked his head, 'Don't worry. There'll soon be help for you.'

For the first time since his father had lifted him from the cell, Harmen spoke, 'Thank you, everybody, thank you.'

The voice was barely a whisper but it was heard throughout the small hold. Quite spontaneously the men began clapping. Tears rolled down Frank's face and he held his son even tighter.

After an hour the barge stopped. *Schipper* Schaaf climbed up the short ladder and raised the hatch. Dawn was streaking the sky and he whispered down details of their location.

'All right men. The first five for Bozum village.' They wearily climbed up the steps and disappeared into the daylight. The hatch was left open and the barge continued on its way. It stopped at another six dropping-off points until only four of them remained.

Frank looked down. Harmen was fast asleep. He gently lowered him onto the sacks and covered him up with his jacket. He stretched, realising just how stiff he had become. Walking towards the ladder he climbed up to the deck. It was a bright sunny day and *schipper* Schaaf beckoned him into the wheel-house. The barge was typically Dutch, long and low in the water. Its blunt bow steadily pushed its way past the grassy banks of the canal. The flat Friesian countryside was like a tonic to Frank. He put his legs over the side and leant back against the hatches. The scene before him was totally peaceful. Friesian cows continued grazing as the barge chugged past. Birds flew overhead and the colours were horizontal green and vertical blue. For a few precious minutes Frank relaxed so much that he fell asleep.

One of the crew-men was tugging his arm, '*Meneer, MENEER!* Go below deck.' He pointed into the blue sky, 'Planes are coming!'

Frank looked around him as he scrambled towards the open hatch. From the north a speck appeared over the horizon. The insistent buzz grew to a roar as the single engined aircraft began to approach rapidly. He fell down into the hold as the hatch slammed to over his head. The sound of the engine came clearly through the wooden hull of the boat. The men looked upwards as the aircraft passed unseen overhead. The deck hatch was thrown open. *Schipper* Schaaf's head appeared.

'You can come up again now. They're gone.'

Frank gripped the rungs of the ladder and stared up into the blue sky above.

'*Heit,* take me with you.' He whirled round. His son was standing against one of the deck supports. 'I need some fresh air. Take me with you.' He tried to stagger forward and was neatly caught by Dirk as he stumbled. Between them they managed to carry him onto the deck.

It was the first time that Frank had seen him in daylight. His son was a mess. The tattered clothes covered up some of the bruises but his face looked in a bad way. The swollen lips revealed two missing teeth and gashes to the gums. Father and son looked at each other. Harmen's face split into a smile. He groaned with the pain of such movement.

'Well, *Heit*, we beat them again, didn't we?' The bloodshot eyes shone through the bloody mask.

'Yes, we did son, thank God.' He put his arm around his son's shoulder and supported him as the sun gained in strength and shone down upon them.

Schipper Schaaf appeared at their side. 'They flew right over us and they didn't come back for a second look.'

Frank was curious, 'Why was that?'

The *schipper* pointed towards the short mast above the bridge and laughed. The German swastika flew at full stretch.

'The *moffen* wouldn't shoot at their own flag, now would they?'

TWO

The barge's final stop was only four kilometres from Bakhuizen. Frank was worried. He had expected to cycle from the dropping off point to the Vissers' house. He need not have worried. Piet had telephoned ahead and the arrangements had been made.

The barge bumped against a little used wharf and a crewman with a boat-hook held the boat hard against the shore. The gangplank extended onto the wharf and Harmen was carried onto land. *Schipper* Schaaf saluted with a smile and the barge cast-off and edged back into the centre of the canal.

'What now, my friends?' asked Dirk. He had changed into old farmer's clothes. 'I suppose we just have to wait.' He looked around him at the open countryside and shook his head. 'I'm worried about sitting here in the open, anybody could spot us.'

Dirk climbed on to the top of a low dyke and stared hard into the distance. He did not have to wait long. Within five minutes of them landing he signalled down to Frank.

'There's a horse and cart coming.' Dirk shaded his face with his hand. 'Two people, one horse.' He turned and scrambled back down the dyke. 'They should be here in a couple of minutes.' He drew his gun, placed it on his lap and waited.

The three men watched the slow progress of the cart. They heard the sound of the hooves and Frank's sharp eyes spotted the identity of the two people.

'I don't believe this: look!' He pointed and smiled. The cart came nearer and drew to a stop.

'Hello, *Heit*. It's so good to see you,' said a smiling Aukje, as she jumped off the cart's seat. Wim beamed down at them as he held the horse in check. Demspey leapt off the seat and barked wildly when he saw Frank.

Aukje caught sight of her brother. 'Oh, Harmen. What've they done to you?' She threw herself to the ground at his side and gently put her arm around his shoulders.

'Ouch! ... Do be careful,' he grunted.

Frank smiled again. His son's condition was definitely improving.

'What on earth is that awful stink?' asked Dirk, with his fingers pinching his nose.

'That,' called down Wim, 'is the smell of the Friesian countryside. It's going to save your life.' He tied the reins to the seat, stepped down and smiled at his friends. 'I'm so glad that you're all safe. Marieke and Hennie have been worried.' He looked at Harmen and shook his head. 'My God, what did the Nazi swines do to you?'

Frank grasped his hand, 'We'll take care of him. What happens next?'

Wim waved towards the cart, 'This is your taxi. We're carrying a load of fresh cow manure nicely mixed with hay. Climb underneath it and then we'll take you home.'

Dirk put his hands on his hips and shook his head, 'I'm not travelling underneath that lot. I'd rather walk.'

'Suit yourself, Dirk,' smiled Wim, 'but, if I were you, I'd come with us. The *moffen* have increased patrols and they've a spotter plane looking for anything that moves.' He glanced at Harmen, 'Make your mind up, because this young man needs moving and a doctor as soon as possible. The muck is not as bad as it looks. It's been thrown over the top of fresh hay. There's a space underneath that's big enough for the three of you.' His head turned as the drone of the returning aircraft reached their ears. 'Come on, get in! Quickly now!'

Wim forked the manure to one side and they carefully slid Harmen into the space. Frank and Dirk quickly followed. Wim covered the entrance hole.

'Oh my God,' shouted Dirk from inside the steaming, stinking heap, 'this is bloody awful. I'll never be able to serve food again.'

The spotter aircraft flew very low skimming along the top of the narrow dyke. The horse plodded on and did not miss a step.

'Wave to him, Aukje, ... WAVE!' shouted Wim.

As the aircraft roared over them she stood up from the seat and waved with both hands and laughed, her mouth wide open. The small aircraft circled and turned back towards them. This time she could see the pilot waving back to her. The wings waggled and it disappeared to the north.

'Well done, Aukje! He was more interested in you than the cart,' said Wim with a wink. 'We should be in Bakhuizen in another half-hour.'

The sun boiled down from a clear, blue sky. The fields were busy with hay-making and the cows continued their life-time task of consuming grass.

Aukje gazed all around her and patted Dempsey on the head. She was absolutely terrified but tried so hard not to show it. Wim concentrated on the narrow track in front of him. They did not speak to each other, this was a dangerous job and they knew it.

They moved off the dyke and onto the tracks that travelled in straight lines between the patch-work of small fields. Wim was aiming for the dense woods that existed in this part of southern Friesland. Once there he knew he was nearly home and the spotter plane would be unable to see them through the dense foliage. They nearly made it. Wim took a deep sigh and pointed in front of them.

'I had a feeling that we wouldn't get away with this. ... Look!'

Coming straight at them, in a cloud of dust, was a patrol of four soldiers on two big BMW motor-bikes. The first machine with a small machine-gun mounted on the front of its sidecar. The leading soldier waved them to a stop. He climbed off the wide saddle and stood casually at ease. His intention was obvious.

'HALT! ... PAPERS!'

As Wim passed the documents down, Dempsey growled and sprang off the cart right into the path of the soldier. The small dog crouched and barked. The young soldier reached down and tried to pat him on the head. He quickly withdrew his hand when Dempsey tried to bite it.

'You should keep that dog under control, it's dangerous,' he said threateningly.

The three other men climbed off their motor-bikes and walked forward, weapons at the ready.

Aukje summed up the situation in an instant. 'Dempsey! Come back here, ... now!' The dog obeyed and slunk away under the cart. She flashed a delicious smile, 'I'm so sorry about my dog. He's not used to strangers.'

She bent down off the seat to check Dempsey. The soldier watched as her thin summer dress gaped at the neck. She bent even lower as his eyes followed every tantalising move. She straightened and pushed her shoulders back, forcing her breasts forward.

'Please, help me down can you?' She smiled sweetly.

He held the papers in one hand and the weapon in the other. For a moment he was unsure of himself. He leant his gun against the wheel of cart and took Aukje's hand. As she jumped to the ground she held onto him for those extra few provocative seconds.

'Oh, thank you so much,' she said quietly, looking the man straight in the face.

Wim became worried. They were a long way from any houses and four Germans would be hard to deal with. He knew that there was a gun under his seat but he would never be able to shoot four of them before they shot him. Instead, he watched Aukje at work.

'It's so warm today,' she said. Standing with her hands on her hips, 'I bet you're really hot in those uniforms?'

The soldier looked from Aukje to Wim and then to the identity cards and then back to Aukje. She looked young, fresh and vibrant. Her sun-bleached, blonde hair bounced in the gentle afternoon breeze. At last the soldier found his tongue.

'*Danke, Fräulein. Ja*, it is a hot day.' He pretended to be looking at the papers but his eyes kept flickering to the summer dress.

'*Juffrouw* de Beer. What are you doing here and where are you going?'

One of the other *Wehrmacht* soldiers came up and snatched the papers away. Aukje noticed the *Feldwebel's* stripes on his arm and the silver gorget of the field-police that hung from his neck. She knew she was in trouble.

He held up the cards to the bright sunlight and rubbed the issuing stamps with his thumb. 'I repeat, where are you going?' Before she could answer he turned and stared at Wim, 'You! Come down here, immediately!'

Wim obeyed and glanced back at the seat. He had no other choice but to leave his gun. He stood at Aukje's side. The stench of the cow manure was overpowering and the stinking steam wafted down over them.

It was a set piece of German organisation. Two men checking and the other two watching. There was no escape from such a patrol.

The *Feldwebel* held the papers in one hand and began to walk slowly around the cart. His nose wrinkled when he stood to windward. He gave Dempsey a second glance. The dog growled. The man's expression did not change.

'Visser, you have not answered my questions!'

Wim shrugged his shoulders and opened his mouth to speak. Aukje interrupted him.

'*Feldwebel*,' she knew enough about army ranks, 'we've been collecting a load of manure and we're on our way to dump it on the other side of the woods at a friend's farm.' She walked up to him and he stared hard at her. With a smile she reached towards the silver gorget hanging from a chain around his neck.

'This is really beautiful. Is it silver?' She held onto the symbol of rank and gently tugged it. Her smile was infectious.

The soldier tried to resist, '*Fräulein* ... ' He froze and his eyes were everywhere. She looked into his face and tilted her head.

'It tells people that I am a military policeman.' She held onto the gorget. He reached out an arm and put his hand on her waist. Aukje let go, he held on. The hand moved up her back and she felt his heat permeate through to her skin. His face was a picture of lust. He smiled and pulled her towards him. She knew she dare not resist.

Dempsey broke the silence as he barked and bounded out from under the cart. His teeth sank into the German's broad bottom and the man let out a howl of pain. Aukje sprang back and the *Feldwebel* managed to shake the terrier free. He swung a kick towards the dog but Demspey was too quick and ran back to his hiding place.

'SEARCH THE CART!' he snarled, withdrawing his bayonet from its scabbard.

The two men walked to the rear of the cart and began to stab the heap of manure with their bayonets. Wim and Aukje were helpless to interfere.

At that moment the horse decided to rear onto its back legs and the cart jerked forward. A huge slab of steaming shit slid off the heap and dropped straight onto the shoulders of the *Feldwebel*. It covered his uniform and dripped down over his breeches and onto the shiny jackboots. He stood stock-still and bellowed at the top of his voice.

Aukje knew some foul words in German but this man used words that she had never heard before. She stole a look at the two men sitting astride their motor-bikes. They were smiling broadly and she smiled with them. The Feldwebel swore for over three minutes and finally threw the documents on the dusty ground and strode towards his motor-bike. The engines started and they roared off down the dusty track into the woods.

For a moment they remained silent and then Aukje began to giggle. Wim joined in. They hugged each other and laughed until they were sore. There was not a sound from within the manure.

THREE

Frank expected the worst. The assault on the prison was a total success. Nobody on either side was seriously injured or killed. They waited for over a week for reprisals and none took place. He met Piet and Dirk in the dense woods two kilometres from Bakhuizen.

'I don't understand it, Frank,' said Piet, with a shrug. 'Nothing whatsoever has happened. Not a sound from SS Headquarters. Not even a round-up, or any reprisals. Joop tells me that the Germans from the prison have been replaced and that's all.'

They were sitting on a pile of logs in the densest part of the woods. Frank knew enough about country life to know that here they would be totally alone for as long as necessary. The slightest strange sound would bring the birds screeching from the tree-tops.

Frank stretched out over an old branch and took in a deep lungful of clean, fresh air. The very thought of freedom made his head swim with happiness. Harmen, according to the doctor, would make a good recovery. A cracked rib and bad bruising. He was a young man and with rest he would soon be active again. For a brief moment all seemed right with the world.

'I think it's because of the Allies,' interrupted Dirk. His voice broke Frank's thoughts. 'They've advanced through France and Belgium. They could soon take Antwerp and then watch out. It's only twenty kilometres from Dutch soil. It could be that liberation is nearer than we think.' He nodded, 'Müller, won't want to upset the Allies. After all, he could be answerable for the terrible crimes that he's committed over the last four years.'

Frank sat up, 'The Nazis don't give up all that easily. They still control an awful lot of Europe.' He saw Piet's questioning gaze, 'I know, ... I know, I listen to the BBC as well. The Russians are through to Lithuania and the Allies have taken Pisa but, ... we border onto the homeland and the Germans will fight like the very devil to stop the Allies advancing. I think they'll probably just bypass Holland and move straight into Germany.'

'I don't think so, Frank,' replied Piet. 'Remember, the Rhine. ... It's important to them. If the Allies take Holland then they control the rivers into Germany.' He shook his head, 'No, no, ... they'll take Holland, believe me.'

'That could be so,' said Frank.

'The only way to find out is to head south and see our people and ask them what's happening,' commented Dirk.

Frank jumped to his feet. 'You're absolutely right! That's the only way!'

Piet saw the look in his eyes and the smile, 'Frank, slow down. I know what you're going to say. It's just not possible.'

'You're wrong, Piet. It's not a long way from the Allied front line. I could be there and back in a few days. The trains are still running, the Germans need them. I could find out what's really going on and that would help us. After all, morale is pretty low at the moment.'

'You know, Piet, he's got an idea,' added Dirk, thoughtfully.

The atmosphere in the group had changed. The sun slanted down through the trees and the men became excited. Piet was more reasoned.

'If you did go, Frank. ... If you did go. The group leaders would have to approve and then ... well, what will your family say?'

Frank was thumping the branch in anticipation, 'Marieke won't mind. I'll go. It's just what we need.'

'He's right, Piet. We need to know what's going on down there.' Dirk nodded, 'We've been through a bad time and this might just help us.'

The majority of the group was enthusiastic about the whole idea. However, other events interfered with the plans. There was a buzz of anticipation all over Holland. The Allies were advancing fast through Belgium. Nightly, every illegal wireless set tuned in to the BBC and Radio Oranje. Life for the people of Friesland went on as normal. Round-ups and arrests continued as though nothing was happening. The resistance groups met almost every day to co-ordinate activities.

They sat in a small cafe in Heerenveen, a town not far from Bakhuizen.

'Frank, you can't leave yet,' said Piet.

'Why not?' he replied, 'I thought everything was clear.'

Piet smiled a look of sheer excitement, 'This morning, all Resistance groups in Holland received an order from Allied High Command. They want us to sabotage the railways all over the country.'

Frank nodded, 'That's wonderful. It's good to hear that something is at long last happening. What're the plans?'

'We've had some idea that this order would come sooner or later and we think it's the prelude to full invasion of Holland by the Allies. The Dutch Railway workers are planning a nation-wide strike. That'll stop the *moffen* using the system for reinforcements.'

'It'll hurt our people. They need the money,' said Frank, worriedly.

'Don't worry about it. The stationmasters hold a month's pay for all workers. They'll just pay out when the strike starts.' He smiled at his friend, 'So you see, you can't travel to the south, yet!'

On the night of the 4th September 1944, Frank was sitting in a large Friesian farmhouse to the north of Leeuwarden. He was in the uppermost rooms with the de Bruin family. He visited them every month to make sure that they were safe. Jan was prematurely grey and had aged ten years in the last two. Tineke, just sat and knitted and her old sparkle had gone. This was their third safe house in the last four months.

'How is everybody, Frank?' Jan looked up from the chair in the blacked-out room. His head hunched down to his shoulders and there was a week's growth of beard on his pale face.

'We're surviving, Jan, we're surviving.' He took a deep breath, 'I've come to tell you that you'll have to move again in a week's time. I won't be here then but Marieke will come and help you.'

Jan shook his head and groaned. 'Oh no, not another move, please. We're absolutely exhausted.' He lowered his voice, 'The people in this house are good to us. But, some are awful and treat us like dirt. They're always asking us for money. I don't know who I can trust.' Tineke continued knitting.

'Frank, it is good to see you. But, ... sometimes, I just feel like giving it all up.' He slumped back in the old chair.

Frank leant forward and grasped Jan's arm, 'Do you know that the Nazis are still deporting people through Westerbork.' Jan raised his head and his friend continued, 'Yesterday a thousand Jews were sent from the camp to Auschwitz. Tomorrow another two thousand will go. Now, my friend, would you like it to be two thousand and three?' Jan wearily shook his head and stared at the floor.

There was a quiet tap at the door. The farmer politely apologised as he entered. 'Excuse me, *meneer*. I thought you would like to hear the latest news. I've just heard on Radio Oranje that Antwerp has fallen to the Allies. It can't be long now before our liberation.' He felt the worried atmosphere in the small, darkened room and swiftly left.

Frank turned to his friends, 'You see, Jan. You've got to hang on that bit longer. Another month and we'll all be free.' Deep down he had his doubts about what he was saying. He knew how tenacious the enemy was. There was no response from Jan and Tineke. He rose to his feet, 'I must go now.' He paused. 'Oh, by the way. Where's David?'

'I don't know, I don't know. He's always out looking for food and helping other people. Tineke worries about him all the time.' Jan raised his hands imploringly, 'I can't keep a young man locked up in here all day and night, can I?'

Frank kissed Tineke gently on the cheek. He smiled although it saddened his heart to see his friends in such a poor state. Neither of the de Bruins said a word as he left the house. He cycled towards Leeuwarden with a heavy heart. Some divers thrived on the excitement and joined in with families. Others collapsed and took it badly. Frank gritted his teeth and pushed the pedals harder. He was due to stay at the house of one of his *L.O.* area leaders and he was already late.

'Hello Frank, come in,' the man said to Frank. The meal was simple and they talked of the logistics of food, clothes and informers. He went to bed late and fell asleep immediately. He slept in fits and starts and eventually a hand shook his shoulder.

'Frank, ... FRANK!'

He shot out of bed staring across the room at the open door and reached for his clothes.

'Don't worry, there's no raid. But there's great news. Hurry up and come downstairs.' He left the room as Frank began pulling on his overalls.

He sat at the breakfast table although by now it was late in the morning.

His friend sat opposite him and his face was alive with excitement, 'I heard on the BBC that Breda in the south is liberated. Frank, that's only thirty kilometres from Rotterdam. They could be here within the week.'

Frank tried to calm his racing heart. With a single finger he tapped his forehead in frustration. 'Wait a minute, wait a minute. ... We've only the radio to tell us this.' He pushed a piece of buttered bread into his mouth, chewed and swallowed. 'I'll believe it when I see the Tommies coming into *het Zaailand* in Leeuwarden.' The conversation died and the two men finished their breakfast in silence.

Frank gave the monthly cash to his agent and left the farmhouse. He was always wise enough to avoid the centre of Leeuwarden. There was still a price on his head. But, today, he quite simply could not resist. He looked at himself. Dirty blue overalls, worn clogs and three days of stubble on his face. As he pedalled down the track he turned sharp right to travel down a road that he had not seen for two years.

The van der Meer Timber Factory looked exactly the same as he had left it. A new sign had replaced the old. He shook his head, it was written in German. He dare not stop outside the entrance but he did cycle slowly past and then stopped in a gap in the hedge of his garden. Tears sprang to his eyes. The garden was totally overgrown and behind it was his house. The windows were nearly all boarded-up, paint was peeling and there were missing tiles on the roof. He shook his head and just stared. The memories of his flight across the roof came flooding back to him.

'Good morning, *meneer*, can I help you?' The man was middle-aged, small, grey-haired and dressed in a crumpled suit. His face was curious.

Frank turned and stared at him, 'Eh, ... no thank you. I was just wondering about that house over there. It seems to be in a bad state.'

'Yes,' replied the man, 'It belongs to somebody and it's not for sale.'

Frank climbed onto his bike and prepared to pedal away. The man caught hold of his arm. Frank turned angrily towards him.

There was a knowing smile, '*Meneer* van der Meer. Don't worry, I'll look after everything. You house is safe and your factory is working well. Wim Visser keeps me informed.' Frank was speechless. The man continued, 'Every week a German officer inspects the factory. He always asks if I know where you are. Naturally, I never do. He says that he knows you. His name is *Oberleutnant* Kraft and he's quite insistent about your whereabouts. Good luck, *meneer*.' Before Frank could gather his senses, the man politely lifted his hat and walked away.

His mind was in a whirl as he cycled into Leeuwarden. Without thinking he went past the main railway station. He stopped his bicycle in surprise. There were small groups of people waiting near the entrance. Frank glanced all around him, there was not one German in sight. Normally, the station was a checking point for all travellers. There was a tension in the air and he felt uncomfortable. For a moment, he thought about retreating out of the town and back to the safety of the countryside. He shrugged his shoulders, climbed off his bike and walked towards one of the groups.

A woman nodded towards him, '*Goedendag, meneer.*'

He touched the peak of his old cap, '*Goedendag, mevrouw.*' The social ice was broken.

He joined the group and watched the scene in front of him. The station was unbelievably busy. Packed full cars rolled forward and disgorged family groups. There were queues at the ticket office. Already other cars were arriving. Horse-drawn carts pulled up and disorderly heaps of luggage began to stack up on the pavement. There was no supervision and the watching crowds began to thicken. Within thirty minutes every inch of space on the station platforms was full. The air was foggy with steam and smoke as trains began to arrive. There were two crowds; one departing and one watching.

The woman laughed quietly into Frank's ear, 'It's the *NSB*. ... They're leaving Holland. They've been going all morning. Look over there.' She pointed towards a black German staff car. 'That's one of their leaders, ... look at him run with his skinny wife.' She chuckled loudly, stepped forward and looked back at Frank, 'Haven't you heard, *meneer*? Rotterdam is liberated and Amsterdam soon will be!' He stood silently, unable to believe what was happening in front of him.

There were occasional rounds of applause and sporadic cheering. Next came a sound that made him shiver and he gripped the handlebars.

The crowd began to sing something that he had not heard in public for four long years.

'*Oranje Boven! ... Oranje Boven!*'

'Long live the Queen.'

Over and over again they sang the well known chorus. Frank found himself joining in and tears streamed down his face. He clapped and shouted and again the chorus of the Dutch National Anthem, "het Wilhelmus", rang out across the station.

He felt somebody tugging at his arm and he pushed him away.

'Frank! ... Frank!' He glanced sideways. It was Dirk.

They both moved to the rear of the group. Dirk pumped his hand. 'Good to see you, my friend. But it's dangerous to stay here.'

'What the hell's going on, Dirk?' he said as quietly as he could with the racket going on all around him.

'The *NSB* are leaving for Germany. They've been queuing all morning. Eight trains have left already, each one was packed full.'

'Where're the Germans?'

'No sign of them. I've heard they're locked in their barracks. To the east of Leeuwarden they say that there're lorries everywhere.' He laughed out aloud, 'My friend, I think it's all over.'

They stood with the crowd for two hours. There was no way of leaving.

It seemed as if everybody in Friesland was in that small space. The woman grabbed Frank and Dirk.

'LOOK!' She pointed at the buildings. The Dutch national flag was appearing at open windows. Streamers of orange cloth were thrown into the street. Frank shouted himself hoarse and nearly lost his bike as the crowds pushed forward towards the station. Somebody prised cobbles free from the road and soon there were flying stones heading over their heads towards the NSB cars. Frank ducked and roared with laughter at Dirk.

'IT'S A DREAM!' He shouted at the top of his voice.

The end came quickly.

'MOFFEN! ... MOFFEN!' was the shout from somewhere.

'Oh God,' said the woman quietly, 'it's the Green Police and the SD. They're coming.' There was the staccato sound of machine-gun fire and the crowd surged backwards and forward like sea water.

'Back to the hotel, Frank! ... Come on, get off the streets.'

It took them twenty minutes to travel two hundred metres. They watched from the windows of the empty restaurant. People were running in all directions. There was panic and total surprise. Squads of heavily armed men moved through the streets and there were cars, motor-bikes and lorries, all packed with Germans.

'That's it, my friend. It's all over,' said Dirk, sadly.

They sat in the office. Frank, in his farmer's clothes, was totally out of place.

'Dirk, I've had my worries about all this liberation talk and, from what we've just seen, it justifies my thoughts.' Frank was sad. He had just witnessed one of his worst fears: Friesians living on false hopes.

'You may be right. But people want to believe that liberation from the Nazis is just around the corner,' agreed Dirk.

Frank sat forward in the chair and his lips formed a thin line, 'We know the Germans. They'll remember today and they'll extract their revenge.' He banged the arm of the chair with frustration, 'The Allies have got to come soon. None of us can live through this for very much longer.'

They were interrupted by a knock at the door. Dirk's manager entered the office. He totally ignored Frank.

'Dirk, you've got to look at the newspaper. It's the "Friesche Courant". Headlines and births are very interesting.' He smiled and left, closing the door quietly behind him.

Dirk flicked the pages over for a full three minutes and the laughter began from deep down. He laughed until it hurt.

Dirk shook his head in wonderment, 'Frank, I just do not believe what our people can do. This is wonderful,' He tapped the front page. 'The paper criticises everything about the Germans in Friesland. What it says would have anybody shot. The births' column gives names of the leading members of the *NSB*, just as though they'd been born yesterday. I can't believe the cartoons, they're really nasty.'

Dirk turned to the front page and scrutinised the main title and the printing details. He looked up, 'It's a fake, Frank. Beautiful, but a fake. Somebody has put a lot of time into this. Did you know anything about it?' He passed the paper over.

Even Frank smiled, 'No, but it's good. ... It's very good. I bet the *moffen* are really mad about this and I bet they're at the doors of the "*Courant*" at this very moment.'

FOUR

That day in September 1944 became known as 'Dolle Dinsdag'.

'Mad Tuesday' made people realise that the occupation of their country was far from over. The broadcasts were untrue, Holland was not liberated. Frank's prediction proved to be correct. The ferocity of arrests and reprisals increased and the Germans extracted a terrible revenge for 'Mad Tuesday'. Prominent people just disappeared. Two outspoken leaders of the Dutch Reformed Church in Leeuwarden went missing in the middle of the night. Their families and the congregations could do nothing.

Frank's plan for the journey to the south was simple. Piet had arranged the documents and the train tickets were delivered to the Vissers' house by Joop Koopman. He arrived in uniform in his police car. When Marieke saw the car pull up, her heart skipped a beat and she raced upstairs. Frank, watching through a spy-hole in the roof, quickly called down.

'Don't worry, Marieke! ... It's Joop!' They met him in the kitchen.

'Sorry about the uniform. It makes it easier for me to travel about,' he said as he kissed Marieke on the cheek.

'Were you followed?' she asked.

'Nobody follows me,' he replied brusquely. 'The swines still trust me.' He pulled off his black leather gloves and flung his peaked hat onto the table. 'I can't stay long. Officially, I'm going to meet the ferry at Staveren. There's somebody from Amsterdam that's got to be taken to SS Headquarters in Leeuwarden.' He snapped the gloves on his leg. 'I'm just a bloody messenger boy!'

Joop took a deep breath, 'Anyway, enough of my problems. I know you've got enough of your own.' He turned to Frank, 'There's been a slight change of plan. Uncle wants you to go to Wassenaar near The Hague.' He gave him a bunch of keys. 'The smallest key is to be handed over to your contact at the main railway station. The key is for a bank safe-deposit box. It'll provide funds for the local L.O. The tickets are from Heerenveen to Amsterdam and from there to Ede. That's not far from Arnhem. You'll have to divert to The Hague and then back to Amsterdam. One of our agents will meet you when you arrive at the station and see you on your way. There's nothing written down. If you stick to the timetable and memorise this telephone number, then you'll be all right.' He reached into his tunic pocket and handed over an envelope to Frank. 'Officially, you're travelling to examine timber contracts.' He winked, 'I think you know a little about that line of business.' Frank flashed a smile. 'Oh, and don't worry about the documents, they're genuine. I stole them myself three days ago. If the *moffen* check anything then they'll contact me. I authorised the journey on behalf of the Friesian Timber Association.' Joop rose and looked at his two friends.

'I know you'll be careful. We need to find out what's happening down there.' He clasped Frank's hand and put his other hand on his friend's shoulder, 'Come back safe and sound. We'll miss you.' Marieke kissed him and he left. They heard the engine start before they spoke.

Marieke was sombre and looked pale and tired. 'Darling, I know you have to go and I can't stop you. Please be careful. You know there's still a price on you head. It would be awful if something happened to you when we're so near to liberation.'

Frank opened the envelope. He scanned the contents and looked up at his wife. '*Liefje*, I know how you feel.' He waved his hand in frustration, 'But, this is something that I must do. I have to know what's happening. I owe it to the local *L.O.* leaders. I'll also make contact with the other groups and see how they manage things. I think we'll need that help in the next couple of months because I'm sure that we're going to have to look after more and more of our people.'

She frowned, 'Frank, I know, ... I know and I pray to God that you'll come back to look after us.'

He held her close, '*Liefje*, don't worry. Harmen and Aukje will help with everything.' They clung to each other and, for a brief moment, he was tempted to stay.

Frank left early the following morning. Wim cycled with him for the hour's ride to the railway station in nearby Heerenveen. They were on the road that skirted the coast of the giant *IJsselmeer* lake. The warmth of the summer was fading and the leaves were beginning to turn brown.

Frank and Wim were used to seeing German convoys. This one was different. The military police waved them away from the road and onto the field.

'Something's happening, Wim,' said Frank, apprehensively, as they waited, 'and I don't like it. I could miss my train.'

They did not have long to wait. From the distance came the sound of wailing sirens. Four lorries full of soldiers drove slowly past. Following them were six massive trailers, drawn by huge diesel-powered lorries. The convoy moved at cycling pace. Frank stared at the low trailers. He could not understand what he was seeing. The loads appeared to be bomb-shaped and as long as a railway-carriage. Each shape was covered by heavy tarpaulins. Blue diesel fumes blasted out from the exhausts of the roaring engines and the camouflaged vehicles stood out sharply against the open road. Ten pairs of heavy tyres to each load. The grinding of the rubber treads on the cobbles echoed back off the trees lining the side of the road.

'What in God's name are they?' bellowed Wim above the noise.

'I don't know,' shouted back Frank, shading his eyes from the glare of the early morning sun. 'They can't be going to the airfield at Leeuwarden, it's the wrong way.'

More military police skirted the convoy. Above them three aircraft circled as the vehicles passed by. It took fifteen minutes for the road to become silent as the escorting motor-bikes disappeared into the distance. For a moment they stood silently and then they climbed onto their bicycles and resumed their journey to Heerenveen.

Wim spoke first as they pushed hard against the breeze, 'It must have been important, Frank. It's the first time I've seen so many *moffen* without them stopping to check us.'

'That's a good sign,' commented Frank. 'Maybe it's an omen for my journey.'

The Amsterdam train was unusually late in arriving at Heerenveen and there were dozens of soldiers positioned all around the station. Wim nudged Frank and nodded towards one of the sidings.

'That's why the train's late.'

Eight flat-bed wagons were lined up on the track. Six were empty, the other two carried exactly the same shapes that they had seen on the way to the coast. They were ringed by heavily armed *Wehrmacht*. Green Police and *SS* were everywhere.

'Move on! ... Move on!'

They turned. Two black-suited men faced them.

'You heard me, ... move on!'

They walked quickly away.

'The whole crowd is here, Frank. I've never seen so many officers in one place before.'

'You're right, I don't recognise any of them. Some of the uniform insignia are strange. I think they're probably from Germany.' Frank was making mental notes all the time and tried not to appear too interested.

Wim turned to his friend and offered his hand. 'Frank, this is a good place to say good-bye and I'll wish you the very best of good luck.' The handshake was firm and there was a gleam in Wim's eyes.

'Goodbye. Look after Marieke and the children.' They both smiled as they quickly parted and Frank was suddenly alone. He walked slowly and deliberately towards the platform.

'Papers.'

The policeman hardly gave him a second glance as he snatched the card and the pass, looked at them and then pushed them back. He was already checking the next person before Frank had moved on.

It was a lovely day, cool and bright with sunshine. The platform was full. A mixture of civilians and military. He leant against the wall at the far end and read a newspaper.

'Papers, *bitte!*'

He lowered the newspaper, reached into his pocket and handed them over. This time the examination took longer. The two Green Police were efficient. One of them produced a list and checked Frank's name.

'Open your suit-case, ... *bitte!*'

He reached down and unsnapped the small case. The man ruffled through it, and dropped it on the ground. The papers were handed back and Frank was left to close the case and compose himself. The two men strolled down the platform checking and re-checking.

There was suddenly a shout and a man broke loose from the waiting crowd and ran across the railway line in a brave attempt to get to the next platform. It did not take long. Within a few seconds he was surrounded, bludgeoned to the ground and dragged away. People diverted their eyes from the incident and Frank gripped the handle of his case until his knuckles locked.

The crowd shuffled forward as the whistle of the train echoed across the station. The black smoke wafted across Frank's face and he covered his mouth. He tried to avoid compartments with soldiers but it was impossible. He found himself sitting with three young members of the *Wehrmacht*. He returned their nods and sat near the window and avoided contact. The train lurched and the station drifted away from view. The rolling green fields appeared and the steady clacking of the wheels on the rails began to lull him to sleep. Somebody nudged him. He jerked upright.

'*Mein Herr*, a piece of bread for you, all right?'

The man was pimply and very young. Frank was tempted to say no but something in the man's face made him take the sandwich.

'*Danke*, that's very kind of you.'

The soldier smiled and took acceptance of his food as a sign to talk.

'Where are you from, *bitte*?'

'From a village in Friesland.' He tried to keep his sentences short and avoid direct eye contact.

'*Ja*,' he nodded, 'I'm from German Friesland, not far away from you. But I don't speak your Friesian language.'

The conversation was friendly and Frank found himself chattering about all kinds of things. Stations came and went. They talked, but never about the war. It was the talk of families and of cows and the countryside. The door to the compartment was flung open as they stopped at a station. The soldier said something and the *SD* man nodded, shut the door and walked away. Frank realised that he was safe with the soldiers. The police thought that he was travelling with them. There was a pause in the conversation and Frank began to doze off.

The train jerked to a halt and he opened his eyes. The platform sign said Amersfoort and he knew he was only thirty minutes from Amsterdam.

Something made him stare across to the next platform. An involuntary shiver passed through him. It was the sight of the brown cattle wagons. There were at least thirty of them silently waiting. He had last seen these transports of despair at Westerbork and Leeuwarden when they waited for Lottie and then he realised that there was the concentration camp here in Amersfoort. It flashed through his mind that Paul de Vries must have passed this way. For a moment Frank closed his eyes tightly and silently prayed. When he opened them, the cattle wagons had gone and for a moment he thought he had been dreaming but he knew that this was not a dream.

The train pulled into Amsterdam Central Station and Frank was surprised when the young man turned and shook hands with him. It was the first time in the war that he had ever shaken hands with a German and for a moment he stared down at his palm.

His papers were checked three times between his carriage and the end of the platform and on each occasion he mentally thanked Joop Koopman.

Frank did not want to loiter. To stand around was to invite attention.

'*Goede morgen*, Frank. Good to see you again.' The woman was as young as Aukje and just as pretty. He smiled. She smiled back at him. 'It's good to see you again.' The young woman threw her arms around his neck and kissed him full on the lips. Her perfume took his breath away and for a moment he was speechless.

'Listen to me,' she said in a quieter voice, 'put your arm around me and walk out of the station for a minute; somebody's interested in us.' He did exactly as he was told.

Frank had not been in Amsterdam for four years. As he walked out of the main entrance to the station he quickly took in the view in front of him. It was just as busy as he remembered it. Bicycles everywhere, the *Damrak* canal full of barges and the towers of the *Oude Kerk* projecting up above the narrow streets and the old canal-side buildings. But in one swift glance he spotted Germans in every kind of uniform. Two of them stood in front of him. *SS*, dressed in black.

The litany of identity began. His new friend took over. She spoke in perfect German as they handed over their documents.

'Gentlemen, gentlemen. Please don't make a scene.' She reached up and kissed Frank again on the mouth. 'Look at my address. He's my favourite uncle and he's come a long way to enjoy my company.'

The two men looked at her identity card and then looked at each other.

One of them grunted, 'It says *Sint Annenstraat*. Is that where you live?'

She let go of Frank's arm and grasped the hand of the man holding her identity card.

'Of course I live there. I'm sure you've been in my part of Amsterdam. If you haven't then just make a note of my address.' Her lips parted wetly for a moment and then closed.

Frank suddenly realised that she lived in the red light district and then he smiled when he thought what Marieke would say.

The two SS men stared at Frank from head to toe.

'No wonder you're smiling. Have a good time, *mein Herr!*' They leered at him and marched off.

'Don't get any ideas, "Uncle" Frank!' She threw her head back and laughed, 'I have a message for you.'

He stood below dark rain clouds as she explained his task. She put her arms inside his jacket and embraced him. He felt her warm hands through his shirt and it thrilled him. She whispered in his ear.

'Frank, I've put your ticket and travel pass in your pocket. Have a good journey. It's been nice to know you. Good luck.'

Before he could reply, she released herself from his embrace, turned and walked away. He followed the lilt of her hips and felt a twist of repressed desire.

The stopping train to The Hague was on time and nearly empty. He had a compartment to himself and quickly fell into a dreamless sleep. Fortunately, he awoke every time the train stopped.

The village of Voorschoten lay to his right as he alighted from the carriage and walked along the deserted platform. The lady of Amsterdam had given him the details and the man fitted the description perfectly. They shook hands and made their way to the station exit. Passes were examined and it was only a short distance to the bicycle shelter.

'Frank, it's nice to meet you. My wife's put on dinner at my house and you're welcome to stay.' His host was smartly dressed and spoke well. There was instantly a feeling of mutual respect. Frank climbed onto the borrowed bike and they cycled to the house.

His judgement was correct. The man was a solicitor. Both he and his wife were still living in their own house. It was beautiful, modern Dutch with a wide drive through rows of mature trees leading to the gabled front door. Frank was made very welcome. The table was laid with the best silver and the starched white table-linen made him feel at home.

'Frank, I'm sorry my wife isn't here, she's visiting friends.' He nodded to the maid as the final course was served to the two men.

'It's so good to be eating in a civilised house again.'

The man nodded, 'I thought you were a diver,' he smiled and his face crinkled. 'I recognise the signs.'

The conversation was as good as the meal. Finally as they stood to leave the table, the man turned to Frank.

'I know you're probably tired but there's something I want you to see.'

Frank followed him outside. There was a gentle breeze blowing and he could smell the sea in the air. The house was a short distance from the extensive sand dunes and woods that bordered the western edges of Wassenaar and Voorschoten. The narrow path weaved its way through dark woods and within a minute Frank was totally disorientated. It was an intensely dark night and dense low clouds obscured the stars. There was no moon.

'Leave your bike here and follow me,' the man whispered.

The foliage and bracken tore at his face as he scrambled through the undergrowth. He climbed up a steep grassy slope and a hand pushed him to the ground.

'Just raise your head and don't move or say anything. We'll talk later.'

Frank was on the edge of a natural hollow some two hundred metres wide. One side was open and he could hear the surf crashing onto the beach. He was hidden by overhanging pine trees. His eyes slowly adjusted to the scene in front of him. Abruptly, bright arc lights clicked on and he closed his eyes tightly. Slowly he opened them and squinted through the brightness. His hands scrabbled in the sand as his mind attempted to comprehend what was he was seeing.

It resembled a vertical torpedo. Its slim shape was delineated in black and white squares and it stood erect and as high as a house. The body rested on four small fins and it was connected to a high steel frame by cables and clamps. Men fussed around its base and there was white smoke everywhere. They moved in and out of the smoke like ghosts. Above it all was the sound of diesel engines and the whine of generators. The bright lights made it look like a stage set for action.

Frank was fascinated. He could not take his eyes away from the scene. With a grim smile he realised what he had seen earlier on the cobbled road near Bakhuizen. There was suddenly the clamour of a klaxon blaring and the men melted away into the shadows. He felt a nudge in his ribs and he stole a glance sideways. The man had his hands tightly pushed against his ears. He nodded urgently at Frank to do the same.

Abruptly there was a jet of flame from the bottom of the torpedo and a roar that blasted through Frank's hands to his ears. The tongues of flame changed from red to white and he saw the ground below the flames glowing with heat. The sound rose to a crescendo of ear-splitting roar and he hugged the ground and cried out with the pain of the noise. The ground trembled and shook and the trees waved above his head. His eyes opened wide as the torpedo slowly moved and began to lift vertically off its launching cradle. The flames became longer and broader and they rippled with pulsating power as the machine rose into the air. It stabbed its way into the darkness above going faster and faster. Abruptly, there was total silence as the flames and the sound was cut-off behind the clouds. The arc lights switched off and darkness returned.

Frank found himself sweating profusely and his mouth was locked tight. He was trembling from head to foot. How he got back to the house he never knew. He lay in a chair close to a brightly burning log fire. In his hand he clutched a hot cup of something as he glanced across to his host.

'Just tell me about it,' he said, simply.

The man took a deep breath, 'They began about a week ago. What we saw tonight was the launching of a new bomb. The Germans call it the V-2. It's the second of their terror weapons. The nose contains high-explosive. The V-1 is smaller and has been used on the south-east of England. This is a pure rocket missile. Once it's been launched, nothing can stop it and it's so fast that you can't even see it and it takes just two minutes to reach London.'

Frank sipped at his tea and nodded, 'I saw four of them in Friesland. There were two more waiting in the sidings at Heerenveen Station.'

The man smoothed his eyebrows with his fingertips, 'Now, that's interesting. I must get this information sent back to London as soon as possible.' His hands relaxed onto his lap. 'Did you see where they were going to?' Frank shook his head. The man left the room and returned with a large map of Holland. He spread it out on the floor.

'It was travelling in that direction,' pointed Frank and stabbed his finger towards Bakhuizen.

'Ah, ... Ah, ... that means that they're targeting somewhere else in England. They can launch them anywhere just by altering the course whilst the missile's in flight. Apparently they do it by radio.' The two men sat back and stared into the embers of the fire.

'Frank, do you think your group could sabotage the V-2's in Friesland?'

'I'm *L.O.*,' replied Frank, 'but I'm certain my local *K.P.* group would certainly give it a try.'

'From what we've learnt in this area you only have to unbalance the damned things and then they fall over. The fuel is so explosive that when they do go up, or misfire, they flatten an area of over half a kilometre, so do be careful.' He nodded and smiled, 'Half of the ones from near here have failed to take off and they always use a wooded area because in that way they can hide from Allied bombers.'

'How much does London know,' Frank asked curiously.

'The Allies managed to capture one not so long ago. But there's nothing they can really do about the damned things because they're so fast and mobile. By the time they've mounted a bomber raid the missiles have moved on.'

They talked into the early hours of the morning and eventually Frank went to bed and fell asleep between clean sheets. He left strict instructions that he was to be woken early. An alarm clock woke him.

He ate a quick breakfast and handed over the bunch of keys to his host.

'Thanks for coming, Frank. It's good to talk to somebody else for a change.' He tossed the keys in the air. 'We need this money badly. Our divers are increasing daily.' He glanced at his wrist-watch, 'I think we have to go. Your train is due in half an hour.'

Both men cycled back down the road to the railway station. They smiled at each other, shook hands and Frank made his way through the security checks to the platform. His mind was whirling with what he had seen the previous night and he wondered how the Allies would be able to deal with such a terrifying weapon of destruction.

He travelled east towards the small town of Ede. Every train seemed to be full of soldiers from every German regiment imaginable and he wondered why the railwaymen still operated a system that so obviously helped the enemy. The train at last pulled into Ede Station and he waited for the compartment to empty.

His surprise was total. On the other side of the ticket barrier was a face that he knew. The two men shook hands and beamed at each other.

'Frank van der Meer, you make a very good Henk de Beer!'

'*Majoor* Hofstra, who would've thought that we would ever meet again?'

FIVE

'What happened to you after Rotterdam, Frank?'

They exchanged stories for the remainder of the day. Marius Hofstra was a diver and leader of *O.D* in his area. He was extremely active and spent most of his time travelling and helping other groups.

'You mean you actually took part in the assault on Leeuwarden Prison?' Frank nodded. Marius beamed, 'Our people down here thought it was a wonderful mission.' He sat back and laughed. 'Who would've thought that a Friesian timber man could've carried out such a precise military operation?' Frank modestly changed the subject.

'Just how close are the Allies? That's the real reason why I'm here.'

Marius stood and began to pace up and down his small living-room, 'You can catch the train as far as Eindhoven or Breda and then everything is closed tight. Apart from the military, nobody is allowed through. Even getting within ten kilometres needs a pass from the German High Command.' He saw the look on Frank's face. 'If you're thinking of going there, forget it, you wouldn't even get a ticket. ... The Allies have stopped at the border. It's the Ruhr they're after. Local feeling is that they'll turn east and head directly into Germany and go for the heavy industry. Our little country will now be forgotten. Remember they took Antwerp, a little tidying up and they've got a tailor-made port. ... Believe me, it'll be some time before we're liberated. Remember '*Dolle Dinsdag*'? If we do anything drastic, then the Nazi swine'll be on us so quick that there'd be slaughter on a massive scale. When the Allies do enter Holland and start moving north, then that's the time for action. At the moment London wants all the information it can get and so, each day, I go for long bike rides.'

Frank took in the information and thought for a moment, 'Marius, when we came to your apartment today I saw that you're living right opposite some German barracks. It's only about two hundred metres from your front door.'

Marius smiled, 'You're right. I like to watch what they're doing. At the moment there's part of an *SS* guard regiment living in the barracks. I don't know what they're doing here. Usually the Nazis use them for guard duty in the camps. Yesterday I saw a bunch of marines walking past. God knows why they're in Ede, resting probably. It is a rather nice area.' He pondered for a moment, 'You know it's interesting. They never check this apartment. I see every kind of *moffen* going past the window but they never stop outside my front door. But, I love it round here. Ginkel Heath to the east is beautiful. Arnhem is only twenty minutes by bicycle and I have enough drinking friends to keep me happy. Look, tomorrow I'll take you to the local *L.O.* leader. He'll be glad to see you.'

'What about your wife, Marius? You haven't mentioned her.' Frank mentally kicked himself. It was the wrong question and he knew it.

He stared hard at Frank and his head dropped, 'The SS took her two years ago on suspicion of being in the Resistance. She's at Amersfoort. I'm not allowed to see her. I believe she's dead, although I have no proof.'

'I'm sorry,' said Frank, 'I shouldn't have asked.' Marius shrugged his shoulders and fell silent.

Later Frank lay awake in his bed for some time and pondered over his position. Maybe Piet had been right, there was little that he could really achieve down here. But he felt better for the journey. He had met other leaders and renewed his acquaintance with Marius Hofstra. He was fast asleep when he felt his arm being shaken. He was instantly awake.

'Frank, wake up! ... Quickly!' Marius stood over him.

Frank swung his legs off the bed and sat up, 'What's the matter?' Dawn was streaking the sky.

'Something's up. ... There's something going on. Hurry up and get dressed.' He dashed away down the stairs.

Frank pulled on his clothes and waited in the small kitchen. Marius came in through the back door. He was breathless.

'Twenty minutes ago I received a coded message. It means that all Resistance groups in this area must begin acts of sabotage. That's all I know.' He tapped his head in concentration, 'Frank, quickly now, butter some bread and I'll make a hot drink. I don't know how long this day is going to be.' As Marius leant over the gas cooker, his coat swung open revealing a large pistol.

There was no time to even prepare the early breakfast. The sound was hauntingly familiar.

Marius glanced upwards, 'Oh Jesus Christ. No! ... Every time I meet you somebody decides to bomb us!'

They dashed outside and stared at the ever lightening sky. The first wave of aircraft passed at low level.

'Mosquito bombers!' shouted Marius.

'I know them well!' Frank shouted back.

The bombs crashed down and then the two men realised what the target was.

'It's the barracks, ... the barracks! ... Grab the bikes and let's get the hell out of here!' screamed Marius above the crash of the bombs and the roar of engines.

Frank automatically ducked and grabbed his bike. Dust and masonry flew all around them as they scrambled for the road away from the attack.

The fast dashing Mosquitoes soon disappeared and high in the sky American Flying Fortresses began to unleash their heavy bomb loads. The crack of anti-aircraft guns joined the ever increasing cacophony of sound. Frank had not the faintest idea where he was going and blindly followed the bicycle in front of him.

They managed to clear the edge of the town.

'Come on, Frank! ... Pedal like hell for the heath!'

They pushed the pedals harder and harder as the flat, open expanse of Ginkel Heath loomed up in front of them. Frank's energy and nerves were spent. He fell off his bicycle into the bracken with his chest heaving.

'You're ... getting ... old, ... that's your problem,' said Marius as he collapsed at Frank's side. He waited for a moment and then turned over into a crouching position.

'My God, ... look at that!' he panted.

Frank turned over and joined him. They both stood.

The bombers were gone, and even from this distance, the damage to the town was obvious. Frank was saddened. He knew that whenever bombers came it was always the innocent that suffered as well as the guilty.

Marius was quiet as he watched the results of the raid, 'Why do you think they attacked this particular target?' Frank shook his head.

There were other people on the heath. Family groups on their way to church on a fresh Sunday September morning. Everybody had stopped and they were staring at the smoke rising into the sky. The stillness was oppressive and the scene was frozen and no living thing moved.

How long Frank stood there for he never knew. Marius was at his side but it was as though he did not exist. He caught a movement to his right, a little girl was not ten metres away from him. She smiled and he found himself staring at her. The mother and father were standing close by and their faces turned towards him. Frank raised a hand and waved at the girl. She smiled again and waved back to him. For a moment he desperately wanted to be home. The little girl turned and her blonde hair caught the rays of the sun. Her mouth fell open and she stared at the sky. Perhaps her young ears were sharper than his and then he heard it as well. The drone of aircraft. He stiffened but his eyes stayed on the little girl. Marius was shouting something. He ignored it. The drone grew louder. He waited for the bombs to fall. There was only the sound of engines. Her small hand pointed into the sky. He heard her voice as clear as tinkling water.

'Look mama, ... it's snowing in September.'

He did not understand until he saw what she was looking at. The sky was indeed full of massive snowflakes. Frank shook his head in disbelief. One of the snowflakes landed near him and it spoke.

SIX

The trip to Sneek was special. Marieke arranged it soon after Frank left for his trip to the south. The small town was only an hour's bike ride away from Bakhuizen. Harmen though it was a wonderful idea as his injuries were almost healed.

'*Mem*, you don't realise what going out means to me. I've stayed in this village for weeks and I'm bored.'

Marieke laughed, 'It's not just for fun. I've arranged a visit to the dentist in Sneek. It's about time you did something about those gums and gaps. What will your girlfriends think?'

Harmen joined in with her laughter and soon Aukje entered into the small living-room to hear what was happening. She was delighted.

'Oh *Mem*! I really do want to go to Sneek. I haven't walked round the shops with you for ages.' A frown crossed her face. 'Are you sure it'll be safe for you? After all you are pregnant.'

Marieke nodded and smiled, 'I think so. I do know a little about having children. We won't stay long, an hour or so and that should be enough. On the way back we can call and see a couple of friends.'

'*Mem*, what about the *moffen*? There's a price on our heads as well,' said Aukje.

Marieke shrugged her shoulders. 'In Leeuwarden they might recognise us. In Sneek, I doubt it.'

It was a fine day but clouds were gathering in the distance. They cycled through the deepest parts of the woods and followed the muddy tracks that led towards the road. Harmen led the way and the autumn leaves rained gently down on them.

Marieke was apprehensive about the trip. It was really to please her children. Nowadays they rarely went out as a family and, with Frank, away she wanted to give them something special. The cool air blew onto her face and she breathed in deeply. None of them spoke as they pushed their way deeper into the woods.

'*Mem*, STOP,' called Harmen. They pulled up beside him.

Marieke saw them straight away. There were deep, freshly made ruts in the path. To the side of the track trees were pushed to one side and their white splintered trunks stared into the sky. From behind the trees two uniformed Germans appeared in front of them.

'This is a military area. Go back!' Their unslung guns reinforced the order.

Marieke smiled and turned to her children, 'Come on. There's another way out of here.'

They followed her. After a few minutes Harmen stopped and stared through the trees.

'Don't stop,' said Marieke, 'they might come back.'

'*Mem*, look over there.' He pointed through a gap in the undergrowth. There was a long low trailer. It was empty.

Once on the road to Sneek they made good time. There was a gentle breeze blowing them along. Marieke began to sing and the three of them sang their hearts out as they made their way past the fields and the odd farmhouse.

They passed the ornate water tower on their left as they entered the town. Sneek is a pretty place, almost a smaller version of Leeuwarden. There were few people on the streets and the shops contained very little. Four years of war was having its effects.

'Dentist first,' said Marieke, as she looked at Harmen.

'We'll come with you for a few minutes, just to make sure you get there,' smiled Aukje. Her brother shook his head.

The dentist was an elderly man and he was expecting them.

'*Meneer* de Beer. Please take a seat.'

Harmen groaned and Aukje laughed.

'We'll come back in half an hour,' smiled Marieke as she left him.

He heard them walking down the small flight of stairs. The dentist began probing around inside Harmen's mouth.

'*Meneer*, there's a piece of broken root still in your jaw. I'll have to remove it. I'm sorry I have no anaesthetic.' He levered a small pick against a tooth. He felt his patient jump. 'Just keep still .... and I'll be as careful as I can.'

The pain drowned out any other sounds and dentist and patient did not hear the heavy footsteps on the stairs.

'Please be careful,' Harmen retorted angrily, 'that hurts!' The pressure on his tooth increased. His eyes snapped open and he tried to close his mouth. He reached up to grab the dentist's hand and he felt his arms pinioned. A new face swam into view in front of his eyes.

'*Guten Tag, Schweinhund!*' The voice was awfully familiar.

He twisted his head sideways and saw the gleam of silver buttons. His heart sank and then he knew.

Obersturmführer Postma stood at his side. There was a fiendish grin on his face. Harmen closed his mouth and his tongue automatically sought out the gaping hole in his gum. He sucked the blood and felt its bitter taste.

There was one place that Marieke always went to. The *Martinkerk* in the centre of the town was one of her favourite places and she always went there. The church was much older than her own Mennonite place of worship and she found great solace in its peaceful atmosphere.

Normally the minister welcomed visitors. She looked around for him but he was nowhere to be seen. Aukje walked at her side and they made their way to the front of the church. They were the only people present and they chose to sit on the front pew. Outside the sun slid behind threatening grey clouds and inside the church the atmosphere was heavy.

Aukje felt a shiver as she closed her eyes to pray with her mother. Marieke heard footsteps and she waited for a moment to finish her prayer. As her head lifted she opened her eyes and glanced sideways. She saw Aukje's face transfixed with terror. Before she could move. There was a coarse laugh in her ear. She whirled round.

There were twenty heavily-armed Green Policemen lined up at the rear of the church. In front of her stood Postma, hand on hips with that smile on his face that she knew so well. Marieke gripped her daughter's hand and stared straight at the pulpit directly over Postma's shoulder. Aukje reached over and clung to her mother.

'Caught like rats in a trap. Nowhere to go and no husband to turn to.' Postma signalled to his men and they rushed forward and surrounded the two prisoners.

He walked casually forward and stared hard at Marieke's face and she matched him stare for stare. Her arms were pinioned to her sides and she was utterly helpless. He reached forward with his black gloved hand and cupped Aukje's breast. His eyes never moved from Marieke's face.

'That's for me, my little chicken.' He squeezed her breast hard and held it whilst he watched Marieke. Aukje went pale but she did not cry out. His mouth twitched, 'I'll pluck you later and then it's your mother's turn. Perhaps you'd like to watch, *mevrouw*. You may learn something new.' He let go of Aukje and folded his arms. There was a smile of satisfaction on his leering face.

'Take them away!' His voice echoed around the empty church.

Harmen felt the handcuffs biting into his wrists as he landed heavily on the floor of the police van. His legs were quickly manacled to a stanchion on the steel chassis. He felt the vehicle move and he watched the two SS men who were guarding him. Their faces were expressionless as they stared rigidly ahead. He expected to be taken to Leeuwarden but the van stopped and he trembled with resignation. He was sure Postma was going to shoot him in some damp field. The doors were unlocked and he blinked in the daylight. His face contorted with horror.

'NO! ... GOD IN HEAVEN!' he cried in anguish.

Marieke was thrown in, Aukje fell on top of her. The doors slammed shut. The two guards leapt on them. Their screams caught at his heart and he shouted until he was hoarse. His hands and legs bled as he pulled frantically at his chains.

They were fastened down at the end of the van. Aukje's dress was torn and her left breast was exposed, it was scratched and bruised. She tried to cover herself and her hands scrabbled at the remnants of her blouse. Her eyes were locked into nothingness. Marieke moaned and rocked backwards and forward. The interior of the van fell silent and the guards watched the two women like a cat watches a mouse.

SEVEN

'Good morning, sir.'

The man was dressed in a uniform that Frank had never seen before. A camouflaged smock, khaki trousers and shiny black boots. Before he could reply the apparition had gone.

Around Frank and Marius landed thousands of parachutes. They stood, surrounded by men falling from the sky. Frank could hear grunts; the swishing of silk; shouted orders; clattering equipment and the never ending drone of aircraft. He looked up. The sky was thick with men.

Marius was thumping his back, 'They're British! ... Just look at them! ... Just look at them!'

They began to dance up and down screaming at the tops of their voices. Two soldiers grabbed them.

'GET DOWN! ... GET DOWN!'

Fortunately they both understood English. The shock was still total and they stood with open mouths. They were pushed to the ground and just in time. Frank looked up as a huge bat-like shadow passed over his head. The word "glider" registered in his brain and he watched it, totally silent, swoop onto the ground with a crunch. Within a minute the nose tipped open and men streamed out. Frank watched with fascination. From the fuselage they pulled out a jeep followed by a heavy wheeled-gun.

'Frank, this is history and we're in the middle of it. Come on, let's help them.'

They dashed towards another glider. Its wing was tipped in the air and the perspex nose was splintered. They clawed at the door. They were elbowed out of the way by a burly man with sergeant's stripes on his smock.

'Excuse me, sir.'

He wielded a huge axe with ease and the door flew open. Men crawled out, some were injured and some were all right. Frank glanced in through the door. The two pilots were dead, their bodies impaled on the controls. He turned away and he heard Marius speaking in English.

'I'm *Majoor* Hofstra of the Dutch Light Division. Can I help you in any way?'

The sergeant looked down at him and his face split into a broad smile. 'I'll take you to my battalion commander, sir. You may be able to help him.'

Frank had never seen so many men, parachutes and aircraft. They came across the flat Dutch landscape in waves and all the time he could hear men dropping to the ground with grunts and groans. The gliders swept over the trees and found the cleared fields. Occasionally he heard the crackle of small arms and the thump of something bigger. A sound made his ears search the collection of men in front of him. He saw two soldiers in skirts come marching across the heath. The wailing of their music cut through every sound around. He laughed with delight.

'Marius! ... Marius! ... LOOK! Scotsmen in kilts with bagpipes!' He stood and stared and the men swirled past him. The sound of the pipes remained firmly printed upon his brain.

Frank walked side by side with Marius as the sergeant led the way across the heath. He could not believe his eyes. Piles of equipment lay in orderly heaps. Men ran and marched everywhere. Shouted orders in unintelligible English rattled backwards and forward. He could smell petrol fumes, gun-oil and something else that was indefinable. It was the smell of battle and to Frank it was invigorating.

'FOLLOW ME!' The soldier bellowed as he pushed his way through khaki and camouflage.

'Frank, I've waited four years for this day. Where the hell are they all coming from?'

'Remember *Dolle Dinsdag*,' shouted Frank.

'Oh bugger, *Dolle Dinsdag*! This is the real thing.'

The sergeant stopped, stood ram-rod stiff to attention and saluted.

The man facing them was dressed the same as his men. He wore no helmet but a maroon-red beret with a single silver badge perfectly aligned over his left eye-brow. The officers' rank was stitched on his shoulder tabs. There was a net scarf in camouflaged colours tied at his throat. The face interested Frank, angular with penetrating eyes and a military moustache. Their eyes met and he knew that this man was a natural leader.

'Good morning, gentlemen.' The voice was clipped English and precise, 'I'm Lieutenant Colonel John Frost, 2nd Parachute Battalion.' The British officer paused for a moment as he sized up the two men in front of him.

'I'm afraid I don't have much time,' he waved his hand around him, 'as you can see we're rather busy.'

Marius saluted, 'I'm *Majoor* Marius Hofstra of the Dutch Light Division. This is my friend Frank van der Meer.' The handshake was cool and firm. 'We're both Resistance leaders and we want to help.'

He smiled at them, 'Thanks for the offer. I suggest that you keep well out of the way. My men know exactly what they're doing and really ... you could end up getting hurt.'

'Colonel Frost, north of Arnhem there are huge numbers of Germans.' He saw the frown but Marius continued, '*SS Generalleutnant* Bitterich is nearby and there are two *SS* Panzer divisions close, not ten kilometres from here. *Generalfeldmarschall* Model is in Arnhem.' He shook his head, 'It could be dangerous for your men if you attack anywhere near the town.'

Two more officers arrived and politely interrupted him. Colonel Frost turned to him. The voice was calm but tinged with impatience.

'Look here, *Majoor* Hofstra. Thanks for your information. Our intelligence is good and we have plenty of men. We're only expecting light resistance. You could help by telling your people to take action against the Germans. Now, I really must leave you.' He smiled, saluted and walked casually away followed by a bevy of officers.

Marius slumped to the ground and stared all around him. Frank knew what was wrong.

'Don't worry. They seem to know what they're doing.' The two men sat in silence and watched the action in front of them.

'Oh my God, Frank,' said Marius, 'they really are going towards Arnhem. Look at them!' He pointed towards the trees and the main road from Ede to Arnhem.

Long columns of marching men disappeared into the distance. Jeeps roared after them and all the time aircraft flew overhead.

'There's nothing that we can do,' said Frank shaking his head. 'At least we can say that they we were here when the Allies took over Holland.'

Their bikes had gone and they were forced to walk all the way back to Ede. It took them two hours and dusk was falling as they reached Marius's apartment. All the glass in the windows was shattered but the building was still standing. Frank nudged his friend.

'Look.'

Out of the partly damaged barracks there came a flood of German soldiers in lorries. They sat stiffly, gripping their weapons. The convoy moved onto the road across the heath and onto Arnhem.

'God help the British,' said Marius quietly.

'And the Dutch,' added Frank.

EIGHT

Harmen remembered nothing about the journey from Sneek to Leeuwarden. The guards leered at Marieke and Aukje and, apart from the roar of the engine, there was total silence within the fast moving vehicle.

They arrived at SS headquarters just as dusk was falling. Postma was taking no chances. The van was surrounded by armed SS and they followed the vehicle as it moved through the rear entrance of the dark building.

The occupants of the van were thrown into sharp contrast by the bright lights in the courtyard. Harmen shielded his eyes as the rear doors were thrown open. Marieke sat bolt upright shielding Aukje. She glanced across at her son and her eyes chilled him to the bone. They were both dragged bodily from the van. He stiffened, unsure of himself. One of the guards loomed up and punched him in the face. The man unlocked the shackles, dragged Harmen out of the van and threw him on the wet ground at the side of his family. He looked at his mother's face. It was bruised and there was a deep gash above her eye. Aukje gazed without comprehension at her brother. There was suddenly total silence and he looked up.

Silhouetted in the doorway stood *Hauptsturmführer* Müller. All eyes were upon him and for a moment he froze, hands on hips. He paused for a full minute, relishing the scene on the ground in front of him. Müller moved casually forward into the bright lights and with deliberate steps slowly circled the three van der Meers. The silence continued and he continued walking round and round. Postma glanced at Harmen. There was no reaction. Eventually he stopped and quite deliberately kicked him hard between the legs. A grunt of pain was the only response. The SS officer carried a short black stick. He raised it above his head and with all the strength he could muster he snapped it downwards across Marieke's inert body. She rolled into a ball trying to protect her unborn child. The sound of the leather on flesh echoed around the courtyard. Her scream ended in a sobbing moan and Aukje choked at the sight of her mother in such desperate pain.

Müller spoke clearly in Dutch and carefully enunciated each word, 'You van der Meer whores will not live through this night, not after my men have finished with you.' He lifted Aukje's head with the tip of his stick and stared into her open eyes, 'I'll save you for Postma, he often talks about you.' He let her head fall back onto her chest. The cold blue eyes flickered and his smile was empty.

Müller straightened up and held the ends of the shiny leather stick with both hands. He was icy calm and his gaze never moved from the three helpless people lying prostrate on the ground. Almost casually he kicked Harmen again, this time at the base of the spine and he laughed as the man moaned in agony. 'You will be executed at dawn. Before that you will see your mother and sister enjoy themselves with my men.' Müller began to walk back towards the door. He called out, '*Obersturmführer* Postma. Put them in separate cells.'

The circle of guards closed in.

NINE

The two men hardly slept on that fateful night in September 1944. They could hear the roar of engines as lorries and tanks made their way towards Arnhem. Aircraft flew overhead continuously and shook the apartment to its foundations. Eventually, Frank and Marius gave-up attempts to sleep and made their way down the stairs.

They looked at each other in the dawn light as it filtered through the windows. Marius prepared a quick breakfast. Frank was the first to speak.

'Marius, I just can't believe it. I've never seen so many planes and equipment in all my life before. I thought the Germans were well supplied, but yesterday proves just what the Allies can do. You know, they all looked so confident and so sure of themselves. And I saw and felt something that I hadn't seen for a long time.' He recognised Marius's questioning look. 'It was their manners. They were polite and just how I expected the British to be. I haven't seen soldiers with smiles and manners since the war began.' They both nodded and began eating.

'I have to make contact with my group,' said Marius as he chewed at a thick slice of bread. 'The Allies will need help and there's no doubt that the Resistance will give it.'

Frank gulped down a mouthful of milk, 'I agree, we'll help as much as we can. After all, it's really what we've been waiting for.' He continued eating for several minutes. 'I have to visit the *L.O.* leader in Tiel. I have his name and address and all I need now is another bike.'

Marius smiled, 'Don't worry, Frank. My neighbour is in the black market for bikes. I'll see him in a minute and we'll collect them before we leave.' They continued eating. Marius excused himself and left the apartment.

Frank felt exhilarated. Through the window and over fifteen kilometres away came the sounds of battle. Black smoke rolled across the horizon and he could see aircraft flying low over the heath. He felt part of what was happening and he knew that he must help wherever he could. As he watched, he saw Marius return with two bicycles. He ran up the stairs. His voice shook with excitement.

'Frank, there's more good news. The Americans are trying to take Nijmegen. There are parachutes dropping at Grave and Groesbeek. That's only five kilometres from the city. They must be trying to link up with the British.' He clapped his hands and his eyes shone with anticipation. 'Come on, let's leave here. I've got to get involved.' He turned to his friend, 'How long do you expect to be?'

'I should be back by dusk. Don't wait up for me.' Both men laughed.

'Really, Frank, just be away for as long as it takes. I'll expect you when I see you.' They looked at each other. In their shabby suits they were indistinguishable from any other person in the street.

The two men embraced briefly and the almost familiar roar of engines interrupted their parting.

'What the hell is happening now?' exclaimed Marius.

They both stared at the sight that slowly appeared in front of them. Another armada of aircraft approached Ginkel Heath. This time Frank could watch it from a distance and the hair on the back of his neck bristled when he saw the parachutes emerge from the twin-engined aircraft. Faster and faster the men dropped through the clouds. The sky above the heath was full of men.

'It's happening again, Frank! ... All over again!' Marius suddenly pointed into the sky. 'Oh my God! ... Look at that! The bastards are firing at them!' Through the early morning air they could hear the rattle of machine-guns and the smoke increased and billowed over the unfolding battle.

Frank tugged at his arm, 'Marius, we've got to leave. Soon, we won't be able to go anywhere.' The two men looked at each other and nodded.

The roads were busy with German military vehicles all travelling in the same direction. Frank was aiming for the town of Tiel and he wanted to cycle there as quickly as possible. The convoys forced him onto the side roads and he had to work hard to find his way. He had little knowledge of the area but the road signs were still in place and he was able to make good time. The sky above him was continuously active and several times he had to take shelter in ditches as fighters streamed over him at tree- top height. He knew he was near something important when one of the fighters let loose its rockets. They whooshed over him and he dived for his life. He gathered his senses and began to climb out of the ditch. His heart missed a beat when he was confronted by a stationary black Mercedes-Benz staff car.

'HALT!'

The uniformed driver held a Luger pistol in his hand pointed straight at Frank's head. He froze and raised his hands.

The car had drawn to a stop because of a crater in the middle of the road. Frank took in the scene. Two men sat in the back of the car and there were no other vehicles in sight. Flying from the high sloping wing of the car was an army rank pennant. The door swung open and a tall man stepped out. Frank jumped with surprise. He immediately recognised the occupant of the back seat. The two men looked closely at each other.

Generaloberst Kurt Student stood for a moment. He was without a hat and thick grey hair lay flat against his head. The bright red stripe down the riding breeches stood out sharply against the *Wehrmacht* field-grey uniform. The only sign of his hesitancy was the raising of an eyebrow. The face remained impassive. He dismissed the driver with a wave of his hand and kept his eyes focused on Frank's face.

'We have met before ...' The *General* let the comment hang.

Frank slowly lowered his hands, 'We have indeed,' he said softly. 'It was at an airfield near The Hague in May 1940.'

'*Ja*, ... now I remember, ... the Dutchman.' He snapped his fingers. '*Ja*, I never forget a name. ... *Meneer* van der Meer, I believe. ... *Ja?*'

Frank nodded and remained silent.

The *General* almost smiled, 'What are you doing here now ... at this particular moment,' he waved at the busy sky above them, 'with all this going on and why are you so far away from Friesland?'

From the corner of his eye, Frank saw the other door of the car open and another officer stepped out into the bright sunshine. His pistol was already withdrawn from its holster and he leant over the long bonnet and carefully aimed the small weapon. In a flash Frank realised that if they asked for his papers then he was a dead man. A story quickly ran through his brain.

'Two days ago I left Friesland to meet a relative in Tiel. It's taken me this long to get here.' He flashed his smile, '*General* Student, may I ask what you're doing here on this country road? You're certainly a long way from Berlin.'

For a moment the German looked at Frank and then his head went back and he roared with laughter, 'Yes indeed. I remember you very clearly. You were just as outspoken four years ago.' He turned, '*Major*, put the gun away. This man will not harm us.' He had instantly judged Frank correctly.

The two men looked at each other and *General* Kurt Student made up his mind, '*Meneer* van der Meer, I'm going near to Tiel and I'd be delighted to give you a lift.'

Frank tied to protest.

'I insist, I would be delighted to talk with you again. ..... *Major* Shroder, take the front seat.' He gave a half-bow and ushered Frank through the open door of his car.

The interior was cool and the deep leather seat extremely comfortable. The driver reversed back to a road junction and drove quickly along the road. The *General* turned his head, 'And how are your family?'

Frank was lost in his own thoughts as he realised what a dangerous situation he was now in.

'*Meneer*, ... '

'Eh yes, ... I'm sorry. My family are well, thank you.' He really wanted to tell this particular German what murdering swines his countrymen had been over the last four years. He turned to look at the man sitting at his side. 'What kind of war are you having, *General?*'

'The Führer has made a bureaucrat of me and for three years I've been sitting behind a desk in Berlin. However, now I'm back with my comrades to stop the Allied advance.'

Without thinking Frank replied, 'I wish you weren't.' The *Major* on the front seat whirled round.

The *General* raised his hand, '*Meneer*, I think I know exactly how you feel and under these circumstances I would feel exactly the same.' He watched Frank's face carefully, 'I am a soldier in the *Wehrmacht*. I think in Friesland you meet more of my countrymen who are in the *SS*. Please don't judge all Germans in the same light.' He pursed his lips and opened his mouth to continue.

The conversation stopped abruptly as the car pulled off the road under some trees. The driver turned round,

'Sir, fighters!'

Frank was the first out as in a flash the car emptied. They dashed to the trees just as two aircraft screamed over their heads.

'Rocket-firing British Typhoons. They put the fear of God into my men,' grunted the *General* from an undignified prone position. He slowly rose, 'It's this damned car. It's like driving a German flag across the countryside.'

They clambered back into the Mercedes and resumed their journey. Kurt Student tapped his fingers on the chrome door handle. His head turned towards Frank.

'Do you know, *meneer* van der Meer? War is a very strange thing. For example, here I have the complete plans of the Allied airborne attack.'

Frank looked at him curiously. The *General* reached down onto the floor and lifted up a big folder and laid it across his lap. It was made from green canvas and two leather buckles kept it securely closed. The *general* carefully unfastened them and threw back the cover. There were maps and plastic overlays. The colours shone out; bright reds, greens and blues. Frank could see numbers and symbols all over the different sheets of maps. He particularly saw the red arrows moving from the bottom of the sheet to the top.

'This full battle plan was found in a crashed British glider. They call it "Operation Market-Garden"', he said quietly above the sound of the engine. '"Market" are the airborne forces and "Garden" is on the ground. He closed the folder with a snap and looked hard at Frank. '*Generalfeldmarschall* Model does not believe a word of it. He says that General Montgomery has no imagination and could not even conceive of such an audacious plan.' He nodded his head and his lips formed a thin line. 'I believe the plan completely.'

'What plan?' said Frank quietly. He was hungry for information.

The General tapped the canvas cover and waited for a moment before replying. 'The British, the Americans and the Poles are planning to take the bridges over the Rhine. They hope to achieve this by simultaneous airborne landings in great strength. Do you understand, *meneer*? If they take the bridges then they are directly on the German border and they can move onto the Ruhr. My job is to persuade my *Generalfeldmarschall* that the plan is true. ... I'm on my way there now.' He laughed again, 'That is, if the damned British will let me.'

'Why are you telling me these things, *General* Student?' asked Frank curiously.

The *General* twisted sideways in his seat and looked Frank full in the face. The smile was almost comradely and Frank warmed to this particular German. '*Meneer* van der Meer, in 1940 you probably saved my life and I've never found time to thank you.' He thought for a moment and his eyes never left Frank's face. 'This is history repeating itself. To me it's almost retribution. During my airborne operation on Holland in May 1940, one of my officers, against strict orders, had taken documents into battle which detailed our entire plans. These plans fell into the hands of the Dutch Army. The wheel of fate has come full circle and I most certainly believe these plans.' He clutched the case with both hands and stared through the window at his side.

Frank saw the countryside flashing past him and he realised that if what the *General* had said was true then he was coming ever closer to the Allied front line. For the remainder of the journey nobody spoke; each man with his own private thoughts.

'Driver stop here,' said the *General*. The car stopped at the side of the road some hundred metres from the nearest house. He leaned across Frank and opened the door. 'I'm sure, *meneer* van der Meer, that your friends would not approve of you being given a lift by a German *General*.' He smiled and raised an eyebrow as Frank left the car. 'Oh, by the way, *meneer*. Be careful on your mission, my men are everywhere.'

The door slammed shut and Frank watched the car drive away towards the main road to the east.

Tiel is a small town on the northern bank of the River Waal, a tributary of the Rhine. He had to meet a man who had established a way of moving Allied airmen back into their front lines in Belgium. It was vital that he found out how this was done, the hidden airmen in Friesland were proving to be an enormous drain on his limited resources. The address was printed on his memory and he made his way towards the brick tower of the Catholic church in the centre of the town. He knew he was tempting luck. His papers were out of order, the dates were wrong. He hoped that with all the air activity above him that the Germans would not have the time to check up on a stranger. He should not have trusted his luck.

'Papers, *meneer*.'

The small policeman was Dutch. The face was expressionless and his eyes were cold. Frank smiled as he pulled the papers out of his pocket. The man scrutinised them carefully. He reached down to his holster flap and Frank steeled himself for the attack.

'*Meneer* de Beer, where are you going to?'

Frank carefully explained. The man kept his hand on the holster, 'I'll take you there. Follow me.'

It took ten minutes to reach the street. The two men aroused no curious stares as they passed by the people in the middle of the town. They arrived at a tiny brick house with thick lace curtains. There was nothing to distinguish it from the other houses that lined the narrow cobbled street. The policeman knocked at the door, said a few words to the man who

answered it and then beckoned Frank towards him. The door closed
silently behind him

'Papers please.'

The man was much younger and the suit was a better fit than Frank's.
He held the identity card up to the light and scratched at the issuing stamp.

'It's not bad, is it?' he said in the local accent, passing the card to the
policeman.

'I think it's genuine,' he replied with a sour face. The policeman squared-
up to Frank and suddenly reached out and grabbed Frank's left hand. He
touched the signet ring on his second finger and bent over to peer at the
initials. 'H.D.M., I suppose that's part of the false identity as well.' He
turned to the other man, 'Johannes, it's good. Just ask him the questions.'

Frank understood completely what was happening. He had done it
many times himself when confronted by strangers.

'What's your wife's name and the names of your children? That is, if
you have any?'

He released the man's grip on his hand, 'My wife is called Kitty and
my two children are Marieke and Hendrik.'

Johannes nodded, 'What's the name of the senior SS officer in
Leeuwarden?'

'*Hauptsturmführer* Edvard Müller.'

'*Meneer*, I think you'd better sit down. I believe you don't drink?' Frank
nodded. 'You took a dangerous chance coming to the town today. Because
of the Allied attack, it's thick with Germans. You're either a fool or a very
brave man. I suspect the latter because even down here we've heard of
the assault on the prison in your town.'

'If you know all that about me,' replied Frank, 'then you know why
I'm here. The sooner I get the information then the sooner I can leave.'

The policeman smiled, 'I'm afraid there's little we can do about moving
your airmen. The Allies have told us that you must keep their men hidden
until the country is liberated. That way there is less risk to all concerned.
If it's supplies that you need then contact London by radio and they'll do
a supply drop for you.'

Frank shook his head, 'Somehow I half suspected this might happen.
Just when is liberation?'

Johannes rubbed his beard. 'Nobody knows, least of all us. It could be
tomorrow, it could be next month.' There was a moment's silence and
Frank felt the atmosphere in the small living-room change. He looked
from one face to another.

'You tell him, Johannes. After all, you got the message.'

'What message?' snapped Frank. His heart sank.

'Frank, I'm sorry to tell you this. Your family have been taken by the SS.'

The details were brief and Frank listened with sweat sheening his brow.

'It must've happened yesterday. I got a message via a courier from
Ede. They knew that you'd come here so the message was sent to me.'

Frank, pale-faced, stood, 'I'm leaving now. When's the next train?'

The policeman put his arm around Frank's shoulder. 'You can't catch a train. Since the landings, the railway workers have gone on indefinite strike. No trains are moving anywhere. I'm afraid you're stuck here until we find a way back to Friesland for you.'

Frank looked around at the room and the faces of the two men. He felt lonely in a strange house and wished that he had heeded Marieke's advice. His voice was firm.

'I have nothing against either of you. I'm going to cycle back to my friend's house in Ede. The Allies are close by and if we are liberated then I will never be able to get back to help my family.' He took a deep breath, 'I can't wait. So if you find me a bike, I'll be on my way.'

The man called Johannes protested, 'Frank, I know you must feel pretty helpless. But to travel without a pass is inviting trouble. The Nazis would shoot you on sight.'

Frank smiled, 'Believe me, when I've made my mind up to do something, then I'll do it. Now, please, which is the quietest way?'

'For God's sake be careful. You know there's a war on.'

'Gentlemen, there's been a war on for the last four years.'

He travelled by night with a box of matches and a small hand-drawn map. Frank knew that his greatest problem was crossing the Neder Rhine, the river that ran parallel with the Waal. All the crossings would be patrolled and the men had told him that the bridges had been closed for civilian traffic since the first airborne attack. As he came within a kilometre of the river, the dark sky to his right was lit up by gun flashes and flares. The sounds of heavy artillery came across the fields and he silently prayed for the British at Arnhem. He pushed his bike across a field and stopped near a low dike. He crouched down and struck a match. The crossing place was clearly marked. The dyke signified the first of the man-made flood barriers that protected the rich farmland. He walked slowly forward across the field. In the nick of time he dropped to his knees and pulled the bike down at his side. Across the top of the next dyke were six men. The patrol was well armed and they walked in single file ranging their weapons from side to side. It was obvious that they were guarding the river crossing. Frank withdrew back to the footpath.

The night was chilly and he could see the path of the river clearly over the dyke as he crept along its ridge. As he moved eastwards, the sound of gunfire grew louder and heavier. Frank shook his head, stared into the darkness and decided to approach the river yet again. As he strode carefully towards the next dyke there was no sign of the patrol. The river was swift flowing and he watched the black waters with a heavy heart. He realised that he would never be able to swim across.

He walked, pushing the bike in front of him. Although he was aware of the danger, his mind kept flickering back to his family. At one point he stopped and knelt by the fast flowing river and prayed with his hands clasped tightly in front of him. Never before had he asked for help so personally.

Ten minutes later he reached a small jetty that projected into the river. He heard it creak under his weight as he walked onto it. Frank could see the opposite shore so clearly and yet it was so far away. He shook his head and turned to walk back along the jetty's short length. His eyes first saw the shape of the bow and as he stared into the shadows the boat swam into view. It was desperately low in the water and for a moment he thought that it had capsized. He leant over and pulled at the rope that secured it to the jetty. The boat floated obediently into his sight.

He looked up into the sky. 'Lord, thank you,' he said out aloud.

The rowing-boat was small, probably built for two people to cross the river. He heaved the bike over the gunnel and searched the flat bottom of the boat. He gave an audible sigh of relief when he found two oars fastened to the keel. He released the leather straps and with a smile, cast off into the river.

The current was strong and it pulled him directly into the centre of the fast flowing stream. He rowed as hard as he could but the strength of the river was too much for him and he found the boat slowly spinning out of control. He whirled round a bend and saw the faint lights of the next bridge. There were searchlights on the water and he realised that he would soon be spotted. He glanced around desperately. The opposite bank disappeared into the darkness. He heaved on the oars until his shoulders ached. The small boat made no headway and it continued on its reckless flight down the river.

Frank dropped his head as his lungs fought for breath. By now he had become used to aircraft overhead. This one sounded different. He stared upwards. He could see it quite clearly. One engine was on fire and long streamers of flame silhouetted the two-engined aircraft against the sky. It circled lower and lower and Frank saw parachutes spilling out of the rear door. It passed directly over his head and went into a steep, screaming dive. Frank found himself shouting at the top of his voice. The sound was swept away by the impact of the aircraft on the opposite shore. There was a dull thump as it hit the ground. The mushroom of flame meant that there would be no survivors. The light from the crash dispersed the darkness and he could see the shore. It now seemed closer than ever. The horror of the crash and the closeness of the bridge made him row harder than ever.

The keel jarred on the fine sand as the boat grounded. Frank leapt into the water and pulled the boat onto the steeply rising shore. Somehow he felt responsible for the small craft and he heaved it as far up the shore as he could. He lifted the bike over the side, made his way carefully up the side of the steep dyke and collapsed in a heap at the top. He glanced at his watch in the light of the dying flames from the nearby crash. It was two in the morning and Frank had another ten kilometres to travel before dawn.

TEN

Everything around him was inky black. For a moment Harmen thought he was dead. The sound of his own breathing made him sit up. Lances of agony shot through his body from the base of his spine. There was some light coming from the passage outside the door. For a moment he smiled. The Germans sense of order prevailed over everything and the smell finally convinced him. They had put him back in the same cell below SS headquarters. The realisation that his mother and sister were also prisoners made him try to stand. It was no good. He fell back onto the floor. He shouted for them at the top of his voice; there was only stony silence.

The cell was damp and this time the light never came on. He crawled round the floor and felt every nook and cranny with his fingertips. He slumped against the wall and folded his arms. He began to shake with the cold that was rising up from the floor and his teeth began to chatter so loudly that he could hear the echo off the walls. Another sound hit his ears and he shook his head. The scream was loud and penetrating. He crawled to the door and listened. In his mind he knew it was a woman's scream and in his imagination he knew it was his sister's.

Marieke averted her eyes from anybody around her as she was dragged from the wet courtyard. Her last lingering grip on Aukje's hand was finally torn away and she felt utterly alone. Marieke felt her arms being pulled out of their sockets as she entered the building. Her legs bumped down the steps to the cellar and then she momentarily lost consciousness.

It was the smell that brought her round. Certain smells the brain remembers and this smell was more than a memory. She knew it was Postma before she opened her eyes. She felt his breath on her face and turned away from him.

'Nowhere to go, *mevrouw* van der Meer, I've got you all to myself.'

She stole a glance at her cell. Dirty walls and wet floors. The smell was indescribable. She had to look at him. In one cruel movement he wrenched her head back by her hair. She tried to fight him but her physical strength was gone.

Postma's face was red and sweaty, the eyes glared. His mouth was half-open and she knew he was going to lick his lips: and he did. Her senses were extraordinarily alive. She saw that he was stripped to the waist and his body was hairy like that of a gorilla. His face was so close that she could see the veins in his eyes.

'Now you're all mine and there's nothing you can do about it.'

Time had slowed down.

Her hair was being pulled so hard that she could feel each individual strand stretching to its breaking point. There came a welcoming numbness. She glanced from his face to her body and saw that her dress was in tatters. She only cared about her child.

'What's the matter, whore? No fight left in you?'

He let go of her and she fell back onto the hard brick floor. She looked up and saw his legs astride her. He was a giant and his face was invisible in the shadow cast by the single light. His voice was punctuated by heavy gasps and spittle ran down his chin and dripped onto her inert body.

Marieke lay immobile and prayed. She begged for peace and she prayed for help. The numbness spread to her whole body and she felt detached from reality. She began to hum her favourite hymn. The sounds of its tune came rushing back into her memory and gave her new strength. She shut her eyes tightly and pictures of everything that she loved flooded her conscious mind.

'Shut up, whore!... Praying won't help you!'

He slapped her hard across the face, again and again and put his hands around her slender throat and squeezed and squeezed.

'I said, ... SHUT UP! ... SHUT UP!'

Frank was with her and at his side was Paul de Vries. They were smiling and pointing at a bright light above them. Marieke looked at it and felt it drawing her closer and closer.

'Wake-up whore! ... Jesus Christ, ... WAKE-UP!'

Postma released his throttling grip and slapped her head backwards and forward like a limp doll. His hands fell to her body and he tore frantically at the tattered dress with clawed hands.

She lay like death.

Aukje saw and felt everything. The two guards dragged her mother away and she heard their shouted commands. She stood alone and clutched her thin dress against her body. Three guards frog-marched her across the courtyard. She held her head high and she was surprised by their total lack of interest. She looked one of the men straight in the eye. He glanced down and muttered something under his breath. She had expected worse.

The cell door was wide open and they pushed her over the threshold and the door slammed closed behind her. The light above clicked out and she was in total darkness. Aukje slept. How she managed to sleep she never knew. The door opening woke her up and the light came on. Two guards came in. They held her by the arms and she faced the open door. Not a word was spoken and they held her tightly but without pain. She looked at their faces and recognised one of them as the same man who had brought her to the cell. Aukje thought no more of that simple fact.

The door frame was like an elongated picture. She stared at the blank space it contained. There was not long to wait. She heard a door open and somebody walking down the corridor. The men held her that bit tighter.

'It's the whore's beautiful daughter.'

Postma stood neatly framed in the doorway. The black uniform filled the space. He smiled at her and she watched him undo his leather belt and it fell to the floor. With that same mocking smile he threw his hat into the corner behind the guards. Each silver tunic button was carefully undone. Postma peeled back the tunic and it slipped off his shoulders. He stood with legs astride, arms akimbo.

Aukje had to look at him. His body was covered with thick hair and drops of sweat glistened on his chest. His belly hung over the black breeches and trembled with the heaving of his chest. She stared, unable to avert her eyes. He took a deep breath and the muscles of his arms rippled with strength.

'You like what you see, don't you, whore?'

Postma's hands dropped to the top of his trousers and with the same smile he undid the top button. Slowly and deliberately he unfastened the trousers. Aukje tried to turn away but the man held her gaze. The trousers fell to the top of his jackboots and he let out a roar of pleasure. His penis was huge and he held it tightly with both hands. His stare dropped to her body and he licked his lips. She closed her eyes tightly but she had to open them again.

'Yes ... it's all for you. But not yet, my van der Meer whore. First it's your mother's turn and then yours.' His laughter cut through her like a knife.

He dragged his trousers to his waist and backed away from the door to the cell opposite. Aukje saw it all. Her mother on the floor and Postma trying to choke her. She heard the slaps and she heard her mother trying to sing.

The horror of the sights and sounds gathered inside her and she screamed and screamed.

ELEVEN

'Frank, it's good to see you and I'm so sorry.'

The last two hours back to Marius's apartment had been difficult. The countryside was alive with Germans. Frank was fortunate, the Germans were more interested in the British at Arnhem than a cyclist on lonely farm tracks. When he was within sight of the outskirts of Ede the reality of the situation facing his family washed over him. Several times he stopped and stared up into the night sky; Frank felt utterly helpless. He collapsed into a soft chair. 'When did you hear, Marius?'

'About an hour after you left. I tried cycling after you but you must've been moving very quickly.'

Frank did not have the energy to explain how he had travelled to Tiel so quickly. 'I've got to get back to Friesland and as soon as possible.'

The room was lit by a single candle and the curtains were tightly closed. Marius had hot soup and bread ready but Frank was not eating

'That'll be difficult,' said Marius. 'The railway workers are on strike and the Germans have closed all roads within fifty kilometres of Arnhem and that means that we're stuck here. I'm sorry, I can imagine how you feel.'

Frank doubted that and tried to eat something. His voice was strained. 'I'll cycle all the way. I could manage it in four days.'

'That's sheer stupidity, Frank and you know it.' There was a sense of annoyance in his voice, 'Your papers are for travel by rail and if you tried any other way the bastards would shoot you where you stood. Forget it and rest here.'

Frank had not a wink of sleep and he lay on his bed fully clothed. He could hear the continuing battle to the east and his mind whirled with the misfortunes of war. Glances at his wrist-watch showed the luminous fingers creeping round the dial. Dawn came quickly and he wearily crept down the stairs. Marius heard him and they soon sat together in the kitchen.

He faced up to his friend, 'Frank, I feel as though I've known you for years. I've some understanding of what the last twelve hours have done to you.' Marius took a deep breath, 'I've got to tell you this. You look a bloody mess. For God's sake tidy yourself up man. Go and take a shower and have a shave. You can have one of my suits, there's plenty in my bedroom.' He wondered if he had gone too far.

Frank heard the words and soon made up his mind. He looked up at Marius and nodded, 'You're right of course. I'm worried sick about my family and I feel so helpless to do anything to help them.'

He jumped up from the table and went back up the short flight of stairs. Marius smiled to himself and quietly left the apartment.

Frank let the piping-hot water run through his hair and he soaped his body completely. The worrying thoughts never left his mind and he tried hard to think of other ways of returning to Leeuwarden. He towelled himself dry and rubbed his body until it hurt. The hot shave was infinitely refreshing. He strode to Marius's bedroom and opened the wardrobe. He was surprised to see the army uniform still hanging from its hangar. It was neatly pressed and he stared at it and felt that his friend was waiting to wear it at the first opportunity. He jumped at the sound of Marius's voice.

'Try the tweed jacket and the grey trousers. They should fit you.'

Frank turned with a quiet laugh, 'I feel better already. Yes I'll try them on.'

Marius returned the smile, 'Hurry up and come downstairs. I've just had some more news.'

Frank needed no second urging. He was ready and left the room but not without checking his appearance in the mirror behind the door.

'I've had a message about your family.' Frank sat up in his chair. 'They're still alive and are being held in SS headquarters in Leeuwarden. I'll get another message later today.'

Frank was relieved. If they were alive this morning then at least they had not been executed. He was still worried. He knew how the Nazi mind worked.

Marius scratched the side of his chin, 'I've been told that the Americans have taken the bridge at Nijmegen and relieved the town' His eyes were alight. 'That means that the Allies have established a line from Belgium all the way here.'

'I know exactly what they're trying to do,' said Frank quietly.

'How do you know?' said Marius curiously.

Frank spent twenty minutes explaining about his conversation with *General* Student. Marius shook his head.

'Frank van der Meer, you always surprise me,' he said with a smile. 'You leave here on a bicycle, meet the same German *General* all over again; arrive at your destination; make it back against all odds and then quietly tell me all about the Allied battle plans.' This time Frank smiled and the two men relaxed. Marius continued.

'But, but, ... there are big problems for the British in Arnhem. They're surrounded by the 9th SS Panzer Division. There's talk of a retreat back across the Rhine.'

Frank was surprised and he shook his head, 'That can't be possible. We've seen the amount of Allied airdrops near the town. Why,' he waved towards the window, 'you can see the planes going over even now.'

'The Resistance groups in Arnhem warned the British and so did we. Frank, you can't fight tanks with parachutes and if, as you say, the Germans have the Allied plans, then it could be a disaster.'

They talked for hours and eventually Frank fell asleep where he sat. Marius placed a blanket over him and left the house to make contact with his group.

Frank woke with a start. He looked around him. The room was dark and a quick glance at his wrist-watch showed him that he had slept around the clock. He felt the blanket and the pillow and knew that Marius had left him to sleep. Pictures of Marieke and his children flashed through his mind continually. However, sleep returned and there were no dreams.

'Come on, Frank, wake-up.' Marius was shaking him. 'There's somebody here to meet you.'

He sat up. His mouth felt dry and gritty. There was another man standing at Marius's side. Frank grasped the extended hand.

'Our friend here has some ideas about getting you home.' He sat bolt upright and threw the blanket to one side.

They were not introduced and the man's voice was deep and cultured. '*Meneer*, I'm sorry to hear about your troubles and I want to help.' He glanced across the room. Marius nodded.

'We believe the British have lost the battle for Arnhem. It won't be long before they are all captured or they all die. Some may retreat across the river but that will be difficult.' He wearily brushed his hair back over his head and Frank saw the haunted look in his eyes. 'The people of Arnhem are having a bad time. The Germans are shooting anybody who moves, whether they're civilian or military. The damage is enormous. I saw the British fighting tanks with Sten guns. It's hopeless. But, there is a possibility that out of this battle there may be some hope for you.' Frank stayed silent and his heart hammered away. The man continued, 'I must return quickly.' He took a deep breath. 'The Germans are forcing the citizens of Arnhem to leave the town. They're herding my people like cattle to railway stations to the north.'

'I thought the workers were on strike?' interrupted Frank quietly.

'They are, but the Germans have brought in their own railway people and some of our men are being forced to work at gunpoint. How can they refuse?' The man paused and his face hardened. 'I was discussing the arrangements with Marius during the night. He explained to me about your situation. When I told him that our refugees are being forcibly evacuated to Friesland and Groningen. ...' He saw the light in Frank's eyes. 'Yes, I know what you're thinking, Marius and I thought the same thing.' For the first time a smile flickered across his pale face. 'So long as you have your identity card then they won't be checking papers. They're just pushing people onto anything that travels on rails.' He raised an eyebrow quizzically, 'Are you interested?'

Frank jumped up, 'Of course, when can I leave?'

'There are details to sort out. You may be able to leave from the station here in Ede. But, I think the best thing is for you to go to the main assembly point at Velp, that's to the east of Arnhem. The problem is that we'll have to get you to the north to bypass the battle and then drop you into Velp.'

'Frank's very good at travelling by night,' said Marius with a wink.

'So I hear!' said the man with another smile. He thought for a moment, 'Yes we can leave about midnight and travel through the woods to the north. I'll have a guide ready for you. There are paths that no German has ever found.' He stood up. '*Meneer*, I'm glad that we can help you. At least a little good will come out of this appalling mess. Good luck to you and your family.' He shook hands and left as quietly as he had arrived.

TWELVE

Through Postma's legs Marieke saw and heard her daughter scream. The legs buckled and he fell heavily onto her.

The cry locked Aukje's eyes stiffly open. Within the door frame another man drifted into view. Her scream was cut off when she saw a pistol rise high into the air and drop to bludgeon Postma at the back of his head. He fell, pole-axed, across Marieke. In a flash the figure whirled round, pointed the gun at Aukje's guards and said quietly.

'Don't move! Let go of her!'

Aukje fell forward into the arms of *Oberleutnant* Ernst Kraft.

He pushed her to one side. The gun never wavered.

'Face the wall! ... Come on now, quickly!'

The guards obeyed and collapsed to the floor as Ernst clubbed them neatly in the same spot behind the left ear. He turned to Aukje and saw the look on her face.

'Aukje, no time for questions! ... We don't have long! Get your mother and I'll find your brother.' He saw her hesitate and he bent forward and put his arm gently around her shoulders.

'We ... don't ... have ... much ... time. MOVE!'

Aukje gazed at him. His *Luftwaffe* uniform was immaculate. She did not know whether to laugh or cry and for the briefest of moments she just stood and stared.

Marieke saw it all. She tried to roll away from under Postma's body. He was a dead weight and he pinned her to the floor. She understood the situation quicker than her daughter.

'Help me! I can't move him!' she cried.

Ernst was at her side. He dragged Postma away and lifted her gently to her feet. For a moment his eyes softened.

'*Mevrouw* van der Meer, I don't know what to say. ....' He straightened, 'Now follow me, quickly!' He turned away from her and rushed back to Aukje. She was through the cell door and waiting in the passage.

Harmen heard, rather than felt, what happened. At first he could not place the voice that came clearly down the passage. When the door flew open, then he remembered.

'Get up ... quickly! We only have a few minutes.'

He forgot the pain and staggered to his feet.

'Kraft! ... What the hell? ...'

'No time! ... No time!'

They assembled in the corridor and looked at each other. Marieke stood erect and her eyes stared hard at Ernst.

'Thank you,' she said with some respect in her voice.

He gave a brief smile and turned towards the entrance steps.

'Follow me and not a word.'

At the top of the steps was another surprise. A uniformed Joop Koopman was waiting for them. Before they could say anything, he put his finger to his lips and beckoned them forward.

It was late at night and the courtyard was empty. A single arc-light illuminated the main gate. The barrier was raised. As they emerged from the cellar, Jan pulled them to the darkest corner of the yard. A black police van was waiting. The rear doors swung open and Piet waved to them.

Although relief was on their faces they had to help each other and it took them some minutes to cross the cobbled yard and climb into the back of the van. Piet started the engine and began to pull away.

'Oh my God ... NO!' shouted Joop.

A bloody Postma, carrying a machine pistol, staggered out of the rear door of the building They could hear him screaming above the sound of the revving engine. Joop skidded the van towards the gate. Postma leapt in front of them and raised the weapon.

'DOWN! ... DOWN!' yelled Ernst.

Piet yanked the steering wheel and aimed the van at Postma. He missed and the side of the van slammed into a brick wall. The staccato sound of the machine-pistol cut through the night air and the windscreen shattered. Before anybody could stop him Ernst jumped through the door and landed in a ball on the ground. He rolled sideways.

'STOP! ... NOW!' he yelled

'NO!' screamed Joop, 'NO!'

Postma's half-naked body froze. With legs braced, he stood between Ernst and the van. Piet made up his mind, gunned the engine and the rear tyres slid on the greasy cobbles for a second, then gripped and rammed the van forward towards the gate.

Harmen saw the scene in slow motion. Ernst rose, crouched and quickly pulled his weapon out of its holster. There was a flat, single crack from the gun and the shot ricocheted off the wall and whined away into the night, missing Postma completely.

Before Ernst could re-aim, Postma was on him. He swept, crab-like, across the short distance, paused for a moment, raised the machine-pistol and swiped it across Ernst's face. With a roar, heard by everyone in the van, Postma, almost casually, put the snub muzzle of the gun against Ernst's head and emptied the magazine in one long burst.

Harmen flinched as the blood sprayed up the wall.

Postma looked up and began to run towards the open barrier. His body was covered in blood and his mouth was wide open in a silent howl.

'LOOK OUT!' shouted Harmen. Piet saw Postma coming and had the satisfaction of beating him to the barrier.

For a brief moment Postma's head, with gaping mouth and staring eyes, appeared at the open side-window of the van. Aukje screamed and punched him in the face. There was a grunt and he dropped out of sight.

As the van charged through the entrance to the yard the sounds of gun fire reached their ears.

'LAY DOWN, ALL OF YOU!'

The black van flashed along the narrow street at the rear of SS Headquarters and soon the streets became dark. Piet slowed down and leant back in his seat. He had time to glance around.

'Is everybody all right?' he said quietly, panting with exhaustion.

Harmen wedged himself against the internal bench seats and looked at the faces.

'Yes, we seem to be in one piece.'

'Thank God. I thought one of you had been hit.'

Marieke rose from the floor of the van and flopped onto a seat. She bent down and pulled Aukje up to her side. They clung to each other like lost children.

The van crept though narrow streets towards the edge of the town.

'Not far now,' mouthed Joop above the sound of the engine.

It was Harmen who asked the question that had been hanging on all their lips.

'Joop, what was Kraft doing in the prison?'

All eyes turned to the police *inspecteur* sitting at Piet's side.

He spoke quietly, 'Ernst saw what war meant to us here in Friesland. He saw what the SS did to our people. Almost since the first day of our occupation he has sympathised with the Resistance movement. I think it was Paul de Vries and the Mennonite Church that finally convinced him.' He turned round in his seat. 'Marieke, he had long talks with Paul and I believe that Paul converted him to peace. Ernst Kraft has been telling Group Uncle about German activities for the last four years. Most of the information that we've used has come from him. By his actions he's saved hundreds of people.' A gentle smile came over his face, 'Tonight, he saved your lives. He planned the rescue down to the last detail. He even removed the guard at the gate before I arrived in this van.'

'Marieke,' said Piet as he stared ahead, 'He never stopped talking about the van der Meer family. But he never wanted you to know that he was helping us.'

There was a silence within the dark interior of the van only broken by the rumbling of the engine.

'This is where we stop,' said Piet. 'We can't go any further.'

The farmhouse was large and at some distance from the outskirts of the town. A small group of people waited for them as they stepped down from the van. Welcoming hands threw thick blankets around their shoulders.

'Hello, everybody. How are you?'

'Lottie! I don't believe it,' exclaimed Marieke.

'Somebody had to welcome you all back to the living,' replied Lottie as she pulled the blanket to cover Marieke's torn dress. She moved away and spoke a few words to Aukje and Harmen.

The other figures in the group came forward.

'You'd better come in, it's cold,' said another familiar voice.

It was Aukje's turn to recognise friends.

'*Mem*, it's the de Bruins. ... Look, ... all of them!' she said incredulously.

Quickly the families moved towards the open door. The room was warm with the old tiled stove radiating heat and the curtains were tightly closed. There were hot drinks and food on the table but nobody was interested. It was a moment of joy and once inside they were able to look at each other. They were free but they were not the people that knew each other four years ago. Jan and Tinneke's hair was prematurely white. He was stooped and the spark of hope had almost gone. It was David who reflected his parent's hopes. He was full of life and had developed into a tall and handsome young man. Marieke watched Aukje smoothing her hair and pulling the blanket around her slim body.

'Now you know just how I felt when you saved me,' said Lottie. She was pale and drawn but her head was held high and she still wore fashionable clothes, even though they were a little worn.

Harmen glanced around the room. His eyes settled on Piet sitting quietly near the door.

'Where's Joop?' Everybody stopped talking.

'Joop is disposing of the van. He's driving it into the canal near town and then he goes back to duty.'

'Surely, the Germans will know he's involved with tonight?' said Marieke.

'I was driving the van and it was dark. There's a good chance that Postma didn't recognise us. Only time will tell.'

'He's taking a chance, isn't he?' said Harmen.

He laughed gently, 'He's been taking chances since 1940. Don't worry, Joop knows what he's doing.' He looked at the clock on the wall. 'Look, I have to go. I'm going to walk back home, Sytske will be worried.'

'Before you go, Piet,' said Marieke, 'whose house is this?'

Piet stood and looked at her. There was a faint smile on his lips, 'The house belongs to Doctor Bergsma and his wife.'

Harmen shot out of his chair, his face was angry, 'You know what that man did to us. He's the one who informed Müller about Kraft being in our house.'

'I know, I know,' he replied sharply, 'we've always known what he did. But since then he's done exactly what we've told him to do. Having a tame doctor is always useful and believe me, ... we've used him.'

'Can he be trusted?' asked Marieke.

'As much as we can trust anybody these days.' He smoothed back his hair and looked at the group. 'Look, ... I have some news of what's happening to Frank.'

Piet told them as much as he knew and they listened silently. As he finished he again glanced at the clock.

'I really must go now. The house is yours until tomorrow evening. Somebody will come and collect you and move you all onto other houses. Marieke, you can't go back to the Vissers in Bakhuizen because the Germans know your identity. Lottie knows where everything is. I think you should sleep in the secret rooms that Bergsma has spent a great deal of time and money building for these difficult times.' He paused for a moment and smiled at them all, 'Have a good night's sleep and don't go outside.'

He left the room and they heard the door closing behind him.

Marieke watched David de Bruin. His big brown eyes never left Aukje and their hands were tightly interlocked.

There was total silence as each person gazed into the dying fire. It was not necessary for them to speak. Each made his own private prayer of thanks.

Without warning, Marieke's head dropped onto her chest and she doubled up clasping her stomach.

'Oh, my God in heaven, ... please, no! ... Please, ... NO!'

'*MEM*! ... *MEM*! ... What is it?' shouted Aukje.

Marieke fell forward onto the floor and began retching from the depths of her body. Lottie took control.

'Stand back everybody! ... Stand back! ... Harmen, Jan, pick her up gently and we'll take her to the bedroom. Aukje, Tineke, bring some cushions.' They followed her instructions.

Marieke was moaning and sweat poured off her face as they laid her gently on the bed.

'*Mem*, what can I do?' Aukje said anxiously.

'Hold me darling, just hold me.' Her voice trembled

'Gentlemen, thank you. Now, please leave us,' said Lottie tersely.

Marieke grimaced in pain, 'Lottie, the pain is unbearable.' She let out a long sobbing moan and Aukje caressed her brow. She looked up at her daughter with anguish on her face, 'Oh, Aukje, I think I'm going to lose my baby.'

Aukje looked desperately at Lottie, 'Please, oh, please do something!'

Lottie nodded her head and left the bedroom.

'How is she?' asked Harmen.

Lottie's large eyes settled on his face, 'She needs a doctor and very quickly.'

He was quick, 'Oh no! ... I'm not having that traitorous bastard touching my mother! Anyway, she would never allow it.' He stood, trembling with anger.

Lottie placed her hand on his arm, 'He's the only doctor we can trust. We're in his house. He'll have to come.' He still shook his head. Her voice was gentle, 'If you don't call him now then she will lose the baby and she could even die. Call Dirk Haan and get the telephone number. I'll speak to Doctor Bergsma myself.' She kissed him gently on the cheek and gripped his arm. 'Harmen, make that telephone call, ... now!

The curfew did not apply to doctors and he arrived in twenty minutes.

Harmen heard the car and opened the front door. There was an icy silence as the two men stared at each other. Doctor Bergsma was the first to speak.

'Take me to *mevrouw* van der Meer, quickly!'

Harmen turned to one side as the doctor walked past. The two men did not speak another word.

Doctor Bergsma opened his medicine case at the side of the bed and placed the stethoscope over his ears. Lottie held Marieke's hand tightly and watched. He used his hand to gently feel the swollen abdomen. As he made the slightest movement Marieke jerked with pain. Her eyes stared at him as a convulsion racked her body. He removed the stethoscope and brought her up to a sitting position and turned to Lottie.

'Pillows, now, ... behind her head and under her thighs.' He reached into the case and laid out surgical instruments on the white bed-linen at Marieke's side.

'Ladies, I can't recommend that you watch this. But if you can, then hold her by the shoulders.' He pulled on a white gown and snapped long rubber gloves over his hands.

Marieke watched his movements and his eyes said what she already knew.

In a smooth movement, the doctor slipped a long hypodermic needle into Marieke's arm and emptied a full ampoule of straw-coloured liquid into the vein. He waited for the drug to have its effect.

She began to moan and her legs trembled and thrashed. He held her and waited for her to subside. Quickly he threw back her skirts and cut away her underclothes.

Her body convulsed again and Lottie and Tineke held her firm. The deep scream lasted almost a minute and arched her body in terrible pain. She collapsed back against the pillows, her eyes glanced around the room and then snapped closed.

The doctor leant over and carefully used one of his longer instruments to complete what Müller had started. With respect he swabbed Marieke's long thighs and cleaned her belly. He nodded to Lottie.

'Yes, doctor,' she said in a whisper and she pulled down the tattered clothes over Marieke's exhausted body.

Doctor Bergsma sat on the edge of the bed and removed his surgical gown and the rubber gloves. He rolled them into a ball and threw them into his big medicine bag. His face was suffused with blood and there was sweat on his brow. Lottie patted the bed clothes comfortably around her friend. She watched the doctor and then reached into the pocket of her dress and produced a delicate lace handkerchief. She refolded it and carefully patted Doctor Bergsma's forehead. He looked up at her and his eyes filled with tears. His voice trembled with emotion.

'I know who you are and I thank you.'

Marieke moved slightly and her eyes flickered open and settled on the elderly physician.

'*Mevrouw* van der Meer,' he paused as he looked at her face, 'I'm so sorry. There was nothing I could do.'

Marieke, even through her grief and aching pain, knew that he was apologising for more than the loss of her child. 'Doctor Bergsma, thank you and I forgive you.' She lapsed back into unconsciousness.

The doctor rose from the bed and tidied away the accoutrements of his profession. His voice was strained and nervous, '*Mevrouw* van der Meer should rest for twenty-four hours and then only be moved if necessary.' He shook his head and left the bedroom.

Aukje's face was set and she clung on to her mother's limp hand and gently wiped her pale face.

Harmen heard the door open and waited. Doctor Bergsma looked around the room and his eyes settled on him. His face was sad and great tears rolled down his face. He shook his head and walked past the three men in front of him. None of them spoke a word and he left the house as silently as he had entered it.

THIRTEEN

The scene at Velp's small station reminded Frank so much of Leeuwarden during the removal of the Jews to Westerbork.

Velp is a small town to the east of Arnhem and even from this short distance the sounds of the artillery battle rolled clearly through the streets. There were over two thousand people waiting in long, silent rows. Each one had a suitcase and the clothes that they stood up in.

'The swines,' muttered the man from Arnhem at Frank's side.

The long line of trains waited. Frank's heart missed a beat when he saw the same terribly familiar cattle wagons. He moved forward and the people all around him edged along with the same reluctance that he had seen so many times. There were German soldiers everywhere, all the time making cursory identity checks.

'Even before the British have left Arnhem, the Nazi swines are destroying the town. Every house is being stripped and blown up.' Frank could see the pain on the man's face.

The guards were on top of lorries and buildings. Occasionally, smoke from the battle blew across the area and people looked skywards as though the war was returning back to them all over again. There was little organisation. As each wagon arrived it was filled to bursting, the heavy door was slammed shut and the line of people moved in a trance to the next wagon. There was no time for food, no time for farewells.

'The trains have been leaving all night. There's little anybody can do. This morning the bastards shot eleven people just for arguing.'

There was a pause on the single platform as a military train roared past the waiting crowds. Flat bed trailers, each with a huge tank fastened down by chains with heavily armed troops hanging onto anything as the train sped along the gleaming railway lines. Thick black smoke billowed over everybody and many coughed and covered their faces.

'Where the hell do they keep coming from?'

'Schnell! ... Schnell!'

Frank turned. There was a huge soldier at his shoulder. The snarling dog completed the scene of horror and compliance.

'Move on! ...... Move on!'

Frank felt the muzzle of the rifle sticking in his ribs and he scrambled forward ever closer to the platform.

'Good luck, meneer, I must be off. There's work to do.' Frank felt a brief tap on his shoulder. When he turned, his helper had gone.

He was conscious of the mass of people all around him. They were forms without faces and personality; merely a mass of humanity. An open wagon door loomed up in front of him and he groaned with terror as the memories of Westerbork seethed through his mind. Frank fell onto the floor and scrabbled his way to the rear of the dank wagon. He climbed to his feet and watched people pile in after him. The desperate worries about his family and the horror of his predicament were almost too much to bear. He struggled to be calm but the mass of bodies began to press in on him and he was pushed hard against the unyielding wooden walls of his new prison. Complete darkness descended and he heard the awful sound of the door slamming closed. It was an eternity before the first jolt of movement began. The train moved and gathered speed.

Clackety-clack, clackety-click, the sound of the wagons travelling over the joints in the rails became monotonous, clackety-clack, clackety-click. There were voices, but no words; there were people, but no faces. Clackety-clack, clackety-click.

Frank was dreaming. He was floating above columns of people. There were clouds of thick black smoke and screams and shouts and barking dogs and children crying and trains whistling and, suddenly nothing. He awoke with a jerk.

'Our Father, which art in heaven, ... '

He heard the voice quite clearly and now he saw the faces.

'.. hallowed be thy name. ... '

There was a woman pressed hard against his shoulder. She wore a hat with a feather in it.

'... Thy Kingdom come, ... '

The prayer was taken up by the people around him. He found himself loudly joining in.

'... Thy will be done, ... '

For Frank, the people in the wagon suddenly became individuals. More light appeared to come through the air grills As the last line of the Lord's Prayer faded away he turned to examine the faces. Although he was tightly wedged in a corner, above the sound of the clacking of the wheels on the rails, he could hear people talking. There was a tremendous feeling of calmness.

The woman looked at him, 'You're not from Arnhem, I can hear it in your voice.'

'No, *mevrouw*, I'm from Friesland.'

Faces turned to stare.

'Then what're you doing here, with us?'

He had time to smile, 'Let's say that I'm returning home, free of charge.'

There was some laughter.

A voice piped up from the other end of the wagon, 'What's it like in Friesland? I hear you don't speak Dutch up there!'

'Well, we're all quite normal. But we do have rather a lot of cows.'

Again people laughed and Frank shook his head, amazed at the strength of his people.

The journey wore on and the train travelled slower and slower. Sometimes it stopped to let a faster train pass.

'More bloody Germans,' shouted somebody. 'I hope their train crashes!'

Five hours later, the stench of urine rose from the floor of the wagon and people shifted uncomfortably against each other.

'I'm so sorry, *meneer*,' said the woman, 'I can't wait any longer. It hurts so much.' Frank glanced towards her, her face was crimson and she was crying. He looked down at the floor. There was a puddle of steaming urine around his feet. He put his arm gently around her shoulders and spoke quietly to her.

'Don't worry, *mevrouw*, I understand.'

The journey seemed to stretch into the whole day and people were silent, each one at peace with themselves.

'I think we're there!' shouted a man.

The train slowed to a stop and the locomotive let out a long drawn-out whistle. Frank heard the familiar sound of dogs barking and swore to himself that he would never own such a dog. The shouts came through the heavy wooden doors.

'*RAUS! ... RAUS! ... SCHNELL! ... SCHNELL!*'

The sunlight was blinding and everybody shaded his eyes and stumbled forward. There were no steps and before they had time to grasp the edge of the door several older people fell to the ground. Frank was the last out and the fresh air was exhilarating. For a moment he thought he was in Leeuwarden and then his heart sank, and he cried out. He recognised the buildings: Westerbork.

He automatically stumbled along the path towards the open ground. The old woman clung to his arm.

'What is this place, *meneer*?' she whispered.

He had the foresight not to spread panic. 'Don't worry, *mevrouw*. It's just a transit camp.' He spoke the truth.

Frank expected the SS, he was wrong. They wore yellow stars but they had the same attitude as the SS. The train was empty and the crowds were herded into columns and then sorted into groups.

'Identity card!'

The man was short and wore an armband with something written on it. The yellow star on his left breast was dirty and hanging by a thread

'IDENTITY CARD! Give it to me, NOW!'

Frank produced it.

'It says here that you're from Friesland. What were you doing in Arnhem?'

Frank shook his head, unsure what to do next. In a flash it came to him.

'Help me, please.'

The effect on the man was instantaneous because Frank had spoken in Yiddish. With a look of intense curiosity he handed the card back, 'Follow me.'

They walked together to the assembly hall.

'Wait here and don't move.'

Frank was surprised. There were still some Jews in the camp. The hall was full of groups sitting or talking and with that same look of quiet resignation on their faces. Frank was totally out of place. He edged closer to the door. An elderly man approached him. He pointed at Frank's coat.

'I see you're not Jewish.'

Frank shook his head.

'Then why are you here?' persisted the old man.

'I'm waiting for somebody.'

'We all are,' he replied with a haunted look.

Frank took the initiative, 'What will happen to the people coming in on the trains?'

The man shrugged and raised his arms to the ceiling, 'They'll be processed and sent out to villages. They're lucky. At least they'll leave here and live.'

The final comment caught Frank's interest, '*Meneer*, why do you say that?'

The old man had long grey hair and his spectacles glinted as he looked closer at Frank's face, 'You have obviously not heard what happens to Jews?'

Frank shook his head, 'Only rumours about the terrible conditions in the work camps in the east.'

The man laughed in such a way that Frank shivered.

'You've not heard about us all going up in smoke then?'

Frank frowned and shook his head, 'Eh, ... no. What do you mean?'

The old Jew took a deep breath and lowered his voice, 'When we arrive at the camps in Germany or Poland, or wherever else they send us, then they sort us out and then kill us.'

Frank leant forward. His heart skipped a beat, 'What exactly do you mean?'

'I'll tell you, *meneer*. They select the young and the fit. All the rest, old women, old men, children and the sick are gassed and their bodies burnt.'

Frank put his hand on the man's shoulders, 'That can't be true,' he said incredulously, 'nobody could do that.'

The man frowned, 'Have you met anybody who's returned from the camps? Have you ever had a letter from Poland?' Frank shook his head. 'Nobody has, believe me, we know what's happening out there. Tens of thousands of Jews are being systematically slaughtered by the Nazis. Nobody has ever returned to Westerbork from the camps.' The frown vanished and he shook his head, 'Soon, I expect to be on the list and then I'll disappear as well.' He clapped his hands on Frank's shoulders. 'When you leave here, and if you can, tell the Allies what's happening. Tell the world.' From his pocket he pulled out a letter and pressed it into Frank's hands, 'Please make sure this letter reaches my daughter in America. It's my last will and testament and she's my only relative who's still alive.' He kissed Frank gently on each cheek, turned, and walked away.

Frank did not know how long he waited. The words of the old man rang through his brain and then the inane logic of all the rumours that he had heard over the years clicked into place. His head spun with the awesome horror of what he was thinking. He let out an involuntary cry so loud that people turned to stare. The dream in the wagon sprang into reality and Frank knew absolutely that the man's words were true.

'Follow me.' It was the same Jew who had met him at the train.

They left the hall and walked towards a smaller building near the main gates. The refugees off the train had been dispersed and Frank saw only a few people walking in the camp. For some reason he worked out that it was almost four years to the day that he had last been inside Westerbork and little had changed. The same feeling of desperation still hung in the air.

At the main gate stood two Dutch policemen. Frank was unsure what to do next and a push in the back made him stagger. He turned and saw an *SS Unterscharführer* staring at him.

'It seems that the Dutch police want you. They're taking you to *SS* Headquarters in Leeuwarden. Enjoy yourself.' He kicked Frank sharply on the shins and he dropped to the ground. The *Unterscharführer* marched away.

The Jew pulled him towards the gate. As it swung open the two Dutchmen grabbed him by each arm and frog-marched him to a waiting black police van. For a moment he thought he recognised one of the men but the thought whirled away as he was thrown into the back of the van. As the doors clanged closed Frank knew that it was all over. Somehow the *SS* now had all his family in captivity.

The van only travelled a short distance and then it stopped. Frank heard voices and his heart chilled. Tears came to his eyes and he straightened himself so that he was standing against the side of the van. He was ready for the end of his life. He fought back the tears and prayed aloud, clasping his hands in utter frustration knowing that he would never see his family on this earth again.

The doors were flung open and he was momentarily blinded.

'No need to pray, Frank van der Meer. Your saviour is here!'

He knew that voice and his heart gave a leap of joy.

'Joop Koopman,' he cried. 'I don't understand!'

Joop was leaning against the open door of a car. His peaked hat was pushed to the back off his forehead and there was a broad smile on his face. His two men had similar smiles. Frank jumped down from the van and then he knew who one of them was.

'Now I recognise you. You're the man in the prison in Leeuwarden!'

Joop walked forward and put his arm around his friend's shoulders. Frank never had time to ask the question.

'Before you ask, they're all safe.'

'Thank God,' breathed Frank.

'But, my old friend,' his face saddened, 'I'm sorry to have to tell you, Marieke lost the baby. She's all right though.'

Frank's head dropped and tears again filled his eyes. For a moment he was silent and then his head lifted.

'Where are they?'

Joop stepped back and took control.

'We can't wait here any longer. This van has to be returned before the Germans miss it. Come on, I'll take you to the house.' He nodded to his men and, before they could leave, Frank strode forward and shook them by the hand. Words were not necessary.

During the journey Joop explained in great detail what had happened and Frank listened in silence. They were stopped twice for checks before they arrived at the farmhouse. Each time at check-points they were waved through at the sight of Joop's uniform. He did not know what to expect as the car pulled out of sight behind an old barn. Joop quickly checked and then waved Frank towards the back door. Before he reached the house, the door was open and Aukje was waiting.

They clung to each other as Joop pulled the door closed behind them. They pulled back and cried together. Suddenly Harmen was at his father's side.

'*Heit*, I ... I... ' Neither of them could speak and the three of them embraced so tightly that it took Frank a few moments to free himself.

'Where's Marieke?'

'She's in bed and waiting for you, *Heit*.'

He dashed towards the stairs and bounded up them two at a time.

Marieke was sitting up and, although her face was pale, her eyes were radiant. He dashed to the side of the bed and then hesitated.

'*Liefje*, can I touch you? I mean are you all right?'

'Oh, darling Frank. Of course I am, just come and hold me.' He stretched out his arms and held her close. Aukje and Harmen saw them together, smiled at each other and quietly left the room.

For several minutes they lay locked into each other's arms. Marieke pushed the hair out of his eyes. He looked at her with sadness.

'Darling, I'm so sorry about the baby, I don't know what to say.'

She stroked his face and said quietly, 'I'm not so sure that I wanted the baby to be born into this world.'

'Marieke, we'll just have to have another baby. It won't be long now, not after what I saw at Arnhem.' She looked at him curiously and he explained to her in detail what had happened to him.

Her eyes softened, 'It's very interesting darling and I assume that's why you smell so awful.'

He pulled away from her and for the first time in days she laughed. Within a moment Frank joined in. It was the laughter of thankfulness and it was so loud that they failed to hear the knock at the door. After a minute Harmen entered and said quietly, 'Is everything all right in here?'

Frank lay on the bed with his arm around Marieke, 'Yes, son, everything is all right.'

'*Heit*, we have visitors. There's quite a few people to see you.'

'Before I see anybody,' said Frank with a smile, 'I'm going to have a bath and a shave.' He saw Harmen about to speak, 'Let them wait. Tell them I'll be a few minutes.'

Thirty minutes later he smoothed back his hair and found a clean shirt in one of the wardrobes. It was a little large and he had to pull it into shape. He glanced again in the mirror and saw a face that was lined with fatigue. He shook himself and turned.

'Oh no you don't, Marieke van der Meer. You're staying right there in that bed.'

She was standing, shaking, at the side of the bed.

'Frank, I've been in this damned bed for twenty-four hours and I need to get up. Now pass me that robe and help me down the stairs.' Frank saw the look on her face and knew that it was useless to argue.

They entered the big living-room and it was full of people. Before he they had time to glance around somebody began to clap. The sound spread around the group as they rose to their feet. They were all clapping, Joop, Piet, Dirk, Lottie and the de Bruins. Frank and Marieke stood rooted to the spot, their faces frozen in total surprise. When the clapping stopped Aukje helped her mother to sit on the low sofa.

'Frank, ... Marieke,' said Piet with a huge smile crossing his face, 'we just wanted to say how glad we are to see you all safe and sound.'

The conversation was never like the old days but for all of them it was an hour of being together, sharing their worries and their hopes. It was Piet who brought them to a halt.

'Frank,' the tone of his voice changed the atmosphere in the room, 'please tell us what you saw in the south?'

He looked at the people gathered around him and decided to stand. He carefully picked his way across the room and stood near the ornate tiled stove. He told his story clearly and simply. Occasionally he had to stop and force himself to continue. Everybody listened respectfully. When he had finished, he quietly returned to his place at Marieke's side.

'Frank,' said Piet, 'the news from Arnhem is not good. Since yesterday the British have totally withdrawn across the river. Their losses are unbelievable. The Germans haven't taken Nijmegen, it's still held by the Allies. Your friend *majoor* Hofstra telephoned me this morning. The Germans are extracting a terrible revenge on the people of Arnhem. This is supported by what you've just told us.' He took a deep breath. 'It seems that the Allied advance into Holland has ground to a total halt. I can't see liberation for some time yet.'

There was a prolonged silence. Harmen broke it.

'Before we're liberated, we've got to kill Postma.' He spoke very quietly but there was menace in his voice.

'I agree,' Piet said quickly. All eyes turned to Frank.

He held Marieke's hand tightly, 'I know what that monster has done to all of us and I understand how you all feel.' He paused for a moment, 'However, I stand by my principles. When we are liberated and,' he turned to Piet, 'I agree with you about it being later rather than sooner, we will deal with the likes of Postma by the due process of law.'

'In the meantime,' said Harmen bitterly, 'the swine goes on killing and torturing people. I still say that we kill him and as soon as possible.'

'Müller would kill half of Friesland,' said Aukje with eyes burning. It was unusual for her to contribute to such discussions and they listened to her. 'I've seen what he can do and now he's got nothing to lose. He'll just round up ten, twenty, thirty or even a hundred people and shoot them. As much as we've all suffered I couldn't have that on my conscience for the rest of my life.'

'Aukje, I totally agree with you and I'll have no part in it,' said Frank grimly.

Joop joined in the argument, 'With Ernst Kraft dead, I no longer have any close contact with SS headquarters. My own position is becoming dangerous and I'll have to lie low for a few weeks.' He rose from his seat. 'I must go. I can't be missing for any longer than necessary and I think that applies to all of us in this house. If the Germans came now then they would execute all of us on the spot.' He smiled and placed his peaked hat back on his head, 'Good luck to you all.' He left the house, later followed by Piet and Dirk.

The de Bruins left and there were tears from Aukje as she parted from her parents. The four people remaining in the room chatted for several hours until eventually Harmen rose from his seat.

'I think I'd better be leaving and this time I don't want any tears.' Frank embraced his son and held him tight. 'In the Lord's name, be careful. We've survived so far and I don't want to lose any more of my family,' said Frank gently as he looked at his son.

There were three of them left.

'I feel as though I'm interfering in something,' said Lottie with a smile as she looked at Marieke and Frank sitting together. She stretched her thin arms, 'I think I'll go to bed. I've had enough excitement for one day.' She bent over to kiss her friends.

'Good night everybody.'

Frank and Marieke retired to bed early. They were both exhausted. Frank fussed around the bedroom.

'What's the matter, darling,' said Marieke from the bed.

He was looking through the wardrobes. 'I can't seem to find any pyjamas.'

'Frank, really! Come to bed without them,' said Marieke with a hint of her old laughter.

They lay in each other's arms and the darkness was re-assuring.

'There's one thing that I find worrying,' said Frank.

'What's that, darling?'

'Here we are near the end of four years of war and our children don't want to stay with us.'

Marieke laughed, 'Why, darling, they're each in love. Can't you see that?'

He turned on the pillow and thought for a moment, 'Come to think of it, I just hadn't noticed. Don't you think they're a bit young for that sort of thing?'

'Frank, Aukje's twenty years old and Harmen is twenty-two. I was married to you when I was twenty-two.'

His arms encircled her slim waist, 'Time moves too quickly. I sometimes feel that I'm losing control of my family.'

She cuddled closer to his chest, 'Darling Frank, you never had control.'

She waited for his response and she realised why he was so still. Her loving husband was fast asleep. She held him even closer and joined his dreams.

FOURTEEN

She was the most beautiful woman that Frank had ever seen. Tall, graceful and with a figure so perfect that it took his breath away.

'Frank, may I introduce Rita de Boer.'

Her hand was warm and slightly moist and it gripped his for a moment. Her green eyes surveyed him and she liked what she saw.

The voice was husky, 'Frank is such a lovely name and I'm very pleased to meet you.' Before he could summon a reply she continued, 'I believe that you're going to look after me?' The pencil-thin eyebrows rose quizzically.

'That's right, Rita. Frank is our local *L.O.* leader,' added Piet.

Her clothes were best Amsterdam not provincial Friesian. She fitted them perfectly and she knew it.

Frank found his tongue, '*Mevrouw* de Boer, it's a pleasure to meet you.' He turned to Piet and smiled. His friend took the hint.

'Rita's from Amsterdam,' Frank was right. 'She's a qualified nurse and worked for one of Holland's finest specialists. I'm afraid she got into a bit of trouble and she's now a diver.'

She sat with her legs crossed and Frank could see her breasts moving slightly as she breathed. She saw his glance, took a deep breath and took a cigarette from a small leather handbag.

'My boss was treating all the high ranking German officers for their sexual diseases and I was passing on as much information as I could to the local *K.P.* group. Eventually, the *moffen* had their suspicions and here I am.' Another deep breath and Piet leant low over her body to light the cigarette.

Frank watched the two people sitting on the sofa. There was something between them that he could not quite put his finger on. He flashed his smile, 'I'll find a safe house for you but it won't be up to the standard that you've been used to.'

'Don't worry about a house, Frank,' said Piet, quickly, 'I've found Rita an apartment.'

There was a moment's pause in the conversation. Frank felt he had to say something. 'You'll need a new identity card, ration stamps and some money. I'll sort everything out tomorrow morning and they'll be ready for you.'

They were sitting in a small hotel to the south of Leeuwarden. It was very safe, Frank had been staying there for some weeks. Piet had arrived at Frank's room for their usual fortnightly meeting and Frank was totally surprised when his friend brought this beautiful woman.

She sinuously rose from her chair, 'Gentlemen, where can I powder my nose?'

Frank was non-plussed and then he understood. He pointed the way.

'It's through that door and first on the left.' She smiled and walked past them. Both men watched her slink across the room. Piet caught Frank's glance and shrugged his shoulders.

'Piet, with that woman I suspect the worst of you.'

Arms raised, he stretched, 'Frank, don't jump to conclusions!'

'I already have done and I don't like what I see,' he replied testily.

'For the past six months things have not been good between Sytske and I and, ... Er ... well, you can guess the rest.'

Frank was angry, 'Piet Bokma, you're a damned fool. She may be beautiful but she's dangerous. I wouldn't trust her as far as I could spit.'

Piet was amazed at his friend's response. 'Now look here. It's not really any of your business!'

Frank gripped Piet's arm and stared him in straight in the eye. He was angry.

'Now, that's where you're wrong. We're totally dependent upon each other and we each hold secrets that could kill hundreds, apart from our own lives.'

Piet's eyes blazed and he pulled away, 'So now you don't trust me, is that it? What a friend you are!'

Frank remained calm, 'You know it has everything to do with trust,' he nodded to reinforce his words. 'If this quite obvious relationship continues, then you open yourself to blackmail and goodness knows what else.'

Rita de Boer returned and sat next to Piet. Her face was a picture of innocence and her lips pouted, 'I bet you've been talking about me? I can tell by looking at your faces.' She tossed her head back and laughed. Her face quickly changed and she became serious. 'I'm not completely useless. You'll find that I'm very good at talking to people. Just point me in the direction of the Germans and I'll find out anything that you want to know.' The open mouthed smile returned and she touched Frank's foot with her toe.

'Frank, I'll need those false papers as soon as possible. Now, why don't you run along and sort things out for me.'

He could feel temper rising within his chest, but he swallowed the anger. '*Mevrouw* ...'

She quickly interrupted, 'No, I'm not married. It's *juffrouw* de Boer, but everybody calls me Rita.'

'Not after tomorrow,' he continued sharply. 'I'll think of a suitable false name for you. And I need a recent photograph.' He rose from his chair, flashed a withering look at Piet and left the room.

She waited until the door closed, crushed out her cigarette and turned to look at Piet. Her voice took on a new seriousness that would have surprised Frank. 'Tell me about this man that you have to kill.'

'He's an *Obersturmführer* in the *SS* by the name of Postma. Unfortunately he's a Friesian. The usual thing, joined the *NSB* before the war, went to

Germany for training, or whatever they do to people over there. He returned in 1940 and he's been here ever since.' Piet looked Rita up and down. His stare caught her off balance and she shivered. His voice lowered and he spoke quietly but with tremendous anger, 'He's an absolute killer and a sadist. He thinks nothing of torture, life means nothing to him. I would think that he's been responsible for hundreds of deaths in Friesland and that's not counting all the Jews that've passed through his hands.'

She crossed her slender legs. The whisper of silk stockings made Piet watch her every move. She sat back and smoothed the dress over her knees staring into his eyes.

'Does he like sex, or is he queer?'

He took such questioning in his stride and found it strangely arousing.

'Postma goes with women purely for sexual gratification. He rapes rather than loves. I know for a fact that some of the women who've been with him have just disappeared. There are stories that *Hauptsturmführer* Müller, he's the biggest swine round here, brings in Polish women for Postma. They disappear as well.' Piet was asking himself why he was talking to this woman. He edged closer to Rita de Boer. 'He needs to be eliminated as soon as possible. He knows too much about our Resistance groups.'

She gently touched his arm, 'By "eliminate", you mean that you have to kill him? Please, Piet, if I'm going to work with you then use the correct words, it'll make my job easier.' He gave a perfunctory nod. Her legs swung over towards him. They momentarily touched and a shock went through his body. He stiffened and moved fractionally away from her.

'Business before pleasure,' he said gently.

She moved back towards him and laid a hand delicately upon his thigh. Her voice resumed its huskiness, 'Business as well as pleasure.' The eyes were wide open and Piet felt himself drawing ever nearer. Again her head went back and the peal of laughter made him jerk upright. She rose from the sofa, stood with legs slightly apart, and looked down at him.

'Knowing Resistance men as I do, you probably want to ambush this Postma and shoot him like a dog.' There was a mocking tone to her voice.

He watched her body undulate as she spoke and he stared into her green eyes, 'I can't think of a better way for him to die.'

She laughed again, 'He'll expect that and he'll be well protected.' She bent down low over the sofa and under the thin silk of her blouse he saw her breasts hang low. She straightened and he watched her. She waved her finger as though talking to a child, 'No! no! no! That's not a good idea. We have to be subtle and do it in a way that hurts him and nobody else.' Her natural smile was, for a moment, replaced with a grimace of pleasure.

He knew the answer before he asked the question. But, this was a woman who needed flattery. 'Rita, do you have any better ideas?'

She lowered herself gently back onto the sofa and her head turned towards him. 'Oh yes, indeed, I do. These swines deserve to die like dogs but there're better ways of putting them down.' He waited. 'I learnt a lot working for my specialist friend in Amsterdam.' A satisfied smile crossed her lips. 'I know of certain drugs that can feign death so that even the best doctor can be fooled.'

'What exactly do you mean?' he said, with interest on his face.

She clasped his hand and he felt her heat, 'A quick injection in Postma's arm and he would die within three minutes. Ah! those three minutes! He would experience pain so intense and yet be unable to move a muscle.' Her voice rose and the green eyes glittered, 'A heart attack will kill him and then your job is done.' She was closer than ever before. Her arms encircled his body and she drew herself nearer. He could smell her perfume and another fragrance that excited him beyond control. Her legs crossed his and he felt himself gripped as though in a human vice. Suddenly she sprang away from him.

'Not yet, not yet, my Piet Bokma,' she said hoarsely as she smoothed her skirt back over her legs. 'Let's work out this plan and then, ... pleasure.'

He took a deep breath to bring his yearnings under some kind of control. She stood, pulled up a chair and sat opposite the sofa. 'Let's reduce our temptations, shall we?' Her smile was controlled. 'I'll need two hypodermic syringes, a phial of cocaine and a room.' She saw the question on his lips and shook her head. 'Most of the SS use cocaine for pleasure. I think they need it to make up for the job that they do.'

'Just where do I get cocaine from?' asked Piet, with a hint of anger crossing his face.

'The same place as the syringe,' she replied impatiently, 'Doctors sometimes use cocaine instead of morphine. After all, both drugs come from the same plant.' Piet shook his head. He was in a new world.

'I think I may have a doctor who could supply your needs.' He thought for a moment, 'Surely when he's dead, the German doctors will spot the mark left by the needle.'

'You're clever, Piet Bokma, very clever.' She laughed again. 'I'll inject the cocaine into him. Swap the syringe over and inject into exactly the same hole left by the first injection. They'll certainly find the cocaine in his body and they'll find the first syringe. But, not the second one, that's your job.'

Piet suddenly realised what she was saying and his voice grated, 'You mean you're going to let that animal have sex with you and then you kill him? I can't believe you would do such a thing.' His passion was subsiding.

The mocking tone returned and she sat back in the chair, 'You're such a moral person. Now sit back and I'll tell you EXACTLY what I want to do.' They watched each other like hawks.

Her voice was precise and loaded with hate, 'I'm a blonde-haired Jewess. Those swines have taken all my family and murdered them. Using my method, I've killed, note the word, killed, the three SS animals who took my family away. As I've already told you, I'm good at talking to

Germans. I speak their language and I know how their brains work.' She rose and shouted so loudly that Piet was worried about somebody else hearing her, 'I would NEVER let those Aryan bastards enter my body, NEVER! Do you hear?' Her face loomed over his and her green eyes bored into him, 'I enjoy killing them and I will do this job for you, because I want to.' Her face was so close to his that he could see each eyelash. 'Do .... you ... understand ... me?' She sat down.

In a flash her hatred vanished and the smile returned. Piet was in a turmoil. He had never met a woman like her and he struggled for self-control. He tried to speak calmly.

'My compliments to you for surviving so long and I'm sorry for insulting you.' She waved away his apology and he continued, 'I like your plan but I worry about you, Surely you understand that fact?'

She nodded and smiled, 'I do, and I worry for myself. The sooner this bloody war is over the better.'

There was silence for several minutes as each examined the other. There was a question that still hung in Piet's brain and he had to ask it. 'Rita, where's the drug that will kill him?'

Her long eyelashes flickered as she looked up. She rose from the high-backed chair and in two short strides reached the sofa. She sat down next to him. Slowly, without looking at his face she drew her skirt above her knees. Higher and higher it went and soon she exposed the top of her stockings. She wriggled her hips and the skirt slipped over her thighs. With one hand she quickly snapped her suspender free from the stocking.

Piet watched her with his heart pounding and soon he saw the V-shape between her legs. Her knickers were as snowy white as the inside of her thighs. He felt her watching him and he glanced upwards. There was a smile on her moist lips.

She spoke in a whisper, 'I keep a small quantity in a special pocket just in here.' She grasped his hand and guided it across her legs.

He felt the velvety smoothness of her inner thigh and she pushed him towards the top of her white suspender belt. His fingers momentarily caressed her pubic bone and he moved upwards. He felt a small hard lump with his fingertips. Her fingers pulled for a moment and a small capsule fell into her open hand. She dropped it carefully onto the floor at her side. His hand remained pressed flat on her belly and she pulled him closer.

A low moan came from within her, 'It's been so long since I was with a real man.'

He felt himself tugging at his clothes and he could not wait to put his hands back where they had been. They fell upon each other in a frenzy of passion that made them roll onto the floor. Their eyes were wide open as their bodies heaved with pleasure.

FIFTEEN

The heavy, lashing rain forced Frank to dip his head lower over the handlebars. It was a pitch-black night and he never enjoyed this particular journey. As the rain penetrated his shoes he knew that on such a night the German patrols would usually be sheltering somewhere warm. To his right loomed the flat grey expanse of the *IJsselmeer*. Even from this distance he could hear the waves crashing on the dyke as he cycled along its crest. Only another five kilometres to go to the hamlet of Laaxum, right on the edge of the huge, inland lake. Although soaking wet, he was happy. On this night and every two weeks, he slept with Marieke and saw his children.

There was not a living thing in sight as he slowly pedalled up the steepest hill in Friesland. He was fifteen metres above sea level with a fine view of the ever distant, unseen horizon. He stopped at the top for a moment and the wind lashed at him, threatening to blow the bicycle out of his grip. He squinted into the rain and could just make out one or two pin pricks of light over to his left. There was not another house for five kilometres. Frank climbed back on his bike and enjoyed the only place in the whole province where he could free-wheel downhill.

Laaxum only existed because of its tiny harbour. It held a few fishing boats and it was full. This trade supported four families and they lived in four houses clustered on top of the dyke and close to the harbour. It was probably one of the most lonely places on the coast and Frank relished its isolation and safety.

He hammered on the door as rain dripped down his neck. Marieke's arms welcomed him as she pulled him over the threshold.

'Frank, it's so good to see you.' Her face was alight with happiness. For a moment, they clung to each other. 'The family have gone across to stay in one of the other houses, so we'll be alone all night.' Frank thought of Piet Bokma and Rita de Boer and he thanked God for a happy marriage.

They talked about families and friends for an hour before there was another knock at the door. Frank leapt to his feet and drew the curtain back. He turned, 'It's Aukje and Harmen.'

They fell in through the door soaking wet and giggling like children.

Harmen was breathless, 'This madam raced me all the way from Stavoren and she won!' There were warm embraces and kisses for everybody.

The hot fire in the big tiled stove dried them out and they lay back in the comfortable chairs looking at each other in the light of the flickering candles.

Frank began, 'I presume that we're all right?' There were re-assuring nods. 'I don't enjoy being separated from you but it means that when we're together it makes it so much sweeter.' He glanced at Aukje. She became more of a young woman every time he saw her. She caught the glance.

'*Heit*, the de Bruins are fine. Jan is working on the farm now and he's looking much better.'

'How's David?' interrupted Marieke with a smile.

'Oh he's happy. He goes looking for food for the divers.' Her face changed, 'I do worry about him though. He takes the silliest chances you know.' She thought for a moment, 'I've got to tell you all. I love him and I know he feels the same way about me.'

'Little sister, don't tell us something we didn't know,' said Harmen, beaming from ear to ear.

'I'm very pleased for both of you,' said Frank. 'But don't think of getting married or anything until this war is over.'

'*Heit*, don't be silly,' said Aukje with a look of annoyance, 'I'm much too young to even think of getting married!' Frank caught Marieke's flash of a smile and he quietly laughed.

'Well, I'm not in love with anybody,' retorted Harmen. 'I'm far too busy working for Uncle. By the way, *Heit*, I've brought the new papers for Rita de Boer that you asked me for.' He pulled an envelope out of his pocket and threw it onto the table. 'She looks beautiful.' He smiled. 'Is it possible for me to meet her?'

'No!' replied his father sharply. Marieke's head shot round and she bent over and picked up the envelope.

'I see what you mean,' as she opened the identity card, 'she is very attractive.' Frank wanted to change the subject. He was not prepared to discuss his friend's sexual activities in front of his children. 'Our big problem this winter, is going to be food.' Marieke relaxed and returned the envelope to the table. 'The Germans are taking massive amounts of food out of the country.'

'It's easy for us, *Heit*,' added Harmen, 'there's enough food in Friesland for all of us.'

After the Allied airborne landings at Arnhem and Nijmegen, the Dutch railway workers had carried out their threat to strike. The German security chief, Rauter, had ordered that no food trains were to be allowed to the west of Holland. The result was starving people and utter chaos.

Frank nodded, 'Rauter has made it easier for us now that he's lifted the ban on the transport of food to the west.'

'Yes, I agree,' said Harmen. 'It's not just the food. The Germans are destroying our harbours and canals. Only last week they blew up one of the dry-docks in Rotterdam.' He saw his father's interest. 'I saw Dirk Haan yesterday and he was telling me all about it. The worst things are the deportations. It's not too bad here but in the west they're taking anybody in round-ups and raids. In the cities you have to have a permit to own a bike,' he shook his head as they listened. 'Can you imagine that? A permit for a bike! Most of the permits are forged anyway so the Germans just take any bikes they see on the streets and ship them to Germany.' Harmen paused for a moment, 'I've heard that people are beginning to starve because of the lack of food. Some older people have died already. They've got food-kitchens on the streets and they're having to feed over a hundred thousand people a day.'

'I've heard the same reports,' added Marieke. 'Some of the men on the fishing boats that call at Laaxum have awful stories to tell. We're so lucky in Friesland, enough food and, at the moment, we're safe. I just don't know when it's all going to end.'

Frank pushed his hair back wearily, 'Yes, I keep hearing things as well. I know that our Government in exile has asked the Allies to liberate Holland as soon as possible. I doubt whether they'll do that until they get into Germany.' He stretched his legs in front of the stove and took a deep breath, 'My L.O. has been asked to get food to the cities. I'll need to talk to the fishermen to see if they can use their boats to take the food across the *IJsselmeer*. It'll be risky, because German patrol boats are everywhere.' He stretched his arms above his head, 'I suppose, as usual, we'll have to be careful and trust to luck and God's help.'

As they listened, the wind howled round the old house and the rain lashed against the small windows. It felt as though they were cut off from the plight of the world around them.

Harmen interrupted their thoughts, 'Don't worry about tonight. I'll sleep on the floor, it's no problem.'

Marieke rose from her chair, 'Frank, it's time we went to bed, I think we're all tired.' She turned to her daughter and smiled, 'Aukje there's a bed made up for you in the roof room. It's a bit cold but you're young enough to keep warm.' She left them.

Frank put his arm around Aukje and held her close. She looked into his eyes, '*Heit*, when will it all end? When will it all end?'

He smoothed his hand through her blonde hair, '*Famke*, It can't be long now. The Allies are so close, I've seen them and spoken to them. They've got to come soon.' He shook his head, 'Our country can't last out much longer.' The wind intensified and he looked up, 'If this is going to be a bad winter, then God help our people.' He released Aukje and kissed her on the forehead. He smiled, turned and followed Marieke up the narrow flight of wooden stairs.

They lay under a huge quilt and soon became cosily warm.

'Frank,' she whispered, 'tell me about Piet and this Rita de Boer.'

He told the story in as much detail as he dared. 'It's the war, Frank. I know that Sytske gets so worried about him. He's always away from home and they live on a knife edge. She told me that they have the most awful rows.' She felt his arm creep around her waist and she moved closer, intertwining her body with his.

'*Liefje*, I could never take another woman like that. I love you far too much.'

'We're lucky, we have two wonderful children and we get on well together. Some people don't, and we have to help them.' He nuzzled his mouth at the nape of her neck and she felt the heat rising from her body. 'I love you, darling,' she whispered into his ear.

'And I love and respect you,' he replied as he felt her mouth meet his.

SIXTEEN

The Dutch winter of 1944 was the worst in living memory. Temperatures dropped below freezing for weeks at a time. The people in the cities died. Infant mortality was the worst for half a century.

Frank managed to organise food shipments from the coast across the lake to Amsterdam. But the amount was just a drop in the huge quantity that was so desperately needed. The stories told by the skippers of the small fishing boats were hard to believe. *Schipper* Schaaf had taken his fully laden fleet of four boats across the *IJsselmeer* to a secret rendezvous north of Amsterdam.

'Frank, it's heart breaking.' His old face was lined with concern, 'In Amsterdam, there's no electricity and no gas. Only the Germans have energy. Food is so short that people are eating anything they can find. You know, the newspapers have told people that they can eat sugar beet. I tried it, it was awful. There's no taste and when you swallow it, it's like swallowing thistles. It hurts like hell.'

They were sitting on the small breakwater wall at Laaxum. It was bitterly cold and part of the harbour was frozen solid.

Schipper Schaaf had his hands deep in his pockets. 'They're eating roasted tulip bulbs and it gives people terrible indigestion. I've seen them being sick all over the pavements.' He shook his head with sadness, 'The *moffen* march round laughing at people.' He snorted. 'Eh! ... They're all right, they get our food and extra rations for the winter.'

Frank listened quietly to his old friend, 'What can we do to help them?'

Schipper Schaaf shrugged and stamped his feet on the frozen earth, 'I don't know. The problem is so vast that I feel utterly helpless to do anything.' He pointed across the dead calm lake, 'If the Germans find me smuggling food they'll confiscate my boats and probably kill me and my men. It's a very dangerous business.' He quickly shook himself and clapped Frank on the shoulder. 'Danger has never stopped us doing anything in the past, has it, my old friend?' For a moment they laughed and Frank brought them back to reality.

'I've a load of grain and clothes that need to be taken. There's probably only enough for one shipload.' He smiled, 'This time I'd like to come with you.'

Schipper Schaaf shot to his feet, 'Oh no, Frank van der Meer! I'm not taking you anywhere. Marieke would never speak to me again. I'll take anybody else but not you.'

'Listen, you old pirate. It takes you two days to get there and back. Marieke will never know and I've just got to do something useful.' A glance at the *schipper's* face was enough for Frank to know that he was not yet convinced. He gave a resigned sigh and reached into his raincoat pocket and withdrew a bottle. 'I don't drink as you well know. But I happen to have come across this bottle of vintage Friesian *Berenburg*. It's been in somebody's cellar since the beginning of the war and they wanted me to find a good home for it.' He gave it to the *schipper* who handled it as though it was an antique. 'It'll keep out the cold going across the lake.'

'Frank van der Meer, I never thought that you would bargain alcohol for a favour.' He scrutinised the label.

Frank pointed, 'Distilled by Boomsma, the very best.'

Schipper Schaaf smacked his lips. 'I know, man, I know! You can't get this stuff anymore. The Germans take it all.' He made up his mind quickly. 'I'll take you. But if Marieke asks, then I'll tell her how you bribed me into it.' He gave a great roar of laughter and it echoed across the icy harbour.

Rita de Boer was restless. The daily grind of helping people and carrying messages for the Resistance was not exciting enough for her. She had stayed in three Dutch farmhouses, all isolated and very rural. She hated the normality of farming life. Her relationship with Piet Bokma had flickered from passion to quiet acquiescence. The apartment he had found for her had proved to be dangerous. An attractive woman on the streets of Leeuwarden caused too much interest and she begrudgingly moved to the countryside.

Dirk Haan was the go-between. With great reluctance, and much against his better judgement, he arranged for one of his rooms to be available whenever Piet wanted to meet Rita. He knew Sytske Bokma well and it broke his heart when he saw the vagaries of war breaking up a marriage. On this particular evening, the *Hotel de Kroon* was full of Germans. There was not a Friesian in sight. Dirk knew there was something different about this assignation; Piet had asked him to be present.

The room was his best. All the highest ranking Germans used it and it commanded the best price of any room in town. It was high baroque, a gold-leafed four poster bed; black silk sheets; red flocked wallpaper and the richest of carpets. Long couches piled with cushions gave an intimate relaxed feeling. There was always an open-fire burning away and even in these hard times the Germans supplied him with coal. He had never wanted to run a house of ill-repute, but to refuse such needs would have meant business suicide. The only redeeming feature of running such an establishment was the rich harvest of information that he culled daily from the people who passed through the hotel's doors.

Rita had entered through the back door of the hotel and was already lying fully clothed on the black silk sheets. She was part of the furniture and she blended in perfectly. Piet was standing with his back to the blazing fire. Dirk was unsure whether he was entering the room after their activities or before.

'Hello, Dirk, please sit down,' Piet waved him towards a high-backed, gilded chair. Rita lay in full view of the men and her low voice came across the room.

'Good evening, *meneer* Haan.'

He smiled and understood why men were so attracted to her.

Piet moved across and sat on a low stool. For a moment he stared into the fire. Without looking at his friend he began, 'Dirk, tonight is special because I'm going to explain to you how we're going to kill Postma.' Even above the roar of the fire he heard Dirk's sharp intake of breath. He turned and faced him. 'Rita and I have been planning it for months and we need your help.'

'I thought you'd both been involved in other things.' He grinned and Piet smiled.

'*Meneer* Haan, really, I thought you were the perfect, discreet hotelier,' came Rita's voice from the bed.

'I'll listen to your ideas but I can't promise anything,' said Dirk his face serious for once.

It took the two of them over an hour to explain the plan. During that time Dirk was conscious of seeing Rita coil and uncoil herself on the bed. It did not help his concentration.

'I'd respect your opinion,' asked Piet quietly.

'My friend, I think we should involve Uncle in this one.'

'Not a chance!' interrupted Piet. 'They wouldn't sanction it. The reprisals would be enormous. Anyway, the fewer people who know about it the better.'

Dirk nodded, 'What about Frank?'

'I approached him some months ago. He's refused any involvement whatsoever. You know what a principled man he is.'

Rita rose from the bed and came to stand at Dirk's side. He was conscious of her magnetism and tried to ignore her. It was difficult, as she was stroking the back of his head.

He tried to appear confident. 'Piet, let me get this straight. You want access through the back door. You want this room for a night and you want me to call SS headquarters when you've killed him. Then I've got to get you out of the building before it swarms with every German in Friesland.' He tried to move his head to one side but the warm soft hand followed his slightest move. 'That's a lot to ask, my friend, and bloody dangerous.'

Her voice was as smooth as silk, '*Meneer* Haan, Postma is evil and he deserves to die.' He felt her breath on his neck as she bent low and kissed his ear. 'Just think how famous your hotel would become. People would come from all over the province to see the place where *Obersturmführer* Postma died. You could become famous.'

He twisted round in the chair and looked into the green eyes. '*Juffrouw* de Boer, I have the feeling that you always get what you want.'

She tossed her head back and laughed. Dirk gave up and thought about what he had just agreed to.

SEVENTEEN

The *tjalk* was ready to sail. The crew was smaller than usual, *schipper* Schaaf, Frank and two other men. They made ready just as dusk approached. The main hold was full of stone ballast, underneath was the food and clothing. The boat had been loaded in secrecy over the last three days. It had taken Frank two weeks to gather up all the donations from his helpers across the province and he was exhausted but happy. His biggest problem was avoiding Marieke in the house not two hundred metres from the harbour. There was a cold breeze from the east and the dark waters of the lake were choppy.

Most Friesians can sail; Frank was one of those who had never learned how to. He wanted to cross the lake and help the people in the cities and he was absolutely terrified. He tried so hard not to show it.

'What do you want me to do, *schipper*?'

The boat was secured at the bow and the stern.

'Undo those two ropes and pull them onto the deck. Don't drop them in the water.' The voice was clear as a bell and full of authority. Frank walked towards the bow and pulled at the half-hitch on the harbour side.

Frank did not notice the slight change in the *schipper*'s voice. 'Oh, Frank, there's something else you have to do before we can leave.'

'What's that?' he said, trying to unravel the knot with cold fingers.

'Say good-bye to Marieke.'

He dropped the knot and looked up. She was standing alone on the quayside side with her hands on her hips. The wind ruffled her blonde hair and her face was calm. Her quiet voice carried across the water.

'Frank van der Meer, where do you think you're going to?'

Schipper Schaaf's voice whispered in his ear, 'We're in trouble.'

'*Liefje*, I have to go.' He called back.

'I've heard that before, Frank van der Meer. This time I'm coming with you.'

'Over my dead body,' muttered the *schipper*. ' I've never had a woman aboard this boat.'

The two crew-men quietly disappeared towards the bow of the boat and waited with patient smiles all over their faces.

'Marieke, be reasonable. I've got to help.' Frank waved towards the giant sail that was already flapping in the wind.

Marieke walked down the hard earth of the narrow path to the harbour, pushed the hanging nets to one side and approached the boat. She was carrying a small bag and Frank saw, with some surprise, that she was wearing boots and heavy corduroy trousers. The men stood and watched her. Without a word of warning she stepped over the side of the boat and jumped onto the deck. Her face was alight with humour and Frank felt a rush of pride.

'Hello, *schipper* Schaaf, it's nice to see you again. Just show me to the galley and I'll cook a meal for everybody. That is, after I've helped you to cast off and we've got under way.' She saw his look and took a deep breath. 'Oh by the way, I can sail, Frank can't, so perhaps it's better if he cooks and I crew!'

The two men stood quite still and she pushed her point home. 'I've known about your little jaunt ever since Frank started collecting food. Anyway, I've watched you loading this boat for the last three nights.'

'*Mevrouw* van der Meer,' the *schipper* spluttered, 'you must ... you must ...' The sentence died on his lips as Marieke picked her way across the planked deck, stood before him and, with finger and thumb, gently pulled his grey beard.

'Now come on, let's get going shall we or else we'll never make it back before the wind rises.' She knew that he could not resist her.

'Frank, cast off,' he said, resignedly.

The *tjalk* moved away from the harbour wall and edged its way into deeper water. As they made way into the lake, the brown sail filled and snapped taut. The deck heeled over to fifteen degrees as the blunt bow bit into the water. Marieke leapt to the sheets and cranked them as tight as a bow string. Frank watched with wonderment on his face.

'Frank, coil that bow line before somebody breaks his neck over it.'

He looked up quizzically.

Marieke was at his side in a flash, 'Darling, pick up that long piece of rope and make it tidy so we don't fall over it.' He nodded dumbly and did exactly as he was told.

The wind freshened, the boat surged forward and the water gurgled past the sides of the squat hull. It was now nearly dark and the horizon disappeared. All lights on the boat were extinguished and Kapitein Schaaf braced himself against the deck as his hands locked onto the long tiller. Frank and Marieke were at his side.

'Would it be easier to use the engine,' asked Frank as the wind blew his hair horizontal.

'No,' shouted the *schipper* above the wind, 'the sound of the diesel carries across the water. The German patrol boats know every sound. This way we can't be seen and we can't be heard.' He pointed upwards, 'Even the sails are a dark colour. Perhaps our forefathers knew something when they designed these boats.' Frank remained silent.

They waited as the boat headed into inky blackness.

'Prepare to go about,' came the quiet command.

Marieke pushed Frank, 'Crouch down. That big beam above you,' she pointed to the big foresail over his head, 'will swing across the deck when the *schipper* changes course.' As she spoke the *tjalk* smoothly turned and the greatbeam swept above their heads and hung over the other side of the boat. Marieke leapt forward and heaved on a line. Frank leant over her and pulled with all his strength. He glanced at her and even in the darkness he could see her face alight with excitement.

'Marieke, where the hell did you learn to do this?' he grunted.

She held the line tight and her head turned to face him, 'When I was a girl my father said every Friesian should learn how to sail.'

The *schipper* sailed by dead reckoning and the boat made good time. Frank was so alive. His body was as taut as the sail and he revelled in the cold, fresh air as it swept round his face. His hand gripped Marieke's waist and they stared ahead trying to see into the darkness. Frank saw it first.

'There's a light dead ahead!' It was a pinprick of whiteness that moved as they sailed closer.

'*Verdomme*,' muttered the *schipper*, 'I think it's a patrol boat. Total silence for everybody. A voice can carry a long distance.' He glanced up at the main-mast and the sail.

'Prepare to come about!'

They hurried along with their set tasks and the *tjalk* edged away from the light. But to no avail, the light became brighter and they heard faintly the roar of engines as the patrol boat came nearer.

'Marieke, come here,' said the *schipper* quietly. The three men joined him as he stood on the deck in the stern of the boat. 'It's time for my secret weapon. Raise the spinnaker.'

'But *schipper* Schaaf, *tjalks* don't have spinnakers,' exclaimed Marieke.

'This one does.' He laughed.

'Marieke, what's a spinnaker?' asked Frank.

'It's another sail that's rigged from the front of the boat. It's huge and can almost double the speed. But I've never heard of a *tjalk* having one. It could rip off the rigging and then we'd be in real trouble.' Frank shook his head and waited for orders.

The sail was huge. It took four of them to heave it out of the forward hold. They fastened it to a halyard and hauled it up the mast. The boat faltered in the water as the *schipper* eased off.

'Let it fly over the front of the foresail, Frank,' shouted Marieke. The two crew men leapt to assist. Again he turned with that same helpless look. 'Grab the sheets!' His face was helplessly blank.

'Oh, for goodness sake! Grab those pieces of rope at each corner of the spinnaker and give them to the men.'

He tried so hard but in the darkness it was difficult to see anything. Slack rigging tossed around the deck and the crack of the loose sails was deafening. Eventually he pulled on something and then Marieke was at his side. She pointed at a smooth piece of wood fastened to the side rail of the boat.

'This is a cleat, tie this rope round it and hang on! Quickly now!' She vanished into the darkness. Frank held onto the wet rope and waited for the next orders. He was enjoying himself and the thrill of it all was new.

'Marieke, grab that oar and push the spinnaker away from the foresail!'

Schipper Schaaf had the tiller amidships and he was peering into the darkness. He waited for a few moments and his voice almost bellowed.

'All right! ... I'm bringing her round! ... Haul in!'

Frank felt the boat heel over and he braced himself against the side of the rail. The sails flapped in the wind as the huge boom swept across the deck and leaned out over the water. He felt the rigging stiffen under his hands and he glanced upwards. The stars were as clear as crystal and he watched them move with the passage of the *tjalk*. He was at peace with himself as the boat surged anew through the water.

To their right the light of the patrol boat had almost dwindled away.

'I think we've lost him,' said the *schipper* quietly. 'They're probably patrolling near the locks that lead out to the North Sea.'

Some of the navigation buoys still operated and the *schipper*'s sharp eyes picked them out. The journey to their destination normally took ten hours and as the first grey streaks of dawn appeared the long line horizon in front of them was punctuated by the tops of church spires and trees. As the boat came closer to land whole buildings lifted slowly into view.

'*Schipper* Schaaf,' said Frank with a smile, 'I can honestly say that I've enjoyed this journey so much.'

Marieke was at his side, 'I think, darling, that you've learnt a lot as well.' She kissed him on the cheek.

The *schipper*'s eyes never wavered from his course. 'The journey is not over yet. We reach Uitdam harbour in about thirty minutes. It's six kilometres north-east of Amsterdam. There's no time to stand around. Stow that spinnaker.' They all leapt to obey his orders.

The island of Marken slipped past on their right and the breeze dropped until it was a whisper through the rigging. The lake was flat calm and the visibility was excellent.

'I don't like this,' murmured the *schipper*, 'we can be seen from the shore and the lake.' A quietness settled over the boat and they watched anything that moved.

'Prepare to come about.' They scuttled away to their relevant positions and Frank now knew exactly what to do.

They were a couple of kilometres from the small harbour when the patrol boat darted out from behind Marken Island and came up behind them .

Schipper Schaaf handed the long tiller bar over to one of his men.

'Frank, Marieke, follow me... Quickly now.' He led the way down to his tiny cabin. They watched with fascination as he pushed an old rug to one side. Frank bent closer. He could not see the slight crack but the *schipper* knew exactly where to look. With a sharp blade on his pen-knife he bent down and poked around in the crack. One plank moved and he pulled it upright. His hand found the lever and he yanked it, hard. A section of the wooden floor slid to one side. The sound of the high revving engines came in through the small deck window above their heads.

'Into the space. I'll close it when you're in. Don't come out until I open it again.'

Without waiting to be asked a second time, Frank wriggled his legs through the hole and waved Marieke in after him. They could just about sit upright. There was a damp smell and it was slimy under their hands as they pushed themselves into a corner. Through the inky-blackness they could hear the water lapping on the sides of the boat. It was not the only sound. The German patrol boat bumped against the hull right behind Frank's head. He held Marieke's hand so tightly and whispered in her ear, 'Caught like rats in a trap.'

Unbeknown to each other they both silently prayed.

EIGHTTEEN

The trap worked. Rita had sat every night in the bar of the *Hotel de Kroon* for over a week. Dirk had to admit that she was good for business and in that week the bar takings increased drastically. Her skills surprised him. She was an excellent pianist with a wonderful voice and for the first time in years the hotel rang to the sound of a woman's voice. Her audience was mainly German officers and men of the Gestapo. She seemed to calm their normally raucous behaviour and they watched and listened in silence, punctuated by the odd roar of approval.

Dirk enjoyed her performances. Each night she always wore something different and he marvelled how she made so much out of so little. On this night she wore a startlingly red silk dress. It was cut very low at the neck and hugged her body everywhere. Her blonde hair was tied in a single bunch and the long strands cascaded over her white shoulders. He found himself watching her every move as her hands danced across the keyboards and her sultry voice cut through the packed bar. Perhaps it was the fact that she was singing 'Lili Marlene' for the umpteenth time that stopped him noticing who had come through the front door of the hotel.

His manager nudged Piet hard. 'Postma's just come in.'

Dirk watched from the corner of his eye as the squat SS officer handed his cap and greatcoat to the reception desk. Without looking left or right he strode towards the bar entrance. Dirk intercepted him.

'Good evening, *Obersturmführer* Postma.'

Postma nodded, trying to peer through the thick glass of the door.

His face was slightly red and the eyes were bloodshot. The hair may have been brown or any other colour but it was shaved so close to his skull that it was just a mere whisper of grey. The black uniform was, as usual, immaculate. The jackboots shone and the creases in the riding breeches were arrow sharp.

Dirk motioned towards the black belt and the holstered weapon.

'Shall I take your belt, *Obersturmführer*?' Postma silenced him with a dismissive wave and pushed the door open. It was as though Dirk did not exist.

Even though Rita had never seen Postma before, she recognised him instantly. For a moment the audience watched him. One or two rose and he waved them back to their seats. He made his way to the front row of tables. Without a word, a *Wehrmacht* officer of higher rank vacated his seat. Postma slumped down into it without a word of thanks. The audience continued watching Rita.

After she played the final notes of 'Lili Marlene' there was a thunderous round of applause and she listened to their requests. It seemed as if Postma was the only man in the bar. Blue cigar smoke whirled and eddied in front of her and the crowd became indistinct shadows. As she burst into her next number she tried to avoid glancing at him but his eyes kept drawing her back. He never blinked and sat absolutely immobile, legs open, arms folded. Again the applause died away and a waiter placed a white card near her left hand. As she stood to take a bow she glanced at the note.

'**See me at the bar after the next song.**'

It was signed with an ornate 'P'.

Rita's heart was beating hard and she worried about reaching the high notes; she need not have worried. She left her piano and realised that Postma's seat was empty. The crowd cleared to let her pass and she swept towards the bar.

He was standing in the middle of the crowd. There was a single space at his side and without thinking she filled it. Any thoughts about his strength vanished when he opened his mouth.

'*Goede avond, juffrouw* Brouwer.'

She recoiled slightly, his breath was awful. Nevertheless, she smiled and perched on the high stool.

'Your voice is superb. Where did you learn to sing so well.'

She knew his mind. He was really asking who she was and where she had lived.

'*Obersturmführer*, I've always been a good singer, I taught myself.' She flirted with her eyes.

'You're new. Do you sing here every night?'

She told him what he really wanted to know, 'I've only been here a week and I have to sing every night. There's no other way to make a living.' She knew exactly what was written in her false papers. 'I used to work in Rotterdam but the pay was awful and there were no,' she smoothed her dress over her legs and smiled, 'shall we say, "extras"?' She almost laughed aloud when he licked his lips, Piet had told her about Postma's nauseating habits.

He wasted no time. His voice was low with a Friesian accent, 'Tomorrow night you do not sing for money. Tell the hotel manager that you're having dinner upstairs with me at nine o'clock.'

She laughed quietly and put her hand on his as it rested on the wooden bar. Postma leant over and kissed her on the cheek. Rita found it hard not to recoil.

She hardly slept for the next twenty-four hours. Piet came into the hotel early on the following evening. They met in the room upstairs.

'Piet, I see what you mean. He's really disgusting.'

Her dress made his heart race. It was made from diaphanous white chiffon that floated around her body like a lost spirit. Her blonde hair was clipped high on her head accentuating the long graceful neck. As his eyes swept down her body the swelling mounds of her breasts made him gasp with anger.

'Rita, you look beautiful, too good for that pig!'

She moved away from him and prepared herself.

'Have you brought everything?'

Piet reached into the pocket of his suit and withdrew a package. He walked towards the small table and carefully laid out the contents. She quickly leant over and covered them up with a small evening bag.

'Two syringes, one full of cocaine and one empty.' He looked up expecting her to search again for that phial. She did not respond. He opened his jacket, pulled out a revolver and laid it at the side of the syringes. They both looked at the gun and then she reached out and picked it up. It surprised him when, in one flowing movement, she checked it and cocked it. Rita saw his surprise.

'When you're a nurse, you learn some strange things.' She glanced around the room, thought for a moment and then placed the revolver under the foot of the bed.

Piet watched her and yearned for her touch. She saw him and there was a sadness about her.

'My darling, I'm sorry, I just can't be near you. Please leave me.'

He left her, alone, and it hurt like hell.

The ormolu clock on the fireplace slowly ticked the seconds away. She watched every minute and every hour. The candles in the gilt candelabras illuminated the room with a flickering pale yellow light. A single knock at the door made her stand and she uncontrollably shivered. The door opened, two men entered. *Obersturmführer* Postma was followed by a smiling *Hauptsturmführer* Müller. As the door closed behind them Postma spoke first.

'Michelle, my comrade is joining us tonight. We have the same interests.' His eyes gleamed and he licked his lips.

NINETEEN

Schipper Schaaf was ready. The fast patrol lay at the side of the *tjalk*.

'*SCHIPPER!* HEAVE TO!' Their intention was obvious.

The craft was twenty metres long. A small wheel house amidships, with a covered dinghy secured to the deck aft. The heavy machine guns mounted on top of the wheel-house were manned by two members of the German Navy. The guns pointed directly at *schipper* Schaaf.

'WE'RE COMING ABOARD!'

The German Second Officer was about the same age as *schipper* Schaaf. He climbed over the side rail and the two men looked at each.

'*Guten Morgen, schipper.*' The German saluted. 'What cargo are you carrying?

'Ballast, nothing else.' The *schipper* smiled politely as he handed over the way-bills. The officer glanced at them.

'Open your main hatch.'

Schipper Schaaf nodded at his crew and they quickly pulled back the wooden hatch cover. The German peered into the hold, nodded and stepped back.

'May we go to your cabin?' The *schipper* nodded.

The officer entered first and looked around. He smiled approvingly and leant against the desk.

'A nice boat, *meneer.*' It gave *schipper* Schaaf the opportunity.

'*Ja*, she's a good old girl. Sails close to the wind and is easy to handle.'

The German tapped the hull with his foot, 'Well built too. I used to sail in one something like this off the German Friesian islands in the thirties.' He clapped his hands, 'By God, I miss those days.' He looked at *schipper* Schaaf with new respect and nodded. 'You're a lucky man.' The two smiled, bonded by the intimacy of sailing ships and the sea.

The *schipper* saw his chance and took it. He opened the drawer of his desk and produced Frank's bottle. The man's eyes lit up. 'Will you take a drink with me? It's the best you can get!' He unscrewed the top and offered the bottle. The Second Officer hesitated only for a few seconds and then took the bottle, raised it to his lips and took a good swallow. He wiped the top with his sleeve and passed it back.

'Whew! ... That's damned good stuff. I haven't had that for a long time.'

The *schipper* raised the bottle and took half a mouthful.

'Are you busy these days?' smiled *schipper* Schaaf.

'Not really, we look out for the Allied bombers.' He nodded towards the bottle. The *schipper* handed it over.

'Go on, keep it. Let's drink to the old days of sail.'

He took the bottle, swigged and swallowed a good mouthful and then stuffed it away in his tunic. 'That's very kind, *schipper* Schaaf. We

Germans don't get many gifts nowadays.' He glanced at the chronometer on the wall. 'I must go now. It's been a pleasure to be on your boat.' He walked to the open door and turned round with a gentle smile on his face, 'Good luck.'

The patrol boat gunned its engines and roared away back towards Marken Island. *Schipper* Schaaf returned to the cabin as the *tjalk* began to make way.

He slid back the floor planking, 'All right you can come out now, they've gone.'

They crawled out, blinking their eyes. 'Thank you,' said Marieke, as she kissed him on the cheek.

'Don't think about it,' He turned to Frank, 'By the way, you owe me another bottle of Boomsma.' Marieke turned with a surprised look on her face.

They dropped sail and moored in the small harbour of Uitdam.

'Oh my God, look at that!' The *schipper* pointed to the quayside.

There were probably a hundred people just silently staring at the *tjalk* as the mooring lines were secured. Men, women, young, old and children.

'Frank,' said Marieke, holding his arm, 'they look awful.'

The crowd edged forward and their faces and clothes shocked the crew. It was the eyes that haunted Marieke.

'We've got to help them.'

'First of all, we've got to clear the cargo and the L.O. should be waiting for us,' whispered Frank.

They waited for several minutes as the crowd watched their every move. A woman emerged from the house closest to the harbour. She was tall, middle aged and walked with a slight limp. Frank knew instantly that she was L.O.

She waited on the quayside and spoke with a strong Amsterdam accent, '*Meneer*, you don't know how glad we are to see you. Will you come in the house for a hot drink?'

Frank shook his head, 'No thanks, *mevrouw*. We'd like to off-load before we do anything.' He glanced round the harbour, 'We do need some help though.'

She waved towards the still silent crowd, 'We've plenty of volunteers. Just tell them what to do.'

Frank hesitated and thought for a minute. It was a strange situation, a ship full of illegal goods, a crowd of desperate people and a single woman in charge. He heard *schipper* Schaaf mutter at his side.

'Frank, I don't like the look of this. Let's off-load and get out as quickly as we can.' He signalled to his two men to remove the hatches.

Marieke, without warning, stepped over the side of the boat and approached the woman.

'Why are these people here?' she asked quietly.

'*Mevrouw*, rumours about food travel fast round here. Go and ask them for yourself.' She hesitated, 'Don't take too long. A German patrol comes past here in another two hours.'

Frank was about to follow his wife but the *schipper* held him back, 'Leave it. She's the best person to go.'

She smiled and walked up to the man at the front of the crowd and extended her hand. '*Goedendag, meneer.*'

The man was about Frank's age, but he looked older. The dark suit hung about him and the shoes were split wide open. His pale face was almost grey and the brown eyes had a hunted look about them. She caught a whiff of his body odour as he moved to take her hand. There was still some pride in his voice.

'*Goede Dag, mevrouw.* I'm from Amsterdam and so are all these people.' He waved his hands in a gesture of helplessness. 'We heard that this boat was coming today and we left the city four hours ago to walk here. Some of us didn't make it.' He was still holding her hand, '*Mevrouw,* we're very hungry. There's no food in Amsterdam.'

Marieke let go of his hand and glanced quickly at the crowd. They were motionless but their eyes bored into her. Marieke took a step forward and climbed onto a cast-iron mooring bollard. Although she spoke quietly, her voice was clearly heard by everybody in the small harbour.

'We bring food and clothes from the people of Friesland. You're welcome to them and we'll try and bring more the next time we come. Please help us to unload. The *schipper* will tell you how.'

The crowd surged forward around her and then faltered at the edge of the harbour. There was a quiet dignity about them and they were unsure what to do. *Schipper* Schaaf took over, selected six men and gave orders. Frank walked past the people and stood quietly below Marieke. She was immobile, watching the crowd, tears streaming down her face. Frank pulled gently at her coat and held out his hand. She took it and jumped down. Within a second she was in his arms and they held tightly on to each other.

'Oh, Marieke! Marieke! ... How long can this torture go on for?'

They stayed there for as long as it took to unload the boat. Somebody was tugging at Frank's sleeve. He turned round. The man who had spoken to Marieke was facing him. Behind were people clutching packages, some were forcing uncooked food into their mouths, and others were empty handed.

'*Mevrouw, meneer,* we would like to thank you for the food and clothing.' He faltered, glanced down and shuffled his feet. Frank knew he wanted to say something else. Marieke reached out and touched the man's hand. His head lifted and his eyes were alight.

'Please, take some of us back to Friesland. There's room on the boat.'

Frank was about to speak and then he closed his mouth. The man continued. 'Some of us here have been in hiding for three years. I'm Jewish and so are my family.' Frank suddenly became aware of the gaunt woman behind him and two small children holding her hand. 'This is only the second time that we've come out of our secret room. *Meneer*, we can't return, the people looking after us haven't enough food to feed us. The Germans are rounding up any men under forty and the searches and checks never stop. There are many here who want to leave Amsterdam and we beg you, in God's name. Please take us, ... PLEASE!'

Frank saw a dozen hands being lifted into the air and then he saw their faces. He did not know what to do. He clenched his fists, closed his eyes and silently prayed.

'Frank, I can take fifty. ... You decide.' *Schipper* Schaaf stood quietly at his side.

A surge of joy rushed though Frank's heart and in one giant stride he leapt onto the bollard.

'We can take fifty. Families, women and children get the first choice. Please hurry up, we can't wait here much longer.'

They finally took fifty-six people. The hold was jam packed and there were eight in the *schipper*'s cabin. As Frank cast off the mooring lines he was desperately happy. He knew Marieke was near him and he looked up. Her eyes were shining.

'Frank, thank the Lord, we've actually done something to help our people.'

'I know, darling,' he replied gently, 'but what the hell are we going to do with them all?'

It was late afternoon when the *tjalk* slipped away into the lake. A slight breeze pushed the boat steadily though the water. After thirty minutes they saw several other fishing boats, no sign of anything else. Frank was leaning against the tiller and watching the brown mainsail pull the boat along. It was the sail that obscured their view.

'Prepare to come about!'

Frank knew the routine and he ducked and reached for the sheets.

'Oh no! ... Look ahead!'

The shape was the same, the patrol boat had returned. There was absolutely nothing that they could do. He watched the boat coming closer. *Schipper* Schaaf kicked a locker door open revealing a squat British Sten gun. He looked at Frank.

'I'm not giving in that easily. This time we have no chance, but by God, I'll take a few with us!' He gripped the tiller and waited.

'HEAVE-TO *TJALK*! ... WE'RE COMING ABOARD!'

TWENTY

For the first time in her life Rita was unsure of herself and she dared not show it.

Müller and Postma sat on the low silk couch and watched her like hawks watching their prey. They had obviously been drinking and their faces sweated profusely.

'Drinks, gentlemen?' She hovered near the cabinet.

Müller nodded and sat with his crossed leg swinging backwards and forwards.

'*Ja*, cognac please. ... Michelle, you're a beautiful girl. Far too good for a town like Leeuwarden.' He turned round, 'Don't you agree, Postma?' The *Obersturmführer* nodded and undid his tunic. Rita saw his hairy chest. Postma saw the glance and gave a wolfish smile.

She filled the balloon glasses and passed two of them over. Postma slipped his hand onto her thigh and squeezed.

'Careful, *Obersturmführer*, don't spoil the goods,' laughed Müller as he gulped down half the cognac.

'Sing us a song, my pretty one,' said Postma.

Rita sat in the chair opposite them and lay back, placing her hands at the back of her head. Such a posture, she knew, would excite them.

'I'm sorry, I really can't sing without my piano.'

'Sing,' hissed Postma through his teeth.

'I'll try, but first let me fill your glasses.' She sinuously stood, picked up the bottle and walked towards them. The glasses were empty and she poured in generous measures. She bent low and let Postma get a good look at her body. She rubbed her hand over his head.

'I love your hair, it's so prickly.' He slapped her bottom.

'Not as prickly as something else!' He guffawed at his own joke.

Rita bent lower and pulled Postma's face closer to hers. She kissed him full on the mouth and he collapsed back onto the couch. His face was a mask. She could taste his foulness and thanked God that the cognac masked the worst.

'I think Postma, that you may have met your match,' said Müller as he rose to his feet. He unclipped his black leather belt and shoulder strap and threw it on the floor. In one smooth movement he slipped his hand around her waist and drew her close. She felt the power of the man as he stared into her eyes.

'I know what you want, madam, and we want the same.' He let go of her and quickly undid his tunic.

She knew she had to regain control and very quickly.

'Gentlemen, gentlemen, I always thought that Germans knew how to treat a lady. Come on, let's fill our glasses and drink to the night ahead.' She pulled off the chiffon top to her dress. Her half-revealed breasts hypnotised Müller and he stepped back, mouth open. She twisted away, filled up her own glass and stared at him over the brim. Her voice was husky.

'There are infinite variations, are there not?'

Müller shook himself and there was an excited edge to his voice, 'Come on, Postma, me first. Let's play this little game. Anyway, I'm enjoying it. We could be having a better night than I thought. Michelle, I've had a busy day and I want to be fresh. I'm going for a bath.' He laughed mockingly, 'I'm sure Postma will entertain you.' He stroked her white shoulders, turned and walked towards the bathroom.

Rita heard the bath running and she knew she had little time. Postma was staring at her with open eyes. She sat next to him, grabbed his hand and placed its sweaty palm on her smooth breast. He grabbed her so hard that it hurt.

'Careful! Careful! I'm not a whore, you know. I just like a good time.'

He began to slobber over her neck and his legs fell over her. She joined him and rubbed his neck. Somehow, she had to control him. Time was ticking by.

She gently pushed herself away from his sweating body and gazed into his bloodshot eyes.

She whispered huskily, 'I've something very special for you. I know you'll enjoy it.'

He said nothing but his grip slackened. She leaned over to the table, pushed her handbag to one side revealing the two syringes. She watched his face, the eyes lit up.

'You're a surprise every minute, you are,' he said as he licked his lips. 'I hope it's the good stuff?'

'The very best,' she filled the first syringe carefully and held it up to the light.

He half-stood, grabbed his tunic, delved into the pocket and produced a small leather box. He opened it carefully on the couch at his side.

'Great minds think alike, Michelle.'

Her heart skipped a beat. The box contained another syringe, half-full of straw coloured liquid. Two phials nestled in the velvet lining.

'Plenty for us all,' he said with his eyes ablaze, 'you give it to me and I'll give it to you.' Postma grabbed the chiffon top, put it to his face and inhaled deeply. He twisted it tightly and threw it round his arm.

'Now, give it me now!' he exclaimed.

She saw the tell-tale marks of previous injections in the heavy artery of his forearm.

'Come on, woman! This bloody thing hurts!'

She bent low and tapped the blood vessel. It bulged with throbbing life. She slipped the fine needle into the vein and watched his face as she emptied the syringe. As she withdrew it he ripped away the chiffon tourniquet. His eyes opened wider and wider and his mouth gaped open.

Grunting sounds came from his throat and he collapsed back onto the couch.

'Now you, my pretty one.'

Rita jumped with shock. Müller had left the bathroom and he was standing behind the couch with an unfastened bath robe around his shoulders. There was a glass of cognac in his hand and he looked stone-cold sober.

'I'll watch you.' He handed the syringe and phial of cocaine over to her.

'Of course, *Hauptstur n,führer.*' She took the syringe from his hand and filled it.

She had taken cocaine before and knew exactly what to do. She worried whether she would be able to control herself.

It rushed to her brain and she felt her body set alight with a fire that raged with such an intensity that she found it hard to breathe. She trembled and her mouth was flooded with saliva. She tried to swallow and could not. The colours in the room brightened to such an extent that she screwed her eyes tightly closed. Her heart was beating so rapidly that she could feel the surge of blood as it ebbed and flowed through every vein. Suddenly, the world calmed and a delicious flood of warmth spread over her. She opened her eyes and saw a naked Müller standing over her.

He carried her to the bed and undressed her slowly and deliberately. The flames of the fire cast flickering shadows around the room and with open eyes she watched the shapes and colours dance. She knew that Müller was entering her and the effects of the drug heightened the sexual sensations, but she felt detached from the awful reality and there was no pleasure.

How long he possessed her for, she never knew. Abruptly there was a change in her body and the draining effect of the drug left her empty and desolate. Müller stood at the end of the bed the robe covering his body. His face wore no expression and he looked down at her. Eventually, he turned away and he disappeared into the flickering light of the candles.

Rita pulled the silk sheet over her naked body and pushed her face into the pillow.

'Postma, get up your lazy bastard. She's yours and she's good. Just wake her up!'

There was a grunt as he rose from the couch. Postma was naked and his hairy body made him appear like a gorilla. He fell backwards with legs splayed and rolled onto the floor. Müller kicked him hard.

'Come on! I thought you wanted her!'

He began to laugh and the sound echoed through the room. Rita heard it and covered her ears as she shook with uncontrollable terror.

'You're a heavy bastard,' breathed Müller as he struggled to lift Postma off the floor. He gave up and flopped back onto the couch.

'Don't worry, my little whore,' he called over his shoulder, 'I'll get him ready for you. He's a real animal. I know what you need Postma, my friend. Another shot of happy juice will do you the world of good.'

Rita's heart skipped a beat and she prayed to the Almighty for divine intervention.

'Where's your box?' muttered Müller, as he scrabbled around the couch.

'Oh no! You stupid bastard!' he shouted. 'You left the lid open and the phials are smashed. Can't you do anything properly?'

Rita turned her face away from the pillow and watched Müller stumble round the couch on his hands and knees. She knew that to speak would bring him back to the bed. The nails on her clenched fists ached and her body was rigid with hope.

Postma groaned and moved.

'Ah! Of course, she has some more. Now where the hell did she put it?'

He stood, walked over to the table and pulled the candelabra closer. She heard him take a deep breath.

'Got it! This'll wake you up.' He bent over Postma's prostrate body and searched for his belt. Rita quietly sat up and watched Müller make his preparations. She found herself speaking and realised that some of her self-control was returning.

'Hurry, *Hauptsturmführer*, I'm getting cold.'

He looked up at her over the couch, 'It won't be long now. In a minute we'll both come and keep you warm.' He turned to Postma.

'Keep still, my hairy friend.'

Postma began to rise from the floor and Müller pushed him down.

His voice was as smooth as honey, 'In it goes. ... There we are. Happy land in a minute.' He stood and walked towards the bed, throwing off his robe as he came closer. In his hand he held the still dripping syringe. 'I've saved a little for you, just to make things more exciting.' He pulled her arm out from under the sheets and single- handedly threw his belt around the upper arm. She saw the fluid squirt out of the needle as he checked the contents. In a second he was on her, pinioning her body with his weight. She felt him quivering with excitement and she closed her eyes.

TWENTY ONE

The brown sails of the *tjalk* flapped in the breeze. Frank and Marieke refused to leave *schipper* Schaaf's side as he waited for the patrol boat to come alongside. The grey superstructure loomed over the wooden sides of the boat. Frank saw the number painted in black on the steel hull. It was the same patrol boat that had stopped earlier and for a moment he felt a rush of hope.

It was the same Second Officer. He jumped onto the deck.

'Good evening, *schipper*.' There was not even a second glance towards Frank and Marieke. The German nodded and looked up at the mainmast, 'I see you've made good time. I wanted to return the favour and so I managed to find this.' He reached into his tunic and brought out a brown bottle, 'It's Schnapps, made in my part of Germany. I'm sorry it's not full, but it's all I could find.' He passed it to over to an amazed *schipper* Schaaf.

'Thank you, ... eh! ... Thank you,' he mumbled.

'We old sailors must stick together. We're a dying breed, you know.' He glanced back at the patrol boat, 'I must go now. There's a strong wind forecasted, so watch out for the next couple of hours. *Auf Wiedersehen!*' He gave a quick salute and leapt back onto the patrol boat. There was a seething cloud of blue diesel smoke and the craft leapt away across the *IJsselmeer*.

Schipper Schaaf unscrewed the top, raised the bottle to his mouth and took a long swig. 'Frank, somebody must be looking after us. That was really close.' He shook his head and a beaming smile passed over his face. 'Really close.'

The hatch was battened down as the wind rose. Marieke showed Frank how to reef the two sails and he thrilled to his new found skills.

'Frank, hold the tiller, whilst I lash it.' The *schipper* threw a length of stout rope twice around the long tiller and secured it to a cleat on the deck. The boat heeled over and the blunt bow pushed its way into the heaving swell. Dusk was upon them and the horizon began to disappear.

'Another half hour should see us back at Laaxum. Hold on to something, it's going to be quite a blow.' The *schipper* pulled his peaked cap down over his forehead.

The flat bottomed *tjalk* was not ideally suited to sailing on rough waters. With no keel it pitched and heaved with every push of the wind. Its two massive side boards were secured in the fully down position and they creaked and groaned as the wind tried to push the heavy hull sideways instead of forwards. *Schipper* Schaaf knew the limits of his boat and he let it slip slowly towards harbour as the wind howled round their heads.

'Let her run with the wind!' he bellowed.

The boat shifted slightly and it pitched and yawed in a new motion that was not good for landlubbers. Frank felt nausea heave at his stomach and he rushed for the side and emptied away his last meal. He felt Marieke tugging at his sleeve.

'Frank, you look green,' she shouted, with a mocking laugh.

His head went down again and he retched until foul bile made him spit with anger. Slowly he stood and made his way back to the stern. He clutched at anything he could find as the slippery deck heaved and bucked under him.

Marieke stood, feet braced against the tiller deck cleats, and watched her poor husband claw his way back towards her. Above the wind and the creaking of the rigging she heard a new sound. It was the cries of their passengers. For a few heady minutes she had forgotten them. *Schipper* Schaaf heard the same noise and shouted across to her.

'Go and tell them another twenty minutes. There's nothing else we can do.'

She fought her away across the deck and reached the hatch. The crew men eased one of the hatch-battens free and a nauseating smell of vomit and excreta hit her nostrils. She recoiled for a moment and then put her head down the hatchway and shouted down the message. There was no reply, only the sound of retching and moaning.

'SCHIPPER, A FLASHING LIGHT TO OUR LEFT!' shouted Frank.

The *schipper* waved, 'YES, IT'S THE OLD LIGHT HOUSE AT STAVOREN!'

'PREPARE TO COME ABOUT!' This time they all worked together.

'LOWER THE MAINS'L!'

It took three of the crew to haul down the great flapping sail and push it into a crumpled heap on the deck. The *tjalk* slowed in the water and the single foresail pulled them along at a slower pace.

'I SAW SOME LIGHTS AHEAD! NO ... THEY'VE GONE OUT!' somebody called. 'WAIT A MINUTE! ... THEY'RE FLASHING ON AND OFF!'

'It's the lights in the houses at Laaxum. Thank the Lord,' said Frank.

Gone was the heaving swell as the boat rounded the corner of the small breakwater.

'LOWER THE FORES'L!'

With perfect timing the *tjalk* creaked its way into the harbour. A final heave on the tiller and it slid silently to its mooring. As the crew jumped over the side to secure the mooring lines, Marieke scrabbled away at the hatches to the holds. Frank helped her and the heavy beams slid back.

'Come up now, you're safe,' she said quietly.

They came out of the hold like ghosts, in single file with not a sound. It was mid-night and dark, but there was a quarter moon that spread some light as the clouds drifted by. A child cried and it was the signal for chaos. They all began to talk at once and again Marieke took over.

'QUIET EVERYBODY, PLEASE!' It had the desired effect.

'Frank, what are we going to do with them all?'

'Marieke, look at the harbour!' He was standing on the rail of the *tjalk*, holding the rigging. For a minute the moon shone brightly. The narrow path to the harbour was full of people. Frank jumped to the quayside and Aukje flew into his arms.

'*Heit*! *Heit*! I'm so glad you're all right!'

He held her tight and exclaimed, 'Who are all these people?'

Aukje stood back, 'Harmen had a message from a woman in Uitdam that "a large flock of seagulls was approaching Friesland". We guessed what it was and all these people have come to help.'

He could see the smiling faces before the moon was blotted out. An oil lamp was lit.

'No lights!' called *schipper* Schaaf. 'It's a clear night. The *moffen* could be anywhere.'

There were bicycles everywhere and on the road that ran along the dyke were silhouetted several carts with horses waiting patiently. Harmen was at his side and he shook his father's hand.

'*Heit*, good to see you. We've thirty people here, let's get them moving'

Both crowds had gone silent.

'All right, everybody,' said Frank loudly, 'two divers per person. Try and keep families together but don't worry if you can't, we'll sort things out in the next couple of days.'

Schipper Schaaf walked with Marieke as she led the children up the path. Voices came out of the darkness.

'Thank you, *mevrouw*.'

'God be with you, *meneer*.'

'I'll never forget what you've done.'

'Good sailing, *schipper*, I'll say a prayer for you.'

'I have no words for what you've done.'

'There is a God after all.'

The words were few but before the people had disappeared into the night every one of them said something to the crew of the *tjalk*. Frank held Marieke very close.

'Tonight, *liefje*, we've done a job worth doing.'

Schipper Schaaf brushed away a single tear from his cheek and put his arms around their shoulders. 'I'll sleep on my boat tonight. ... You sleep well, you deserve it.'

Before they could reply, he walked away down the harbour path.

TWENTY TWO

The scream penetrated her consciousness and for a split second she thought it was her own.

'What the hell's the matter with you, Postma?' grunted Müller as he forced her legs wider. A silence dropped on the room like death and she knew that her prayers had been answered. He rolled off her and dropped to the floor and was at Postma's side in a moment; he kicked him sharply on the leg.

'Come on move, you fat pig!'

Postma was locked rigid and his eyes bulged in their sockets. The veins in his neck stood out like whipcords and the hairy body was bright red. Müller stared at him coldly.

'Stop fooling around! Come on, ... GET UP!' He tried to drag the inert, naked body into a sitting position, but to no avail. Postma was very heavy.

Rita slowly sat up and watched Postma dying. A smile spread over her face and she dropped back onto the pillow.

Müller stepped back and grabbed Postma's head and slapped it once, twice and backwards and forwards. He dropped to his knees and jammed his head against the chest. There was shock on his face as he stared at the body.

His voice was incredulous and he said in a coarse whisper, 'He's dead. The silly bastard's dead!' He sprang to his feet, ran over to the fireplace and jabbed the bell-push.

There was a quiet knock at the door. Müller ran to the bed, grabbed his robe, searched for his belt, found it, and pulled out the gun.

'COME IN!' he shouted.

Dirk walked through the door, saw Postma sprawled naked on the carpet and then his eyes swivelled towards Rita, spread-eagled on the bed. Müller was directly in front of him and the hand clutching the gun was levelled at Dirk's head. A snarl came from deep in his throat.

'Get a doctor, NOW and get me to a telephone.' He pointed at Rita with a quivering finger, 'And watch her. See the bitch doesn't move a muscle.'

Dirk summed up the situation in an instant and his voice was steady, 'Of course, *Hauptsturmführer* Müller. The telephone is down the corridor and turn right.'

Müller elbowed him out of the way and ran down the corridor.

Rita quickly sat up, pulled the black sheets round her bruised body and said in a loud whisper, 'Dirk, find the syringe. It's on the floor at the side of the bed. Quickly, hide it before he comes back. Get the other from the table and put it near the bed.' Her eyes were dark and lifeless. She dropped back onto the pillow.

Dirk was at her side tenderly smoothing the damp hair away from her face.

'Oh my God! What's the Nazi bastard done to you?'

Her eyes stared at him and she grasped his hand, 'Do as I say, please! Or Müller will kill both of us!'

He dropped to his knees and searched in the flickering light of the candles. His arm reached under the bed and his fingers just touched the glass tube of the syringe. He pulled it towards him and rolled into a sitting position.

'I've got it,' he said triumphantly.

'Dirk, be careful. Don't touch the needle. Now, empty it into the fire and hurry.'

In a single bound he reached the fire and jetted the contents into the dying embers. There was a puff of smoke and a flash of purple flame. Swiftly he pulled the white handkerchief from his top pocket, wrapped the syringe in it and stuffed the bundle inside his jacket. He lifted his head as he heard Müller screaming down the telephone. Dirk found the other syringe. He glanced at it and threw it down at the side of the bed. He remembered the gun, found it, and pushed into the waistband of his trousers. All this he achieved in one minute flat.

'It's done,' he whispered across the room. Just in time as Müller strode through the door.

'Get that doctor, NOW!' he snapped.

Dirk inclined his head, 'Of course, *Hauptsturmführer*.'

As he left the room he heard the scream of sirens as Müller's men approached the hotel. Dirk ran down the corridor knowing that he had to get back to Rita as quickly as possible. He grabbed the telephone and spoke quickly to the hotel's operator.

The message was conveyed and Dirk slammed the receiver back on its cradle and hurtled back down the corridor. Before he turned the corner, he paused for a moment near another door, used his pass key and pushed it open. A white-faced Piet sat on the bed.

'What the hell's going on?' he whispered loudly.

'No time to explain.' replied Dirk brusquely as he pulled the handkerchief out of his pocket and removed the syringe, 'Get rid of it, and this.' He pushed the gun into Piet's hand and then saw the look on his friend's face. 'Don't worry, I think everything'll be all right. And for God's sake go down the fire escape and get to hell out of here!'

He was back in the room and saw Müller pulling on his uniform.

Dirk's voice was icy calm. '*Hauptsturmführer*, the doctor is on his way.'

'Haan, put this woman in another room where nobody can speak to her. She'll be guarded. After the doctor has seen Postma, this room will be sealed off until the SD have examined it.' Müller's face was a mask of coldness. He patted his uniform into place, walked to the door and switched on the lights.

Dirk saw the room as though it was a scene from a stage play. Postma's body lay rigid on the carpet. His eyes bulged out of their sockets and the massive fists were locked solid over his chest. Almost as a symbol of surrender, the white chiffon top lay across his genitals.

Rita was sitting on the bed, her eyes staring fixedly at Dirk. He flashed her a quick smile and she visibly relaxed.

The sound of heavy boots on the stairs prompted Müller into action and he straightened his back and walked to the open door. *Sturmscharführer* Hofmann of the *SD* stood rigidly to attention.

'Ah, ... Hofmann. Wait outside. Tell your men to search the hotel from top to bottom. Interview everybody.' He noticed the doctor standing respectfully in the corridor. He crooked his finger at him.

'Bergsma, examine *Obersturmführer* Postma, I want the cause of death.'

The old man came into the room, glanced at Piet, slightly lifted an eyebrow and lowered himself onto the carpet at Postma's side. He flipped open his medical bag and withdrew a stethoscope and a small torch. He clipped the instrument over his ears and put the listening tube against the chest. He listened for a few moments and carefully moved the tube to several places. He felt the neck with his fingers and took a deep sigh as he turned to look at Müller.

'I pronounce this man dead, ... '

'I know that, you idiot!' interrupted Müller, impatiently. 'The cause of death! How did he die?'

The doctor saw the broken syringes on the floor, reached down and picked up the empty phial and sniffed it. He wrinkled his nose and put the phial back on the carpet. He reached across to Postma's arm and examined the marks and bruises near the main artery. He came very close to the bulging eyes and, with his torch, peered into them. He then moved down to the legs. Moving the chiffon slightly he compressed the calf muscles, delicately re-adjusted the chiffon and eased himself to his feet.

'Well?' said Müller, tapping his belt with his right forefinger.

Doctor Bergsma squared his shoulders, put the instruments back in his leather bag and snapped it closed. His voice was clinically precise.

'The evidence is quite clear. I'm absolutely certain that *Obersturmführer* Postma died of a massive heart attack as a result of taking an overdose of cocaine. He didn't stand a chance. When he injected himself with the fatal dose he was rather careless. I would say that some air was also injected at the same time as the drug. He really ... just killed himself.'

Dirk saw Rita blanch.

'Thank you, Doctor, that'll be all. Now leave us.'

As Doctor Bergsma left the room he slipped a sidelong glance towards Dirk's impassive face.

Müller's voice grated, 'Haan, take that woman out of here and find her another room. She's not to leave the hotel under any circumstances. Do you understand?'

Dirk nodded and turned towards the bed. Rita looked up at him and tried to move. 'Keep still, I'm going to carry you.' He rolled her to one side and gently wrapped the sheet round her body. With ease he lifted her body and carried her from the room. Müller stared after him.

TWENTY THREE

The awful winter of 1944-45 ground on without respite. Holland was slowly stripped of everything that was useful for the German war effort. Friesland was lucky, it was self sufficient in food, but a lot was given away or traded to the suffering people in the cities of the west. The black-market boomed and the Resistance had to fight hard to overcome unscrupulous people. In Amsterdam fuel was scarce and the proud citizens cut down the trees in their once beautiful parks. Coffins were unobtainable and the dead lay in the streets until they could be thrown into the canals to float away and block up the fresh water system. Still the Germans rounded up every man under the age of forty and continued in their relentless hunt for the hidden Jews. The people of the cities flocked to the provinces in their search for food. They walked for days to reach Friesland to buy food with anything that they still possessed. Diamonds and gold were exchanged for bread and bacon. Many farmers showed only moderate compassion for their starving people and drove hard bargains. On all the major roads stood the dreaded *CCD*, the controllers of food organisation. They were entitled to confiscate any food transported by private persons. The Germans controlled them and they were inevitably corrupt. Soldiers even raided Dutch houses in The Hague to confiscate clothes for the Russian Front.

Frank and Marieke were kept busy with hardly any time to think. They smuggled food, passed on forged documents and tried to survive. It was a meeting with Piet and Dirk at Laaxum that forced another decision on their lives.

They met by candle-light as the electricity supply had long been cut-off for non-essential users. The days were lengthening slightly but the winter still retained its freezing grip. Piet began the conversation on another topic.

'I've just come from a meeting of group co-ordinators. Something terrible has happened at a village north of Arnhem.' He saw Frank's interest. 'The local Resistance group wanted a car, so they ambushed a German vehicle on the main road in broad daylight. Our comrades exchanged fire with the occupants and found that the car was carrying Commissioner Rauter, our "Lord High Executioner". They seriously wounded him and the Germans took him away to a hospital. He'll survive.' He leant forward in his chair, 'The incident happened two days ago. Yesterday Schoengarth, Rauter's deputy, executed 400 people as a reprisal. He had 117 of them dragged to the spot where the ambush had taken place and shot them.' There was a feeling of anger in the small living-room that made him pause. After a moment Piet continued, 'The Resistance is losing men and women every day. Some are tortured and then shot. Others are just shot or disappear.'

'Oh my God,' said Marieke quietly with her head in her hands. Frank put his arm round her.

'We've lost two very important men. Jan Thijssen, leader of the Central Resistance Council and, I'm sorry to say this, Frank, because I know that you knew him, ... Walraven van Hall.'

'Oh no!' exclaimed Frank, 'not van Hall, he was banker for the *L.O.* He was a good man and he'll be missed. God help his family.'

'I'm glad to say that there is some good news. Limburg in the south has been liberated and the Allies broke out from Nijmegen and took Goch. Which means that they're in the Fatherland.'

'That's good,' said Harmen. 'Soon they'll be over the Rhine and then they can free the rest of Holland.'

'I doubt it,' said Frank, with his usual caution, 'you know my feelings on that matter. We're too far away from the Allies. Friesland and Groningen were the first to be occupied by the Germans and we'll be the last to be liberated by the Allies.'

For a full minute everybody sat silently. They knew that Piet had another reason for coming to them.

'After we killed Postma.'

'After you killed him,' interrupted Frank quietly.

'All right, I understand,' replied Piet, impatiently. 'After Uncle killed him. Müller suspects Rita, although he can't prove it.' He turned to Dirk, 'I think you'd better explain the next part.'

Dirk's face dropped and he nodded. 'She's been in the *Hotel de Kroon* now for seven weeks. She hardly ever leaves the hotel and her room is guarded day and night. She even has an *NSB* woman to do everything for her. When she does go out, it's in a German staff car with two *SS* guards. Müller visits her twice a week, regular as clockwork. Piet and I are worried. She knows a lot about our movements and where we are.' He slowly stood and walked around the room. 'Both Piet and I believe that she puts us all in great danger. Müller is absolutely unscrupulous and he could torture her at any time. Believe me, my friends,' he said with a grim smile, 'I can feel that swine closing in on us.'

Frank's eyes bored across the room straight at Piet and anger was in his voice. 'It's happening all over again isn't it? First of all, it's, "let's kill Postma because he's getting close to us." He's been killed and now you want to kill Rita, who did your dirty work for you.' He shook his head, 'God in heaven, we're as bad as they are.'

Piet was stiff with anger, 'We're telling you this, Frank, just in case the Germans come here and take you and all of your family. At least then you'll know who informed on you.'

Frank spoke so sharply that Marieke was surprised, 'I want nothing to do with it, nothing to do with it, AT ALL! I wash my hands of the whole damned thing.'

The room fell silent again.

'There's obviously nothing more to be said here,' said Piet as he turned to Dirk, 'I think we should leave.'

They left into the darkness and Marieke joined them on the track on top of the dyke. 'He'll calm down in time. He's got a lot on his mind, you know.'

'Haven't we all, Marieke,' replied Piet as he kissed her gently touching her shoulder.

They cycled together the long way back to Leeuwarden. For the first hour they rode silently to gather their thoughts.

'Dirk, I'll have to kill her. I'm the only who can do it.'

'Nonsense,' replied Dirk breathlessly, as he pushed hard against the head-wind, 'I can see her whenever I want to. I'll do it.'

The argument went backwards and forward for the next hour until they crept into Leeuwarden in the early hours of the morning. They entered the hotel through the canal entrance and sat together in the small cellar. The two friends were obviously depressed.

'I've been thinking, Dirk. It'll have to be poison. To shoot her will bring the guards in.'

Piet wrung his hands, 'What are we saying? I'm beginning to think that Frank is right. Four years ago I would never have thought of even hurting somebody, never mind murdering them.'

'Thank God, we still have a conscience. That's more than the Germans have,' replied Dirk. 'Why don't we wait until the Allies come? It can't be long now.'

'That's no good,' answered Piet, shaking his head. 'She could tell her secrets at any time and it could lead to hundreds, if not thousands of deaths all over Friesland. No, ... I've got to do it and as soon as possible.'

They parted and went their separate ways.

Doctor Bergsma provided the poison and Dirk thought that it was strange how fate intertwined around their lives. Rita had killed Postma with poison and now she was about to die in the same way. He managed to convince himself that the best way to do it was to take her a drink late one evening. Occasionally, the bored guard would let him stay for a few minutes.

Rita had never felt so lonely in her life. Seven weeks in the hotel and she was already totally subjugated to Müller's routine. What had really surprised her was that he never wanted sex, just to talk. It was as though Postma's death had somehow dirtied her. She lacked for nothing and ate and drank only the best. Contact with the outside world was limited. She tried to talk to Dirk, but he never wanted to talk to her. That was why she was so surprised when he entered the room carrying a small tray. His voice was friendly.

'Hello, Michelle, I thought you may like a cup of cocoa.'

She was sitting on a low chair near the window. The curtains were wide open.

'Why, *meneer* Haan, you really do amaze me. Why am I suddenly so popular? And cocoa, why cocoa? I thought it was totally unobtainable?'

He stood close to her as he lowered the tray onto the table. Dirk felt her magnetism and smiled. 'Being a hotelier does have some advantages.'

She waved her hand towards the chair. 'Do sit down and join me.' She glanced at the tray, 'although I see the hotel can only provide one cup.'

To prepare himself he had drunk half a bottle of his best *Jenever* gin and his heart hammered away under his ribs.

'My word, you have been drinking. I can smell it on your breath.' She moved closer to him and the fragrance of her perfume wafted across his face. Abruptly her attitude changed and she leant over and whispered in his ear, 'For God's sake can you get me out of here? I think Müller's a madman.'

He wanted so much to help her. 'Michelle,' he kept up the charade of false names, 'of course I'll help you, but do drink your cocoa before it goes cold. I wouldn't want to see it wasted.' He gave his most charming smile and handed her the cup.

She took it from him and raised it to her lips. It must have been a flicker of something that passed over his face and the whiteness of his knuckles as he clenched his fists. Something instinctively warned her and she lowered the cup. Her eyes opened wide and her voice was like a whiplash.

'You drink it! I don't like cocoa.'

He wavered for a moment and took the cup from her hand. He trembled from head to foot. She tossed her head back and laughed.

'You swine, Haan. You were going to kill me. Is it the same poison I gave to Postma?'

Her outburst made him drop the cup and his composure was gone. 'Rita, we're worried about what you know ...... and ......eh .... well you can guess the rest.'

Her bright red lips compressed into a firm line. She stood, looked down at him and spoke in mocking tones. 'Oh, you brave Dutchman. You made your little plan to kill me and it hasn't worked.' She thrust her face closer to him, 'You think I've enjoyed being locked up here with that idiot Müller?' Her voice lowered and she put her hand on his. 'You bastard, I'm going to surprise you. You know what I really am?' He shook his head and she gripped his hand even tighter. 'I'm an agent of the Dutch Section of the SOE. You know, the British Special Operations Executive. Although I doubt whether you've ever been close to a real spy.' She sarcastically snapped her fingers, 'Oh I forgot, Mata Hari was born in Leeuwarden and the French executed her and you thought you were going to execute me!'

The shock showed on Dirk's face, 'I don't believe you, ... prove it!'

She folded her arms, 'Get on van Hamel's radio transmitter, you know, the one that you hide in the organ in the Mennonite Church, and contact London. Use the code-word 'Windmills' and see what they say. When you've proved my identity, tell them I want to leave and they can come and take me out of Holland. Müller has told me a lot that London would like to know.' She patted him on the head. 'So now run along little man and obey my orders.'

Before he could reply, there was a single knock at the door. Rita rose from her chair, gave Dirk a look of total disdain and walked slowly to the door.

'*Fräulein*,' the SS guard was elderly, 'your guest must leave now, I'm sorry.'

'I don't believe it!' exclaimed Piet. 'An SOE agent? She can't be!'

'If you think about it, then it fits,' said Frank excitedly. 'How else would she know about van Hamel's transmitter in the church or indeed about van Hamel? There are only three people who know about its location and we're all sitting here.'

They were in a safe house on the outskirts of Leeuwarden. It was now taking Frank a full day to make the journey. Even with another new identity he was always in extreme danger. Following the decree issued before the end of 1944, the Germans were still taking any men under the age forty for labour duties in the east of Holland. They were preparing a defensive line on the German border and labour was short. Frank had papers to prove that he worked on a fishing-boat and as such he was exempted from call-up. The Germans had photographs of him and his family and it only needed a keen-eyed policeman to spot him and that would be the end of everybody. With this in mind he always cycled along the quietest of routes, through fields, over small dykes and never near houses or villages. Anybody who knew him in 1940, well dressed and young for his age, would never have recognised him now in 1945. Old clothes, a grey beard, clogs and a fishy smell that never left him. Frank realised that he would rather look different than be caught and shot.

'If we have to get rid of her then let's do it her way,' suggested Piet with a wry smile.

'Be careful, she may be laying a trap for us,' said Frank. 'I think we ought to contact London and check her story.' He turned to his friend, 'Piet, when's our next transmission?'

'Tomorrow at mid-day. I've got several messages together and I'll include "Windmills".' He saw the expression on Frank's face. 'What's the matter, don't you agree?'

'I've not been in the church since Paul de Vries was murdered.' He scratched his beard. 'This time, I really would like to do the transmission myself.'

Dirk was worried, 'Frank, that would be taking a hell of a risk. You were a strong church ... '

'I still am a member of the church,' interrupted Frank quickly.

' ... I'm sorry, but you know what I mean?' Dirk took a deep breath, 'It's almost as a big a risk as leaving Rita de Boer in Müller's clutches.'

'Dirk, I think you're wrong,' said Piet quietly. 'Frank takes risks every time we meet. I think we should all agree with his request and help him as much as possible.'

Frank smiled, 'Thank you, Piet, I really appreciate that.'

Dirk laughed and shook his head, 'Well my friends, we really are amazing people. We argue every time we meet and yet we're still alive.'

'Just,' added Frank with a wry smile.

It was the first time that he had walked alone through his town for over three years. Frank left his bike near the station and strolled down the narrow streets. For some reason he felt invulnerable and carefree and smiled at every face that passed him. Little had changed, the buildings were the same but the shops were almost empty. He saw only two patrols and they totally ignored him.

He knew he was tempting fate when he walked past *SS* Headquarters. He grinned when he saw the stone building, draped in long black and red swastikas, and laughed aloud when he remembered the day when the Royal Air Force nearly bombed it. As he walked past on the opposite side of the road, there was a sudden movement near the main door and he paused for a while to see a car draw up. Curiosity got the better of him and then he watched Müller walk down the steps. For a moment the head of the *SS* in Friesland stopped, held the open door of the car, and stared around him. For a fleeting moment their eyes met and there was no recognition. He jumped into the car and it sped off towards the railway station.

Frank passed a shop window and briefly saw himself in the reflection and he stopped in amazement. He suddenly realised why the Germans were not interested in him. He looked more than fifty years old rather than just forty. Frank shook his head and walked on.

The rear entrance to the *Doopsgezinde Kerk* was through a small, secluded park. The gate was surrounded by thick bushes and Frank had to push his way through. He burst into the tiny courtyard and memories came flooding back. It was here that he had first met Marieke. There was a small social gathering late on a summer's evening and it had been a mutual attraction for both of them. He leant against the high brick wall and placed his hands deep in the pockets of his baggy trousers. The years had gone so quickly and it only seemed like yesterday since they had stood in exactly this spot holding hands. Frank looked up. The sky above the enclosed courtyard was cloudy and he felt distant from the realities of life. The cultured voice made him jump.

'*Goedendag, meneer*. Can I help you?'

The man was young, dressed in a neat suit and shiny black boots. The rear door of the church was ajar and he stood with arms folded, a slight smile crossing his face.

Frank jumped. 'I'm sorry, I was lost in thought. *Goedendag.*'

'Do come into the church,' he pushed the door open. 'I'm *dominee* Sipma and you're very welcome.'

They walked together into the side door of the committee room and Frank stared hard at the leather chair that he had always sat in. The *dominee* led him through into the church and Frank followed. The interior was unchanged and the same smell of polish and candles still hung in the air. But there were no flowers. Marieke had always made sure that there were flowers. The quiet peacefulness of the church made Frank pause for a moment and gather his thoughts. Without thinking, he walked quickly to his customary pew and sat down. He bowed his head and found it difficult to pray. Pictures and thoughts flashed through his mind and tumbled together until they were all a blur. He quickly opened his eyes and felt the *dominee* at his side.

'I'm sorry,' he mumbled.

'Don't worry, *meneer* van der Meer, there's plenty of time.'

Frank jerked round and his eyes opened wide.

'Oh yes,' continued the young man, 'I recognised you when you first entered the courtyard.' He smiled, 'When Paul de Vries was *dominee*, I used to preach here quite often. I remember your kindness and, indeed, your wife's smile.' He laughed aloud and Frank worried about the noise. The *dominee* saw his concern, 'Don't worry, *meneer*, Germans never come here.' Maybe it was the *dominee* that was tempting providence rather than Frank, but, at that precise moment, the main doors burst open and in marched two *SD* policeman. Frank's heart stopped beating. He bowed his head and clenched his fists. The *dominee* was icy calm and turned to meet them.

'Gentlemen, you're welcome in this church. Can I help you?'

His courtesy stopped them dead. One of them walked forward to the end of the pew where the *dominee* and Frank were sitting. They pointed at him and ignored the *dominee*.

'Papers!'

Frank fumbled in his pocket and handed over the grubby identity card and two other documents. The guard wrinkled his nose as the fishy smell reached him. Without a sound he thrust the papers back into Frank's outstretched hand, turned, and both men walked out of the church.

'A bit of divine help, I believe,' said *dominee* Sipma with a broad smile.

Frank let out a sigh of relief and this time he did pray.

'I suppose you want to use the radio transmitter?' This man kept surprising Frank. 'I've known about it for years. I know I'm not supposed to, but I do know, because ... this is my church.' He shrugged his shoulders. 'Uncle Group find excuses to get me out when they want to come here. I play their game and I enjoy the antics they get up to. I help the Resistance in my own way.'

'I know you do,' said Frank. 'The *L.O.* receives your gifts with thanks and much appreciation.'

The *dominee* thought for a moment and his voice was sad, 'when do you think it will be over, *meneer* van der Meer.'

Frank shook his head, 'I really don't know. Our people can't stand very much more. We must believe that the worst is past.' He turned round and glanced at the balcony clock. The *dominee* caught his intent.

'I'm sorry, I know you've a transmission time to keep.'

They both rose from the pew and made their way to a small door behind the tall, oak pulpit. It creaked open and Frank crawled into the tiny space.

The *dominee* thrust a tall, flickering church candle through the door. Frank coughed with the dust as he took the candle in his hand and crawled forward. Slim shafts of light came through from the organ pipes above him. He raised the candle and saw the air brick, pushed it hard and it fell backwards into the hole. He reached up and groped with his free hand. He touched the leather case and found the handle. With a grunt and a heave, he dragged the case from its resting place and lowered it to the rough wooden floor in front of him.

By the light of the candle he opened the leather case. The label "**Pye of London**" stamped inside the lid brought more memories flooding back and for a moment he thought of Lodo van Hamel. He shook himself, pulled out the aerial and unwound it, hooking the slender wire to the air brick and then around the walls of the small room. He flicked the power switch and the single green bulb glowed on the control panel. Taking off his boot, Frank peeled back the sole. Inside was a small piece of paper. It was his code sheet. Flexing his fingers he put the Morse key on the floor. He smiled to himself when he remembered the difficult Morse lessons that he had learnt so carefully when van Hamel left the radio for Uncle to use. Frank clamped the earphones over his head, pushed the transmission button and the set hummed into life. He glanced at the code paper and began the transmission. First was the Group Uncle code, second the secret code letters that had to be correct or else in distant England the listeners would know that the Germans were transmitting. Knowledge of such codes had caused the death of over a hundred Dutch agents at the beginning of the occupation.

Frank had no idea what he was sending because only Piet knew the code. He sent the three pages of six-letter groups and then stopped. Any longer than two minutes and the German radio locator vans would find him. He waited for the acknowledgement and pushed the button to stop the carrier wave. Frank sat back and waited for the minutes to pass. London would send their signal when they were ready with their messages. After a few minutes he flicked the switch and listened, nothing, and so he switched off. At the third attempt the signal came through against a background of static, making it hard for Frank to hear. He scribbled down the letters, sent the acknowledge signal, the code and switched off. He placed the papers back in his boot, swivelled the sole over the recess, reached up and pushed the radio-set back into the air cavity. The brick fitted perfectly and Frank blew out the candle, tapped on the door and waited.

The *dominee* said good bye to him back in the courtyard. '*Meneer* van der Meer, I'm proud to have met you. I hope next time that we meet under happier circumstances.' They shook hands and Frank scrambled back through the bushes.

He made his way back to the safe house without incident and for every road that he walked past there were memories.

De-coding the messages did not take Piet very long. He sat scribbling for several minutes, occasionally glancing between the leather covers of an old family bible.

'Gentlemen, Rita is quite a lady,' he tapped the notepad. 'She's absolutely who she says she is and the British will take her out the day after tomorrow. They're going to use our old hunting ground on the Tjeukemeer. A plane will land at three in the morning.'

'Not again,' groaned Dirk.

'They say that lightning never strikes in the same place twice,' shrugged Piet with a smile.

Frank was thoughtful, 'How are we going to get Rita away from the hotel without casting doubt on Dirk or the rest of us?'

Rita solved the problem with Dirk's help. He met her in the cupboard in the ladies' toilet on that same night.

'Dirk Haan, this is a very strange place to meet a lady. What would your friends think of you?'

'It was my friends who suggested it,' he replied with a wide grin.

She listened carefully, 'It's easy, I'll climb down the drain-pipe, somebody can collect me and take me to this lake, ... whatever it's called?'

'The Tjeukemeer and it'll take us about two hours to get there on bicycles.'

She made a face, 'I know I'm Dutch, but I've always hated the damned things. They're so undignified.'

'I hope you can ride a bike?' said Dirk worriedly.

She tussled his air and laughed, 'Of course I can, don't be silly!'

Rita thought that Müller would never leave. For the hour that he spent with her he said very little.

Eventually when he left, he held her hand and said quite simply, 'Michelle, have a pleasant evening.'

She slipped off her high-heeled shoes and replaced them with something more suitable for climbing down drain-pipes. As she pulled the curtain to one side she thought for a moment and returned to her dressing-table. Swiftly, and with a smile, she scooped up a handful of perfume bottles and stuffed them into her shoulder bag.

It was a chilly night and without a breath of wind. Rita stepped out onto the small cast-iron balcony. She glanced around her. The black-out was almost complete and without a moment's thought she pulled up her dress and threw a leg over the balcony rail. She stretched out her arms and found the thick drain-pipe. Pulling herself up, she stood on the rail, grasped the pipe and stepped out into space. Her legs dropped sickeningly and then her arms took the strain. She grunted with pain and her feet scrabbled for a purchase on the brick wall and the pipe brackets. For a moment her hands lost their grip and she began to slip. There was another grunt as finally her foot found the bracket. For a full minute she clung like a fly to the pipe and the wall and then slowly her feet edged downwards. Rita looked at her hands clutching the black pipe, she lessened her grip and slid down half a metre. Her feet found the next bracket and so she progressed in a series of fits and slips almost to the courtyard at the back of the hotel. As she glanced down at the last two metres, her eyes caught a shadow against the wall below her. She froze and tried to calm her breathing and relax her aching arms.

A voice whispered up to her, 'Come on, jump!'

She trusted her instincts and let go. Frank caught her neatly and lowered her onto her feet. For a split second he felt her warmth and then it was gone.

She stared into the darkness. 'Frank van der Meer. I remember you.'

'No time to talk. Just follow me and not a sound.' They padded across the yard and onto the narrow back street. Apart from them, nothing moved. Within a minute they reached a canal and Frank drew her towards the edge of the street. He pulled a rope and a small rowing boat emerged out of the darkness of the canal.

'Jump in, sit in the stern,' he whispered.

He rowed as close as he dared to the steep walls lining the canal. The oars dipped rhythmically as he propelled the boat carefully in and out of larger moored boats. There was the sound of a car and he steered under the welcoming darkness of a swing bridge. He waited for several minutes and then quietly paddled on. The occasional dog barked and, somewhere in the distance was the sound of a siren, but he continued the journey.

'Frank, where are we going?'

'Shush! ... Be quiet.'

She shivered in the evening chill and drew the thin coat closer. The dark shape in front of her smoothly pulled the oars and she felt his presence. For nearly an hour Frank rowed. The town slipped away and the flat fields slid into view. She watched the odd cow lift its head as the boat came close to the canal bank. There was a quiet thud as it touched a low jetty. A bulky figure reached down and grabbed the prow and pulled the boat closer.

'Climb out, please,' said Frank, quietly.

She stood and the small boat rocked precariously. A hand reached for hers and drew her onto the jetty.

'Hello, Rita.'

She let go of his hand, 'Piet, you're the last person I expected to see.'

He stood back and looked at her, 'It's good to see you safe and sound.' He took a deep breath, 'But now we have to leave. There's not much time.'

Frank walked towards the side of nearest the field and pulled the shrubs to one side. His voice broke their thoughts.

'A bike for each of us. Come on both of you, let's go.'

There was no moon but Frank knew the way exactly and they made good time. Two windmills loomed up in the darkness and they read the signs and cycled on.

'Please stop, I'm not used to cycling.' They pulled off the farm track under a bare tree. She looked at them and pushed her blonde hair back out of her eyes.

'I suppose you two were also involved in the plan to kill me.' It was not a question, just a statement of fact.

Piet looked up at her, 'I was, Frank would have nothing to do with it,' he said quietly, without taking his eyes off her face.

She thought for a moment and her voice was sad, 'I just want to say that under the circumstances, I would have done exactly the same thing and I certainly wouldn't have waited seven weeks to do it.'

Frank sensed the moment and climbed back onto his bicycle, 'Another half hour should see us there. The plane's due in an hour.'

They cycled on with Frank in the lead.

He remembered the spot so well, the path to the lake, the clump of trees and the bushes.

'Rita, they'll circle once and then taxi as close as possible to the shore. I'm afraid you're going to get wet,' said Frank.

She put her bike against the bushes and turned to him, 'Don't worry. It might wash some of Müller's filth off me.'

Piet approached and put his arm around her waist. She smiled and held his hand. Frank fumbled in his coat pocket and produced a sealed package and held it out for her.

'Please would you take this to a member of our Government in London?' He saw her quizzical expression. 'It's a list of our needs for divers and other supplies that Uncle needs.'

She took it and opened her handbag. Frank heard the clink of bottles.

'A quick drink for the flight?' he said with a smile.

For the first time that night she laughed and they all visibly relaxed. She showed Frank one of the bottles 'Oh no, it's perfume. They won't have these in London.'

'And not in Holland either,' he replied, with a shake of his head.

She laughed again, 'Of course not, how stupid of me. Müller got them for me, as you can see, best French.' She put her hand to her mouth. 'Frank, take this one for your wife. That is, if she likes perfume, and knowing you, I suspect that she will.'

'Really, ... I ...eh ... couldn't.'

She leant over, kissed him on the cheek and pushed several bottles into his hand.

'Take them, they're more use to her than to me.'

'Frank,' said Piet from the bushes, 'listen, I think it's the plane.'

The low drone from the west carried easily across the Tjeukemeer and Piet pulled a large torch out of his pocket.

'Right, over to the edge of the lake. Quickly now, before they miss us.'

The single engined aircraft swooped low over the water and completed a lazy turn over their heads. Piet shielded the torch with his hands and flashed three times into the darkness above their heads. The engine note changed and the aircraft made a perfect landing to their right. It taxied rapidly towards them as the pilot blipped the throttle.

'Into the water and swim like hell,' whispered Frank loudly as they jumped into the freezing cold waters of the lake. The aircraft came as close as it could and the noise was deafening. Frank saw the door open in the fuselage and a helmeted face peered out. He pushed Rita forward and she fell into the black waters. She gasped as he pulled her to the surface. The shout surprised Frank. It was in English.

'COME ON NOW, LADY! GET IN! ... HURRY!'

The pilot seemed younger than his own son, and instinctively Frank pushed Rita over the float and into the cabin. He reached out and the gloved hand grasped his.

The smile was friendly, 'GOOD LUCK SIR! THE WAR WILL SOON BE OVER! SORRY, WE HAVE TO GO NOW!' The door slammed shut and Frank and Piet were knocked flat on their backs into the water.

He rose spluttering and gasping and watched the aircraft take-off. He found it hard to believe that within two hours the aircraft and its occupants would be in England and free.

TWENTY FOUR

'Frank! Be quiet, I can't hear.' Marieke crouched low over a hole in the floor of the house in Laaxum. The long-hidden radio was quietly broadcasting the latest news from Radio Oranje. This time the message was something that they had long been waiting for.

> *'His royal Highness Prince Bernhard, wishes to send a message to the people of Holland who are still suffering under the German yoke of oppression.'*

There was the usual crackle of static and then the familiar voice could be heard so clearly,

> *'Citizens of the Netherlands. The day of freedom for all our people is close by. The Allies are making advances on all fronts and the Dutch forces of the Princes Irene Brigade are at long last fighting in their own country. Time is running out for the German occupiers. To all our people I give the orders of the day.*
> *Firstly: Under no circumstances, are you to take any actions upon your own initiative.*
> *Secondly: Keep up the strictest discipline. At this time great military operations are taking place with the greatest consequences for our future.*
> *These are important times for us all; I trust that soon the hated invader will leave our shores for ever.'*

The message clicked into silence and the music returned.

'Frank, is this it?' said Marieke rising from the hole eyes shining.

'I really don't know,' he replied. Before he could continue the door burst open and a breathless Harmen ran into the room. He stood for a minute, panting with excitement.

'Listen, everybody, I've just heard. Deventer and Zwolle have been liberated.' He grasped his father's arm. '*Heit*, that's only seventy kilometres from here! We could be free tomorrow!' Harmen flopped into a chair.

There was a silence where nobody could speak.

For two days messages and rumours flowed thick and fast throughout the province. Nobody knew what to believe. Frank was in the nearby village of Makkum. He was with Jan de Bruin, who more and more was helping other Jewish families in hiding. Some of his strength had returned but he was still thin and his face bore a haunted look. They were sitting before a grave in the local churchyard. Germans, apparently, rarely spoke to people who were visiting the dead.

'I wonder what it'll be like?' said Jan as he lay on his back looking up at the spring sunshine.

'What?' replied Frank.

'To be liberated. I mean, will the Allies just come marching into a village and say, "Right that's it, it's over!" Or will leaflets come from the air? Or just something else?'

'I've never really thought about it, to be quite honest. It's been so long I still can't believe it's ever going to happen.' Frank leant against a gravestone and looked around. A fresh wind blew off the *IJsselmeer* and the small town was quiet. 'I don't trust the *moffen*. I think they'll fight to the last man.'

Jan was thoughtful as he watched the clouds scudding by, 'I never thought that my family would survive this long.' He turned over to gaze at Frank, 'You know, without you and Marieke, we'd all be dead.'

The single gun-shot stopped their conversation and they scrambled to their feet.

'What the hell was that? ... Quick, into the church,' cried Frank as he grabbed Jan's arm and pulled him through the graveyard.

They pushed open the heavy door and dashed into the vestibule.

'Close the door, quick!' Jan slammed it shut and Frank rammed the bolt home. He dashed up the stairs of the bell tower with Jan hard on his heels.

The single bell hung centrally and the four apertures in the tower let in blasts of cool air. Frank peered over the parapet at the small village of Makkum spread out below. The *IJsselmeer* sparkled in front of him. The coastal road on top of the dyke stopped as it reached the small, red-roofed houses. The streets were totally deserted and, for a moment, Frank thought that he had been hearing things. He scanned up and down the canals that interlaced the narrow streets and squares. He caught a movement to his right.

'Frank! Over here, quick!' exclaimed Jan.

He scrabbled his way to the next aperture. It was a scene that he had seen before and hoped that he would never see again. He counted a row of about ten people, young and old, men and women. They were aimlessly milling around in the corner of a small, cobbled square. On the opposite side to them was a thin line of half a dozen German soldiers, their weapons pointing at the group of people. Jan grabbed his arm.

'Oh my God, they're not going to do it, are they?'

'They will,' replied Frank grimly.

As though from heaven the two men watched and, before they had time to gather their thoughts, there were ragged muzzle flashes from the rifles and the people fell before their eyes. Only then did the sound of the explosions hit their ears. Jan twisted away, holding his head in his hands.

'Why?' his voice rang out. 'In God's name, WHY?' His chest heaved and he clung to Frank's shoulder. 'Will it ever stop?'

Frank watched the men march back to their wagon and climb into it. He heard the engine start and it made its way out of the town and sped off northwards on the dyke road. He waited until it dwindled to a speck on the horizon and only then was he conscious of the crowds below him.

'I'm going down there,' said Jan with tears on his face. He pushed past Frank and vanished down the steep steps.

Frank clutched the weathered sill of the tower and stared to the distant horizon of the *IJsselmeer*. His heart was beating so fast that he became breathless and suddenly the world blacked-out as he slumped forward over the stone sill. How long he hung there for he never knew. It was only a cool cloth on his forehead that brought him round.

'Frank, you're all right now. Come on, wake up!'

There was a mist over his vision and objects swam before his eyes. There was something to look at but he could not see it. He tried to stand and fell back on the hard surface beneath him. The coldness on his head returned. In the distance he heard a voice.

'Sit him up. Put his head between his knees. Careful now!'

With a jerk everything sprung into focus. He flailed his arms and felt them gently pushed to his side.

'What the hell is happening?' He heard his own voice as though it belonged to somebody else. Jan's face loomed up in front of him.

'Frank, you must have fainted. ... You're all right now. ... Just take it easy.'

There was a small crowd around him in the churchyard. He felt the hard gravestone behind and managed to lever himself upwards. Everybody began talking at once.

'*Meneer*, it's all right now, don't worry.'

'He nearly fell out of the tower, you know. I saw him hanging over the edge.'

'Lucky the Nazis weren't here.'

'I think I know him. He's helped some of our divers.'

Frank slowly stood and looked around him. The attentive crowd watched as he shook his head.

Thanks, everybody. ... I'll be all right now, thank you.'

The crowd edged away but one man remained. He walked forward and grasped Frank's hand.

'You were lucky, you know. Five minutes earlier and the Germans would have taken you.'

As his head cleared completely, Frank looked more closely at the man.

'I'm the minister of this church.' He placed his hand on Frank's shoulder, 'Come on now, be careful. Just walk slowly. My house is over there near the gate.'

With Jan on one side and the minister on the other, he made his way out of the churchyard.

The three men stopped and watched.

The dead were scattered like chaff on the cobbled square. The villagers stood in silence. Others gently lifted the dead and carried them back towards the church. The minister pointed towards a small house.

'That's where I live. Please go in, I have work to do here.' He left them and turned to help with the dead.

The square was quickly cleared. Four old women appeared from the houses nearby with buckets of water. One stood silently and prayed whilst her friends sluiced away the blood that ran across the cobbles.

The living-room was small and sparsely furnished. Jan and Frank sat down. Neither of the two men spoke. Frank's vision began to blur and he grabbed at the chair. Jan guided him down onto cushions.

'Just keep still for a few minutes.'

The minister returned. There were tears on his face and he brushed them away.

'That's the second time this week. ... Sixteen people slaughtered for no reason whatsoever.' His voice choked with emotion. 'Let's pray together for their souls.'

Frank stood up and the three men remained silent for several minutes. The minister looked up. 'Amen.'

'Amen,' intoned Frank and Jan.

'Are you feeling better now, *meneer*?' He laid a cool hand on Frank's forehead.

'Thank you, minister. Yes, I think so. I really don't know what came over me up there.'

'It's called war,' said the man quietly, 'I've seen it before. Poor food, worry, lack of hope and pure unmitigated terror.' He sat in the chair opposite Jan and Frank. 'I've seen more and more of it.' He smoothed his thinning grey hair back over his pale scalp. 'It makes people give up all hope. In the last two weeks there have been two suicides in Makkum.' He shook his head and clutched a bible in his hands. 'People can't believe that it's nearly over. They can't cope with it. Somehow they just melt away.' He was silent, staring at the bible resting in his hands.

Frank looked at Jan. 'Minister, we must leave now. We have to get back to our homes.'

A slow smile came over the minister's face. 'Yes, I understand.' He rose from his seat and Frank and Jan turned to leave. 'Before you go, can I thank you for all your help?'

Frank was non-plussed, 'My help?'

'Yes, I was told by the people in the square that you're the provincial L.O. leader.' He made the sign of the cross over Frank's shoulders. 'God be with you and may he protect you at all times.'

They cycled back to Laaxum and the spring sunshine warmed their backs. Frank felt light-headed and he frequently stopped to rest.

'You've got to relax for a few days, Frank,' said Jan as they sighted the small harbour. 'You just can't keep going on and on all the time.'

'I know, I know, but there are so many things to do and so little time to do them in.' They were silent as they covered the last five hundred metres.

Frank saw Marieke outside the house and his heart jumped with fear. He pedalled even harder and Jan caught his mood.

'What's the matter?' he shouted, as Frank pulled away from him.

'Something's wrong, I know it!' he called back over his shoulder.

Marieke's face said it all.

'They've got David!'

Jan skidded to a halt and dropped off his bicycle.

'We got a telephone call from Joop Koopman. David was taken in a round-up. We don't know where he is, Joop's trying to find out.' Marieke's face was streaked with tears and she reached out for Jan. 'Tineke is in the house with Aukje.'

Jan touched her and flew past up the short path.

Aukje had stopped crying and was holding Tineke tightly in her arms. Their faces pale with shock. Jan stumbled towards them and they parted. One look from Tineke was enough and tears rushed from his eyes as he held both of them tightly in a grip that was part-rage and part-terror. Nobody moved or spoke for a full minute. It was Frank who tried to bring them out of their shock.

'The war is nearly over. They'll probably just hold him until the Allies arrive.'

Jan snapped back, 'Not after what we've just seen in Makkum. If they find out he's Jewish then he's already gone.'

Marieke looked at Aukje and pushed her long hair away from her face, 'Oh my darling. I'm so sorry. I know how much you love him.'

Aukje was dead calm and her body stiffened as her mother touched her. 'I've been waiting for this to happen. He took far too many chances. I was always warning him and telling him to be careful.' She looked at Marieke's face, 'There is hope you know. He could still just be locked up somewhere.' Her face expressed her real feelings and suddenly her body heaved with emotion.

TWENTY FIVE

The round-up centred on houses outside the town centre. Each street was cordoned off and everywhere was searched. Anyone suspected of anything was herded into the yard at the back of *SS* headquarters and there lined up in rows for further checking. Every identity card, pass and paperwork of any kind was scrutinised by the *SD*. Some people were released, most were pushed into the back of trucks and driven off for imprisonment.

It was a warm, late spring day and the sun shone down from a cloudless sky. Müller came out from his office high above the yard. He strolled down the rows of men and women remaining and looked at each of them closely. David de Bruin stood out from the crowd. He was the youngest. The *Hauptsturmführer* stopped near David's shoulder and stared hard at his face. He nodded to the nearest *SD* policeman and David's identity card was handed over. Müller looked at it carefully and his eyes flickered from the photograph to the face and back again. He returned the card without comment and raised a finger towards David. The *SD* man leapt forward and grabbed David's arm. He pulled him out of the line, kicked him across the yard and threw him into the back of a black car. David protested loudly and the result was a punch in the face so hard that he was knocked unconscious. Within the next ten minutes six men and two women were bundled into the waiting cars. When the yard was finally empty Müller waited for a few minutes, glancing at the open blue sky above him, clapped his black-gloved hands together, turned and walked back into the building.

'David is in the prison in Leeuwarden,' said Joop Koopman with sadness in his eyes. He was with Frank in the cellar of the *Hotel de Kroon*. 'The Nazis have taken eight people to the prison. They're under the heaviest guard, only *SD*, no Dutch allowed in at all. I only found out because one of my men saw them being taken through the main gates.' They both stood near the open window and he saw the look in Frank's eyes. 'Sorry, there's no way that we could get him out. I think the best thing to do is to wait until the Allies arrive.'

Frank looked exhausted, his face was drawn and gaunt. He had cycled through the night for this meeting. All the way he had seen convoys of German vehicles flying along the narrow roads and always moving to the north of the province.

He put his hand on Joop's shoulder, 'Thanks, for letting me know. We just have to hope that he can be saved.' He shook his head and rubbed his neck, 'It seems so stupid that after five years he should be taken when the end is so near.' Joop nodded grimly.

The door flew open and Piet stepped quickly into the small room. Joop whirled round. 'You're early!'

Piet laughed, but with no humour. 'And with good reason. We've just received messages that on Friday the 6th April all resistance groups must join together to sabotage German lines of communications. The Allies want us to give them details of important bridges including their size and weight carrying capacities. They must be able to carry tanks weighing forty tons. They also want to know where all German strong-points are located and where their troops are day-by-day.' Piet's face glowed with excitement and he clenched his fists, 'Frank, Joop. This is it! It's only a matter of days before we're all free. Can you believe it?' He slapped both men across the shoulders, 'Freedom! Freedom! At long last.'

Frank was quiet but his brain was in a turmoil.

Piet stared at him. 'Why so miserable? Isn't it the news that you've been waiting for?'

'Yes Piet, it is and I just can't believe it. When the occupation is over there's much to do. Who will govern us, who ...'

'Frank, forever the pessimist,' interrupted Piet. 'Let's get the Nazis out of our country first and then we'll talk about politics.'

Joop glanced at his wrist-watch. 'Look, ... I'll have to leave. There're things happening all the time and I can still be missed. These bastards don't let up you know.' As he left, Dirk bounced into the cellar with a huge smile on his face.

His voice was calm and yet his voice trembled with excitement, 'My friends, amazing news. The *Burgomeester* has declared that *Groningerstraatweg* is closed to all traffic.'

Piet jumped up from his seat, 'That's the main road to the east.' He clapped his hands in delight. 'This can only mean one thing. The bloody *moffen* are leaving Leeuwarden.'

'No,' replied Dirk, with an edge to his voice. 'It means that they could be bringing in re-enforcements.'

Frank nervously walked up and down the small cellar. 'I just can't sit here. I've got to go outside and see what's happening.'

'That could be dangerous,' said Piet, his face becoming serious.

'I've come to the conclusion that everything is dangerous,' Frank said exasperatingly. 'Who's coming with me?' Before anybody could answer, he strode through the next cellar and up the stairs to the hotel foyer.

There was an atmosphere in the town that Frank could cut with a knife. He had the feeling that something was happening and yet he was unable to work out exactly what it was. He threw caution to the winds and walked out of the hotel towards the town centre. The first thing that he noticed was the absence of any German uniforms. The streets were full of people, all milling around aimlessly. Frank stood near the *Doopsgezinde Kerk* and just watched the people around him. There was an excited expectancy in the air but it was tinged with fear. He saw the same old lady twice. She was dressed in her Sunday best and she paraded up and down the main street. Suddenly, all was confusion.

A voice shouted stridently. 'They've left the airfield. It's empty.' The crowd froze and stared around in amazement. Panic began as the wail of police sirens reached their ears. They were running as fast as possible away from the town centre as rifle shots echoed against the buildings.

Frank felt a hand pulling at his coat sleeve, 'You're taking a chance, *meneer*, come with me.'

He turned to see *dominee* Sipma standing just inside the gates leading to the entrance of the church. Frank ran towards the open doors of the church as the gates were solidly locked behind him.

He held Frank's arm, 'Stay here for an hour. By then the panic will have lessened.' It was sound advice as the two men waited inside the doors and watched the crowds flooding past the church.

'It's been like this for the last two days,' said the *dominee*. 'Crowds one day and dead quiet the next. I think it best if you stay out of the way.'

Frank nodded as he watched the street become calm again, 'Yes, I see what you mean.' He turned to look at his helper, 'Just what's going on? Have you got any idea at all?'

The young man smiled, 'I believe that we're seeing the death throes of the Third *Reich* in Holland.' His face changed to that of sadness, 'Unfortunately, they won't let go all that easily. This morning they raided the summer houses near the outskirts of town and rounded up over two hundred people. I don't think it's over, quite yet.'

The two men waited for some time before Frank spoke, 'Again, I must thank you for your help. But now I've got to get back to my family.' They shook hands and the *dominee* opened the gates for Frank to leave.

He was tempted to call at the hotel but then he saw crowds of Dutch NSB. He quietly collected his bicycle and cycled away in the opposite direction.

The journey back to Laaxsum was uneventful, primarily because he saw no Germans whatsoever. It was a warm afternoon and for the first time in many months he relaxed. The fields were spring-green and the cows were grazing contentedly. Occasionally he passed other people cycling along the farm tracks but nobody spoke a word and they averted their gaze as he glanced at them. For the last five kilometres Frank saw not a living-thing as he pushed his way through the woods and onto the high dyke.

The house was quiet and Marieke was waiting for him. He shook his head and held her close. 'All we know is that he's in the prison. *Liefje*, it's impossible to do anything about it. This time the guards are all *SD* and Joop says there's nothing we can do.' He thought for a moment, 'How's Aukje taking it all?'

Marieke shrugged her shoulders and gazed through the window at the still harbour below the house. Her voice was calm. 'She's all right now. I think she's been expecting it for such a long time that in her own mind she knew it would happen.'

'Where is she?' asked Frank.

'She's gone to help a family in Makkum. I expect her to be away for the night.'

'I don't like her being away. These are difficult times and the Germans shoot on sight. She's a beautiful woman and they could do unspeakable things to her.'

Surprisingly Marieke smiled, reached out and touched Frank's face. 'Aukje is as stubborn as you are. I can't stop her doing what she has to do.'

For a brief moment they laughed and embraced.

Frank sat on the low harbour wall, utterly frustrated. He knew that the time was near and yet for the last two days there had been no contact with Group Uncle. The wind was fresh and it blew across the lake and into his face. He shivered and drew his old coat round his shoulders. He took a deep breath and let out a long drawn out sigh. He jerked as Marieke touched him.

'Marieke, you made me jump.' He smiled and grasped her hand.

'Frank, what're you thinking about?'

As great white clouds rolled above them he thought for a minute. 'I know that the Resistance is at this moment waiting to sabotage goodness knows what. I would love to be with them.'

Marieke sat down on the harbour wall at his side and tenderly stroked his hair. 'Darling, I know how you feel. But you've always said that you would not be involved in violence.'

'You're right. But this is not killing people. It's ... eh ... well, you know, ... blowing up things and cutting cables.' He laughed aloud. 'I remember so much about that time when Piet and I cut the cables at the airfield. It was wonderful!'

Marieke laughed with him. 'Frank, that was a long time ago and I think it's too late to start doing that sort of thing all over again.'

He nodded, 'You're right Marieke. I hope that those times will soon be over.'

They both heard Harmen shouting and they turned to meet him. He was cycling along the dyke at full speed. Frank stood and ran up the path to meet him.

'Heit,' he said breathlessly, 'a message has been broadcast.' He swung his leg off the bicycle. 'Oh I've got to sit down. I'm exhausted.' Frank led him to the sea wall where Marieke was waiting. Harmen flopped down at her side.

'Radio Oranje has transmitted the signal, "the bottle is empty." It means that within thirty-six hours all sabotage must begin.' He wiped the sweat of his face. 'There's more news, Heit. Piet and Group Uncle want you and me to help blow up the main railway line from Leeuwarden to the harbour at Harlingen. The Allies want us to cut off the Germans' retreat.'

Frank smiled. There was some of the old excitement in his eyes and he looked at Marieke with a broad smile, '*Verdomme*, I've always wanted to blow-up something.'

'Yes, darling,' she replied with a mocking smile on her face.

Frank rubbed his hands, 'Well, my son, when do we start?'

'We've got to meet Piet in five hours at Dronrijp village. That's eight kilometres west of Leeuwarden.'

'I know, I know,' said Frank with a smile, 'I've lived in Friesland longer than you have.' They both laughed.

He thumped his father on the shoulder. '*Heit*, we'll have to leave in the next half-hour if we're to get there in time.' Harmen stood and walked slowly back up the path towards the house. His parents followed him, lost in their thoughts.

It was a good three hours cycle ride to Dronrijp. The weather was warm and they made frequent stops to drink water and eat thin slices of bread that Marieke had managed to find from somewhere. Food was still difficult, even in Friesland. Frank felt good as he passed through the small farming villages. The streets were empty as though the people were waiting for something to happen. They saw one German patrol waiting quietly at a cross-roads. It was easy to avoid as they diverted across a field and back onto the cobbled road. Dusk was falling and they reached the hamlet of Rewert only a kilometre away from Dronrijp railway station.

Piet was waiting inside the windmill. Frank was surprised at his appearance. He was wearing blue overalls with a leather military belt fastened tightly around his waist. A gun sat snugly in the canvas holster. A forage cap sat firmly on his head and immediately Frank's eyes were drawn to the red, white and blue armband around Piet's left arm. The letters *NBS* were clearly printed in big letters around the band.

'Well, Piet Bokma, I've heard about the *Nederlandse Binnenlandse Strijdkrachten*, but I didn't know that you were in it.'

Piet laughed. 'Yes, our Dutch Interior Forces now have a uniform of sorts and we even have our own military command structure.'

Dirk emerged from behind a pile of sacks. He was dressed in the same uniform and a British Sten gun hung casually from his arm. Frank grinned and said, 'You two really look the part. Dirk, where on earth did you get that machine-gun from? And, are you sure you know how to use it?'

Dirk flung the gun into the firing position and drew back the cocking-lever. 'Yes indeed, I know how to use it. This young man gave me lessons.' He waved theatrically to the pile of sacks. Another man strolled into view carrying the same weapon.

'Hello, *meneer*, how are you?' said Richard Johnstone with a great beaming smile.

Frank clapped his hands and let out a roar of delight. 'Flight Lieutenant Johnstone. Where the hell did you come from?' The two men embraced each other.

'From the sky above you,' said Richard. 'I parachuted in yesterday, only about five kilometres from where you're now living.' He stepped back and stared hard at his friend. 'Frank, you're definitely looking a bit older but you've still got that sparkle in your eye.' He turned, 'Harmen, you were a boy when I left you three years ago and look at you now.' He beamed at his friends. 'Now then, how are the family and all my friends?'

Frank took a deep breath, 'We're all fine and just waiting for this damned war to end.' The two men smiled at each other.

'Richard has been sent to help us,' said Piet quietly. 'He's brought explosives and weapons. There are specific targets all over Friesland for the *NBS*.' He smiled at his friend and produced two armbands from his pocket. He offered them to Frank and Harmen. 'We'd like you to join us.'

Harmen took the armband and looped it around his arm. Frank paused for a moment and shook his head.

'I'm sorry, I'll take the armband but I can't wear it, or the uniform. Naturally, I'll help you to blow up things but I can't belong to an army, even if it is to free my country.'

'I know that, Frank, and I understand how you feel.' Piet's face beamed, 'Anyway, let's go and blow up something, shall we?'

There were eight of them cycling in the dark towards their objective. Frank was the only one not wearing the *NBS* uniform but he felt part of the group and elated by the thought of their action. It was a still night and one of the men guided them through the village and close to the railway line.

'Leave the bikes here. We'll have to walk the rest of the way,' whispered Dirk.

Richard had a heavy rucksack slung over his shoulders and he followed the guide through the lush spring grass. It was only twenty minutes walk and they soon reached the railway line. It gleamed dully in the moonlight and stretched away, dead straight, on either side of the group.

'Seems a pity to blow it up,' said Dirk quietly. 'It's a perfectly good railway line. The Allies may have need of it after the liberation.'

'There won't be a liberation if we don't blow it up,' growled Piet. 'The Nazis could use it to get to the coast and escape by sea back to Germany.'

Frank rubbed his hands together, 'Right, Richard. What do we do?'

'Frank van der Meer, or whatever your name is nowadays, I think you actually enjoy doing this sort of thing.'

Even in the darkness Frank felt himself blushing, 'Well, ... eh, yes, I do actually.'

Richard pulled the rucksack off his shoulder and placed it on the ground. He unbuckled the flap, withdrew several packages and laid them out on the ground at the side of the track. He hefted a brown paper parcel in his hand.

'This, gentlemen, is called plastic explosive. It's totally inert and can only be used when it's fitted with a detonator.' He threw the parcel at Frank who deftly caught it and frozel, unsure what to do. 'Don't look so worried. The real danger lies in these babies.' He took out a small wooden box and laid it very carefully on the ground. 'The long ones have an hour's timer and the shorter ones have five minutes.' He took the parcel from Frank's hands, rammed the pencil-like detonator into the paper covering and handed the package back to Frank. 'Now, all you have to do is to stick it hard under the railway sleeper. Pile up gravel around it, that confines the explosion, and twist off the cap. Then you've got five minutes to run like hell.' He laughed quietly and tossed another packet to Piet. 'Stick that under the other line.'

Piet and Frank glanced at each other.

'Frank,' he called softly, 'it's just like the good old days.'

'Yes, but don't forget to run,' he replied.

The two men crawled near the line and scrabbled away at the gravel under the heavy wooden sleeper. Frank was the first to finish.

'I'm ready, Piet. I'm going to count to three and then I'll tear off the cap. One, ... two, ... three!'

They turned and ran like hares back across the field.

'This should be far enough,' whispered Richard to the group. 'Now sit back and watch the fireworks.'

Five minutes seemed like fifty but suddenly there was a thunderclap of an explosion and a blinding flash of white light. Gravel rained down on them and they covered their heads.

'I suppose we should have gone a bit further away,' muttered Richard as he rose to his feet and ran back towards the line, followed closely by the remainder of the group.

The two lines were bent upwards above head-height. Frank grabbed hold of one of them.

'VERDOMME! They're red hot!' he shouted as he let go and shook his hand.

'It's the power of the plastic,' said Richard. 'I should have warned you.'

They all stood in a circle around the railway line. There were two deep pits cleared of gravel by the explosions. Three sleepers had disappeared completely and the railway line itself was buckled beyond repair.

'That was wonderful,' said Dirk. 'I don't think I've enjoyed anything so much for years.'

Frank laughed and something of his old excitement returned, 'I think that the Germans could repair this bit. Let's blow up another stretch further along the line.'

'Frank,' exclaimed Richard, 'you're worse than the rest of us. But, it's not a bad idea.' He drew two more packages from his rucksack. 'It's Dirk's turn to play with plastic now.' There was quiet laughter.

During that night the group not only blew up the railway line but sets of telegraph posts and three road bridges over canals. They all enjoyed themselves.

Frank slept in the barn of a farm near Leeuwarden, deliciously exhausted by his efforts. His body tingled with excitement and he yearned for Marieke.

'Go away,' he pushed the hand from his shoulder, 'I said go away.'

'Wake up, Frank. Come on man, wake up.'

He sat up, instantly alert. Piet, bent on one knee, faced him. 'Frank, good news. The Poles have pushed through to the coast east of Friesland. That means that the Germans are cut-off from the Fatherland. It also means that their only escape from Friesland is west, past us, to the coast. Detachments of the *NBS* are going to stop them.'

Frank pushed the straw away from his body and jumped up. 'Where the hell are the Allies?'

'At Dokkum,' said Piet quietly.

'DOKKUM!' exclaimed Frank. 'That's only twenty kilometres north-east of Leeuwarden. That's east. What's happening in the south?'

'Latest reports say that French parachutists have taken Meppel.'

'That's too close to my family,' said Frank with a worried frown. 'Only sixty kilometres from Laaxsum. Piet, I've got to go there.'

'That's why I told you. I've managed to get transport for you. It'll be here in twenty minutes.' Frank slumped back onto the straw, shaking his head. 'How are things in Leeuwarden?'

Piet nodded, 'Good, so far. Our men have told our people to stay off the streets. All telephone lines have been cut and the Germans have locked themselves into their barracks. Before you ask, I still don't know anything about David de Bruin or any of the other prisoners.' He thought for a minute and snapped his fingers, 'Oh yes, I nearly forgot. The Canadians have liberated Westerbork.'

'Thank God,' breathed Frank.

'It seems that there were still nine hundred Jews waiting there to be transported.' Frank's eyes lit up. 'I don't know about David. But, there could be a slim chance that he's there. We'll just have to wait'

The sound of an engine came through the thick walls of the barn. The men rushed through the doors with weapons ready. It was a German BMW motor-bike with one man revving the engine. He lowered the stand, climbed off the machine and spoke a few words to Piet. His face dropped and he walked across to Frank and Harmen. They knew by the expression on his face that it was news of the worst kind.

'He's just told me that all eight prisoners in Leeuwarden were shot this morning in reprisal for last night's sabotage.' Piet put his hand on Frank's shoulder, 'I'm so sorry to have to tell you this, but David de Bruin was one of those killed.'

Frank's face froze and he walked away from the group. He walked back to the barn and kicked the heavy door over and over again.

With his back to the men they heard him say, 'Oh my Lord, will it never, never end?'

They stood silently for a minute before Piet walked over to Frank and spoke quietly, 'You'd better leave, Frank. I've got to get into Leeuwarden and take charge of Uncle.'

Harmen stood near his father, 'Please go to *Mem* and Aukje. I have to go with Piet. There's much to do.'

Frank lifted his head, tears flowing down his face. 'All right, son, I understand. Just come to us when you can. Please be careful, I don't want to lose anybody else.'

Straightening his back he looked at the BMW and shook his head, 'Is this my transport?' Piet nodded. 'I've never driven one of these things in my life before.'

Richard stepped forward and put his Sten gun on the ground. 'Frank, it's dead easy. If you can ride a bicycle and drive a car. Then you can drive a motor-bike. Look, I'll show you.' He climbed onto the broad leather saddle and explained the controls.

'All right, I'll try it. But I think it's more dangerous than dodging patrols.' There were quick smiles from the men. Frank kicked the starter and the engine roared into life. He clicked the motor-bike into gear. Richard was at his side and he shouted into Frank's ear.

'LET THE CLUTCH OUT SLOWLY AND MOVE OFF IN FIRST GEAR.'

The bike stalled and ground to a stop. Frank looked over his shoulder.

'Try it again, a bit slower this time. Don't worry, you'll soon get the hang of it,' said Richard, with a grin.

'Have you ever driven one of these things?' asked Frank.

Richard stopped smiling, 'Well, no ... I haven't actually, but I've seen soldiers driving them.'

Frank grunted, started the engine, slipped into first gear and roared away down the road.

Somehow he managed to use all the gears and he soon thrilled to the exhilaration of speed. The roads were clear of traffic and he threw caution to the winds and travelled faster than he had done for four long years.

Marieke heard the engine as she put out washing on the clothes line. She watched the motor-bike become clearer as it raced along the road on the dyke. With her blonde hair streaming in the wind, she ran down the path as she recognised Frank. He managed to brake to a stop at her side. He lifted the goggles and drew her close before she could say anything. There was grit in his mouth and he spat it out. She knew what he was going to say.

'I could feel it, Frank. I just knew that it was going to happen. Oh, I'm so sorry for Tineke and Jan. I'll tell them.' As he climbed off the BMW, they clung to each other.

'*Liefje*, I can't stop crying,' said Frank. 'It seems that every day something awful happens.'

'Darling,' she said with big eyes, 'at least we've survived this far.

That's why I worry about our children. Aukje's in Makkum with the de Bruins and now you tell me that Harmen is in Leeuwarden.'

They returned to the house and sat together in the small living-room. The door was open and a cool breeze blew in. It was late in the afternoon and Frank was dog-tired. Within a minute of sitting down, he pulled his legs onto the couch and dropped off into a deep sleep. Marieke threw a blanket over him and left him alone. It was hours later when she closed the front door and climbed the stairs to bed. She tossed and turned all night trying to sleep and shadows rushed across the room and brief images of faces flashed across her half-conscious brain. Suddenly Frank was at her side and she thought it was a dream.

'Marieke, wake-up.' In an instant she sat up and it really was Frank.

'What is it?' she said hoarsely.

'I can't stand this waiting any more. We've got to find our daughter and tell our friends about their son.'

'You're right, oh yes, you're so right.' She stumbled out of the bed and drew on her clothes.

Within ten minutes they set off for Makkum. With only one bicycle between them, they decided to walk. Using the motor-bike was out of the question. There were still Germans in Makkum. They strode as quickly as they could along the dyke road. The sun was well up and there was the promise of a fine day. Neither of them spoke for twenty minutes as they breathed deeply and made good time.

Marieke suddenly stopped, 'Frank, enough. I've got to have a rest.' She sat down heavily on the side of the road with her legs dangling over the side of the dyke. He sat down beside her and pulled her close.

'Darling,' she said, 'just look at us. You in that old blue overall and three days of stubble on your face. And me in this awful linen dress. We used to have such beautiful clothes.' She lay back on the grass and stretched her arms above her head.

Frank lay over her and played with her hair, '*Liefje*, I love you so much and don't worry. Soon life will get better and you can buy as many clothes as you want to.'

He felt the warmth of her body and his arms slipped around her waist.

She smiled as she looked up into his eyes, 'Frank, I think I've got my breath back now. We really should move on.'

He lifted himself away from her and laughed, 'One day, there'll be time for us.'

With new heart they resumed the walk.

TWENTY SIX

The de Bruins were hiding in a comfortable house on the main street in the centre of Makkum, a village famous for its pottery and fishing. Hard on the coast of the *IJsselmeer* it was normally prosperous and proud of its traditions. Its church, built solidly on its protective mound, loomed over the neat, red brick buildings. Unfortunately, it was one of the last villages in Friesland to be garrisoned by the Germans.

Frank saw the windmill and read its message; it had been the same signal for five long years. They crept through the town as most people were starting their breakfast. Frank moved down one street and then waved Marieke to follow him. The *SD* headquarters was in the centre of the village and the safe house was directly opposite. That was what had made it safe for so long. The streets were totally empty and not even a cat or dog was out.

Frank froze to the wall of a pretty gabled shop, its shutters were firmly in place. He peered round the corner. The safe-house was in the next street. The early morning sun cast long shadows and he hid in the corner of the square with Marieke crouched at his side.

'One quick dash and we're there,' he whispered.

'Why don't we wait until people are about?'

'They won't be, not today,' he replied with his arm firmly round her waist.

Frank grabbed her arm, straightened and casually they made their way across the square. He swore he could feel eyes boring into the back of his neck but he kept walking and very soon reached the house. For a moment he thought he saw a curtain move and then he was at the door. He tried the handle only to find the door was locked.

'Frank, what are we going to do?' said Marieke.

He answered her question by using the door-knocker. The heavy door creaked open five centimetres. He put his foot at the bottom and pushed hard. The door flew open and they tumbled through.

A pale-faced old woman in full traditional Makkum costume stared at him and then babbled something in Friesian. She tried to pull him back towards the door. Frank gently got hold of her arm and said with a smile, 'I've come to see your guests.' He pointed with his finger at the ornate ceiling above her and nodded. She peered into his face, yanked her arm away and waved towards the stairs.

'Thank you, *mevrouw*,' he said with a slight bow and Marieke followed him up the stairs.

The de Bruins were in a first-floor room and they heard the footsteps on the wooden stairs. Jan opened the door and let them in. His face was streaked with tears. Tineke stood quietly at his side.

'Frank, I think I know why you're here. Before you say anything, I was told yesterday that the Germans shot the prisoners in Leeuwarden prison.' His sunken eyes stared upwards, 'Please God, tell me that my son was not one of them.'

Marieke stepped forward and put her arm around his neck, 'Jan, I'm so terribly sorry.'

He closed his eyes and shouted, beating his fists on the wall. 'Oh my God, NO! Why should it happen now? Why now?' He turned and Tineke held out her arms. He fell into them and they both cried and cried and cried. Frank and Marieke tried to comfort them, but they were lost in the depths of their grief.

The room had tall windows and the heavy brocade drapes were pulled back and the window was wide-open. Frank stepped across the room to close it. He grabbed the heavy cast-iron stay and pulled. The window refused to budge. He pulled harder and then saw why it refused to move. It was secured from the outside by an old-fashioned latch. He took a deep breath and leaned out of the window. He heard Marieke's cry of warning, but it was too late.

'YOU! ... YOU UP THERE!'

Frank looked down and his heart skipped a whole beat. An SS *Unterscharführer* stared up at him. The rifle was aimed straight at his face. At the man's side was a younger soldier.

'STAY WHERE YOU ARE! ... IF YOU MOVE, I'LL SHOOT!'

The *Unterscharführer* turned to the other man. 'Go into the house and bring him out. Come on, quickly now. I think I know him.'

The soldier pounded on the heavy door with his rifle butt and Frank heard the old woman turning the key in the lock to let him in. He glanced at Marieke. She was frozen in shock and her face was pale with terror.

He looked down. The rifle did not waver a fraction. There was a smile on the German's face.

'I KNOW YOU!' was his shouted comment.

Frank thought of pulling back away from the window, but the decision was taken away from him as the other soldier burst through the door into the room. He was young and very nervous. His rifle moved in a short arc covering the three people standing in the corner.

'COVER THEM! ... I'M COMING UP!' bellowed the voice from the street.

Frank knew that he was dead and he smiled grimly to himself. He thought it was a dream and then another thought flashed through his mind which made him think that he was already dead. It reminded him of Arnhem: and people always said that your life passed across your consciousness just before you died.

It was the sound of bagpipes. He shook his head.

'KEEP STILL I SAID!'

No, it was bagpipes. Frank could quite clearly hear them. He knew that there was no other sound like bagpipes. He looked up and down the street. The German stood rooted to the spot and a puzzled look spread across his face. His eyes turned away from the rifle sights and glanced down the street. A shadow of fear rushed across his face. He shook himself and the rifle still pointed.

Frank saw the man first. He was small, with bandy legs and big black shiny boots. He saw his legs because he was wearing a kilt. Frank laughed out aloud. The man marched down the street totally alone. He had a tartan Tam o' Shanter hat sitting squarely on his head. The navy-blue ribbon hung over his left ear. The soldier's face was bright red and his cheeks were swollen like small crimson balloons. The wail of the bagpipes echoed back from the deserted streets in a way that both thrilled and stilled the heart.

Frank watched the scene unfold. The lone piper marched right up to the German. He stood a metre away from him and still the pipes wailed. He was much shorter than the blonde SS man. To Frank, the scene was comic in the extreme and he laughed so loud that tears streamed down his face.

The rifle fell with a clatter to the ground and the German raised his hands slowly above his head. Events happened quickly. The sound of marching feet came from Frank's right and he saw a whole column of men marching, with kilts swinging to the lilt of the pipes. They carried rifles at the slope and their uniforms were neatly pressed khaki. As they marched precisely in column-of-route towards the piper he felt them coming, took two steps sideways and continued marching but this time at the head of a long line of men. They marched round the German like water round a boat and he just stood, frozen with his mouth wide open in shock.

Frank watched for a moment and then turned back into the room. The young German soldier held the rifle pointed at Marieke's heart. Behind her Jan held Tineke close. Marieke had always surprised him. He watched a slow smile spread over her face. She reached forward, gently pushed the rifle muzzle carefully to one side and then, almost in slow motion, kicked the German hard between the legs. He grunted deep in his belly, dropped the rifle and collapsed onto the floor. She turned to Frank, her face flushed with excitement.

'Darling, I think we've been liberated.'

TWENTY SEVEN

'Good morning sir, ... madam. I'm Lieutenant Gordon Mcdonald of the Royal Canadian Dragoons. Can I be of any help?'

The officer was tall and looked as though he was fresh out of school. His uniform was neat and the dark colours of his tartan kilt shone out in the early morning sunshine. He carried a sub-machine gun casually crooked in one arm and his other hand executed a crisp salute.

Frank and Marieke stood in the street and gazed in amazement. He remembered his English. 'Good morning, Lieutenant. Yes, you can help. My wife has something for you.' He nudged Marieke. She walked back into the house and dragged the German out of the front door.

'I'm afraid I kicked him a little too hard but I think he's all right.'

From nowhere a sergeant in khaki appeared and the German followed him as meekly as a lamb.

'Hello, Frank, how are you?'

He whirled around. Marius Hofstra stood casually at ease with a huge smile on his face.

'I presume this beautiful lady is the one that I've heard so much about.' The smile stayed on his face.

Frank's mouth dropped wide open and his face was split by a huge smile. He could not take it in. He just stared and stared at the scene around him. Behind Marius, the streets were beginning to fill with the good citizens of Makkum. Orange flags appeared at windows along the street. Cheering rang round the small square and then came the roar of engines. Slowly squat armoured cars appeared. The heads of the smiling drivers stuck up from the open cockpits. The stubby barrels of their twin machine guns pointed skywards. The small vehicles were soon covered with happy men and women. Marius had gone, carried away by the crowds.

'HOORAH! HOORAH!' shouted Marieke over his shoulder and soon the crowd joined in.

Frank was unable to move. His emotions were overloaded and the scene before him began to swim before his eyes. He felt Marieke nudging him.

'Frank, ... look, ... look.' She pointed at a massive tank that was just lumbering into the square belching out blue smoke from its rear. The tank-tracks clanked across the cobbles in front of them. What really surprised him was Aukje. She was standing on the turret gripping its open lid with both hands. Her face was alight with excitement and her long, blonde hair blew in the breeze. Suddenly, she noticed her parents and she lifted a hand to wave. As she waved to them, she glanced at the first floor window and saw Jan and Tineke de Bruin. Their faces told the story and she clambered down the steel sides of the tank and jumped lightly to the ground.

Aukje threw her arms around her mother but there was no happiness.

She released her and flew into the house. Frank moved to stop her and Marieke caught his arm. 'Frank, let her do it her own way.' He nodded and stepped back towards the crowds.

The column of men and equipment had nearly passed and there was a sudden commotion that caught Frank's attention. Behind the last man were a dozen or so Germans of all ages and ranks. They staggered along with heads hung low as they were kicked from all sides by angry people. The leading soldier was the man who had seen Frank through the window. His face was covered in slimy spittle but his eyes flashed fire as he caught sight of Frank. They stared at each other for a brief moment and each knew that the day of reckoning had arrived. The Germans quickly moved on, pushed along by six well-armed, grim-faced Canadian soldiers.

Frank found Aukje standing at his side, oblivious to the occasion. He smiled and put his arm around her. She placed her head on his chest and her pale face was damp with tears. Frank held her tightly.

'My *famke*, I'm so sorry but at least we're free.'

Her head came up and some of the light returned to her eyes. She straightened her back and kissed him gently on the cheek.

'I love you, *Heit* and life must go on.'

The three van der Meers held onto each other until the crowds had gone and the square became strangely silent. Soon the de Bruins joined them and they stood together. Marieke was the first to speak.

'I know where everybody has gone to.' She pointed down the street. Small groups of people were slowly making their way towards the church. Soon it became a steady stream as the houses began to empty and the joy of the last hour had its effect on emotions.

The church was packed full and there was only a slight murmur of sound. Frank knew that there was no minister for this church. He had been shot in front of the church doors not a week ago. The people were content just to sit in freedom. There was a sound at the rear of the old building and faces turned to see what was happening. The Canadian lieutenant and Marius Hofstra passed through the tall archway and made their way quickly to the front of the rows of packed pews. A silent anticipation descended over the assembled people.

Frank thought to himself how relaxed the two soldiers looked. They were well-fed and their gilt buttons shone. They wore smiles that pleased everybody and soon there were nodding heads and then people broke into spontaneous applause. Frank joined in and stood up to cheer. The noise was deafening as it echoed and re-echoed around the rafters of the beautiful old church. How long it went on for, Frank never knew but then Marius removed his beret and raised his hand. Quickly, silence descended and people sat down.

Marius wiped his forehead with his beret and began to speak. He spoke quietly, his voice choked with emotion. 'Friends,' he glanced quickly at Frank, 'citizens of Makkum. I'm *Majoor* Marius Hofstra of The Princes

Irene Brigade.' There was a quiet round of applause and he smiled again. The clapping stopped. 'This officer at my side is Lieutenant Gordon Mcdonald of the Royal Canadian Dragoons. Our men have liberated Makkum and the surrounding area.' There was yet again a deafening cheer. Frank glanced over his shoulder. There were now crowds outside the open doors of the church and everybody was pushing forward. Marius continued, raising his voice for the people outside. 'I'm happy to announce that Leeuwarden is liberated.' He paused, expecting some sort of excitement. This time the people were silent. 'All German forces in Friesland have now capitulated.' There was another cheer that seemed to echo in to the church from the whole village. 'However, I must warn you that there are some members of the SS still in hiding and my men are searching them out. I must tell you that if Germans surrender to you then hold them in a secure place and inform the local NBS. The Allies are offering free food for every German handed over.' There was laughter and people looked at each other and smiled. 'The occupation is not yet over. The western part of the country is still in the grip of famine and, at this very time, His Royal Highness, Prince Bernhard, is negotiating with Seyss-Inquart.' There were hisses of disapproval and Frank for a brief moment felt a wave of hatred from all around the church. Marius paused as the Canadian said something to him. 'There's a relief column of food waiting on the outskirts of Makkum. I ask you to take only what you need. Most of the supplies will be needed for our troops.' The man in front of Frank turned round and nodded. He quickly faced the front of the church waiting for the next words. 'Until the government in exile returns, the province will be governed by a military committee. They'll need help and certain people will be called upon to assist.' Marius shifted on his feet and scratched the side of his face, a mannerism that Frank knew so well. 'Lastly, I come to the matter of dealing with Germans and with Dutch traitors. Orders have been issued that prevent citizens from taking military law into their own hands. All prisoners, both civilian and military, will be dealt with by the due process of law. We know who the collaborators and traitors are and they will be rounded-up when it's practically possible.' His voice became louder and changed tone, 'Do not, I repeat, do not, take part in any acts of retribution, as you may find yourself under arrest by the Allied military authorities.' The audience was absolutely silent. Marius smiled, 'And now, all I have to say is 'Long Live the Queen.' Everyone jumped to his feet and shook hands and hugged everybody near to him. The venerable old building had never witnessed such scenes. Somebody starting singing the national anthem and it was taken up by the people and the strains of *"het Wilhelmus"* rang around the brickwork and the lofty oak beams of the church roof.

Sometime later they sat on the side of the road and watched people singing and dancing around them. Frank had his arms around Marieke and Aukje and they just sat in silence, letting their freedom sink in. Jan and Tineke were near them, lost in their own thoughts. Occasionally the two families glanced at each other and smiled. The day was warm and sunny and there was a gentle breeze coming off the lake. To Frank it seemed as though nothing had changed. The fear and the worry would take a long time to leave his consciousness.

'Hello, everybody, nice to see you again.' Marius appeared magically in front of them. Even whilst he stood, people kept rushing up to him and pumping his hand. 'It's been like this for the last month you know, my arm aches day and night.' He laughed, 'Frank, please introduce me to your family and friends.'

Frank stood and carefully introduced everybody by name. Marius politely shook hands with them all. There was a moment when they did not know what to do next and then he embarrassingly delved into the pockets of his tunic and produced a handful of gifts.

'I'm sorry it's not something really special but I thought you might like some English chocolate.'

They all stared at the foil wrapped bars that lay in his hand. Nobody moved.

'Well, I'm sorry ... '

'I would love a piece,' interrupted Aukje with a grin. 'It's my first real chocolate for three years.' She took one of the bars from his hand. Carefully undid the wrapper marked "**Food Supplies, English Chocolate (sweetened)**", folded it and placed it in her skirt pocket. 'Souvenir,' she said with the same grin. With a shaking finger nail she slit the silver foil and unwrapped the chocolate. It lay there in her palm, eight small pieces formed into a single dark brown slab. She stared at it for a full minute, relishing its simplicity. There was a crowd round her.

'Go on, eat it,' somebody said.

Aukje shook herself, wiped one hand on her dress and then carefully snapped the chocolate into its separate pieces. She looked up.

'*Mem*, you first.' Marieke shook her head, never taking her eyes of the chocolate. Everybody else also shook his head.

'Oh, all right, I'll have the first piece.'

With finger and thumb she selected one of the small oblongs and lifted it to her mouth. She licked her lips once, opened her mouth and popped it in. The crowd watched her cheeks suck in and again she licked her lips. This time her pink tongue left a thin, dark brown line.

'Mmmmm! ... It tastes wonderful.' The small crowd roared with laughter and soon the chocolate bars had disappeared.

Marieke kissed Marius on the cheek. Aukje kissed him on the lips leaving a few flecks of chocolate on his cheek.

The day drifted by and Frank was lost in an excitement that left him utterly exhausted. His arm was aching with shaking so many hands. The day quickly drew to a close and he gathered his family and the de Bruins around him.

Frank said, with a happy smile, 'Let's all start off for Laaxsum, shall we? It's a long walk and it'll be dark before we get home.'

Aukje smiled, '*Heit*, just give me five minutes, please.' And off she ran down the street towards the centre of the village.

She returned in less than five minutes sitting in a Jeep at the side of a smiling Marius.

He stood up above the windscreen, 'I can't have my friends walking, can I!' he said with a huge smile. 'Climb in and I'll take you home.'

Frank shook his head and helped everybody to clamber into the small vehicle.

'Sorry, my old friend,' said Marius, 'climb on the bonnet and hang on.'

He revved the engine and roared off down the cobbled street. People waved and cheered as they sped out of Makkum and onto the dyke road.

Marius had to leave them to return to his men who, by this time, had left Makkum and were liberating smaller villages up the western coast of Friesland.

Frank left the house and walked to the harbour. The sun was blood-red as it set low on the horizon. The three fishing boats moved easily on their moorings and the gentle slap, slap of the waves on their wooden sides Frank found comforting. His mind was completely at peace and the only nagging thought was for the safety of his son. A seagull swooped low and landed on the path in front of him. The gull fixed its beady eyes on Frank and they watched each other for a few seconds. With a flapping of wings the bird flew away. To Frank it was somehow strangely symbolic and it made him concentrate his thoughts on the future.

'Lost in thought, darling?' He jumped. Marieke was standing behind him.

'Yes, *liefje*, I was. The problem is that I just can't believe what's happening.'

'I know, I feel the same way. It's happened and we have to deal with it.'

'How are the de Bruins?' asked Frank. 'I'm sorry I didn't stay with them. I just wanted to be alone.'

'They're fine. They've just gone to bed in Aukje's room. I managed to find some pillows for Jan to sleep on. I think they're totally worn out.'

For a minute or so they watched the sun set and, as darkness fell, it grew chilly and Marieke shivered. 'Frank, let's go back in now. I don't want to catch a cold on the day of liberation.'

They walked hand-in-hand back up the path to the house and Frank turned to face her. 'Look, Marieke, as soon as possible, the three of us are going to find some bikes and then we're going to Leeuwarden. I want to find our son and see our friends.'

Marieke gripped his hand more tightly and her voice softened, 'You're right and I want our house back and I want it just as it was.'

'Somehow, Marieke, I don't think our life will ever be the same again,' he said wistfully, as he kissed her full on the lips.

TWENTY-EIGHT

They cycled together along the main roads through a spring-time Friesland, without any worries about identity cards or German patrols. However, they did have to look out for high-speed convoys of Allied vehicles that seemed to rush in both directions and with no particular purpose. Everybody, either people on bikes, or soldiers in Jeeps, waved and shouted at each other. The villages that they passed through were full of people singing or just sitting in the sunshine. The whole province was awake.

'Marieke, Aukje, there's one place that I want to call at before we get to Leeuwarden,' Frank called, as he led his family down one of the roads.

Marieke glanced across the handlebars of her bicycle, 'Frank, I know where. It's Roordahuizum and it's Lottie Cohen.'

'How did you guess?' he shouted back with a smile, glancing over his shoulder as he pedalled away from them.

The village of Roordahuizum is just one street with two shops and a small church. Frank skidded to a stop outside the butchers. Before he dismounted from his bike, Lottie came running out of the door.

She wore an obviously French dress, all velvet and lace. 'Oh, I'm so glad to see you all,' she said, with a smile on her pale face. 'Do come into the house.' Behind her stood the butcher and his wife, both with red faces and hearty smiles.

Frank hugged her and noticed the perfume. 'I'm sorry, Lottie, we can't stay. We've got things to do in Leeuwarden.'

'Do you know,' she said happily, 'tomorrow I'm going to Westerbork to look for the records about my family.'

Frank felt a stab of concern for her. 'Let me know if I can be of any help, won't you?'

Marieke and Aukje arrived, breathless. They kissed Lottie gently on both cheeks. Marieke spoke first, 'Lottie, you look tremendous. And, may I ask, where do you get clothes and perfume from at the end of three years of hiding?'

Lottie gave her giggly laugh, 'Listen, Marieke van der Meer, when you've had years with nothing to do, it's surprising what you can find in wardrobes.' She looked them both up and down. 'You can't go into town in those clothes.' She folded her arms and said firmly, 'Now, come into the house and I'm sure I can find something better than those awful things that you're both wearing.'

Frank shrugged his shoulders, swung the stand down on the bike and walked towards the house. He was not surprised that he had to wait an hour. He knew his wife and daughter only too well.

Frank sat with the butcher in his big living-room and they chatted about the war and business. Their conversation was interrupted.

'Frank, we're ready to go now.'

He turned with an unspoken word on his lips and his mouth fell open. Lottie stood at Marieke's side with a smile on her face. Marieke had washed her hair and it was flowingly coiled, neatly framing her face. Her blue eyes shone with pleasure. The pale green skirt swirled around her legs and the woollen jumper of a lighter green fitted her perfectly, showing off her slim figure. His eyes turned to his daughter. Aukje had dressed herself in a deep blue cotton dress with a short coat thrown round her shoulders. Her smile was dazzling. They were clearly mother and daughter and a stab of pride left him breathless. After a moment, he found the right words to say.

'You both look wonderful and I'd be proud to take you into town.'

Marieke put her hands firmly on her hips, 'Oh no, Frank van der Meer, not in those horrible blue overalls and those disgustingly dirty clogs.'

The question was on Frank's lips and Lottie laughed, 'Yes, I've even collected suits.' She walked across the room and took Frank's hand, 'Follow me please.' He meekly obeyed.

She had quite a collection in the small room and he tried on four or five suits before he found one that more or less fitted him. He saw a small bottle of cologne on top of a cupboard. With a guilty feeling he grabbed some and splashed it onto his chest and under his arms. It was sheer luxury and he felt wonderful. The shoes fitted as well as the shirt and he found a reasonable tie. With a rueful smile he flung the overalls into the corner and strode out of the room. He somehow felt that what they had represented was now in the past.

Lottie clapped her hands, 'Now, that's much better. You look like the real van der Meers that I used to know. Have a good day in Leeuwarden and please keep in touch with me.'

Frank thanked her and the butcher and his wife. They had been looking after Lottie for the last two years and without a single word of complaint.

They reached the outskirts of Leeuwarden and found their way barred by a road-block. Marieke's smile vanished and the old fears returned.

The man was tall and wore the make-shift uniform of the *NBS*.

'We need to know where you're all going to.'

Frank was angry, 'Where we are going to has nothing to do with you. Now out of my way!'

The man was armed and his face flushed, 'I'm sorry, but we have to check everybody. We're looking for collaborators.'

Two other men appeared from a house. They walked slowly towards Frank and blocked his way. It was an impasse and the three men stopped him moving.

'Have we not had four years of this?' said Frank, his whole body tensed with frustration.

'Can we see your identity cards, please?' asked the man.

Marieke came to husband's side, 'Frank,' she said quietly, 'patience, in their own way, they're only trying to help.'

He pulled out the identity cards and the red, white and blue armband fluttered to the ground. The attitude of the three men quickly changed. The man's voice was polite, 'I'm sorry, I didn't know you were *NBS*. You're free to go. But, *meneer, mevrouw*, be careful in the town. We have groups looking for traitors.'

Marieke smiled at them and guided him back to his bicycle. 'Don't look back. They may change their minds.'

Frank looked around him as they cycled through their town. There were Allied vehicles everywhere. Jeeps, lorries, motor-bikes armoured personnel carriers, and men in uniforms of all colours imaginable. Three massive Sherman tanks, engines running, were parked outside the railway station. Armed British Tommies formed a line in front of the ticket office. There was a queue of men and women waiting for tickets and they all carried a single suitcase. A crowd of laughing children threw stones at the queue and people ducked to avoid the missiles.

Frank pulled up and watched the scene in front of him. An old man with a walking stick saw him stop and carefully walked over to stand at his side.

'They're *NSB*'ers going to Westerbork.' He saw the surprise on their faces. 'They were rounded up this morning and we make them pay for their tickets.' He chortled and tapped his stick, 'First-class prices for first-class traitors. Look, *meneer*,' he pointed towards the end of the platforms with his stick, 'with first-class carriages.' He roared with laughter and walked away. There was a line of the familiar cattle trucks. The doors were already open.

Frank shook his head, 'I've had enough. Let's go to the *Hotel de Kroon*.' Marieke and Aukje followed him, pushing their bicycles to avoid the crowds.

The hotel foyer was full of chattering people and they had to fight their way through the entrance and across to Dirk's office. He saw them coming and threw open the door.

'My friends, am I glad to see you. Congratulations on being liberated, or whatever we're supposed to say after five years.' As he moved to one side, Marieke saw the other man in Dirk's office.

'Harmen,' she shouted and flew across the room.

'Hello, everybody,' he said, with a huge grin.

She stared at the heavy bandaging round his shoulder and it stopped her dead. 'What's the matter? What's happened?' She gently eased him back into the leather seat and brushed the hair out of his eyes.

'Your son is a hero,' laughed Dirk. 'I know he won't tell you, so I will.' He waved his friends to a long couch set against the wall. 'Two days ago the *NBS* took over the town. The *SS* tried to disguise themselves as soldiers of the *Wehrmacht*. Harmen here and three others got to *SS* headquarters just as Müller was about to leave on a bike.' He laughed again, ' Can you believe it? The *Hauptsturmführer* on a bike! Anyway, your son here rammed him with his bike and jumped on the bastard. Oh, sorry, Marieke.' She smiled. 'It was a good fight until Müller pulled a gun out from under his tunic. He managed to let off one round before Harmen swiped him across the face and laid Müller out cold. He arrested him and they took him to the prison. He's there with his other cronies, that is apart from Hofmann. He was shot by somebody, we don't know who. Good riddance, I say. The Allies want Müller, but we've refused to hand him over. We want our people to deal him when the rest of the country is liberated. Meanwhile he can rot in hell.'

Harmen spoke for the first time. His voice was strained, '*Heit*, he's in exactly the same cell as the one he put me in. I went to see him last night. He hasn't said a word since he was arrested. He just sits in the corner staring at the ceiling. People want to shoot him, but I don't.'

'Why not, son?' said Frank gently, with his eyes on Harmen's face.

'It's what you said sometime ago. Let's deal with them by the due process of law. Our people need to see him dealt with properly.'

Frank smiled and he knew that his son had learned something during this awful war.

The room was silent for a moment and then Aukje said, 'I suppose you've heard about David?'

'Yes,' replied her brother. 'We found the bodies, including David's, in the cellars of the prison. They're all in the church waiting for burial. Aukje, I'm so sorry.' They embraced and Marieke and Frank watched their children with respect.

Dirk chose the right moment, 'Look, I know what you want to do next. I've contacted the man in your house and he's waiting for you. I've even got a jeep to take you there.'

'Where did you get a jeep from?' said Marieke.

'Piet arranged it. He's the deputy Town Mayor'. He saw Marieke's questioning face. 'Oh yes, You don't know do you? The Town Mayor is a Major J.G. Robinson. He's Canadian and a really good man. Piet, as leader of Group Uncle, is his deputy and I'm glad, Frank, to be the first to officially inform you, that as leader of the L.O., you'll be a deputy as well.'

Frank shook his head, 'Sorry, I'm not ready for that yet. Please tell Piet that maybe in another couple of days I might feel like doing the job. First of all. I want to go home.' He thumped Dirk on the shoulder, 'Oh, thanks all the same. We don't need the Jeep. I think we'd rather go on our bicycles.'

Dirk nodded, 'Frank, I understand. I think I know how you feel.'

'What about Harmen?' said Marieke. 'He can't use a bike with that arm.'

He slowly stood, 'I'll walk most of the way and then my loving sister can put me on her luggage carrier.'

The door opened and a waiter came in bearing a loaded tray. The aroma wafted across the office.

'It's coffee,' exclaimed Frank, 'real coffee.'

'My friends, I've been saving it for this day. I know you don't want any of my hoarded champagne and so I've kept this especially for you.'

'Dirk, two days ago I ate real chocolate,' said Aukje, sipping at her cup, 'and now I'm drinking real coffee. I can't believe it.'

Marieke glanced across to Frank, 'All right, darling. I know you want to go and so do I.' She stood, placed her cup on the table and turned to Dirk.

'That was the most delicious coffee that I've ever tasted, Dirk Haan. Please save some for me the next time that we come to see you.'

'That might be sooner than you think,' he said with a wink.

Dirk reached over his desk to pull open a drawer. He found a small package and put it into Marieke's hand. 'Here's a small sample for you to take with you. Let it be the first drink that you all have together in your home.'

Marieke held his arm and kissed him on the cheek. Her blue eyes sparkled, 'Dirk, you're always so thoughtful.'

He blushed, 'Think nothing of it. We all have much to celebrate.'

Together the family walked past the familiar places but recognised nobody. As they turned the corner of *Nieuwe Stad* there was a large crowd gathered outside the police station.

'*Mem*, keep walking, please,' said Aukje, impatiently.

Shouts reached their ears and suddenly they were caught up in the crowd that surged onto the street. Frank used his bicycle to push a way through. A gap appeared and they found themselves watching the reason for the shouting.

'*MOFFENMAIDEN!* ... *MOFFENMAIDEN!* ... *MOFFENMAIDEN!*'
The chant got louder and louder as more people joined in.

By the side of the canal bordering the *Nieuwe Stad* there was a row of ten wooden chairs. In each one sat a woman; their ages varied. They were surrounded by groups of chanting, hysterical people. Two of the women already had their heads shaved close to the skull. Most were white-faced and some were angry. The hair-clippers were ready for use by anybody who wanted them and there was no shortage of volunteers.

'Serve them right,' shouted somebody. 'They shouldn't have gone with the Nazis. They're worse than whores!'

'*NSB* BITCHES!'

The first shorn woman was distraught. She rushed from side to side against the jeering crowds and her face was full of uncontrolled terror. Marieke saw her eyes and her heart went out to her but there was nothing she could do. The crowd edged closer and closer and eventually two other women simply pushed their victim into the canal. There were cheers and the crowd crowed for more.

Frank grabbed Marieke and said desperately, 'No more of this. No more of this. Come on, let's get away from here.' He pushed his way clear through the crowd of chanting people and eventually they all reached a deserted back-street. Frank paused for a minute and there was incredulity in his voice. 'How can people do that to each other?'

'*Heit*,' said Harmen, 'it'll take a long time for the war to go away. I understand how they feel.'

'Revenge is not the answer,' replied Frank quickly, as they walked away from the noise of the crowds. It seemed as if everybody was in the centre of the town and they walked quickly along deserted streets.

Harmen saw the first of many posters that had been plastered all over walls. He stopped, 'I've got to read one of these, I've seen so many.' He began and his family listened.

WELCOME ALLIES

With yearning, often difficult to restrain, have we awaited your arrival. And now that you have liberated us, delivered us from the most cruel tyrant, we welcome you with all our hearts. Full of sincere admiration we have followed your self-sacrificing struggle from day to day, from hour to hour. Your successes, were for us, a time for rejoicing, your set-backs, cause for much grief. We know how much you have already sacrificed and are still sacrificing on the battlefield, also for our country's sake. This is irretrievable as well we know, for has not also in our midst many a brave man fallen in the uneven struggle against the all powerful enemy, we must needs believe that the ordeal that we had to go about together, has not been in vain, but was for some ultimate reason. It is the hope of the Dutch people that you will tell the bereaved relatives of your friends on your return. We shall give you what help we can, to terminate the war, that you may soon go home and your stay here we shall make as welcome as possible. But remember, the enemy who occupied our country has oppressed and plundered us. The Dutch population has been reduced to begging so that materially our help may not amount to much.

But the Netherlands will rise again!

And for that we owe you so much and we are indebted to you!

In the name of the thousands of inhabitants of the Netherlands.

The editor of the illegal papers.

"Je Maintiendrai"

15 April 1945

'That's wonderful,' commented Frank as he read and re read the poster.

They walked all the way to their old home, down roads they had not seen for three years, past empty and deserted houses.

'Frank, stop here for a moment, please,' said Marieke as she produced a key from her pocket. They stood at the end of the short drive leading to the de Bruins' house. 'Will all of you wait here? There's something that I have to do.'

She walked up the path towards the farmhouse. The garden was totally overgrown with dense weeds and paint was peeling off the boarded-up window frames. It took both her hands to turn the key in the lock and eventually the door creaked open. There was a musty smell in the air and, because the curtains were closed, there was little light. Marieke waited for a minute, remembering all the good times that had happened in the room and then she reached into her pocket and slowly pulled out the fading, yellow star. She looked at it for a moment and then placed it on the dusty table. Marieke quietly recited a Jewish prayer that Tineke had taught her.

She took a deep breath and walked out of the house securing the door behind her.

'What's the matter, *Mem*?' said Aukje noticing the sadness on her mother's face.

'Nothing,' replied Marieke, squeezing Aukje's hand, 'just something I promised Tineke.'

For the remaining fifteen minutes walk nobody said a word.

They turned the corner and the factory faced them. Nothing had changed. It was exactly as they had left it. They dropped the bikes in the bushes and walked past the closed doors. Frank gripped Marieke's hand, took a deep breath and prepared to walk the last few steps. Before he could even lift his feet, the factory door crashed open and a stream of people rushed out. The van der Meers stopped in their tracks and turned round in astonishment.

The same familiar faces with the same familiar smiles. A small, suited man stepped forward. There was worry on his face and a frown on his forehead. He quickly removed his trilby hat and held it close to his chest. The men behind him became silent.

He cleared his throat, '*Meneer* and *mevrouw* van der Meer, on behalf of the men and the Friesian Timber Association may I welcome you back to your home and your business.' He made a nervous gesture with his hat and from behind the group emerged a beaming Wim Visser and his wife. She carried a huge bunch of flowers and with a few quick steps she faced Marieke.

'These are for you and your family with all our love and best wishes.' Wim nodded, smiled and waved his cigar in the air.

Marieke took them and her eyes were wet with happiness. She glanced all around her and tried to speak but it took a few moments before she regained her normal composure. 'I would like to ... oh dear.' She buried her head in the flowers and tried again, 'just, to thank everybody.' She fell into Frank's open arms.

The man began again, '*Meneer* and *mevrouw* van der Meer. My wife and I have not lived in your house.' He glanced towards Frank, 'As you know, I had the windows boarded-up and we looked after it for you.' He opened his hand and there in his palm lay the key to the front door. He looked expectantly at the faces in front of him.

'Frank,' said Marieke in a whisper, 'you take the key.'

The man led the way and they followed him. Frank was surprised. The garden, although a little overgrown, was neat and tidy. He stopped and looked at the house. The paint on the woodwork was fresh and the shine reflected back in the sunshine. Marieke dug him in the ribs. He smiled and strode towards the door. The key turned easily in the lock and the door opened without a sound. He turned to Marieke.

'I suppose I should carry you over the threshold.'

Marieke handed the flowers over to Aukje and threw her arms around his neck. He stooped and picked her up. Together they walked into their house.

As he lowered her to the ground, he looked into her face. '*Liefje* Marieke, I never thought that this moment would ever come.' Aukje and Harmen gently put their arms around their parents and for a brief moment they were locked in a family embrace.

Marieke separated herself and walked into the living-room. It was almost as she had left it. She walked around the room touching objects that she knew so well. Frank watched, his eyes alight with happiness. Aukje linking his arm on one side and Harmen on the other.

Frank suddenly pointed to the wall above the fireplace and exclaimed, 'It's the de Hoogh landscape. How on earth did it get there.'

'Ask your son,' replied a smiling Aukje.

'Well, Er ... *Heit*. It's like this, you see,' he rubbed his aching shoulder, 'after we caught Müller, I went back into SS headquarters and remembered that Müller had the picture on his wall and so I ... eh, ... took it. Wim here, put it back on the wall.'

Frank held his son very close and laughed. Everybody joined in.

Aukje walked over to the Friesian clock. There was a huge grin on her face.

'Do you have to?' said Marieke, with a concerned expression on her face and her hands on her hips.

Aukje opened the door of the clock, delved down into the depths of the long-case, and scrabbled around for a moment. 'Got it,' she exclaimed, withdrew the gun and held it by the barrel. Harmen leapt across the room and took it away from her.

'Where the hell did this come from?' With a practised hand he withdrew the magazine. 'And it's loaded.' He looked at his mother curiously.

'Frank, I think I'd better explain.'

'Yes, I think you'd better,' he said, curiously.

They all sat and listened to the story that had happened almost five years previously.

'And now, Frank, I know what I'm going to do with it.' She took the gun carefully out of Harmen's hand, walked across the room threw open the French windows and disappeared into the garden. She returned a few minutes later rubbing her hands. 'It's in the river, but for a moment, just before I threw it, I couldn't help thinking about poor Ernst Kraft. Without him, Harmen wouldn't be here.'

The Vissers were in the hall and the men were outside. Frank stood in the doorway. The air of assertiveness had returned to his voice and his back was straight, 'Everybody, can we please go outside into the garden? I would like to talk to you all.'

They all gathered on the grass near the river. Before they had quietened, Marieke suddenly gasped.

'Look, Frank! I can't believe it!' All eyes turned towards the river.

The *tjalk* had crept quietly along the waterway and was just about to moor in its customary position. *Schipper* Schaaf stood in the stern and waved. Within five minutes the boat moored and he stepped onto the quay. Marieke ran forward to greet him.

'I can't believe it. How did you get here just on time?'

He grasped Marieke's hands, 'Good planning, but I've had help from one or two friends.' Through the open hatch emerged a smiling Piet followed by a grinning Richard Johnstone. The assembled crowd burst into applause, but the surprises were not over yet. Richard stamped his foot on the deck. A stream of people emerged from the hold. First was Lottie, then the de Bruins and finally another dozen people

Frank folded his arms and watched silently as they jumped onto the quay and joined the party. He recognised them all. The first man walked up to Frank and firmly shook hands.

'Mr Levisson,' said Frank, 'it's a long time since we stood in the cellars of the *Hotel de Kroon* and prayed together.'

'*Ja*, a long time and it's thanks to you that we're still alive. *Meneer, mevrouw*, when our synagogues are open again I will make sure that a Kaddish prayer of thanksgiving is said for our people on your behalf.' He turned to look at the people behind him, 'And all these people owe you both an eternal debt of gratitude.'

Frank recognised them immediately. It was the family that he had taken off the street near to the railway station. He shook his head in amazement and said, 'I can't believe it.'

The queue continued winding its way past the family. Marieke suddenly gasped, 'You're the man from Uitdam,' she grasped his arm, 'but you're looking much better than the last time we met.'

'*Ja, mevrouw*,' smiled the man, 'good Friesian food and a safe place to hide. May I introduce my family and friends.'

Frank and Marieke shook hands with everybody and bouts of crying were interrupted by roars of laughter. Frank found himself standing near to Piet and Dirk.

'How did you manage to organise all this? We only decided to come to Friesland yesterday.'

Piet gave a great smile, 'There wasn't much to do really. When we knew that liberation was close, most of the people here,' he waved his hand around at the crowd, 'said that they wanted to do something special to thank you and the Resistance. After that it was easy.'

'But,' said Marieke, with her eyes wide open in amazement, 'we left the de Bruins and Lottie only this morning. How did you manage to get them here so quickly?'

'In the jeep,' said Dirk with a smile. 'Piet collected people as you left Laaxsum and Roordehuizum. We know you both so well and we assumed that you wouldn't want to use the jeep. After you left the hotel, we took everybody to the *tjalk* and here we all are.' His smile turned to laughter, 'Although, I've got to say, that without your children it would've been difficult.'

'Aukje, Harmen, you're wonderful,' said Marieke as she held them close. Frank was still shaking his head as soft drinks and food appeared like magic from the factory.

After an hour Frank raised his hand, 'Ladies and gentlemen.' They stopped talking and formed into a semi-circle. For all the best reasons Frank was nervous. He looked round at his friends, cleared his throat and pushed back his greying hair.

'I really don't know where to start. So many old friends and so many new. I must thank all of you for today and for this welcome back to our house.' He closed his eyes tightly for a moment, 'I don't want to make a speech. There will be time for that later. But I would like us to stand in silence and thank God for our deliverance from tyranny.' There was a murmur of agreement and people stood with their heads bowed. Marieke held his hand tightly.

It was a quietness that only nature interrupted. The breeze ruffled the new leaves on the trees and the rigging of the *tjalk* cracked against the main-mast. A blue, clear sky and the sun shone with a brightness that dazzled.

'Amen,' said Frank quietly.

TWENTY-NINE

Their invitation to the national ceremony in The Hague arrived and Marieke opened the envelope. They had been expecting it and all the plans had been made ready for the journey. Frank had obtained petrol from somewhere, Marieke suspected that the Resistance still had stocks hidden away somewhere. There was a look of surprise on her face when, with a toot of a horn, a car appeared round the corner of the factory wall. It was the Austin and as it braked gently to a halt. Frank stepped out with a huge grin on his face.

'You didn't expect me to throw it away did you? It's a perfectly good car.' Marieke laughed and, with sheer pleasure, clapped her hands.

They were waved away by friends and the men from the factory. Frank took the same route that he had taken nearly five years previously. This time the weather was wonderful and they bowled along with the engine happily purring away. The chatter was of friends and family and normal everyday life. There were no road blocks, no *NSB*. But, as they passed through the cities there was desolation and people thin from famine. Some stared at the car with hate on their faces. Most just ignored it. Frank was silent and drove with a single-minded intensity that was felt by his family.

As they approached the centre of The Hague, the atmosphere changed. There were road blocks and each time the car and the invitation were checked, but this time with welcoming smiles.

There were no fenced off-areas outside the medieval town hall. Dutch flags were hung everywhere with long streamers of orange bedecking every building. Thousands of people had gathered to take part in the ceremony to celebrate the final act of the liberation of their country.

It had taken another month before Holland was completely liberated and then not before the Allied bombers had changed their loads from death to life by the dropping of hundreds of thousands of tons of food on the starving people of the west. Liberation finally did come, although far too slowly for many people.

They walked together towards the area designated for Friesland. All their comrades were waiting for them. Seats were laid-out but the conversation was of the past and, at the same time, of the future. There was an air of expectancy and every few minutes people glanced at the great stone steps of the town hall. Representatives of the exiled London government were already seated and, every so often, other famous men and women sat in their allotted places. There was every kind of band playing every kind of music, from provincial tunes to Glenn Miller melodies. White carnations and flowers of all kinds were given to everybody in the square.

Other sights away from the ceremonies of state were less glorious.

Food and cigarettes dropped from the skies had appeared on the black market at dazzlingly high prices. The number of prostitutes increased and the Dutch saw their brothers and sisters making themselves available for their uniformed liberators. For most, liberation was an anticlimax. The country was economically and socially ruined but Dutch heads were still held high.

Frank leant over and whispered, 'Look on the steps. It's *burgemeester* de Monchy. In May 1940 he was sacked by the Germans and now he's been re-instated. It's good to see him again.' Marieke nodded, not wanting to miss a second of the occasion.

'Frank, I think the ceremony is going to begin. Listen!'

The crowd heard it as well. It was the deep thump of a military bass drum. The crowd refused to sit in their seats and pressed forward to see what was happening. The dignitaries left their seats and walked down to the cobbled road and waited. The steady beat was hypnotic and it stilled the crowd. From the steps of the town hall a young Jewish girl walked to the side of the road and waited quietly. In her arms she held a bouquet of flowers. The crowd was transfixed and all eyes watched her. She was dressed in a simple black dress, black shoes and her long dark hair flowed over her thin body. Even though it was only as a big as a rose, the yellow, six pointed star pinned to her breast stood out like a beacon.

The Princes Irene Brigade was formed in England from Dutch men and women who had either fled at the outbreak of war or joined it as escapees from the mother country. Its commanding officer was Prince Bernhard, the German-born husband of *Princes Juliana*, the eldest daughter of Queen Wilhelmina. He marched at the front of the Brigade with measured tread and in a relaxed manner that no German would have appreciated. Frank nudged Marieke; one row back marched Marius Hofstra. He wore the rank of *luitenant-kolonel*. The brigade marched steadily past the saluting rostrum followed by its transport vehicles and the flags of liberation. The crowds cheered until they were hoarse and the air was thick with flowers thrown onto the road. The drum beat slowly faded as did the noise of the people and a silence descended.

The girl turned and faced the burgemeester. She slowly walked forward and thousands of eyes watched her firm step. She stood one pace away from him and with both hands presented the bouquet. There was not a sound. The elderly man accepted it with a slight bow of his head and, with a slow movement of his hand, he carefully removed the yellow star. The girl stepped back and melted away into the people on the steps.

Frank found himself crying. When he looked around so was everybody else. Marieke smiled up at him and his children stood close to him, arm in arm.

Not a word was spoken until the *burgemeester*, still clutching the yellow star, walked to the microphone. After a moment's hesitation he said, 'The

Netherlands has regained its freedom.' He had to wait another moment because the crowd erupted in one long drawn out roar of cheering, clapping and shouting.

After the emotional and highly-charged ceremony, the Frieslanders gathered in a well-known hotel in The Hague. There was just enough food for everybody and plenty of drink. People ate little. Old habits, born from adversity, die hard.

Frank found himself standing strangely alone. He looked around for his family. Marieke was talking animatedly to Tineke de Bruin and Lottie Cohen. Harmen stood at his mother's side, smiling. Frank's eyes swept round his circle of vision and then he saw Aukje. Her long, blonde hair was coiffeured high on her head and held in place by a silken orange band. She was standing with her hands on her hips in a pose copied from her mother. The dark green dress was so simple that it looked like high fashion. Her face, devoid of make-up, was radiant and happy. Her pale blue eyes danced from one man to another. On her left was Squadron Leader Richard Johnstone in the blue uniform of the Royal Air Force. His gilt dress-sword was pushed casually to one side and his hand was gently touching Aukje's shoulder. His eyes were glued to hers and she looked at him with a hint of interest. To her right was *luitenant-kolonel* Marius Hofstra of the Princes Irene Brigade. His maroon beret was tucked neatly under his shoulder epaulette and his hands were just reaching to touch Aukje's other shoulder. Frank breathed in sharply. Suddenly Marieke was at his side.

'Darling, I think Aukje has found her freedom.'

'Yes,' said Frank, kissing his wife gently on the cheek, 'the freedom to choose.'

Somehow Prince Bernhard managed to visit all the hotel parties. When he reached the Friesians it was already late in the evening. There was a moment when he separated from the crowd and walked away to step onto a low platform. The audience became silent as he glanced around the waiting faces. His steel-framed spectacles glinted in the hotel lights and he smiled. The voice had just a trace of a German accent and he spoke quietly, but everybody clearly heard him.

'I have heard a great deal about the people of Friesland and you were one of the last provinces in the Netherlands to be liberated. I know you have suffered greatly and that is recognised by all of our people. Tonight it has given me the greatest pleasure to meet all of you and I share your hopes and desires for the future of our great country. All of you here tonight have contributed in some way to the liberation. In time, those contributions will be recognised and rewarded. Some of you here have lost members of your family and close friends. They died tragically in the pursuit of freedom and now that freedom is finally with us today. Her Majesty Queen Wilhelmina has asked me to read a message to all of you. It is a message that sums up how difficult I find it to speak on this day.'

He straightened his spectacles, reached into the breast pocket of his khaki tunic, produced a single sheet of paper, and began,

> *'"Our language has no words for what goes on in our hearts in this hour of liberation of all of the Netherlands. Finally, we are again master of our house and hearth! The enemy, from east to west, from south to north, is defeated. The firing squad, the prison, the torture camp, have disappeared. Gone is the unspeakable oppression by the persecutor, who for five years has tormented you. Gone is the horror of famine. Freedom is yours."'*